Symphonie Fantastique

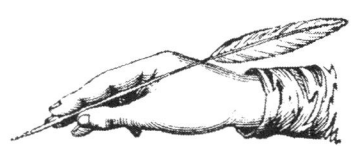

By
Mark Seinfelt

Symphonie Fantastique

Four Movements/ Four Haunted Individuals/ Four Novelettes of approaching death, heightened consciousness and ungainly obsession. An elderly writer who begins to doubt the validity of his life's work as his world begins to come apart at the seams. The persisting influence of a domineering, overprotective, and long-dead father upon his agoraphobic son who remains glued to his television during the first Gulf War feeling that the enemy has secretly targeted not only him but everyone else watching at a distance in supposed safety. Another young man experiencing the irresistible force of *Frau Minne*, transfixed and smitten in an *Augenblick* at first sight of the Beloved and of the constant and agonizing pain of the suppurating and bleeding Kundry-wounds occasioned by her departure and her subsequent reduction to the status of ghost in his life. And finally an individual shattered into slivers and fragments, an omnium-gatherum of alters, nightly revenants, spectral visitors or the illusions thereof.

All persons and places in this book are either fictitious or are used fictitiously.

To the three woman in my life:
my mother Laura who told me my first stories
my sister Bronwen, to whom I told my first stories
and, of course, Mindy at whose call and summons
I first seriously put pen to paper
But also for my three great teachers:
Paul, William, and Frederick William.

At Last The Distinguished Thing

OR

The Two Masters

Table of Contents

The War Cripple

The nicest thing the gentleman did during his recent illness and period of confusion was to once or twice apply his surname to my Christian own, as if I stood his brother or his son. For that but not for that alone, for everything else as well, I'll forever remain loyal to him, will perform the most menial service with the utmost dedication and sympathy.

Yesterday I held a white basin all garlanded with bright blue forget-me-nots for him to retch in. Propped up by his pillows he lay in the mahogany four-poster. We had changed the sheets and the two nurses had dressed him in a newly laundered nightshirt. "What a beautiful thing," the gentleman, rasping, finally said after catching his breath, "to serve such a base function." His face had such a sorrowful, suffering expression, the one eye open and staring at me, the lid of the other drooping over the ball except for a small sliver of white at the bottom, as he did not have strength on that side of his body even to lift his eyelid; I could have shed tears for him, right at his bedside, had I not steeled myself beforehand. The lady from across the Atlantic would not stand for any unseemly show of affection from a menial. She observes me with a very cold eye. Yesterday, she sat on a horsehair divan opposite his bed attired in layer after layer of frilly bombazine, her large masculine face framed by her thatch of white.

My gentleman's days stand numbered; his suffering will soon cease. I pray I could do more for him now, not just scrub his urinal, or bring his food tray. Despite his impairment, he seems to enjoy meals, still delights in eating if not quite with the old hearty appetite.

I would gladly sit and keep him company, hold his hand, the dear man, but I am pushed back, not given much access to him, now that she, the sister-in-law, has arrived and taken over. She presides over the show like a Queen appointed from on high, stage-manages the old man's death just as she did her husband's own six years ago in America, for I went there with them, accompanying my gentleman, his brother and his wife across the ocean to the brother's home in America, the greatest adventure of my life until my experiences, my ordeal, in the present war.

In 1910, the brother and the Missus had sailed over the ocean for an extended visit with my gentleman. The master despondent and sad for some time for no apparent reason other than the great God Dumps had decided to precipitate him down to the blackest pit and bottom. True, he did have several attacks of gout then also, but he had

had them before and they had in no wise plunged him into such dark despair previously. I hoped the arrival of the relatives would cheer him, would snatch him out of his sullen mood. It must have been a premonition of things to come (the year that followed was a very hard year for him) that had haunted him those last several months.

His brother, suffering from a heart condition for years, aside from visiting him would also take the cure over on the continent.

The Missus took charge of things then too, presided over Lamb House as its resident queen, its visiting dignitary. But the brother's condition was so impaired he could hardly walk. His presence rather added to than subtracted from my master's sense of doom and gloom; medical Doctor that he was, the brother didn't admit the gravity of his own condition but contented himself to addressing my gentleman's melancholia only, which he termed "simple." The gentleman, on the other hand, blamed his diet for his gloom.

Still in a black mood, on his bench of desolation, my master (with me in tow) accompanied his relatives to Switzerland, where the brother seemed to worsen daily. In Geneva the news of the death of another brother in the States reached us but my master and his sister-in-law didn't disclose it to her husband. Well, we returned to England, and after the first night spent in his rooms in the Reform Club, my master's mood improved—his depression left him for a time. His brother received treatments in the city, and I noticed that as the gentleman, as was his wont, crossed the days off on his calendar with red and black x's, there were more red crosses, thank Heaven, than black.

After the brother's course of treatment ended, we returned to the country for a short stay at Lamb House, where the brother rested for our impending voyage over the water. He had severe chest pains in the night. It became clear as day that he wasn't long for this world and both the master and the Missus wanted to get him home. Naturally enough the gentleman's black mood returned. His respite had been short-lived. As sad as the situation was, I was still very excited about my first trip across the Atlantic. I had feared seasickness but we had an exceedingly peaceful crossing, a succession of sunny days and smooth ocean. From the deck I espied both porpoises and whales.

The brother did not last long once we reached the new world. In awful pain, he simply had no will left in him to fight. He died in his sleep at his home that August. We stayed the winter, did not leave until the following July. The master loved the lakes and forests and as he termed it, "the delicious orchardy," surrounding his brother's country home but we soon removed to town where the widow employed a succession of mediums in an attempt to converse with her husband's spirit. He had taken an interest in spiritualism during his lifetime and made his wife promise to try and contact him after he passed. My master thought it all cheap conjurors' tricks. Tapping on tables did not signify a ghost. Only in literature did spirits roam through the dusky halls of ancient castles or inhabit a certain haunted room. But one after the other, the Madame admitted to her parlour a succession of ladies in black shawls and bonnets who claimed to have a special ability to communicate with the departed. The gentleman just to appease the

Missus held hands with the others around the séance table, but they did not have any real success as the master could tell from the very beginning.

Over the years, my service to *him* has been so light, especially when compared to the assistance I so shortly rendered the King over on the continent in Belgium, stepping up to the firestep, and pulling the trigger on the machine gun. My pneumatic riveting machine which fired through a camouflaged net curtain to keep my position hidden. I saw so much carnage and myself mowed down numerous Germans as they came charging out of their trenches in the direction of our wire, but then a shell exploded over my position. Shrapnel entered my body in over thirty places. My skin pierced, I bled. Jerry hit nothing vital. I would have a lot of little scars where the hot metal particles entered my flesh but that was all, or not quite all. I was totally deafened in one ear while the other was damaged as well, but I could still hear if I had that ear cocked in the direction of the speaker or if someone shouted, if I was spoken to loudly enough. In the mornings, the moment that I awake, some times I don't realize where I am and I start up in a panic but then I see that I'm in the by-now old and familiar servant's room and I sigh with much relief.

Before the Madame's arrival, his typist blonde, blue-eyed Miss Bosanquet, I and the little maid Miss Minnie Kidd, quiet and self-suppressed as always, took charge of the gentleman, and of course followed the two doctors' instructions to the letter. In fact, Miss Bosanquet hired the first nurse—a male orderly later dismissed. We carried on very well ourselves until the Madame's arrival.

Miss Kidd had entered the dining room early that Thursday morning (December 2nd), suspecting nothing was at all wrong when she heard the master moaning and calling out for help. She burst into my quarters where I had just finished making my toilette, screaming that the master lay on the floor of his bedroom unable to rise. I followed at her elbow, rushed into his room, where it took both of us, Miss Kidd and myself, the master being so large and I so diminutive not having really grown much since I was fifteen or sixteen, to heave the gentleman to his feet, carry him to his bed and tuck him in. After catching her breath, Miss Kidd left the gentleman's apartment, made her way on foot down the lime-tree-lined avenue, turned onto Lawrence Street, and ran up the steps of Miss Bosanquet's flat to solicit her aid, for we had realized our employer had suffered a stroke. We hoped a light one. Before Miss Kidd left to fetch Miss B., I had the presence of mind to have her first telephone Dr. Des Voeux. He had quit his residence but had not yet arrived at the hospital. She left a message for him there. Usually it is impossible for me to decipher what is being said at the other end of a line, yet when she and the typist returned I informed them that the doctor would arrive presently. I had caught that much. I had been standing next to the telephone waiting for the call. Afterwards I returned to the master's bedside. He was conscious and strangely calm. After the doctor confirmed the diagnosis of minor stroke, the gentleman thanked him, and the doctor promised to stop again that evening, the master dictated a cable to his relations in America, informing them of his illness. He had just finished a letter to his niece the day before. He would have posted it himself that morning had he not fallen ill.

By the next day he had taken a decided turn for the worse and lay in bed babbling, not seeming to know who he himself was. Miss Bosanquet felt his forehead and realized that he had a high fever. Finally the doctor's carriage arrived. Des Voeux examined the patient thoroughly, then pronounced he had had a second, much more severe, stroke and that nurses would need to be engaged at once. The paralysis was far more extensive, he added. Within the hour, Des Voeux had called in a specialist and that authority—Sir James Mackenzie—confirmed everything that Des Voeux asserted. We had to be prepared for the worst. The patient's condition was quite grave. Miss B. fired off another cable to America and also one to Mrs. Wharton in Hyères. Two neighbouring ladies, acquaintances of the gentleman, stayed the night on the chance they would be needed, but the master fooled them. Quite himself the next day, he called out for a thesaurus to be brought to him. "Surely there must be a better word," he said, "than paralytic to describe my present state." Apoplectic perhaps?

He seemed himself for a while, but presently we saw that he was confused to the point of being, well, quite unhinged. During the days that followed, before Madame's arrival (within the week we had received her cable that she was en route), the doctors came and went, the male nurse was hired then discharged and the two female nurses recommended by Dr. Des Voeux retained. The master didn't seem to know where he was and would ask us again and again to tell him. We tried to calm him. One day he stared at me, then turned to Miss B.

"Burgess is to accompany me to Lady Hyde's. We are running quite late already."

"Sir," Miss Bosanquet interrupted, "You are home. At your chambers, No. 21 Carlyle Mansions."

"How very curious," he replied. "I was sure No. 21 was Lady Hyde's address as well."

I witnessed his confusion firsthand, for prior to the arrival of his sister-in-law I sat at his side for many a long hour and conversed with him, and, of course, shaved his whiskers each morning as always.

Before the war, while we resided at his home in the country, if he could not sleep for any reason and wanted to converse, he would use the pull bell to summon me to his rooms (oh if only I could hear a bell today how I would run to answer it, but alas someone must come and fetch me if I am needed) and we would chat, not as master and servant, but old man and young, though sometimes we would discuss the practical matters of household business as well. More often we would speak more personally, matters on life and goals and such. The pressures of his daily work made sleep difficult for him, he said, but my conversation and soothing manner he claimed helped him to relax, enabling him to submit to the night. We engaged in pleasant and uplifting discussion at the end of our busy and responsibility-laden days. If I could only be with him now to soothe him into submission with the sleep of death! But she has cut me off.

I never shall forget the day upon which that august, triple-chinned woman made her grand entrance at Carlyle Mansions, stepped onto the premises for the first time. She had visited us both in the country and at his old London rooms, but never here.

The coachmen took twenty minutes to bring in her voluminous luggage, all those suitcases and trunks which had crossed over the Atlantic with her. She came, to her credit, despite the warnings of German submarine attacks on the English liners. But the first thing she started doing after going in and checking on the gentleman's condition for herself, was to compile an inventory of all the house's furnishings to determine which items would accompany her, her son, and daughter (for those two would follow her, would later and separately appear) on their journey back to America after the master finally made his end and breathed his last. I have been in the man's employ since fourteen years of age. Other servants have come in and out of service, but I, until I enlisted (with the gentleman's approval of course) into His Majesty's armed forces, had always remained at his side.

I shall never forget the day when I, then such a young wee-sized bit of a lad, was first inducted as houseboy into the master's service. I climbed up the steep road to the great redbrick house. I knocked at a certain time at the large entrance door and was ushered in by the butler, a man with goggling bloodshot eyes. "Natcherly ye're sich a boy wha' the gentleman hissel received a ledder from the lady?" "Jes' so, sir," I answered, "Aye." "I don't like the sicht of you. Ilka nicht you'll be trouble. I dinna ken. Well, come in. Git a gaen." So I crossed the threshold, and the man lifting me up by the arm the while, marched me up the first flight of stairs, then first rapping on the study door, opened it when the man within shouted "yes" and shoved me forward into the dark room (the curtains inside were drawn and outside the sun had just been so bright) and into my prospective employer's presence. The man sitting at the room's end in a large plushly cushioned chair (later I would hear him call it a bergère) wore a high cravat and a waistcoat as red as a veritable robin's breast and a dark overcoat with tails. A fantastically tall black satin top hat fitted his huge knee very snugly. He, perhaps as nervous as I, kept removing the hat then putting it back on his kneecap before crossing his other leg over that knee at last, but then he switched knees, put it on and off the new one. This bald, burly giant had just moved to our town from the London metropolis.

"Child, what is your name," he asked as I stood before his chair in his study, cringing like a cat.

I shook and said, "Noakes, sir."

"No, no lad." He glowered down at me from his perch in the high-backed chair. "What is your given, your Christian, name."

"Burgess," I answered simply.

"Well, Burgess, you come highly recommended. The matron writes that you are a boy of cheery disposition and good habits. That you are diligent in the performance of your duties, seeing things through to their proper finish. Is that all true?"

"I hopes so, milord," I said and bowed. "I hopes everthin' she wrote int it's genuin." He smiled, no snorted, sniffed, at my words. I started stammering. "I'll satisfy ye, sir, so I will, there hisn't a thin' which I canna maister if I put my mind to it partikler." "I see I will be called upon to teach you the correct use of your language," he said. "But yes, you'll do, lad. You'll do." And he did indeed keep his promise. I listened to him, he made sure that I did, and learned how to properly pronounce all my words and to speak grammatically.

What good it did me! For now I have to turn my head so my good ear faces the speaker and even so if he doesn't loudly intone or distinctly enunciate, I still can't make him out. I have seen how deaf people speak, how they shout out whatever they have to say, not realizing they are speaking at the top of their voices. It is funny. People laugh. My speech will have as much a defect now as it did then when I was a mere stripling. A different defect but one every bit as noticeable, it will proclaim to the world my handicap as my youthful speech proclaimed my lack of education, my station and class. Not hearing distinctly will now be my bane, or so the doctors say, for the rest of my life—I am frustrated everyday because I simply can't make out what people are saying.

That was a very ungracious train of thought, Burgess, I chide myself.

No, I'm very grateful for all he taught me. I should be. He needn't have, but he did. My first year in his employ, he made time for a lesson almost every day. We kept a very strict schedule at Lamb House. Master and servant alike confirmed to his personal ritual.

Each morn I would ascend the stairs to his bedroom, carrying hot water, a towel and his strop razor. The first several years, he performed the rite before his mirror himself, but as I grew and began having to shave myself he let me take over the task for him. He would sit still as I lathered his cheeks and not say a word until I finished. I never nicked him once. Then I would draw his bath water. He liked it steaming hot. After his tub, he would dress and again I would assist him. Vain as any London lady, he took a full fifteen minutes to decide what to wear, which jacket and waistcoat to don. Dressed as if going out to make some important diplomatic call, he would descend the staircase for breakfast at nine. As he ate, he issued the day's instructions to the housekeeper. Shortly thereafter the typist would arrive and he would accompany him or her whichever the case might be out into the garden if the weather was seasonable or else upstairs to his study. He would not need me again until the afternoon when visitors might begin to arrive. Often I would read a book from his library. This habit started several months after he gave me my first rudimentary lessons and continued throughout all my years in his service. The lessons would come at night, after the work of the day was done. He said that I learned quickly, had an ability to take things in, but that I would have to serve out my apprenticeship which would be rigourous. He had me writing in several weeks' time. We were both proud of my accomplishment. I showed him total dedication in performing my duties as his houseboy, he told me some weeks after the lessons had begun. Therefore it would be remiss on his part not to likewise show total dedication to me as my teacher. Long after the lessons ended, I continued to learn from the gentleman if only by a sort of osmosis. Not only did I read several of his books; I overheard so much intellectual discourse, of a proper proprietary nature of course, in his house that I apprehended and perceived something new almost daily. And as I said earlier I was glad to serve him though certain of the other servants were resentful and lackluster in the performance of their duties. I am thinking especially of the Smiths. They had been in the master's service for many years when I first entered it, having come to the country from the metropolis with him. They had ministered to the man at De Vere Gardens, my master's former residence in London, Mr. Smith as butler, Mrs. Smith as cook, and now they performed the same duties at Lamb House. It had been Smith who had raised me up by the arm and had led me up the precipitous steps for my first interview with the gentleman.

The rest of the staff at that time consisted of MacAlpine the first of the master's three typists and the only male in the trio, and the gardener Mr. George Gammon. The gentleman later replaced him with a woman also, Miss Muir Mackenzie. Shortly after I commenced service at Lamb House, Fanny the parlour maid was hired. In all my years in the master's employ, I never had any complaints about my treatment, only the highest praise. The Smiths didn't have any grounds for complaint either. What happened to them was their own fault; they were great drinkers, and always had been I later learned from the gentleman. He said that in the early years of their employment they had been wondrously proficient, but then he was constantly crossing over to the continent and when he was away they treated themselves, he was certain of it, to prolonged gin holidays, weeks upon weeks of heavy drinking. Here, in the country, longer periods of uninterrupted service ensued. Besides he always entertained, which kept them even more active. They did not seem to like the country and took recourse to drink on an almost daily basis. It seemed the more they had to toil, the more they wanted to imbibe and they ran up quite a liquor bill during the tenure of their stay in Rye.

He had always been good and generous with them. Once long before I entered his employ, he even allowed a sister of Mrs. Smith's to recuperate after surgery in his London apartment. She had cancer, the same disease that had taken the master's own sister shortly beforehand. The Smiths had been properly grateful at the time for the courtesy shown them, but later they forgot themselves completely, letting things slide and slide until finally at long last they went to their inevitable doom, preordained and implacable. I was there to witness their downfall. Smith had begun the third day of a drinking spree when the gentleman's sculptor friend Hendrik Andersen and several other guests on their way to London stopped at Lamb House. Smith had been drinking gin since six in the morning. He served the visitors lunch then staggered out of the dining room and fell to the floor, blind drunk. The master managed to hide his menial's disgrace from his guests. He ushered his friends out of the house and set them on their way to the train station. But the Smiths' tenure had, if not abruptly, indeed come to an end with the butler's fall to the kitchen floor. Mrs. Smith begged the master not to cast them to the wolves.

" 'E's a good man, my husband," she said, "when he ain't in the stews. Please give us another chance. If not, at our advanced ages you'll be as much as puttin' us aneath." But the gentleman remained adamant. Off they must go. "Please do somefing," she begged of me, then turned again to the master, "What have we doon?"

Later she whispered in my ear on the stair in utter perplexity, " 'Is 'ighness caint jest give us the 'eave 'o." But that is exactly what he did. Both of them had deserved their dismissal for years. Only the kindness of the gentleman's heart had kept them in their respective positions for so long. Other masters would have drummed them out much earlier, or at the very least upon the occasion of Smith's catastrophe, then and there, but the gentleman summoned the local doctor to treat Smith first. A week passed before he had them out of the house. Smith's wife proceeded to get stinking herself during the days her husband convalesced, but at last Mrs. Smith's sister arrived to help the couple pack up their belongings and they were loaded into the dray with their little bit of property and were on their way back to London town.

The master even bestowed two months' severance pay on both husband and wife and settled their bills at all the Rye wine-and-gin shops, but he finally, thank Heaven, got them off his hands. For a time he took his meals at the local tavern while he inquired of his London friends for a suitable housekeeper and cook. Finally he settled on Mrs. Paddington, a portly middle-aged woman whom he referred to in strictest confidence to me as "Our Lady of the Gorringe's costume." The matron treated the other servants much more severely–Fanny found her highly temperamental–than her immediate predecessors, but she performed much to the master's satisfaction which in itself endeared her to me. He simply raved to the point of becoming rhapsodic about her cooking–"up to the wildest want or fancy"–and her thrift and economy: "My tradesmen's books go down and down." He found her agreeable as well as sensible, and she clearly enjoyed being in his service. As did I. I am sorry to say that she is no longer with us. She did not follow the master to Chelsea in 1913 when he moved to our present lodging at Cheyne Walk, his London Flat No. 21 Carlyle Mansions. The tall and efficient Mrs. Anderson has replaced her.

I remained in the gentleman's employ for fifteen years before I gave him notice in September 1914 and joined up. I was sorry to leave him then for he had had a long stretch of illness and was taking the war very badly. He had little appetite and was as morose as I had seen him ever. The slightest little thing ruffled his feathers. He kept declaring the worst has happened, the very worst. His friend Mrs. Wharton had come from Paris where she had been when the German army had invaded Belgium. She sat with the gentleman in the upstairs study when I got up the courage to approach him and make my declaration. Readily he gave me his permission to enlist. The day before we had watched the local recruits as they drilled and paraded together on a farmer's field at the outskirts of town. I myself was healthy and athletic, quite fit for service.

"It will be like losing an arm or a leg," he said, "But go Burgess with my consent and blessing." He paused a moment and then added: "And your job will await you on your return, rest assured." I thanked him and bowed. I overheard Mrs. Wharton say that she would send him one of her menservants. I was glad that he would be well taken care of in my absence.

He wrote me on an almost weekly basis while I was in Belgium. If it were socks that I would most want, he would keep me well supplied.

On another occasion I opened a letter to read: "What things you are seeing, and perhaps will still more see, and what tremendous matters you will have to tell us! I think it wonderful for you to be able in the midst of such things to write to us all, and we are very grateful."

Yes, I did write back to him and to the other servants, but not with the same frequency as he wrote me. Of course, like the rest of the recruits, I tried to be plucky and nonchalant, easy and unruffled, in my missives home. They were meant to display my "sang-froid," so none of the horrors that we men faced almost daily in the trenches found their way into my account. I didn't write about the new shell holes each morning in our boardwalk, the fact that the German guns had us in their range, that daily the sandbags caved in and someone smothered or that our communications with headquarters in the rear of the lines were forever being interrupted, especially during action. In a way my letters and those of the other men were as great lies as the German films then being screened in New York (or so we read in the papers) which showed smiling Jerry soldiers rushing to the aid of old and infirm Belgian refugees as the latter crossed over debris and mud puddles in one of their wrecked and burning cities. It wouldn't be sporting, Captain Harval said. He had appointed me his batboy, so I was still pretty much of a valet the first several months of my martial career though of course my Captain was much younger than my gentleman, much closer to my own age though I in fact was his elder. The war had interrupted his education at Cambridge. Dutiful and punctilious, I performed any task he asked of me. Besides, he warned, the censor would let defeatism slip into our letters as little as any military secret. However (I thought) the censor would not detect the change in my handwriting whereas my old teacher, I felt reasonably certain, had. Often I would be in the middle of a letter when a bombardment began and the movement of my hand grew jerky. What I wrote almost became illegible. Could the censor even read it? Nonetheless I did my duty, expressed only the most proper and fitting sentiments. The master wrote back that I must be under a great deal of stress my letters to the contrary, though he was sure that I would do my best, meet any challenge half way. Indeed there were many challenges. The trenches were filthy, filled with contagion, and the food was inedible. Friends died daily in the bombardments and the gas attacks, and I, who in civilian life, had an aversion to shooting birds let alone a deer (though, as a prize-winning bantamweight who took the local championship at twenty, I had grown used to seeing my opponents bloodied—yet we contestants fought fair, never struck low blows intentionally) must do my duty and drill down my fellow men, which at first I admit did not seem so hard after seeing our own men, my Captain included, fall. His body remained tangled in the wire where the Germans had machine-gunned and put paid to him until the shelling ended and the enemy's advance had been repulsed and our position was again secure. Then I and two or three others went out and retrieved it. I washed and laid out the corpse, had my officer looking the best he could for interment in the ground. I performed this duty with great care unlike some others. There were many dead. I had, after all, been his batboy.

So for a time, I gladly pulled the trigger on my Vickers, killing Germans left and right. Yet when the heat of the engagement passed, I would feel remorse. They after all served their country as I did mine. They had mothers, fathers, and sweethearts, just like us. Why did the world inflict such carnage on itself? Yet during the next firestorm, despite my conflicted feelings, I stepped up to the front line and performed my duty again, mowed the enemy down. I was wounded and invalided home in mid-1915, early in my service. The gentleman came to see me while I was in hospital. He sat at my bedside then. Not six months later our roles would be reversed and it would be I tending him.

"You have clearly been very bravely through very stiff things," he told me, "but have paid much less for it than you might. Keep up your heart—there are many so much worse." Shortly after his visit—I am sure he had a hand in it, that he had turned the proper screw—I received word that by special dispensation I would be allowed to reenter my gentleman's service and not, as I expected, be assigned to desk duty on the home front.

Now my master is going to die so shortly after my return to him. The three of us—Miss Kidd, Miss B., and myself—tried to do everything we could to make him as comfortable as possible. Miss B. had him for herself a number of hours each day, for the gentleman still wanted to dictate and as ever she pecked at her machine, taking down his each and every word. His identity, his sense of self, came back to him right away, but we quickly saw that his brain had been damaged. He didn't know where he was. Forever confused as to time and place, he tried to accustom himself to his condition, to his surroundings nonetheless. He feared that he had gone mad, that he had a complete mental collapse. He grew horribly frightened at moments and was as affecting as a lost little child. Above all else he didn't want his friends and visitors to detect his "madness." He trusted Miss B. and myself, took us into his confidence as his co-conspirators. He would admit his impairment but then beg us to give him our word that we would not divulge his secret to anyone else. He asked us to help him keep it hidden, instructed us not to answer the doctors' questions or to speak about his case where the nurses might overhear. In his mind he kept traveling from place to place. One morning at breakfast he asked Miss B. and me how we were enjoying our stay in Paris, then at supper he bade me engage a gondola—so he and I could be ferried through the canals and past the marble palaces, not straight to the Piazza, but once there that we might take an ice together at Florian's. Then he muttered incoherently about his "old friend the Russian" down on his knees before "the horrible old man." I did not follow him. On another day I heard him say, "The weather is quite chilly for this time of year in Rome," then only a couple minutes later speak about his being "for some time now" in New York. The very day the Madame reached us he was maintaining that several of his manuscripts had been stolen or else that they had been inadvertently sent to Cork. The Irish city, he said, was now adjacent to Chelsea.

His sister-in-law arrived on the thirteenth of the month, the niece and nephew shortly after the New Year. Our guardianship of the master ended with the appearance of his relatives. When the sister-in-law entered the sick room I was attending the master. He patted her hand and said: "I don't dare to think of what you have come through to get here." Then he asked her if he were in California. I couldn't make out her reply (I swear she would purposely lower her voice in my presence) but later I recalled that she and the master's niece had traveled there before the outbreak of the war and sent the master post cards from Yosemite and elsewhere. The next morning when I tried to shave him, he kept insisting that we weren't in London, though later in the day after having been told over and over again by his sister-in-law that he was indeed presently in the city, he finally acquiesced and agreed. When a number of us were assembled in his presence one morning he said rather crossly: "I have the curious sense that I'm not the bewildering puzzle to all of you that you are to me."

His disposition and mood wavered sharply. Often he became despondent. The tears ran down his cheeks, and he trembled head to foot, his body racked by sobbing. The name of Mrs. Wharton came up in our talk and the master became very excited. "I hope she does not know of my state." We had to reassure him that she did not. The fear of revelation continued to besiege him. At all costs disclosure of his malady to anyone must be prevented.

He became angry with all of us—relatives and servants—at one time or another, and would often grow quite unmanageable. At Christmas he threw fit after fit, would not cooperate with anyone. He bellowed at the nurses, would not take a bite of food or a drink of water, cursed God and thrashed about in his wheelchair as if he were engaged in a death duel. The next morning it seemed that some movement had returned to the left side of his body. He was able to wiggle his fingers and toes. Several days later he again went into hysterics, crying so hard that I at first could not make out what he was saying. I wiped his nose and then he said, "Farewell Burgess, farewell." All day he was bidding everyone in the house adieux. "I won't be here much longer," he said.

His condition improved somewhat the first week of January. His niece had now arrived as well. He seemed less confused and became much more manageable. He ate more and seemed content to sit at his window and watch the barges on the Thames. The Madame had him sign a power of attorney form so (so she told him) she could take care of all the bills. The nephew arrived next and she dispatched him to Lamb House to make an inventory of the gentleman's belongings, his manuscripts, there. At about this time too, she and Miss B. had their falling out. She denied the typist access to the gentleman. She or the niece would now take down what he dictated. Occasionally they would deign to admit Miss B. to the master's presence. She still calls each morning but most days she is turned away. She had met his relatives six or seven years ago and seemed to get on famously with the Madame and the niece then, but now they seem to be at sixes and sevens. My presence the sister-in-law endures more readily than Theodora's, but I am called only to perform my various tasks and duties. I am no longer able to linger in the master's presence. I cannot always make out Madame's instructions; she speaks both quickly and softly. She always seems to want to shoo me off. A half-deaf servant, I guess she feels, is practically useless. Of the master's three original caretakers, quiet self-effacing Miss Kidd is now most often in his presence. I am in it long enough though to see that his confusion has returned. One morning after his shave recently, the gentleman asked me if I would accompany him back to Rye. The next time I saw him he smiled up at me from his chair at the window and said how nice it was to be back at Lamb House. Then he asked if his madness was a subject of mirth to the people around him. Before I had a chance to reply the Madame interrupted: "Never, no one wants to smile." I'll never forget the gentleman's reply. At that moment he had such a resounding stentorian voice that I caught every word: "What is this irrelevant voice from Boston, Massachusetts, breaking in with remarks in my conversation with Burgess!" Needless to say after that my presence, my service, is even less in need. Instead of being called in, I am increasingly sent out on errands. The master now has several days' growth of beard.

Just the other day Miss Kidd informed me the gentleman thought he traveled on a boat. Again he had been looking out the window at the barges. He asked for me and the Madame replied I was out shopping. "How extraordinary that Burgess should leave the ship to do that," he said. In truth, my gentleman is indeed embarked on a voyage. I hope to a much better place than this one. Each day I expect to hear news of his decease. And I know what will happen. The nurses will wash and lay out the corpse but it will be I who will be called in to give the master his last shave. Once more his face will be shorn and made to look respectable. I shall perform this last solemn duty, soon to be laid on me I fear, with love yet profound sadness, for when all is said and done this man was more a father to me than my natural own and I love him far more than even my late Captain, whose body also I had to prepare for the great earth to swallow.

Theodora and Other Voices

A smart young girl must have gumption, must see her chance then spring on it, and seize the opportunity for herself. It helps if she is somewhat boyish in appearance; then it seems a little more natural—that she is *properly* assertive and aggressive. Such a chance came my way and I indeed pounced when eight years ago I learned that such a distinguished writer as my present employer needed a lady typist. At the time the opportunity presented itself, I had already found myself a position in the secretarial office of Miss Petheridge's employment agency where at the time my assignment had been to proof the very dry and dull (not to mention enormous and interminable) 1907 Royal Commission on Coast Erosion, marking in commas and semi-colons, circling a typist's error—the accidental misspelling—with my red and blue pencils. There before my desk with its sloping adjustable top, I sat very businesslike lost somewhere in the middle of a seemingly unending sentence filled with all sorts of technical terms I was not familiar with, hot and uncomfortable in my office girl's uniform of white blouse, green tie, black belt and scratchy wool skirt (also green to match the tie) when I heard a man's limpid voice accompanied by the familiar staccato of one of the girl's machines, emanating out from the open door of Miss Petheridge's office and into the lobby. From my position in the adjacent main work hall, I could not quite catch every phrase. A number of other girls worked in their cubicles, but none seemed to attend to the purling cascade of words, several girls even stupidly staring out the large (regretfully unopened) windows into the London street.

He sounded as if he were reciting poetry. His voice had a cadence and a beat like some curious musical composition. Later I would learn that when he dictated he strode back and forth, rocked on the balls of his feet every so often inhaling and puffing out smoke from his just nervously lit cigarette, like a great dragon, all the while speaking in tempo with the typewriter, as if it provided him with his metre. But as I said, the first time I heard that voice I could not make out all the words, but it was clear from the start that what issued from this man's lips, the little I caught, was not dry and academic—that a chapter of some fiction, story, novella or novel was being set down, I did not know which. Yet I knew right away that this *was* a literary gentleman. I myself had pretensions in this line even though I was a mere girl. As of yet I am only potential and promise. Nothing's been fulfilled though someday I would like to write my own book on the poems of Paul Valéry—I so very much admire them.

As soon as I heard that voice, I wanted to know who the man was, and to my surprise I learned he was one of the most celebrated writers of the day, and that he was currently in search of a full-time typist because his former employee—a Miss Weld—had wed on him while he was away on his latest American tour.

He had come to our agency in search of a replacement and before settling on one dictated his latest work-in-progress to various of our office girls, using anyone available, even those not interested in the position. Whoever he ultimately hired would accompany him to his country estate several months later. He had other business in London to detain him until then. This was not a position for a run-of-the-mill girl, I don't care how trained a secretary. The ideal candidate, I realized immediately, would possess greater sensibility and more intellect—she must appreciate the writer's artistry, the loveliness and the spell of all his periods. I was such a girl. While I had not yet learned how to type, I, as opposed to most of the other women, had taken a degree, had attended both Cheltenham Ladies' and University Colleges, and I confess had a secret avocation to write. I had dabbled, produced some verse of my own and an essay or two. So I immediately commenced to learn all the secrets of our modern writing machine, developed a new skill, taught myself to type, so I could try for the position. It took only a matter of weeks. I truly applied myself—almost as never before. Miss Petheridge told me that she would be sorry if he chose me. None of the other girls could proof nearly so well. I had become—had made myself—essential to her office. However, being a fair-minded person and realizing that my ability to serve and please, indeed to satisfy, so famous a gentleman would no doubt redound well for her agency, she agreed to procure me an interview with her most distinguished client. It was my great good fortune that none of the better typists desired to remove to the countryside. They all had either families or else beaux or swains in London. I must admit that during the interview I seemed timid and abashed though very, very docile. I did not display my literary aspirations or flaunt my degree.

The clash of the gentleman's clothes startled me. His kelly green breeches did not at all go with his blue-and-yellow checked vest, and the overcoat he donned was surely meant to be worn with matching trousers, was of a very formal cut. I imagined that he would be much more circumspect about his dress. Bald except for a dark patch above each ear, he appeared overweight and perspired profusely. I stood directly in front of his chair after Miss Petheridge summoned me into her office, the agency's "inner sanctum." Immediately his gray eyes fixed on me. He asked if I would mind spending most of the year in a distant though scenic corner of the country far from the bustle of the great city. I would be integral—basic—to his work, so he would not be able to spare me for long intervals. Years ago he had written everything out in longhand but by now he had quite gotten used to dictating to an amanuensis. If he engaged me it would be with the understanding that I signed on for the long haul. He would be very upset if I'd depart his employ anytime shortly after committing to him, as a good typist was now, as he said, indispensable to him but also very hard to find. "The value of the process for me," he went on, "is in its help to do over and over, for which it is extremely adapted, and which is the only way I can do any more at all." In the past, he related to both Miss Petheridge and myself, he had made changes when he read the proofs sent to him by magazines on both sides of the Atlantic in which his works were being simultaneously serialized. Then before the entire book was to appear between two covers—at long last in final form, he would also make alterations, but now with a typist he could revise on a daily basis, read proof perpetually as it were. He went on to say the town of Rye would promise me very little in the way of amusement or diversion and that sometimes his work progressed at a very slow pace. He could foresee many days which his typist's work hours would be filled with nothing but a steady ennui. She would sit for several hours in front of her machine—the brand-new Remington—while he would construct and develop at the most, say, only several sentences, maybe a mere hundred words altogether. So little to show for a morning's toil!

I assured him that I had no objection to country life and that I would be happy to remain at his side for however long he needed me. Moreover, becoming just a little more outspoken and self-assured at this point in the interview (just prior to its termination), I told the gentleman that I had chosen not to wed, that I wanted a career for myself. I would remain eternally grateful for the opportunity to serve him. I found out the next day that I had been engaged.

Everyday at the appointed hour, he became the great singer and I his little staccato-ing accompanist, an automaton at his disposal, for his use. It seemed as if I took down dictation from God himself, though on one occasion, one occasion only, he did admit to me in the course of our table talk that, yes, at times he felt himself a mere medium through which the Universe gave utterance, that on those rare occasions, it came all at once as if it spoke to him, as in fact it was to me by him. In my mind I occasionally pretended that I was the artist, the vehicle through which the Gods spoke, that the words were mine. But afterwards all alone rereading (not hearing his voice ever-so-slowly reciting or at most in my own head) any given passage that he had previously dictated, seeing the perfection of its construction, I of course knew then, at my moment of greater rationality, that it could not possibly be mine, it was too perfect, too *recherché*, and I despaired. He loomed over me like a giant. I felt so small and defenseless in my inadequacy. Yes, I had been privileged to accompany him on his journey to heights which I alone could never aspire to. I saw the top of his mountain of achievement because I had stepped upon his magic Persian carpet which was indeed able to get us *there*—and accompanied him for the ride. In comparison to his, my poor brown crazy patch could scarcely rise off the ground—would just sit lifeless and unmoving on the floor. I got to the apex via him, for which I am grateful (that sight is not vouchsafed to everyone) but mightn't I also be allowed to air a little of my own private suffering, the loss of my old sense of worth after realizing his? My too close proximity—my propinquity (to use one of his words)—to genius wounded me like the flame it is drawn to scorches the moth, because it forced upon me once and for all a most painful recognition.

Usually he stood hands clapped behind his back and eyes tightly shut. What vistas must he behold, must he lay bare before his inner scrutiny, as the words pour out of him! He bends them to his usage with such involuntary, almost reflexive power! He holds sway over form itself! Something beautiful is born. He has told me that he deliberates and ponders his sentences in his head for hours before I sit down before him, my fingers at the ready at the keys. They are often long, of an almost bewildering complexity, and though he frequently pauses, when he does commence dictating again, he resumes purposely at a consciously slow pace (this extra reflection, this additional expenditure of brainpower and energy and, I'm sure, headbirth pain for him, to fashion or at least to try to fashion something flawlessly) the interrupted sentence, which as often as not, unfolds as naturally, as bewitchingly, as a flower opening its petals to the sun in all their rich colour and perfection of form. The next day he may alter it—usually by adding something to it, rather than the reverse. A brand new metaphor comes to him and he introduces it into one of his finely polished seemingly already complete sentences. He has a compulsion to revise (if I dare say such a thing maybe to over-revise; sometimes I feel he quite spoils a sentence by twisting and turning it around until it is all out of shape).

Of course, I shall never regret my decision to accompany him to the country. I arrived that autumn of 1907. He had found lodgings for me in Rye with a landlady who had five or six other boarders. He met my train and we rode in a hired victoria to my new address, our conversation very constrained. The rooms he had found for me were very pretty and nicely furnished but I felt out of place. For this, I thought, I gave up my dear London flat? The next morning, after clambering up the old cobbled street, I arrived at Lamb House at the appointed hour—ten in the morning. He met me at the door and gave me a quick little tour downstairs. What choice objects were in each dusky and only half-illumined room. Mantle garniture of Sienna marble. Chairs of finest mahogany upholstered in an array of rich colours. French Empire porcelain on inlaid bureaus. A marble-topped pier table with an astral lamp with pendants at its center. Walls adorned with gilt mirrors and paintings fantastically framed. He conducted me up the stairs to his study. "This Miss Bosanquet," he said, "is the Green Room, the chamber of our conjoint labours." I sat down at the oak desk with all its carved decoration where I had a view out the draped window into the garden with its numerous peach trees and rolled a piece of paper into his Remington. He took a seat in a plush chair in the centre of the room but later sprang to his feet and trod the carpet.

That first morning he dictated at a very considerate pace as well as spelled and punctuated, yet I was still abominably slow and clumsy. Although he remained very polite those first few hours, he did say that he hoped my skills would develop somewhat in the coming weeks so as I could type just a bit faster. I wrote in my diary that evening: "He assumes complete ignorance of any literary knowledge on the part of his amanuensis" for in the course of that first session, he told me that *The Newcomes* was a novel by Makepeace Thackeray and that the surname was one word, not hyphenated. Then he added that I would do well to read it!

Subsequently, after one or two more sessions, I was not nearly so nervous and I also developed a feel for his particular typewriter (each machine is so different) so that I made fewer mistakes and was able to type much more rapidly. Calmer now in his presence I even thought about offering a word now and then at one of his lengthy pauses when he was so clearly stalled, but I knew better, sensed somehow that collaboration of any sort, even the smallest suggestion, would not be looked upon kindly by him. The quickness and accuracy of my fingers counted more than any original thought in my own head! He complimented me at the beginning of the second week on my increased speed though first told me that his production had also improved: "Ah—it's coming better today—I don't mean the dictation—though as to that I have great pleasure in saying that I'm extremely satisfied, Miss Bosanquet. You seem to have picked things up so quickly and so intelligently." I had my chance here to show him both my admiration (which of course was very great) but also and more importantly that I, Theodora Bosanquet, was more than just ten nimble finger stubs, that I too had a portion of mind, that I was in fact full of feeling! I told him that I was so fascinated by his writing whether it was a new preface to one of his older volumes for the forthcoming collected edition in which he theorized on various aspects of the writer's craft (in the nine years of my service the composition of these prefaces would take up most of our time together) or an essay or a story or even just a letter in his voluminous correspondence. I always wanted to do my absolute best—for what he did was so interesting and so important. He seemed genuinely touched and replied: "Among the faults of my previous amanuenses—not by any means the only fault—was their apparent lack of comprehension of what I was driving at. But you—you comprehend. Even anticipate." Thereafter he treated me with even greater consideration. Once he said that he regarded me as an initiate. Every evening I would write down in my diary some of the off-the-cuff statements on his vocation that he had made to me earlier in the afternoon but even weeks later sometimes something else he had said which I had momentarily forgotten might burst into my mind. Just today I recalled, for example, him saying sometime late last November that his true descendants would be those who read his books and appreciated and learned from them. He would be a future great-granddad to many a fledgling author. Those not yet born would appreciate his worth. And then he made a statement on the duplicity of art. I have it here somewhere in my notes. Ah there it is. If we lived today in a more tolerant and liberal society, it would certainly be reflected in our works of art, which are shackled by ankles and wrists to today's convictions. What he wouldn't do if he was free to adopt a more open manner. It wouldn't be pure excrement like Pierre Louys. Yes, he could envision the hard and brittle book he would under those conditions indite. But society surely shouldn't change for it was better as it now was. He certainly could not envision himself living comfortably in a libertine age where such books would be the order of the day. To hide, to imply tantalizingly, that was his preferred path. What isn't seen, what isn't heard, is far more seductive. Whatever is cloaked and disguised remains behind its decorative screen much more mysterious and attractive.

On days we worked late (which we never failed to do if things were going well, "moving apace" as he said) he would offer—no force upon me—pieces of the choicest chocolate after first removing himself their gold or silver foil. He tried to be attentive. If I ever became ill and missed a session he would order flowers to be sent me at my landlady's, but he did not observe closely. One Christmas he purchased me a glove box though he never once saw me wearing long white ladies' gloves and then repeated the same useless gift twelve months later!

All nine years I remained in his employ, unbeknownst to him, I kept writing myself but I never tried to publish unless only something anonymous defending women's rights in a ladies' journal. Before entering his service I must admit that I had entered some poems in a literary competition, but of course did not take the prize. Over the years he very kindly gave me more and more time off, bestowed on me all sorts of extended vacations. One summer I took a long holiday indeed—at my request he granted me three whole months! The Parson's daughter, a Miss Lois Barker, took my place for that period of time. He said that she was a good girl but just not up to snuff. Burgess would usher her into the house and upstairs at the appointed morning hour, and yawning and grumpy, he would trudge across the hall and into the Green Room, inevitably late for the session (on several occasions, Burgess has informed me, still dressed in robe and pajama bottoms!) whereas he greeted me at the door himself most punctually (and needless to say properly attired) and we mounted the steps to his study together. I am very glad you are back, he said the first day of my return. There is ever so much work for us to sit down to. Since I the partner of his labours had abandoned him, very little indeed had gotten done, as I shortly found out. Edith had come across the channel and swooped down on him. She pulled him by his great lapels and forced him to go out motoring with her. Yet he was grateful. He smiled. He positively beamed at this point in our conversation. I had treated myself to a lark, so why shouldn't have he, even though he had to pay Miss Barker her usual rate despite no work (for the duration of Mrs. Wharton's stay) having been done?

At long last in 1915 I met the lady when the master lent me out for the day. She had wanted to drive him to Qu'acre to see Howard Sturgis, but he was indisposed, had been suffering from palpitations of the heart. Of course by now we had made the move from the country back to the city. How I loved Chelsea right from the start of our stay there. For over half a century, our neighbourhood had been frequented by a succession of great writers and painters. There were so many famous haunts. Each day I passed during the course of one of my walks a great stone pile of a house where some lion of literature once resided. Oh if the buildings themselves could speak and tell us tales. As he says, every house has its story. Some I am sure have several. Carlyle, Hunt, Swinburne and Meredith had lived at one time in Chelsea, all within several blocks of each other.

I made my way to her hotel just a little bit flustered. Today, I told myself, I would be taking dictation from a successful woman novelist, and, yes, I must admit the prospect excited me. One of her menservants let me into her room where she stood, dressed only in a pink negligée and a cap of écru lace. Excuse me as I thumb through my diary. Here, let me read you the entry I made: "Her arms were very much displayed, coming from very beautiful frills of sleeve, and they were good arms, not either scraggy, or too fleshy, but just the right plumpness and ending in hands most beautifully manicured." I remember that she wore a very strong perfume which was a bit off putting. What's this? I can't believe now that I wrote it. Here, go ahead, read it for yourself: "I wasn't as much charmed as I ought to be. She so evidently depends on fascinating people all about her, her sole effect makes one continually conscious of it." Tsk tsk, that is a little harsh but is no doubt an accurate record of my impression at the time. Though when I found out the real reason she had summoned me, I couldn't help liking her a great deal despite the airs she put on. Our mutual fondness for the master drew us together. His welfare concerned her so. She didn't want to dictate; she wanted to "pump" me for information on the state of my employer's health, asking me if I knew of anything she could do to lighten his burden. During the course of the master's present illness, I have kept in constant communication with her.

No, I don't think that I would care to be any other literary man's or (even for that matter) lady's amanuensis—it is time that my own voice emerges. Though years ago I must admit, I did enjoy taking down a page for the master's brother. I found him at my Remington, typing with two fingers—the second digits of each of his hands. I liked him immensely—he was a small, thin and cheerful man though even then quite ill. He looked ten years older than his actual age. As initially I also admired his wife and daughter. I laugh now as I remember how my employer introduced us. "Theodora," he said in his most factitious, affected, and highly amused manner (I remember his mocking tone quite distinctly), "may I present my eminently practical brother and his equally eminently practical wife." It amused me watching the two brothers, both such famous men, as they quarreled just like little boys. My employer caught his sibling peering over the garden wall at his neighbour Mr. Chesterton, the elephant with crimson face and oily curls, as we called him. Positively incensed at his brother, he called his spying despicable, then ordered his gardener to take the ladder inside. His brother then strode out the gate in a huff.

I found the mother and daughter much alike. The girl took quite a liking to me back then and we often walked together, conversing about the coming emancipation of the female sex. Even at that time, Peggy seemed a bit dull. She hadn't a sense of humour at all, was always so serious just like her mother Madame Alice. At the time of our introduction, I never would have guessed or predicted that they could have turned on me in the way they have recently done. Presently our relations are quite strained. I am now *persona non grata* at No. 21 Carlyle Mansions, and really I don't know why. I had been somewhat perturbed at the widow's nonchalance when the government awarded the gentleman the Order of Merit. She was positively cool to the King's representative and did not read to the master many of his telegrams of congratulations. Perhaps some hostile expression I wore on my face at the time set her against me. I was awfully surprised when I found the note written by Peggy to her brother lying open on the secretary. I thought it might be my instructions for the day so I picked it up and read it. I don't make it a habit to read other people's letters but I saw my name. Peggy wrote that I was acting above my station and that before their arrival that I had managed things in a heartless sort of way. Nothing could be further from the truth! I did everything I possibly could for him. Oh how he hated this war! He never could abide violence of any sort. It's funny but I am reminded of how he acted years ago when he accidentally killed his chameleon, flattened it one day with his foot while it scampered through the tall grass. He had found it one morning sunning itself on his front step. Enthralled by its ever-changing colours, he kept it for a pet but then one day it darted out of the jar and into the lawn and he stomped after it, could not find it, kept looking and looking for it until he felt its spine snap under his shoe. Sick and morose for a whole week, he cried and cried. "Why, oh why, could I not be content to let it go free!" Of course that incident stood as nothing compared to the effect the current violence has had on him. He became so dispirited after the war had broken out that he could not write. He tried to extend for a little while the fragment of a novel he had begun in 1904 about a young American historian awaking in the house of his London ancestors to find himself imprisoned in the past where he has become one with one of his forebears, but he could not continue very far. Instead of composing fiction, he threw himself into relief work and other war-related activities. Just before he fell ill, he dictated to me a preface he had agreed to write for a posthumous book by Mr. Rupert Brooke, who had died of blood poisoning while serving with the navy. I thought when Miss Minne Kidd burst into the drawing room of my flat that December morning that the master had died—that he had suffered a heart attack in his sleep—she so white and out of breath. It turned out that he had a slight stroke. " 'E said the beast 'as sproong," Miss Kidd whispered at last. She explained that she heard a muffled call for help from his room early that morning and answered his summons immediately. On her opening the door and entering, he turned his head to face her while raising himself up on his elbows from where he lay on the floor, and said those very words: the beast has sprung! I drew my shawl over my shoulders and put my tam on my head after lifting those items from off my hall tree and followed Miss Kidd out into the street. Quickly turning the corner, we reached the portals of his flat. We clambered up the stairs and entered his rooms, rushed through the hallway and into his bedchamber where we found him propped up on a mountain of variously cased pillows, calm as could be. Burgess sat in a chair by his side. I knelt down on the other side of his bed, a great four-poster. "I have had a hemorrhage," he turned his head to me and said composedly. Later when Burgess and Miss Kidd had both stepped out of the room for a moment (Burgess to wait to usher in the doctor, Miss Kidd to attend to some other chore) he said that he had tried to ring them when he collapsed but had only yanked the electric wiring of his bed lamp and not the bell cord. He had remained on the floor for hours. Within one more, the Doctor arrived and gave instructions. The master was to have complete bed rest.

Two days later, he had a second stroke, and things looked very bleak. I sent cables to both his sister-in-law and to Mrs. Wharton, who was then at Hyères and thus unable to come immediately, but in twenty-four hours he had rallied and, for the present at least, was out of danger, so when Mrs. Wharton cabled back that she could come if advisable, I sent back word that she needn't. I took things in hand until the arrival of his brother's widow. Dr. Des Voeux brought in the two nurses. The master had grown disoriented. He did not know where he was, kept imagining himself in this or that country and city. He grew feverish. Des Voeux diagnosed embolic pneumonia due to the formation of a clot in his lung. No longer the singular genius I knew, he became, degenerated into, simply a sick man. Yet within a week, he again seemed more himself. The proofs for the Brooke preface arrived, and I read them aloud to the invalid.

During the height of his fever, he decided that he wanted to write. He asked first for pen and paper but then he wanted to dictate so as of old I sat down before the typewriter. I don't know if he meant for this paragraph to be recorded, whether or not these observations were made just for my benefit; nonetheless I determined to set down everything that issued from his lips. Posterity would thank me. He spoke very slowly with breaks and pauses much longer than usual. He discoursed about his illness and his recent recuperative abilities, how he had rallied back from the very abyss. It seemed all in the way of prelude. The meat of his dictation would come after (or so I thought). But no, he abruptly broke off—perhaps he grew too tired to continue, to start after all—just when I thought that he was really about to commence. Here is the document. Let me hand it to you:

> I find the business of coming round about as important and glorious as I have had occasion to record, by which I mean that I find them as damnable and boring. It is not much better to discover within one's carcass new resources for application than to discover the absence of them; their being new doesn't somehow add to their interest but makes them stale and flat, as if one had long ago exhausted them. Such is my sketchy state of mind, but I feel sure I shall discover plenty of fresh worlds to conquer even if I am to be cheated of the amusement of them.

Yes, to my surprise, he did not dictate anything further. "For now," he said, that is quite enough." But several days later on December 11th—I have the entry dated in my notebook—he again called for me.

It seems, looking back at what I recorded that day (often missing one word or even several, not able to drive my modern mechanical "quill" fast enough to get it all down; the ellipses were both his and mine; he was disjunctive jumping half way through a sentence into another but I too missed words later adding those I was sure of in brackets) that what then came forth from my employer's mind was pure music, the old rhythm and cadence came so naturally to him, but the meaning of the passage is as illusive as a set of piano variations by Schubert or Schumann. What fearsome arpeggios took shape, were born, at my fingertips, *du bout des doigts*. Sense it had some—but all in all it was a very obscure poem. I think that he recalled the war, our world thrown into upheaval, in the second paragraph, but what he had been reading for the last several months—accounts of the Napoleonic wars—also fed into the passage. Again, let me show you the page, so you can read it yourself:

...the large old phrase into the right amplitude...we simply shift the sweet nursling of genius from one maternal breast to the other and the trick is played, the false note averted. Astounding little stepchild of God's astounding young stepmother!

...on this occasion moreover that, having been difficult to keep step ...we hear the march of history, what is remaining to that essence of tragedy, the limp?...

...mere patchwork transcription becomes of itself the high brave art. We...five miles off at the renewed affronts that we see coming for the great, and that we know that they will accept. The fault is that they have found themselves too easily great, and the effect of that, definitely, had been, within them, the want of long provision for it. It wasn't why they [were] to have been so thrust into the limelight and the uproar, but why they [were] to have known as by inspiration the trade most smothered in experience. They go about shivering in the absence of the holy protocol–they dodder sketchily about as in the betrayal of the lack of early advantages; and it is upon that they seem most to depend to give them distinction–it is upon that, and upon the cranerie and the rouerie that they seem most to depend for the grand air of gallantry. They pluck in their terror handfuls of plumes from the imperial eagle, and with no greater credit in consequence than that they face, keeping their equipoise, the awful bloody beak [of] that vindictive intention, during these days of cold grey Switzerland weather on the huddled and hustled after campaigns of the first omens of defeat. Everyone looks haggard and our only wonder is that they succeed in "looking" at all. It renews for us the assurance of the part played by that element in the famous assurance [divinity] that doth hedge a king.

The following day, December 12th, I would perform my duties one last time. Again he fixated on Napoleon Bonaparte. Ever since the war began, he kept reading on and on about the French General, that nation's old victories a source of comfort for him. Several months prior to his falling ill, his Roman acquaintance the Count Primoli–a Bonaparte–paid him a call and photographs of Princess Victor Napoleon had also appeared pretty constantly over the last several months in the papers. I think that day, he thought that he himself was the Corsican. First he dictated a short passage (after which we shared our luncheon) then he followed it (and our meal) with two short letters. In the first of these, he affected to be Bonaparte, pretended that he himself was the great dictator—he had the disposition and temperament of a King that day—and in the second he addressed his own dead bother and his wife Alice, who was currently in transit, on her way here across the choppy and submarine-infested waters of the Atlantic. He confused his family with that of Napoleon's, I think, in all three passages. Earlier in the morning, before the session began, he spoke about traveling to Europe as a boy in the company of his now long-dead father, how they had come to Chelsea and had paid a visit here to Carlyle. For the last several days he said over and over again—maintaining the truth of what he averred against all opposition—that Cork and Chelsea were now adjacent to one another. He grew worried, he had said, because several of his manuscripts had been sent inadvertently to Cork. Then he also recalled how he and his father had met Makepeace Thackeray and how that noted personage had taken a particular fancy to the burnished gold buttons on his little boy's coat. When I sat down at the Remington, my hands at the ready, he spoke perfectly clearly and coherently. I think in the passage he first dictated to me (which in point of fact ended as if it were a letter though it did not begin as one), he recalled his own dead sister and desired now to see her elevated. After our lunch though he clearly became the General. He insisted that I use the Corsican spelling of Bonaparte's name in the superscription to the first epistle. In the second missive (which he signed with his own name), I realized that he wrote to his deceased brother but I am not certain if he addressed this brother's living wife or the dead sister I referred to above. Both women bore the same first name: Alice. Nonetheless, in this second letter, he told the two people he communicated with that he had done what he had set out to do in life and was now inviting them to share in his triumphs. After he finished the second letter he appeared quite content and shortly thereafter fell into a peaceful sleep. All three texts fit neatly onto one and one half single-spaced pages. Here, I hand them to you, certain that you are interested in reading them as well. As I say these lines were the very last I was able to record:

> The Bonapartes have a kind of bronze distinction that extends to their fingertips and is a great source of charm in the women. Therefore they don't have to swagger after the fact; fortune has placed them too high and anything less would be trivial. You can believe anything of the Queen of Naples or of the Princess Caroline Murat. There have been great families of tricksters and conjurors; so why not this one, and so pleasant withal? Our admirable father keeps up the pitch. He is the dearest of men. I should have liked above all things seeing our sister pulling her head through the crown; one has that confident... and I should have had it most on the day when most would have been asked. But we jog on very well. Up to the point of the staircase where the officers do stand

it couldn't be better, though I wonder at the souffle which so often enables me to pass.

We are back from ...but we breathe at least together and I am devotedly yours...

Dear most esteemed Brother and Sister,

I call your attention to the precious enclosed transcripts of plans and designs for the decoration of certain apartments of the palaces here, the Louvre and the Tuileries, which you will find addressed in detail to artists and workmen who are to take them in hand. I commit them to your earnest care till the questions relating to this important work are fully settled. When that is the case I shall require of you further zeal and further taste. For the present the course is definitely marked out and I beg you to let me know from stage to stage definitely how the scheme promises and what results it may be held to inspire. It is, you will see, of a great scope, a majesty unsurpassed by any work of the kind yet undertaken in France. Please understand I regard these plans as fully developed and as having had my last consideration and look forward to no patchings nor perversions, and with no question of modifications either economic or aesthetic. This will be the case with all further projects of your affectionate Napoleone

My dear Brother and Sister,

I offer you great opportunities, in exchange for the exercise of great zeal. Your position as residents in our young but so highly considered Republic at one of the most interesting minor capitals is a piece of luck which may be turned to account in the measure of your acuteness and your experience. A brilliant fortune may come to crown it and your personal merit will not diminish the harmony. But you must rise to each occasion–the one I now offer you is of no common cast, and please remember that any failure to push your advantage to the utmost will be severely judged. I have displayed you as persons of great taste and judgement. Don't leave me a sorry figure in consequence but present me rather as your fond but

not infatuated relation, able and ready to back you up,
your faithful Brother and Brother-in-law

After her arrival, my employer's sister-in-law was at first very civil with me, and he, on his part, seemed very glad to see her. She said that she had a very bad crossing—that the ocean positively churned the whole time, as did her stomach. He answered that she had gone through a great deal to come and see him and that he was appreciative of that. Naturally, I relinquished all control of the gentleman and situation to her, but they allowed me to remain in the writer's presence, at least initially. I showed myself willing to render her any service and at first she seemed most responsive and grateful. So for yet another three weeks (until Peggy's arrival on the scene shortly after the new year), I observed the horrible, tedious, and slow process of the man's dying. He grew increasingly muddled and was often baffled and perplexed by the most trivial things. Once, I remember, he complained of the lack of male society, "with the negligible exception of Burgess and the doctor." Again and again he asserted that we were in Cork. His sister-in-law clarified that mystery. She said that he was remembering his mother's death. He had visited that Irish city only once. He had stopped there on his return to Europe shortly after his having attended the maternal funeral. For short periods, he would become unresponsive. His eyes would glaze, and he would not answer when someone called his name, sometimes not even if his shoulder or hand were tapped. He did not ask to dictate, but he would make movements with his hand as if he wrote with a pen and sometimes would make large flourishes in the air. If he would grow agitated, I would tap on the machine. The pecking noises always seemed to calm him. On occasion, he would sit up in his wheelchair perfectly silent for a long time, and then suddenly he would address you. I recorded in my diary how once he abruptly called out my name as I sat opposite him on the chesterfield: "Miss Bosanquet, this place in which I find myself is the strangest mixture of Edinburgh and Dublin and New York and some other places I don't know." Just before Christmas, he looked, I remember, desperately ill. If ever a man appeared dying, he certainly did, but again and again he would slump down only to rebound once more. On the holiday itself, he went into a momentous rage, became the image of old Lear railing on the heath. The next day quite a little movement had returned to his paralyzed side; his exertion had yielded positive results. He kept saying that he had gone completely insane, but he made all of us swear—take a solemn oath—that we would not reveal his present mental state to anyone. Miss Wharton's name came up. I had posted her all along on the progression of his illness, but he said that he particularly did not want her to know the extent of his deterioration, to which the Madame quickly assented. I kept writing anyway. One of his dearest friends and greatest admirers, she had every right to know.

My difficulty with his American relatives really began after the niece joined her mother. From then on, I found myself, each day to an ever-greater extent, ostracized by the two American ladies. Very quickly I received the impression that they no longer extended me their welcome, that I was being given, as the Americans say, the cold shoulder. I already mentioned how shocked I was at how lightly the sister-in-law took it when the King conferred the Order of Merit on the dying man on the first day of the new year January 1st, 1915. I remember some dignitary brought the insignia to the master's bedside, and how he had appeared so gratified to receive it. He told Miss Kidd to "Turn off the lights as to spare my blushes." Peggy arrived only several days later and only a short time after that I received that horrible jar when I picked up and read the note she had written and left out on purpose, I am sure, so I would find it. That same day the gentleman said to me to tell Edmund Gosse that his powers of recuperation were very great and that he was making progress towards recovery without withdrawal. Peggy's brother appeared shortly after her. I wrote in my diary a description of him: "Nearly white-haired but still black-moustached, he has a tremendous chin—the most obstinate-looking jaw." His mother dispatched him immediately to Rye for he had been made his Uncle's executor and the master's manuscripts had all to be inventoried. Peggy's and her mother's animosity towards me continued to increase. One day I inquired if I should write to the gentleman's agent Mr. Pinker, and Mrs. William snapped at me that she would write if and when she found it necessary. As I jotted down in my diary, the presumptuous secretary was put in her place. She slunk out of the presence of righteousness. For the rest of January and now into February, though I call almost everyday, the two ladies tell me that there is nothing that I can do. Some days they are a little friendlier than others. On several occasions I have been allowed to go in and see my old employer, but always only for the briefest of intervals. I have kept in communication with Mrs. Wharton and some of my present dolour must have seeped into my letters for recently she offered me a position with her. She wrote me and said that I could serve as her secretary. Of course I declined. I wrote back that I was not proficient in French which is an out and out lie, as anyone who knows me and of my penchant for the poems of Paul Valéry will attest. No, now that my gentleman is about to die, I must finally begin my own work. I will not serve as another person's secretary.

Several days ago, Miss Kidd let me up into the master's drawing room. Two or three other visitors had been admitted and Mrs. William and Peggy were both out. The master sat at the window, touching his finger to the pane. Burgess came in and swung the wheel-chair around so the invalid would face his guests. He raised his good hand high into the air. The tip of his long fine forefinger touched the end of his thumb to form a perfect ring. "This is a desperately long tunnel I see," he said, "but I do make out a gleam of blue at its far end."

I have not seen him since. It has been close to two weeks now.

Miss Kidd

What's a serving gerl te do? The answer's simple, serve, don take charge! I allays tuk my orders straight frem the lips of the Guvnur. I hurd it from 'is ain tung. But now 'e's all in the derk, 'as made uh real pother uv 'imself an 'as turned all bitterish. I don noe if we can stand 'im as 'e iz now—any maur. 'E's nasty with everyone, spec'lly the nurses. 'E 'as even thrown ah plate uv fud at won of 'em after calling 'er ah filthy nime, but 'e's lost his mind. The things thet cum out uv 'is mouth don make sens. 'E assed me won day if the plumers 'ad made the propper alterashins in the bathroom. I begged 'is pardon and said thet no plumers 'ad te my nawledge been called in, and 'e burst into a rage and called me an ingrate. "I shud dismiss you ferthwith," 'e said. I cried into my 'anky all day. We stay, the servants, becuz we love 'im and r'member 'ow 'e used to be. Now 'e's furi'us angry with everyboddy. Burgess says no matter 'ow much abuse 'e 'eaps on us jest to smaiul an try an do all we can fer 'im.

After the Guvnur fell ill, Miss Bosanquet took over running the 'ouse and we all defurd t'er. In fact it was I who fetched 'er. I went straight over te 'er Lawrence Street apartment and told 'er that the master 'ad uh stroke and she 'ad better come raite an. She maide all the more impertant desicishns. We abdehcatd all 'thority te 'er, served 'er in fact, carried out all 'er many wims and wishes jest like she wes our new Mistress. She determined who the Guvnur could see an for 'ow long. Many visiters—old frens of 'is—ped calls, but the docters sed he must not tire 'imself, that 'e 'ad te get plenty of rest, so she 'ad te limit access te 'is bedchamber. Now that 'is kinfolk 'ave arrived frem across the water, it's they that must be defurd to and not 'im nor 'er. A good servant disappears into the background. That is a pint Miss B. jest didn't get, despite her being so natcherly bright and talented. I wish I could read and rite wurds like she. What wes she thinkin' then puttin' on airs like she doon? Nae in the whole wide wurrld would I do sech a thing. I don think it wes a conshus fault or shortcoming on 'er part. She wes simply too kind and preposed to take too much on 'er ain shoulders. Whether assed or not, she was always off'ring 'er pinions on evry subject under the sun and val'nteer'ng to do this and that. They jest found her too meddlesome and self-important. Uppitish is the word the Madame used, and that's not a propper way for uh servant te act. Ye do as y're told. You sit down immediately in the rush-bottom'd chais if thet's the command of your betturs! The Guvnur caint write me no ref'rence—not in 'is present mad state. No it's up te 'is sister-in-law te extol my worth to eny future employer. Fur me te find a position today in thes present 'ard times, she must say thet I'm really a very profis'ent maid. She'll 'ave to lay it on thick and 'eavy, I'm efred. My 'erbert says I 'ave to keep uh position if we're ever te git married.

It wes I after all who found 'im on the bedroom floor. The first thing he said looking up at me from where 'e lay on the carpet wes thet "the beast 'ad finally sproong."

I'd stay now even if I was te get nuffin'. For when my muther fell ill recently, the Guvnur kindly fuhted 'er bills, even though 'e was under no sech oblegeshn. I'll never furget that kindness. If 'is relations wern't seein' to 'im propper, I'm sure I would res Cain, even if it would be to no purpose, but they are so selicitess, they look after 'is each and evry need. They duhserve three cheers fer attending te 'im so. Now te be fair, Miss B., befor the 'Merican lady arrived, 'erself was a very gud caretaker, but she jest wouldn't step aside grasf'ly. And that wes 'er downfall. It's not that I'm no longer being respec'ful or that I'm purpes'ly trying te shun Miss Bosanquet. I like 'er, thank y'kindly. After all I let 'er in thet one time when both the ladies, muther and daughter, wes out. But I noe 'ow te act t'ward my betturs and she don't. A gud servant is jest like a little chaild, bet'er seen than haird, I says. The Guvnur—'e 'as both his gud and bad daiz now. It's 'is weeping and sobbing that's so 'ard fer all of us, family and servants both, to take. But when 'e's sitting in 'is wheelchair at the window, so contented and peaceful staring out over the chimneypots down at 'is boats on the river, we jes let 'im be—for 'ours at a time.

Dr. Des Voeux

I have never seen a patient with a more tenacious grip on Life than my present literary man. The process has begun and the conclusion, I am afraid, is quite inevitable. It is only a matter of time. The question of *exactly* how much time is what's difficult to predict accurately. Having been caught so many times before, I hesitate to venture any guesses though if prodded and pushed I will hazard that it won't be another two months, the time that has passed now since his initial attack December 2nd. True, he has great reserves of strength but surely those stores must soon be depleted. Nay, now must be utterly exhausted! The man has a very strong will, that is what has kept him going up to now, but his body is just giving out; he is winding down like an old clock. The spring is about to snap. I have seen it before. However, as I remarked when I first began to attend him back in 1913, this particular patient does have extraordinarily great powers of recuperation. We have witnessed these abilities over and over again during his present illness. After his second stroke December 3rd, I didn't think he would last out the night, yet within several days he sat up in his chair calling out for one of his books. During the Christmas holidays, he grew so irate at the world, his present diminished condition, the war or what have you, that he struggled in his chair, thrashed about as if an invisible foe cudgeled him. His systolic blood pressure had to have risen well above 200. Surely such actions upon anyone else's part would have brought on a third and fatal stroke, but not in his case. He fought his way out of—at least partially—his state of paralysis. A good deal of movement returned to his up-to-then frozen limbs. Still I am quite confident informing his relatives that his death will soon be at hand. The process sometimes is cruel, tedious, and long whereas in other cases death can be mercifully quick and sudden, totally unexpected. I have witnessed in my career many, many deaths. No two are quite identical in progress and even process, though all are the same in conclusion. Early on I predicted that, as he held on with both hands, as it were, dying, in his case, would be sadly a quite protracted affair, and I have been proven right in the issue. He knew years in advance that stroke or heart attack would fell him. He had a family history that condemned him finally to such a demise unless the hand of God (or his own hand for that matter) intervened. He did not meet his death in some accident, nor did he put a bullet in his brain, so nature in the end will have its way with him; the familiar motif would sound once more. He informed me in 1913 after suffering his first fainting spell that his mother had died quite unexpectedly at age seventy-one, that her heart simply stopped all of a sudden, and that his father after several strokes became clouded and confused yet was quite happy and becalmed withal believing that he was about to enter into his spiritual life where he would be reunited with his wife. Moreover two of his brothers died of heart attack, including the eminent physician and philosopher. True, he *did* have a sister who died of cancer, but she was the exception that proved the rule. It would be his heart, my patient was quite certain of it. He said that he had begun experiencing chest pains at the very time when his brother had his last attacks. He said that he had heard of bushmen whose wives were in labour who feigned they gave birth as well, but in his case, the attack was real and not the proper subject for any psychological investigation. I doubt, however, if his late brother would have been of the same mind.

A family pattern remains imprinted in all our brains like a sort of pre-set heading. Perhaps we fit ourselves to the paradigm unconsciously, carry our deaths *in ovo* and *in mora* within us. Something triggers the mechanism and the death process, up to then held in check, activates. Perhaps in the end we will and desire and lust for nothing more than restful sleep? I've seen many a patient retire happily to his deathbed. Paradoxically my client desires and wills for both life and death. He remains of two minds and thus his present struggle, manifested at Christmas by his thrashing in his wheelchair as if he tussled with an invisible opponent, is also internal, fighting itself out within him.

Joan Anderson

My joints ache. The rheumatism runs through my whole body today, yet work is much more demanding, much more taxing, than it's ever been since I joined the staff as 'is cook. Not only do I 'ave to follow the doctor's orders concerning 'is food—none of 'is dishes are to be seasoned with salt; I'm to cut off all fat from 'is meats—but there are all the meals to be prepared for 'is relations not to mention the two women in starched whites, and Burgess and Miss Kidd. Though to be fair in all my years of service, the last two have never once complained or found fault. That slip of a girl fears me. She knows our respective stations in this household and she knows I know her secret, that she has grown to marriageable age but that she does not know how to read and write. When I put a book in front of her and made her try, she struggled and struggled trying to sound out words until she was finally brought to tears. I may drop my aitches, but I can read my Bible. She can't read her betrothed's letters. Why the man is old enough to be 'er father. A reprobate and a drinker but he can write. I 'ave to read 'is letters to 'er and write 'er answers back. She wants to keep 'im in the dark about her great failing until they're married. But the master's family, the blighters, they have their ways and wants! They all are, 'specially the lady, very particular, and that's the God's truth! She's always sending perfectly good dishes back. She never can be placated or satisfied. When I agreed to come work for 'im, I thought it would be an easy job. And it was, but ever since 'e fell ill, he lingers, lingers, lingers. I wish 'e'd make done with it and die forthwith, so I could at long last retire. One of my daughters will surely have a room ready for me. My career as a domestic will be over. I'm simply too old now. I'm paid very well, so I must stay and not give my notice, even though death 'as entered the place and I would feign be gone. I must look it straight in the face once again, as I 'ave done many time afore. It is a 'ard thing, for I know I'm not getting any younger; I realize it will be me that's struck down next. I don't dare to 'ope that I'll get up. Muckle good watching him die will do me, and the Americans like I say—they run me ragged. The sweat pours out of me. I am forever wiping my brow in this hot kitchen. All their lives these Americans have been waited on 'and and foot. We owe our service, but isn't it shameful how they treat us? The lady barely deigns to recognize me. She expects us to disappear into our duty. We're all interchangeable to 'er and she believes 'erself so far above us I suspect she thinks us all as illiterate as Miss Kidd.

Oh how I wish 'e'd git his dyin' done! Bless me I've even thought about 'elpin' 'im to 'is just reward by pouring cups of salt into his soup. If I 'ad access to the doctor's bag I'd mix something into his gruel to put him under and do 'im in. It's bound to 'appen anyway, so why prolong it? Aye, I'd put an end to his suffrin', so I would. Is there wrong with that might I ask? Live as long as you can then die peas'bly at your own 'and or someone else's. No, they don't 'ave to worry. He don't mean enough to me, 'e's not my 'usband or father, that I risk the peelers cuffing and 'auling me off to 'ang for 'aving putting paid to 'im. If the doctors want to keep 'is poor dying soul alive for a little longer, if they want to lengthen 'is suffering who am I to gainsay it?

Mrs. William

Alice, I told myself, you better see if Angel attends, so halting at the first period, I looked up from my Bible (I had begun with five or six psalms but had moved on to the first chapter of the Book of John) and stared at my poor brother-in-law, such a sweet and kindly man his entire life, but now positively a demon at times. In his nightshirt, the covers torn off him and kicked to the floor, he sat at the head of the bed, a pillow between his back and the headboard, one pale white leg raised, the knee pulled upward to his belly, the other extended straight ahead with toes pointed at the door. His privates would be exposed to anyone opening and entering right now, but the way he constantly turned it was no use asking him to put his leg down, he'd only move into another awkward position in a few minutes, and I had already covered him several times in the last hour, only for him on each and every occasion to kick off the sheets, quilt and blankets. My last attempt I tried only the sheet and one blanket, thinking that maybe he had become too warm, but he still pitched and lurched in bed all the same.

I sit beside the four-poster, the bureau behind me, with a pleasant view, across his midriff out the window, of skyscape. When I asked him half an hour ago if I might read to him, his eyes shut as usual, he nodded his assent. The way he thrashed under his blankets made me, as I've already said, stop several times to recover him. At each break I asked if I should discontinue reading out loud, if he was tired. His eyelids still lowered, he barked out a "no no go on go on" whenever I inquired. But now I notice that he is of a sudden still. His breathes slowly and peacefully. Relaxed, his eyes open and he stares at the polished black door. Suddenly I become aware that a cross is "hidden" between its four squares, a thinner raised and beaded rectangle protruding from each. The cross stands in plain view but I only saw it now. I blink. It remains. It prevails. The right half of its horizontal beam terminates just under the knob and keyhole. I again look at my brother-in-law, then back and forth several times. Yes, he stares at the cross! Once more I begin to read from the word of John, every so often glancing out the parted yellow curtains at the stunning sky, saucer blue in shade.

On just such a bright winter day as this in 1882, our eccentric Angel took his well-composed farewell letter to the graves of his parents and I gather unrolled it like a scroll and declaimed for twenty minutes to the marble headstones. On neither occasion did he arrive on time, being in Washington when his mother Mary expired unexpectedly in January of that year—I had wired him that she ailed and that he should come at once—and eleven months later, at the time of his father's falling desperately ill, he had just returned to London from a long ramble on the continent, where my husband William, on sabbatical leave, having abandoned me so soon after the birth of our second boy, remained even then. That December, as I recall, Bill resided in Paris studying I believe with Charcot at his Salpètrière clinic. The sons agreed that only one of them should sail to America. Angel took passage home and my husband afterward crossed the channel and insinuated his way into Henry's apartment in Bolton Street to await word. But the old man died and we buried him the very morning Angel's ship moored in New York. My father-in-law's last thoughts turned to his recently departed wife. He called out he would join her soon and for that reason his sickroom became a place of great joy and gladness.

Yes, on just such a day the maid admitted Angel to my house, and he visited with the two children and me for a couple of hours. He told me what he had done, how under the bright sun he stood a solitary figure in the cemetery amid the drifts of snow looking at the fields across the Charles River, and read on and on. Staring at the two stones, he said, he gazed into the eyes of Medusa herself. Life could show no uglier face. Oh how he was mistaken! The whooping cough felled my darlingest little youngster and sent him off to heaven. What could be worse, pray tell, than the loss of your child? If the boy hadn't died, we would have reproduced an exciting duplicate of the family of my husband and brother-in-law and their siblings and parents. We would have had five sons and one daughter just like Mary and Henry Sr., but my last little boy perished and we buried him. The years went by, Father, Mother, my friends, and finally my beloved husband—William—passed. Again and again you have to watch those you care for exit this life, and now—an old woman myself—I alone am left to minister to poor Angel, he has no other family to see him through. When my time comes, when I am called to an afterlife (we are not allowed to make contact with those who have preceded us; Heaven isn't vouchsafed to mortal eyes: we must have faith that it exists), my four children Harry, Billy, Margaret, and Alex will I hope stand round my bed. I am lucky. *We are not allowed to make contact*, I repeat to myself. Due to William's final injunctions, I tried and tried, never meeting with sure success. It's just because I have grown tired from staying up nights to soothe him when he awakes from dreaming that this has happened. I also hallucinate—not just my poor brother-in-law! I know it! But I must cease with these pointless speculations.

Yesterday February 24th was a red-letter day—he seemed so like his old self— but a very bad night followed. So this morning, I feel wearier than I did upon my arrival after the rough Atlantic crossing. What happened remains ever so shocking! As usual, after luncheon, I pushed his wheelchair over the blue Wilton, with its pattern of yellow diamonds, to his favorite window. Peggy had just gone out for, she said, a long walk. When I launched him up to the glass, he quietly addressed me. "Alice," he said, "would you kindly take some dictation?" "Certainly," I replied. He spoke slowly and at length. His clearness of mind amazed me.

"By way of preface," he began, "let me state right away, though I realize of course that you won't believe it—at least initially—that my memory has become almost superhuman."

He hung fire for ten slow seconds, then it came out in a rush: as if he read from a prepared speech, so I hurried my pencil over the lined paper in my amazement, occasionally not keeping the words between the two ruled lines, several of my sentences slanting downwards across the margin. I would have rapped my pupils' fingers for copying so sloppily. One or two of the things he said I didn't like right as they came out, just as soon as he uttered them, but I didn't concentrate primarily on the content of his words. I directed my energy instead into putting his words on paper, catching them, as if with a net, then spreading and pinning their fluttering wings down onto the satin, before slipping them under glass.

"Through intensely recalling prior events," he said, "I find that I relive them, that I can travel into the past. That may in part explain to you my confusion of the last several days. Or is it longer? It doesn't much matter. At any rate, do you now understand, bewildered by the puzzle as you have been up to now, that though I seemed out of place and lost to you, as if I didn't know where I stood or sat, that actually my sense of place grew keener than yours. I just happened to be at another spot than you: one that I was revisiting as it were. Now I remember details from years gone by that I had previously forgotten, every word of ancient conversations for example. I can summon the world all back, as if I simply sat down, opened an old book and reread it. Everything stored in my brain, events now repeat themselves, echoing and reverberating at my direction and will. I relive something past and dead but—*basta!*—I cannot alter it. I keep falling asleep and waking up somewhere else. Everything always changes, so no wonder I seem confused! I keep praying for clarity, Alice dear. I don't wish to be fooled. I will work myself out of this maze. The solution will come to me. But all the while I keep taking jaunts back into my deceased life. At times, I seem to have returned to the youthful body I once resided in, and I look out into the world from it. At others, I remain on the outside, watching myself act in the world as if I were indeed captured on motion picture, as if the Henry I see is a different person than me, a character in one of my books, someone whose existence remains totally independent of mine, another individual entirely, a he instead of an I. But then whenever I become engrossed with what happens to this character, when I get caught up with what goes on, I become him. I enter his body all over again. The he changes over into the I. Do you follow me? Yet I have been aware—part of me at any rate—of what occurs all the while here at Carlyle Mansions. Yes I recall your arrival, how you said the ocean was choppy and that you retched several times. Then you asked me if I remembered Mr. Bruce Porter from San Francisco. I didn't then, but I do now! I met him at Robert Louis Stevenson's widow's. He's an architect correct? He hoped to win the commission to sculpt Stevenson's memorial in that city. But he also wrote verse and believed that Shakespeare had woven secret ciphers into all his plays. Fancy such rank stupidity! Stick to landscape gardening I told him. But the day of your arrival, you said he and Peggy became fast friends on the basis of their love for me, and I replied: 'A pretty feeble basis.' After dinner you wanted to brush the little hair I have left and I told you that ardent brushing would not mitigate my troubles. Then in the days that followed, I instructed you not to speak of my condition before the nurses. Do you remember how I told Theodora Bosanquet in your presence that I needed someone whom I could ask if my extraordinary state of utter dependence upon the good offices of these quite well meaning ladies didn't strike them as uncanny in the same way it struck me? If I am not mistaken—correct me if I err, Alice—she replied that I was ill, that I would understand what was unclear to me now when I got stronger and that I needed to eat to become stronger. You know Alice, you behaved quite naughtily when you expelled her. And, of course, I believe you recall the night I thought one of my plays, *Guy Domville* I believe, was being produced, and, quite worried, I asked you, 'What effect will my madness have on the house?' You see my complete recollection Alice? I can also remember verbatim words, sentences, paragraphs, pages of what I have written. Some of the material is decades old. Did you ever read 'The Jolly Corner,' my tale concerning a man and, horrible Hun word, his *doppelgänger*? When Spencer Brydon sees that the door hitherto locked has sprung open, and that a staircase descends from it into the darkness, he rushes through and plunges down the steps. As he goes down, the shades at its foot coalesce. Something takes form. He sees the ghost that is himself and yet not him. To impress you, I'll recite the last couple sentences, the description of what he sees ... his planted stillness, his grizzled bent head and white masking hands, his queer actuality of evening dress, of dangling double eye-glass, of gleaming silk lappet and white linen, of pearl button and gold watch-guard and polished shoe. No portrait by a great modern artist could have presented him with more intensity, thrust him out of his frame with more art. Yes, "The Jolly Corner" remains a fine bit of work. Superior, since his name came up earlier, to Robert Louis Stevenson's *Dr. Jekyll and Mr. Hyde*, or for that matter to that horrible Wilde's *Portrait of Dorian Grey*. No the word portrait was in one of my titles. He used the more generic term: picture. Alice I wanted to be William, but I find out that I'm able to stand apart from him. I'm my own entity. The ghost story that I could write now would exceed—would far outdo—my old tale about a man pursuing his *alter ego* and finally pinning it down, encountering and defeating it. In that by now quite passé and precious piece, my character Brydon had been abroad for thirty years but returned to the States to renovate a Manhattan property he had inherited. Staying at another place, the house he grew up in on lower 5th Avenue, he wonders what he would have become if he had never left New York. His friend Alice Staverton tells him that by now he would be a millionaire. I chose the friend's first name very carefully, my dear; I'm sure you recognize its antecedent, your name and my sister's too. Peggy's counterpart, the sole girl as opposed to the quartet of boys. He thinks about whom he might have been, paces through the rooms of his house at night, holding a fluttering candle aloft to light his way. Then he goes down the secret stairs. The ghost he confronts will be as nothing compared to the spectre in the new tale. Yes, the Huns have been brutal! The martial character of Germany's people is as cliché-ridden and bombastic as its loud operas-the sets to one of which the friend of my youth designed, the Russian dilettante Paul von Joukovski—shall I spell his name for you? Do you keep up? I made a point of finding out all I could about that—use quotation marks—"music drama," because of the involvement of my friend in the first production of the work, even though I hated the composer-in-question's music...."

On and on he went, discussing pomposity and grandiloquence in Art. I wrote down his words diligently, not daring to ask my so-suddenly revitalized brother-in-law for the spellings I wasn't sure of. For the life of me, I wouldn't break his train of thought. Later I would check my orthography with a dictionary and recopy. However, he began criticizing his own writing, which unfamiliar with much of it as I am, I did not like to see him do. Again he spoke about the story he wanted, intended, to write, but his thoughts which up to then had so admirably hung together began wandering elsewhere. Tired and worn out, he told me, that he must continue composing. The words ceased. I looked up. His head had fallen to one side. His eyes had drooped shut, his lips a lopsided pink comma wiggling, trying to straighten. He slept several hours, until dinner when we awoke him. He took little food. The pimply-faced midget and the large cross-eyed buck-toothed nurse, what's her name, Milly, shifted him out of his chair and into bed. He kicked and tossed and turned and woke up screaming four or five times during the night. I sat up with him till dawn.

The sun had risen when I got out of my chair at his bedside to go to Mrs. Anderson's dreary breakfast (not seasoning a dish with anything but salt and pepper is the least of her crimes; each meal is poorly prepared, ever only half-cooked and rarely served on time), that I thought I heard William speaking through him. Their voices for a moment sounded so much alike, that, for several seconds, I thought Angel had become his brother's medium. "Stay with me, Alice, stay with me," he pleaded, and I did—I had to obey my husband's voice—taking Henry's hand into mine and squeezing it. Siblings in their everyday verbalization often sound alike, I afterward told myself, trying to put a stop to the direction my thoughts were taking, to prevent any more wild ideas entering my head. A natural enough phenomenon brothers and sisters speaking similarly, something observable in every village and town. My being without sleep had also played its part: Tired and susceptible, I recollected that forty-eight hours had passed since Henry said to me on the 23rd, "Beloved Alice, tell my brother I come to join him in two days' time. Relay it to him, helpful creature to both William and me." Then I thought that he had a premonition of his own death and that he asked me to notify William that he would shortly reunite with him on the Other Side. I would be his conduit to the dead! As if I were in communication! But, no, contact is not vouchsafed to us. After letting go his hand, I asked if he would like me to read from the Bible. He kept his eyes shut but nodded affirmatively. Every few minutes he turned kicking in bed. But now he looks at the cross shining—positively throbbing—in open declaration between the four ornate squares in the door. He breathes deeply and contentedly as I continue to read scripture to him.

At the sound of the knock I stirred. "Not yet," I said, bounding up from my chair, tapping Henry's knee and making him put his right leg down and extend it straight like the left. I then tugged his nightshirt to his ankles to make him look semi-presentable.

"Enter," I said, resuming my seat. It's either Peggy or Miss Kidd. Ah, I see it's the latter. Such a lithe little young thing, she bows her head and gives a shake to all the blonde curls coming out at the back and sides of her cap of muslin and lace. "Anything needful, mum?" she asks me.

I told her she might brew me some tea, and she replied, yes, mum, and left the room even quicker than she had come into it. With the possible exception of her, I cannot tolerate any of the domestics here. The Anderson woman is old and on her last legs, yes, but that does not justify the perfunctory manner in which she performs her duties, her slapdash style in the kitchen. Maybe she nods over her pots; everything remains either under or over done, just like this morning's breakfast: half cooked bacon and egg served with burnt toast and cold coffee. Then there are the hired nurses Anne and Milly. They try hard but are certainly not used to working with a demanding and belligerent patient: Anne screams and runs from the sickroom whenever Angel rages; I have found her sitting on the stairs, both hands to her face, hysterically crying. A big girl, Milly can and will hold him down but she remains tentative about everything she does. They both seem right out of school. Des Voeux assures me that both are quite competent, but then, fakes and charlatans, European doctors lie perpetually. None of those we visited on the continent or in England helped my poor William. This Des Voeux is just the same. He chiefly wants to appear learned to us, which is not difficult for he is: very. However he receives bad marks in the practical application of his art. I can't see that he's doing anything for Henry other than examining him as if he served as a specimen in some experiment. He keeps predicting how long his patient will last. Angel does his best to keep outdistancing his guesses, simply won't oblige him and give up the ghost on schedule, much like a woman unable to go into labor and carrying past her due date. To achieve the desired result, the physician will in the one case have to administer a morphine injection and in the other break the bag of water. It would be better for Henry if right now he were in the hands of one of our American country doctors instead of those of this British theorist, someone who, in his long practice, in the course of his many house visits, has brought hundreds of souls into the world and has helped an equal number to depart the very same life. But to return to the domestics. I have even become disillusioned with his two favorites (the very individuals I had never presumed to find fault with, who heretofore had not once given grounds for dissatisfaction) the valet Burgess Noakes, whom I have known and liked for many years and Angel's typist Theodora Bosanquet, who practically became Peggy's best friend four or five summers ago and whom my late husband also thoroughly liked. Disposed to esteem these two as I was, it came as quite a shock when their true natures were revealed. Oh, not at first or all at once, but remember I have been here now for two months, and that which is rank and rotten will always surface. Shortly after my arrival, in fact, I witnessed such a touching scene in my brother-in-law's bedroom: little Burgess sitting in the chair beside Angel's bed, squeezing his hand, his face held very close to my brother-in-law's, as he struggled to make out the words Henry murmured, but Burgess hardly ever responded when I called out to him. He ignored my repeated solicitations. The typist and Miss Kidd said his inattention was due to his war injuries, so I was inclined to be charitable, but then one day unable to find him anywhere, I knocked on the door then entered his servant's quarters, and discovered all those smutty French post cards (dancing girls performing in beaded headdresses and garish costumes, kicking their legs high, some brazenly bare breasted!) scattered on his dresser. The same day Brother-in-law coupled our name with that of this servant's, called him Burgess James. Yes, the gnome is completely devoted to him, but I found Henry's making him one of us rather sickening and disgraceful. Only his illness excuses it. The pimply Onan does not deserve the elevation. I speak my mind, and I've got a practical philosophy of life. I don't care if I'm labeled heartless and unsentimental. I must get down to the matter at hand right away. What needs done will be. Items have to be tallied. His possessions must be cataloged. It is not that he has any great treasures at either Lamb House or Carlyle Mansions, though he does own a few choice pieces. We had much better furnishings at both Chocorua and Irving Street. I remember quite well that on his first inspection of his brother's Rye property (in '99 was it?) my husband had not been that impressed with either the house or its furnishings, but Angel's many belongings are stored and displayed there. The task simply has to be undertaken and completed. We can't hope that he'll ever get well, so it's best to determine right now what furniture shall be shipped to America. It is right that the choicer pieces remain in the family, with those who still bear the name. No, I say, never put off or procrastinate. Face everything squarely. Whatever looms, look it in the eye and meet it as it comes, never shirk or turn away. You can always find the fortitude inside yourself to stand up to any challenge.

But let me continue. Theodora, on the other hand, made me feel uncomfortable and on my guard from the day of my arrival. She seemed so firmly in charge; it appeared that I stood in the way. Positively, she did not want to place the reins in my hand. And then she made no bones of the fact that she kept a journal of Henry's end (something I also had decided to do), so we became as great competitors as if we worked for opposing publishing houses or city newspapers. I determined that my version would make the superior document, that it would have the greater ring of truth. It stood against my best business interests not to dismiss her immediately. Then the story would remain exclusively mine. She wouldn't witness Henry's death, and thus would have nothing to record. Of course, however, I couldn't deny her access on those grounds. That wouldn't be ethical. But when I heard from Peggy that contrary to my expressed wishes, the girl continued apprizing Mrs. Wharton of Angel's condition, I realized that she herself did not have a very high moral character and I could toss my own scruples to the winds. She got, as Peggy said, "a bit above herself." For that, because of her obvious care and concern for Henry, I could forgive her, but not for her continued intercourse with Mrs. Wharton. The minx brazenly disobeyed me; she regarded that Wharton woman so highly. I wouldn't want any young girl of my acquaintance to associate with that wanton. I certainly would not leave my Peggy alone in her company. Such a corrupting influence, especially for those still innocent. I must admit, however, that even in her banishment (for from the moment of Peggy's revelation I began excluding her), Miss Bosanquet still shows an interest in the well-being of my brother-in-law. She comes around almost every morning to ask if she can do anything for him. Most often we turn her away, though I will allow her every now and then to look in on the patient. He still asks for his amanuensis. Her presence seems to calm him, so I allow him little doses occasionally. I, however, am through with her. She reminds me of a character in that ridiculous book of Angel's which since coming over to tend him I have again taken a stab at reading, of the wicked penniless English girl Kate Croy who pretends to befriend the ailing and naive American heiress only to work against her, to use and manipulate her for the furtherance of her own ends: she covets Milly's money so she will marry her off to her lover Merton Densher. After the girl's death the spoils will fall to them.

In fact, I took several of his novels down from the shelf and browsed through the first pages of each. One *What Maisie Knew*, I gathered, he told from the point of view of a little girl. No doubt for him to have given it to his young heroine, the name must have appealed especially to Henry. His books *were* in fact his children. He, the constructor of verbal mazes, was indeed, in word, her father. Every time I open one of his creations, I take a deep breath to overcome my reluctance and to steel myself. You know in advance that it is going to be a hard go, worse almost than a bumpy Atlantic crossing. I've managed to slog through some of his shorter volumes, the ones he wrote when younger, but I have never been able to get very far, much less finish, those three last monsters. It seems strange to me, the notice and regard shown to his work by the British public. I can't deny that he hasn't made a mark in his chosen field. He was important, William always said so, but I previously imagined that the British people would pretty much ignore him, preferring their own Dickens, as I must admit do I. Books should entertain. One should not knit one's brows over them! My hands would sweat. His prose made me so uncomfortable and fidgety, so befuddled and lost. It goes without saying that I skipped the unreadable sermonizing prefaces! But the English adore him and stand in awe of his work. I will always think well of our Angel: not in his author aspect but for all his numerous kindnesses. For me he will forever remain humble 'Enry, my husband's highly eccentric but amiable little brother. I had come to know him long before we actually met, he figured so prominently in my fiancé's recollections of their shared boyhood.

Bill gave me an account of how they had run races through the halls of the Louvre, as young children! Their father had started the madness–this taking of mere babes to Europe. William would emulate him. Our family too would go, even though the children remained much too young to appreciate anything the first several times. From a very early age, my husband and his brother never really got along. William confessed to me all his childhood sins against his littler sibling, the many slurs and taunts, the occasional blow. Nonetheless Henry always tried to court his brother's favor, but William constantly rebuffed him–called Henry a sissy and refused to play with him, for my future husband was much too proud of his position as older brother. He associated, he said, with tougher, bigger boys who weren't afraid to swear. He mockingly taunted the younger son. He teased constantly, teasingly shouting "Angel, Angel, Angel," their mother's nickname for him, later our term of love and endearment. Even so, Henry still tried to emulate him in everything, but Bill would never let him catch up, would move on ahead to something else whenever Henry came up close on his heels in an attempt to overtake him. Perhaps the nearness of their births—only fifteen months separated them—explains their extreme jealousy and competitiveness and why Henry identified so closely with his older brother. He simply had to. They might as well have been twins. Years later whether he realized it or not, Henry still always attempted to copy my husband.

As a boy, he stood in awe in front of William's easel and even gaped sometimes at pencil sketches in his notepad. He wanted to become a painter too, but William said he couldn't be, for he had gotten there first and had beaten him to the punch. Henry didn't take up painting (and later William abandoned it) yet he entitled his water-to-wine novel *The Portrait of A Lady* after all. The brush had been denied him. He never produced aquarelles or fine oils. So he had to resort to the ink pen, his medium words. I don't think that they ever ceased fighting from the moment little Henry entered William's nursery. I wonder? My own children were not nearly so combative—more time stood between them—as, I gather, my husband and my brother-in-law had been. As youths, those two had shared the same life experiences—reached the same point of development—simultaneously, not a good thing. No wonder they grew so close, yet acted so aggressively, in such a dog-eat-dog manner, with one another.

A young mother, I finally met Angel. He did not come over for the ceremony in '78. He could not be faulted; we had simply decided to take prompt action and wed almost immediately. When notified of our engagement, he wrote back to William that he had long wished to see him married, and that he believed almost as much in matrimony for other people as he believed in it little for himself. Oh how I long for those times, my hair a beautiful dark brown and tied in a bow, not white as now. I was by far the prettiest and most practical girl Billy ever fell in love with. Back then someone always turned his head and put him down on one knee, from which position he declared his undying affection. The first who said yes, I also came from good enough family for his parents to accept and to welcome unconditionally. My entering Bill's life had been the best possible thing for him, for I turned my love straight, whipped him into shape, got him out of a rut of ten years' duration, one of his very own making. With me, with what I supplied to his life that up to then he lacked and needed, his career as philosopher and psychologist could begin in earnest. At the time of our marriage he finally had inked his first publisher's contract. He had fallen sadly behind his younger brother in terms of production. Their careers never ran parallel, one's high point invariably the other's nadir.

As I said, William and I wed after the briefest engagement. We received a strange letter full of hurt from his brother after he heard from their mother of our nuptials. He wrote that, as he was "divorced" from us by an untimely fate on the occasion of our wedding that he could at least write us to repair the injury with the most earnest words that his clumsy pen could muster. The scolding tone, the icy irony of the letter, stood readily apparent, and then within the year his novel *Confidence* began appearing in serial installments in *Scribner's*. Henry issued it in book form in December of '79 but afterwards called it his worst production. "Have no fear, Alice," he said to me on a much later date, "that wretched piece of drivel will certainly not find a place in my collected edition." The work in question was sandwiched between from my point of view two of his better fictions, *The Europeans* and *Washington Square*, though William also considered both those novelettes slight.

My husband always had spoken fondly of Henry prior to our betrothal, but he grew enraged when he read *Confidence*. "There is something shamefully effeminate about our Harry," he said. He had allowed me to read the first two installments, but not the third. He kept it and the subsequent issues hidden from me. Later that year, I secretly procured a copy of the complete book from the local lending library.

The novel deals with two close friends, obviously patterned on William and Henry himself, the one scientific, the other artistic. They're named, as I recall, Gordon Wright and Bernard Longueville. The William character—Gordon—wishes to wed, and introduces Bernard, the Henry character, to his intended, a lady named Angela. Her name an obvious feminization of William's teasing appellation, "she" too is Henry, a female version of him. Bernard promptly falls in love with his feminine analogue, himself, and wins her away from Gordon, who then weds another young lady, presumably me. Of course by then, the two former friends have become estranged, a great gulf which can never be bridged now forever between them. I assume that Henry's making a woman out of himself and causing William to vie for her hand is what Bill found so unsavoury. Years later I learned from Henry that his original intention had been to kill "me" off, that his William character would so hate his new wife that in a fit of rage he would murder her, but he changed his mind, decided that he would allow William a happy wedded life, but only after he lost the former object of his affections to the Henry persona. In other words after the masculine Henry brought off his own marriage to his feminine self.

After the fiasco with the book, I didn't know quite what to expect meeting Henry for the first time late in '81. I gave him my hand at the family home in Quincy Street in the presence of his stooped and haggard dam; her husband, his still energetic though visibly aged father; and his sister, the other Alice, who had arrived at his parent's home only a few days prior to him. From the first, Angel and I got on famously. Shy and secretive, not nearly as vigorous and exuberant as my Willy, he behaved in a perfectly obliging manner to all of us ladies, deferring to our wishes in most things, quite the opposite of his brother my husband. Willing to help whenever requested to do so by his mother or sister, Angel would perform any household task with alacrity. Never grumbling or complaining, he continually accommodated: would drop what he was doing and come to one's aid, sometimes without even being asked, as once I observed him, after first laying his book aside, stand up and cross the room to where his mother sat at the window, remove the needle from her shaking hand, thread it for her, hand it back, then not saying a word return to his seat and resume reading. "Women's work," Bill would sniff, "did not interest him." By definition, he'd be unable to do it. So why even try, he argued. He knew he could not perform to satisfaction.

No, I couldn't help cherishing our Angel. He endeared himself because he fussed eternally with William's and my boy. He'd bounce Harry on his knee, let him crawl all over him, even pull his hair and thumb his eyes. He asked our delighted son if he wanted to romp and play. "Little Henri-*trois*, shall we?" he inquired. He called him "Our Royal Prince." The toddler would run to him with arms flung open, and Angel would catch him up and hold him high in the air. "Your Highness," he would say, "What is your command and will? Your Uncle stands ready to obey." For weeks after Angel's visit, when we asked our son to tell us who he was, he would invariably reply, "My Uncle Harry's fascinating little nephew." Angel's homecoming would be sad. He irritated William by saying his choice already had been made years before and it was for the Old World. Bill said America might be raw and shrill but it remained a far better place with a far better form of government than could be found in any of the desiccated and decadent European nations, including his, Henry's, adopted island. Angel protested that he stood a firm democrat, but William countered that he had never even visited Washington. So with Christmas over, Henry left Cambridge, returned to New York then traveled to Philadelphia and from Germantown went on to the Federal City. From there, I summoned him when his mother had a bronchial attack and her heart suddenly gave out.

He set sail for Europe in May, leaving ship at Cork to spend a week in Ireland, the land from which his father's father had emigrated immediately after the Revolutionary War. My husband received a year's leave of absence from Harvard in September of the same year. Our second child Billy had been born only a few months before, but William remained firm in his resolve to leave us behind. He had determined to go to Europe and observe the working methods of his fellow psychologists there. I had made it perfectly clear to Bill that I did not want him to go, but he paid me no mind. After his departure, I began receiving letters of condolence from Angel. Of his numerous kindnesses over the years, the writing of those letters perhaps meant most to me.

Earlier William had corresponded from Germany. He recounted how he had recently observed several peasant women striding like men through the streets of a city, pulling their baskets behind them unmindful of the stream of luxury and vice around them. He wrote that all the mystery of womanhood seemed to him incarcerated in their ugly beings and ended the letter with the words, "the Mothers! the Mothers! Ye are all one! Yes, Alice dear, what I love in you is only what these blessed creatures have." I cried for days. I had been reduced to what I was by gender and nothing more. My whole identity had been horribly abridged and shortened. Any other woman who had a fertile womb would have done just as well. How could I possibly mean so little to Bill, I wondered. Henry wrote from France. Altogether on my side, he found my situation quite unnatural, and wrote that he greatly pitied me. He hoped that the company of my two little children was some comfort. He described William as being in bad temper upon his arrival in England—he had met his train in Eustace Station. William did nothing but complain. He tried to nettle me, Henry wrote, by claiming Europe was just the same as it used to be in our dreary boyhood. He concluded the letter by saying he thought of me with tender sympathy, and that he believed William's abandonment criminal.

Suddenly their father was dying, having suffered in a matter of a few days several strokes. Henry came home, but did not arrive in time to sit at Henry Sr.'s bedside.

He read his farewell to his parents at their graves, replaced the letter in his pocket, and visited the two children and me. He cradled the baby in his arms and called him "a most loving little mortal." Angel was definitely the gentler, the more considerate, of the two sons. I never could have loved him like I did my Bill, but I appreciated his amiability and unselfishness. He became as much my brother—and I cherished and fancied him as such—as his biological sister's, whose name I shared! Years would pass before I would see him again.

I think now of all those back-and-forth trips from America to Europe that William, the children, and I made. When traveling we would see Henry: when we sailed over there, or else when he crossed to our side as he did in 1904. Of course, we wrote to each other quite regularly, but years could go by before we again stood in the same room with Angel and once more saw him in the flesh.

In the summer of '92, William took another sabbatical leave. This time all four children and I accompanied him, Peggy and Alex entirely too young for the trip, Alex just a baby. We made straight to Switzerland, where Bill's father had taken his family in the fifties. We stopped in Lausanne. Henry wrote from Venice that he would join us there. I hadn't seen my eldest brother-in-law for nearly ten years. A decade had almost passed since his father's death. I had given birth to three more children, but the whooping cough had felled one of my babes.

That summer Angel had been enjoying himself in Italy—he left the company of good friends to come north, and checked into the Hotel Richemont. Unfortunately, Henry did not receive the reunion he had hoped for. He wanted to see Harry and Billy again, but we had boarded them out with a pair of Swiss pastors. Knowing that his brother was in transit, William had nonetheless quit Lausanne for a walking tour in the Engadine, while I remained behind in a Vaudois pension, tending to our small daughter and the baby. I'm afraid that I didn't prove a very entertaining host.

William, our daughter Peggy, and I visited Europe again in '99, my husband's health already in rapid decline. After Bill took the water cure in Nauheim, Germany, we visited Henry at Lamb House, which he had only recently bought. Bill enjoyed traveling through the autumnal English countryside. He said that he found much to please his old painter's eye. Not much impressed with his brother's acquisition, he nonetheless rather liked the ancient seaport town with its endless brick houses, all or at least most with adjoining gardens. Standing in each other's presence seemed to make both of them nervous and on guard. Bill remarked to me that his brother's life must be lonely here. Again William felt a horrible tightness in his chest. He appeared in very great pain. We hurried up to London where we lodged in Henry's rooms in DeVere Gardens. The specialist put my husband on a no-starch diet, and we later traveled to Malvern where Bill underwent more hydropathic treatments. He grew worse. The frigid waters in the baths made him catch cold. We returned to Rye briefly. Just before our departure, Henry also complained of chest pains. William dismissed them as psychological.

I next saw my brother-in-law in 1904, during his American lecture tour. He spent a fortnight with us in Chocorua in September. He had his own suite of rooms and complete privacy. If I remember rightly, he had been quite fidgety and unsettled. He made several day trips away from our summer home during the two weeks he spent there. Yet he wrote us in 1909 that he fondly recollected his single visit to Chocorua and felt he had been given a beggarly snatch of all the place offered. As the time of year of his visit came round again, he wrote that the yearning but baffled thought of being with us on that woodland scene and at the same season once again tugged at his sensibilities and was almost too much for him. He disclosed that he lovingly recalled the many small lakes, the woodland scene with its assault of forest, the smell of summer's end. He spoke of my beautiful "rustic" hospitality and of squash pie and ice cream in heroic proportions. Oh how he longed to return, he wrote. He would get his chance the following year, but Chocorua was hardly a place of cheer then. Later that fall, he quartered himself for awhile in an upper story of our house in Irving Street. He commented to me how strange he now found Boston, how everything had changed. For the most part, he and William kept out of each other's way. They had taken walks together in the woods at Chocorua, but on the whole they did not spend much time in each other's company. During the first months of the new year, Henry traveled both to the South and the Mid-west, and William decided quite on the spur of the moment to set sail to Greece.

My husband and I visited Henry twice more in Europe, first in 1908, then our last trip in 1910. On the first visit, we became acquainted with Theodora Bosanquet, and there had been that terrible incident with the ladder—Henry and William fighting again just as if they were little boys.

We came over in 1910 because we felt Henry to be badly depressed. William gathered this from his brother's letters and, as ill as he himself was, determined to go over to cheer and distract Henry. He'd also travel again to Germany for hydropathic treatments. We reached England in April. The brothers presented a sad sight. William could hardly walk, and Henry could not smile. Angel traveled with us to Bad Neuheim, and then on to Switzerland, where once more the brothers visited the cities of their youth. Word of Robertson's death reached us in Lucerne. Henry and I both felt it best to keep the news from William. We returned to England from the continent and William received further treatment in London. After spending a few days in Rye where William rested up for the impending voyage, my husband, my brother-in-law, his man Burgess, and I sailed for Quebec on the *Empress of Britain* August 12th. The seas weren't at all stormy. We had a long peaceful lull, yet William became so weak he could hardly get up from his chair. He spent a long part of the voyage in bed. Harry awaited us at the pier in Quebec, a day's journey from Chocorua. Billy met us with the car at North Conway, and we ferried William back to his beloved country house, where he died on the 26th.

Angel helped us greatly then, God bless him. He stayed nearly a year, accompanied the family to Irving Street in the early fall, and attended my futile séances. While staying with us in Boston, he accepted an honorary degree from Harvard. William would have been quite happy to have seen him so honored. Now, as only right, I tend to him in his last days.

I have sat here for quite awhile having stopped reading out loud to the patient some time ago. Alice, you should know better than to leave your thoughts wander off, I chide myself. Minnie Kidd will arrive any minute with the tea things. Maybe Henry has fallen asleep? He did not complain when I stopped reading and entered into my own recollections. No, his eyes remain open. He lies there so still and silent. Could he be—no he is breathing, his chest rises and falls as he draws in and expels air. Henry, I say, but he remains unresponsive. I repeat his name several times, wondering if he can hear me. He has had periods like this before where no type of stimulus will arouse him. They have lasted anywhere from several minutes to as long as twenty. Even though I have seen him like this previously, I decide to ring for the nurses. They will want to keep abreast of his condition....

Harry

I have left with Mother's blessing. In fact she believes that she has empowered me on her behalf to perform a mission which she considers just as important as my previous commitment—to see to the disposition of all Uncle's worldly possessions, his chattels and his gewgaws. But the task he set me clearly, oh-so clearly, takes precedence over hers, is far, far, more consequential. I am honor-bound to do it well. What Mother herself effects perhaps equals it in importance. She dutifully fulfills her promise to Father: his deathbed request that she see after and tend to Angel if he ever became mortally ill. Grandmother first called Uncle that, so reliable sources tell me, yet it quickly became Father's favorite name for his brother.

Even though Father always tried to cut Uncle down to size as Uncle did him—both of them delighted in playing a sort of cat-and-mouse game with each other; a twinkle of complicity glimmered in both their eyes—and leveled criticism after criticism at his work, attempting to deconstruct with aplomb what he so beautifully built, his remarks were never what I would call derisive, contemptuous, or scornful. His quite brilliant criticism, as usual, always hit the mark. There was plenty of validity to all his comments and suggestions. Yet speaking with anyone else but his brother, he praised his brother's work profusely. He spoke to me many times of Uncle's quite momentous achievement. He remained simply our first man of letters though (I must agree with Father) he always did mire himself in a maze of long and over-complicated sentences (Father said he would have preferred a more vigorous, masculine style and sunnier stories with less rapacious heroes and heroines) and so many of his political opinions were from Father's and my points of view nothing short of detestable. It's Mother's task with Peggy there to aid her to see to all his bodily wants and to make his passing as pain-free and comfortable as possible. I breathe easier now that I no longer stand in his presence, for Uncle has lost all his brilliance. His senility and feebleness have reduced him to a mere dying body gasping a few final breaths. Spared, I do not need to watch him expire. He entrusted me with something far more important when he appointed me caretaker to his voluminous literary remains. He commissioned and entrusted me with them just as Grandfather, the man for whom both Uncle and I were named, did Father with his. Surpassed by two of his four sons, what presence, what character, that old Irish American must have still possessed, that man who lost his leg yet traveled on one across the entire European continent with his young family, an author and philosopher in his own right. After his decease, Father demanded that public justice be done to his works, though while Grandfather lived, he could poke fun at them, even designing a tiny woodcut for the title page of Grandfather's essay on the Physics of Creation, of a little gnome belaboring a dead horse with an iron rod. I intend to perform my duty as diligently as did he, my task, however, that much more enormous and important, as Uncle outdistanced Grandfather by many miles, both as to quality and quantity. I think it infamous that they presently take down his dictation. Oh yes, by all means, humor the man, write out the words or better still pretend to, but don't publish. If that was what that Bosanquet woman had in mind, Mother correctly showed her the door. But both she and Peggy have followed suit. They jot down everything he says. If the man stood in his right mind, he would shudder—positively shudder—with disapprobation. He would never wish these last inchoate senile mutterings put before the eyes of his reading public. I can envision how offended he would be with me for not disallowing the spectacle. While acting as his own agent, he left nothing go to press unless he was absolutely, supremely, satisfied with it. If Peggy's handwritten pages ever fall into my hands, if they come under my governance, as Uncle's literary executor, I shall order them destroyed—see them put to the flame. That is what Uncle would want—I'm sure, and it would be an injustice not to follow his dictates. Hugely disrespectful.

Peggy

When I first met her, Theodora Bosanquet very much attracted me. We took long walks together through the Rye countryside, and she discoursed on a wide range of subjects, foremost among them suffragettism—the enfranchisement of women. But she also read me poems and spoke about the gentlemen who had plied her with their suits and how she had inevitably rebuffed them. I grew eager to hear her opinions on everything, she seemed so intelligent and worldly-wise. She could offer me all the benefits of her vaster experience. I would sit at her knees like a star-struck pupil. No, to be truthful, I can't say that we engaged in meaningful conversation. There existed no give and take, for I did not feel that I had anything to offer and was content merely being the receptive (and grateful) ear into which she could always feel free to empty and pour all her myriad thoughts. She, however, quickly grew bored with me, did not consider me her equal (which of course with respect to intellect neither did I) and upon my later visits to England, treated me rather coolly, disregarding my advances just as if I were one of her smitten swains! She must have let a word drop to Uncle for in between correcting my English grammar as he always did whenever more than one or two words issued from my lips and disgusted at some mistake I repeatedly made, he said that, yes, he must agree with his amanuensis that in my stubbornness and intractability I stood *sui generis*. Of course, since that moment, I have harbored ill feelings toward my Uncle's servant, an insolent working girl who thinks she can—is destined to—rise above her station. If the chance ever came my way, I determined right then and there, I would set her tumbling down. Now, all these years later, my opportunity has at last arisen. I heard about the faces she pulled when the British King awarded Uncle that trinket, and Mother didn't fall on her knees and prostrate herself for very joy. I realized that friction already existed between her and Mother, but did not know how to exacerbate it. However, when I found out that Miss Bosanquet kept in constant communication with Mrs. Wharton, I saw that I held my trump card. Mother harbored a great antipathy for the female authoress whom she felt lived a very immoral life. She had come to that conclusion after reading her book *The Reef* in which Mrs. Wharton (at least according to Mother) positively celebrated adultery. Mother did not like that Uncle and she were good friends, not in the least. Mother absolutely didn't want the typist communicating about Uncle's condition with the lady novelist. She forbade it, especially as Uncle had said in his confusion that he hoped Mrs. Wharton was not aware of his present state. Since he has fallen ill, Uncle has become quite the paranoiac. Miss Bosanquet had not been aware of Uncle's revelation to me, for she now pretended we remained fast friends and that she could confide in me. I certainly did nothing to disabuse her; in fact I feigned that I was the same old dull Peggy that she had formerly known and gave her my toothiest smile whenever she desired my ear. Oh I acted the part quite well and fooled her thoroughly. She expected nothing. When she told me that despite what Uncle said she knew that he would in his right mind want her to keep in communication with Mrs. Wharton, who in truth remained one of his dearest and most concerned friends, and asked if I would consent to her disobeying Mother's stricture on that matter, I gave my permission immediately, only to inform on her the moment her back turned. Mother did not want her in the house and with malicious joy I laid out my letter to Harry where I knew Bosanquet would find it. Being a woman, I realized that she, also a woman, would not be able to forbear reading the missive in which I wrote that before our arrival while *she* managed things in her heartless way, the, and I underlined the word, *faithful* servants had been slaving under her overseership to the absolute breaking point. Yes, I had my revenge. Mother, for all intents and purposes, banned her from Carlyle Mansion, and I got to tell her through the planted letter exactly what I thought of her—returned slight for slight. Since her virtual departure, her duties as the recorder of my Uncle's words have fallen principally to me, although Mother also keeps a diary in which she, too, takes down some of dear old Uncle's sentences. I have supplanted Miss Bosanquet. She was not nearly so essential as she thought.

It is frightful to see Uncle as he is now: at bay. The memories of him I will treasure will certainly not be of his last months. Although he remained critical of my speech (he criticized most everyone's), he treated me (and most people for that matter) very kindly. I remember when I had reached my twelfth year and father had already started ailing and traveled to Europe for his health with mother and me in tow, how after Daddy took the water cure in Germany, we visited Uncle at his newly acquired country home in October of (it must have been) 1899, and how concerned Uncle became when Daddy's chest pains returned. Daddy had been critical of Uncle's purchasing the house several months before and Uncle had grown very angry with Daddy then, but with Daddy now so ill, Uncle refused to return to the subject, even when Daddy tried to goad him into a conversation. Shortly thereafter, Mother took Daddy to London for treatment by a heart specialist and then both my parents wintered at Rye. I spent Christmas there also, but afterwards they sent me to Harrow to attend an English school. I boarded with the Thatcher Clarkes, friends of Papa. My parents had decided to cross over to the continent. Uncle told me then he knew what it was like being an American child apart from its parents in Europe. He patted my hand and told me that I had worlds of discovery awaiting me. Mother said that the school I should attend must offer moral and spiritual training, but Uncle replied that with my New England background and upbringing, that I could be "raised on almost solely *cultivated* 'social' and aesthetic lines." He suggested a school in Wimbledon, but Papa wanted me to continue living in a family setting, so he selected Harrow, a compromise. Daddy's friends lived there, and I could lodge with them. I think it largely due to Uncle's strenuous arguing that my parents did not immure me in some religious institution! Still I remained very lonely and unhappy. Uncle wrote me regularly–tried to cheer me up with his pen. He said that he missed me very much and took interest in everything I did and all that I experienced. He even came to visit me at Harrow and took three of my schoolmates as well as me to London, to see newsreels of the Boer War at the Biograph Theatre. I learned then that Uncle's political opinions were a bit queer, certainly very different from Daddy's. In response to my question he told me that most certainly he was not pro-Boer. Later we learned that the pictures had been faked. By spring, my parents had moved on to Rome where Papa decided to so-journ in an attempt to regain his health and strength. They remained on the Continent come Christmas, so Uncle invited me down to Lamb House to spend the holidays with him. He gorged me with candies and fruit, then sat me down in a plush chair and gave me Walter Scott novels to read, and I remember that I completed four or five of them. We also took long walks together, Uncle's white-haired fox terrier Nick barking at our heels. Before New Year 1901, we traveled to London, where the old Queen lay dying. He bought a black mourning hat for me to wear when the aged Monarch at long last expired. I watched the funeral procession from a window of one of his London friend's home. To my astonishment the coffin on the gun carriage was quite tiny. It looked like that of a little girl's. During the years that followed, I saw Uncle on a number of occa-sions: when he came to America or when I traveled to Europe, and his kindliness never wavered, though he often would make critical remarks about either me or my traveling companions. As I grew older and began reading Uncle's books, I realized that poor Daddy had assessed his writing correctly. He gave me one of his later volumes. I made a go at it but found it, I'm afraid, damnably difficult. "All you say, and your manner of say-ing it," I told him, "is pirouetting and prancing, and beating the air, very charmingly, but still once in a while we readers crave a strong simple note." He replied that he detested anything simple and that if he found a different and more elaborate way of pronounc-ing his own name, he would most certainly do so. Yes, he was so good to us, especially to Mother and me, when Daddy passed away back in 1910, staying with us in America for many months until we arranged everything and got the estate in good order, that it gladdens me that we can help and see him through now. He remains quite confused true, yet he has moments of lucidity as well, as yesterday when he recognized the blouse I wore as one he helped me pick out when we shopped together nearly one year ago. He seems to have two distinct personalities, one clear-headed and content, the other dreary and vague and either vehemently angry or quite mawkish. He sobs a great deal. To see him crying breaks my heart, and occasionally something he says brings tears to my own eyes, as when he confided in me one day quite recently that he hoped my father would arrive soon—"He is the one person in all Rome I want to see." I wonder if he was recalling (if he returned in the course of his mental wanderings back to) the time when my father actually convalesced in that city and he befriended me, at thirteen a mere slip of a girl, marooned and left behind in a dreary, isolated corner somewhere in the bleak English countryside. If he thought the past had become the present.

The fragments I set down all leave off abruptly. Weird maxims of a broken mind, I call—define—them to myself, after having given them close scrutiny: the careful attention of several slow readings. Uncle's brain dies faster than the rest of him. His bloated body lags behind. It still lives, a far bigger carcass than that of the tiny yet ancient Queen I saw pass on the caisson as a maid of thirteen. Today Mother said that just the day before, Uncle had his most lucid period in weeks, that he returned for awhile to being the same old Henry we remembered. She said that he told her he thought that any truly sapient reader upon examination of the works in question would surely judge his tale "The Jolly Corner" superior to Mr. Stevenson's *The Strange Case of Dr. Jekyll and Mr. Hyde* or Oscar Wilde's *Portrait of Dorian Gray*, whereupon according to Mother, he suddenly became furious. How dare Wilde use—copy—that word, he asked, but then he laughed and corrected himself. What am I thinking, he said. Wilde didn't use it. The title was *The Picture of Dorian Gray*, not *The Portrait of Dorian Gray*. Mother said that he then spoke about of all things a strange ghost story he wanted to write, after which he returned briefly to the subject of the present European war and delivered a short philippic against the German character, the *loudness* of its operatic music. Finally he broke off and nodded in his chair. Mother said that he had been coherent for twenty minutes and that she was able to set down several long paragraphs. I write down all he says when I am in his company but I surely wouldn't call him coherent.

The final time I took dictation, several days before his last session with Mother, he muttered about souls crossing borders, stated that men and women should move down the road of life with unfailing admiration for everything they saw but then warned them that there would be many sordid problems for everyone. With me too, he also alluded to Stevenson, called him, if I remember correctly, "one of the earliest consumers of the great globe." What he said next was obscure and hazy, something about a visitor at Vailima. Then he aimed a barb at us, Mother—and me too perhaps—about acquiring pious antiquities and dead men's domestic annals. He knew he wasn't making much sense for he said that these words of his might have some interest to the world, but a highly competent person, or several perhaps, would have to go through these dictations and carefully edit them, or as he put it, "furnish such last offices." The nurses had warned that all day his temperature had been steadily rising, but now he said that he felt tired and unwell. He didn't want to work further. He complained that he never dreamed such onerous duties would be laid upon him. His final fading words to me were: "This sore throaty condition is the last I ever invoked for the purpose." After that nothing.

Mrs. William

Harry has wired from Rye to say that he has completed all his inventories. In turn he asks that I should destroy the dictations Peggy and I have taken down since December. He wants to prevent their future publication. He says that it would be Henry's wish. Peggy is adamantly against our doing so. She says the last words will have an archival importance. No they don't have to be immediately released, but they should be kept for future reference in some safety-deposit box. The words she took from him are half-baked—and so often dark and impenetrable—Harry is right, their release might prove embarrassing to my brother-in-law's literary reputation, yet if Peggy feels they should be preserved, I won't gainsay her. As I understand the will, Harry can prevent publication as his uncle's executor but he cannot force his sister to relinquish her own property, which indeed is what her notes are. The two of them can squabble if they want to over those few handwritten pages. On the other hand, most of the material I scribbled in the writing pad I am determined to destroy, especially what I set down on his recent lucid afternoon. During the last several days (with Angel almost totally unresponsive and quite unable to speak any more) I have read and reread those paragraphs. At the time of the dictation Henry's renascence so excited me that except for one or two items that gave me pause, I hardly noticed what he said. Also he spoke so rapidly I had to hurry to get it all down. So nothing had time to really sink in. But now it is quite obvious to me (no reason to show the pages to Harry, I can see clearly myself) that their content would do great damage and to a whole lot more than his literary reputation. Yesterday, the 26th, even though he had not spoken intelligibly to anyone for over twenty-four hours, I pled my case in his presence, asked if our last session was something that should really be preserved for posterity, but he just looked up, stared straight into the heavens or rather at the ceiling impeding his upward view and did not answer.

No, I did not like at all the doubts he declared himself as having concerning Christianity and the afterlife. I must admit I revolted against those ideas as soon as he expressed them. I am sure he couldn't truly have meant what he said. Besides the next day before he lapsed into unconsciousness again he struck me as reverently contemplating the cross concealed in his door as I read passages from the Bible to him. After taking time to study the material, I find more than those remarks objectionable. He's proved himself partisan enough already concerning this war. William would not have shared his position, so why advertise it further? In addition, the world should never know that he depreciated his own work. Perhaps it was natural that he should have qualms and reservations about what he had written, but why air them? Also he expatiated at length about that German composer, hardly a fit subject to devote so much time and space. His last spoken thoughts, I think, should have been about his niece and nephews. And finally what did he mean about suppressing certain truths about himself? Could William have been right all those years ago when he expressed his reservations about "that thoroughly bad novel" *Confidence?*

Having said my piece to him and not having received any sort of reply, I walked out of the room, closing the door upon my unfortunate brother-in-law, not a vacant shell quite yet, his eyes still open for all the world to flood into. Maybe he could still see and hear.

This morning I scanned the pages once again before making up my mind and placing the first two in the grate. The destruction of the third had to wait until somewhat later, for they called me back to the sickroom. My brother-in-law had difficulty breathing and his body trembled, as if he underwent convulsions. I sat beside him until his pulse and temperature returned to normal. Again and again he tried to speak, but his mouth no longer could form words. He merely grunted and moaned despite, upon his part, a positively Herculean effort, struggle, to verbalize. Eventually he tired himself out and slept. Only then did I destroy the last page of the document. I'll never now forget the gist of those final words having read them over and over again these last two days. I remember him speaking them ever so clearly.

"Yes," he continued, "I always wanted to be a serious practitioner of my craft—my art, certainly not one of those sham artists like my fellow Celt, that not-worthy-of-my-contempt George Moore or that monstrous assailant on all the arts with his fusion, his "total art," the loathsome Wagner. One of the very few good things about the present war is the fact that his works are now banned in England, though it appears that the Germans are now winning. Wagner seems to be in the ascendancy. I certainly hope that he will be checked and rebuffed by the forces of civilization. However, I also compromised myself. Yes, I wrote a vast array of fine short stories, but, I must confess, they were for the most part bread-and-butter works intended for the popular magazines, not originally written for a unified collection within solid library bindings of the best buckram, of finest linen, goldstamped. Too, I was drawn from the novel, the novelette, and the literary essay to the fascination of the current London stage, surely at its furthermost point from the glorious outpourings of the Shakespearean age, and how many mysteries did I write? Yet even there didn't I create a serious art work *The Turn of the Screw* while appealing to the Saxons' simple, never failing love for a good scary ghost story? It has come, at long last, the truly distinguished thing and all that will be left is my literary remains. Ghosts do not exist. There is no such thing as a soul. I hardly think Jesus awaits, still young, handsome, physically perfectly formed, lovingly greeting me with open arms, and I don't think my destination, perish the thought, is the sheltering bosom of a black, hairy, Fagan-albeit-Lincolnesque-nosed Abraham, of definite Old Testament vintage. But whose voice, then, did I hear saying that the moment had arrived? Can I create a solution to the riddle, provide an answer to my own question, construct yet another character? Perhaps the voice could be made to belong to a vibrant and angry personification of all the things I suppressed about myself, that over the years I swept under the carpet and would not permit my Puritan character and singularity to admit as valid and acceptable either for my craft, my art, or my own personal life or even for investigation into the makeup of some of the more flawed characters in my writing?

"Could this personification be waiting for me now? Is he up there on the ceiling? Do I see him in that shadowy corner where the candlelight flickers and is more subdued? Does he await his final victory over me, the enemy I long wrestled with and thought I had vanquished? Will truly liberated writers follow me? Oh, surely not. Even Wagner remains superior to all his slavish followers working with shreds or fragments extending from their master's *oeuvre*, no *werk*. I must write. There is still so much to compose!"

One more day has now passed and my brother-in-law remains with us, the living, no longer. The struggle terminated at long last. This morning he could not take any nourishment whatsoever and his ankles and wrists began swelling as if someone pumped air into them through some secret nozzle. His face had turned ashen and bloated-looking. At four in the afternoon the doctor summoned me. Henry's breath came in short little gasps. Des Voeux said, "This is the end," but we still had to wait two hours more. At six, he took three long sighing breaths, separated from each other by several seconds, the last very faint. He departed—without a shadow on his face, nor the contraction of a muscle. I left the room immediately. I had no satisfaction in my role, the task laid upon my shoulders, but I saw the stern necessity of it. If the torch had been passed to me, if I, William's widow had been crowned queen, as some might say I had been, though by blood I am not a James, I found the weight of the family crown quite burdensome, yet I realized that I must quickly determine what the "last words" of the world famous writer would be. No I never dreamed that such an onerous duty would be laid upon me. The final line Peggy set down, "the sore throaty condition is the last I ever invoked for the purpose," would certainly not do. No, I could not place the final period there. Henry's words should otherwise terminate. I realized that I could manufacture something better. We will give the press its bone, a few lines which I'll contrive but say he spoke to me at the last, words that all three of us—Peggy, Harry, and myself—can feel satisfied with.

No one save Peggy perhaps, to whom I told something about Henry's and my last conversation, will ever have knowledge of my actions today. I'm sure that some would say that any crime by Thomas Bowdler paled in comparison, for not only did I expurgate, omit and modify, I also *invented*. But I did what I considered best. His last thoughts should have had something to do with his family—the living Jameses. Indeed sitting down at his desk, taking up his pen and steeling myself to indite the first few words, I thought that, yes, I acted properly, for I, a Howe Gibbens from Weymouth Massachusetts, a Boston school teacher and a lady, I hope, of considerable charm, had turned, had become, James by marriage. I had joined with them, our blood intermixing (mine of the old New

England stock) in the children: the future Jameses. I had attached myself to the first family of American letters. And despite his recent gesture—though I am glad William didn't live to see Angel relinquish his American citizenship; he certainly wouldn't have approved, even though he would have realized (as I do) that Henry had meant it as a symbolic act only, as he wanted Wilson to get us into the fray, the very thing that I (and William if he were still with us) would not wish to see; I admit that I profess isolationism; let the Europeans fight their own internecine wars—Henry remained ours. The British would never be able to claim him, reverence his works as they might, for he remained American through and through. To be a James means to be American, and *through* my children, I will play a major role in the future of the tribe, in the ensuing generations of Jameses, who like their forefathers before them will remain in the forefront of their young nation. It's entirely proper that Henry's last thoughts be of them. So sitting at his desk and holding his pen between my two fingers, I began putting words to paper.

I wrote that in conversation he asked me if his nephew Billy had friends on the continent and that he then said that he wished one of the boys had connections in England. "You are their connection with England and Europe," I wrote, I replied. Our fictive dialogue continued as follows:

"Yes," he went on, "I know, but I should say, without being fatuous, with the future?"

"With the future always. They will try to follow you."

"Tell them then *to follow, to be faithful, to take me seriously.*"

It was here, with a smile on my face after expending a great deal of energy to come up with something appropriate, that I decided his words should cease.

Envoi

I

His counterpart surrounded himself with beautiful objects, became a connoisseur of fine furniture, but how utterly now did *he* hate chairs and couches as types for all inanimate things which endure while we rot. They are never conscious of how they are used, if they are sat upon or not, because they were never blessed with discernment—not even the polished wood in the invalid chair, which came from a once living plant. Yet is the woody part of a plant even alive? I should know this but due to my madness I forget. Certainly there is a difference between green and dry wood. One stokes one's fire with the latter to be sure. And aren't parts of us dead all along too? Our hair. Our nails. Our bones. Yet the spongy interior of our bones lives when we live, does it not? Our bones grow. We drink milk as children so as to have a healthy skeleton. Yes they grow. The dead words from his pen also accrue. He thinks they're alive. He thinks they will have permanence, poor deluded fool. But despite our dead parts, our hair our nails our squiggles on the page, we have apprehension and wakefulness. The consciousness of a living plant must be quite limited. The merest glimmer or glow. A phantom awareness. A ghost-like cognizance. Yet with apprehension and wakefulness at least in our case if not in the peony's or the rose's, if not in the hawk's or the elephant's (though did not Kipling write somewhere that the sight of the rotting carcass or skeleton of another elephant would deeply distress that animal, that like us it was also cognizant if only in a rudimentary way of its last end?) comes the foreknowledge that one day one will be bereft of them, that one will become less than dog, rooster or mealworm. Less than a daisy or an oak tree. As dead as a chair. A doorknob. A page of *prose choisi*. Or for that matter a line of doggerel. Words are insensate, they don't know if they are being read or not. No matter how artfully they are arranged. Just as a chair does not know it is sat upon. But if his counterpart was presently at some stage in that process of reduction, he had burst his bonds—had finally come out. So.

Leave me all gloomy deliberation, he adjured and charged. *Here it is.*

He remembered when they had met he had said, "*At last, the distinguished thing!*" For years he had battled to make his presence known, to come forth and confront the Master face to face. But now he sees him in bed or sitting up in a chair, a feeble old man who very clearly has been run through the mill and as a result has suffered unspeakable torments, his eyes glassy and vacant, his face ashen, his cheeks bristly with a day's growth of new beard, his mouth contorted in a perpetual grimace, a scowl of pain and extreme repugnance, and his skin mottled and stippled with an assortment of little malignant growths. Pink, brown and a few black, hairy, moles sprout like mushrooms on his neck, his armpits and pubis. A variegated crop. Small red elevations of the skin with inflamed bases containing pus dot his face. Which of us is more of a corpse, a ghost? I dare ask. In bed his feet stick out from under the covers like a dead man's. In the chair when they have him up at the window, his head droops to the side of his body which Medusa has looked upon (his left) and which as a result has hardened and frozen. He still speaks, but when I concentrate hard staring at him I can see his eyes cloud. Then I am no longer looking down at him from above but instead view the world through his old rheumy eyes. And it is I who control the hand making the writing motions. He took my dictation as Peggy did his, in longhand, a few days ago. But this morning I am again on the outside. Someone randomly taps pianistically on the typewriter keys, because the sound seems to soothe him. He is composing in his head. He sees bright colours. Purple and ruby triangles. Green spots. His own personal kaleidoscope. He watches the colours skirl, dance, and mogrify and practices his sentences the while, thinks he spins living tissue, that he is in travail, labour, that the moment of parturition is at hand and that he is delivering something animated and vital. Not merely dropping word-turds. So he hopes. So he prays. Indeed he thinks *"laborare est orare"* then resumes dictating yet another letter to his dead brother William and to his dead sister Alice. He recalls the war. Napoleon Bonaparte figures in his reminiscence. Prominently. *Obliquely*. He calls him forth to conquer. To defeat the enemies of culture and civilization. To ride down the *Allemand* and sees him mounted on his great white horse wearing his famous hat. I listen. Beautiful things come forth: "Individual souls, great of...on which great perfections are if one does ... in the fulfillment with the neat and pure and perfect, to the success or as he or she moves through life, following admiration unfailing ... in the highway problems are very sordid."

Ah how he loved to dictate to his various typists. He could be a performer—a stage actor, an opera singer. Finally, at long last. The distinguished thing. Miss Bosanquet had been a most appreciative audience. "An impressive resuscitation," she would compliment him. His greatness outstripped that of a mere actor. How the rabble booed and hissed his *Guy Domville*. No memorized speech issued from his lips as he stood, eyes closed, and dictated. Gave birth. A composer forming and fashioning. But an original piece. Something new. Not part of the world before. Something added to the sum total of creation.

Yes, for years and years I have been attempting to break through his barriers and make contact. Finally I made my presence in a flash known to him—made my way to the distinguished thing, our meeting. He heard me! He was falling to the floor, his leg having given under him. Having a stroke in the most approved fashion. He had tried to summon the servants. I knew what he thought as he lay on the carpet. With his good arm he yanked on the electrical wiring of his bed lamp. He thought he rang for his maid and valet. He knew by pulling he could summon them. He needed help. He was in distress. He tugged repeatedly then everything went black. He never realized that his hand didn't clutch a bell pull.

He should have known, why am I lying, for a long time he did know, what was coming. Henry I am nothing if not truthful, as you well know. You did discern that in your cosmos turned abattoir the hammer had lifted to deal you the death stroke. You willed that the blow would fall soon; the weight of the world had grown burdensome on your shoulders. It was a nightmare, this crash of your civilization. A nightmare from which there was no waking save sleep. *Sans death.* Even before everything that was yours was undone, before the War erupted, you were on edge. Was not that mad suffragette attacking you when, wielding a meat cleaver, she went at your portrait (your lovely, lovely portrait)? She shattered the glass then slashed the canvas, put a gash through the left side of your head, another through the right side of your mouth all the way down then through your shoulder. And now not only the world, but you too, Henry are undone. And in a most retroactive way, alas. I've been outside looking on, observing these last few months. At first I too had lost all my memory. From what the other people here have said—Miss Bosanquet before she left; our relatives Mrs. William, Peggy and Harry; Dr. Des Voeux—I have pieced together some of what has happened. Your maid and the war cripple your valet Burgess, who by special dispensation was allowed to reenter your service after receiving thirty shrapnel wounds and being deafened in the trenches, found you on the floor and helped you into bed. You recovered most of your faculties, were your old chipper self. That is probably why I have no memory of those days. I made contact; our wills struggled with each other for dominance and as usual you gained the upper hand. You cabled Harry and received Mrs. William's reply that she sailed at once. But then two days after your first attack, you had a second seizure. Your left side was paralyzed. I remember looking at your face, your piteous bloodshot eyes, your gaunt cadaverous cheeks. Tears welling up, you attempted to speak but all you could say was "mmm, mmm." Terrible. But your will was still great. You rallied a second time. However, you thought you had gone mad. Maybe your madness was merely my presence, for now I was awake too, looking down at you from above. However, I did hear the doctor say that you ran a high temperature, that he had discovered a clot in one of your lungs, and that, yes, there had been some brain damage he was not sure how great the extent, that while you were oriented as to person, at intervals you were disoriented as to time and space. I on the other hand didn't recognize the feeble stricken babbling old man in the bed and chair. Nor did I know what to call myself. I knew where we resided though, at your London flat No. 21 Carlyle Mansion. Someone gave the address and number over the telephone. But I heard you say that you were in Cork one day, in Edinburgh on another, and on yet a third you claimed to be home in New York! Then you said that the place where you now found yourself was the strangest mixture of all the places you had ever been. Gradually your identity dawned on me as did my own. I heard people say your name but it did not mean anything to me. As you grew stronger I became weaker. But as you declined, my powers waxed. My memory returned to me and I was suffused with warmth. I recalled everything. Our relation became clear. Yes, for some time, you had known that the hammer had been poised to fall. After war had been declared, you had been unable to read much less write. Everything seemed black and hideous. You wanted to avert your face from the whole monstrous scene. You regretted that you had lived to see the downfall and utter collapse of your civilization. Part of you began wishing for extinction that summer, the most beautiful English summer conceivable. But you determined to do your part, to live on and fight for the just cause. You joined the committee for Belgian relief, spoke French with the Belgian maimed and wounded, also visited the English soldiers at St. Bartholomew's, brought them pocket combs and cigarettes, tried to pull the conversational cart uphill for them. You hobnobbed with the PM Herbert H. Asquith, played the part of diplomat, met Generals, Viscounts and the First Lord of the Admiralty Mr. Winston Churchill, whom you instantly disliked. You met at 10 Downing Street in December 1914, then again in January 1915 at Walmer Castle. Jealous at the attention you the cynosure received, he interrupted you constantly and used slang words purposely to nettle you. Yes you knew the end was near. That same month you learned that your favourite tree in your garden at Lamb House, the giant mulberry under which you and Hendrik Andersen sat all those years ago, had been overturned in a tumultuous winter storm, and you wrote: "He might have gone on for some time in the absence of an *inordinate* gale—but once the tempest really descended he was bound to give way, because his poor old heart was dead, his immense old trunk hollow." You were the tree and the war was the storm. But still you persisted. Would not give up the good fight. You accused your old enemy Wilson, who while president of Princeton called your style laborious, of leg dragging. Finally as a last gesture, you determined to relinquish your US citizenship and become a British subject. You did not like your status as resident alien. Four people had to testify to your character and literacy! The PM as a personal favour obliged as one of the four. Yes you knew. You had had heart problems for years, seen many doctors and specialists. William died of a massive coronary. So did Robertson. You knew what was in store, and you wanted to rub me out, expunge me like a bad sentence. You determined not to leave the slightest trace of my existence behind for posterity. You made that special trip to Rye, to Lamb House, with only one purpose, to burn all incriminating evidence, correspondence or photograph. Your privacy had to be kept at all costs. You wanted to make your life a cipher for the future biographer. You destroyed all Andersen's letters. But you did not have the heart to commit Joukovski's missive to the fire. You had not seen each other in years. The tone of the letter was affectionate, yet well within the bounds of the socially acceptable. Yes, the chemical components of page after page of your correspondence went up your chimney as smoke. Years before you had gone through Fenimore's papers. You feared that she might have squirreled away some incriminating letters of yours, so you offered her sister your assistance in ordering her estate. You determined that the only record of your life would be your books, your vast self-portrait in words. When anyone criticized your writing it was far, far, worse, much more criminal than the act of the old militant suffragette. She didn't slash you. Only Sargent's oil portrait. How William's words about *The Golden Bowl* stung. He cut into the living flesh. He attacked the book in a letter to you after your great American tour in 1905. You had no reason to hate the Germans then. For your crossing you took a cabin on the North German Lloyd liner *Kaiser Wilhelm II*. You shed tears at leaving behind in England your German *Hund*. Your red dachshund Max, "with a pedigree longer than a Remington ribbon." With a tongue just about as long. You even let Max lick your face, did not turn away. The affectionate beast loved you. Yes? Unlike William, who wrote: "Why don't you, just to please Brother, sit down and write a new book, with no twilight or mustiness in the plot, with great vigour and decisiveness in the action, no fencing in the dialogue, or Psychological commentaries, and absolute straightness in style. Publish it in my name, I will acknowledge it, and give you half the proceeds." Ah, if William's words hurt, just think of the pain my words could elicit. But fortunately for you, your mind is now unhinged, you have retreated into the past. I'll do more damage to your great self-portrait than Mrs. Wood did to Sargent's canvas. For I possess the key. I can reveal to the world the figure in the carpet.

And I desire to set down the great confession. Then I'll burn all those dead words, for the creation of which you sold your soul to the devil—traded your life, my life. Yes, Henry, you never lived. You stood on the sidelines and observed. You never allowed yourself to love. You forsook love in order to create, in order to arrange lifeless words on a page. The dead, the embalmed things, you made will be all that remains of you. You will become your words. Damned to be nothing but your words. Extinguished.

I can enter your body—all it calls for is a moment of supreme concentration. I ingress, catching you saying just as I nudge you away and take your place that the absence of the male element in your entourage perplexes you. I see that only ladies attend. I call out for my glasses, pen and paper. Of course they think it is you. I see his hand move over the counterpane, while he sits at the window looking out at the river, as if he were writing. But I have complete control over that husk. I blink my eyes. It is my will which commands. I look down at my arm, the youthful arm of Henry, his well-shaped hand, not your old dead one covered with liver spots, plying pen to paper. He is full of strength having just dined on *rosbif saignant*. Is this an illusion? Am I living in one of his interminable fictions? A young American walks into Mansfield Square, the house of his London ancestors, and finds himself in the past. Entering the family house, he sees a strange portrait. Only the back of a man's head. The name on the oval plate on the frame that of one of his forebears. Glancing up from the name to the portrait, the American sees that the figure in the frame has, in the interval his eyes were averted, faced forward. To his consternation and chagrin, he beholds his own countenance! Was it an hallucination, a trick of the light, some sort of *trompe d'oeil*? The young hand I so clearly see, which at this moment takes my dictation, is it also an hallucination? For that matter, am I an hallucination? Do I actually exist and, if I do, will I die too? With him, with old Henry? Finally free, having more power than I ever expected thrust into my hands I can make myself young again, my will is so puissant. I achieve something he only dreamed of. I hope that I'm not a mere chimera, a byproduct of the dying disorientation and confusion of the stricken ancient. That my existence is not due, how did Dickens put it, to a slight disorder of the stomach. An undigested bit of beef, a blot of mustard, a crumb of cheese, a fragment of an underdone potato. Old Henry Scrooge there is almost gone. I, pray God, hope to linger on. To survive him. Tired and overburdened by the news of these dark times he welcomes the balm of sleep. He escapes from this awful war by lapsing into that natural recurring condition of suspended consciousness by which the body rests and when he does I wake. Yet I too dream. Perhaps like the oracle I see into futurity. He still every so often stirs, returns to the present from the past, and then I am banished elsewhere. At one such moment, I find myself transported from Carlyle Mansion to Italy.

I open my eyes and see Hendrik's colossal statues finally put to use there and I shudder, this is a nightmare—I wish to awake—as a new Caesar enters Rome, not my Rome, a Rome akin to that of Nero yet in a future foretold by Nostradamus. A time yet to be. I blink. I am somewhere else, a concert hall I think. Why it's "dearest darlingest" Hugh but he's aged a little. His latest protégé, a beefy young Dane who sings, stands beside him. Compositions by that monstrous man! But then again I wake and see that I am writing. I'm glad to be residing in the younger Henry where I can outperform William at his streamlined, fluent best, write with such concision so as to be sure to gain his approbation. My performance will please him thoroughly, for Henry Jr. had a more vigourous, masculine style. Much more to brother Bill's liking than the interminable, laborious *Wagnerian* manner of the late Henry. But look over what you have written. Read. Recite. The dying Henry James now doubted the validity of his work, felt the full futility of life, as he saw Germany emerge as a world power then the war he had long predicted actually break out, all of British society immediately imploding as a result. The Titanic sank yet again, the whole world lighting up in flames all at once. Anguished struggle and disorder prevailed. Caught up in the hysteria, the great masses gleefully bared their bosoms for the rifle bullets. The uppercrust professionals, those with the stiff upper lips, shrugged their shoulders, resigning themselves if needs be to have recourse to their own swords, to fall on them if it came to it like the great pagan nobles of the past. Old Brutus. Old Mark Anthony. All their lives they had been secretly steeling themselves for this. To their great delight, they could now depart this world in cork-popping good style. In positively heroic fashion. All of Britain had gone mad. Not just he. The old and expiring man had heard the death knell ring for an entire way of life, for a whole generation. He witnessed the solemn passing, the violent spasm and death gurgle, of a once great civilization. His own. A second time, the Goths and Visigoths seemed destined to bring down Rome. Albeit the Rome or should he say Romes of the modern day. The French Republic and the British Empire. A new dark age loomed and Henry fancied himself as he lay prostrate a second Marcus Aurelius, his case surely on a par with, as painful as, that of the stricken emperor. Yet there lived others of his age and sensibility.

Was it any consolation that the remaining select few of his tribe, the last of the Mohicans as it were, the hangers-on with the most tenacious grips as it turned out, would now all go down together? Perish in the general shipwreck? *He however had his afterlife: his words, his collected edition, if future people still read that is.* That his surviving peers would not have to perish one at a time, individually, any longer? So many of his people had already crossed over. So many deaths had already crippled and weakened him. Isn't life composed of endless little or partial deaths stitched together? The brave die only once says the Bard. Mostly young men die in war say I. Yet this new generation perplexed and angered him and he couldn't help but feel the world deserved its doom.

His nemesis Wagner, over thirty years dead, had a mass, a popular, following, whereas he, Henry James, did not. He had his disciples, a coterie of course, but he would remain a novelist's novelist. Another Meredith. Above all, he recalled the friend he had lost to the nemesis. Paul had proposed again and again that he meet with the master. Adamantly, however, Henry refused. *Create the scene now on paper.* Wagner would play his Jesus role to the hilt. He was the Saviour of Art calling young men to abandon their worldly tasks, their own puny attempts at artistic creation, lay them aside and take up His cause. Use their own meagre talents to further his ends. To glorify him. Henry wouldn't feel the call at all, of course. He had hoped to pull back Paul and it seemed for awhile that he could, but then Paul misunderstood his intentions. No, Herr Wagner held no attraction for Henry. The supreme vampire demanded that young men kneel down and submit. Even a prince had to bow low. Ludwig II of Bavaria. So how could good old Joukovski have possibly resisted his blandishments? Henry's natural snobbishness, his partiality and bias to all things French—German is such a monstrous, such a cumbersome maladroit language, it dully and stiffly plods, it stumbles, has none of the sprightliness, none of the concinnity of the French tongue—disincline him to have anything to do whatsoever with the mad, raving Dutchman. He would never have taken much notice of him although indeed he was a cultural phenomenon—would have remained blissfully ignorant of his accomplishments, had it not been for his friend Joukovski. In Paris, shortly after making Paul's acquaintance, Henry Jr. had attended lectures on the composer, piano performances of his work, at his new friend's request.

An utter chauvinist and hater of all things French, his nemesis had nonetheless even found adherents in that most blessed of nations and had a deleterious effect on her literature, namely on Proust, who despite all his great gifts as a society painter and as a master at description was also an infinite bore. His novel *Du Coté de chez Swann* (which Edith had sent on for his perusal) was so glacially slow paced it put all but the most refined and most stimulated asleep. Though he thought he knew the original of Dr. Cottard. Sargent had painted his portrait in oil. Perhaps this young Frenchman also had but in words many years later. Although he would have merited mention had he or rather had old Henry *père* lying on his deathbed there read him in time—would have deserved several long paragraphs in fact in an article on the new novel and younger generation—the author upon final analysis had to be held up as an appalling and insufferable mutilator of his mother tongue, of French, of all the languages the most pithy, the most sparkling and concise. He wasn't writing it anymore; *he was making French into German,* destroying it by creating his own signature style. Like the sorcerer from Saxony, he had to leave his own distinct thumbprint, impress it into the putty of his medium. A dog marking its territory, raising its leg and p—g so that others would trace, detect, its scent. W. had been there. What had started out as sweet strains in the naves of Europe's stone cathedrals, as the wholesome and deserving nay even divine art of St. Cecilia, ended in the depravity and abasement of his Faustian experiments, his aural achievements, rather one should say atrocities and outrages. His music a derisive travesty. Burlesque and caricature merely. An over-blown, over-orchestrated, over-ripe, stomach-turning, sickly sweet concoction. A witch's brew. A pestiferous sillabub. I wretch at the prospect of tasting it. Take the bitter cup from me. No, Henry had no inclination in the direction of Wagner worship whatsoever but his sworn friend the young painter Paul Joukovski could not resist the siren call, fell under the sway of the Dutchman. *The painters he loved as personalities always remained dilettantes.* Stunted, they could not grow beyond a certain point. Paul then Hendrik, whom he had hoped was a younger Henry. A protégé. A son. An heir. An Henri-*trois*. He struggled for Paul but lost to Wagner. Would Joukovski have fared better if he had attached himself to me? The larger tree always blocks out the light for the seedling struggling upwards to the sun but unfortunately under its branches. The wood in the chair shall outlast me. All ancient Henry's dead words shall outlast him. But come now, I won't accept this final revelation foisted on me probably by the mocking spirit of my brother William that my late manner is in all its intricacy, its balance and sentential mastery—William would say its mendacity, its utter duplicity and falseness—Wagnerian. Yes, yes, during those times of doubt, despair and disillusion that all artists from time to time experience, I sometimes felt as if I were perpetrating some vast comprehensive fraud, and I almost wanted to break out laughing. Of course I could restrain that impulse. Henry always could restrain himself. And indeed he enjoyed puzzles, not only finding figures in the carpet but figures in the figures. He reveled in complexity yet he spun the finest gossamer threads. Very early on Willy complained of over-refinement, of too much elegance and elaboration. Too *tarabiscoté*, he said, employing on purpose a Henry word. You go on and on. Revelation follows upon revelation. You remind me of a vulture, a buzzard endlessly circling its prey! Why don't you just pounce down and seize it. You don't need to observe a situation from all possible angles. We need greater forward momentum, a quicker pace. There are far too many gallicisms in your prose.

For a full five hours, Herr Wagner arranged and rearranged a mere handful of motifs into countless different patterns. He stretched his medium to epic lengths.

Am I as colossal a fraud as he? As guilty of padding?

My dear beloved older brother William had learned German, so naturally I the second son who so badly wanted to be the first had a predisposition against the tongue. A double second in fact because I was also the second Henry: Henry Junior. I loved but deep down wanted to supersede my father and namesake just as I wanted to best William. Although as a youth I had spent time in Bonn and enjoyed my studies there. Father wanted us to have an education, took the family to Europe, where we were to absorb French and German. In fact I lived only a few blocks away from the Beethoven *Geburtstaghaus*. And I also enjoyed day trips to the Drachenfels across the Rhine and picnics on the Venusberg. When

I returned to the continent in '72 squiring Alice and Aunt Kate, I had further experience of the country. In comparison with Italy it had very little to offer. Verona was much more to my taste than Nuremberg, though the latter city was preferable to Munich, a nightmare of pretentious vacuity. How did I frame it then, that I must listen to the voice of the spirit and cease hair-splitting but treat myself to a good square antipathy? Well I went back later on, spent ten weeks one year in Bad Homburg and five weeks in another in Baden-Baden. The dullest days in my life. I left the spa in early August and took a Rhine journey into the Low Countries. *Roderick Hudson* gestated in my not-yet bald dome. In 1890 the Curtises persuaded me to accompany them to the Passion Play in Oberammergau. The mountain scenery was truly splendid but the play was so very primitive and the town so distastefully commercial. I also was summoned across the channel to attend the funeral of my young agent Wolcott Balestir in Dresden—his sister later married pubescent Kipling—and stood at his grave in a tawdry green cemetery. The poor fellow swallowed tainted, defiled water. Only a few months later and dear Alice would be dead. Why had the Germans reverted to barbarism? Were they all intoxicated with, were they all drugged by, Wagner's music? I tried to be fair and even-handed. In the past I had written rather sympathetically about Germans. An aristocrat Count Vogelstein narrates "Pandora." His name, the name I gave him, a combination of bird and rock, a hurled weapon which sings! My diplomat, this "Featherstone" (heavy and light, vapid and turgid at the same time, such is the paradox of the German character) meets the heroine of the title on board a ship bound for America and then encounters her again in Washington at a social gathering where he sees her charm the President of the United States and obtain from him a post for her fiancé. Vogelstein is amazed at the girl's temerity and develops a new admiration for American ladies. Not a negative portrait. No, not at all. Merely a truthful one. And in "Collaboration," admittedly one of my lesser more inconsequential efforts, I wrote about a French poet and German composer who were so taken with each other's work that they decided to write an opera together even though their collaboration has costly consequences for them both—as the Frenchman loses his fiancée whose father fell in the Franco-Prussian War because her mother cannot tolerate him working with the German and the composer loses the support of his patron brother who also has an aversion for the former enemy. But enough. I hear William's voice accusing me of digressing. But no, I must persist. I even wrote kindly about Wagner, about his Wedding March. In *The Bostonians*, I think. Certainly nothing so condemnatory as John Ruskin's review where he labeled the German's music as bête, clumsy, baboon-blooded stuff. Worse than railway whistles. Adjective after adjective. Affected, sapless, soulless, beginningless, endless, topless, bottomless, topsiturviest, togs and boniest doggerel of sound he ever heard. In "Crappy Cornelia," I used his phrase "Music of the Future" to describe my vision of a coming America where everything was homogenized, exercised, sanitized and manicured, where civility amounted to taking the amused ironic view of those less initiated than oneself. But in *Wings of the Dove* what I wrote about his music rings complimentary. Well, if not altogether complimentary, I recognized the music's force and grandeur. How it overwhelms, conquers, triumphs, takes no prisoners, dwarfs. "But the great sustained sea-light had drunk up the rest of the picture, so for many days other questions and other possibilities sounded with as little effect as a trio of penny whistles might sound in a Wagner overture. It was the Wagner overture that practically prevailed up through Italy, where Milly had already been, still further up and across the Alps...." His death came in Venice where the dove of my novel the young American millionairess Milly Theale dies and where Fenimore, dear Fenimore, took her life.

No I won't accept William's criticism. Wagner's art and mine are not the least bit alike. True, when his works were performed in Drury Lane, they were excoriated in the newspapers, found to be impure and repulsive. He was accused of worshipping animal passion. My morality also offended. The world was worse off for my decadence, someone once wrote. But aside from charges being made against us both for producing immoral art, we are so different! Wagner engrossed all the groundlings as well as the élite intellectuals, pandered to them. *Shaw lauded his operas not my dramas.* The throng heckled *Guy Domville.* In these apocalyptic times the entire Germanic nation venerates him, is inspired by the blackguard to prevail over their betters and to feel as if they have been criminally persecuted at our hands. He succeeds as artist. Only a few hear my voice. It dies out.

The soldiers I saw in the long wards knew that the portly gentleman who sat down at their bedsides was revered by the nobs, those in the know. But they did not revere him, had never read any of his books. Thanks be to Zeus, I have the force of personality, however, to make an impression on them, lock an image of myself into their brains. I don't deign or condescend, act the part of the superman or God. I quietly pay homage to them within proper bounds—while observing all the proprieties of course. I honor them. I am another Whitman. Twice a Whitman, for at the start of America's epic four-year confrontation Sargy Perry and I visited convalescent troops at Portsmouth Grove along the Rhode Island coast. But then because of the injury I sustained to my back fighting a barn fire I had been unable to enlist, had been reduced to a stay-at-home, although both Wilky—he came very close to giving up the ghost—and Robertson did, Wilky in fact joining Gould Shaw's coloured regiment which attempted to lay siege to Fort—my God—*Wagner.* No we say Wag not Vog. Though Wagner is nothing if not a rogue fully deserving his waghalter, though hardly a wit, a sport. In Charleston Bay. Most of the men including Gould Shaw—or was it Shaw Gould?—were gunned down or bayoneted, but Wilkinson only took a ball in the ankle. They brought him home on a stretcher as pale as death. Yes the Civil War occurred all over again. Only this time it was Europe being torn apart, being visited by destruction, and not the United States.

Ugliness. To have lived to behold such ugliness! And years ago Paul fell in love with the spook this master swindler was then unleashing, the ghost haunting us all now, his galling art!

Once more old Henry strives to displace me. He wants me to stop talking. He says civilization, Napoleon, will triumph. Right will prevail, as will he. His work. *His* ghost. After he's dead, men and women will still read his stories, his amusettes and his novels for he has produced a long list. They (his future readers) will share his consciousness. Entering one of his books like a soul transmigrating into a new body, from the very first page, they will bring life, their life, to his sloughed off words, into his literary remains, and reanimate them and thereby he will gain new life as well. He will win adherents while not even in the flesh; his ghost will woo its own. Good. Let it. Then I won't have to share those I'm enchanted by now, while I live, with his Frankenstein's monster. I can keep them for myself. For me. Jocelyn Persse, for instance. He's all mine. There existed, there exists, an exquisite accord, a complete agreement in feeling, between us. And now he is off to fight, to struggle to the death with the Hun!

I was, I became, a batty older brother for Persse. I gave him *The Ambassadors* to struggle through although I knew he probably wouldn't read more than twenty or thirty pages if that, but I didn't care. Persse likes me so much as a person. In the flesh. Even though I'm bloated and long in the tooth—made that way by, the product of, those thousand and one days, more many more in fact, of writing six and eight hours at a go. Henry was destined to turn into his creation, to live on in his texts after he went back into the ground, this future self the true Henry. He sacrificed a life in his ghost's creation. Clearly he had felt that the ghost was more important than he, but Persse didn't love the ghost, would never view it. Maybe he would get a quick glimpse if he dipped into *The Ambassadors*, into Lambert Strether's tale: the ghost would be visible and then in a flash be gone. Persse would rub his eyes and dismiss it as an effect of shadow and light. No reader, he valued Henry in and of himself and I was enchanted by him. Much earlier Paul had also been such a friend. We adored each other like brothers but then he fell in love with the German's spectre, his monstrous art. I can hardly help but feeling the tug and pull of all the paths I didn't choose. In retrospect their allure is greater now because once they were rejected. Paul and I could have bonded together had I not been so inhibited when I was young. I had difficulty befriending both men and women. As a youth I couldn't tempt women to the essential thing. In later life I'm sure I could have. Many ladies were susceptible to my charms but by then I didn't have the slightest interest whatsoever though I would wittily discourse on any subject that interested them, enjoyed them as friends. I wanted so badly to be Joukovski's friend, and he was a second son, a younger brother to a tee. A perfect companion for me. I could play the William part. I wouldn't be cold and aloof rejecting all overtures of brotherly affection with superior, scornful disdain. Oh how I suffered at William's hand as a child. He was so cruel and malicious. Every time I reached out to him he would smack my hand away. I'd be responsive and broadly demonstrative in my love. He'd be my dear darlingest Henry. I would protect and look after him. But how tell him? I had lived my whole life in a cage. My timidity prevented me from making an open declaration. I blushed when I thought of unburdening myself. I erected barriers and put impediments in my way, kept myself cocooned. Often I wanted to be invisible. To disappear out of sight. I strove to always keep my private feelings hidden from view. I felt like a fly imprisoned in a bead of amber. I couldn't pass through the transparent resin which seemed to be of my own making. A substance which oozed out of my pores as a protective response to outside danger. My sap hardened round me. Kept anything hurtful from penetrating and getting through. I didn't like to be touched. No, never. I felt safe behind my screen, my arras. Poloniously observing the swelling scene but forever cut off from it. Yet I wanted desperately to burst the bubble and befriend Paul. All that I desired was brotherly love and affection. I found it tremendously difficult to approach and sound him. However, I fought through my reticence and let him know how fondly I regarded him, told him he should not sell himself short, that he could be an artist in his own right and not a mere disciple. But he misunderstood, thought my affection was perverse, of an unclean nature, and responded—No, Henry won't let me say it—as if I had given him an invitation!

Ancient Henry, stubborn to the last, is again pushing me out. I am almost gone. I hear his voice. Again he venerates Napoleon. He is dying. His mind is disintegrating, yet he still wants to dictate to Miss Bosanquet. The nemesis drew his first breath in Leipzig in 1813, as French forces fled across Germany, pursued by Tzarist troops. If only Napoleon had taken on the role of Herod, found the young male baby and had its throat cut. But I am missing what he is saying: "These final and fading words. Some interest, some character. Should be extracted by a highly competent person only. Invoke more than one kind presence. Several could help...."

II

I have been asleep I don't know for how long but when I open my eyes I see a sheaf of papers. Now a single sheet. Words formulate in my head. I see them appear on the page.

Mother died in January 1882. Afterwards I again sailed to Europe and stayed for a little while in Ireland, left ship at Cork. *I mothered Burgess, sent him socks when he went off to fight the Kaiser, Victoria's grandson.* Father passed in December 1882. I took that role on for Hugh Walpole. Became Henry Sr. indeed. He called me *très cher maitre.* As a green youth I could have called Turgenieff my master, yet I must say that I feel I surpassed the great Russian, as I certainly outstripped my biological father. He and brother Garth Wilkinson both gave up the ghost in 1883. The year also of the nemesis' end, of his black heart's ceasing—at long last—to beat. Alice in 1892. Of breast cancer. Henry, one of your crimes was that act of suppression. You insisted that her journal not be published in your lifetime. *She urged me to marry Fenimore before she died.* She understood yearning for the beloved. She realized Fenimore longed in the same manner as she, with the same intensity. Alice coveted Kate Loring and struggled with her beloved's own sister for her affection. They both wanted to possess her wholly, heart and mind. They needed her kindly ministrations, became ill so they could have her at their sides. It had been a fairly evenly matched battle. The nemesis' pull, his power of attraction, on the other hand, was far greater than my own. He tugged Jou away from me into his orbit. Though at the time of our separation, our final rupture, I, aged thirty-five, had published *Roderick Hudson, The Madonna of the Future & Other Tales,* a collection of essays on French writers, *The American, Daisy Miller, The Europeans, Confidence, Hawthorne,* and *Washington Square,* as well as numerous short stories, reviews, and articles in both American and British periodicals. I had just commenced writing *The Portrait of a Lady.* Yes, my decision to go to England had been the right one. I felt still too much of the foreigner in Paris to make my permanent residence there. Once I crossed over, my writing career really bloomed and took off. I brought a book out every year, met everyone of consequence, in short became a literary lion. William would say I developed my massive self-sufficiency, but I am digressing. Everything is muddled. Bob died in his sleep of a heart attack. William expired August 26 of the same year. 1910. His heart burst as well. He had problems, little intuitions, for years. His death marked my ascension to the Jamesian throne. I became undisputed king and monarch of the clan. But now my heart dies inside me. The Jameses will be no more. My life nothing but a fraud, I committed great crimes during its course.

Like Wagner, I was a vampire. *Not with men surely*. Aside from the painful case of Howard Overing Sturgis. I suppressed him with my thumb. Squashed him like an insect by what I said. I didn't intend to destroy, to nip his flower in the bud. I wanted only to be helpful when he brought me the galleys of his novel. Golden-haired, small-footed, fastidious Howdie. He traded his pen for a knitting needle, returned to the tacking and tucking, to making antimacassars to protect sofa backs. Never before did I express a dislike of furniture, rather I appreciated it, or the workmanship that went into its construction, but is it not just a turn of the screw from love to hate? There exists an inner naysayer—a rebellious negator— in us that dislikes and tears down what we as individuals seemingly most especially esteem and prize. I found his work very promising but flawed. I was also very critical of anything that came from Hugh's pen. My remarks never stemmed *his* flow, blocked his output. I saw the crack in, if you'll pardon my use here of my own singular metaphor, "his" golden bowl and could not resist, deny myself the pleasure, of pointing it out to him. But I also saw the rift the fissure in my own productions. Perfection of form does not compensate for lifelessness. How could a man who never lived write? Such was the charge I leveled against myself, the flaw I pointed out to Howdie far less devastating. Nonetheless, after my revelation, he ceased to compose; yes, he'd take a carpet and a high-backed chair and place them on the lawn in front of his lodging, in his private park. He brought a basket filled with balls of yellow thread outside with him. His dogs would gambol in the sun, chase squirrels and rabbits through the grass, as he worked, hours at a time, on his bulky composition, laden with all sorts of patterns and motifs. Some sort of tapestry, some sort of antimacassar.

Yes, the sexes feed upon each other. I must admit that I was something of a bloodsucker with women, took their life breath and fed and battened upon it, that that was one of my secrets, though I more than hinted at my sin in various of my works. A figure in the carpet that should be visible to any discerning, disinterested, reader. No male reader would have to contemplate marriage to another man's widow—who knew the solution to the riddle (as was the case in my story)—in order to have the secret revealed, the figure pointed out. For years and years I looked askance at my romantically entangled acquaintances. Whenever friends grew infatuated, I observed with a kind of distain and hauteur. Their strength would be sapped by some succubus assuming the female form to make the beast with two backs in order to siphon off their youth and vigour, their wit and intelligence, to make them grow soft and addlepated and causing them to act silly and inebriated. I drained the life out of my cousin Minny Temple, didn't I, grew strong as she declined? Poor Minny dead so long ago. We loved each other but I could not approach her. I could only look on from some far distant periphery, as if from some far shore across the waves. I, the malingerer, the shirker, did not show to advantage when compared to the veterans John Chipmann Gray and Oliver Wendell Holmes. After her early death, she took up residence in my mind and often, many times over the years, I have inserted her ghost into some of my pages. She became Isabel Archer and Milly Theale. My Milly would die in Venice where dear Fenimore ended her life, leaping out of the second-story window of her *Casa* and falling to her death in the little side street. I made her acquaintance shortly after being disillusioned with Jou. The grandniece of James Fenimore Cooper, three years older than myself and anticipating my future valet Burgess, deaf in one ear. A lady novelist. She developed a passion, an ardour for me as both writer and man. As always I remained frosty, detached and dispassionate. She recognized the worth of my work and because of her insight, her obeisance, I developed a great affection for her and took her under my wing as a sister artist, a gentlewoman of some sensibility. A curious companionship we shared, she always publicly declaring her great esteem for my fictions, my great gift to the world, to mankind. But at the same time she was also horribly jealous. She worked indefatigably, yet despite her dedication to the craft, her works did not deserve the praise I—more than partial—bestowed on them. Yes my superiority was evident to her, my first draft far more interesting than her sixteenth or seventeenth. But she also offered me a gift which I could not take. She told me that I didn't understand how women thought or felt. One made oneself lovable by loving. A simple truth. I offered to collaborate on a play with her. The only time in my career—I was such a solitary artist—that I agreed to share writing duties with anyone, this to recompense her for a failed union elsewhere. The power which resides in little words like if. The beast never sprang from its crouching position in the thicket and the possibility of a deeper alliance vanished with her Venice death. The capacity for further growth and development in our relations ceased. *If only* I had acted differently. *If only* I had not been so inhibited. *If* only I had taken the chance and accepted what she proffered me. When something can no longer be realized, when an opportunity is lost forever to us, we mourn. *Will I be mourned?* The significance and worth of a thing increases when it becomes impossible, when it can no longer ever be actualized or consummated. Kindred by choice, she wanted more, what I felt incapable to ever give. When revising my work, my hand was ever poised to strike anything perfunctory and second-rate, anything unseemly and indelicate. I wanted my prose blemishless. Nor, of course, do I want any personal lapse or failure on my part to come to light. Therefore through ruse and misdirection, I gained access to her posthumous papers. I told her sister I would find all the best gleanings, all the choice chestnuts. I proffered my services. The professional would separate the wheat from the chaff with an eye toward future publication. Truthfully, I went through her papers to find and destroy any in-the-heat-of-their-composition ill-considered and injudicious letters of mine which she might have kept as precious mementoes, as well as anything that she might have written about her unhappiness at our equivocal relations, how Henry escaped all the various snares she laid for him. I wanted no one, certainly no future biographer, to know the particulars of our sad story. After all "The Aspern Papers" was written while we resided in adjoining chateaux in Florence, she at the villa Castellani, I at the villa Brichieri-Colombi. The palaces had both been erected on the Bellosguardo, a Florentine hilltop. I had heard about several indelicate Byron letters in the possession of a niece of Claire Clairmonte, curios for future voyeurs. Those supposed letters sparked the idea for my novelette. It would be ironic in the extreme if some future scholar got hold of some incriminating document about me, especially one dating from that time period! I wanted to destroy, if it existed, any such evidence about my and

Fenimore's sad and problematic situation. Afterward I could claim that I only realized belatedly that I had unwittingly trifled with her affections. Privacies had to be kept safe, to remain private. Most of all when one planned to hide them in the guise of one's fiction. While perusing her papers, I, of course, came across then skimmed the entry in her notebook, her idea for a story about a man who never gave fully of himself, never experienced what was best in life because he never allowed himself to love. I saw immediately that I could do something choice with that theme. *Admit it, you stole her story idea. Even after all that happened. You could write it so much better than she. That was your justification. Another of your crimes.* Ah, but remember, too, how that silly American adventuress Emilie Grigsby implied that you had turned her into a fictional character—into Milly Theale—when you hadn't at all, because of a supposed infatuation on your part, a love she did not return. I had been introduced to Miss Grigsby once or twice and after that saw her in public only six, at the most seven times, and never did I say anything untoward or suggestive to her. Yet the little schemer, she let it be known—told the American papers—that I had actually gotten down on my knees and proposed marriage. To the redheaded model of my dying heroine. Absurd laughable assertion yet the press circulated the rumour, let it reverberate like an fff cord. Preposterous, fantastic, that I would ask for a woman's hand, especially at my ripe age, let alone hers. Silly goose. Yes, Fenimore, I too was a victim. Moreover your claim that I never loved women is quite untrue, for I cared deeply for Mother, Alice, and Cousin Minny and yes in my own peculiar way for you. In my youth, I enjoyed sitting at the knees of elderly women and listening to them talk about the past and make it live for me. Old stories I would thus pick up which could always be reworked, remolded, into new fictions. I loved to be carried backward in time. I learned, for instance, about days gone by sitting as a young man at the feet of the great Mary Ann Evans. And yes Fenimore another lady writer began to reverence me after your departure from this our vale of tears. We took long rides in her Panhard, motored across the French countryside. *Today it's littered with the corpses of men and horses, spent shells lying everywhere! The world's on fire, expiating its sins.* I could satirize her in one of my stories without the least fear of offending; she would even pronounce what I wrote really good; she remained loyal and true to me though I refused to write her a preface. No *pouf* from me, Edith dear, not that you don't deserve one. But it would sap a little of my precious strength. All of which must now go into writing down my version of the past, so that it will never be lost.

III

William again says that I became what I hated. Yes I admit that in later years I could appreciate being Master, of having a select coterie of young disciples who took me as an oracle. Just as the nemesis had his cadre of male admirers. Funny pictures of us both appeared in the newspapers, my style so universally well known, it was parodied everywhere.

I could also dismiss a rival author, another artist some would say. I knew better: a dilettante. Someone like little Georgie Moore for instance, another nemesis venerator and like the always-facile Shaw of the Irish variety. *American Celts like myself aren't nearly so susceptible, Heaven be thanked.* "Unimportantly dull," I opined about Moore, every bit as acidly as the man he and G.B. reverenced, the oh so vulgar Herr Wilhelm Richard Wagner could discount and depreciate a contemporary composer, a peer of his such as Brahms or Verdi. We could both dispatch a victim with equal celerity.

But I, unlike him, pay homage to men who can't fully appreciate me and tolerate—and usually only barely—any devotee from the various literary cliques who falls down on his knees and grovels at my coattails, who dutifully bows, scrapes and makes obeisance. Well, if the boy had merit, if I adjudged him as truly deserving, truly worthy of being admitted to the secret inner sanctum, I might accept him as an acolyte. If I saw that I had inspired and sparked an interest in him. If I saw for once that the seed I scattered in all directions had not fallen on fallow ground. If I saw something take root and sprout in him that came from me. If I detected a transference and transubstantiation, I would have to resignedly accept him as a novice of my order. But I would remonstrate with him constantly; show how grudgingly I granted his admission. How provisionally for the time being. Many higher degrees would have to be conferred and many deeper mysteries penetrated before he could ever presume to knighthood. Yet to remain truthful, many of my hangers-on charmed me. Balestir. Bourget. William Morton Fullerton. Sturges. Harland. Bennet Brewster. I retained deep affection for them all. Others, those without merit, without depth, I brushed aside—cut. That haughty hun Hueffer, for instance. However a totally naive and unaffected young man without literary pretensions who merely demonstrated affinity and liking for me as a person provided that I also found him attractive and agreeable—if he had force of personality and charm—might, just might, have the capacity to excite and pull my heartstrings in a way that the most reverent, the most deserving disciple of the master could not. No matter how talented, how literate he was.

Hendrik Andersen differed from Persse in that I also saw him as an artist. He had the personality but not the gift which disillusioned me to a very great extent. I tried to encourage him but the fact that he didn't measure up, that I could not lie to him when he sought my wholehearted approval and approbation put too much strain and stress on our friendship. Art entered in where it shouldn't have.

He seemed so promising when we first met that summer in Italy, the same one as I encountered the Bacchus boy, Aristodemo, his name honey on the tongue, frolicking in the strawberry beds adjacent to the temple ruins on the shore of Lake Nemi. I could have written that experience up into a majestic novella but was too afraid of being misunderstood, of being labeled a leader of an abominable life like that horrible most Roman of men Oscar Wilde. The lake, below, blazed blue as a Nordic iris. We crossed the ancient viaduct. Staring at the sun reflected in the lake's lapping waters I blinded myself for several seconds. Mrs. Humphrey Ward and her two daughters accompanied me on this ramble, Mrs. Ward accepting the offer of my arm, to behold where the Pagans practiced their mad and frenzied rites, their holy mysteries. Relics strewn on the ground could be seen protruding up through the earth in the berry fields to our right and left. An excavation was supposed to be in progress at the site below. I felt glad to have my hat to shade my eyes from the sun's brilliance, my armpits stained with sweat. Before coming on the boy, up above, taking our eyes off the lake for a moment, we saw—Mrs. Ward pointed it out to me; I still blind from staring at the reflected sun in the water squinted and squinted but could not find it for myself—the ruins of Diana's temple, and Mrs. Ward said an ancient spring—Egeria's holy fount in fact—had once bubbled from an embrasure in the temple's wall. I gasped once or twice, had to pause and rest but bit-by-bit we made our way down toward the temple when we encountered the dark-eyed youth.

Never before had I seen so beautiful a child, thin and lithe, agile and loose, head aureoled by curly black ringlets like those of the Assyrian God, skin olive-hued, both sides of his face as proportionate as any statue's, he could have grown into Michelangelo's young David. At most he was eleven.

He ran right in front of us, out of the recently ploughed strawberry pastures. I asked the frisky little specimen his name and he told me it was Aristodemo. I repeated it several times, such a lovely old and noble Greek name. I walked at his side, alas not nearly so nimble as he. I couldn't keep up, so he stopped, and I asked him if he ever found any artifacts in these fields and he said that they uncovered many, that the ground was replete with them. They lay at our very feet at this moment. Once he found a marble head. A bust or a decapitated statue, I wondered, unable to shift my eyes from his beautiful visage in which the blood of the ancients still coursed. He stood as straight and comely as a little soldier. I saw perfection, purity of form, the loveliness of life in his little sparrow limbs. The cream, coming on him during the jaunt along the blue lake down to the temple, red strawberries growing as far as the eye could see.

I was no dandyish Count Robert de Montesquiou-Fezensac, no fey Oscar, or crusaderish John Addington Symonds with a hideous human history. As a favour to Sargent, I once acted the part of London guide for the French Count, unique extra-human that he was, along with two other visiting Frenchmen. He sported waxed moustaches and all the time he wore a strong cologne. A pungent perfume. And Symonds? Asked to write an appreciation of him as we both had a passion for Italy, I sent my regrets, having learned of his inversion. They remained without exception fell rutting animals, who enjoyed smelling each other's excrescences and ammonia odours. Little gigglers who had not brought their bodies under control, who could not abstain, whose brains they suborned to their hairy genitals, always standing to attention, always at the ready. Able but false, that is what I had to say about Wilde's writings. I on the other hand could practice the love that Jesus taught: the extent of my affection for Aristodemo, for Persse. Hugh offered to lay his head in my lap. *I can't, I can't,* I told him. That didn't mean I was not sympathetic to his human weakness, as I should have been to Joukovski's, that I couldn't forgive and absolve them. Then I was so young, so infernally callow, stiff. I told Hugh that for him it was healthy, inevitable, he young and curious. He shouldn't have any guilt, as long as it came but in bouts and brief convulsions. I remained the understanding father figure he needed. His real father wore the collar. He could expect no acceptance from that quarter. I told him one needed to live in order to write, that we must know what we are talking about if we expect to create beauty on the page, to depict truthfully the human comedy. He saw me for the tolerant Puritan I was. I would not damn others for doing what I had the strength not to do. His own sense of morality amused me. Outraged at a Catholic priest who suffered the same affliction as he, he wrote to me of immorality on stone floors. With prayerbooks in their hands! I replied coolly would the exigencies of the situation permit of the manual retention of the sacred volumes?

Yes, Hendrik Andersen stood a gross miscalculation on my part. Charmed by him like no other, I so wanted to be his father. I felt that I was his father, he my Roderick Hudson made flesh, the purest expression of the blond Nordic type. He wanted to erect gigantic statues just as did my fictional creation, my real son. I visited his Rome studio that summer and bought a terracotta bust. A terrible tease, I chose to overlook his faults. He bloomed before my very eyes. I saw him in his prime. I had deteriorated, become bald and obese. I wanted my youth back. I wanted to be him. He had the world to conquer, but alas he suffered from *la folie des grandeurs.* He used me shamelessly. Had he been successful in his career—as I had been in mine—I would have forgiven him, would not now be ashamed of my weakness. I wouldn't have minded using my watering can, had he sprouted, but the waste of the water on him now pains me. He sat under my tree and as I looked into his eyes I so badly wanted him to succeed. He only occasionally came into my orbit, but we exchanged those disgusting *billet-doux.* Unfortunately I teased back, silly game that we played, called him my dear boy, wrote that he condemned me almost never to be near him but that he felt my arms around him, my hands soothing, sustaining, positively healing in the quality of their pressure. I'm sure he burned my correspondence as I tactfully destroyed his letters back to me. Yet he failed, failed miserably as an artist, sent me a circular appealing for funds for the City of World Peace which he hoped to build himself somewhere in the Midwest. I could not indulge his mania for the colossal.

Persse I could love more purely, for the life in him. I loved that life, but I denied myself it in order to devote myself entirely to my art. Persse lived and did not create, but his "art" beat mine hollow. He relished it all: fine cigars, a good brandy, the joy of the hunt with all those braying hounds. He made love to women which I never permitted myself to do. He delighted in eating whereas I often bolted my food, didn't even taste it. Oh, the life he allowed himself to lead! What wouldn't one do for the privilege of standing in his shoes? All of us men need to belong to a monastic order. We would all benefit from journeying to some pure and elevated spot—a site of purification where I'd feel comfortable even if several of our worshippers, our acolytes, were to place their hands on me (I feel fingers cupping my closed eyes; another pair of hands squeezing at my knees). Others would prostrate themselves in front of my person. There would exist no exigencies of the moment. I would remain free to meditate. Oh the joys of being one of the elect, of belonging to a secret society. Suddenly the light pressure on my eyes is gone. The acolyte has removed his fingers from off them, yet I still do not choose to lift my lids. Do I smell incense? I will open my eyes on a Roman bath. I am at peace not looking on, a fat Buddha sitting here.

Oh I failed. I failed at so many things. I contemplated writing a tale about an elderly writer falling in love with a young boy but despite the keenness of my desire, would not allow myself to succumb to it. I had been unable to complete my novels *The Ivory Tower* and *The Sense of the Past*. Both of those abortions could have been molded into memorable, momentous manuscripts had I only had the time and the will.

I started *The Sense of the Past* at the turn of the Century after shaving off the beard I had worn for decades. My young historian protagonist fled from the present, as perhaps I did even then. The clock indeed remained on my mind, but after six or seven months, I abandoned the book to take it up again fourteen years later in 1914. Again I could not get on with it. Wish fulfillment on my part taking up the manuscript then, for *I* wanted to flee backwards into the past as I saw the Apocalypse approach. Wagner's art seemed right for the times, this barbaric era coming into being, whereas my works belonged to the civilization being supplanted.

Even more than my unfinished books, I lament all those forks in the road, the turns not taken, in my life, and also my many mistakes and oversights, my often dull incomprehension, my quickness to find certain things vile and repulsive. What did I tell Walpole, I didn't regret a single excess of my responsive youth, I only regretted, in my chilled old age, certain occasions and possibilities I didn't embrace. That is right. Now I can open my eyes. And I know where I'll stand when I again look out on the world.

What! I can't change anything. Who says this? I can go back to observe—to see—but I am the past's prisoner. *Shocked*, the voice says, *you will again pack your bags and leave Posillipo, hiring a calèche at an extravagant price to drive you to Sorrento.*

Then I won't bother opening my eyes, I reply.

Yes, says the voice. You will.

He felt, that winter, the need to escape the narrow confines of London town where he spent the better part of each day inside sitting at his desk at very taxing work, like a gem cutter. It thoroughly, altogether, exhausted him. Pale from standing out in the sun, chubbier this year than last, he bellied up to the scrolled roll top, the place of his Herculean labour, every morning feeling full, so overstuffed with roast beef, kippers, tea cakes, pudding, potatoes and gravy, that he wanted to jump deck, to abandon his English ship, his lodgings, most of all the food, all the standard fare, and for a goodly length of time. He overindulged. He took port with his meals. The life of a man of seeming leisure could be very unhealthful, but he produced and produced and produced (his study *Hawthorne* was finished as was his novella *Washington Square*); then every night he had an invitation out. He was a gentleman, refined and educated, cut from the finer cloth. An eminently respectable up-and-comer, but he longed for a little anonymity. The continent would furnish it to him. England having been cold and blanketed with snow the entire winter, for months he had craved the sunny climes of Italy, longed to take the trip there which he had had to forego on account of the weather in December (for he had managed a visit to Paris the previous autumn and had begun *Washington Square* there), but just before he was due to depart France for Italy, where he had planned to pay a call on his old friend M. Paul Joukovski, who then lived near Naples, the blizzard struck and he had to postpone. He crossed the channel and waited for the spring, working feverishly but not on the novel he had promised to write William, the book that would be to his earlier productions as wine was to water. He knew that it had to be written or at least begun in the homeland of great Virgil.

In 1878, William had married and he felt completely cut off, estranged from his brother. Did Fate doom him forever to remain a solitary? William called his work trifling and superficial, and complained that he wrote increasingly about the weaker sex, that he had a preference for heroines instead of heroes. I want, William said, a great big fat tome, and Henry promised to deliver it to him.

For many months, feeling hostile toward his brother, he had been struck by wave after wave of nostalgia for Paris and for Paul. During the entire summer of '79 he had pined for the Paris world he had left half a decade earlier during his salad days. How doubly glad he stood now that he had overcome his fear five years before and had paid his respects to the great Russian writer, his idol Ivan Sergeyevich Turgenieff, a year after receiving in Baden-Baden an invitation from the man to call at the Paris home of his friend Madame Pauline Viardot, Turgenieff's own residence while in the French capital. The Russian introduced him to the notable and to the not so notable—to charming dilettantes such as his countryman Paul Joukovski, son of a famous poet and tutor to the Tzar, who had a wonderful engaging personality, and to the greatest writers of the day. He had met Flaubert, who in turn had presented him to many of his own adherents, notables and future notables themselves—de Goncourt, Zola, Daudet, de Maupassant. Henry had been doing only prentice work up to then. He learned from the French. Flaubert's little coterie stressed style. A novel must be well written. That was all. But in Paul he had made a friend like no other before him. He had absented himself from his friend's society now for five whole years, but soon they would see each other again in Italy, after yet another postponement of three months. He remained quite excited. All that winter, he kept catching himself going into reveries about those Paris days when he and Paul had kept in each other's company weeks and weeks at a time. He thought about their nightlong conversations over an open bottle, both of them smoking stale yet very pungent cigars. Paul could be a William replacement for him now. He wanted to see the Russian again ever so badly, even more so because William's new wife had come between his brother and himself. Unlike William, he would never marry. I resolve to be a bachelor for life, he wrote his newly-wedded brother, even though in England women of all ages liked him because he saw them as they saw themselves, that is to say in a favourable light, though he himself preferred the society of elderly spinsters for they remained his windows on the past.

Shame on you Bill for marrying, but I should not tsk tsk (it is your destiny, your task and function now, to carry on the James family name, where mine is to create works of high art) although your plight saddens me because she will become an encumbrance for you, interfere I'm sure with your academic work, check you ambition and now I am irrevocably abandoned and left alone. I crossed the Atlantic so as to be out of earshot of all your carping yes, but I remained ever fond of it, and we maintained contact via letters, yet now I truly feel truly divorced from you. William had been so much a part of me, another self almost, a twin as it were, though my mother gave birth to him fifteen months in advance of myself, but now the tie severs. We all need a nemesis. Someone to hone ourselves on by perpetually trying to overcome and surpass him. William had been mine.

Five years before in Paris, Henry and Paul had visited together all the famous salons. Henry had loved them although he did not care for the interminable music, one thing from those Paris days that he did not wax nostalgic about. He had heard assorted divas, tenors, and string quartets. Once at a grand ball to which Henry was invited, Johann Strauss himself led the orchestra through several of his waltzes. They did not grate on the ear, puncture it as with a pin, but he (Henry) reeled in agony on another occasion, when he sat in the audience while Giuseppe Verdi conducted his *Requiem*. He could not abide the singing, especially that of the females. He had already heard enough, really, before befriending the young Russian. Paul had been raised at court, a perfect little prince who spent his boyhood in proximity to greatness! However, after making the young man's acquaintance he simply couldn't refuse him his company and would be dragged to numerous concerts and what's more to bloody Wagner evenings. There was something of the blue blood, the silk stocking about Paul yet dilettante that he was, he had the zeal of a visionary. He had lived in Venetian palaces, but his enormous Parisian studio remained the true abode of his soul, his rooms laden with Italian statuary and other works of art. Two large canvasses of his stood on display, that spring, in the Salon. They did not impress me, but he himself remained much to my taste. A poseur Paul, yet also a flower of Civilization, a dying, almost spent blossom.

Tall, he had pale blue eyes. He had already lost hair from his forehead, and his long face tapered to a goateed chin. His lips pursed in a perpetual whistle. He looked a little like William Shakespeare but with more beard. Animated at all times, he threw his hands outward, wiggling and drumming his fingers as if he himself hammered on a piano. He seemed shockingly naive on occasion, innocent, incorruptible, but the next minute he would wink or whistle and his eyes had that sly glint to them. We would speak in French for hours about art. He had taste; he was truly the connoisseur, the collector of old Italian prizes. Pampered all his life, every desire every craving indulged and overindulged by his various retainers in both Russia and Italy, he remained a young man of independent means and he remained endlessly diverting, a gabbler, a prate. Like William he could speak and read German. As well as being half orphan—his father the poet was deceased—he was half Hun, his mother an *Allemande*. On the card he sent me in Paris when I first wrote concerning my approaching visit, he gave his name as Paul von Joukovski, an affectation on his part which I did not appreciate.

I left March 22nd. We agreed to meet each other in Posillipo after all this time. After a five-year separation, I would go to him, to his villa just outside of Naples. He had taken his residence up there to be near at hand should his master need him. Oh, I wished that the third person, the other star in our trinity, would have been my friend Turgenieff instead of that opera composer Richard Wagner, as had been the arrangement in Paris five years before. Paul wrote to me that now I would have the opportunity to meet the greatest man of the century.

He had become such a hero worshipper! I never got down on my knees before Turgenieff. I prized and esteemed him. For me he became a father figure, stern and implacable, looking over my shoulder at my fledgling efforts, finding all the faults, drawing a neat line through all that must be excised, passage after passage. In fact, I could adopt his persona and Ivanize myself. I would look down at what I had written through his eyes and expunge and rewrite, polish sentences incessantly, never satisfied, the painter with his sponge and varnish bottle, or I could make him mouth William's or even my own father's criticisms! Too *tarabiscote*, fancy and ornate. Not manly enough. Are you an old woman sewing? In truth, I learned a great deal from reading the Russian—in French translation, of course, and he respected me, a much younger man, as a fellow artist. He told me that his characters came to him long before the plot of the story he would eventually put them in, that it didn't matter in the end what direction your novel took. It unfolded before you, like landscape on a train, as you wrote it. You just had to keep at it, keep writing. It was all right to remain in the dark as to where it all went. We understood vastness, both of us exiles from such huge sprawling countries, he from Russia, I from the United States of America, yet we also understood art, how everything should be connected, tied together. His works, many of them, seemed flawless, his sentences, at least in French, written down copperplate. Yet, despite my sincere admiration for his art, I recognized his all too human weaknesses. Madame Viardot led him around by the nose. He obeyed her every command. It was idiotic to see him participate in her games of charade. He had an expansive softness. We could disagree with each other, something I think M. Joukovski incapable of doing with his idol, the German composer. My mentor thought Tolstoi the greatest of the Russian writers, whereas I would award the palm to him. Tolstoi is just a vast reflecting pond of life. Turgenieff and brother William agreed in their high appraisal of Tolstoi; at least in one thing they concurred, William even going so far as to say that *War and Peace* was the greatest novel ever written. A large but artless work, not at all self-conscious, a vast reflector, a mindless mirror. Even if he did not know the direction in which his plot eventually headed, Turgenieff wrote in a very controlled fashion. He moved his characters as if they were chess pieces. Mind—artistic consciousness— stood behind everything he wrote. No, one could not dismiss Turgenieff as a mere mirror.

The duration of my stay at Posillipo had not been determined (at least by me) upon my arrival. The invitation had been open ended, and when finally I reached my destination, I thought I would surely stay a week or two, perhaps longer, maybe months longer, if I recaptured what I had lost in Paris five years beforehand. Certainly I intended to remain longer than the three days I actually spent.

Paul met me at the Naples station. Effusive and high-spirited as ever, he grasped my proffered hand and clasped me on the shoulder at the same time, then standing eye to eye with me, he slapped my upper extremities excitedly with the palms of both his hands. I managed a smile and quick nod. "Henry, Henry, it's so good to see you," he said, still clapping my shoulders which under my thin jacket must now be bright red. His hairline had receded by the several inches his beard had grown and now silver threads stood in both his beard and hair. He remained still exceedingly thin and lithe. We would take *déjeuner* together he said, after engaging a carriage to take us out of the city and into the suburbs, to the village of Posillipo and my baggage on to his villa.

Arriving at the town, he and I dismounted at a pension, sent the carriage on, and sat down at an outdoor table in the little courtyard. The day was brilliantly warm. I stared at the grassy hills in the distance. A balding gray-headed waiter brought us a plate of cheese, a loaf of freshly baked bread, and a bottle of wine and two glasses. Birds twittered in several nearby cypress trees. Not a fleecy cloud moved in the eggshell-blue sky though I felt a slight breeze.

Over the table, as we partook of the light meal and the sun shone down on us, Paul spoke fervently about the German's new opera. The *Meister* worked on a sacred festival stage play, *ein Bühnenweihfestspiel*, for the Easter season. He, Paul von Joukovsky, would design and paint the sets for the world premier at the *festpielhaus* in the town of Bayreuth in Bavaria, would have a share in the production of this transcendent work about a Christ-like figure. I interrupted him, asked if he was labouring on any of *his* canvasses at the moment, and he just shook his head, you could see the five years in his face, the wrinkles under his eyes, the wanness of his countenance. Those cheeks once had been rosy. Dabbler that he was, never before did he seem such a sycophant, such a hollow shell. To my surprise, he seized my hand and implored my person; I must meet the *Meister*, his villa only a pleasant carriage ride distant. Oh, be yourself Paul, I so badly wanted to say, but suppressing myself, I replied that our tryst would be of little value for either the composer or myself because I could speak only a few disjointed fragments in the composer's tongue, whereas he did not know mine. Moreover, although he surely knew some French, he would not speak the language, or so I read in the press. Paul gladly volunteered his services as translator. He smiled in such a self-serving and insinuating way I felt thoroughly disgusted. Did I want to hear about the new opera? I did not, but I decided against being rude. Maybe he would purge it all out of his system if I indulged him here. Then perhaps we could discuss other more pertinent matters. I had not gone into this in the dark, after all. In Paris he claimed that Wagner was the wisest of all living men—the supreme musician of this or any other century. True, I accompanied him to the Wagner sessions in the salons, attended the ones he sponsored in his own beautiful studio, but we did other things as well. We used to go to the museums together to view the antiquities, where I loved to hear him discourse on the development of the fine arts. In those days, I could effectively move the conversation to subjects other than the German composer. *Perhaps now I can persuade him to renege on his pledge off to Bayreuth to march.* Yes, at that former time, just to please Paul, to indulge his whims, I would go to the concerts, knowing full well that anything and everything could be found in Paris, a city of endless variety. She would compensate me in other ways for the pain I endured; the time I lost to Herr Wagner remained slight when compared to the rich hours and days Paris afforded me in my pursuit of the finer thing. Even after Turgenieff left for Russia where he hoped to finish the manuscript of *Virgin Soil*, I continued to drop in on Flaubert and his *cénacle*, where I sat not at the knees of a master but at his side and where I learned many of the lessons of my chosen craft, engaged in worthwhile, fruitful pursuits. Paris offered manifold diversions. I hoped Wagner would not be the only topic of conversation here in Posillipo. In the past, between us, Paul and I developed a sort of *quid pro quo*. I hoped the old rules of conduct still stood in effect. So I let him expatiate at length on the opera.

The world would acknowledge it as a cornerstone of civilization, he said, the composer's most sincere, soul-searching work. At the present, the *Meister*, imbued with religious feeling and assurance of the immortality of the human soul, was setting his libretto to music, lingeringly goading it into existence. It would stand as his crowning achievement and would never be desecrated by contact with any profane stage, but be performed only at Bayreuth. The *Meister* had penned the libretto, years before, after reading the romance by Wolfram von Eschenbach, the historical figure he had brought into his own *Tannhäuser*. The *Meister* had even earlier intended to write a Biblical opera on the lives of Christ and Mary Magdalene, but after reading Eschenbach, he saw how with *Parsifal* he could transform the Semitic Jesus into a medieval Aryan knight and the Jewish Mary Magdalene into the still Semitic Kundry. This would be his Jesus Christ opera. As always, as with the *Ring*, the *Meister* improved on his sources. His Parsifal developed in directions never conceived by Wolfram.

Paul continued to go on at length. He related the strange, exotic, story, prefacing the tale by saying the instruments of evil in the opera were the brunette temptress Kundry and the Judas-like Klingsor, the pure and godlike characters the blond, blue-eyed Parsifal and presumably not much less Teutonic Gurnemanz, Amfortas, and Titurel. Then he provided me with an extended synopsis. I wanted to drum my fingers on the table so very badly, but out of tact and politeness, I checked the impulse.

"The first act takes place near the Castle of Monsalvat," he began, "where the Knights of the Holy Grail defend and shield the holy relic. It is dawn. On the edge of a small lake, the elderly knight Gurnemanz narrates to two squires how the order's leader King Amfortas, who presently lies ill and prostrate, fell victim in the magic garden of the evil sorcerer Klingsor, to a seductress of great comeliness.

"Klingsor had at first been a fledgling knight in the order of Monsalvat which Amfortas' father Titurel had founded to uphold the guardianship of the consecrated grail and spear. Distressed by his own lustfulness and impurity, he had resorted to self-castration only to undergo the scornful disowning of his fellow knights."

I cringed at the crudity of Wagner's plot and could not help interjecting: "*Mais mon chèr Paul, ceci est très ennuyeux.*"

"Пожа́луйста́, *chér Henri . . . bitte, bitte schön. Il faut que tu écoutes attentivement . . . ainsi, je reprends . . . je résume encore.* In bitterness, Klingsor schemed to ravage the order and ruin the holy cleansing attributes of its hallowed relics. He had recourse in his extremity of dishonour and debasement to the forces of darkness. Consequently, the knights of Monsalvat were summoned individually to his mysteriously materialized castle and to Kundry and the flower maidens, to their remorse and mortification.

"Because of the beautiful woman's beguilements, Amfortas laid aside the sacred spear which had pierced the side of Christ at Calvary and along with the Grail had come under the knights' protection. Klingsor then stole the spear, stabbing King Amfortas with it. It was written that only an innocent fool, illuminated with faith and empathy, could heal the stricken King's wound."

I determined to make amends for my previous impoliteness, so one once again I interrupted Paul: "*Bien, peut-être maintenant ici ton sommaire commence d'avoir un peu d'intérêt, Paul.*"

"Хорошо́, *gut, bon. Je reprends encore.* Only an innocent fool could heal the King's wound. A strange wild woman whom we later learn is the very enchantress who brought about the King's downfall, arrives at the lake and offers Amfortas a balsam for his injury, which only temporarily lessens his pain. A swan drops to the ground out of the sky, pierced through with an arrow. A youth emerges looking for the slain swan. Gurnemanz informs the boy that on this holy land even the animals are considered consecrated and hunting is forbidden.

"He then asks Parsifal where he came from, his father's name and his own, and Parsifal replies '*Ich weiss nicht,*' I don't know, to all of his questions. Kundry excuses Parsifal. He is uninformed of the law, as he was brought up by his mother Herzeleide to be guileless, so that he would not meet the same end as his father Gamuret, who fell in combat. Kundry tells him that his mother has died. Recalling the prophecy, Gurnemanz hopes that Parsifal can heal Amfortas. He summons him to the grail chamber to witness the love feast of the knights. There, at the command and behest of his importuning father the ancient warrior Titurel, Amfortas once again unveils the grail in all its blood-red luminescence. Parsifal comprehends little, so he is unable to pity the wounded King who desires only death. Frustrated and depressed, Gurnemanz shoos the untutored youth away."

At least, I thought to myself, it is shorter this way than one's having to sit for four or five excruciating hours in the opera house. How many scenes would each act contain?

"Act Two," Paul continued, "focuses on Kundry's and Klingsor's schemes and designs to bring about Parsifal's defeat and undoing, assisted by their coterie of flower maidens, perhaps all Eastern and Semitic, or perhaps some Christian women as well, proselytized by Kundry and Klingsor to lives of sensuality and sin."

The German's mania, his hatred, here enters his opus, I thought.

"Part of her strategy to entice the boy is to recount to him her mystical intelligence of his youth, of how his mother had raised him deep in the forest believing she could deliver him from the world of men which was liable for his father's passing, and how she perished in heartbreak after he became exhausted with her tender custody and neglectfully forsook her. Kundry calculates on his contrition and his immediate requirement for motherly solace and succour to win her to him. Parsifal is at his most susceptible when Kundry declares her sorceress vision of his mother's death, and indeed she does achieve in persuading him to take her kiss."

As he spoke, Paul rocked back and forth in his chair like an Eastern mystic in ecstasy; his head tossed first to one side then the other, his almond-shaped eyes rolling back behind their heavy lids, one of his hands clutching the arm of his chair. After a moment's pause, he straightened up, then once again proceeded with the story.

"Kundry's success is of fleeting duration however. Parsifal withdraws, his original response changing over into pity, compassion for all suffering creatures—the mother who had passed away in anguish when her son had deserted her, sorrow for Amfortas and all the other knights of Monsalvat whom Kundry and Klingsor had shamed, and even pity for Kundry. Despite the surface strength and faith Kundry had gained from the necromancer Klingsor, she had profoundly implanted in her soul the shame of spitting on Christ when centuries earlier he bore the cross on his shoulders. Parsifal grows Christlike in his responses to her and she in her hysterical arguments becomes high-strung and frantic. At the close of Act II, the young innocent knight has utterly defeated and driven her back and also overcome Klingsor. He has reclaimed the holy spear that the wizard in choler heaves at him, and as he makes the sign of the cross over it, the enchantments and supernatural might of Klingsor and Kundry cease forever, the fair garden turns to a desert, and as Parsifal departs, the castle itself fades into nothingness. Only Parsifal withstood the maidens' alluring enticements and managed to loose the chains and fetters with which Klingsor had bound them in loyal service. A eunuch by his own hand, the magician himself had been impervious to the charms of the women in his domain. He became bereft of all feelings of love and compassion and the ability to forgive. Evil took him over completely and instead of serving goodness, his life's sole aim became to destroy it."

I had crossed one leg over the other and had repositioned myself several times in the chair (a dull American would say I had ants in my pants, I suppose) but I had listened. For a while the expression I had worn on my face must have been one of open (and utter) boredom, but either Paul did not notice, or he was oblivious to the twitching corners of my mouth. At one point, I closed my eyes, and just attended to Paul's squeaky tenor, the music of his voice and not the words, *but I realize now that there were things about this opera narrative that intrigued me!* I did not lie to Paul when I said that the music drama had its interest.

The opera was set "in the days of yore," yet there were some disturbing modern elements in Wagner's version. Act Two resembled the Legend of Temperance, Book II of *The Faerie Queene*, in which Sir Guyon visits and destroys the Bower of Bliss. Wagner's bombast would, of course, in no wise compare to the exquisite verse technique of Spenser with all its colour and warmth, the silvery music of the eclogues, where poet-shepherds converse all day on the hillside, the lull of their solitude invaded only by the falling of streams and the jocund voices of the birds, but both poets deliberately employed archaism in their language. Paul told me that Wagner purposely antiqued his German and had a decided penchant for alliteration in his verse. I yawned not for the last time as Paul once again took up the thread of his narration.

"As Act III of *Parsifal* commences, an aged Gurnemanz once more rescues a penitent Kundry, now trounced and vanquished and nearly frozen after her exposure to a long and difficult winter. It is Good Friday. Somewhat less understanding and willing to overlook her faults, if ultimately still able to forgive her than he had been with the faithless woman before, Gurnemanz chastises the sorceress strongly. Now for all time released from Klingsor's evil magic and truly remorseful, she bends her head downward and pleads in a harsh and raspy voice, '*Dienen, dienen!*' To serve ... to serve!

"Titurel has died, and Amfortas refuses to uncover the grail. The radiance of its holy splendor has been lost. As Kundry fills a water pitcher in the spring, she notices a distant stranger. It is Parsifal, who brings with him the spear with which a Roman soldier had pierced Christ's side at Calvary on the first Good Friday and with which Klingsor within his castle many centuries later had also pierced Amfortas' side in finalizing the effects of her seduction.

"Kundry washes Parsifal's feet and dries them with her hair. Parsifal, whose possession of the spear destines him to be Amfortas' successor, is anointed by Gurnemanz. The wound that Amfortas took back with him to Monsalvat had never mended, and as the years advanced the triumph of Klingsor over all the knights who had aspired to regain the holy spear had disheartened the order. Parsifal, however, places the spear on the wound of Amfortas and it is at long last healed. A humbled, unprepossessing Kundry falls dead, and the opera ends with Parsifal's uncovering the Holy Grail from its long inactive state, and the newly cleansed knights are once again able to pray without scruple. Спасибо, *mein lieber* Henri."

Paul looked me in the eyes when he finished, expecting some reaction. Was I to fall on my knees, now having seen the light at long last? I determined not to be discourteous. So I obliged with a comment, one not outwardly snide, yet revealing to Paul how I felt, for I had heard in Paris how obsessed this German was about matters of race, how he execrated the Jews, an easy target; tawdry Disraeli seemingly relished being insulted, so happily I obliged him, called him a garish Son of Abraham. Certainly no one would consider me a virulent anti-Semite though I too could if not pummel, at least direct a verbal blow or two at a cringing Jew.

"Interestingly enough," I said, "this opera is set in Spain, a land whose tradition included the combining of diverse ethnic groups, Basque, Aryan, Celtic, Latin, and Negroid Moorish elements, but evidently at a point just prior to the mixing of these separate streams into the one national river."

In other words, I implied, evil triumphed, the race of the grail knights became polluted. They failed. But as I was greeted by such a look of absolutely bovine incomprehension on Jou's face, I became more forthrightly foul. "Your master's theme of celibacy attracts me, I must admit, Paul. This is the same man who made a habit of carrying on intrigues with his friends' wives? He is now professing abstinence and celibacy, the man who wrote that long whine, that bacchanalia to physical love *Tristan*, who fathered illegitimate children on Liszt's daughter while she was still the wife of that pianist and fellow Wagner worshipper and sycophant Bülow?"

Paul looked very angry. He threw his napkin on the table. I had gone too far. "I am an artist," I apologized, "I must scrutinize a subject from all points of view. I'm also captious critic, a spirit of negation, as it were. You know that surely. I am a student of human weakness. I do not mean to offend. I realized that even the most flawed character can also have a measure of greatness. You hold this man up so high; I must undercut you just a little. Moreover, I'm not a professional musician. Others are more qualified to judge the man's merits and I realize that the *cognoscenti* esteem him greatly. I too give the man his due. But it is good to see you! I didn't come all this way to meet Herr Wagner. I wish him great success. However, I want to spend my time with you. I'm as jealous as the Hebrew God. Five whole years have elapsed since we last met. Please forgive a bruised and muscle-cramped traveler who has sat on an uncomfortable train for hours. I'm tired, yet the day is so *recherché*, so glorious with its sunny beams as if Art and Nature had assembled here all pleasure for which man's heart could long, that I feel like walking. Let's knock about a bit."

He smiled, then whistled, then smiled again. "It is good to see you too, Henry, but you are being very unfair, you know. You have an opportunity to meet the great man, the musician of the future. You've been introduced to every one else of note in Europe. It would mean so very much to me...." He pled and beseeched until I promised him that I would reconsider, but today, I insisted he must make me his sole occupation. I required his presence for myself.

"This afternoon and evening I am all yours," he interrupted me, "but tonight after dinner a few of my countrymen will be stopping in. They're already invited."

"Well, we must make the most of our allotted hours then." After settling our bill, we took a stroll out into the nearby hills and into the sunshine, two balding bearded men, one a little stout, the other quite thin.

"So Henry," he said. "I hear you are the talk of London." I demurred, shook my head. Don't make application to my vanity now, I told him, and he remained perfectly pleasant for the rest of the afternoon. We had our idyll in the countryside, in the Italian fields under a warm yellow sun. Finally, we sat down in a meadow, chit-chatting for a quarter of an hour about numerous subjects. I yawned and said I really must rest, I had not slept for a full twenty-four hours, so we headed out of the hills and back toward town, the little village. He pointed out his villa, plainly facaded, barnlike in its size, and stuffed he assured me with treasures: the finest furniture, large mirrors, distinguished works of art, sculpture and painting. I did not have time to admire the parlour rooms but right away, telling Paul not to rouse me for dinner, mounted the marble staircase to ascend to the guest chamber. Turning the latchkey in the ornate shieldshaped keyhole escutcheon, I about-faced and looked into the wide room with framed oval oils on the striped walls, and saw my baggage neatly stacked at the foot of a princely four-poster. I proceeded to unpack, hung several shirts and jackets in the wall closet and then trans-ferred the rest of the contents of my bags into the bureau drawers. A white pitcher with ornate blue flowers within a fleur-de-lis'd and bestudded basin, equally white, sat on a stand. There was one spacious, ornately curtained window. I didn't bother changing clothes but stretched myself out full length on the bed.

When I awoke, I heard voices down below; a soirée was in session. At first I didn't know where I was, but then I remembered Paul saying that he would be entertaining tonight. I heard women's and men's voices in cadenced verbalization, the men speaking in a tongue I didn't know, but could quickly identify as Russian. I felt groggy and thick-skulled, so I shook my head and gazed out the window. I knew without looking, that hours had elapsed since I was last conscious, but I wanted confirmation, so I found it, for indeed there was a greenish moon in a corner of my windowpane. I had sat up in bed, but after several seconds' hesitation, I once again reclined (I guessed that it was far too late for myself to make an appearance), so I got underneath the covers for I hadn't as yet unmade the bed, only wrinkled it, and rested on one side, my head cushioned on an overstuffed pillow. I shut my eyes knowing full well that the voices wouldn't go away, but I'd let the strange tongue draw me back into sleep. I ignored the little snippets of French spoken by the ladies, tried not to listen to them, but one woman spoke louder than the others and what she said caught my ear. To my disbelief I heard her say that her master wanted to emigrate to America, to the state of Minnesota, but that this would dictate considerable remuneration from across the Atlantic. For the tune of one million dollars—for that was his asking price—he, at his advanced age, would move with his fam-ily to the New World. Annual festivals would be held. He would found a school, and *Parsifal* would be staged there and not in Bayreuth. The association to provide him with the needed funds, he said had already been formed. The woman broke off just as the thought occurred to me that we would reverse paths over the ocean, he going to the U.S., I having traveled here, both of us exiles from our native hearths. I heard someone else, a man—Paul perhaps?—say the composer after completing his sacred stage work wanted to write an opera on the Buddha and compose ten symphonies, one more than Beethoven. He is still full of vitality, I heard him say, but nothing more. Blackness overtook me. Later I dreamt about fire. I saw fields ablaze. I stood at the conflagration's centre en-tranced by the flicking orange, yellow and blue flames, yet it was not a deep sleep for part of me could still hear words being spoken below. This was a most pleasant type of inebriation. I dreamed but my ego still held everything in control, I could stage-manage the direction of this dream. I controlled the movements of all the dangling puppets, the myriad strands of fancy. Then I watched a city in the process of igniting. Row after row of brick buildings crumbled into ash and debris, and then it seemed that I had a quick succession of little mirages, none of them related, all odd but each evaporating just as soon as I dreamt it. When I awoke a second time, my bladder full, I couldn't recall what I had just imagined. Everything remained disjointed. I found the door, discovered that it was locked, then fished in my pocket for the key, finding then turning it, and staggered into the hallway. I headed for the steps, first striking a lucifer and lighting the wick of the candle I had retrieved from off the bureau in my room. As I went down the staircase, I saw that tapers still burned in the parlour, so I stepped into the room hoping to find Paul to ask directions to the lavatory, when I came across several of my friend's guests. A man attired all in black with a cadaverous face and purplish circles about his eyes, staggered by me, then said something in Russian which I did not understand. I asked in French where his host was, and he jerked his thumb in the direction of an adjoining room. Inside it, a black bearded man with a full head of hair, wearing a black dinner coat, white shirtwaist and red bow tie, stood talking to a woman with corkscrew blonde curls and a slight nose, dressed in an elaborate skirt and a white muslin shirt with pearl buttons and abundant flounces and ribbons on the front, discoursing in French about Wagner purging Christianity of its Jewish genesis, that the poet had written that the Teutons had sprung from the Gods, whereas the inferior races had descended from the monkey. And I, Harry James, had in London made Dr. Darwin's acquaintance. Zola had read and understood the doctrines of the new science. Had also this Wagner? I doubted it. The man said: "One of our party, Sergei, although he's blond and blue-eyed is also one-fourth Hebrew, but he's the most slavish follower of all, the greatest Wagnerphile." I did not see Paul. Feeling the inner pressure to the utmost, the breaking point, backtracking through the rooms, I hurriedly headed for the front door. I know these details are indecorous. A character in one of my novels would never have such an experience, never be a slave to necessity and bodily function. In fact they had no bodily functions whatsoever. But here I do not create; I merely record what in truth happened. The exigency of the situation precluded any other solution. I would hemorrhage internally if I did not soon relieve myself. While alleviating the pressure, around the back of the house, in the bushes, I heard muffled noises from inside. Suddenly a room illuminated as someone lit a gas jet, and I beheld something altogether repulsive. Through the window, I caught a glimpse of a tall blond man dressed in the costume of a Russian dignitary (he had epaulets on the shoulders of his red frockcoat and a long blue sash across his shirtwaist) sit down on a couch beside another man, brown bearded and rotund, and whisper something in his companion's ear, and then proceed with curled tongue to lick his fellow's cheek and ear as if he were a kitten! Then his companion turned his head in my direction and stared out the window, his eyes wild and bloodshot. With jagged teeth he bit on his own lip as he looked into my face. I turned away from the window, my shoulder tearing through the bush's opposition, my coat, face and hands whipped by the branches. Paul's friends were the most decadent of bohemians. True, they did not know they were being watched. They did not intend to be blatant. Nonetheless, I was horribly shocked. Entering the house, as fast as I could, I made my way up the stairs and back into the room, where I again turned the key in the lock. I spent a restless night. I finally drifted off to be awakened by someone's piano playing, a selection I had heard before in Paris, something I think from *Tannhäuser*. After the music stopped I counted my heartbeats then awoke in a sweat. Someone had toppled me into an abyss and I fell. I had lost control of the progression of what must have been a prolonged hallucination. Had I been in command, I would have sprouted silver downy wings and changed my course from descent to ascent and soared upwards. I wondered if I had only dreamt that I looked into a window earlier in the night.

The house remained quiet. The sky had lightened almost imperceptibly; birds chirped outside. Again I dozed. When I finally climbed out of bed it was after midmorning. Descending the steps, Paul's Italian valet greeted me. He ushered me into the kitchen where my breakfast stood ready. He handed me a note from Paul. It stated that he was needed at the Villa Ungri. I was welcome to follow him. First I was led into the washroom where I made my toilette. I would remember its location. Afterwards, I again went upstairs and rummaged through my portmanteau for a fresh suit. As I again rounded the head of the staircase, the valet appeared and offered to have a carriage made ready, but I decided that I would take a stroll first. I must get him away from here, I told myself. I already felt very uncomfortable in this environment and would flee it shortly with or without him. Already a sentence formed in my head to my friend Mrs. Grace Norton to the effect that the manners and customs of a little group of Russians I had just been observing was about as opposed to Cambridge, Massachusetts, as anything could well be.

Striding outside into the already warm Italian air, I wandered through the village until I came to the *pension* where Paul and I had lunched the previous afternoon. The waiter, bald friendly Italian, waved to me, and I asked him directions to the nearest stable. I hired a conveyance after first asking the mustachioed driver if he knew where the Villa Ungri was located. The composer Herr Wagner makes his residence there, I added by way of explanation. The orange-headed Italian bowed, the ends of his dark mustache bobbing with the motion of the head.

I had the man drive past Wagner's villa. Then, a mile or so distant, I disembarked. Pulling a watch from out of a vest pocket, I told the driver in Italian that I wanted him to wait here for me, that I would be back in a quarter hour's time. We had gone up a slight incline. Grey olives dotted the hillsides, stood out against the bright blue of the sky. I saw several other villas across the brown road below me in the many-hued coulée. They had yellowed walls, some mottled with ivy.

I would reverse myself, head down the road I had just ridden up in the carriage, and make a quick reconnaissance. I didn't think the sorcerer could entice me within his gates, but who knows, I said to myself. My curiosity was wetted though I certainly hadn't let on to Jou. Was this German really contemplating a move to the States?

As I approached, I thought about going in, making the grand entrance. I would say that I wanted to leave my card, but presumably I would be invited in. Paul would be happy. If I budged, made an appearance, maybe he would listen to me later on, when we were back home when I would do my best to inveigle him—to convince him to quit this venomous, this positively poisonous, environment. Would I make a sacrifice now, I asked myself, for the success of my task, the duty that I saw laid upon me? For even then I realized that I must take on the role of evangelical, convert Paul to another life, one in which he would not be the flunkey, the bootlicker, to a German *Meister*, but himself would be a creator. I would take him away from here, probably somewhere in the French countryside, where in front of a brook, a little rivulet, I would set up an easel. The serenity of his surroundings would make him serene also, and he would begin to daub, put the sunspilling sky, the landscape surrounding him, onto the canvas with ochers, reds and yellows. A specific green shade.

But no, my initial plan remained best, to sneak by as unobtrusively as a ghost, probably seeing nothing, going away with my curiosity still unsatisfied, returning to my waiting carriage post haste. I simply could not go against my own principles, Paul be damned. I would get a look for myself if I could, but do nothing to please him. Moreover, thereafter, he wouldn't listen to what I had to tell him; my putting in an appearance would have the contrary effect of tightening his resolve. It would be showing your opponent a weakness. He would try to exploit it. He would be the one trying to convert you!

I saw the villa before me as I descended the hill. I had stopped to remove my top hat and wipe my brow with the initialed hanky I fetched from a waistcoat pocket. The waistcoat was plum coloured and had a flower motif stenciled on it. My overcoat was black as was the silk top hat which I quickly replaced, then strode onward. I was approaching Wagner's residence from behind. A series of high cypresses stretched in a straight line behind the villa's turnstile of iron. I saw no gate in it, though, of course, there would be one in the front. The villa had high walls and tall, narrow windows. I could see that much from where I presently stood. After taking a few deep breaths, I made for the cover of the trees. I reached out and gripped the iron bars as I looked into the courtyard, at the end of which (some thirty yards distant), on a sunny terrace abutting the house, four or five people were sitting on porch settees. From my vantage point under the trees and behind the fence, I recognized the blond man of the night before, no longer in his epauletted uniform of that night but instead attired in a tasteful green velvet jacket, his hands thrust into the ample pockets of his checked breeches. A dwarfish potbellied man with white hair and sideburns running all the way under his chin discoursed from a stool. He had on a dark coat but light trousers. A watchchain crossed his vest under the silk puff tie. I fancied that I beheld Daniel Quilp, that the fiendish, ferocious dwarf had stepped right out of the pages of Dickens' novel and stood before me. So here was Paul's idol starting to speak to his disciples. What great teaching would he, from on high, Christlike, bestow on them? I strained to hear what he would say. Despite what I told Jou, I did understand a little German, but then, before the little man uttered a complete sentence a commotion arose in his audience. Someone stood up. Immediately I recognized Paul's slender figure. Apparently several of the Russians did not speak German, so Joukovski was called upon to translate Wagner's comments to his fellow Slavs. He did so in French, and I could make out what Paul said. It sounded much more guttural and earthy coming out of the composer's lips in German, but even in the beautiful French language what the man had to say was terribly repugnant. I listened as he disparaged the Jews in a vile half-educated manner. He seemed to me thoroughly underbred. And there was Paul, his lickspittle, faithfully translating for his master. I turned my heel when I heard Paul say, "The effete Frenchmen were all sons of Sodom." I turned around once again for now Wagner was shouting, spewing forth his hatred like an insane man. He thrashed his arms wildly in the air and stamped his foot on the ground. With this image of him locked in my brain, I headed up the hill.

I grew angry enough on my trudge back to the carriage to depart from Posillipo without saying goodbye to Paul, but I calmed down somewhat as I drove through the muggy afternoon air into Naples—I took the walking tour through the Museum, visited the blessed antiquities for solace to my soul, walked through and also around the Gothic cathedral and across the quadrangle of the university in this city that had been founded by the Greeks—then drove back into Posillipo to Paul's villa. When I had a chance to speak to him on his return home much later that night (for even taking my trip into Naples, I got to his villa hours before him), circumstances still prevented me from announcing my incipient departure. I had decided that I would pay him one final courtesy. Spend another night with him in Posillipo, but then I'd make my bound to break away. That afternoon, I arranged with my driver to meet me at Paul's gates, at three o'clock the following day. He would take me to Castellammare and then to Sorrento. For time and convenience's sake I acceded to the fabulous sum he asked.

Upon entering Paul's house, his valet asked me if I should like to dine. His master had given him instructions that he should serve me well. Most probably his employer would remain away until well past the dinner hour. He stood at my service. I said that I was not hungry, that I had eaten earlier in Naples. I asked the valet to relay to Paul upon his arrival home my message: I was at his disposal.

Back in my room, after I had repacked my suitcases and was once again lying down on the four-poster, I began outlining a travel essay in my head. Several good sentences swam by, their word combinations bound for oblivion, for I knew that I would forget them if I did not momentarily pen them down, but I did not have the strength or will to bother.

It was almost dark when Paul finally returned. After receiving my message he called out for me at the foot of the marble staircase until I emerged from my room. I saw immediately that he was not alone but was sandwiched between two of his countrymen, the blond Jew in his green jacket, and the bearlike Ivan with the jagged teeth, full beard and bloodshot eyes. All three of them were drunk. Even those he claims to hate worship him, I thought to myself. "Come," he said, "I want you to meet my friends Peter and Sergei." I replied that I was just about to go to bed, and that I would see him in the morning.

I went back into my room and shut my door. No one disturbed me for the rest of the night. The following morning I heard a knock. I had been up for over an hour, and had fished a book out of my bag and was reading. I opened the door and Paul, his beard wagging, waltzed into the room. I saw again how much hair he had lost at the front of his head.

Shutting my book as I stood there I said: "Paul I'm leaving you today. I have other calls to pay. Other spots to visit. And I think that I must tell you that you should follow on my heels. This atmosphere, this heady milieu, is no good for you. Would you come to France with me? We could rent a cottage in the countryside. You could paint and I could write. Again I must reiterate my opinion that this place is not conducive to your, and I underscore the word, art." I saw the look of rage on his face and tried to modify my tone accordingly. "Paul," I pleaded, "I am telling you for your own good."

He burst into his tirade anyway, said that he was making in his own way a small contribution to art. He was assisting Wagner! Then he said I always called him a dilettante and a dabbler. Tears formed in his blue eyes as he said this, a show of emotion on his part resulting because of my tactlessness, due in part to the high brutality of my good intentions. Suddenly I felt the old tenderness for him swell within me, all the old pity and empathy. "I love you like my own brother," I said. "Come away with me."

"Do you mean it, Henry?" he asked, standing in the frame of the door, dabbing his tears with his wrist, and I replied that of course I did. I had recently discovered the kind of company he presently kept, but I never before guessed that he himself had a penchant for unclean things, but because, I think, of the vigour of my courtship of him, he responded as if I had invited him to take the utmost liberty.

The physical always repulsed me. I never liked touching anyone, but standing in that guest room, I had such a sudden surge of pity for Paul, seeing him standing there broken, that I put my arm around his shoulder. He sobbed and I patted him on the back. Then he lifted up his head and pressed his lips against mine. I froze, paralyzed in my shoes, where I stood within my skin, the shock was so great to me. Then, it must not have been long, only seconds afterwards, I pushed him away and called him an insect, storming out of the room into the hallway and then down the stairs to the entrance of his villa. My man, I shouted upwards, would call for my bags.

So I drove from Posillipo to Castellammare, and then onto Sorrento.

There, while looking out from my hotel window at the Bay of Naples and at the pyramidal truncated cone of Mount Vesuvius rising above the sea, I again felt in my own element. For the last five years, ever since quitting Paris for London, I had believed that Paul and I had formed a lifelong association with each other, that our friendship would be carried on indefinitely.

How sadly I had been mistaken. So many deathblows to the picturesque.

Of course by the time I took the jaunt to Naples to fulfill my promise to visit him, I knew that all of us have masculine and feminine sides to our character, our personality. To my advantage, I had learned to utilize my feminine sensibilities in my work, my artistic creation. I put those parts of myself into my fictional heroines, the very ones

William complained about. Jou's inversion, his desire to act out the part of the woman repelled me completely. For all my life I have been nauseated by the prospect of sexual relations between anyone and myself. Yes, even with a woman, where a child can result, a transformation of oneself into another being, a son or daughter.

It's much more recompensatory to recast oneself in words than to make the beast with two backs.

I would continue to deny myself to anyone, though I would form more friendships. Now not only William but Paul also was as if dead to me, but Fenimore loomed on the horizon.

I would flee out of Paul's arms into hers. Out of the frying pan and into the fire.

IV

I don't want to observe the young Harry any longer, so I close my eyes to see only blackness then after a moment's pause open them wide to again look down at the old man in bed. I watch as he extends his forefinger and traces little waves on the quilted coverlet, as if he were writing. I blink. A white piece of paper lays in front of me and I have a quill in my beautiful young hand. I can continue working, setting it all down on paper. Yes, Paul wanted to be Wagner, in other words, an extraordinary personality. I never saw his painting, *The Holy Family*, but someone once described it to me who had just returned to London from the continent and had seen it hanging at some German exposition.

Jou had *la folie des grandeurs* just as would Hendrik Andersen. Perhaps it was all in his name. Paul, the apostle, the convert. In his painting, the boy Jesus has the visage of the composer's young son Siegfried, a boy of about fourteen. Shown in profile sitting down, the youth plays with a wooden planer. Hans von Bülow and Cosima Liszt's daughter Daniela lends her face to Mary the mother of God. Blandine, Eva and Isolde (Cosima's other daughters by Bülow and Wagner) become angels performing on various instruments, and the artist paints himself as Joseph, the earthly father of Jesus, I mean Siegfried. What a revelation the description of the painting occasioned for me. Joukovski portrayed himself as what he desired most to be, Siegfried's father, i.e. as a Wagner surrogate. But he did not have the talent to rise above his own mediocrity.

Wait! I again sit in the invalid chair, blankets draped over my chest and knees looking out the window at the Thames, at the ornate street lamps going down the entire length of river. I've returned after retreating into my past, of all things traveling back to that sordid Neapolitan episode of my late youth, where I first became aware of the sickness inside myself and watched how I conquered it, only to return again to this squalid London room in which I am dying. Oh how I wish someone stood on that far shore, there to greet me with open arms. I hurt and I need to be healed, to be made young. Oh if my innocent fool, my Persse, could await me there, I would not miss you Jesus. William wanted there to be an afterlife, had faith that there was one, defended the right to believe in the myths and fairy tales told to us as little children. But in all my wisdom I know that there will be nothing. All the varieties of religious experience are but earthly phenomena; they have a firm psychological basis, fill a vacuum, a gaping need for something, anything, to believe in. But one of us, the counterpart or myself, speaks and I note that Mrs. William, my sister-in-law the former Alice Howe Gibbens—the second James lady to bear the name Alice (I stood at the death bed of the first who in her agony urged me to wed Fenimore), sits at my bed and takes down whatever I or he utters. It still astounds me that my brother wed a woman who grew as stout as myself. She wears a boa around her neck and a hideous polka-dotted strawberry-coloured monstrosity with large, flouncy ribbons, on her head. No, that was when she first arrived, not yesterday or the day before when I began dictating to her. But that moment has also passed for I lay in bed alone. No one is with me. Neither Alice, nor Persse, nor Jesus.

The counterpart and I keep changing places. Now it is he who is dead, and it is I who look down at the old man's corse laid out for public view. But then I lay dying while he watches the spectacle like some besotted Nero, and I hear him comment that it will be his image of himself that will survive and that mine will be buried with me. Only his books shall last, he says. That is why I hate them. Why I would commit them to the fire. His civilization itself is in the death throes. He could detect all too present and palpable a canker in the rose, a crack in the golden bowl, something diseased about everything, about himself, his work, the time in which he lived, the beautiful things he surrounded himself with, the empire furniture, the ornately framed paintings on the wall, the ornamental gardens he loved to stroll through, the New York Edition of his collected writings sitting snug in the bookshelf. All of it should pass away into nothingness. The counterpart and I are in truth one, both facets of that singular enigma known as H.J., he the part of me that has longed for love and human involvement, a part of my nature I always repressed. In my current work of fiction, the one I now write, at the moment I had my first stroke, this other self emerged from the confines of my body to look down over it. It had tried to make its presence known for years. Yet I realize, have always realized, that I write on the windowpane, no not even on it but now on the coverlet of my bed, and that it will all be lost, that in truth nothing has been set down. So be it. But I must carry on anyway, describe (if only to myself) this distinguished thing called dying. Fine. The past over and done with, I must remain an artist to the end. I must write what happens to me here and now. The challenge of challenges. To put the distinguished thing into words. Like England I shall be heroic to the end. I am England, or at least as an American, side with her. I see what stands in the cards, for I have lived through so much I can accurately predict what will happen in all futurity. Germany shall go down in defeat and England shall emerge triumphant! The unfolding of history resembles a landscape rushing before one's eyes while one rides first class, full tilt, some locomotive. But on that first fateful day in the month of August 1914, the train ran off the rails. Yet to be truthful I had foreseen the eventuality years before, had written somewhere though I am sure there will be those usual castigators and doubting Thomases claiming that lying here on my deathbed, I had forgotten the words, had fallen completely into the darkness and despair of the last several months, yet now, dying, I can clearly recall what I wrote: that the rest of Europe would take advantage of the high pitch of civilization in England, the basic humanity of the Britons which precluded their shedding a huge amount of blood for any vain cause. Because they were reluctant to take up arms, I wrote, they would be put to the test by the other nations of Europe and yes would arise to the occasion, would plunge clumsily and unprepared into war. Laid on her back she, England, will exhibit—in her colossal wealth and pluck—an unprecedented power of resistance. She will prevail though I shall now not live to see it.

Persse, Persse, come to me. Heal the old man of his wound. So he can see Albion attain her proper glory. Both Joukovski and Fenimore upbraid me. Jou laughs and says that however much I despised the Master that I have become a combination of his lowly creations Amfortas and Klingsor. Like the King I have been horribly wounded and like the evil sorcerer I emasculated myself. "By not allowing yourself to love," Fenimore chirps in. Wagner himself now rebukes me, calling me the wicked dwarf who has forsworn all human affinity. So come and heal me. I wait and wait yet you do not arrive. Perhaps we all need a nemesis. Well let us fight then. Let us struggle. I feel my fingers on your throat, Herr Wagner. Even with that ridiculous purple beret on top of your head, I still tower over you and shall squeeze your infernal windpipe so no more air shall ever flood into, and inflate, your lungs. They will collapse and flatten out because of me. Your hat falls to the floor, you drop to your knees, yet you look at peace, the expression of your features unaltered by all my fury, by all my shaking and choking. I see a pursed little smile on your face which does, now that I further study it, look slightly pressed-in and drawn-together about the eyes and nose, the latter now no longer so big and Semitic. It looks squinched and compressed, as if you mentally resisted the pain I inflicted, held back, trying to make it look as if it had no effect on you. Even in death though, your face remains leonine with that great shock of white hair and sideburns running under the chin which I in my anger could now pull off. You currently lay prostrate on the floor. I loosen my grip, thinking you are dead, but suddenly there is life in the corpse! You arms lash back and forth, but I again have you by the throat and I begin to crush your Adam's apple with my thumbs, but now it is not him, but *you* whom I am strangling, with you grizzled goatee which once had been a jet black beard. Your hair has thinned considerably on top, William. Performing an appropriate brotherly function, you put your hands around my neck and squeeze, as I likewise choke you. Well, all our lives we've engaged in cheery rivalry—were a set of feuding fraternals, opposites, I the reverse of you, you my obverse, one incomplete without the other. You believed that utility and practicable workability were the measure and gauge of all things and you put the paramount importance in the worth and merit of man. I, on the other hand, saw all the evil in the species, how we constantly exploit one another for personal gain. We were all after the spoils and in competition with each other for them. We would do whatever was needed, even if it meant working to the detriment of one another, to get what we desired. You, too, soiled your hands for gold, William. Without question. At any rate, that is how I viewed the sorry spectacle of humanity, of the relation of brother to brother. You, on the other hand, filled with your wide human sympathy, explored the varieties of psychical and mystical apprehension, used drugs purely for the pleasure and the experience, and wanted to explore the realm of the dead, the phenomenon of extrasensory perception, the world of mind readers and mediums. You bloomed late (when you finally brought out your *Psychology*, a fourteen-volume collected edition of my novels and tales had already been issued), whereas I saw my destiny to write rather early on in life. First you wanted to be a painter, then you took your medical degree at Harvard and became an instructor there in physiology. Under the influence of German science, you explored the relations between physiology and psychology and at last began to publish. Your interest shifted to philosophy, Pragmatism, and you thought it best to express Truth in unceremonious, even colloquial terms. Opposite, competing sons which of us was more like Father? Since we are both facets of him, he must have been a fusion, a union of antitheses.

We forever disagreed, even in our politics. I remember the border dispute between Venezuela and British Guiana in '95, when the possibility of war between England and the United States loomed large, President Cleveland threatening to invoke the Monroe Doctrine. I wrote to you that "one must hope that sanity and civilization, in both countries will prevail," while you maintained England alone was in the wrong. During the Boer War, I, of course, stood for Albion while you struck your anti-Imperialist pose and declared yourself pro-Boer, indoctrinating your daughter, my niece Peggy, with your anti-British sentiments. Surely, however, we would stand united in the present struggle against the forces of barbarism. You would rise with France and England against Germany. As steeped as you were in the traditions of the Hun, you believed in the worth of greater mankind. You would oppose tyranny and inhumanity. I remember how you replied to their request to join a committee for a memorial to Schopenhauer: "I really must decline to stir a finger for the glory of one who studiously lived for no other purpose than to spit upon the lives of the like of me and all those I care for." You despised the German, his alienation and pessimism, his solution to the problem of life the annihilation of personal selfhood. For you to pay homage to Schopenhauer was akin for the Parisians to raise a monument to Bismarck. You said I was too liberal with my gallicisms but you certainly could throw out weighty Dutch terms like *Weltanschauung* and *Auslassungen* in your prose, much of which was too technical for me to judge, yet I admired enormously what I could rate, the craft with which you put your sentences together. Your criticisms concerning my work often wounded me yet I will always be your Beloved 'Arry. You have crossed before me to the far shore. Let our conflict finally cease. Both of us, on the count of three, shall release our grasp on each other's throats. I love you William. But whom now am I throttling? Paul? No, the one he slightly resembled, the other William. I see his domed head, the black hair hanging to his shoulders, the thin long tapering mustaches and short beard under the slightly recessive chin. Something of a dissipate, I judge looking at the bags under his dark lively eyes, a gold ring depending from his ear. Well, it is fit that we should contend, test ourselves upon each other, for indeed I have mastered my craft to such a degree that, yes, even the Swan of Avon would feel uncomfortable because one capable of surpassing even him had appeared on the scene. Who cares about Shakespeare the man? If Bacon, Oxford or someone else wrote the plays under a pseudonym? I care nothing about his personal history, for he has become the imagination itself, or at least a metaphor for it, and it was as that incarnation as the imagination itself that I hymned him in my short story "The Birthplace," where the tour guide knowing no true facts about the master's life makes stories up out of his own head, substitutes personages he actually knows for the historical originals and archetypes. That is how I want to be remembered—for my writings, my collected works, the products of my imagination, my reincarnation in words, a thing of beauty molded by my own hands. Yes. Through my own efforts, I have become the William of the novel, even if my works for the stage have failed miserably. But old man, I hear myself say, you are so puffed up with pride and conceit you should hemorrhage to death slowly. The blood should be drained out of you drop by drop, for you deserve an agonizing end, your head whipping back and forth in torment on your pillow. How dare you rank yourself with *him*?

Indeed your head does shake back and forth as I throttle you. I sit on your chest, riding you, choking you in your own bed, old man. You, too, are bald yet you are also very fat about the jowls and chubby cheeked; the remaining hair you have, now turned white, is trimmed very short. You have a Roman length of nose, and wide Negroid lips, 'Arry. I'd like to drown you, hold your head under water and watch the bubbles coming out your nose and mouth as they rise to the surface and break. But I'll just finish you off here. In bed.

You were a failure, I tell you. A complete utter failure. Oh 'Arry, how I loathe you. I so enjoy doing you in. And now you are gone, I have finished you off, only to become weightless and to rise above you. I am stopped like a helium balloon at the ceiling. My head, my back, my gouty legs all scrape against it and I stare down.

Again I look at you lying in the mahogany four-poster. But I still try to ascend upwards, to float away and dissipate utterly, but the ceiling blocks me. I'm glad the bed didn't have a canopy or tester, an extra obstacle for me to overcome. But I hear myself addressing myself. I say:

"Tolstoi, Wagner, and you Henry were all alike in that you all were stupidly excessive in your productions, you and Wagner particularly susceptible to the sin of too elaborate orchestration. Your works, Henry, bloat just like your body. Tolstoi remains a vast reflecting pond of life true; but in the end despite all those hidden little connectors, your books likewise endlessly meander, are as tediously repetitive as one of Herr Wagner's operas. The three of you are also alike in your sanctimonious desire for purity. All hypocritical old men! Look at the works you produced: 'The Kreutzer Sonata,' *Resurrection*, Guy *Domville*, 'The Great Good Place,' *Parsifal*. Yes, admit it, various novels went out of control, spinning in directions not at all contemplated at the outset. *War and Peace* certainly, but also *The Wings of the Dove*. Your later style is as false and artificial as Wagner's manner of composing, admit it! All he did was arrange perhaps twenty of his so-called leitmotifs into an endless succession of different configurations. Weren't your rearmost sodomitic novels, as opposed to your frontal earlier ones, likewise corrupted by a bid to fathom more than they actually accommodated and held? True, you have infiltrated genuinely into the mechanism of your characters' minds, but weren't those processes necessarily repetitive and prolix? Your late novels wanted the resoluteness and compression of your initial endeavours. You have to admit that."

I do not want to hear myself talk, so again I close my lids upon my eyes and travel inward, vanish somewhere else. I choose to leave London. I want to be in the country. So I will return to Lamb House. But actually I have retreated only into myself. What I see is not real, it is the product of my mind, an illusion. My brain burns itself up, combusts into nothingness, into word not found. The wick extinguishes when the flame runs its length. Likewise my brain shall soon be spent. Parts of you die. Bit by bit. One piece at a time. Like a star I wink out, vanish forever from the night sky. I must say goodbye to everything I ever loved. As it dies. Soon I'll be dead, less than even a chair. Nothing of me will remain. My brain expires as I write.

Yet even now I journey from No. 21 Carlyle Mansion, London: my final residence. From this spacious L-shaped apartment with its five bedrooms and its two large front rooms overhanging the river, my dining room and study, I ascend, looking all the while down at the fabulous embankments of the mighty artery. I see the River Thames in all her glory, the barges floating down her. I scrutinize all of London, the homes of so many great personalities all lying within a few square miles of one another. For the last time, I take in all the views and prospects my countryman Whistler painted within the city's confines. I say goodbye to Chelsea, and to Westminster. In my youth I paid a visit to the home of Mr. Dante Rossetti. Somewhere near my present quarters in Carlyle Mansions. I see old London Bridge, the Tower, and St. Paul's, and to think over and over again fire ravaged so much of the city; during the seventeenth century all of it came close to burning. Yet I turn my eyes, and now I am in the town of Rye in Sussex. Again I wander the streets of this ancient Cinque Port looking at all the redbrick houses. I walk down a cobblestone road with the name of Mermaid and once more I am journeying backward into time, into history. I pass shops with signs indicating the owners' professions hanging outside them. I spy the square tower of the old Norman church and stare at the houses, some of them dating back to the reign of Queen Elizabeth. Reeking oil lamps protrude from their fronts.

A strong and sturdy three-storied redbrick Georgian manor with numerous chimneys, owned for generations by the Lamb family, stands on a loop at the top of one of the precipitous streets. My beloved home. I purchased it despite William's advice against. He felt that it wasn't practicable for me to acquire the property, yet I had determined that I would realize my dream of the great good place. I liked coming to this town. I made the right decision when I traveled from the city out into the country but also, when I came here, backwards in time, into England's agricultural past.

By the time of my occupancy the bricks of Lamb House had turned a russet colour. Again I approach the house from the outside, then enter through the front door. As I walk in and see all the beautiful things which I owned, now indeed for the last time, again I feel revulsion. But I am here to say goodbye to my rooms, to my favourite articles, to all the objects I surrounded my person with, and, of course, most of all to the volumes of my New York Edition slumbering on the shelf. I must remember that in truth I am not in Sussex, instead I am rambling through the corridors of my mind, through my mental extrapolation of Lamb House, not the actual building. I remain stoical. I realize that very soon, when I am indeed at last dead, that I won't be able any longer to haunt these halls, much less the real ones. They'll continue to exist long after I am gone, for things endure. Going round the balustraded oak staircase, I walk through the oak-paneled parlour and stop at the door opening onto the garden and look outside at the huge mulberry Hendrik and I sat under and also at my numerous greenhouses and peach trees.

Then I turn around, retrace my steps, and mount the stairs. I traipse through the Kings' room facing toward the old Roman Church, lined with wood paneling in the shape of crossbars from floor to ceiling. George I and George II had both slept here. They were long dust, but Lamb House still stood, and shortly I will be reduced to ashes as well for yesterday didn't I hear Mrs. William say that she would cremate my remains, then transport them to the family plot in America, where staring at my parents' recently occupied graves back in '82, life first showed me her Medusa face? I cross the hallway from the Kings' chamber to a small square paneled room looking onto the garden, and stare at the detached tawny-bricked assembly hall of the Lambs, and think about the parties, the all-night banquets, that the long-dead hosts had once presided over there. Turning around, I exit that space and returning to the top of the stairs, enter my study, the so-called Green Room. There I take leave of my writing desk and of my library. Other people will soon make their residence at Lamb House; I must vacate the premises; however, now I must also say goodbye to all the other places I loved. No other novelist up to my time had moved his characters from so many locales, for indeed I had traveled the globe, from New York to London, to Paris, to Rome.

First I will return home, across the ocean, to the United States. During my lifetime, I have crossed and crisscrossed the entire continent, but now choose to return to Cambridge, to again cross over the Charles River from Boston and walk once more through the grounds of Harvard, then I return to the city, visiting the graves of the notable Brahmins Emerson, Hawthorne, Longfellow.

Of course I must next head south and visit New York. Again I will tour Wall Street and then once more I'll perambulate around Washington Square. From there I will depart for Paris.

My earliest memory of childhood is of the Place Vendôme and the column commemorating Napoleon's victories in that fair city. As boys William and I wandered through Paris' streets. He carried a large sketchpad and was constantly drawing figures on its pages. We traipsed through the Louvre whose magnificent parts arched over us in the wonder of their endless gold riot. But even as I stand in the Louvre of my mind looking once more at all the myriad canvasses, Italy beckons, and I am in Rome, where the early spring has filled the air with bloom and perfume, and I stroll around all those mounds of mossy ruin with all their monumental inscriptions, and suddenly I am in the middle of the awful arena, the Colosseum, and it is midnight and the atmosphere, as it was for my poor Daisy, is likewise for me a villainous miasma. The plague is in the air. I close my eyes and stepping onto my mind's magic carpet, I am swept from there to of all places, venerable, variable Venice, every building a museum, the city itself a work of art, yet the water of the canals was foul smelling. Venice perched atop a sewer and was slowly sinking into the lagoon. All who visit there detect the crack in the golden bowl. I see the two main sections of the seaport divided by the Grand Canal, the Piazza of St. Mark's and the Campanile. Next I glimpse the Bridge of Sighs, but I must take a side canal to Fenimore's *Casa*. Floating in the air, I pass over the singing gondoliers. If I couldn't join you in love Constance, I will join you in death. I see you there, standing on the balcony.

You wear a black shawl; your hair is pinned up in a bun, and a black ribbon is tied around your aging throat, the front of your frock adorned with gay bows and fancy ruffs. Let me join you, Miss Woolson. Hurtling downwards together with you, my dear, will be the great moment of shared experience for which we always awaited. At last we shall be free, yet I hesitate. What if hell exists? Will I finally be able to stop writing or will I be forced to do this eternally as my punishment for never having let myself live? I have been a worthy son and brother, haven't I?

Father, William, testify to the truthfulness of what I aver. Take my hand Fenimore. We will take our swan dive together. Over the ledge we tumble and drop. Yes, we are falling, and soon, very soon, we will be at peace. The abyss yawns, and the extinguishing thing approaches at last.

Steiglitz's Folly

I

What would Da have said? Had he lived that is? Voyeurs got what they deserved? That the American spectator urge dated far back in the nation's history, and not contrary to an ever-recurring phenomenon in this living-breathing echo we term the present, the past (though not without deviation) repeated itself? In most cases it would—make up a word—reloclone. *A wrong term in this instance for relo isn't apropos* even though every other time, virtually, it would be apt. For this type of duplication arose much less frequently. Hardly ever at all. Lions got loose in the crowd just as they had in 1861, yes. But *in the very same spot. Lightning struck twice.* Perhaps in a prior manifestation, or future reverberation, something very like took place (or will transpire) elsewhere. There is recurring, and there is recurring. Some oglers paid the ultimate price then. Others will now and again. Yes, it happened afresh in July of 1973. And maybe it would occur more than once even in the

Opening shot.

You stare at the wide movie screen and see a director's chair. The overseer with the megaphone sitting there (a large predatory bird both old and fat) shouts: "Action!" Next a blackboard on rollers and a man with a piece of chalk appear in the middle of a meadow. He lectures not only to us (his via-the-camera augmented audience) but also to a large group of tourists right there on location with him. Country bumpkins, for the most part.

"The area surrounding Sudley's Spring and the dirt road running from the stream south and over which Burnside's brigades paraded, was for about a mile from the ford densely wooded. Then backtracking, to the right of the thoroughfare for about the same distance, the terrain split between woods and fields. Finally, continuing in reverse direction and going back the way the Union troops came in, the country on both sides of the road opened for about one mile. The Federals marched through the wide rolling fields which extended down the Warrenton turnpike, crossing what became the field of battle, through the valley of this small watercourse, a tributary of Bull Run."

Calling attention to itself, the camera shifts up and down then moves horizontally in one great big panoramic sweep. We see the meadow, stream, turnpike, farmhouse and, again, the pack of people surrounding the spokesman. Then the lens zooms in on two men in the crowd, father and son (but we don't know this yet). All we see: a middle-aged man and boy in his early twenties. They, like everyone else, look at Chalkman. Our eyes become theirs.

Thin with snub nose, bushy eyebrows, and dark mop which (father thinks) needs cropped, the studio's appointed mouthpiece attired in an expensive Italian suit, drones on, arrowing his battle diagram with the chalk. A young puppy (voice over narration, Da's deep baritone). More accurately the runt of the litter. Yes, precisely (we see Da smile at the aptness of his metaphor). A pup performing parlor tricks in front of a crowd of (he turns his head over his shoulder) delighted fat ladies, bored red-eyed teenagers, flower children, this decade's androgynes. Before hicks from the sticks trying hard to simulate a false façade of interest. In front of. He shades his eyes with one hand, squints right and left. Whom else? Hotsy-totsy Rotc nazis chop strut about. Brainy when compared to the homegrown National Guard type, a Cro-Magnon to be sure, several specimens of which also floated by in bloated slow motion. Their eyes now like everybody else's (except Da's) turned toward the hill with the farmhouse on it. He remembered seeing those anthropoids as he and Billy cut their way up front. They now stood in the very first row. The studio spokesman irritated him. He should succeed or fail in front of an open mike in some comedy club. He wants to entertain instead of inform. Yet he spouts facts as if he's an expert. I'm afraid I'm going to have to expose him, to trip him up. They should at least have the decency to set someone before us who is genuinely knowledgeable. Who has a deep, thorough, understanding of his chosen topic.

Since we are not reading a book we must wonder (since we can't delve so deeply into his consciousness)

Had Pup noticed Da what would he have deduced about him from his appearance? Maybe Pop did catch his eye and mouthpiece ignored him purposely? Yes, sweat beads on Pup's brow. Zoom in and focus on his face then point of view shot from Pup's eyes. We see

An athletic-looking man wearing glasses (Da) lifting his hand in a partial fascist salute. The sun's in his eyes. He can't see so he averts his head but still holds up his arm. But the speaker does not call on him. Instead he continues his own rote recitation. Chalkman:

"The battle took place three months after the fall of Fort Sumter. Imagine that you lived then. Were a Union soldier, say. What's going on up North and down South? Well, let's see. The Army of the Potomac has assembled around Washington while the Confederates are massed at Richmond. Some fear that the Southern forces might march on the capital. Bored and demoralized, you and the rest of the Northern troops sit and do nothing. Just wait for the inevitable explosion. The people back home are indignant. They demand action, angered by bold forays against federal soldiers near the city of Baltimore. The demolition of telegraphs and railroads by Southern troops, the seizure of the Norfolk naval yards by the rebels and the Southern practice of confiscating Northerners' assets and holdings in certain secessionist states. Sumter still smarts in peoples' hearts and minds. There're loud cries, repeated over and over again, for some sort of advance. Many maintain that the rebellion should have already been checked, so finally General Winfield Scott ordered the Union Army to move forward on July 2nd."

I should have checked you by now, Pa thought.

Just as he was about to lower his arm, the man saw that his son Billy was looking over at him. Never accept defeat my boy, he thought. Then he silently addressed himself.

You must set an example. You will be rude. You will shout out whatever it is you have to say, interrupt the mouthpiece.

Pay back's double. So often had his students broken in on his lectures with their stupid comments that he had the right to push himself forward. Intrude. Yet something inhibits him. He can't get the words out. Oblivious of Da's raised hand, Chalkman continues to orate:

"The first division receives orders to march forth at half-past two a.m. so as to reach the lines early in the day and avoid the heat. But its regimental commanders dawdled in moving out causing other divisions to fall between two and three hours behind schedule. Tyler began firing at 6 a.m. The enemy did not counter. Heintzelman held one of his brigades in reserve in case it would become imperative to reinforce Mile's unit, but Burnside's division proceeded to ford Sudley's Spring. The men, however, crossed slowly, stopping to drink. Clouds of dust from the direction of Manassas betokened the advance of a large Confederate force. Frightened that these fresh troops would charge the crest of the column before the division could all get over, the officers commanded their subordinates to detach from the column and advance separately as fast as possible. Tyler received orders to press forward, as large numbers of enemy troops went by him to attack the brigades of Burnside's division which had already begun to ford. When the first of these reached the open space, the Confederates opened fire. These men sustained the brunt of the initial attack, but soon they received support. Other corps and a regiment from Heintzelman's division forced the enemy back far enough so that Sherman's and Keyes's brigades could cross from their position on the Warrenton Road."

I would like to ask "That's Tecumseh Sherman, right?" Da thinks to himself. See if he knows. Billy's great-great-great grandfather Jacob Kemper served under Ambrose E. Burnside. But not until the St. Petersburg siege, three years later in 1864. But in November of 1863, the Corl brothers fought briefly under his command, the whole Union army in Virginia did, before Hooker in turn replaced him after the fiasco of a battle on December 13th. For when at the command of the President, Burnside relieved McClellan, the paunchy General determined to move on Richmond by way of Fredericksburg. At that time the Fifth Reserves the Corl brothers William and Prosper's regiment came under his authority, and he ordered them across the Rappahannock in one of a series of desperate attacks. As Da still does not interrupt him, Chalkman pivots to the left, extends his arm and points across the meadow:

"Beyond the Warrenton road, to the left of the path down which the Union troops had marched from Sudley's Spring, stands a hill. From here you can see it clearly and the farmhouse on it. Across from it observe the other knoll. Behind it the Confederates positioned several vexatious batteries. During the fieriest part of the fray the opposing forces contested with each other for the control of the hill with the house. Many brigades joined in the assault. The federal troops confuse a Confederate regiment for one of their own and let it advance. It disables the battery then strives to take it, but three different corps repel it in rapid succession. The third corps forces the Rebs down the hill and out of sight. The Union troops feel the day is theirs, but the Confederate line on the hill holds its position, turns them back with its musket and artillery fire, and then enemy reinforcements arrive from the railroad train. They open a fire of musketry from the woods to the Union troops' right and to his rear. The federal troops break and retire down the hillside. Efforts to rally them are fruitless. Only a battalion of regular infantry moved up the hill opposite the one with the house on it and supported the other troops as they got down to, then across, the turnpike on their way back to the positions they held that morning. Retreating troops covered the plain. The retreat became a total rout. McDowell gave the necessary orders to protect the withdrawal but all organization was lost when the troops reached the Warrenton Road. Confusion and chaos reigned on the field that day, for Confederate and Union uniforms weren't uniform. The New York Zouaves, in fact, wore Frenchified shakos. Both sides made mistakes, fired on their own men. But when the Confederate reinforcements—General Johnston's men—arrived, the battle was lost. Not all Union troops retreated willingly. In review," (he looks at his watch) "the forty-five thousand man Union army...."

Fadeout.

Abrupt transition: close-up of the seasoned Bird of Prey (his face that of Ari Onassis or Joss Ackland). He speaks to us, tells us the footage we just saw was from the fourth day of shooting, that the battle took longer to restage and film than it had originally done to fight. He claims to have often and bitterly complained to the producers about the open set. But did they listen? He gestures with his hands, a sarcastic expression on his face. No. Certainly not. Bystanders kept getting into his shots whichever way he panned his cameras, and finally catastrophe struck on the fourth day, the last on location in Virginia. All he had left to film was the uncontrollable panic of the Northern troops and spectators, the 1861 spectators that is. So he cordoned off the meadow and farmhouse, pushed the 1973 onlookers way off to one side. Two days later, had things proceeded as planned, he would have finished filming in Atlanta where he was scheduled to shoot a Southern choir in period dress singing a *Te Deum*. The final few shots would showcase a jubilant South.

No, the day didn't begin auspiciously (as he said before, it had been a very taxing shoot). That morning, prior to shooting the new footage, he swore like a longshoreman while reviewing rushes from two days before. Drawn in, caught up in his work, the illusion worked. He actually stood there, Matthew Brady with a moving picture camera and colored film. Sound. "Retreat?" said the blue belly, "That ain't what we come for. We come to give them a shellacking!" Sulkily the New Yorkers start to fall back but just then the Black Horse Guard (a splendid cavalry corps, all the horses of which were coal black) charges at them from across the field. The line breaks. Horses rear up and are received by the firemen upon their poised bayonets, but Zouaves are also cut down. While reviewing the raw footage, Bird saw the finished product in his mind's eye. The completed edit with all the special effects added. He'd splice in a close-up here. Half of one blue belly's face would explode, turn into bloody mush. Another volley follows, and the horsemen break, their sabres flashing. The Union riflemen ramrod and reload. Several seconds pass. Time, of course, would telescope in the movie. The Black Guards reappear, their forces doubled. Again they gallop with frantic yells at the mad, frenzied Zouaves. But this time the horsemen bear Old Glory and a number of the Zouaves think for an instant they had fired on friends whom they had originally mistaken, but the flag's thrown down, the horses hurl themselves upon the regiment and the slaughter begins anew. Yes, the blood and guts would be added later. The reenactors used only blank cartridges. But the cannon charges looked realistic enough. Smoke covered the battlefield. Again, he envisions the final form the film would take. No hesitation, no quavering, interrupts the infuriated, death-dealing blows of the troops as they engage each other in mutual desperation and hopelessness. Men crumple and collapse but no quarter is given. The ranks fill up. Sabers, bowie knives and bayonets glint in the sunlight. Horse after horse goes down, shot out from under their riders. The Confederates break, regroup, and are about to charge again. But then. Before they can be repulsed for a third and final time.

Vulture shouts to the projectionist to halt the carnage. Freeze frame, he cries while waving his arms. The film stops; he points to the tree line, to the Ugly American in purple Bermuda shorts holding his own camera. A Brownie Hawkeye. They run it back but rewind too far, and the director slaps his forehead at an even earlier point (blue streak excised—BEEP) as he spots a thirteen-year-old boy in blue but not a drummer boy, a cub scout. It won't happen again, he tells everyone. He makes up his mind right then to send out the mouthpiece to lecture to the tourists but also to keep them the hell back. Several hours later, sitting in his chair, he speaks on several telephones to his numerous assistants as filming resumes. He and one or two aides look into several (but not all ten—between them they don't have enough eyes) video monitors on the control center's wall. Time telescopes again. Next Ari stands before a clerk in a courthouse and swears to tell the truth. He takes his seat in the witness box. Close-up of his face. He waits as his assistants set up the three movie projectors. In succession, each will be turned on as Ari reads his statement (prepared and rehearsed in advance of course) into a microphone clipped to his lapel. The lights dim. I had to shout myself hoarse due to all the deafening noise, he says. For three miles swarms of extras merged in one disorganized rout, were escaping through the meadows and woods on either side of the road. We had an actor in mind to provide voice-over narration, to inform the audience that the men had all separated from their regiments.

I had ten camera crews filming from various angles that day. A team shot footage from a helicopter. From that hawk's point of view, army wagons, sutlers' teams, and private carriages obstructing the way out were to be photographed toppling against each other in billows of dust. Other cameramen recorded the sights and sounds up close.

Suddenly on the screen we see footage from the first projector. Ladies in crinolines scream and clutch their umbrellas to their corsets as their picnic lunches are knocked over. Hacks containing unlucky spectators (really stunt people, the Bird of Prey informs the hushed courtroom) smash and collide, their occupants flung from the vehicles onto the meadow. Blanks whiz overhead. Cannons boom and flash. More gunfire. Ari: "The bombardment was staged. There were no actual cannonballs, only smoke and special effects." Horses flying wildly from the battlefield join the stampede. "The script called for some of the animals to be mortally wounded, to be seen in the death throes," Ari explains. "Of course, your Honor, we didn't sacrifice any steeds, but the illusion had to be created." *The second projector switches on*: Foot soldiers try to grasp riderless horses. Two or three do, then mount and ride them bareback. Several dozen actors portraying wounded men lie stretched on both banks of the stream. They signal with raised arms to other actors riding horses—implore to be heaved behind. Only one benevolent cavalryman stretches out his hand to a not too badly wounded man and lifts him up. Then after several more bursts of Confederate artillery, Union horsemen gallop down footmen without mercy. A stuntman darting between the prodigious front and back wheels of a massive carriage, hangs on with both hands and feigns that he's trying to jump up on the buckboard, but the driver spurs the horses and the coach bounces from the roughness of the hill leading down to the creek. The man loses his grip, falls under the great wheels, which would crush the life out of him the next moment. Or so the footage led the audience to believe. Ari: "But then the real" *Not reel* "catastrophe took place. The helicopter filming the retreat began to have engine trouble." A man flicks on the third projector. A giant lemon-green dragonfly hovers in the air. Its engines spluttering and choking, it aims its head at the ground, tilts its tail up. Freeze frame freeze frame catch it there hold it up in the sky forever. Accelerating in its downward trajectory like a ballistic missile, the yellow insect explodes into the field just beyond Chalkman's blackboard.

The screen goes black for a second. Then once again we see footage of the 1973 crowd. Pup, the studio spokesman, is winding up. Filming will commence momentarily. Chalkman looks down at his wristwatch, clears his throat, and says: "In review, the forty-five thousand man Union army was under the command of McDowell and officered by Generals Tyler, Hunter, Richardson, Heintzelman, Patterson and Miles. General Beauregard commanded the Confederate division entrenched at Manassas Junction. Thomas Jonathan Jackson, commonly called Stonewall Jackson, earned that nickname here at Manassas, his men holding back the main Union assault on the hill. In several months time, he would be promoted from brigadier to major general. Finally we mustn't forget General Johnston, the commander of the Confederate brigades in the valley of the Shenandoah transported here by rail—an important first in modern warfare—to serve as Confederate reinforcements." *Which Johnston*, Da thinks: *Albert Sidney or Joseph Eggleston? That could be my query.* Albert, whom President Buchanan, blue-and brown-eyed Jim, dispatched to Utah in 1857 to put down a Mormon insurrection, or Eggleston, veteran of Indian and Mexican wars, whose strategic retreat in Georgia in 1864 is considered one of the most skillful war maneuvers ever executed? He doubted if Chalkman would know the right answer. Pup read his lines dramatically but couldn't vouch for their accuracy. He merely read what the bosses put before him, was no real Civil War expert. But Da wouldn't get the chance to embarrass the fake for the reenactment of the retreat was scheduled to begin (Da glanced at his Bulova) in only a few minutes' time. The crowd hears the initial cannonade, and everybody but Pup and Da, who continue their mutually antagonistic scrutiny of one another, watches the reenactors preparing to withdraw down the hill. The helicopter flies overhead, its shadow cast on the meadow, on the people, below. But there is a lull on the field, a pause in the action. Some momentary snafu. The mouthpiece's lucky I didn't divulge his ignorance, show him up, Da thinks. Dammit he acts like he grasps everything, knows the answer to any question, but I'd gamble just about anything that he does not. Facts, numbers, reveal the bare minimum anyway. And I've conned more facts than he has. Still I know next to nothing. Forced to rely on my imagination because they, my protagonists, all dead in dole do lie, I could only guess, approximate, yet I forged on bravely, wrote up for Billy the adventures of Pete, William and Prosper Corl, Percy McCalmont and Jacob Kemper. His forbears. My wife's. What all had Da committed to memory? What other facts about Bull Run, or as the Southerners preferred to call the battle, First Manassas, did he know that Pup did not? Again Chalkman starts to speak but breaks off in mid-sentence. He would not be heard now due to all the explosions. The reenactors begin flying down the hill. Again Da winks. From this distance, he can't differentiate the men playing Confederates from those portraying Union troops. He sees a number of cameramen and other technicians on the distant battlefield. Then time slows down, stops. The helicopter approaches overhead.

People point, look up, then turn around and begin to run. Those up front push and shove their way back though the crowd. And—

Next we see a succession of still photographs. Wreckage, twisted metal, charred remains. Injured people prone on the grass. Paramedics. Emergency Personnel. A makeshift morgue. Body bags. Dead the seven men in the helicopter as well as twelve people on the ground including Chalkman and Billy's Da. The boy sustained first, second, and third degree burns but he had run like a track star and had outstripped his father by at least forty feet.

II

Billy's father Franz Steiglitz, one of the nineteen men killed during the restaging of the federal retreat, came to the United States with his parents at the age of six. Affluent Austrian Anglophiles, the Steiglitzes continued to lead as lush and extravagant a life in America as they had previously been accustomed to in Vienna, Berlin, and London. Franz attended the best of schools (Catholic and private) and like his father before him chose medicine as his career. He returned to Europe in September 1945 as an International Red Cross doctor, but when he came back to the States in 1947 he abandoned his medical practice (to all his friends' and colleagues' incomprehension and regret) and thenceforward earned his livelihood and supported his family by teaching graduate and majors-only Biology courses at the Pennsylvania State Teachers' College in Slippery Rock until his death in 1973.

Steiglitz came from a long line of doctors. His grandfather Wilhelm served as an army surgeon during Austria's two-week war with Prussia in 1866. The Prussian Generals made a thorough study of the American Civil War. Austria lost because she didn't grasp the significance of the railroad and telegraph and because the Prussian Kaiser had outfitted his infantry with breech-loading rifles which could fire six shots to every one from the outmoded Austrian muzzleloaders. At the conflict's end, Hofrat Wilhelm Steiglitz resigned his commission and until his death in the late 1890s, carried on a private practice. In 1872 he became director of surgery at a celebrated tuberculosis sanatorium in Innsbruck, where he met his wife Margretta Eigert, daughter of a Leipzig banker and patient at the facility. During the course of a long and distinguished career, Franz's father Alois Steiglitz, a famed neurologist in Vienna, operated in hospitals in London and Paris as well as at home. Additionally Alois' wife Carolina's father Joachim Matzelot had been a chaired professor of medicine at the Imperial University in Wien. However, an amateur ornithologist, he devoted more time to his hobby than to his chosen profession. His wife Magda (nee Markwort) Matzelot received significant attention, was even more highly esteemed by the general public than he, at least during their first years together, for a month prior to their 1878 marriage, Joachim's wife published a short book of lyrics—her only work—for which she received very favorable notices. A reviewer in the *Frankfurter Allgemeine* went so far as to pronounce her "a female Heine." In spite of the many predictions and forecasts of great things to come, she never produced a second volume. A failure of the will. Try as she might, nothing more would flow from her pen. Her husband Joachim Matzelot never suffered from any such impediment. He wrote a number of tomes not only on the human nervous system but also on the migratory habits of European birds. But the verdict of even his intended audience, the professional experts in both fields, was that his books were unreadable and dry. In 1911, Dr. Alois Steiglitz assumed a permanent post at a London sanatorium, and two years later became a British citizen. A year prior to America's entering World War One, Franz's father accepted a teaching position at the University of Pennsylvania, and he, his wife Carolina, and their son Franz arrived in New York aboard the HMS Mauritania in 1916.

Prior to his military service during World War Two, Billy's father Franz Alfred Steiglitz married Carol Alice Corl—his mother, a young nurse at one of the Philadelphia hospitals at which Dr. Steiglitz had admitting privileges. The last scion, along with her brother Roger, of the illustrious Corl family, she had a bloodline which—at least according to her lifelong prejudices (partialities inculcated since childhood) compared, vied, with Franz's own. The first child of Ben and Libby McCalmont Corl, she had just turned twenty-two when she and Franz married in '43, her husband eleven years her senior. Entering Ben Corl's house, Franz immediately noticed the framed, elaborately designed Family Tree above the mantel amongst the family portraits and noted the excellent calligraphy on the part of the register of the births and deaths, the handiwork he assumed of a long dead ancestor of his wife's. Many sonorous names had been inscribed there. They came so trippingly to the tongue: Eliza Abell, Percy McCalmont, Susanna Woodle, Cyrus and Marilla Helfenfuss, Anna Ebler, Benjamin Corl…. Men and women whom Fate had drawn together so they'd charm and captivate each other, then cross-pollinate, recombine their DNA, to which pool he would now add his genes as the other half of the equation to produce a new life. He had wanted a family but then the war intervened and he changed his mind.

Germany was one vast bombed-out landscape, having suffered the heaviest continued air attack in all of history. The major cities reduced to rubble and ruin—to shells of their former selves—entire sections of the country lay in ruin. Contagious diseases such as cholera and enteric fever broke out at all the refugee camps affecting many individuals at the same time. Franz traveled back and forth between twenty such aide stations treating displaced persons and cared for many prostrate patients with eruptions of rose-red spots on their chests and abdomens or suffering from overwhelming dehydration brought about by severe diarrhea and vomiting. Eventually emergency hospitals opened in the skeletal cities. Franz supervised the operations of several and himself performed numerous surgeries. In a civilian infirmary in Frankfurt, he confronted an East Prussian family which had made it to the American zone from the Russian, a husband and wife and their unconscious, pregnant, seventeen-year-old daughter. From a hiding place inside their house, the parents had watched the Russian soldiers, eleven or twelve of them, violate their child. The door of their outbuilding had been kicked off its hinges. The Russians knocked their daughter down onto the door, pinned her arms and spread open her legs, then drove nails into the wood through her palms and each of her two feet. The men took turns, waited in line. When the last of the men finished, they set fire to the cowshed, lifted the door and the girl crucified to it and tossed them inside the blazing structure and then departed. Only then could the father and mother rush to her rescue. They had nursed her back to health. She had made the journey westwards, but ever frail she became febrile two months before, five months after the attack, and fell into a coma. Dr. Steiglitz felt her life might be saved if the baby was aborted. Her parents begged him to perform the procedure. He waffled, knew he must make a choice, had to decide which life was worthier of being saved. He had toured Buchenwald and had seen pictures from the other death camps, but thought that the innocent babe in the unconscious girl's womb might be the second coming of the Lord Jesus whose latest entry into this world, whose newest incarnation, would be in a German body (what people had more need of redemption?) for He would want to take their sins upon himself. Yet lying on the hospital bed, the mother seemed as sweet and innocent as the Virgin Mary or his tubercular sister Hannelore, who, born in America in 1919, had died at age twenty in a Vermont sanatorium. Two weeks after becoming the physician of record, he decided to perform the procedure. The mother's life came first. The girl's parents' arguments persuaded him. *And perhaps the German people should not be vouchsafed an opportunity for salvation. He would slay the Redeemer in the womb, hazard the role of Herod.* He scrubbed down, feeling hatred in his heart for his own people but also for atheistic communists of the bookish Russian type. For while he could imagine that most of the brutes who assaulted her were anthropoids, there had to be among them an officer, a leader, who dreamed that he was a neophyte Lenin. Franz worked for the Führer at last. But the mother died after he executed, bungled, the surgery (in his mind an amputation, a removal of cancerous, gangrenous, tissue). He became one of the happy guilty or the guilty guiltless. Not only did the child die but also a few hours afterward so did the girl. Yet his decision had been the correct one. Had he attempted a Caesarian, he would have doomed the mother to certain death, and the chances of a baby delivered before term, in only the seventh month, surviving would have been very low. *Not if it had been the new Christ child. But then could he have performed the procedure? Would not hosts of Angels have held back his hand?* The odds for survival had been higher for the mother. Moreover, he had heard the horror stories. How the Russians lined up children in front of their parents and machine-gunned them down (bread for bread, blood for blood) in reprisal for German atrocities in the Soviet Union. Scores of women, ages ranging between twelve and eighty, had been raped by the Russian soldiers. All the Fraus and Frauleins and even the dear little Mädchens feared to hear the words *Frau komm.* At that very time, even in the American, French, and British sectors, German women still worried about being attacked. He had noticed that many had let the hair on their legs grow. Did they hope thereby to quell any carnal urge on the part of a would-be violator? To dissuade him by disturbing his aesthetics? They wouldn't succeed. Battle had hardened most of the soldiers, turned them into brutes and animals. Not Circe's swine but ravenous boars. Few could be deterred. Yet he felt that it was only right that Hitler's master race was corrupted and fouled, the Aryan blood sullied by intermixing with all the others. He wanted to say like the majority of American doctors that the

Fritzes dished out their fair share so they damn well deserved what they got, but part of him recoiled, held back by his own Germanic blood and by his common humanity. The refugees' plight elicited his sympathy. All sufferers might apply to him for aid. He had sworn an oath to aid and succor all men regardless of nationality. Since his German was impeccable he did most of the interpreting, heard the refugees' stories from their own lips. His ears pricked whenever one middle-aged dame from Saxony, a Frau Schilling, whose two sisters had died in the Dresden bombings, mentioned the British Prime Minister by name. She pronounced it incorrectly with open defiance, garbled Sir Winston's surname Churchill with the German word for monster *Scheusal* (Joycean word play, but a dreadful slur). Talk about removing the beam from your own eye before taking the mote out of your brother's.

During Franz's stay in occupied Germany, the allies had begun gathering evidence to prosecute the Nürnberg War Crime trials, and the military and civilian authorities had asked Franz to examine Nazi records of medical experiments on inmates in the camps. To his disgust and horror, he read about the gas gangrene experiments performed on Poles, Dr. Josef Mengele's use of one identical twin as a control while he butchered the other, injecting dye in her eye or operating on her without an anesthetic, usually to remove a healthy organ. To determine the effects of hypothermia, they buried naked camp inmates up to their necks in the snow, used them as human guinea pigs. In the camp dormitories, the bald heads in the bunks rose row upon row—the prisoners hardly had space to turn. Many starved; others worked until they dropped as slaves in German factories. And the Nazi rationalization? They simply facilitated, sped up, the process of the natural selection. To enhance the survival of the fittest, degenerate elements had to be weeded out—without pity— starting with the grossly handicapped and the insane. Did not the Jew Stefan Zweig write that there are two kinds of pity and that one should beware of the first, the weak and sentimental kind, which is really no more than the heart's impatience to be rid as quickly as possible of the painful emotion aroused by the sight of another's unhappiness, that pity which is not compassion, but only an instinctive desire to fortify one's own soul against the sufferings of another; whereas one should embrace and adopt the second kind of pity, the only pity which counts, the unsentimental and creative kind, which knows what it is about and is determined to hold out, in patience and forbearance, to the very limit of its strength and even beyond? Why waste plentiful human resource material? If the highest authority decreed their doom, if they were going to be systematically destroyed anyway, why not conduct research on selected untouchables, selected damned, which might prove beneficial to the Reich, as the knowledge of hypothermia would be to army physicians on the Eastern Front? *Fiat experimentum in corpore vili.* The Nazi doctors committed the most appalling crimes. One handed out toy balloons to the Jewish children right before his aides and underlings administered fatal phenol injections at the rate of ten children per minute, inserting the needles of their syringes directly into the little boys' and girls' hearts.

After a two-year sojourn in war-torn, defeated Germany, Franz Steiglitz returned to the United States having already made his decision to abstain from active medical practice forevermore. Hired to teach advanced physiology classes at the state teachers' college in 1948, he (to his mind at least) disappeared entirely from view. He let former acquaintanceships slide. He began a new life, having put space first between his former colleagues and friends and himself. Although his wife still wanted children, he for a long time couldn't stomach the notion of fatherhood. In fact he considered Carol a sort of first child he had to mold initially. Not until 1953 did he at last relent, and she bore him a son—Billy—and in 1955 the Steiglitzes had a second child Miles. When the boys were both still quite little, Father set to educating them. He taught Billy to be proud of his American heritage and wrote up for his son Civil War tales collected and culled from all the various branches of his wife's family. Every year they visited one or more battlefields.

Although Franz remained very vocal in his rejection of all things German (the music, literature, scientific advances had all been tainted to his mind), he had the archetypical Teutonic personality. Quite hawkish, unmerciful on his students, he believed that an instructor must be very hard on the pupil if the tyro was to develop into anything that was not average, or into something more than a closet dilettante. Billy would be his Beethoven. Consequently Bill became afraid of his *Vater*. That was to be expected. For Da remained unsociable, a dogged individualist. He had nothing but contempt for his fellow educators and their petty office politics, wouldn't go to department picnics, faculty cocktail parties, etc. He liked to be alone, to escape into his own world of intellectual interests, where few could follow him, a dark wood which was his homeland—the territory of his heart—where he knew each and every contour of the landscape, and how to skirt any and all pitfalls. Where he felt completely safe. Away from the sharks.

He had a den, a "bunker" in the basement. This was Franz's area. Access was strictly *verboten*, off limits to the children, even to Carol. He had a credo: **Act like you're at war with everyone, for you in fact are.** Since each person they might encounter was potentially and probably in fact hostile and antagonistic, he counseled his boys to always be on the alert. Simultaneously, he warred with the Department, his students (how he hated them!), his wife, father-in-law, and his young sons, going so far even as to launch preemptive strikes on them whenever they tested his patience. He tried to impart or implant his philosophy into Billy. He succeeded somewhat (his son became very competitive) but failed partially too for Bill wouldn't accept all points of his father's dogma, would not engage in battle if not first attacked. He reposed trust in people. Franz, alas, also undertook the education of Miles, who rebelled completely, but thanks to his father developed a real inferiority complex. At the age of seventeen, the boy committed suicide. Always last at everything, (he never got good grades or excelled at sports or with the girls, Pa called him a stupid mortal), he decided to experience death first (find out the answers to those persistent, nagging, ontological questions before his father and everyone else did). At last he could be first at something. Maybe he hadn't experienced death earlier than his Grandma Corl. Indeed many, many others had preceded him. But at least he would get there before Da, Ma, and Bill. They found him hanging from the crossbeam at the top of the attic staircase—as far from the basement as possible. After her son's suicide, Carol Steiglitz became mentally unhinged, attempted suicide herself by swallowing sleeping pills and therefore had to be committed to a state institution. She responded to therapy, and after several months no longer needed medication for severe depression. But her protracted final illness began, her husband was quite certain, while she was institutionalized. At our mental and emotional low points, we have the power to will our deaths. The causes of cancer were psychosomatic. Freud, Jung, Groddeck, and Stekel would all agree. Mrs. Steiglitz succumbed during Billy's sophomore year at his father's Alma Mater. She had battled valiantly. It took the cancer four years. She had tumor after tumor cut out of her body, endured radium treatments twice. Despite her evident pain and nausea, she drove herself to choir practice after chemotherapy, after first putting on makeup and a wig. But finally she grew so tired, she just gave in. During the final weeks, she could not get out of bed without assistance, did nothing but sleep. The disease consumed her, or she digested herself, fulfilling her most ardent desire at the time of the disease's inception—to die. She went gently into that good night but only after a long period of turbulent strife. For two years she did not give in, had convinced herself that she wanted to live after all, and kept herself alive, although the doctors said she could go at any moment. Her time finally came. Standing in black suits at the gravesite, Billy and his father were at long last alone.

III

The Civil War stories about the three ancestors on his mother's side that his maternal grandfather Ben Corl related to him as a child and which Franz Steiglitz later wrote down for his son in the form of a pamphlet fascinated Bill from the time he first heard them, but his interest peaked on his fifteenth birthday when his father presented him with the opening pages of the booklet. Although Franz Steiglitz knew the results of war—its horrible reality—he romanticized past American wars (especially the Civil War) in his presentation of family history to Bill, for he wanted to instill a certain attitude into his son. He wanted Bill to love his country. Franz determined to raise a real American patriot. Yet during the Vietnam conflict, when Bill enrolled at the University of Pennsylvania majoring in Pre-Med, his father made sure that he got college deferment after college deferment.

The first tale set down by Franz Steiglitz was, of course, that of the Corl brothers: William, Prosper, and Peter Corl. He gave Billy the typescript on his fifteenth birthday. Although much of the material he retold had come down by word of mouth, had been divulged to him by his wife Carol and his father-in-law Benjamin, Franz spent many hours searching through libraries and archives for additional information. He uncovered, ferreted out, many new details on his wife's forebears. He tried to put flesh on the skeletons by digging up all the statistics and facts which had been buried, lost in time. He would go on to write numerous pages on the Corl, McCalmont, and Kemper families while he included only a brief ten-page sketch on the Steiglitzes, Matzelots, Eigerts, and Markworts. However, of his wife's many forebears, the material on the Corl family took precedence. His father-in-law had already done some initial work, so naturally he began where Ben left off.

Shortly after Billy's direct ancestor (his great-great grandfather) Peter Corl turned twenty-eight, he was appointed a policeman of Philadelphia, more accurately a member of the City Night Watch, by the Mayor's office. Every year from 1848 to 1867, the city council nominated and elected him to this position. Assigned to duty in the North East District, he resided in South Mulberry Ward at 144 Juniper Street, two doors down from his parents Henry and Susanna Woodle Corl. A butcher by trade, Henry Corl hailed from Wales and had crossed the Atlantic as a young man whereas Peter's maternal grandparents, Benjamin and Wilhelmina Woodle, were respectively of English and German stock, the grandfather a cooper by occupation and a member of the Society of Friends, his forebears having come to America with William Penn. The Woodles lived on Arch Street, a center of business and a residential site at that time, then moved to Germantown where Benjamin Woodle built one of the first brick homes.

Peter August Corl had remained under the parental roof until he reached his twenty-seventh year. His early education had been rather limited. At the age of seventeen, he began serving an apprenticeship to the carpenter's trade with one Compton Templeton, a contractor and builder of Philadelphia, receiving a wage of forty dollars and board per year. On attaining his majority, he started out as a journeyman, and remained so employed until twenty-eight years of age, when he accepted the post of policeman, which position he acceptably filled for twenty years. In May of 1848, he wed his cousin Luella Spohn Woodle, Billy's great-great grandmother. Both Corl and his wife entered this life and embarked on their pilgrimage through the wilderness of the world, in 1820, the husband several months the bride's junior.

In the course of his researches, Franz Steiglitz secured copies of several pages of *Journal of Select Council, Philadelphia, Penna.* "wherein the convention of the council did proceed to nominate persons for the Marshal to select as policemen." The Marshal hired the men on an annual basis and the Select Council had to renominate candidates yearly. Every year for twenty years, Peter Corl received the same appointment. A man of good character and sterling qualities (Ben Corl had always said that much had been passed down), he diligently and conscientiously performed his duties as watchman. But (a revelation to the family, Ben Corl himself hadn't known) in a September 7th, 1854 entry of the above-mentioned journal which listed the total police force at that date, not only could Peter's name be found there, so could those of his two younger brothers: William and Prosper. The former saw the light of day in 1824, the latter in 1827. All three Corls remained on the force for the next four years. Then the two younger boys resigned, taking up brass fitting and carpentry. The following year the younger Corls left Philly, taking up residence in Clearfield, Pennsylvania, in the center of the state where they became engaged in the express business and in lumbering: cutting down pine forests, harvesting the tall trees for ships' masts.

The two younger Corl brothers enlisted as Union soldiers in Clearfield County in May of 1861. They served in Company C of the Fifth Regiment PA Reserve Volunteer Corps, also known as the Thirty-Fourth PA Volunteers. Recruiters had signed up the volunteers making up the other companies comprising the Fifth in Lancaster, Centre, Huntington, Union, and Bradford Counties, among others. The men arrived at Camp Curtin, near Harrisburg, PA, on June 20th, 1861. The very day they reported to bivouac, the Pennsylvania Governor (Franz Steiglitz ascertained this accidentally one morning at the county historical society research library, while leafing through an old dusty volume) had received a telegram from Lieutenant General Winfield Scott, importuning Curtin to send troops to aid, assist, and strengthen the Eleventh Indiana at Cumberland, Maryland. It surprised Franz Steiglitz to learn that none other that Col. Lewis Wallace commanded the Eleventh, the same Lew Wallace, who in '62 would move "to retake the heights late lost at Donelson" and be celebrated in Herman Melville's famous war poem, who himself some twenty years later would pen that hugely popular Biblical novel *Ben Hur*, and who as Governor of the New Mexico territory would order Pat Garrett to bring in Billy the Kid. The Fifth, together with the Bucktail rifle regiment, and Captain Easton's battery of the First Artillery, were at once dispatched, the whole under the command of Colonel Biddle of the Bucktails, but after arriving in Cumberland, the Fifth participated in only a few minor skirmishes, but most days drilled monotonously afternoon after afternoon, forever it seemed, in camp after camp.

The brothers first participated in a real battle at Mechanicsville, also known as the "Seven Days in front of Richmond" and later saw combat at second Manassas, Chantilly, South Mountain, Antietam, Fredericksburg, and Gettysburg. At the Fredericksburg fray in December 1863, Prosper Corl lost the hearing in his right ear, the only injury he sustained in the entire Civil War. William Corl fell in the line of duty at Gettysburg, his body later interred with all due honor in the battlefield cemetery.

Ironically, in the center of all that carnage and bloodshed, William was the only soldier in his company mortally wounded. A week prior to the battle, Hooker resigned his command and Lincoln promoted General George Meade to the leadership of the Grand Army of the Potomac. The Fifth Regiment, together with a brigade led by one Colonel Fisher, joined the Fifth Corps.

Headquarters held the brigade upon its appearance on the field for a time in reserve in the vicinity of Little Round Top. It did not see action until the second day of the campaign July 2nd, 1863. That morning the adversary, realizing that the high ground was the key to the Union position, strove hard to gain possession of the smaller Round Top. The Third Brigade of the First Division of the Fifth Corps under Col. Vincent had been ordered to march on the double quick and hold the hill. Vincent's men had scarcely taken up positions on the eminence, when Hood's division of Longstreet's Corps—tall lanky Texans, for the most part—came rushing on with deafening yells in three battle lines. With the strength coming from urgency and dire need, the Confederates toiled to unblock the rugged sides and carry the heights. If they could seize and secure Little Round Top, they could enfilade the entire Union position. Failing to take the hill from the front and to the left, they teemed through the little valley between the Round Tops, doubling the left flank of Vincent and menacing his rear. At this critical moment, Colonel Fisher and the Fifth Regiment charged to the relief of Vincent's hard-pressed brigade. Hooraying and yelping, they went forward at the double quick, bolted up the hill, gaining the summit in time to share in the victory, the loss to the regiment in the action two wounded and one killed, the man killed Billy's namesake William M. Corl. His sacrifice had not been in vain. During the night, Union troops advanced to the summit of Big Round Top, and the two hills were joined in a strong line of breastworks constructed of loose boulders. The following day, at Lee's insistence, Longstreet ordered a direct attack on Cemetery Hill, the strongest part of the Union center, with Pickett's, Pettigrew's and Trimble's division. The Civil War had reached its turning point.

After William's death, Prosper continued the fight. He participated in the Wilderness Campaign on May 5th –7th, 1864, an indecisive three-day affair in which Lee outmaneuvered his opponents, but also the half-deaf Prosper Corl's great moment of glory, for he single-handedly captured three stands of enemy colors for which he would receive the Congressional Medal of Honor. Ben Corl saw the medal as a young boy, then in the possession of Martha Corl, Prosper's daughter, the principal of a girl's boarding school in Bellefonte. Prosper Corl received his discharge from the service and mustered with the other men for a final roll call on June 1st, 1864. He later held offices in both the local and state GAR.

Billy's direct ancestor Peter Corl had just turned forty when the War Between The States began, old enough that he did not have to serve in the army like his two younger brothers. He kept his policeman position and stayed out of harm's way. The war came home to him first with the death of his brother William and then shortly after Lee's surrender at Appomattox, with the assassination of his President, for he stood watch when the funeral procession of Abraham Lincoln passed through the city, having been assigned by the Marshal to the honor guard.

Thousands of Philadelphians viewed the procession. When the cortege passed where Billy's forefather stood, a few flowers fell from the caisson bearing the body of the late president. Corl picked up the yellow roses and preserved them. At the time of Franz Steiglitz's death, Billy's grandfather Ben Corl had them in his possession. He also had handed down to him a large oval-framed photograph of Peter Corl in his police uniform, Peter's wooden whistle and his wooden law rattle which could also serve as a billy, as well as two miniatures of Peter's brothers Prosper and Will. After Ben Corl's death of a stroke in 1976, the United States Bicentennial year, the effects were turned over, as had been stipulated in Ben's will, to Bill's Uncle Roger.

The billyclub resembled a miniature baseball bat with a handle on one side. A center section of the "bat" rotated, and the notched top made a loud clattering noise, when the constable spun the rattle. A brass piece had been fixed to the tip of the billy—engraved on it Peter Corl's initials and his police number, thirteen.

After his retirement from the police force, Pete Corl served as the first assistant engineer to one of Philadelphia's early fire departments. Ben Corl had one of the company's fire markers. Homeowners placed this brass symbol above the door of their house to show that they had purchased protection from a particular fire company. The First Fire Brigade would put out fires only in buildings displaying its marker, the owners having paid the company's annual fee. Numerous brigades competed with each other; each had its own marker or plaque.

When Franz commenced his research, as stated earlier, only a few records of Philadelphia's Night Watch remained in existence; he discovered these by enlisting the help of several city archivists. They could tell him little other than that the city council appointed the patrolmen on a yearly basis and that the practice of electing officers annually continued for more than a decade after the department's incorporation in 1850.

A professional researcher Franz had hired to comb through the old city ledgers unearthed several interesting items, including the 1867 dismissal notice of Peter Corl's friend and fellow officer (they walked, it turned out, the same beat together),

Francis X. Boulanger, whose superiors not only drummed him out of the police force but also demanded that he leave Philadelphia after he nearly killed a grave digger at the I.O.O.F. Cemetery at 24th and Diamond Streets. Several years previously, the bodies of a number of the officer's family had been moved there from St. George's Methodist Episcopal Cemetery. The records indicated that Peter Corl not realizing the unfortunate incident which would ensue because of his revelation had informed his fellow watchman of the sale of the entire I.O.O.F. cemetery to make way for the construction of a railroad and that the remains buried there were to be removed to a cemetery at 16th and Coates Streets. Hearing that the ashes of his loved ones would be disinterred a second time and only such a short spell after they had originally been disturbed, Boulanger went to the graveyard while the vaults were in the process of being opened, and he and the gravedigger got into a heated argument because the officer thought the gravedigger treated the skull of the officer's grandfather, a hero of the Revolution, with disrespect (apparently he tossed it rather cavalierly out of the pit). They scuffled, and the officer struck the gravedigger on the head with his billy, this offence occasioning his dismissal and forced relocation from the city. He withdrew to the town of Rallingsburg in Rallings County, Pa, to what fate Franz Steiglitz couldn't ascertain. The incident intrigued Franz for two reasons. One, another of Bill's ancestors Frederick Wilhelm Kaempfer had been one of the twelve original settlers of Rallingsburg (as also had been Francis Boulanger's grandfather the Revolutionary War soldier, an interesting coincidence that two different forebears of Bill's would have interaction with the same family, for in the course of his researches Franz learned that Kaempfer and old Boulanger had been fast friends) although Kaempfer moved back eastward after only a short period of time. And two, because of its similarity to an event which happened to the corpse of Jacob Kemper, Frederick Kaempfer's heir and grandson. Like two of the three Corl brothers Jacob had served as a Union soldier during the War Between The States. Years after his death, Jacob's family had his casket exhumed in one cemetery for reburial in another. The lid of his coffin somehow sprang open, and, exposed to the air, the skin on the dead man's face crumbled and dissolved in front of the eyes of the horrified burial party.

At the time of his grandfather's death, Bill would not step a foot out of the house. He knew all along that Roger would take possession of the Corl heirlooms, but he didn't feel that that was totally fair or just. He could have preserved the family relics at his parents'—now his—home. He would have made a place on the wall and mantel to proudly display them. How he would have loved to have had the pressed yellow roses. Maybe his grandfather hadn't willed Bill the items in question because Bill hadn't passed a test administered to him in his youth? But no it was Ben Corl himself who had taught Billy his first lesson about loss and had comforted him as he sat on his lap crying, a dejected little boy. He said that forfeiture and foolish waste were part of life, and told Billy how he, Ben Corl, and his daughter, Bill's mom, had in their time lost, damaged or broken valuable items, that Bill was hardly the first person to do this. Recalling his grandfather's lecture, Bill gave it a name: "The Story of the Tooth, the Banana Bug, and the Blue Willow Pitcher."

In his whole life, Billy had never forgotten about the tooth. According to his grandfather, he would never forget about it. The month before school started (that year he would have been entering the third grade) as they did every summer, he and his parents and his younger brother Miles spent several weeks at the home of his grandparents in the small Eastern Pennsylvania town of Stony Run, a six-to-seven hour drive from Slippery Rock (where the Steiglitzes lived and where Billy's father taught college) taking the backroads route they always had, although Franz knew at least three other faster ways, a travel plan, an itinerary that (despite the length of the car ride) Bill had practically memorized they had made the trip so often. When they got close to Grandpa's, he sprang up excited as a little puppy and directed his father at each and every turn in the road, but after the fun of getting there, as always, the vacation came to an end almost as soon as it started, or so it seemed, but this year both Bill and his mother brought home mementoes, Billy the four-inch fossil dinosaur tooth Pappy Ben had given to him, his mother a set of her mother's best china. The tooth had come from Pappy Ben's memento drawer in the cabinet in his den where he also kept Peter Corl's rattle and whistle, and the miniatures of William and Prosper Corl. Peter Corl's portrait hung on the wall above the roll-top cabinet. The tooth had belonged to Ben's daddy, who had found it in a coal mine when a young man of seventeen or eighteen. Billy admired it so much that his grandfather gave it to him. The very day they got home, he had to take it outside and show it to all his friends. He said that he had found a dinosaur's tooth. They passed it around then handed it back to him and he pocketed it, but when he came home he no longer had it in his possession. He panicked and ran back out to look for it. But it was lost, gone. When three months later at Thanksgiving, Grandfather Ben asked him what happened to his tooth, he broke down and cried, simply went to pieces. Grandpa lifted him onto his lap, his own eyes watery, and said that he had lost things too, how when he was a boy his Uncle Albert Corl had brought a dead banana bug all the way from Panama, where he worked for Uncle Sam digging the great canal. Albert made a present of it to him, but he traded it at school for a marble or something else he couldn't remember and had regretted it ever since. "And Carol," he said, "You know what your mother Carol did at her Grandmother McCalmont's when she was a little girl?" Well, she broke the antique pitcher with its pretty blue birds and pavilions—demolished it, destroying not only the pitcher alone but because it had been part of what up to then had been a carefully preserved sixteen-piece set, also considerably depreciated the worth of the remaining fifteen pieces. "You have to get used to losing things, Bill," he said. "For in the course of your life, many precious things, not only objects but more importantly people too, will be lost to you. And if you don't become inured to it, in the end they'll cart you off to the crazy house. Son, you just have to grin and bear it, that's all. So keep a stiff upper lip, my boy. As for the tooth. It came out of the ground and now the ground has swallowed it up again and reclaimed it."

Billy had always enjoyed looking in Grandpa's memento drawer. He stared at the old photographs—looked up at the proud countenance of his forebear Peter Corl hanging on the den wall. Perhaps Roger would make him copies. He'd gladly pay whatever it cost.

In his youth, he repeatedly glanced at the old daguerreotypes of all three Corl boys. If photographs had existed of his two other ancestors who served in the Civil War, his Grandma Libby's grandfather Percy McCalmont and her great-grandfather Jacob Kemper, he had never seen them. They had been lost or had been passed on to distant relatives of his grandmother, with whom his branch of the family had long since lost touch. But the Corl visages he had seen. Billy knew the lineaments of the long dead Corl faces. They were not lost to Billy Steiglitz. At least not yet.

His father had devoted more pages to the McCalmont and Kemper ancestors than he had done to the three Corls. Franz had known less about them. He had to dig in all sorts of unlikely places to come up with the few facts he did know, but those facts were not enough for him. Not content with merely reporting what battles the two men participated in, he wanted to tell two vivid exciting stories. To give the illusion of fluid reality, he invented and imagined, put flesh on the bone and created characters and personalities, made the men almost come to life in his pages. Did his Percy McCalmont and his Jacob Kemper resemble their originals and prototypes? He could not be sure. He tried to adhere as best he could to the facts of their lives, as he knew them. He had not been overly free in that regard, but as far as ascribing individual traits and qualities, motivations, driving forces and incentives, who knew? A merchant of the untrue, he had taken liberties to be sure, his aim to create a high degree of impressionistic accuracy. But Franz also wanted his Civil War tales to be illustrative. He'd use them as covert pedagogic tools to convince his son that he lived in a dangerous world, a world in which at all times someone or something waited to strike out at you. "Yes, Bill, we are all targets. You, me, everyone." The McCalmont and Kemper stories would drive that point forcefully home to Bill. In fact, the tale of Percy McCalmont and his unfortunate wife epitomized his point that even close family members, kin, can become your enemies, trouncing and smiting you when you least expect it.

Yes, even now, years later, Bill could remember those three faces. Framed behind glass in an ornamentally carved wooden oval, the portrait of Peter Corl was three to four times as large as the miniatures of his two younger brothers, the old photograph almost sepia tone, a tan, brownish hue. The subject sat in a chair, his cap on his knee. He wore a vest, watch chain, and outer garment with prominent brass buttons, his outsize police shield displayed prominently—obtrusively—on his coat. His face lean and long, he seemed to stare down his nose at you (perhaps only because the picture hung high on the wall and Billy had to look up to it as a boy) despite his jaw's being thrust out and his eyes (if you took the picture down from the wall and examined it closely) looking squarely, unflinchingly at the camera—in other words straight ahead. One huge ear cocked toward the photographer, Peter had curly black hair and a full beard but no mustache. His uniform (there was no way of telling from the black-and-white photograph) one assumed had to be blue.

More classically handsome than his elder brother, Prosper Corl, photographed in his Union uniform, wore a mustache like General Custer, his hair dark and of only moderate length. He had a medium-sized nose and dark, penetrating eyes. a globular face with a cleft chin. He too sat, photographed from the waist up.

William, however, stood, dressed in civilian clothes. A squat man, broad of brow and shoulders and wearing a knee-length coat and bow tie, he positioned himself elbow on banister at the stairhead, standing on a plush carpet with a fancy geometrical pattern.

He was clean-shaven, his chin a bit recessive. His copious hair bunched out to both the right and to the left sides. He had come to his nation's call, and paid the full price: his life.

IV

Why did he try to instill his ideas into his son's head? Because he loved him? Surely. But as his wife and all members of her family averred, you love each of your children just the same. He tried, and, although Miles at first perplexed then angered him because of his perverse, finally intolerable, conduct, in his heart of hearts he did feel affection for them equally for he could recall them both as babies one, two, and three days old, when mother and father could not help but feel all the intoxicating aftereffects of the birth, the issuance of new life into the world, when they both experienced the exultation of shaping something new out of that which was primeval and immortal, a feat so exacting that the father feels like a champion salmon. He had to swim against the current and jump up a whole series of waterfalls, but he succeeded by God, and the perpetuation of the species had thus been insured. But to be truthful during the years that followed he showed (it was obvious to anyone) all the signs of a marked favoritism. He had to confess it. A decided preference had developed. You worked the field which bore the most promise of bearing fruit. Miles dead-ended. In each generation of the mad Darwinian struggle a similar tragedy played itself out, God's Steiglitzian variations. Until finally one day they'd all die together in their last remaining avatar. The line would come to an end. *Punct.*

William and Miles reenacted the archetypical sibling struggle. Inevitably one son had to subordinate himself and live in his brother's shadow. Survival of the fittest again.

Well Miles lost out. To hurt the family, he took his life, hoping that the residual grief would pull the beloved enemy down as well, inspire another suicide. Bill's. I doubt he foresaw the effect of his miserable action, his perverse desire to do away with himself having gained the ascendancy over any decent scruple or impulse in him, on my wife, his mother. Of course all members of the surviving family share in the guilt. I too bear some of the blame. I admit my responsibility for the deaths of three children, one of them my own. Only a venal sin—a small guilt—that when compared to the enormity of my killing Madonna and child in post-Adolf Deutschland. William must remain strong. He will fight back. I will make him want to resist, want to tussle and skirmish. Example upon example I will lay before his eyes until he realizes the truth of all I say. He must prepare himself to parry and riposte attacks from all directions. He has to learn to outwit and outmaneuver his opponents whoever they might be. He has to survive and carry on the Steiglitzian cycle.

He won't wilt and collapse with my example before his eyes. My strength and will shall become his, he too will want to outlast his time, make a memorial to his existence, strive to effect some sort of advancement, it doesn't matter in which field. As long as he achieves his set goal, he'll gain fame, there'll be a luster and an aura to his name. People will remember him. Yes, William will make his mark and he will be mine.

Now to prepare. First I must pick up my car—it has just had its annual tune up—then turn in my grades and retrieve my paycheck. Then I can be off. I'll pick up Bill in Philly, then we can head south, and I'll let him take the wheel and enjoy the scenery as he pilots us, and while he drives I can talk to him. I'll ask about his finals and how he thinks he did in his courses this semester. I hope you'll make me proud of you, I'll say. If you didn't waste time and screw up and through your own laziness hurt yourself, and more importantly if you didn't mouth off but showed respect to your teachers, acted as if not only you could learn from them but that you were grateful for the opportunity of so doing, things I'm sure will have gone well enough for you. Sometimes Bill could be a bonehead. It remained very tempting, but, no, you must never hit slow child even though—be truthful—it stood in concordance with your deepest, innermost, wishes. Yes, you must refrain. However if the child feigned intransigence and just didn't want to learn, became sulky and uncooperative, well then—let your wrath descend on him. I remember the "fun" I had teaching Bill to drive. He put off getting his permit. Unlike most willful, cocky, boys that age who wait and suffer several years for the magical birthday to arrive so that they can run and get their licenses, he didn't really care one way or the other, show any desire to learn. This didn't bother me because at that time he worked diligently at his studies, did very well in high school, and I commended him for applying himself so assiduously. I thought he would approach me in the summertime. Surprised when he did not, I let him alone until he turned eighteen, but then we had our obligatory little scene, a tempest in the teapot if you will. We fought. I won. The next day I marched him down to the police barracks to apply for his permit, and we got started. He shook like a leaf. I saw the sweat as it ran down his forehead. I had to shout, call him to attention, when he crossed the line right in the path of the oncoming truck. I yanked the wheel in my direction and punched the horn just in time. After swerving back into our rightful lane, I made him pull over and twice cuffed him on the back of his head with my right hand. My left still clutched the wheel. He began crying like a little child of course, and I had to suffer it. Some of his friends worked with him, and now he can drive better than I. He says that I brake too much. Every time I go round a curve. And (get this) that I slow down whenever I approach a green light because I'm afraid it will turn red. I do apply the brake much too often. My driving is jerky. Whereas his is smooth. He cruises at a set speed. And I do not distract him. He can still concentrate even though I am talking. I entrust my life to him and freely admit that he's the better driver, now, of us two.

Won't Bill be surprised? He-he. I hope he hasn't read a publicity notice in the *Inquirer* or any other newspaper. That he doesn't know about the filming of the Civil War reenactment. Or he'll guess my intentions. If as I expect he's been too busy to notice, I'll tell him that our destination is Washington, Nixonville. And that we're going to hear, I've got tickets for, a performance of Beethoven's *Missa Solemnis* at Kennedy Center. In Philly, we'll get on 95, motor south across the tip of Delaware into MD, bypassing Baltimore down through Silver Springs to DC and onto the beltway. Then I'll tell Billy that Kennedy Center is not our true destination, and we'll drive through Bethesda and Arlington and Vienna (how fitting a Wien in VA) and on towards Centreville (Bill still in the dark) then down at long last to Manassas. Where we'll step onto the set and watch the reenactment of that bloody war's first major battle Bull Run. Where (don't fear; I've studied this; have all the salient facts, here, in my noodle) Confederate General Jackson the former professor—no wonder he made such a good soldier, such a born leader—the former professor of artillery tactics and natural philosophy at the Virginia Military Institute, Lexington, acquired the sobriquet of Stonewall, his troops, his men, having held off and repelled a strong Union assault. He had read about the shoot in a reenactors' newsletter. At first he thought it some full-blown Hollywood production but quickly realized that the film was only a documentary for public television, fact not fiction. But that remained just as well as they didn't make movies today like they had under the old studio system, movies which if they seemed a little saccharine and romanticized (such as *The Santa Fe Trail*, for example, starring Olivia DeHavilland and Errol Flynn) nonetheless left one satisfied, wholesomely entertained, and morally uplifted—yes despite maybe even partially because of their ridiculousness and historical inaccuracy. No, today the films relied on shock value: nudity and vulgarity, gutter realism. We didn't want naturalism back in the thirties and forties. We wanted escapist fare. The movies, aside from jazz, stood as America's greatest contribution to world culture. Every week we went to them. Now whom would I cast to play Stonewall Jackson? Randolph Scott maybe. And his Union opponent? The in-decline Henry Wilcoxon perhaps. Just like the stories he had written up about Billy's ancestors, the Hollywood films for all their unreality their glossing over the war's ugliness, the Auschwitz-like skeletons discovered at Andersonville victims of starvation and how fitting that camp, that Southern stalag, had a German (well all right, Swiss) commandant—Wertz, wasn't it? I'm not sure of the name. I'll have to double-check. They hanged him, precedent for Nuremberg. Of that I am certain. Yet those films (American studio kitsch, pabulum put out by MGM and the brothers Warner) remained well acted, had fine production values and, more importantly, were chock full of American conventions and ideals or should I say Judaic-Christian ethics and standards? We didn't need to delve into the prurient to be entertained like they do today. We accepted the fact maybe we even giggled that all married couples in the current-day stories if not in the historical dramas slept in neat twin beds. If we read the book, we grew even angrier, the censorship was sometimes so contrived and silly. The villain had to get his just deserts in the end. Bette Davis couldn't get away with murder in the film version of *The Letter*, so the Malaysian wife of her victim in turn murdered her, but her murderess couldn't get away with it either: the police nabbed her in the last few frames of the picture! *Kitty Foyle* stood as another good example of studio compromising or should I say fudging? In the Christopher Morley novel, Kitty was a tough, modern secretary of the 1930s, who had her illegitimate baby aborted by a "back alley" doctor, but in the Ginger Rogers movie, she got married to her society boyfriend from Boston, then had her marriage annulled after meeting his snobbish relatives, then found she was pregnant, refused to consider abortion, then had a miscarriage! Four artificial plot elements foisted on the story so the film would get the seal of approval from the Legion of Decency. My God, the Johnson and Hays Office Code volumes had more pages than the Washington Congressional Budget. Yes, the Catholic Church policed Hollywood for us, told us what to see, wouldn't let those materialist Jews running the entertainment show exert any sort of corrupting influence. So the moguls hired smart-assed lawyers–probably Jewish most of them–who contrived thousands of ways that plot elements had to be resolved so everything would come out legal, properly whitewashed, so as not to financially jeopardize a film Messrs. Mayer, Goldwyn, or Cohen had sunk their much-prized monies into. Yes, the Catholic Legion of Decency had power in Hollywood. It forced the studio heads to make all sorts of compromises. Thank God, it didn't have authority over America's publishing houses or Broadway Theater. But the Church did compile a list of forbidden books; it told the faithful what and what not to read. You risked hell fire, the priest said, if you even glanced into or skimmed one of those proscribed volumes. I often wonder whether Hitler would have exterminated the Jews if Charlie Chaplin hadn't made *The Great Dictator*? Disney switched from German stories and themes to English and Danish subjects for its animated features after the Second World War. But *Snow White* remained the greatest film ever made.

Yes we had had a healthier society in those days. We had collective values. So maybe the Church was right to take on the role of policeman. And the movies were better then than they are today even if they often contained silly preposterous compromises. I have to stand for those old ideals, pass them onto Will, my son. I believe in the bedrock American values. Like that other college professor Mr. Jackson, I will hold the high ground against the onslaughts of all our blitzkrieging enemies. I will protect you, Bill. We will repel them. You will. But just like my stories, Hollywood fashion, we'll sugar the pill for mass consumption.

V

Percy thought that he had put the worst behind him in his early thirties, that nothing that life could deal out to him in his middle years and in his old age could compare with the dark days back in '64 when drafted into the Union Army, he served in the Forty-Fifth Pennsylvania. Even now well into his seventies, he could not help but feel that in his thirty-third year, he had broached Hell itself but somehow had made it back. You'll face nothing as terrible or as bad as what you've already been through, he told himself numerous times. Halt in one leg, he finally returned to Pennsy proper after participating in the Grand Review May 23rd, 1865, after marching down its (yes Pennsylvania's) Avenue in Washington City and parading past President Johnson, Lieutenant General Grant, and Secretary Stanton, who stood and waved in the flag-draped reviewing stand. How he had managed that he didn't know. The leg tormented him ever since. He had suffered so much on account of it. He remembered that he drank two whole days at Saurbaugh's Tavern in Alexandria. On the 17th, he reached that town by ordnance. The nonwounded in his regiment marched via Petersburg to City Point and moved by water to Alexandria two days later (he waved to the boys from his cot when they marched into the barracks that night) and kept on drinking in camp but also stood and walked, worked the lameness out of the limb. For he had made a vow. Prior to leaving for Alex, lying in the battlefield infirmary outside of Petersburg, he had burst in tears when he had gotten word of Lincoln's assassination, but right then he determined to strive even harder to gain back all the former elasticity in his leg, and by the time of the Grand Review, one month later, he could (albeit he grit his teeth the entire time) keep in step and march in file. Then in July his company mustered out.

On April 2nd, 1865, he had been wounded (grape shot or canister he didn't know which) several inches below his left hip. The doctor said that it was only a flesh wound albeit a serious one, but it tormented and caused him pain ever since and moreover the leg never worked right afterward, still did not work all these years later. Even now in 1907 he walked with a limping gait, and today, as he sat on the gallery in front of his son-in-law's Enoch McEwen's house, he felt the old ache and familiar pang radiate out from the old lesion—that long pink scar—he could see it even with his eyes closed whenever he repositioned himself on the settee, moving his leg only the slightest little bit. Every several seconds or so he experienced another twitch, prick or goad.

Nonetheless he considered himself lucky, lucky to have survived and prospered, fortunate to have escaped with his life from Hell. Fort Hell they called it even though its real name was Fort Sedgwick. Thankful that he had not been called to serve in Company A of the PA 45th earlier than October of 1864. That month, the one in which he reported, the regiment numbered only ninety-two men before being filled with sub-stitutes, recruits, and drafted men—one of them McCalmont himself. The 45th had seen action since the beginning, since '61, having fought at South Mountain and Antietam and participated in the Vicksburg campaign, the siege of Knoxville and the Battle of the Wilderness, and having sustained heavy losses in all those contests. When they'd write his obituary they'd say he was one of the brave boys (his daughter Jane would quote him word for word, not knowing he stretched the truth when he said it) who voluntarily shouldered their guns and went to the front in the defense of their country during the war of the Rebellion. Yes, he had been brave though his heart beat so fast in his breast, nervous and frantic, shuddering and perspiring, he might have very well poo'd up his backside. Though one grew accustomed to it, the fear, every engagement afterwards it was almost as bad, yet he never shirked his duty; he acquitted himself honorably. A brave boy, he was that—yes. And he did go to the front to his country's defense, but he had been a conscript not a volunteer. He hadn't admitted this fact to anyone who hadn't already known the truth. After he mustered out, he returned to the family farm near Shirleys-burg in Huntington Co., where he had passed the days of his boyhood and youth. About a year afterwards, he and his lifelong sweetheart Miss Eliza, daughter of old Fritz Abell, wed. Then with the money from her dowry combined with his savings and a generous loan from his father, Perse purchased one hundred fifty-six acres of land in the vicinity of Sinking Valley, also in Huntington Co. He immediately commenced to clear and im-prove the same even though he walked with a noticeable limp and had to use a cane. He also engaged in lumbering and rafting on the river and other profit-making ventures and had become a leading and prominent farmer in the section. But today he was destitute due to the villainous machinations of his other son-in-law Wilbert Asbury.

He and Mrs. McCalmont had a family of eight children. Two of their daughters Effie and Ida died in infancy, victims of diphtheria, while another daughter Gaynell died of pneumonia at age thirteen after the ice underneath her cracked then gave way as she crossed the pond. Eliza saw from the upstairs window and called to the boys. He could have gone to, had it not been for his lame left leg. Rosewell, their oldest son, charged down the steps, ran like the wind, and plunged into the icy water and out to her. Allen, their youngest, followed him, and they brought her in; miraculously she kept her head above, out of, the water until they got out to her. But the fever came, the doctor couldn't prevent its onslaught; he arrived that afternoon an hour after they brought her inside, but she didn't live out the week, her spirit taking its flight to realms eternal three days later.

His eldest girl the mousy not too pretty Edith wed Wilbert Asbury, a railroad man, the conductor whom the company brought in after Perse, already wealthy or at least well off, discovered an excellent grade of coal underlay his land and the mining engineers Samson and Son offered to pay him a handsome royalty to work his lands. He only allowed them to tunnel under the back fifty acres, preserving the heart of the property around his farm which he kept under a high state of cultivation and which over the years he improved with good and substantial buildings, which (he felt) stood as monuments to his thrift and enterprise. Jane the third child, even less pretty than Edith, married the son of a neighboring farmer, slow Enoch, a modest man content to live off the land. Rosewell never chose to take a bride. He died unmarried at the age of thirty-eight. Percy and Eliza, his old shriveled parents had to put another of their children in the ground, Rosewell expiring of a short but excruciatingly painful bellycrab. The next boy born Herschel left Pennsylvania for the West, Nebraska, where he and his family (he already had two sons and a daughter, his own farm here, and another child on the way—his wife showed early—but still he decided to sell his land, take the risk, he and his family head out westwards) relocated, he saying his goodbyes to everyone including his parents in May of 1892. Allen, the baby, Eliza's lastborn, wed a Tamaqua, Schuylkill Valley girl, Marilla Helfenfuss, the daughter of old Cyrus Helfenfuss, a regular scoundrel some folks said, a drunk and a lecher, but a captain in the war who (so the rumor went) on a veteran's furlough seduced the girl's mother, a Cressona lass whose own Pa had also gone off to the fight only several months before. The townsfolk said that Marilla's mother Miss Doris Kemper accompanied the Captain back to Virginia disguised as a boy from his outfit.

Yes he considered himself lucky to have escaped hell, where he could envision men in blue and gray battling each other for all eternity, a Valhalla where one killed and one's enemies struck one down in turn, but only for one to be immediately resurrected to fight anew. Yet now in his old age he found himself once again in the Devil's Den! He had experienced sorrow after the war, he cried and cried when the two baby girls died, and years and years later, at Rosewell's funeral he saw himself as a second Job. He found it unbearable to bury a son at his age. It should have been the other way around—Rosewell should have been a pallbearer lifting his—Perse's—casket. Yet he pushed through his pain, and eventually enjoyed life's simple pleasures again. Death remained a natural part of life. You grew used to seeing people dying especially if you saw so much of it in your youth. But even if you didn't fight in a war like he did, you encountered death again and again as you aged. Maybe first it would be a pet then one of your parents' friends then maybe a distant relative. On and on, someone was always dying. But a difference existed between the two kinds of death, the two types of expiring. God called his infant girls and the thirteen-year-old Gaynell and his son Rosewell, a grown man approaching middle age, home. Man, on the other hand, killed his own brothers, his sons, and his fathers in the Rebellion. They died at each other's hands. None of his relatives as far as he knew fought for the South, but he had heard all sorts of stories of families divided against themselves. As his family was at this very moment. His stupidity in trusting Wilbert Asbury and his resultant impotence once again infuriated him. How could his son-in-law have been so cruel? Why did not his own daughter Edith do something, right the wrong? Wicked girl! Betraying her father as did Lear's two eldest. I signed the property over to him. Did I even realize what I signed? I had no idea that Wilbert would do this. I handed him power of attorney because I had decided to retire from active business. I'd let him manage the farm and collect the royalties from the mines. How could I have foreseen it? He promptly sold my land, didn't even tell me in person. There was more money to be made in mining, he said afterwards when I finally confronted him. Eliza and I could move in with them, come to town, or stay with the McEwens, if we preferred. He gave us notice that we had to vacate the premises. And Jane, darling Jane, my Cordelia opened her doors for us. I could accept if not forgive my son-in-law's actions but not so my wife. At first she refused to leave her house. Jane, Enoch, and I had to compel her physically. Overwrought she braced herself in my Oddfellows chair, wouldn't get up. Jane felt her mother didn't move and had become frightened because she couldn't understand. They had such trouble communicating with her due to her hearing loss. Quite deaf in her right ear and the left going bad, getting progressively worse and worse, but she could still hear out of it if one got up close to her and shouted. She had just turned seventy-four. Percy himself was now seventy-six. Both he and his wife had lived their three score and ten. They took her in the McEwen wagon into the town of Sinking Creek and then on out of it to Enoch's place, a mile or two beyond the burg. That morning he had slept late and he woke up to find out that she had just left her son-in-law's and daughter's home for the purpose of going to the post office to mail a letter to her sister. They lived just a short distance away from town; Eliza was used to taking a long walk every morning on the farm. They both remained very active, could outwork people younger than themselves. And it had been and remained a fine August morning, the sun resplendent, birds twittering in the trees. Not too hot though a little humid. Jane saw no reason not to let her go, but Percy worried. Yesterday his wife had been in a high state of agitation. Today she seemed calm, Jane said. Almost glad at moving in, for now she would have her daughter for company. Maybe things would turn out right after all if only Wilbert would make proper financial restitution—pay them what he owed. The money he had cheated them. But because she had resisted so defiantly just the day before, Perse thought the change had come too fast. He didn't believe it. He had a foreboding. He just knew despite what his daughter said.

He had settled his weight into the porch settee and waited for his wife to come back. He could have asked Enoch to go fetch her. He could not walk two miles, but he could have ridden with Enoch in the buggy. But maybe that would anger old Eliza more than anything else. You mean you can't trust me to walk to town and post a letter? she would say and shake her head, moving her old eyeballs rapidly to and fro, back and forth from side to side in a most apoplectic manner, her white hair filled with long black ribbons, her head shaking as if she had the palsy. Of course he would have to shout his denials several times before she could make sense of them though she could read certain people's lips, slow talkers. He was not one. But he decided to say nothing to his son-in-law. To just sit and wait on the front porch, and as he stared into his son-in-law's pasture and at the not-too-distant turnpike to Sinking Valley which his wife had taken, and watched the two brindle cows grazing, the hogs wallowing, the pony whinnying and the black shepherd dog dancing, he twiddled his thumbs and chewed his mustache then twisted its end with his thumb and forefinger. Every so often he took his watch out of his vest and looked at it, pocketed it again, and then reached up and pulled down his slouch hat. To shade his eyes from the sun's slant. No, he did not volunteer the fact that he had been a conscript to anyone, let them believe whatever they wanted. During the post-war years he had prospered in business and always went to town attired in a brand new black reefer suit and a tall hat. And when he stepped into the Frenchman's place, the town general store, or went to the Shirleysburg Lodge 121 I.O.O.F. and sat with the boys, if he told any stories about the war they were amusing anecdotes about the vicissitudes of camp life, never a true account of the carnage and death, the fear and confusion of battle, but something witty, something to get a laugh. He even had a favorite tale from his soldier days that the boys would ask to hear again and again. During his year of service, on four different occasions, his regiment marched through, occupied, or billeted alongside of the town of Alexandria, and Perse regaled himself at Saurbaugh's Tavern. A different daughter of old man Saurbaugh was hostess each time. On the first occasion, shortly after he entered the service, the next-to-eldest girl Donna Saurbaugh served his beer, whiskey, and vittles. As he wolfed the food and downed the amber liquid, the staff of life his father always called it, and then the brown firewater, he ogled the petite blonde girlwoman with finely turned wrists, wearing a green dress coat with fancy frills, white neckerchief and a bejeweled breastpin—overheard her speaking to another customer, an elderly man bearded, balding and fat, an old friend he could tell by the way she leaned over and talked to him. He had gained her trust. She said that her sister Phyllis had reached her ninth month and that for the past two days she had taken to her bed. Because of her small hips, the doctor expected a difficult delivery. And for the last twenty-four hours, Phyllis remained convinced that she had gone into labor, but the night before she had eaten applekraut, pork, and mashed taters, and she was experiencing nothing more than an attack of gas. Poor girl. Mother and Lucinda the eldest sister, Clea the youngest, and the adopted Indian girl in the middle Catharine all told her horror stories of breach births, of women who underwent three days' worth of birth pains. Phyllis had been the last of the daughters to marry and this would be her first baby. The man interrupted her. And what about you? he asked. Have you been telling tales to frighten your poor sister out of her wits? Shame on you, Donna. The barmaid smiled and shrugged her shoulders. I guess I stand just as guilty as everyone else, she said. Yes, between us, we've scared the girl silly. But you know Andy, each night I pray that she'll have an easy go of it when her time comes.

On his second trip to the tavern (the regiment returned to town a week later) tall Lucinda with her enormous brown eyes and long lashes, her bow so anxious and diligent to each and everyone of her customers, waited on him the first hour, then the narrow-eyed, high cheek-boned Catharine, inscrutable and mute, replaced her. Having drunk his fill, he rose to his feet and prepared to leave when Lucinda rushed in and said to all the customers that it was a boy. Phyllis had come through her trial—and it was a sore one; she had shrieked for three hours, repeated over and over again that she would welcome death—that it would be preferable to this. But now she cradled the little man in her arms and had a rapt, radiant, spiritual expression spread across her pale, fine-featured face. What travail! But she had come through and held a healthy boy in her arms.

The third and fourth occasions Percy graced Saurbaugh's with his presence did not occur until almost a year later after Lee surrendered the Army of North Virginia, at Appomattox, to the victorious Grant, when the work of death and carnage was at long last finished, and he, ahead of the PA 45th, had arrived by ordinance in Alex. He had gotten permission to leave the barracks, had hobbled into town and had proceeded to guzzle more hooch than Noah did after the flood. For two days straight, he consumed the liquid bread and the firewater. That first afternoon dainty Clea with her narrow forehead and her smooth blonde hair reaching down to her shoulders, tied in the back with a bright bow, brought him the house fare. During the evening he again overheard a conversation, this time between the hostess and a handsome corporal from New York, concerning Miss Phyllis (by now he felt himself a Philistine; he felt he knew the girl, had become an old friend, although he never had the pleasure yet of actually meeting her). Apparently she had given birth, only two weeks earlier, to another child: this time a baby daughter: and she had another hard time of it. Clearly Clea was jealous of all the attention the family showered on her older sister. Of all Saurbaugh's daughters Perse had yet seen, Clea was the most beautiful. The youngest child, she would have been daddy's favorite. However she didn't have abnormally thin hips like her sister. She had just given birth to her fourth toddler two months before. But because at the time Phyllis was also again with child, it seemed to Clea that her parents, her siblings, even her own husband Hubert hardly noticed her in her equally bloated and overweight condition. The birth of her boy didn't bring everybody to her bedside. The whole family, on the other hand, pampered her sister. Phyllis, she claimed, had put on a show, stretched everyone's shirt-sleeves. She liked being queen to a bunch of fawning servitors. Percy stopped in again the next day hung over—crapulent, as the sergeant would say—and lo and behold Phyllis herself acted as hostess. Old Andy, Donna's friend, gently taunted her. Perse's ears pricked when he heard that familiar first name. Were her birthing struggles really that horrible, old Andy asked. Perse took notice, stared up at his hostess in her white blouse and black hoop skirt. Her aspect, tired facial features, rheumy eyes, indicated extreme duress. She looked like she had been through the Wilderness Campaign. That bad. Pudgy yet pale and hollow-eyed with a slender little nose, beautiful white teeth which flashed whenever she opened her mouth, a tired smile, her lips chapped, raw, and bluish, she nonetheless pertly replied, retorted, that neither of her two pregnancies had been difficult, that her sisters had been telling him stories, fibs, her son and daughter had just popped out effortlessly. Blind drunk as he was, Perse could not help cherishing and adoring this woman as she rebuffed poor Andy though he knew in all likelihood after tonight he would never see her again and anyway she wouldn't recognize him—her knight; her servitor; her Philistine—from Adam. But he loved her because she had suffered so much to bring new beings, new souls, into this our God-given garden. Taking life had meant so little such a short time ago. Perse himself had been guilty of slaying his fellow men. A sharpshooter he took pride in picking off Rebs and knew that he killed at least four men and wounded up to fifteen others. As he stared into Phyllis' green eyes, he felt remorse—bitter regret. Life beginning this way, with a mother's rarefied spiritual love, should not be lightly cancelled out and nullified. It was just too precious a commodity....

Perse McCalmont blinked then closed his watery eyes. He felt the sun on his face. The pleasant perception of warmth never left his cheeks and forehead even when he started to nod, but then he fell asleep, started to dream, and as the hours passed he kept right on dreaming: going far, far afield (though he snoozed in the same chair, spot), carried off by sweet siren sensations—terrible yearnings!—from his subconscious, back to those days of his turbulent youth when he had been present at one of the great moments in history, at one of those significant hinges, turning points, every subsequent event for the next fifty years would not only be able to claim as its direct cause, as its basis and *raison d'etre*, but would also probably be accurate in so doing! Something so momentous, so grand that the mind of an average man could not fully comprehend it, even if he had stood in the midst of it and took part, effecting in his small way the general course of human history. His participation, to however slight an extent, had to have counted somewhat—adding its insignificance to that of all the other men dressed in blue regimentals, who added theirs, to build up a force with the requisite strength, might, to turn the tide, to win, to defeat the tired-out, all-but- vanquished Army of North Virginia.

It had been a prolonged siege. On December 10th, the 45th regiment transferred with its division to the defense of the Fifth Corps, which collected intelligence, made an advance reconnaissance, to the Weldon Railroad beyond Nottaway Courthouse. It came back on the 12th and held its place on the right side of the army until the closing attack on the rebel positions in April. Perse's regiment occupied Fort Rice, near that familiarly known as Fort Hell, though its real name was Sedgwick. The 48th Regiment of Pennsylvania Volunteers, Jacob Kemper's unit (McCalmont never met, encountered, him, but both men had been there, so close to one another, in the same general vicinity, the grandfather of his future daughter-in-law Marilla Helfenfuss Jacob Kemper and himself) had been sent to occupy Sedgwick early in December and had defended and laid siege from it (the Confederate works in front were equipped with eight and ten inch mortars; the Rebs shelled the Fort almost daily) until April 2nd , 1865 when they advanced to attack the rebel Fort Mahone. For the last several months, the declining fortunes of the rebellion were evident, unmistakable, to be seen on all sides. Command issued orders to storm the enemy's lines on April 1st, 1865. The 45th Pennsylvania marched to the rear of Fort Hell the following day. The shelling began along the entire line of the corps at four a.m., and at half-past four the troops made their assault. The Confederates welcomed them with a storm of musketry, grape, and canister, but throughout the lethal tempest the men steadily advanced. Nothing could block their progress. The boys ripped down and scattered abatis, scaled walls and parapets, and in the end carried the Confederate works in the face of a withering fire. The 45th kept to the extreme left of the line and captured a six-gun battery. In this sparkling proceeding, Captain Cheesman, commanding the regiment, forfeited his right leg—it was blown half off on the battlefield, then in hospital the dangling dead portion surgically removed, the stump cauterized. Among those prominent for gallantry and nerve, Lieutenant Robb, collapsed fatally wounded, shot straight through the eye during the initial charge, where Percy McCalmont took, received, a flesh wound to the left leg. Brought howling and screaming to hospital, he missed the excitement which followed—did not march into Petersburg City. The final night bombardment of that place prefatory to a general assault the next day had occurred two nights before on March 31st.

Lee thought it rash and unwise to keep his ground, because his troops had drifted out of position and could no longer defend the main Confederate fortifications and Warren's corps had come up to the line and now menaced them. So he ordered the retreat to Five Forks. Sheridan followed Lee at dawn, but Warren's two divisions encountered him midway between Dinwiddie Court House and Five Forks at Seven a.m. April 1st. The action left the Confederate line, from Appomattox to Hatcher's Run, sparsely garrisoned as the calls for troops to strengthen the right flank thinned the Confederate ranks, leaving only one man positioned at every five yards of breastwork. As the medics carried more wounded men into Perse's battlefield infirmary, he heard all sorts of strange rumors, purportedly the most recent news from the front: what had happened thirty-two or forty-eight hours beforehand at this point on the line and at that further on down.

It was not a strategic requirement to contest and skirmish at Five Forks to achieve the capture of Petersburg; Grant and Sheridan desired the apprehension or destruction of Lee's army in order to preclude its breaking out to join Johnston, more than they did to liberate the city. As the battle of Five Forks came to an end on the 31st, the troops before Petersburg opened fire, shelled the city in a savage night blitz. From the Federal lines, the barrage of bursting shells lighted the sky over the soon-to-be vanquished town. The shelling kept up from nightfall on April 1st to four a.m. on the morning of the 2nd, when Parke, Wright, and Ord charged the Confederate lines from the Appomattox to Hatcher's Run. And Percy played his part, stormed the Confederate fortifications and, shot in the leg, got carried off the field and brought to hospital, so he didn't know what happened next but wished to have quick intelligence. And gradually it came in. After abandoning their successive defenses, the Confederates retreated within the inner lines of works around Petersburg. Rebel General A. P. Hill, in a thwarted lunge against the Ninth corps, fell mortally wounded off his charger's saddle. The Army of Northern Virginia made its last feeble feint in the defense of Richmond. Robert E. Lee, however, preserved his position waiting for darkness to cover his design to forsake Petersburg and Richmond. Lee withdrew the entire Confederate front by the north bank of Appomattox River, and at Chesterfield Courthouse rendezvoused with the troops holding the Bermuda Hundred front. He ordered the entire Confederate Army westward, and, before dawn of Monday April 3rd, they had put sixteen miles between them and Grant's forces at Petersburg. Only when the mists lifted that morning did the Federal troops learn of the evacuation of the city. That same gray morning, Union soldiers beheld the sky above Richmond lighted with a lurid glare from rapid explosions and shell bursts. Throwing forward his cavalry, the Federal Commander General Weitzel entered undisputed into the city and hoisted the United States flag on Jeff Davis' former capital.

Yes, shortly after dawn on the morning of the 3rd, the advance skirmish line learned that the adversary had deserted his former positions round Petersburg, so the corps entered the outpost of treason—and at five a.m., subordinates informed the commanding general that it had surrendered. Following the withdrawing foe, Percy's regiment (he learned this from a friend carried in on the 11th) participated in all the movements of the brigade from Petersburg to Farmville. It encamped on the evening of the 3rd at Sutherland's station, on the Southside Railroad. The pursuit continued on the following morning when the Ninth Corps was ordered to move to the Coxe Road, and guard the rear of the pursuing army. By April 4th, Lee's forces had attained Amelia Courthouse, thirty-eight miles to the west of Richmond, and to their great chagrin discovered that the commissary stores, by the confusing of an order from President Davis, had been shipped to Richmond and doubtlessly had been obliterated in the firestorm. This compelled Lee to scavenge for stores and supplies and retarded his withdrawal giving Sheridan time to bring up a cavalry force of eighteen thousand men, against which the Confederate commander could not hope to make a successful stand. On the night of the 5th, Lee withdrew from Amelia Court House, Grant's entire army in full pursuit. The Confederate scroungers were apprehended. Sheridan and Custer pressed the attack continuously, kept up a running engagement on the 5th and 6th; and although Lee's army continued to resist, conceding ground only by the inch, the likelihood of escape steadily diminished then disappeared altogether, and on April 7th Grant opened communications with Lee, who while Grant waited on a reply continued to retreat, and gained a night's march. On the 8th Grant pursued the chase. Sheridan reached Appomattox station, cut off Lee's supplies as well as his way out, and on the 9th Lee asked for a suspension of further conflict and for an interview with General Grant to discuss terms of surrender.

Perse's regiment remained on the Coxe Road until Lee's capitulation. On the 17th, Perse left the hospital, transported with a wagonload of other wounded, their destination Alexandria. On the 19th, his regiment marched via Petersburg to City Point, and from thence moved by water also to Alexandria, where Perse already awaited them.

Even though he slept heavily from early morning into the early afternoon, a part of him realized that he didn't stand outside Petersburg, that he only heard his own voice reciting all the facts he knew about the great armistice, what he saw, felt and experienced. But then he drifted off and found himself in the thick of it again. Toppled and burning dwellings, scattered bricks, pocked walls, splintered doors, cannon smoke obscuring everything. Great clouds—billows—of smoke and gun thunder everywhere. In his nostrils the sickening smell of sizzling human flesh. Shrieking shells above him hissed their high demonic whistles. Corpses everywhere illuminated by the lethal fireworks of this All Fools' Day in aich, eee, double toothpick. Friends fell to his right and left but the men blessed by the gods, unhit by ball or shell, charged on, a human battering ram, into the Confederate fortifications until they gave, then he himself was winged, taking iron shrapnel in his leg and he didn't know what would happen and now he began to awake, heard voices round him, someone saying, "Wake up Perse wake up." He hadn't dreamt about the Civil War for a long time. All that happened years and years ago. But what did he wake up to? Disoriented and groggy, he opened his eyes and saw that a group of concerned townspeople, men, women and children, surrounded him, and then, looking round, not sure of his current location, he realized that he was not at home at the farm. As his memory rushed back to him, he sat, straightened up, in the chair then looked down, saw his slouch hat at his feet. He became quite frightened when Catlett, the Sinking Valley Post Master spoke his name in a hushed solicitous tone. "Your wife has met with a terrible accident," he said. Perse reclosed then opened his eyes, saw where the sun rested in the sky, thereby quickly determining the time. Shutting his lids with ferocity, he willed himself back into his dreams, back into Hell because he preferred Hell to this. "The train ran over her, Perse," Catlett said. "She had just come into the office to post a letter. But she didn't give it to me, for at the window she discovered that she was a penny short for the stamp. Overwrought she seemed and nervous. Through the back window, I watched as she commenced to walk on the track. Being quite deaf of course, she did not hear the train backing out of Sinking Valley mine, No. 15, and not being observed by either the engineer or fireman on account of the tender being ahead of them, she stepped in front of the locomotive and was instantly killed, her body terribly mangled. I don't know what happened to the letter."

No, it couldn't be true, Percy thought. Like Orpheus, he would enter Hades and attempt to bring out his bride, his darling Eurydice. No she couldn't be gone. God wouldn't let him outlive her! Why didn't he listen to the warning of his inner voice which prompted him to follow her and bring her back? No it couldn't be true. He dreamt right now. Did he even recognize one of all these faces surrounding him? Where was slow Enoch? Where was Jane? He rose to his feet, hobbled through the six or seven men and women gathered on the gallery, down the porch steps and out a short way into the meadow. Asbury bore all the guilt. Asbury was to blame. He had to be the conductor. Catlett grasped the railing with both of his hands. She had delivered him the letter addressed to Wilbert Asbury, esquire. Immediately he became suspicious when she said in the trumpet-like blast common to the deaf who weren't dumb but could communicate with their vocal cords no matter what happened he (Catlett) should deliver her letter. He promised that he would, but then he saw her looking up at him in the window (the train tracks and mine stood directly behind the Post Office, almost at the direct center of the village). The train whistle blew and the cars began backing out of the mine. She still looked at him, then abruptly turning her head, she stepped directly in front of the car, the hem of her coat caught, pulled under, the giant wheels and she with it. She didn't scream, or, behind the glass, right then also deaf, he could not hear her. He ran down the steps and outside. A crowd gathered at the scene of the accident. The train had halted, the conductor and fireman appearing on the scene, then the constable and coroner. Catlett turned back to his office. He would shut it down, get in the buggy and ride out to the McEwen farm and inform Jane and Enoch of the terrible event. But when he got back he immediately noticed the cream-colored envelope and couldn't resist tearing it open. He took out the single sheet, uncreased it, then read the following: "Your recent actions already did me in. You didn't care. But now that you've *in fact* killed me you might possibly change your mind—your attitude. Know now the full extent of your crime!" What good would it possibly serve to deliver this letter, Catlett thought, and fumbled in his coat pocket for a match, found one, struck it on his thumbnail, and put the letter and the cream-colored envelope he had taken it from into the flame and dropped them into the ashcan to burn. The obituary read: "Eliza, seventy-four-year-old wife of Percy McCalmont and descended from one of the first settlers of the Valley met her death yesterday afternoon by being crushed under a coal train, of which her son-in-law Wilbert Asbury was conductor. As she was stone deaf, she didn't know for sure which track to step onto at the switch, and mistakenly stepped onto the wrong one and into the path of the oncoming locomotive."

VI

The death of his father had a profound effect on Billy Steiglitz. It drove home with a vengeance Da's point that the whole world stood at the ready to strike out at one. Billy didn't want to accept his father's credo but after the accident in Manassas he felt that he had to embrace it. However he grew too afraid much too afraid to continue fighting the good fight. He caved into himself. Frightened to go outdoors, he stayed inside his house for the next eighteen years.

When he first shut himself in in 1973, the television anchors began their nightly newscasts with stories about the Watergate break in and the withdrawal of US troops from South Vietnam. The next several years sped fast for Billy and every night it seemed something significant and breathtaking occurred in the world; the pictures appeared in rapid succession on his television screen. One by one they flashed by: Nixon resigned and with both hands signaled V for victory as he mounted the steps of the Marine helicopter, Ford selected Rockefeller as his Vice President, North Vietnam invaded the South, encircled Hanoi, and the massive exodus from the capital began, the pull out of US embassy personnel, the airlifting of desperate South Vietnamese, and the purposeful splashing of our own helicopters. Billy often thought about leaving the bunker, would say to himself that maybe today he would step outside for a brief walk. But weeks, months, went by and he still made excuses for not going through those French and foyer doors and into the front yard. In the 1860s, he mused, the United States waged war to keep a country from breaking in two, but in the 1960s it fought to keep two halves of another nation Vietnam from joining together. Still more time passed. The country celebrated its two hundredth birthday, Jimmy Carter defeated Ford and became the new President, and Bill's grandfather Benjamin Corl passed away and still Bill didn't go outside. Carter initialed the Panama Canal treaty and the Camp David accords. Egypt made peace with Israel and the United States returned sovereignty of the Canal Zone to the Panamanian people. The Shah fell from power, Iranian students stormed the American Embassy and seized hostages whom they held captive for hundreds and hundreds of days but not nearly so long as Bill remained inside, cut off from the world without. No, he could not bring himself to step outside his house.

After the first four or five months back in '73 most of his friends had gotten the point. Billy brought it home to them one by one that he had dropped all his old friendships, that he didn't want to have anything to do with any of his former acquaintances. He had the phones disconnected first. He didn't answer the door and had his food delivered, pretending that he worked at his residence, that he served as the personal nurse of an elderly bedfast man. But that first year he had to endure the presence of the workers who remodeled and soundproofed the den in the basement—his soon-to-be occupied lair, his place of future habitation—having to put up with the hirelings for two months, the time it took for them to refit the den to his exact specifications but when they finished he realized immediately that all the aggravation and annoyance had been a small price to pay, the remodeled basement worth both the wait and the trouble. He paid the workmen. They quit the premises for good and he could begin moving downstairs. He had his stereo and books brought down to the dungeon. The UPS man always stepped in the foyer, rang the doorbell and left the box or package at his inner doors, formerly the front door before he had the foyer built onto the house. Only after he thought enough time had passed and that the delivery man had definitely departed would he open the door and retrieve the package. That was, if he was upstairs for some reason and *heard* the doorbell, for usually he remained in the bunker most days and only at 4:00 am would he venture surfacewards—mole man that he had become—and fetch yesterday's mail. For he had everything he needed downstairs. He had the porcelain crapper installed the same time as he had his father's den soundproofed. He bought and brought down the kit out of which he put together his new brass bedstead for his new room in the house's basement and as one by one the next eighteen years passed he added extra amenities. The CD player replaced the stereo and he could wallow in even more glorious sound. For he loved his music loud and he could play it at all hours of the night without worrying about whether his neighbors would complain. He read his newspapers, watched his TV, had all the settlement checks direct deposited. He could live and live well. From the court decision he had funds so large he could comfortably make it off the interest alone. He had the UPS man deliver his computer and all his video game tapes, including the one he sent to Austria for *Camp Commandant* where the player earned bonus points ingots molted out of gold fillings for every five thousand Jews he eliminated. Yes, most of his friends had gotten the point. In fact all his friends had except for Rutger who persisted in sending him letters imploring him to come out into the light of day once more and who after failing to elicit him through the post adopted sterner measures to try to root him out, but failed like everyone else. Visiting his parents in Slippery Rock he walked to the Steiglitz home, knocked on the door. Bill didn't answer and then later attempting to ring him Rutger discovered the old number to be no longer in service, that Bill had changed it and requested an unlisted line. They had been best friends, Rutger and Bill, since Kindergarten, Rutger's Da like Bill's a teacher at Slippery Rock. Both competed in the public schools but Billy received slightly higher marks. Always in each other's company folks took them for brothers indeed Bill felt much closer to Rutger than he ever had to Miles. They challenged and encouraged each other recognizing all the time their superior intelligence and the incredible stupidity of everyone else, even corresponding after they left home for different colleges. Rutger later served as pall bearer at Franz Steiglitz's funeral along with Roger Corl and three university colleagues of the deceased. After making his own discoveries and hearing about his friend's strange behavior from others, Rutger even went so far as to smash Billy's living room window, then unlock and open it and break in.

He searched the house eventually making his way to the basement where confronting Bill face to face he told him how worried about him everyone was and that he would have to snap out of it and he finally slapped his friend twice across the face. Get out you fucking faggot. No, Rutger said. Not unless you come with me. Then I'm calling the cops. Bill proceeded to dial the number. I'll make you get a restraining order. I'll force you to come out even if it's only to go to court to put me in jail. The police came. Bill let them in and Rutger left voluntarily but said he'd be back. The officer in charge told him to be quiet, clutched him by the elbow and urged him to the door. I don't care if he is mentally ill or not it is still his property and you're trespassing. But true to his word Rutger showed up once again. He staked the place out waited outside until he saw someone open the foyer door, step inside the enclosed vestibule and drop something off. He followed suit, went in the door after he observed the man go out, and sat in front of the inner doors, the old front doors. In other words the French doors Billy would still open to step into the foyer, the farthest from the basement he would come. He didn't dream of passing through the screen door of the foyer to the outside. Rutger waited for him to appear then caught him by the wrist when hours later he finally opened the door. If you're bound and determined to retreat from the world I guess I can't stop you but it deeply saddens me. If you ever need me for any reason don't hesitate to get in touch. I'm you're true friend. I want you to remember that. All right I'm leaving I'm leaving I'm gone I'm history but make sure your fortifications remain up to snuff for at any time I might blitz your lines, declare total war and force you out of your godamned hiding place! You hear me, boy! After the second encounter Rutger never encroached on Billy's space again but his words of caution—his threat—rang over and over again in William Steiglitz's head. Heed me boy I might pounce on you unexpectedly at anytime. Bill took the words to heart and even dreamt once that Rutger carried his threat through and Bill applauded him for it, for in the nightmare Rutger tossed a cocktail Molotov through the bedroom window, set the house on fire, thinking that he'd smoke Bill out. But he had mistaken his adversary. Young Steiglitz had made up his mind to stay though it would surely mean his death but oh what a glorious apotheosis. He smelt the dream smoke, inhaling it with relish deep into his lungs. Why didn't Rutger do it? He wanted—he deserved, Bill did—a most spectacular immolation. He knew what it meant to be burned, had hideous scars on his back and on his right arm from the helicopter crash. But he didn't care. He'd pour gas on himself anyway if someone else would only strike the match.

Not long after he made his resolution to stay inside, Bill became a full-fledged vidiot—sat in front of the box the boob tube for twelve or fourteen hours a day watching whatever happened to play. He found one station as good as another and then the American people elected that old hambone Ronald Reagan President. Da would have enjoyed, commented wryly on, the ascendancy of a B movie star to the nation's highest office and the next thing you knew war erupted in the Falklands. Argentina wanted the Malvinas back but England said no Argentina tried to invoke the Rio treaty but the US had of course to support its dearest and most trusted ally but England's old enemy France America's first ally during the war for independence from the motherland had already sold exocets to the Argentines, some of which they would use against the Brit ships. From the news reports he took in over the years, he came to the conclusion that the country of his nativity supported right wing dictators wherever communists stood the chance of coming into power. So the Reagan policies in El Salvador and Nicaragua came as no surprise to Billy Steiglitz. He only had to recall the Nixon-sponsored coup in Chile. Next came Beirut, Grenada, the bombing of Libya. The Russians of course had also occupied Afghanistan. Wars raged in many locations on the globe. He abhorred these military conflicts but what he saw on the tube riveted his attention; he couldn't look away. He didn't mind not having a woman for he had magazines, video tapes from the late sixties and early seventies like *Deep Throat* and *The Devil in Miss Jones,* and he even went so far as to mail order a solid life-size love doll with vac-u-suc vagina but after four or six years in seclusion he began to tire of having sex with himself and stopped looking at the tapes the magazines took Sue up into the attic where his brother Miles had com-mitted suicide pulled off his belt tied it around the neck of the love doll and suspended her from Mile's crossbeam and for all he knew she hung there still but he had merely traded one vice for another he started consuming great quantities of food like a neutered cat yet he had been right to wean himself first from having sex with others and second from having it with himself occasionally he would dream have a nocturnal emission but this happened very seldom only irregularly almost never at all. According to Da a woman a lover could turn into the most dangerous enemy one would ever have to face because she appeared to one not enlightened, to one deluded, still in nescience, lost in the vaginal folds of Maya, as the most loving creature in the universe, one half of a split self, a mir-ror in which to view one's inner face for the first time, an affecting and bewitching soul mate. Needless to say she could inflict the deepest of wounds, soul wounds as it were. Also he saw photos of the sex organs of men and women with venereal diseases most of which could be cured but not herpes and he began to equate sex with illness. The Eliza-bethans were right. For them the phrase to die meant to have an orgasm. Actual inter-course should be abolished from the face of the earth. Humanity should perpetuate it-self with test tube babies, fetuses grown in incubators. His abstention adumbrated that of many others for suddenly a new STD—Aids—appeared. A case of the clap could once again be deadly, in fact Aids was almost always fatal. On one of the television shows, Bill watched people walk in front of a hospital and he felt lucky he didn't have to be in the same vicinity the same place they stood that he remained inside safe secure and hidden in his basement bunker. They might step on a needle and catch the dread disease. Yes he merely traded switched one vice for another—gluttony. Bill became outrageously fat. In 1973 when he locked himself in, he weighed one hundred sixty-nine pounds. In 1991 he pushed three hundred. To be exact, he weighed two hundred eighty-five. In the eight-ies he mail ordered exercise bikes, weight sets, belly busters, indoor rowers and other exercise kits a Nordic Track but the pounds wouldn't come off no matter how he ex-hausted himself at the machines. Like other rich men he profited during the Reagan years yet he secretly thought the President a dolt hoped that a shadow government ex-isted with Reagan the star of *The Santa Fe Trail* a mere figurehead then the Iran Contra story broke on TV and he felt that the fiasco would bring down the oh-so-avuncular and commander-like Ronnie as the Watergate scandal had brought down King Richard in '74. Actually he had liked Nixon more than he did Reagan, considered him, introverted and paranoid as he was, a perfect foil for the Russians and the Chinese, a brilliant Realpolitiker. His own father had lauded Nixon's abilities profusely. William considered Ronnie Raygun a lightweight media creation all surface polish not a true pol like Tricky Dick so Bush a Nixon protégé an insider with an intellect but lacking his predecessor's personal appeal had his attractions for Billy Steiglitz. The new President reminded Bill somehow of Da. An expert in many fields with a great foreign policy background, plenty of experience there, and skilled in all intelligence matters from his days at the CIA Bush would be a take-charge a hands-on president. Bill felt sure that he wouldn't delegate authority like Ronnie. Yes Bush would certainly make a much more informed and discerning commander-in-chief than the Hollywood actor. But his human all too human personal flaws would also be continuously on display. He did not speak with Reagan's eloquence. He had no flair or style in his delivery. In fact he often mangled the language, talked like a yokel or a country bumpkin. Yet Bill had high hopes for the new administration and at first those hopes seemed justified. Bill witnessed the fall of Communism on his TV. As much as he was loath to do so, he felt that in fairness' sake he had to credit Reagan somewhat for the earthshaking events taking place in the Eastern Block. The Russians couldn't keep up with the Jones. They couldn't afford Star Wars. A pragmatist Gorbachev realized the importance of reform but who could have foreseen that circumstances would force him to grant political freedom to all the former Soviet satellites in Eastern Europe—that the Berlin Wall would come down? Bush had every reason to bask in the glory of unfolding events for the iron curtain fell during his watch. The President resembled Billy's Da, the smartest man Bill had ever known, in that he too was a man with a wealth of knowledge and experience, someone who deserved the highest esteem and adulation. But in stark contrast to Bush's flatfootedness as an orator, how well Billy's father could write! Bill recalled the family history Franz Steiglitz had set down in such vivid language. According to Bill, Da wrote so well because he had been bred to it, his parents, his entire family, having a history of appreciating great literature which reached back to the poetical matriarch Magda Matzelot, the original and archetypical literary lady herself. Da considered written composition a greater art than music which like Bill he adored. However he deemed all German music after Beethoven and Schubert corrupt and even these last two he found suspect though he would have ultimately voted for their acquittal at the bar of justice. He claimed that the only German composers completely guilt free lived between the times of Bach and Mozart. He also admitted the greatness of Goethe and especially the freedom-loving Schiller but had hated all the philosophers after Kant especially Schopenhauer and Nietzsche preferring the ancient Greeks to the Teutonic moderns. Bill's Da even encouraged his son to listen to jazz and ragtime as well as to French, Italian, Russian and English music. His library full of books by scribblers from all around the world, the works of Latin American, Egyptian, Russian and Eastern European writers, Billy's Da read on a daily basis for hours and hours at a time. His volumes sat on the same shelves even now. Bill had kept them all. He knew that his father had a strong preference for all things British and that like his father before him had styled himself as an Anglophile. Perhaps he even experienced a slight feeling of inferiority when in the company of someone of pure British stock. Of all the world's authors, he loved the English writers best and here Bill had to agree with him. Great Britain had produced the greatest body of literature on the planet. However, his father had also professed English madrigals and Elizabethan virginals superior to German *Lieder*. He preferred to listen to the works of Purcell, Shield, Stanford and Corder to those of any German composer. Despite this aberration in his father's taste, Bill would still have to acknowledge him an authority on music. But Da also understood the workings of the stock market, interested himself in American and World politics, and studied philosophy and world religions. An expert on Hollywood films from the 20s through the 60s, this polymath had also devoted much time to American History and had researched all the battles of the Civil War. He spoke four languages but insisted that Bill develop speaking and writing skills in only one: English. Like Bush, Da was also an athletic man. Bush ran and Dad swam. Yes, Bill had high expectations for the Bush administration but then the Commander-in-Chief ordered the invasion of Panama to capture drug kingpin Manuel Noreiga. *Welcome to the Jungle* became the official tune of the American invasion force. Of course Manuel asked for it the way he taunted Bush and waved that saber over his head like a crazed lunatic but Bush gave the go-ahead for the invasion not from noble motives but for reasons of political expedience. In order to silence his critics on the far right. So they couldn't call him a wimp any longer. Out of the charity of his heart, Bill forgave him. Yes, Americans had short attention spans. They forgot yesterday's news as soon as something else hit the airwaves. What supplanted Panama? The democratic uprising and attendant bloodshed in Romania. What he saw on the tube sickened Bill. The two thousand civilian deaths in Panama seemed almost insignificant compared to the wholesale slaughter taking place in the Eastern European nation. All the poor orphan children with acquired immune deficiency syndrome in the adoption houses and orphanages where pregnant women sold their older children for $10,000 each. Then he saw the opulence of the presidential palace. Several weeks later when he turned his head in disgust at the sight of the bodies of President Ceasu□escu and his wife riddled with bullets he could not help but think of those earlier images of his palace, where that hypocrite commie had lived like a European monarch. And next came more good news. In Nicaragua the people voted the Sandinistas out of office and surprisingly they relinquished power. Again one had to give credit to Presidents Bush and Reagan. And Bill bestowed such credit willingly. But his esteem for Bush once again would plummet, for he couldn't abide "the first television war," the U.S. war with Iraq. Horrified at all he saw, he felt scud missiles would come straight through his television set to strike him. He couldn't stomach the scenes of carnage beamed to him by satellite. He had endured the Falklands, Grenada, the bombing of Libya, and the invasion of Panama but with the Gulf War he reached his saturation point. He felt manipulated by the media and believed the reporting one-sided. It seemed that the American television news coverage of the war consisted of nothing but jingoistic propaganda. Did the Iraqis really pull babies out of incubators in Kuwait and throw them on the hospital floor to die or did a United States public relations firm invent the story to sell the war to the American people? Sure Saddam Hussein was a tyrant who deserved beheading but he had been our tyrant our stooge our bulwark against Iran and Islamic fundamentalism. We had armed him to the teeth, so now we had to defang him. This the only justification for the war that Bill could accept. The dissipated sheiks in Kuwait weren't worth fighting for. Our troops didn't risk their lives for liberty or freedom but for jobs and yes Bill had to give George credit for his great diplomatic skill and inventiveness how he masterfully put together the coalition then sought and received the UN sanction before the military assault began but the hypocrisy of the allies sickened him. Didn't Kuwait and Iraq once belong to a greater Islamic nation? Didn't French and English diplomats dismember that nation then draw the new borders? The nations condemning Hussein had all seized territory themselves, Russia the three Baltic States did they have any intention of leaving of giving them back—no—nor would America return the Southwest which rightfully belonged to Mexico. In fact European settlers had dispossessed the Indians of virtually the entire continent. England wouldn't relinquish Northern Ireland. How could one justify dividing an island? There should be only one border, the natural boundary of the sea. Yet every day he once again turned on his television and watched the planes taking off from the aircraft carriers, the smart bombs dropping from the bomb bay doors of those black triangles which conventional radar could not detect the STEALTHS, and the cruise and Tomahawk missiles launched from the decks of the Navy ships. As he watched the special reports on CNN, Bill realized that military censorship would prevail over the press corps. Standing at his podium attired in a gray pinstriped suit and red-white-and-blue tie, a yellow ribbon in his lapel, the Pentagon spokesman Pete Williams appeared a dead ringer for Chalkman. His hair blow-dried like David Stockman's, he wore designer eyewear. Maybe it is he, Bill thinks. Maybe Pup didn't die back in '73. But no he's far too young. Could Chalkman possibly have a son? The big beefy general whose last name in German meant blackhead reminded Billy of Hermann Göring or Ariel Sharon or even the PBS director who recreated the first battle of Bull Run back in '73, whom Billy watched testify at the civil trial for the wrongful deaths of his father Franz Steiglitz and eighteen other men and women. The news coverage remained irresistible. He sat glued to the set all day....

VII

He had lived. He had come through all that, unscathed. More importantly he had put his mining experience to the use for the benefit of his nation and yes he had survived, had come back home—only to die when the roof of a Pennsy coal mine collapsed on top of him not even a year later. How horribly unfair! Once again Lionel Kemper sighed at his father's destiny and shook his head, whipping his sun-gilt locks. What mocking good luck, bad fortune, he thought and smiled ruefully. Over the years, he repeatedly bowed his head in merry befuddlement over his father Jacob's fate. To have gone through all that, he mused. Only to die in a totally unnecessary mine accident—it should never have happened—once he returned to his home in Pennsylvania. Lionel could recall that day in February 1864, when the men on veterans' furlough from the 48th came home to Pottsville and his father first learned of the suicide of Lionel's elder brother Edmund. Jacob's three oldest sons Herman Joshua, Felix, and the above Edmund had enlisted together in the 48th Regiment, PA volunteers in July 1861. The outfit mustered by directive of Governor Curtin, in answer to President Lincoln's summons for nine hundred thousand men to serve for three years, issued in July 1861. Colonel James Nagle, of Pottsville, Schuylkill County, to whom Curtain relayed the order, resolved to amass a regiment solely of Schuylkill County men. He recruited Companies B, C, D, G, & H in Pottsville, Company A in Port Clinton and Tamaqua, Company E in Silver Creek and New Philadelphia, Company F in Minersville, Company I in Middleport and Schuylkill Valley, Company K in Cressona and Schuylkill Haven. Governor Curtin presented two stands of colors to the men on September 20th. The recruits armed themselves with Harper's Ferry muskets.

Edmund put a bullet in his head during the train ride home after he reenlisted, after he bowed to peer pressure like all the others. He and all the men who bravely reupped had left for home from Kentucky on the train, but Edmund knew that the serenity he then experienced could not last for long, for they would have to go back to the front all too soon. After the deaths of his two elder brothers, he had grown morose. When he first made his mark, crossed his x, to join up back in '61, he had just turned fifteen, the same age as the eldest drummer boy. He served as a private in the infantry and fought bravely for not quite two-and-a-half years, but he just couldn't continue fighting. He knew that death would find him on his return to the battlefield, that when he made his mark on the reenlistment papers he had actually signed his death warrant, that the reaper had touched his brow, had cut an x in his forehead with his scythe. So why delay and put it off? He determined to face the reaper right there and right then and be done with it. His comrades said that he had grown weak, that he had become physically and mentally exhausted, plumb wore out. If only he could have gone home not for a short respite but for a longer period in order to rest and recuperate, but command had granted the veterans only eight weeks' leave. So he decided to end it right there on the locomotive and felt happy to at last be out of it. The forge man Jacob learned of his boy's death when the soldiers from the 48th who had received veterans' furloughs when they reenlisted in Kentucky reached home—Pottsville—by rail. Several boys from Cressona came to the forge, informed him of what happened (Lionel would learn of Edmund's cowardly act also but not from the lips of his father but from those of a school chum several days later). When he heard what had happened, Jacob Kemper, on the spot, immediately enlisted in the regiment in his son Edmund's place at the rank of sergeant. Three of his sons had died for their country in the 48th. He could make just as extreme a sacrifice, his life if necessary.

Herman and Felix fell in separate battles. Along with the crowd, Jacob Kemper had always come out to wait in line to see the bulletin on the public board in the center of the wafered square. To read the names of the sons that had fallen—to see if one of his three had reached—had gone through—his final apotheosis.

Lionel remembered when his brothers left home back in '61. The regiment moved by train via the Northern Central Railroad for Washington City, where it received orders to advance immediately to Fort Monroe. At the time, the mails still remained trustworthy, missives from the boys got through. Herman Joshua wrote that having attained Baltimore on the 25th, the men set sail on the steamer Georgia and alighted at Fortress Monroe. On November 11th, the 48th embarked on the steamer S.R. Spaulding for Hatteras Island, North Carolina. On his promotion to the office of supreme commander, General McClellan dispatched divers brigades and regiments on divers futile campaigns and crusades to make beachheads at various locations on the Southern coast. He appointed General Ambrose Everett Burnside to lead the division to which the 48th belonged and ordered the paunchy general to hold and occupy the coast of North Carolina. Eluding the hazards of shipwreck from the tumultuous weather experienced at Cape Hatteras, the 48th went ashore and the men realized an important triumph in the liberation of Roanoke Island. But long periods of inactivity followed that signal victory. Time passed, nothing but the occasional skirmish broke the monotony of the passing days. Felix wrote home to say he was bored to tears. More time elapsed. Lionel didn't recollect what happened in between. The next thing he could remember all those years after reading his brothers' letters was that suddenly it became necessary to evacuate the Peninsula in order to mount a rescue mission to save the army of General Pope. The 48th reached Acquia Creek and then traveled by rail to Fredericksburg. The regiment fought at Antietam where Felix fell and then took part in the offensive on Fredericksburg—Jacob's oldest son Herman gave up the ghost there—on the 12th. The men crossed over pontoon bridges spanning the Rappahannock, and bivouacked in the streets on the right side of the city. On February 11th, 1863, the 9th Corps separated from the Army of the Potomac, and advanced to Newport News where it sojourned until March 26th, when it received orders directing it westward. Embarking on the steamer John A. Warner, the 48th sailed to Baltimore and thence, traveling northward by rail, passed through Harrisburg and Pittsburgh on the way to Cincinnati. Fording the river at Covington, Kentucky, the 48th marched on to Lexington, where command detailed it to provost duty.

On December 7th, 1863, the brigade advanced from Rutledge to Pleasant Valley, where it nestled down for the night. Here a large proportion of the men reenlisted and received veterans' furloughs to date from January 14th, 1864, and within days commenced the march back to Lexington. The men arrived there on the 23rd of December, two days before Christmas. Proceeding by rail they reached Harrisburg February 2nd, and the following day Pottsville.

That day in February, Jacob came home and spoke to his oldest living son, the then thirteen-year-old Lionel. He remembered looking up into his father's old harried face. His dad had a very thin and long nose and a bearded chin but no moustache. Totally bald, he had eyes of a beautiful hazel color. Muscular and thickset, he had a high-pitched eunuch's voice. He reached out with his arm, stretched it to its full length, and put his hand on Lionel's shoulder and told him to take care of his big sister Doris, his mother, the infant toddlers, and his baby brothers but most of all himself, for he must grow up, marry, and have children of his own to carry on the Kemper name. He instructed Lionel to remember all this in case he didn't come back from the war.

Jacob Kemper first opened his eyes to the light of day in 1820, his wife Martha Salford two years later in 1822. Martha had just turned eighteen at the time of their marriage. The couple had ten children, eight sons and two daughters. Jacob's grandfather Friedrick Wilhelm who had originally spelled the surname Kaempfer and who hailed from Hesse-Cassel had fought in the American Revolutionary War, a British mercenary and one of those Hessians captured by Washington at Trenton, Christmas night 1776. A funny old genius but a little piggish withal, he lost a stocking full of money and a flask of fine schnapps at Trenton but he had expected to meet something still worse. He believed that "dem Chankees" planned to roast and eat him and his fellow captives, for the British officers had informed them that if they ever fell into the hands of the rebels that the Americans would flay them alive like so many swine. But instead Washington's men invited them to partake of everything they had, and, when the war ended and his captors released him, Kaempfer decided to make his home in America, to settle in the new land.

Lionel's father worked as a mining engineer and foreman and as a blacksmith. He was one of the Pennsylvania miners who, in July 1864, dug the tunnel under the Confederate trenches outside of Petersburg and filled it with explosives. He told Colonel Pleasants that six or seven tunnels should be dug, but the Colonel opted for just one. The explosion terrified the Rebs, but the Northern troops waited an hour before ordering a charge. A *Negger* regiment stormed the Confederate lines, but the men charged down into the crater instead of around it. The Confederate soldiers saw that the *Schwartzes* were trapped and gleefully picked them off from around the lip of the crater. A brilliant stratagem failed in the execution. The men bungled the advance. He told Lionel the entire story upon his return to the hamlet of Cressona. After the war, Kemper ran a sawmill, but times remained hard, and he made little money at lumbering. Several months after his return home, his brother Bennet Boyd Kemper induced him to come to Port Clinton, and he returned to working in the mines. Jacob worked two weeks, then died when the ceiling above him collapsed. Jacob and his brother Boyd worked in the same room when the accident occurred. Jacob noticed that the rock above where Bennet stood slipped and teetered, so he pushed him out of the way and the ceiling collapsed on him instead. Jacob Kemper expired as a result of injuries received by a premature sudden fall of rock and coal. Although both Jacob Kemper and his wife lay buried in Cressona, Jacob had originally been laid to rest in a cemetery in Port Clinton. When Mrs. Kemper died twenty-three years later, the eldest of their five surviving sons Lionel Ludwig Kemper had Jacob's body disinterred and the coffin removed to Cressona. The old casket accidentally opened, and the son viewed his father's body before its reburial in the Lutheran cemetery. When the lid of the coffin popped up, the skin on Jacob's face crumbled and dissolved in front of his son's horrified eyes.

Yes he had made his way through to the other side of a pretty amazing gauntlet. Only to die back home. They had him, Martha, Doris, his brothers and himself, until March 14th. That day the regiment, filled with new recruits, departed from Pottsville and marched on to Camp Curtin, where the new men Jacob Kemper among them secured Federal uniforms, regulation boots and other supplies. The regiment remained in camp until the 18th, then began their excursion to Annapolis by way of Philadelphia. In the City of Brotherly Love, the 48th reunited with the 9th Army Corps, and was allotted its old place in the First Brigade of Burnside's Division. On April 23rd, the Corps marched out of Annapolis and on the 25th passed before the lanky bearded President dressed all in black as if he were in mourning, at the capital.

And then the fun began, and Jacob had been in some of the worst of it. On May 5th, the 9th Corps spanned the Rapidan at Germania Ford and took part in the Battle of The Wilderness. During the days preceding the battle at Spotsylvania Courthouse, the men continued to march and tramp through the countryside. Since crossing the Rapidan, the unit had lost one hundred eighty-seven men killed and wounded. The regiment fought at Cold Harbor June 3rd and there lost seventy-five men killed and wounded. It then resumed its trek, forded the Chickahominy on the morning of the 14th, crossed over the James on the evening of the 15th, and on the 16th challenged the Confederates before their works in front of Petersburg.

The most memorable event in the war for Jacob Kemper—the one repeatedly referred to in his polite conversations afterwards—had to be the mining of the rebel fortifications before Petersburg. But oh what hell and horror he had gone through to arrive there. His regiment did all the digging, excavating, and mining, and his expertise and experience helped the 48th complete its difficult assignment. Used to going deep under the earth, he had worked on and off in the mines all his life.

Other regiments attacked the Confederate lines after the explosion but not the 48th. They just watched the stupid *neggers*, no the (he had to admit) intrepid colored regiment, as it ran down into the crater instead of around it and became canon fodder for the startled Rebs. Yes, the Negroes made easy pickings.

Directly after its appearance at Petersburg on the 16th, the PA 48th attacked the enemy works but the Confederates quickly repulsed the unit. Just before dawn on the 17th, the 48th and the 36th Massachusetts of the 1st Brigade, negotiated their way through a bog in single file and entire hush and quiet. The two regiments attached themselves to an advance position occupied already by men from the 2nd Brigade. Launching a surprising and unanticipated assault, the Blues overran the rebel lines and captured the men behind them. It came as a complete shock for the Johnnies. The enemy fled their forward positions and hunker-down sites in mass confusion. The men seized four artillery pieces and one thousand five hundred rifles, and captured six hundred prisoners, but the 48th paid a high price—sustained seventy-five men killed and wounded. At dawn the regiment advanced and threw up entrenchments which the Rebs shelled but made no serious bid to retake. During the star-filled hours of the night, the rebels retreated as far as the outskirts of Petersburg, which became their fixed position until the city's surrender and abandonment a year later in '65. Early after daybreak on the 18th, the men made an abortive attack on the Rebel works. They succeeded, however, in capturing the Norfolk and Petersburg Railroad, and stretching the Union lines right up to the brink—the very edge—of the enemy's advance positions.

The two lines stood less than two hundred yards apart when headquarters made the decision to undertake the mining of the Confederate fortifications. Across from the ground held by the 2nd division of the 9th Corps, the Rebels had erected a sturdy bulwark just below the summit of Cemetery Hill. To take this redoubt by a forward infantry charge would dictate an awful sacrifice of Union soldiers' lives. Northern and Southern troopers applied their powers toward bracing and reinforcing their posts and stations. In other words, they dug in and fortified their positions. On the 21st, Jacob's friend (Kemper had known Henry since the latter had been a young boy, years before the present conflict) Colonel Pleasants thought up the notion of quarrying a mine below the rebel Fort which loomed up so defiantly in front of them. They would pierce the enemy works by means of a powerful explosion. On the 24th, Pleasants declared his conception, made his scheme known to General Potter, who in turn submitted it to General Burnside. At a resulting conference with the two generals at which Pleasants again put forth his plan, the paunchy, oft-drunken first wearer of sideburns ordered the Pennsylvanian to put the plan into execution

Between June 25th and July 30th, no major offensive took place at Petersburg. In fact, the Confederates did not know that the 48th PA Regiment tunneled under their fortifications until late in July. Colonel Pleasants was an accomplished engineer. Years earlier on several occasions, Kemper had looked after his future commanding officer when the latter was still a boy as a favor to Pleasants' father. Now he served under Henry's command. When digging ended July 26th, the excavation which began beneath the Confederate advance rifle-pits stretched below Taylor's Creek and terminated one hundred seventy yards farther at a point known as Elliott's salient. A horizontal passageway ran to the right and another to the left, each thirty-seven feet in length. The men filled both passages with explosives: with eight magazines, containing about eight thousand pounds of powder, equally distributed. It had taken the Pennsylvania regiment to which Jacob Kemper belonged heart and soul one month to tunnel out and mine the galleries.

On July 26th, General Hancock's Second Corps and two divisions of Battlin' Phil Sheridan's cavalry forded Deep Bottom, with directions to advance speedily to Chapin's Bluff to annihilate Lee's pontoon-bridges there which shortened the route between the army at Richmond and the troops stationed at Petersburg. Sheridan led his men toward Richmond with the object of seizing the sparsely manned lines in front of it. Lee challenged General Foster's control of Deep Bottom. He dispatched a large squadron from Petersburg, which forced Sheridan backwards and halted Hancock in his tracks. General Grant resolved, in Lee's absence, to attack Petersburg. Hancock withdrew quietly from his position on the north side of the James, and again settled down secretly at the very place he had slipped away from on the 18th. His men gathered together at Deep Bottom, whereas Sheridan received orders to advance against the Rebel right and to occupy all the roads leading south and west to Petersburg. The troops kept pontoon-trains handy, and command assigned engineer officers to each corps. Fifty thousand men besides and beyond the cavalry, made themselves available for the attack on the city. On July 28th, Pleasants received orders to explode the mine. Afterward the attack would commence.

The tunneling of the shaft was an amazing technical feat. The 48th achieved something many others dismissed as hopeless and impossible. Colonel Pleasants strained under handicaps and obstacles which would have discouraged a man of less drive and ingenuity. All the ranking officers and corps commanders except those from his division showed a complete lack of faith in the success of the undertaking. The army also blundered by not furnishing Pleasants with the instruments necessary to the success of the operation within a reasonable time period. The men of the 48th—and only its men—lugged and toted the dirt out in cracker boxes slung between wobbly poles, as no wheelbarrows had been available. Headquarters even denied the Colonel the use of a new tool to compute the necessary triangulations. General Burnside had to send to Washington for an old-fashioned theodolite. Both General Meade and Major Duane, chief engineer of the Army of the Potomac, voiced their opinion that Pleasants' plan was unfeasible, derided it as claptrap and nonsense. Such a long length of mine had never been excavated in military operations in the past. The operation would fail for it attempted the impossible.

When the 48th began excavating at midnight June 25th, the requisite tools and lumber had not arrived. The men had to make their own mining picks out of the materials at hand. They procured wooden beams by disassembling a bridge and obtained planks from a sawmill six miles away. They loaded the dirt and carried it out in wooden boxes. The digging proceeded at a fast pace until July 2nd, when the men reached an exceptionally soaked and waterlogged section of ground. The wooden beams snapped and the ceiling and the bottom of the tunnel almost touched after the cave-in. The soldiers had to redig and retimber the passageway. They began hauling out dirt once again. Next they ran into a stratum of marl. It had the consistency of putty. Progress went on at a snail's pace. Pleasants started to dig on an inclined plane to avoid the marl. The tunnel sloped upwards for about one hundred feet. On July 17th, the men finished digging the principal passage. It ran five hundred ten and eight-tenths feet in length.

The Rebs received intelligence, got wind of the mine and began looking for it. The men had managed the excavation with such secrecy that for almost a month they kept the venture concealed from enemy eyes. Command had not briefed the other Northern brigades in the vicinity about the mine. Accounts, however, circulated among the troops about the Union undertaking, but most of the soldiers dismissed them as wild rumors. No one thought that the tunneling operation was actually afoot. A private in the fortifications, by whose station a ventilating shaft aerated, told his fellows who shook their heads and laughed it off that, "Each night a great many men work below me and are up to some mischief or other. I hear 'em digging and talking all night long." To prevent a breach of intelligence by the Union infantry and pickets, to avert any chance confrontation of federal soldiers with the Johnny Rebs, where the mystery and puzzle of the mining operation might be unwisely revealed, Union riflemen fired perpetually in the direction of the Southerners in a never-ending fusillade.

Warned that the Confederates had learned of the excavation, Pleasants stopped operations for several days. The digging recommenced on July 17th in the left lateral passage. At 6 p.m. July 18th, the slow hollowing out of the right gallery resumed even though the miners could plainly hear their nemeses walking over them in the Fort. They dug the tunnel out a little beyond the Confederate lines in a curved concave heading. The left lateral passage extended thirty-seven feet long when excavating ended at the stroke of midnight July 22nd. The men finished the right tunnel by 6 p.m. July 23. The soldiers next dug a culvert to drain the mine, added extra wooden supports to prevent another cave-in and finally set the gunpowder magazines in proper position. The men could light the fuses now at any time, whenever they received the order. Initially, the men aerated the tunnels by allowing the fresh air in along the main passage as far as they had dug out and timbered it, forcing the air contaminated with all the gasses released from the earth in the mine to waft back to the surface through a square pipe made of pine wood. This pipe led toward a perpendicular shaft twenty-two feet high to the outside; the vitiated air escaped upwards through it. The men fashioned a grating at the bottom of the shaft below which they kept a fire continually flaring and flaming, which rarefied the ventilated air and sent it spiraling upwards. Later on, as digging progressed, Pleasants caused the fresh air from outside to flow down the above-mentioned square tube to the extremity of the mine, and the "used" air to escape down the main gallery of the mine and up the shaft encircling the square pipe, placing a partition to prevent its exit by the mine entrance. This was an improvement because the fumes and vapors had a shorter distance to travel before dispersing into the air outside. As the excavation progressed, every soul in the regiment—all four hundred men—helped to haul out the soil, eighteen thousand cubic feet of material in all. During the entire operation, the greatest difficulty Pleasants had to surmount was to obtain the exact distance from the entrance of the mine to the enemy's lines and the direction and contour of their positions. He made five separate triangulations all within one hundred thirty-three yards of the enemy's line of sharpshooters. The men worked like mules for a month hauling out all the muck. Kemper's back ached and his legs buckled under the weight of the loads he carried out and dumped. He wiped his brow constantly on his shirtsleeve. Once the roof started to collapse above him, but he hurled himself backwards to avoid being pinned and trapped in the cave-in.

Headquarters issued the directive to explode the mine on July 27th. The men packed additional powder into the galleries from 4 till 10 p.m. The explosives included three hundred twenty kegs of powder, each barrel holding twenty-five pounds or four tons. The miners placed the kegs in eight magazines linked together by wood shafts half choked with the black powder. These tubes met at the ends of the two lateral passages branching off the main gallery. The man had earlier laid down three lines of fuses for a distance of approximately ninety-eight feet. Not having squibs as long as required, the soldiers had to splice two together to make up the mandatory length of each of the three separate lines. The men finished tamping on July 28th. They packed powder into both galleries for a distance of ten feet and then filled thirty-four feet of entrance passage with additional stores of potassium nitrate, charcoal and sulfur. The stretch between the ammunition dumps they left clear.

Colonel Pleasants received the command to spring the mine at 3:30 a.m. on July 30th. He lit the fuse at a quarter to 4 a.m. and waited until a quarter past before determining that something had gone amiss. A brave Lieutenant from Company B and Jacob Kemper from Company K volunteered to drop down into the mine and discover the reason for the failure—the cause of the lag and holdup. They found that the fire had extinguished itself. The fuses had guttered out where they had been spliced together. Sergeant Kemper relit the extinguished squibs, ran down the tunnel as fast as his legs could take him, reached the entrance, and pitched forward, his arms tracing wide parabolas in the air as he fell. He came down flat on his face outside the mine. Sixteen minutes before 5 a.m., the charge exploded. After the smoke cleared, a tremendous rift appeared. The size of the actual crater was two hundred feet long, fifty feet wide, and twenty-five feet deep, but the breach extended on both sides. Pleasants and Kemper positioned themselves on the Union breastworks to observe the blast. It took their breath away. The entire breach spread almost four hundred yards. The sleeping rebels in the redoubt roused from their slumber, terrified. For over an hour their artillery fired not a single shot. Elliott's salient was the immediate scene of the blast. A simultaneous outburst of artillery fire from all the Federal batteries accompanied the explosion and cut through the Confederate positions on either side of the gap. Two entire South Carolina regiments fell to their deaths when the ground collapsed under them. As the smoke continued to lift from the site of the explosion, Federal troops advanced. But not the 48th. The men who dug the galleries stood on the sidelines and watched. The blast had divided Elliott's brigade in two. Fear and dread gripped the Confederate soldiers rudely awakened by the detonation. They rushed from their beds in all directions. Their officers, however, prevented a general retreat, and General Beauregard trained the undamaged guns of his batteries toward the besieging Yankees running down into the crater. Federal artillery opened all along the line, concentrating its fire to the right and left of the crater. Beauregard ordered his men in the eventuality of any breach to concentrate their firing at the hole which would then open up. Hand-to-hand battle ensued. The Federal soldiers reached the parapet and main trench, but a crossfire of Confederate riflemen on either side of the crater promptly drove them back. As they received no support, circumstances compelled them to withdraw. The Federals occupied the crater for two hours, and Burnside now thoroughly drunk kept throwing more and more troops into the fray. He commanded General Ferrero to force his way through the gap and take Cemetery Hill with his Negro division. Ferrero's men passed through the crater, advanced toward the crest, where they met a fierce artillery and musketry fire, but then broke in disorder. Afterward Ferrero partly reorganized them, but many soon broke again, fleeing in wild confusion into and out of the crater, back to Burnside's outlying lines. This stampede effactually disheartened the remainder of the party who, gathered within the crater, were exposed to a murderous fire from both the left and right. General Grant, who had ridden to the scene of action and saw how the Confederates mercilessly cut down the Union men, hollered: "These troops must be immediately withdrawn. It is a slaughter to leave them there." Returning to Meade's headquarters, Grant issued an order to withdraw the troops, which, however, Meade modified so as to leave to Burnside's discretion the time of the withdrawal, so that he could pick the most favorable opportunity for the men to depart with the smallest loss of life. Burnside received the order to suspend operations at 9:30 but Burnside let the men keep fighting. At 11:30, General Wright's regiment, of Mahone's division, forced the Federals back from the trenches to the right side of the crater, from ground they had just taken, but the Federals mounted a counter attack, and again made headway. The Rebels fixed all their free rifles on the crater and contiguous ditches and furrows and readied both Mahone's and Johnson's brigades for a charge; but as the rifle barrage had already virtually cleared the crater, the Confederates slackened their fire. In the end, they captured thirty men and three stands of colors. Thousands of men lost their lives on both sides, but the Confederate positions held.

His father participated in other battles after digging the mine, but he dismissed his involvement as ordinary duty where he served like any other soldier as a common infantryman. In front of Petersburg his mining skills and expertise heightened his worth to his commanders and the union cause. So in consequence he thought the siege the high point of his military service. On August 2nd of 1864, the PA 48th now under the command of Major Bosbyshell received a temporary commission to the 2nd Brigade of the 2nd Division. Lionel's father fought at the battle at Poplar Spring Church, his first priority living through it: saving his own skin. Lionel remembered his father's account of that particular bloody engagement for his mother received a long letter from his father directly after the skirmish which she shared with him. Lionel remained hazy and unsure about Jacob's whereabouts and activities after that engagement. All he knew for certain was that during the last months of the war, the 48th occupied a redoubt known as Fort Sedgwick. The regiment remained at that location until April 2nd, 1865, when marching out of the bulwark on the double quick they departed, ordered to attack—to make a breach in the Confederate lines—at Fort Mahone. On the morning of the 3rd, the Union troops advanced and occupied Petersburg without opposition, and after the surrender of Robert E. Lee on the 9th, they received orders to tramp to Washington, where before being mustered out of the service, the men marching in their regiments and companies participated in the Grand Review. After his return home Lionel's father relayed a cautionary tale to his son. At a Washington brothel (he did not cheat on his wife, only went into the establishment to drink with the boys), Jacob Kemper encountered a man he knew from his hometown Robert Elder chewing and swishing a cigar in his mouth as he stood in the raw, a *poule* under either arm, both ladies also *in flagrante*. He told the startled Kemper that elated the war was over he would now put a plan into execution which he had resolved on before enlisting, namely to desert his wife and children. The war provided him an opportunity to escape, to unloose the marriage and family bonds, to start anew. He thought that he would surely die each time he faced combat, but now that he had made it through, let them think he had died! He wanted to bow from the scene forever just as if he had kicked the bucket and given up the ghost. He had decided that he would head out to California. He came from old pioneer stock, he boasted, thumping his chest like an angry ape. His grandfather had left Scotland, his family of nautical engineers and shipbuilders who owned mammoth works at Cowden on the Clyde, near Glasgow, and had come to the new country. For adventure. To explore. He felt the same wanderlust. Elder enjoined Kemper not to go home to his family but to instead accompany him west. Why not? he pleaded in his drunken stupor. Never again will such a perfect opportunity present itself. Kemper declined, morally disgusted at his comrade's proposed action. He could imagine the suffering of Elder's poor offspring. After he joined the army, Elder's family never heard from him again. He had cut all ties, had not written a single letter. His wife and their four children—two boys, two girls—endured many privations after Robert Elder left home. Of that Jacob Kemper was quite certain. At the brothel, Elder even showed him photographs of the children, pulled them out of the breast pocket of his uniform. Kemper took what was proffered him, glanced down at the pictures, and shuddered. He could see into the future. The wife and children would never have very much to live on. At a very young age, the kiddies would have to plant the crops and tend the fields, fend for themselves. Sink or swim. Life is a battle, he told his son afterwards when he got back home to Cressona. You must remain strong and steel yourself to endure a long siege, a war of attrition ... for that was what life was. Every fellow homo sapien, even one's own father, could turn into a potential foe. You cannot trust your left hand from your right. Nothing could be more detestable, however, than shirking one's duties or walking out on one's loved ones, one's family.

No Sergeant Kemper wouldn't under any circumstances have deserted from his regiment. Nor would he ever abandon his wife Martha, his daughter Doris, or Lionel and the other boys. He would always provide for them to the best of his ability, see to it they never suffered from want or privation. He had the rest of his life before him and he planned to enjoy it to the fullest. He would die at age one hundred in his own warm bed. He had much, so very much, to look forward to. He would see his daughter and his boys married and hold his grandchildren and even his great-grandchildren on his lap, bounce them on his knee. Yes indeed, he had everything to live for. When he returned home in July, he threw his hat in the air, spent the rest of the summer celebrating his survival. So happy to return to his forge and mill in Cressona, Kemper did something the boy had never seen him do before—after crossing the threshold of the old family farmhouse, he took a drink. The fields had gone to seed. It was too late to plant a crop, but Jacob hoped that patriotic citizens of his town would patronize his forge. Several months after his return, it caught fire and burned to the ground. Jacob Kemper didn't know what to do for his sawmill didn't provide him with a sufficient income, but then his brother Boyd came to his rescue, got him a job in the mine at Port Clinton. They worked in the same room when the accident occurred, when the ceiling crashed down on Jacob Kemper. Yes, he had gone underground one too many times. Miraculously Boyd received no injury whatsoever. After her husband's death, Martha Kemper and the children experienced extreme financial hardship. The family broke up. Various relatives of their mother and their late father took in the younger boys or else persons other than relatives adopted them, whereas the teenage sons including Lionel bonded out as apprentices. Over the years his mother resided with different members of the family in various locations in Schuylkill County. She stayed a number of years in Pottsville with her sister Rebecca. But after her death—a sudden heart attack—she crossed the County to Silver Creek where she kept house for her brother-in-law Silas Weaver, the husband of another sister Harriet, who had recently suffered from an effusion of the brain—a stroke or a cerebral hemorrhage—and now remained bedfast. Harriet had a reputation for being spic and span. She always made the folks who came to her house take their shoes off before entering so that no mud would be tracked onto her carpets. Fanatical in her war on dirt, she always kept her house immaculate. And her war on filth and grime extended beyond the confines of her home. Between the farmhouse and barn ran a wooden boardwalk. Every week Harriet would get down on her hands and knees and scrub the entire length of it. When the seizure felled Harriet, her husband was at a loss. Martha needed a place to stay, and like her sister she was a very tidy woman. Silas needed a housekeeper and an attendant for his wife. Probably only his wife's sister could answer his high standards, but even Martha I'm sure found it difficult to step into Harriet's shoes. Silas could be a very authoritarian taskmaster and her paralytic, dying sister resented her presence, she could tell. A second stroke took her and Martha stayed on, but Silas became quite remote, morose and bitter, mean even. He demanded more and more from her, drank large quantities of alcohol, and often leered at her. She felt unsafe. She stayed for maybe a year after her sister's death then left for Tamaqua and took up residence at her daughter Doris Helfenfuss' home. But feeling unwelcome there also, she again removed after obtaining a position in a hotel in New Philadelphia where she worked for several years as a maid and cook. Finally she retired back to Pottsville, where several of her sons resided, including her eldest Lionel, now a blacksmith and farmer like his father. But for the life of him, he would never work in a mine. The Widow Kemper maintained her own residence on Tenth Street. She died of heart failure at the domicile of another son Willie, whom she was visiting for several days, her age sixty-four years and ten months. After she died, Lionel laid her to rest in Pottsville and afterward decided to exhume his father's body from the memorial park in Port Clinton and rebury him at the side of his wife. He supervised the second interment of Jacob Kemper's casket. Two powerful horses drew it across the county in a hay wagon. The gravediggers had already opened a grave on Lionel's newly purchased lot. His wife and twin sons, his brothers, several married several not, their families, and Captain and Mrs. Helfenfuss awaited Lionel and the coffin's arrival at the cemetery. Just as they approached the gravesite, for some inexplicable reason the horses reared, the wagon whirled and the casket tumbled off. Flipping as it fell, the box landed top down. The driver leaped off his perch. The gravediggers ran to his aid. They turned the casket over but then the lid sprung open. All the living children of Jacob and Martha Kemper once again saw the face of their father. The casket must have been airtight, for he looked just the same as he had twenty some years before when they first shut him into the box. But after a few moments, a terrible transformation occurred. The face fell inwards. The skin, cartilage and bone sank in, crumbling into powder—dust—as it collapsed into the bowl of the skull—of the death's head—like the roof of an old abandoned mine at long last giving way, drawn inexorably all these years by mother earth's mighty attraction, her pull and tug.

VIII

Some time had passed since the signing of the armistice, and the celebratory victory parades had already all taken place. He had watched quite a few on the tube. Everyone waved yellow banners and hoorayed hysterically, and Billy Steiglitz himself exhibited some marked signs of regeneration. Bored—inexpressibly bored—by the hubbub and celebration, tired of the whole proceedings, he wanted to leave the confines of his house, for he felt suddenly claustrophobic. His reaction to the war had been fascination coupled with extreme abhorrence. Yet after the country's victory, he sensed that his wounds had finally healed. In the twilight of his thirties, approaching the big four-o, he suddenly had the courage to leave his fortress, his home. He wanted to take a walk through the woods. True until the war ended, he couldn't tear himself away from his TV, where he saw a dead ringer for Chalkman, the Pentagon spokesman Pete Williams. Indeed he mistook Williams for Chalkman the first time his image flashed up on the screen. But the Pentagon spokesman looked like the studio mouthpiece had in 1973. Maybe Chalkman had a son? At any rate if someone ever made a movie about the making of the ill-fated Civil War documentary (a movie concerning another movie) and the helicopter accident which had caused the death of Billy's father, Williams could take on the role of the studio spokesman, General Schwartzkopf the character of the megalomaniacal director, and George Herbert Walker Bush even though he wasn't a professional actor like his immediate predecessor the part of Billy's Pa. Dad would have been pleased as punch that an Anglo-Saxon took on the character, the guise of an Austrian American. Of course Bill's notion was far-fetched and ridiculous, but not any crazier than a lot of his father's caprices had been. His dad had often compiled an ideal cast for a film version of some great work of literature. Pretending to be the motion picture's director, he'd cast stars from the thirties and forties (at their age then) alongside contemporary actors. Put the dead on the screen alongside the living. Humphrey Bogart with Sean Connery, for example. Or Clark Gable with Michael Caine. Several nights before Billy made up his mind to actually go through with it—to actually leave his house and come out of his tomb—he dreamed that the structure collapsed on itself. Also things laid to rest suddenly rose from the ground in his nightmare. His dinosaur tooth. The skeleton of his dad Franz Steiglitz. The mummies of Iraqi soldiers entombed alive by coalition forces under the dunes of the desert. The Confederates at Petersburg. He had to admit that at the commencement of hostilities he had opposed the war. The United States, however, had won a signal victory. What right had he to carp and criticize! He had grown as rotund as Marlon Brando when Brando took on the role of Colonel Kurtz in Frances Ford Coppola's *Apocalypse Now*. Yet when

Bill finally decided on his course of action, he bravely went ahead and pushed open those French doors, crossed the vestibule to the new screen door leading outside, and stepped into the sunshine. Feeling a bit like Rip van Winkle, he walked down the street, surprised by the look and size of the new cars. Of course he had seen all the new models advertised on TV, but the vehicles were much more compact, smaller than he imagined. He saw a group of teenagers with shaved heads or purple and green colored streaks in their hair and did a double take. He wouldn't have given ten cents for the music issuing from their portable sound system—aptly named a boom box, he recollected from television. A sort of tribal chanting, percussive and harsh.

He walked past them, didn't turn around to look when one of the young punks accosted him, just continued straight ahead. It took him ten minutes to cross the residential area, then he cut through Davis' yard (at least the Davises owned the property when he last pranced across the greensward as a teenager years and years ago) and reached his destination. It gratified him that the enchanted meadow and cornfield of his youth looked much the same as he remembered it. As a little boy, accompanied by his dog Shep, he had often made his way through the ears of corn to Duncan's Pond. Fred Duncan had owned this land and the big red farmhouse down the highway, small in the distance from where Billy Steiglitz stood. Or at least he had owned it. Billy didn't know for sure if Mr. Duncan still lived. The pond at the center of the property, sad to see, had disappeared. Rows of corn grew across where it had once lain. Shep's waterhole existed no more. As a kid, Billy had caught countless bluegill and bass from out of it, but the pond had been filled in. He walked right over where it once had lain. Another surprise awaited him when he reached the last row of Indian corn. Instead of a poplar grove, he saw a housing development. Civilization had encroached this far into his old haunts.

He now began to puff and sweat profusely. His lungs heaving, he had to stop. The roll of fat on his belly bounced obscenely under his white Nike sweatshirt. He coughed so hard he had to barf. He emptied the contents of his stomach between the two closest cornstalks. He staggered on a few paces then sat down under a shade tree. He leaned his back against the bark and scratched it by rubbing his shoulders and spine against the trunk. He shut his eyes and drifted off into unconsciousness for a quarter of an hour, then he awoke, sprung to his feet, but his right leg hurt. He had a cramp, his muscles unused to this level of exertion. Yet he determined to move on. He limped like his ancestor Percy McCalmont or as if he had a club foot, hobbling out of the meadow and into the new street and then down it past the newly constructed split-level, ranch and two-story houses. As he trudged on, he saw pickup trucks parked in driveways, children running and screaming, gigantic satellite dishes tilted back to receive a thousand signals from the blue sky. He went up the hill beyond the last lot. Someone had marked out future parcels and plots beyond it, but as yet no one had felled the trees on the separate pieces of ground. Part of his old woods remained intact though dirt roads now traversed the woodland both lengthwise and across its width indicating the direction of future development. Bill fingered the flaky bark of a great pine, threw back his head and filled his lungs with the crisp, sweet-scented air. He hurried on, though to anyone else, his pace would have seemed quite slow—that of a much older man. He reached a summit, passed over it, then went downhill until he came to a brook. He hopped across several large stones protruding out of the water to the other side then sat down and listened to the plashing water. Aside from the gurgling, he experienced perfect silence. Then he made out a distant birdcall. He felt the wind lashing his cheeks, the sky the same shade of pale blue he always remembered in late spring, early summer: just the color of a robin's egg. He heard more chirping, birdcalls of several different species.

Yes, he had come through the gauntlet.

Now his life could begin once again.

IX

It took quite some time for the weight to come off, for Billy Steiglitz to slim down. He started swimming Monday through Friday at the local YMCA. Again he emulated his father, for Dr. Franz Steiglitz had always taken care of his body, had always maintained a reasonable weight, followed a sensible diet and exercised daily. He both swam and walked. Every morning during faculty swim at the university natatorium (then and only then; he'd never go during the "open" hours and share his lane with students), Dr. Steiglitz would propel himself through the water, kick and glide, ninety or one hundred pool lengths.

Not long before his death, he had tabulated the number of miles he had swum since coming to Slippery Rock and had discovered that he had traversed the span of the Atlantic Ocean once and that he had reached one third of the way back across it, that he had swum over four thousand miles. He crowed about his accomplishment to everyone, including Bill. A very long time would ensue before his son could boast of anything even approaching that, but you had to begin somewhere. At least, he had started, taken the initial step. Now success or failure would depend only on his perseverance.

Almost a year had passed after the Gulf War ended, however, before Bill took out a membership at the Y. During the first six or seven months after he emerged from his self-imposed isolation, to make up for all the time he had spent inside and to test his resolve, he traveled across the country. He flew to Hawaii within a week of coming out of his house and stayed there a month, spent the days on the beach tanning his corpulent swollen stomach and the nights in a four-star luxury hotel. He had certainly managed his money well. He could afford to be extravagant and improvident. On the return leg of his journey, he stopped over in L.A. and toured Hollywood. Then he turned in his plane tickets, having decided to return to Pennsylvania by rail and really see the country, get some idea of the vast distances the nation stretched. Whenever he felt like it, he'd leave the train and tour. He spent several weeks in the desert, surveyed the Grand Canyon for the first time, went sightseeing in a lot of out of-the-way places, ran up bills on his various credit cards. He had learned to use plastic during his eighteen years inside: had mail ordered on an almost daily basis—books, CDs, computer software, exercise sets, whatever at the time he decided he had to have. And as the courts awarded him eight hundred thousand dollars in his wrongful death suit, the charge card companies set no limit on his credit, issued him the gold cards reserved for their most select clients, but he had always squared his bill monthly and so never paid any usurious rate of interest. He knew how to buy on credit before ever leaving his house and now that knowledge stood him in good stead.

After returning home, he visited his Uncle Roger at his home in Philly. His mother's brother seemed quite surprised and shocked to see him, their only communication in years Billy's written request that Roger make him copies of the Civil War photographs of the three Corl brothers which Roger had done. After answering the door and inviting Bill in, Corl asked his nephew what he now did with his life. Right now, Bill replied, he traveled. His uncle told him he needed to find an occupation—to do something meaningful with his existence. Bill told him that he'd make him proud yet, and they parted amicably. His uncle's surprise in no way prepared him for that of his old friend Rutger when unannounced he showed up one day on his friend's front porch step in Fort Lauderdale. It had taken Billy some time to locate him. His parents had moved from town years ago. Even the neighbors had lost touch. Billy had to locate the Poells through the University; they now lived in upstate New York. He telephoned, told Dr. Poell who he was, that he and Rutger had lost touch with one another and that he now wanted to reestablish contact with his old friend. The day after receiving the information, Bill boarded a plane for Florida. He had asked Rutger's dad not to let Rutger know in advance, that he wanted to surprise him, and that he did. At first his friend didn't recognize him and then when he dropped the bombshell, told him his name and removed the blinders, Rutger stared at him open mouthed, with wide-eyed incredulity, and at least thirty seconds passed before his senses came back to him, and he invited him in. Billy never felt more like Rip van Winkle, the bibulous Dutch settler in Irving's *Sketch Book* put under a spell in the Catskills, than he did at that moment. Rutger had become a successful lawyer with a large practice; he had married fifteen years before and now had three children the oldest of whom had just turned thirteen. Introduced to his friend's family, Bill sensed just how much he had missed in life, perceived all that his existence lacked, and felt a bitter pang in his heart for all the time he had let slip by, not recapturable now, forever lost to him. He bounced Rutger's youngest daughter on his knee and felt his own biological clock ticking. Would he remain the last of the Steiglitzes? His father had inculcated to him how imperative it was that the line continue. Having children, he said, remained the only way to defeat death, the only way that one's ancestors could live on after one's own passing. How lax he had been in his duty. Well now he could strive to make up for the time he had squandered. He wanted not only to explore his own country from coast to coast but also to cross the oceans, travel the globe. After a few days in Florida, he flew home and applied for a passport.

Upon reentering his parent's house, he feared a setback, an eddy or countercurrent that would reverse the progress that he had made. Inside its walls, he suffocated and choked. He would have to move into another dwelling. Yet he might become as much a prisoner inside a new building as within his parents' old residence. The outside world must hold no more fears for him. He would have to grow strong enough to confront all his old demons. He set himself a supreme test: to go to a Civil War reenactment on the Gettysburg battlefield. If he could force himself to attend it, he would face his fears head on and conquer them. He arrived there on a painfully hot and humid day. Tourists combed the town, none of the local hotels had any rooms to rent as sightseers and vacationers had booked them long in advance, so Bill had to commute from Heidlersburg. He hired a driver for the trip. His license had expired years and years ago and while he knew himself an excellent driver (like riding a bicycle one never forgot), he did not want to break any law. He had it in his hands to remedy the situation, but as of yet he hadn't had the time to see how one went about getting one's license renewed, reinstated, or whatever. He would make that one of his first priorities on returning home; but for now he would have to suffer the indignity of public transportation, or else simply hire a man: after all he could easily afford the three hundred dollar a day limousine fee. He did feel rather sick and not just from the heat when he trudged across the battlefield and lost himself in the swell of humanity: people of all ages and colors, women with baby strollers, men of the cloth, young boys who misbehaved and caused their parents no end of grief, Gulf veterans wearing their dress uniforms and sweating profusely, elderly fat people sticking together with their own group, one of many such that had disembarked from the numerous tour buses parked in front of the battlefield museum and park entrance. He had seen them unloading all morning. Upon reflection, Bill smiled that he had not sat behind the wheel; the streets of the little town became so congested, so choked with traffic, that driving would have become most unpleasant. Now as he elbowed his way through the crowd, he felt like a lemming, an ant, an extra in a Cecil B. DeMille film. As he made his way forward, the staged battle began. His legs buckled when he heard the initial cannonade and he felt as if he would swoon, so he held his breath, shut his eyes, and counted to ten, then feeling his resolve deepen within him, his anger at God, the world, and himself burn like a red-hot coal in his bowels, he drew himself up, opened his eyes and as spryly as a condemned man mounting the gallows, put one foot in front of the other. If William Corl, the brother of his ancestor, could find the strength within himself to march straight into the arms of death on this very battlefield in 1863, his namesake could do no less in 1991. Bill succeeded in slaying his dragon; he got close enough so he could see the Confederate reenactors make their fateful charge, observed the cannons explode from the Union positions on Cemetery Hill. He felt a tightness in his chest, but continued watching the millipede-legged lines as they advanced. One after another, he saw the marching men cut down, but still the drummer boys beat their rhythmic tattoos, even as the flag bearers pitched forward, their colors fluttering in the sweltering air one last brief moment before falling to the ground for someone else to pick up, who would in turn fall: on and on all day. But Billy had seen enough. No helicopter would drop out of the sky this afternoon. He remained free to go. If he left now, he'd beat the rush. He turned around and made his way back through the crowd, found his driver where he had left him, and they departed.

Several months before he took out his YMCA membership, he succeeded in selling his parents' home. Though he thought about it, he decided not to put the house on the market right after returning from Gettysburg. First he'd find and buy a new pad, but it would take some time to locate a house that suited him, and, as he could not bear going through his old doors ever again, he rented an apartment as soon as he returned home. He considered this a stopgap measure, for he needed a large house to store his many possessions, and besides he didn't like noisy neighbors on the other sides of his walls or above and below him. However, he wanted a palatial crib of a fireside, as he now desired to show the entire world that he had money coming out his ass. During the years he suffered from agoraphobia and that he never strayed from his bunker in the basement, only a few people realized his net worth but now he'd make up for lost time. Everybody in town would see that he had grown wealthy, and not just by his house. Before he started the long, complicated process of getting his license back, he purchased a seventy-thousand-dollar Porsche. He ordered it straight from the factory in Germany. It took him more time to find his future abode, but at long last he located his dream house: an old Victorian mansion or, as the realtor had said, a Steamboat Gothic manor, on the west side of town. He signed the papers at the realtor's office and took possession of the keys. Several months had passed since he moved into the apartment, but he still could not bear to return to his parents' home. In fact, since returning from Gettysburg, he hadn't reentered the womb, the eggshell he hatched out of, even to retrieve his clothes. He had bought himself an entire new wardrobe after coming out. He felt that he did not have to watch and supervise the removal of his beloved possessions. He'd pay someone to cart all his things out to the new house instead, but then he remembered Sue, his love doll hanging in the attic, and thought that he would have to go back to dispose of her, so he set out one morning, walked across town to his old address but couldn't cross the threshold—he turned away from his parent's place trembling from head to toe—not even to save himself the embarrassment of the exposure of his vice. He read the want ads in the newspaper, found a college kid willing to do odd jobs and paid him two hundred to get rid of Sue and also dispose of all his pornographic books and videos, then called the movers to pack up and transport the rest of his belongings to his new residence. Only then did he place his parental home for sale. He told the realtor to get rid of it quickly, to mark the price way down if he must. From thenceforward he studiously avoided Meadowood Village, the residential area where he grew up, and the house that he hadn't left for eighteen long years. After taking out his YMCA membership, he began swimming every morning from 10:00 to 11:00 during the "adults-only" hour. He also worked out in the weight room and spent hours burning off the fat in the sauna. He felt like a snake sloughing off his old skin. Everyday he stepped on the scales to see if he had lost any weight, and gradually the air went out from the tire circling his waist; the jellyroll constricted and shrank. He lost forty-five pounds in the first three months. Don't quit, he told himself. If you retrogress now, you will only have yourself to blame.

He had seen many good-looking girls in skimpy bathing suits at the Y. They dangled like sweets and candies just out of his reach, inspired and drove him to push harder in his endeavor to resculpt his torso. If he continued working out, one day his physique would return, and he could again strut and prank and would once more possess the resources, the wherewithal, to tempt one of those fine ladies to amorous or wanton play, to dalliance and fondling.

One summer morning, his destiny rose out of the pool like a naiad out of a mountain spring. At least ten years younger than he, she wore an indolent and unhurried expression on her face, her hair tucked up under her bathing cap. She smiled at him. She actually turned her head in his direction, looked straight at him and smiled. She had piercing blue eyes, slim arms and round legs and full breasts. After stepping up the ladder onto the deck, she took off her cap and shook out her dark, damp curls. Then she pulled her orange towel off the wall rail and draped it around her shoulders. She shot another quick glance at him—the artery in his neck began throbbing, as she did—and then disappeared into the women's locker room. It relieved Bill that he stood in the water at the time and had not climbed out onto the deck because his member had grown tumescent. He continued swimming until he once again became flaccid. Then he too left the pool. He hoped that he would have the opportunity to meet this girl who had caught his eye, or rather he hers, as she had spotted him first. He had not held a woman in his arms for almost two decades. Not since his adolescence, since his college days at the University of Pennsylvania when he had a few casual encounters with equally young, equally curious, coeds. Those first tentative explorations in the back seats of cars or motel bedrooms had been his only ventures into the world of eroticism, aside from mounting his love doll while looking up at the adult movie on his television screen. But Sue's bloodless embraces had quickly grown stale, the films tedious and time-consuming. While he had outgrown his voyeuristic tendencies, the sex urge had not shriveled up inside of him as he had thought it had done. It had only gone to sleep. Now those fires blazed up again—all the stronger for his repressing them so long—and conquered him wholly. While he remained deathly afraid of venereal diseases, he knew if the opportunity ever arose for him to bed a woman, his basic instincts would overpower him. He could not check them. He'd catapult into the naiad's bed in an instant. To truly live one must walk hand in hand with death. He found it essential to take risks. If you caught the virus, you did, end of story. You had to welcome your fate, embrace it like a lover. You must leap into the pool of life, not just put a big toe into the water, and then stand paralyzed and frightened at the pool's edge, not knowing whether to jump in or stay out. For years, he had opted for the second, cowardly choice but now he wouldn't even bother sticking his toe in to test the temperature first. He'd leap without looking. It wasn't just a craving or yearning for sexual gratification—an itch that he had to scratch, a gnawing hunger he had to satisfy—that he now experienced though desire for physical pleasure did, of course, factor—and factor strongly—into the equation. But in addition to it, he felt a procreative urgency as well, a need to beget and sire. Something he had first perceived while bouncing Rutger's daughter on his knee. He wanted a woman to stroke, tease and squeeze him but he wanted children to result from the stroking and squeezing. Bill felt all his forebears trapped inside him—Corls and Steiglitzes, Matzelots, McCalmonts, and Kempers—banging on the prison gates of his body, desiring to issue forth from him into other frames, other forms. They wanted to be refashioned and remade into countless children—to be poured into endless new molds. They had grown comfortable in him, had settled down into a sort of sleep or lethargy. Time had paused for them just as it had done for him those eighteen years he spent, snug as a bug in a rug, inside his parents' home, but now they had grown restless—the spirits—had reawakened out of their long slumber. They had gone into hibernation, had drifted off into limbo, the land of shades and had almost died that second, final death. They had almost doused themselves in Lethe's waters and accepted annihilation and oblivion. However, at the last moment, the graveness of their position had suddenly come home to them. They emerged from their trance-like state at the point of plunging into the river and awoke hell bent on prolonging their being and entity in numerous daughters and sons as yet unborn, but soon to be fathered, they hoped, by Bill. Franz Alfred Steiglitz called on his son not to let him die again, as he made excuses to all the older forebears for the boy remaining so dilatory in carrying out his obligations.

Yes, Franz agreed, it was high time that "their current avatar" got down to business and founded his own family. Then pivoting away from the other spirits, he asked Bill what, if anything, he had accomplished all those long years that he had shut himself inside his cocoon? He didn't give him time to answer. Not a thing, he declared. Bill opened his mouth but couldn't get a word in edgewise. You spent your days watching television. What you saw on the screen became your life—you had no other. Da turned once more to the ancestors and apologized for his son's "interminably long gestation period" but stated that wing buds now sprouted from Billy's shoulder blades. That a sense of mission and duty had developed inside him and that his own personality had started to coalesce at long last, that his ancestors could now rest assured that Bill would find the strength, up to now latent within himself, to accomplish great things. Besides he, Franz, would goad and prick him until he located a womb into which to plant sons and daughters—not only his own but also *their* reincarnations.

Bill received his license by the time he accepted delivery of his car and found incredible reserves of pluck and courage in himself that he never before even suspected existed. He took the car up to one twenty the first time he got behind the wheel. He wanted to hurl, to propel himself forward into life, to squeeze all the juice from his existence then drain the cup of his lifeblood to the lees. He desired to apprehend and intuit all Being, to undergo the whole gamut of man's manifold experience from A to Z, to lay hold of and grasp mentally all the secrets of the Universe, for the third eye of apperception to slowly open on his forehead, for it now struck him full force that all life including his, lasted but a short time, remained transitory and ephemeral, and that he had better enjoy to the hilt his time, the few hours allotted him to sprout in the sun's rays and effloresce, before sunset and oncoming night. He had lost eighteen years, but not another day. The already numbered, only-so-many-still-left, ever-so-few palpitations, beats, of his ticker before apotheosis, judgment day, that still remained before all the sand ran through the neck of his hour glass—the rest of his life in other words—he vowed not to spend idly. He would relish every minute and cram each day with new experience as if he had metamorphosed into great Goethe's Faust. He vowed never to remain satisfied, never to remain slaked. He would not waste what little he had left of that short stretch of consciousness—a tiny burst like that of a shooting star, a lightning streak—between the two big nothingnesses: Before Birth and After Death.

Most mere mortals wasted the sum and entirety of their allotted time—relinquished and misspent whatever amount they still had, lightly, as if it meant nothing, as if they regarded it as something of little worth, something easily forfeited. Their lives sank into routine, into repetition and rut. Doomed to do the same things over and over, they accepted monotony as their fate or even welcomed death and non-entity. Yes, they lowered their necks like slaughter cows, as meekly as Marie Antoinette or Anne Boleyn. They walked slowly in long lines to the gas chambers, not daring to run away, to at least try to escape, not willing to storm the guards *en masse* and wrench the machineguns out of their hands. Billy had once acted as humbly and submissively as they. Not any more. If they strapped him into the chair, he'd fight the whole time, shout out that he stood as innocent as Jesus and why oh why did they want to shed his blood? He would never again passively accept his fate. He welcomed—embraced—risk, and knew his life a gift ever available for the fates to cut short and snuff out, that he might wreck his car because he drove it too fast, but he decided he'd rather live a short happy life than a long unhappy one. But more than anything he wanted to father sons and daughters and until he fulfilled that duty, he had better decelerate. After that he could dance all he wanted on the cliff's edge, fall off if he had to, if he must. He felt two impulses at once inside himself. At the same time he wanted a hearth and home—bovine domesticity—he desired to set out to sea, to embark on fabulous new adventures. Odysseus' dilemma on finally reaching Ithaca, at least according to Dante and Tennyson, now became his own. Both roads had their allure and again he felt paralyzed, couldn't make up his mind which path to take. Steiglitzian folly, he thought and laughed. The tribe's characteristic desire to have it both ways. To eat their cake and keep it too. His father's obsession with, his love for, the old Hollywood movies even though he laughed—scoffed—all the while at their contrived plot elements, their happy endings, their inherent falseness and artificiality. Yes, Da loved that fantasy world where the good received their reward and the unjust a proper and befitting punishment. Franz would have exchanged the actual cosmos for the fantasy one in a flash. And just as he had a double reaction toward Hollywood films, Da saw war one way with one eye while he regarded it in a wholly different manner with the other. The second had to compensate for the first, to balance and counter what the first eye saw so nakedly, the hellish brutality of combat, the stupidity and insanity of battle, its function to clean up, to sanitize, war in order to justify it and make it palatable. No Billy couldn't father a child then abandon it, as he thought he might do just a few minutes before. He could not turn into a second Robert Elder. That solution wouldn't work for him because he wanted to be as good and exemplary a father as his own had been. Molding a son would become his life's work. A responsibility he couldn't shirk or pass on to others. If he decided to father a child, he'd have to forego dancing at the edge of the cliff. Well, he didn't have to make up his mind today. Not just yet.

He did know one thing for sure, though. Driving his car down the country roads around Slippery Rock, Billy Steiglitz decided that the next time he saw his naiad that he would start up a conversation with her, charm her with the full force of his personality. If he found the courage to walk out of his parents' house after eighteen years, the courage to step onto another Civil War battlefield during mock combat, he certainly could approach a girl and ask her out. He had glibly used whatever communication skills he had at the time to lure and tempt college girls at age eighteen to "do the wild thing," as they had then called it, so he could certainly sweet talk a woman at age thirty-nine. He hadn't forgotten how to drive, had he? And besides he'd make a fine catch for any gal. He was loaded, had money to burn. If she didn't find him attractive, if he still weighed a little too much for her taste, what more could she do to him other than say no? Besides she remained younger and less experienced than he as well.

With these and such like thoughts, Billy steeled himself to speak to the girl who had smiled at him at the Y. Yet the next time he saw her, he couldn't find the strength within himself to walk up and approach her. His hands became clammy and sweat beaded on his brow, and he just knew if he opened his mouth that he would become tongue-tied. They both stood in line at the front desk to turn in their locker keys and to receive back their membership cards. He hung his head in shame, but after sliding her card into her wallet, she turned around and spoke to him.

"You must have swum a good sixty or seventy laps this morning. You've really got get up and go."

"No. Not really," he stammered.

"We haven't met or should I say been formally introduced?"

"No, we haven't."

"Well, I'll rectify that right now. Hi, I'm Cindy." She proffered him her hand. He took it.

"Nice to meet you. My name is William Steiglitz."

"I'm really glad to finally meet you, too, Bill."

They said nothing further, but several days later, he saw her walking down the street while driving in his Porsche. He tooted the horn and waved. She smiled and signaled back. As he drove past her then on out of town and into the boonies, he had already begun contemplating their future life together. He would bow down before her, her body an altar at which he would worship. He'd place his lips on her feet and smother them with his kisses. He'd totally abase himself and throw himself down like a carpet in front of her and wouldn't complain if she walked over him. He wanted her to! And, of course, it went without saying that he would support her in any enterprise she'd embark on, take up, and, most certainly, they would have children together. A loving mother, Cindy would always place her children's interests above her own. Both parents would take elaborate pains over their kids, cultivate and foster self-confidence in them, instill the belief that they could accomplish any task they set for themselves. He would read every night to his sons, introduce them at an early age to both music and art. In fact after Cindy became pregnant, he'd have her hold a stereo speaker up to her womb and let those little ears forming inside her experience the shimmering tones of Debussy, the ingenuity and intricacy of Bach. And he wouldn't make as stern or forbidding a figure as his own father; he wouldn't retreat from life, disappear into some bunker into which his wife and children had no access. Like Da, he'd want to mold his children into

Beethovens, but he'd go about it in entirely a different manner—with love and sympathy and positive reinforcement—not by fear and intimidation. No, he'd never call any child of his a stupid mortal, Da's epithet for poor Miles. And while he would teach his girls and boys to stand proud of their American heritage and let them read his father's stories about the Corls, Kempers, and McCalmonts, he'd also instill in them an appreciation of their Austrian ancestry. If anything he'd teach them to be leery and skeptical about American nationalism. Not because he believed the United States an inherently evil country but because they lived in America and he found patriotism and flag-waving in any state dubious and questionable—highly suspect—because those in power could easily exploit such healthy sentiments and transform them into jingoism, fanaticism, and hatred for those who differed from the norm. Why did the human race continually divide and categorize itself? Don't we all live on one planet? Shouldn't we see each other as brothers and sisters? Chauvinism creates an us-them mindset, a vulnerability that any unscrupulous leader can easily turn to his advantage. He remembered all the propaganda posters he had seen in his father's books—the twisted distorted animalistic features of "the enemy" in all his countless incarnations, and shuddered, gripping his steering wheel as tight as he could. Even the name of the antagonist had to undergo a sort of depreciation—a cheapening. Germans became Huns; Japanese, Nips; Vietnamese, Gooks. The propagandists weren't stupid; they deemed it essential to dehumanize the enemy. If they turned him into a monster, the soldiers on the front line would find it a lot easier to kill him, would not engage in soul searching or suffer any moral doubt about pulling the trigger. Bush knew which buttons to push, and push them he did. He sold his war to the American people, called Hussein a second Hitler but neglected to tell them that the United States considered this Hitler a trusted ally only a few months earlier. True, numerous television commentators related all the facts, even the ones the administration wanted kept quiet, but the vast majority of Americans didn't listen—or only half listened—to them. The herd instinct prevailed. People rallied around the flag. Closed their eyes to anything which might compromise the president's or the coalition's position. The administration put out disinformation too. The Iraqis never threw babies out of incubators, allowed them to die on the hospital floor, so that they could ship the medical equipment back to Iraq, a distortion worthy of Josef Goebbels. Of course our smart bombs didn't kill any Iraqi children. Nor did any die now, a year after hostilities ceased, from lack of food and medicine. Our pro-life president wouldn't want the blood of babes on his hands. The military had learned from Vietnam and banned television crews from the battlefield, allowed only its own cleaned-up footage to appear on TV. Nor did Bush wish us to recall that during the Iran-Iraq war, the United States vetoed the U.N. resolution condemning Iraq's use of poison gas. Most Americans would conflate Iranians with Iraqis anyway, wouldn't care if we killed them all dead. If they knew that our navy shot down an Iranian 747, while in the Gulf to protect Iraqi ports, the departure points for their oil exports, they should kindly forget all about it, for SH was AH now. And he succeeded. Bush convinced the easily swayed that Saddam Hussein was evil incarnate yet he remained quite acquiescent with dictators from other nations when he felt it in the United State's best interest to look the other way. It took him far too long to recognize the independence of the Baltic States.

Thank God the Soviet Union had dissolved, that the communists had been ousted from power, the Commonwealth of Independent Nations formed, Bill thought.

Nor would Mr. Bush support the student democracy movement in China. A Real-politiker to the core, he refused to censure the Chinese leadership after the Tiananmen Square massacre. In the realm of foreign affairs American ideals of democracy and freedom apparently did not always rise foremost. Other considerations superseded them.

But when it came to supporting the archaic feudal regime in Kuwait—to protecting U.S. access to Middle Eastern oil—the President chose to commit American firepower and to hoodwink the population with all the old truisms and verities, those noble conceptions of justice and honor, God, country and apple pie. And the American public was complicitous. It allowed itself to be hoodwinked!

Willingly most citizens shut their eyes to what truly went on, accepted the cleaned-up sanitized military-authorized version of events. Billy called the President the Great Homogenizer, for George Herbert Walker Bush knew how to increase digestibility! Instead of confiding in the American people, instead of telling them the truth—that we fought for oil, period—he not only maintained that we combated aggression (which we did, but only because in this instance we found it in our best interest to do so), but also that we fought for liberty and freedom. What bunk, Billy thought. What complete and utter hogwash. The descendants of the minutemen who defied the tyranny of King George III fought to put a Kuwaiti Sheik back on his throne, to protect the Saudi royal family who had refused the common people any real rights and had given sanctuary to Idi Amin, the butcher of Uganda. Nor would Bush support the Kurds in their abortive uprising against Hussein. That might upset his Turkish and Russian allies who had large Kurdish populations of their own. He called for the people of Iraq to overthrow Saddam, but when the Kurds took him up, he refused them air cover and support. U.S. and coalition troops sat on the sidelines while Saddam slaughtered all his internal enemies. Bill shook his head in disgust, sickened by his government's dishonesty and double standards. He would teach his children not to observe passively and robotically, not to simply watch their televisions and cheer their "team" on or to blindly deck their homes with yellow ribbons and giant flags. Yes, support the troops, most of whom came from the lower classes (how many senators and congressmen had children in the Gulf?) but not a cause unless it proved truly a just cause. He recognized his former hypocrisy on this score, confessed it to himself and remained shamed by it. He remembered that during his years at the University of Pennsylvania, he had stood a model scholar, conservative and unassuming—the farthest thing from a longhaired war protestor. Happy and secure in the bosom of Academe, he had rejected the counterculture and hadn't feared the draft at all. He realized, too, that had he been a Chinese student in June 1989, he would not have stood in the ranks of the democracy movement but almost certainly would have remained an exemplary young Maoist. Now he looked on the anti-war demonstrators, the so-called radicals, as heroes. Yes, Da had been right. One could characterize life as a horrible Darwinian struggle. But it also remained something more, as well. He'd make sure that his children would see that "more" (he didn't know what to name or call the additional factor: the beautiful? the transcendent?) so that they'd savor and relish their time on this planet. His father had not tried to blind him toward this other component or convince him that it didn't exist. He had merely pinpointed it in a spot just as dubious as the place where he had said it had completely absented and negated itself. Da saw things too simplistically. He viewed England and America as repositories of goodness, Germany and Austria of evil. When Bill first realized that the United States did not live up to its high ideals, he suffered extreme disillusionment, wrote off the whole world, mankind, and retreated to his bunker, but now since emerging from his dugout, life's other element again made itself known to him. He wanted *his* kids to recognize the beautiful, the transcendent, in life, to become cognizant of, and to appreciate, the eternally questing side of man's nature accountable for the eternal symphonies, the great paintings and all the lauded plays and poems; for the pyramids, the acropolis and the Gothic cathedrals of Europe; for the world's scientific and technical achievements and for the advances in medicine. One could find this positive, vital force working everywhere, in all nations, in all people (though, alas, it often lay dormant). His father had been wrong to build an altar to yet one more false God: the United States of America, for Billy now experienced almost as deep a feeling of disappointment, of disenchantment with his nation, a land he dearly loved, as his father had with Germany and Austria. Yet within earshot of his children Bill would never call the United States a morally bankrupt nation—would never say that it lay beyond the powers of redemption—as his father had said about Germany and Austria. Da had been right to warn him that life consists in competition and conflict, and he would not try to shield his children from existence's darker realities. What remained glorious about man was that he persevered and endured in spite of those darker realities.

Yes, he'd teach his children that the Germans and the Austrians did not stand alone in sin, though their crimes remained particularly despicable, maybe even unique in modern times in that Hitler had wanted to wipe out an entire race. No advocate of cultural relativism, Bill would teach his children that the German leader's minions systematically carried out a diabolical policy of racial extermination. Yet he'd make sure that they knew about the atrocities of other nations as well, abominations which did not receive nearly as close scrutiny as did those of the Third Reich. How many Americans realized that Mao butchered twenty-five million people? At least in the 1950s *Time* magazine claimed that he ordered the liquidation of so many. Perhaps one could write off the report as red hysteria and government propaganda, another instance of the big lie in the U.S. The Chinese government of course disputed *Time's* findings. But if indeed Mao had killed so many or even more, as Presidential candidate Pat Buchanan maintained in a column from the late 1980s which Bill happened to read, it remained little publicized. Historians did not proclaim or widely disseminate it in their writings like they did the Holocaust. But then the United States wanted to maintain good relations with China. Richard Nixon had shaken hands and had drunk toasts with perhaps the biggest mass murderer of all time (if *Time* magazine and Pat Buchanan had their facts straight). Billy didn't know what to believe. Both explanations seemed plausible to him. We lied, or the Chinese did. One of the two.

China, after all, had joined the nuclear club. Nixon and Bush would insist that it remained an incumbent duty of any President to preserve and repair relations with a nation to which one out of every four people currently living on the globe claimed citizenship. Realpolitiks raised its ugly head once again.

Yes, Bill thought as he rounded the curve and came out of the tunnel of trees roaring, just about every American, even the most illiterate and uneducated, had heard about the Holocaust. Far fewer ordinary people—the men and women he met with on a daily basis—knew about Stalin's liquidation of twenty million (this despite all the new revelations coming out of Moscow since Glasnost), or cared about thirty million babies aborted in the United States since 1973. A lapsed Catholic, he couldn't say for sure if he still believed in God. Nonetheless he felt that the deaths of all those unborn children a crime against humanity and saw the abortion protestors as the John Browns of the present era. At least here, Bush and Reagan occupied the moral high ground. He also liked Bush for supporting the Palestinian quest for statehood. But as he continued getting himself even *more* lost in a remote corner of the county (he had no idea where he drove), he recalled again why his faith had lapsed and recollected the numerous crimes committed in the name of the church, how the Spaniards under Cortez destroyed the Mayan and the Aztec civilizations in Mexico, how the priests burned all the written documents of the former, destroyed the literature of an entire people in the name of Jesus. He recalled the crusades and how the "noble" knights had rounded up the Jews of Jerusalem and burned them in their synagogues. The Protestants did not fare any better. If not the first German to call for the extermination of the Jews, Martin Luther nonetheless maintained that they should be all put to the sword if they did not convert to Christianity. He wrote in *On the Jews and their Lies* (*Von den Jüden und ihren Lügen*) that the Jews are "base whoring people, that is no people of God, and that their boast of lineage, circumcision, and law must be accounted as filth," that they were "full of the devil's feces …which they wallow in like swine" and called their synagogue "an incorrigible whore and evil." He advocated the burning of all their places of worship and wrote "all who are able" should "toss sulphur and pitch" and that "it would be good if someone could also throw in some hellfire." He also demanded that "their prayer books, their Talmudic writings, also the entire Bible be taken from them, not leaving one leaf" and ended his little book with these words: "There is no other explanation for this than the one cited by Moses—namely, that God struck the Jews with madness and blindness and confusion of mind. So we are even at fault in not avenging all the innocent blood of our Lord and of the Christians which they shed for three hundred years after the destruction of Jerusalem, and the blood of the children they have shed since then (which still shines forth from their eyes and their skin). We are at fault for not slaying them. Rather we allow them to live freely in our midst despite all their murdering, cursing, blaspheming, lying and deforming; we protect and shield their synagogues and houses, life and property.

In this way, we make them lazy and secure and encourage them to fleece us boldly of our money and goods, as well as mock and deride us, with a view to finally overcoming us, killing us all for such a great sin, and robbing us of our property (as they daily pray and hope). Now tell me whether they do not have every reason to be the enemies of us accursed Goyim, to curse us and to strive for our final, complete, and eternal ruin."

One by one, Billy tallied all the religious wars he had ever read about and recalled the slaughter done in the name of God, the us-them syndrome in another of its disturbing manifestations. He remembered the rivers and lakes of blood shed as a result of the Reformation, due to Catholics and Protestants seeing each other as severed doctrinally past all dreams of rejointure. And even at this late date, they still slew each other in Northern Ireland! Nor did he forget the mutual blood letting of Moslems and Hindus who had worked hand in hand for India's independence in 1947 but who, as soon as they achieved that goal, turned on one another and slew each other left and right. More than five hundred thousand perished in those disorders and more than sixteen million fled for safety across the newly created borders of India and Pakistan. Nor did he forget the internecine struggle of Israelis and Arabs, horrible crimes committed on both sides initiating lasting hatred and suspicion between the two parties despite the fact their religious texts taught them that they both descended from Abraham, that they both shared the same blood. Not able to tolerate the presence of each other, unable to live in peace, the two sides would carry the conflict on, generation after generation, in perpetuity.

Then Billy reeled off the deity's own crimes against humanity (if despite what the scientists tell us, the deity did in fact exist). At least the ones that he had witnessed through the medium of television. Driving his car, he had a long flashback—saw again all the horror stories he had seen on the tube the last few years, the disasters of various types and kinds—earthquakes, typhoons, floods—and all the terrible diseases human beings, even little children, suffered from. How, he asked himself, could any thinking man believe in a benevolent father in Heaven? Yes, he could make the leap of unfaith. He believed in a cold, mechanistic, godless universe and saw the planet as one large killing field. Yet despite all life's horror, man's creative spirit continued its upward flight. His father knew about man's resourcefulness and potential and had even made Billy aware of it but only as a matter of peripheral importance, as something of small account. Yes, it did exist, but could it ever compensate for all the blackness? He, on the other hand, would convince his kids that this relatively negligible and nonessential thing (at least according to his father) belonged to all mankind, the entire species, that on the contrary, it existed somehow in the very essence of our being—in one's self as well as all others—and that we should cultivate it like some beauteous, abundantly flowering plant.

But his father would say that to give their own particular plant more air, room, and space, people would out of jealousy always tramp down and destroy the flowerings of others, that one had to fight and compete so that one's own plant would survive. Bill couldn't compete, so he withdrew indoors, but now he had grown stronger. He stood ready to battle for his future sons and daughters so that they could participate, strive and struggle, so that they could feel within themselves man's unsatisfiable questing spirit, his eternal aspiration to raise himself higher and higher....

Eventually he found his way back to town, though the sun had set six or seven hours prior to his reaching his driveway. He pushed the red button and the garage door groaned then began its slow rise on the rollers, and he drove the car in, stepped through the screen door into the old pantry off the kitchen of his big, many-roomed house, but he went directly up the stairs and slung himself onto the bed and within an hour or two slept. He awoke early in the morning, a morning not special in any way though the day would turn out to be a red-letter day and would mark his great conquest. He, of course, had no foreknowledge of what would happen later that afternoon or when he awoke he would certainly have bestirred himself in front of his mirror and faucet. He just squinted at his reflected image not wanting to really look at it, either inwardly envisaging a more becoming countenance—a face still not double chinned—or else trying to avoid a good glance at his twin because if he looked at him full in the face he'd start making faces at him, start grinning and grimacing like a bald albino ape, and he would have to laugh, even if he would never stop once he started. It happened at the mall. Shortly after noon, he visited Waldenbooks and National Record Mart but didn't buy anything. Cindy Daughenbaugh made the trip to purchase a pair of new shoes. They bumped into each other in front of the splashing fountain where older people and mothers with young children sat on wood benches and watched the water, either taking a breather and resting before resuming shopping or waiting for someone else, the person they came with, to "get done and finish up" so that they could go home. She asked if he had any free time and when he answered in the affirmative wondered if he could help her with a problem at home, so he followed her to her apartment, his car bumper to bumper with hers: a red Corvette. She needed to change the lock on her doors as she had lost a set of keys. She stood beside him as he knelt on her red tiles with a Phillips screwdriver. It took him some time to figure it out. "Basic mechanics is not my strong suit," he said—a feeble attempt on his part at a quip or a witticism. But in four or five minutes he had the old lock out and the new one in. He stood up and wiped his brow. She asked if he would like a glass of wine. "Why thank you," he answered. "Sit down, sit down," she said. So he sat back in one of her chairs just beyond the red tiles of the entryway. He could see her in her kitchen in front of the small range standing on tiptoe to open a cupboard, out of which she removed the wine glasses. He made himself comfortable as she reached over to pull open her refrigerator, then she suddenly stood opposite him with the bottle in her hands, taking her seat on the other side of the glass table. They talked. He didn't really tune into what she said but played his role of courteous listener to the hilt, appeared attentive and interested. Suddenly she sprang up and turned on her TV. How could she stand to live in such cramped quarters, what they called an efficiency? His interim address, the apartment he had moved into before purchasing the large Victorian dwelling with its spacious veranda with fancy intricate woodwork—especially the ornate corbels supporting the overhanging weight of the porch roof also upheld by columns—had been much more spacious. He had paid much higher rent of course; nonetheless he found all her furniture modern and stylish. She flipped through the channels and told him to go ahead and pour them each a glass. He reached for the bottle. He hadn't taken a sip of alcohol in years. In the past, during his years in the bunker, he had ordered beer delivered to his old address now and again. For a period of time the bottles had come in weekly, but for the last four or five of the eighteen years he spent inside, he hadn't sampled or downed any adult beverages whatsoever. Eventually he had grown bored with drinking. He had a protracted fling with the bottle but in the end gave up the habit, as he disliked the morning hangovers and pissing all night.

A Presidential candidate made a stump speech on the tube. Bill hoped she wouldn't bring the conversation round to politics as his might not agree with hers. He believed one party as corrupt as the other and found the system dishonest and morally bankrupt. He could have thrown her set off the stand and smashed it. Since his rebirth, he hadn't watched any news stories though he did read the papers. He had been addicted to staring at a television for so long that he never wanted to waste time in front of one again. But he didn't dare destroy her set. He remained non-committal but extraordinarily polite when she queried him about the coming election—so, oh so very interested.

She kept refilling his glass. Really lit after the second and third drink, he nonetheless determined to keep right up with her, as she showed no signs of slowing down. Suddenly her face came up close to his. Their lips grazed. His heart beat rapidly in his breast, but he forced himself to hold back—at least for a few seconds. But then she brushed his cheek with her fingertips, and he leaned into, entered, her kiss but only to again draw back but not so quickly. He started and shied out of hesitation, but she soon overpowered him and wouldn't let go or unloosen her grip. She drew him down to the rug. He closed his eyes, opened his mouth, and her tongue entered it. Totally passive, his head propped up against the foot of the chair, he let her bite the lobe of his ear then her lips descended to his throat and neck but when she started undoing his shirt buttons he pushed her away and said no. He had terrible scars on his arm and back. She pulled his head into her shoulder, cradled him in her arms for he didn't know how long. It seemed an eternity. At last he felt ready, and suddenly he became the aggressor. "Only if you take off your shirt," she said. "I won't with you dressed." So he surrendered his garment, let her take it off. She brushed her hand across his scarred back. He shuddered as she planted her lips on his shoulder and kissed again and again the area of his injury, the mark of his near immolation.

After that day, for the next three or four weeks at least, they kept in each other's company a good bit of the time. Cindy Daughenbaugh, he learned, had just turned twenty-four years old. She worked as a part-time secretary for a Real Estate agent but also took classes at the University as well, where she had changed her major so many times in the three or four years she had been enrolled there, several colleges had written her off. Her latest faculty advisor said that she flitted like a bee and would never graduate. Yet she persevered. She came from a flyspeck town one hundred twenty miles distant, where her dad had worked as a guidance counselor, senior history teacher, and track coach. The local New Life Center had also elected him as a church elder. She said that she thought of herself as "a kind of born-again Christian," though unlike some of her friends, she didn't consider the Catholic Church a cult. She granted that Catholics were Christians too. She shared her generation's passion for openness and freedom and passionately believed in a woman's right to an abortion. Bill cringed when she confessed that like many other girls circumstances had forced her to have a termination. She announced this fact to him very early, a sort of test or challenge. And no she had never told her father or family, it was really none of their concern or business, only that of the man who was then screwing her. He told her to have the abortion, that he didn't want to get married. He was older than she and (she later learned) already wed. A sweet talker, he had spent a lot of money on her. She continued talking but Bill had stopped listening. If she could spare her father and not disclose this to him why could she not do the same with him? He didn't want to know about her past, but now that he did, he'd have to deal and make terms with it. Her revelation would forever tinge the way he'd think about her. A part of him could not help but see her as a modern-day Medea. If he ever deserted her for someone else, he wondered, would she kill the children, her rival, then set torch to the palace and flee into the night? On the rebound from Gil, the married man with lots of bucks, she married Trevor MacNeil, a bricklayer whom she met in her father's church, but he hit her, so despite her parents' objections they divorced and she moved here and studiously avoided men until she met Bill. She had learned how not to get pregnant the three years she spent with Trevor. Thank God she didn't have any children to the man....

At long last she exhausted herself—wore herself out talking—and stopped. He would have liked very much to have told her to do so a half-hour before. He refrained out of tact, again realizing the part of the solicitous lover, the humble good man understanding to a fault. During their first months together, however, he experienced only a few such awkward and painful moments in her company. Her body still arrested him and offered him recourse for his boredom. On a basic, animalistic level, they suited one another quite well. Also he found their outings together, when they went some short distance away—usually to some rural spot not too far from Slippery Rock—adequately diverting. Together they enjoyed the local color and visited many picturesque places. He dreamed about taking her much farther away to Germany and Switzerland. She said that yes she'd travel but not just quite yet. "Just how much money do you have?" she then asked. "Quite enough to keep us comfortable," he said, and the interrogation began. She dug for all the particulars of his life story. Reluctantly Billy opened up. One by one he drew back all the curtains hiding his privacies. He didn't like divulging his secrets. Again he felt uncomfortable and queasy. But as he still lusted and yearned for her attractive, ample and generous body, he submitted and answered briefly and concisely all her questions—underwent torture comparable to the extraction of teeth without anesthetic, praying that she would have done with all her questioning soon—that they would get the cross-examination and grilling behind them as quickly as possible.

They kept in each other's company constantly, did everything together. In eight weeks' time, he had met numerous friends and acquaintances of hers and found himself playacting in front of them, too, assuming his role of smitten lover and perfect and flawless boyfriend. Even if he found an individual boring or tedious, he did not let on. He did not want to come across as rude or arrogant to anyone whom Cindy liked. Alas, she did not only have female friends. Kurt Kovacs behaved like a brother to her. Or so she said. They had grown up together in the same town. Bill found him very good looking and wondered why she picked him over Kurt. Kovacs had the superior build and was her own age. He displayed his athletic prowess on all occasions, and he and Cindy often exercised together. Cindy reassured him again and again that he was her friend, nothing more.

Eventually they reached the point where they could stand to be apart. Alone in the tower of the Steamboat, Bill remembered how his father had once in conversation advocated (perhaps in jest, perhaps in earnest he was not certain) the highly regulated existence and monastic manner of life that men and women had led to a large degree in the Middle Ages, how he applauded the perpetual segregation of the sexes. He considered their mode of life, he said, of the best possible design. The sexes lived without complaint. Indeed that day he argued that men and women should for the most part deny themselves and practice abstinence. But the system, he winked confidentially, a real twinkle of joy in his eye, was also contrived to maximize those exquisite and rapturous moments of sinfulness associated with the occasional breaking of one's vows, of denying, disavowing, allegiance to one's own sex, to dally with the other. Da remained a man of contradictions, someone who always saw both sides of a question, for in other conversations he of course argued the importance of the family unit and carrying on the line of descent. While he deeply loved Bill's mother, he also warned Bill to regard women as potential foes—as especially dangerous enemies.

Apparently, Bill thought, the men and women of the Middle Ages whom Da spoke of could taste of the forbidden fruit once or twice and then forswear it, renounce and give it up. But could Billy? He didn't think so. He wanted to just keep eating. If he saw through Cindy's simulation and charade, he refused to acknowledge it. He wanted her, badly and continuously. She satisfied all his needs, so he had no trouble putting blinders on. He gave her the benefit of the doubt. He suspected that she didn't tell him the whole truth concerning her relationship with Kurt Kovacs, yet deep down he remained glad of it. He didn't wish to pry into her prior life—wouldn't question her as relentlessly as she had questioned him. He always gave the best possible construction and interpretation to any and all of her actions. He tended to idealize her and to accept and shrug off any little white lies she told.

Did Cindy want to entice him into marriage? Did she think him easy to deceive and dupe? *Does she boast to her friends that she can wrap me around her little finger? That she finds me malleable, compliant, and acquiescent?*

Bill had to put his own needs foremost. Again he felt conflicted. Abstinent for so long, a part of him wanted to service any and all comers. He dreamed and fantasized about finding himself standing within a budding grove in the shadow of young girls in flower. He wondered if he should play the field and court several women simultaneously. He understood why one might want to establish a redundancy, an excess or superabundance of women. The Mohammedan saw the advantage of keeping numerous wives and concubines, his harem a sacred place, forbidden to infidels. William also saw the genius behind the Indian practice of purdah. In an ideal world, he would maintain his own walled seraglio and make all his women wear the veil. He would play one against the other in order to obtain mastery over the entire group. A single mistress can break her lover and gain her own way by withholding sex, but by taking many wives the Mohammedan stripped such power from the hands of all, for if one wife became difficult he could always find solace in another set of open arms and parted legs. He doubted if the wives and concubines would ever band together in solidarity. They would remain jealous and competitive with one another for such was woman's spirit and disposition, her innate character. Alas, however, Bill remained a child of the West. Perhaps Cindy was not his perfect match but she had chosen and accepted him and he availed himself of all that she offered and did not now want to go without. Perhaps no other opportunity would arise, build hougongs and castles in the air as he might. Moreover he wanted to sire a child. If she would agree to that, he could overlook almost anything, for he wanted to silence the demands of Da and the other forebears.

Then he met Cindy's former hubby Trevor MacNeil. One day he rapped on the door of Cindy's apartment, and she let him in. He asked to borrow money. Cindy had none to spare, so Bill paid him out of his own pocket so that he would leave. On the scant evidence presented him in an exchange lasting at most ten minutes, Bill judged MacNeil a know-nothing and boor. Born and raised in Altoona, he had later moved to Cindy's hometown. His reserve unit had been called up to fight in the war. He boasted that he had been stationed in Saudi and that he had helped put down the aggression of one of the worst tyrants in history. He wanted to make damn sure that Bill knew it, too. William felt certain that "the anthropoid brute" (to use one of Da's expressions) standing before him didn't know anything about the exterminations of Stalin, Mao, or Pol Pot. *The illiterate doesn't realize that we bankrolled Saddam for years and years.* William wanted to shake his head in exasperation. Once more he vowed that he would teach his children to have morals and not to become cheering or worse indifferent spectators, sleepwalkers blindly playing follow the leader. He chatted to McNeil but remained well mannered and affable if also reserved through their entire brief encounter. With types like him walking about Billy found it hard to retain his hope in humanity or to see life as anything more than a mad, Darwinian struggle.

As for Cindy, William looked the other way. If she wanted to fool and outsmart him, he'd let her. He would accept any cover story she came up with as the Gospel truth.

Did he feel that a crisis impended? From his father's writings about his maternal ancestors, he had learned that we all stood doomed, but he did not care to stare into the abyss any longer. He would face whatever fate awaited him when the time came. He didn't know what he would do or how he would react when the hammer blow finally fell, but until it did, he would rejoice in his life. Henceforward he would not look to or consider his end. He would make do. He would put on his rose-colored glasses and find consolation in Cindy's arms.

How he loved looking into her face. He could stare at her, he claimed, for hours at a time. Her hair stretched all the way to her shoulders and he enjoyed running his fingers through it and bringing his face down and sniffing its fragrant scent after she stepped from the shower at first light. Often she would ask him to comb and brush it, her cobalt blue eyes sparkling and her small, shapely chin outthrust. She continued to captivate and delight him as she made her morning toilette, applied her cosmetics and hummed the tune of some country music song. As they breakfasted together, he told her that she looked beautiful: good enough to eat. She smiled or laughed but constantly looked down at her watch for most mornings she found herself running a little late. William knew to stay out of her way as she packed her lunch and readied her school and work things. He looked on lovingly, drank her in with his eyes, as she made ready to depart. He wanted to absorb her image and sop it up, he said, so that a part of her would remain with him when she left, so that he could still hug her close when she went out the door. She kissed him a final time. He returned to their bedroom and lay back down. He smelled her hair oil on the pillow. Desire clutched him, but he closed his eyes. Often he would succeed in drifting off but first he would luxuriate in an interrealm between sleep and waking. Memories of their lovemaking the night before would flood and fuel his reverie but then blackness would overpower him and pull him down like a drowning man. He would find himself fighting the darkness and striving again for the light and at last he would achieve consciousness but feel benumbed and hung over although he hadn't been drinking. He would lie for a time blinking, the light streaming in at his windows even though the Venetian blinds were closed. Clutching his pillow he would again Cindy-meditate. Once more his internal seas would begin to churn and roil ahummer and afroth with whitecaps and he would thrash and twitch in torment. A moment before all remained placid and becalmed but now long breakers humped muscled backs and raised trembling combs that tipped over at the greenest summit, and he felt divided from his heart. Again he felt the muscular urge and the blending, again he engaged in a form of intimacy that he found the sweetest surrender. Time was canceled and annulled. Again they lay beside each other and again she initiated him in Eleusinian mysteries. Again he worshipped at the altars of Demeter and Persephone. Once more he tasted the maternal mystery below the belly.

He recalled how he unbuckled and unzipped her pants and how every so often, she lifted her hips so that he could glimpse what he tasted. The folds of her sex, the small pout they made, fascinated him. Again she sloshed against his face and he tasted the seed that he had spilled there.

Yes, he recognized all her flaws and faults. But he refused to acknowledge what he saw. She offered him too much in recompense. He would never contradict her, and, if they disagreed in their political opinions, he would only seldom take issue with her and often would feign agreement instead. Indeed he tried to see matters from her perspective.

He found himself capitulating on all fronts. She said that she only wanted one child. He wanted to have three or four children. They would have to broach that matter at a later date. Except for one occasion he had faithfully worn prophylactics, so the matter could be deferred for the time being. He knew her stand on reproductive rights, and, well yes, he had to admit her arguments had some moral suasion. He didn't like the idea of an intrusive fascist government intruding in what needless to say was a very personal decision. But this he had to weigh against the slaughter of all the innocents. She constantly told Bill that he didn't take enough interest in the upcoming election. She said that she always voted Democratic and that she hadn't made up her mind between Jerry Brown and Bill Clinton but that she leaned toward the latter. Once he made the mistake of saying that reproductive rights weren't a burning issue for most of the electorate.

"Oh no," she said. "You're wrong there."

"No I'm not. The state of the economy, the recession, trumps everything."

"Maybe for you men."

"Yes, yes. It should remain only your decision."

"Whom does the responsibility ultimately devolve upon? Answer me that?"

"I should say it falls equally on the shoulders of both parties."

"There you are wrong, Bill. The baby feeds off of the woman's body, receives its nourishment from her blood. It is she who in the end always has to make the sacrifice. You men do nothing but gewgaw over your little ones. Most of you are totally inept when it comes to caring for a child. Ninety-nine percent of the burden falls on the mother. Don't even start to tell me what it's like carrying a baby in your belly. You just don't know."

Swimming, eating, sleeping, doing everything imaginable with her—glad when she stood beside him but sometimes relieved when out of her presence—he nonetheless now and then still experienced sudden and quite gnawing suspicions about what she did when out of ear-and-eye shot, especially during her longer absences—if she stayed away and didn't contact him for two or three days at a time. Once when she said that she would be visiting her mother for a week, he followed her to the flyspeck town but at its lip could not proceed and made a u-turn at the last minute instead. What if she saw his car and thought that he spied on her? He decided to camp out at a state forest some ten miles distant. He paid six dollars for a site, watched the kids swimming in the dark water and then looked off in the distance at the canoeists, the paddle and pontoon boat operators, at swallows diving under a bridge from which fishermen cast their lines. At his side, at the docks, an old woman in a floppy hat fed fighting mother blue-wing teal ducks and their omnivorous little ducklings. The two dams repeatedly tried to chase off each other's chicks so that their own could eat all the pellets, bullets of bread. All the ducklings tried to outswim each other and reach the floating crumbs first. They squawked and pecked at their own brothers and sisters as well as the other chicks. Each rushed to gobble up the new handfuls of bread the woman tossed before other ravenous bills could arrive and nudge theirs to the side. As the day wore on, the sky clouded over and at nightfall it started raining and William decided to leave the campsite and find a motel. As he drove down the winding, curving road back to town in the dark, the woods lit up in the light-ning flashes. Fat frogs or toads (he didn't know which) hopped across the road to the other side but also straight down it. He slowed his speed and tried to steer around them, not wanting to flatten their plump, leaping bodies with his tires. Patches of mist rose off the macadam as the road ascended and he rounded curves both to the right and left. Then it began to both hail and rain at the same time. He could barely see when a truck came careening around an elbow. High beams to his face, Bill closed his eyes. He opened them after the truck had passed him—and blinking could still not see. The rain started falling in streams, and Bill began to feel a little scared and frantic. His heart started thud-ding in his chest and his face perspired. He had prided himself on his driving, but he lost confidence in his ability under these circumstances and conditions: motoring on a dark and unfamiliar road, his visibility greatly impaired due to a spring storm. All the faith he had in his skill as a driver evaporated, and he wanted to pull off to the side and wait it out, but a vehicle—he couldn't tell for certain but probably a jeep or pickup—came right up behind him. The other driver would have to remain content to follow at a snail's pace. He'd be crazy to pass, but a high-performance sports car inching ahead of him at ten or fifteen miles an hour would probably make him chuckle. Billy pushed away the rear-view mirror, got the pickup's headlights out of his sight, and continued driving. At least the deer would stay huddled deep somewhere in the forest and he wouldn't have to worry about one of them jumping out in front of him. Uphill, downhill, the road seemed to roll and stretch on forever. Finally the rain started to slack, and soon it only drizzled. Bill then put his foot down hard to show the guy in the pickup, left behind in the wet, what his car could do. Then he passed out of the woods entirely, rounded a curve by a hospital and went down a last hill into town. He had had quite a scare. He felt several belts of alcohol would steady him, so he looked for a bar, found one, but the street it sat on had parking only on one side, so he had to go around the block. He turned onto an adjacent street, saw an empty place and took it, deciding to hoof it back to the bar. As he approached the bar—a blue neon sign, The Oasis, blazed in the window—from across the street, he saw two people going in, and he recognized Cindy Daughenbaugh and Kurt Kovacs. He quickly ducked back around the corner. He couldn't believe it but there they stood. His eyes hadn't lied to him. His desire not to know, he realized, outweighed any curiosity he had. He didn't wish to subject himself to nagging doubts and all the rigma-role attendant to the silly, stock, run-of-the-mill situation in which he suddenly found himself. And why shouldn't he take her word? She had said that she and Kurt had known each other for years, that they had practically grown up together. If they both visited home at the same time why wouldn't they go out for a drink? He did not want to waste time, that precious quantity given to us all in such unequal portions, uneven allotments, making recriminations or becoming jealous.

No, he didn't wish to feel sick and rueful about her. Nor did he want to feel mad insane rage boiling up inside him. He did not tend to the melodramatic anyway. Could she push him toward the edge? Only if he permitted her. But he had the strength and power to shut his dark suspicions out, not let the evidence of his own eyes bother him or rather not make mountains out of molehills. Naturally he had grown a bit queasy about her past association with Kurt, but he brushed his misgivings aside with a brusque sweep of his hand. And then one night several weeks later, she said let's make a baby. He again took her without wearing anything, and his skin rubbed against hers in fricative ecstasy.

He wouldn't have it any other way thereafter. But what if she actually did become pregnant? He didn't care. He stood that committed to their relationship. In fact, it would make him happy. Six weeks later she came rushing home to him in the Steamboat and announced with a smile that her home pregnancy test had turned out positive. Marry him? Yes, of course she would. He enfolded her in his arms, and, from that moment on, he started daydreaming about his future life with his wife and son. For he knew the baby would be a boy. He had won out, for she agreed to become his wife and even if he still harbored undisclosed, private doubts, if he secretly feared that she might be carrying Kovac's child instead of his own or that she didn't know herself which of the two had fathered her baby, it didn't matter. If she married him, he had won. Henceforward, he would have her all to himself. He wanted and needed her, for she completed him and made him whole, and he would eventually father a child on her. Next time she became pregnant he would make certain that the baby was his, for her resolve had crumbled, her resolution had given way when at last he showed some spine and told her that he wanted at least three children and that he'd only marry her if she would agree to have three. And she said yes.

So he had to meet her relatives, present himself to her father and mother. Unlike him she still had hers on this side. They prospered and throve whereas his mother and father had both died long before. He liked and tried to impress his future in-laws and did everything which he could on his part to make the wedding less burdensome, less onerous for them. He agreed to wed Cindy in the sanctuary of the New Life Center and to have their minister Dr. Allport H. Weiler conduct the service. Her parents both believed that one took marriage vows for life. They took literally "for better or worse," but they had lately come to reconsider their position. MacNeil had proved a selfish brute and if he hit her then she stood well within her rights to demand a divorce. They should have supported Cindy more fully in the past. It saddened them that they had failed to stand by her in her hour of need. They'd do anything to make up for that now.

Bill started arranging their honeymoon trip to Europe. They would tour nine countries and he would finally visit all the places he had only read about or else seen images broadcast from on his television set or as the Germans dubbed the device, *der Fernsehapparat* or "far-away seeing apparatus." A quite literal name. But the English verb broadcast conveyed an equally primary meaning. To make available for everyone. To cast or scatter in all directions as seed from the hand in sowing, as signals sent from a television transmitting station, as bread crumbs tossed or thrown into the water for hungry and aggressive little ducklings.

They would fly to Frankfurt, take a cruise up the Rhine into Holland where they would embark, set sail, for England and then after several weeks in the British Isles they'd cross over the channel back to the continent to Normandy. Then they'd travel on to Paris, spend some time there before trekking to Switzerland and over the alps into Italy and down the whole length of the boot to the port of Brindisi and the blue waves of the Adriatic and on across the water to the isles of Greece. How nice it would have been to take a train up through Yugoslavia straight to Vienna, but war had erupted yet once again in the Balkans. He had read in the newspaper that chaos reigned in Yugoslavia and that the country would likely split into three nations, that Serbs, Croats, and Bosnians warred against one another, so they'd fly to Austria from Greece and from there proceed back into Germany. She would have to apply for her passport (he already had his) and they would both need a battery of shots, for they planned to travel to the Mediterranean as well as to northern Europe. Bill had a thousand and one things to do and arrange to make the trip an actuality. He sat for hours on the phone speaking to travel agents and would continue to do so for the next six weeks, the entire interval between the present time and their somewhat hastily settled-on wedding date. He wanted to book all the hotel rooms in advance. Whatever it cost, he could cover—foot—the bill, for he had the necessary reserves of capital. Cash always smoothed away difficulties and expedited things. Still he had a great deal to set up and coordinate, plenty of troubling and annoying fine points to work out. If he took responsibility for planning the honeymoon, the wedding itself fell on the capable shoulders of Cindy and her parents. He and Cindy met only infrequently as each had much on their hands with their separate undertakings. He wondered if she had told her parents Sam and Ellen about the baby. Of course, she didn't show yet and wouldn't in six-weeks' time either. Or did she feel her pregnancy as private a matter as her termination? He wondered if knowledge of their daughter's condition would change their opinion of him? If they didn't know now they would soon enough. She could hide her pregnancy for only so long after all. At least he hadn't taken her virginity, but would they still accuse them of grave sin, of committing fornication and adultery? Because of their beliefs they might feel a little hurt and troubled, but even so they must realize what a catch their daughter had reeled in. If for no other reason (and although he did like them, he didn't doubt them any less venial and small-minded than the rest of the common lot), they'd appreciate and esteem him for his money.

Rutger would act as William's best man, and he would invite only one relative on his side, his Uncle Roger Corl. That pleased his future father-in-law Sam, a big hulking man, in fighting shape for his age. He had a vice-like grip and he liked to slap you on the back and talk football or basketball. Despite his height, girth, and general robustness something stood out or hung about his features which made him look slightly infirm and sickly. Bill had trouble putting his finger on it. His future father-in-law had a thatch of snow-white hair and a very light complexion, very pale skin, but that was not it exactly. It was something about his eyes. His irises seemed colorless—gray—and his lips, instead of being pink, had a purplish hue. Cindy's mother, on the other hand, tried to hide her age by dyeing her hair a dark-reddish brown which seemed as out of place as scarlet lipstick or green eye shadow would be on her much worn and wrinkled, still heavily freckled face.

Pa had thrown Cindy one big wedding already where he invited everyone, his aunt and uncle. He didn't think it appropriate to do that again, but he insisted on a church wedding—he felt anything less undignified for his daughter. He would restrict the invitees to her immediate family and maybe a few select friends. It pleased him that Cindy had finally found someone who recognized her value and worth. He felt great confidence in Bill, and knew that he would cherish, protect and provide for his daughter. Everything settled, they shook hands, and he requested William to share a bottle of wine with his future dad. Billy graciously accepted his offer, but as he raised the glass to his lips, thought: *No you never could replace my Da. But then no one could.* After many glasses, many toasts to each other's health and good fortune, Sam began to drunkenly ramble on about what a real SOB Cindy's first husband Trevor had turned out when at last he showed (and they for the first time saw) his true colors. That bastard really had everyone fooled. Mr. Daughenbaugh paused then enunciated the next word slowly, with relish: "Buffaloed." They had thought him a sincere Christian who believed like they did, and well he had to confess that, despite all that happened, he still thought the boy displayed some admirable traits. He had proved himself a hero in the Gulf. But Cindy was just too fine-grained for him. He remained too earthy and she too ethereal. That's all. But he never should have raised his hand against her. Nothing could justify that. Oh he understood how someone like Cindy could really infuriate a man. She's matured a lot since then, but as a girl she never did anything, didn't help around the house, and her mother proved a perfect angel and let her get away with it. Back when she and Trevor became engaged maybe she knew how to boil an egg or cook spaghetti but not much else and as a teenager she always left her room a mess, clothes and underwear on the floor, a ton of junk under her bed, pushed there in a hurry to get it out of sight. If he expected a cook and homemaker, Trevor no doubt felt sadly shortchanged. And she could be so selfish and willful. He supposed that she still remained stubborn about certain things. Oh in public, at a school or a church function, she appeared the proper young lady to a t, but at home, in private, she often pulled ferocious temper tantrums. She fought viciously not so much with him but with his wife, her mother. He lowered his voice. Sometimes she even went so far as to call her own flesh and blood an effing bitch. He shook his head. He would never have said such a thing to his mother, nor would his wife have dared to say such a thing to hers. They respected their elders. He didn't know where the young folks picked up their manners these days, certainly not from them—people, that is, of his generation. Yes, his daughter had a mean streak and in addition, to tell the truth, he often found her wild and rebellious. Yes, he understood how she could provoke someone like Trevor. Early in their marriage, he discovered just how hard she could make things. Arguing with her, he felt like he ran into a brick wall. He couldn't cope with her obtuseness. Mulish and intractable, she wouldn't do anything around the house, let the dishes stack up, never volunteered to run a load of laundry, et cetera, et cetera. If he didn't address her in a nice enough manner, right away she'd start. She'd begin to sass and insult him and wouldn't let up until she unleashed a torrent of abuse. Finally it reached the point where he could not stand it any more. She wouldn't shut up, and he became so angry he snapped and slapped her a good one, the only defense, he said, open to him, the only way to make her quiet. He felt ashamed afterward, came to him, her father, and confessed what happened, and we knelt down and prayed together in the living room. We told them to enter Christian counseling, but Cindy grew hysterical and said that she wanted a divorce. We did everything to dissuade her at the time and even agreed to foot the bill for the counseling and then all the expenses of the divorce if afterwards she still wanted to go through with it. She owed the marriage that, we said. She had made a commitment at the altar, and he had only struck her once hard across the face. I guess that's why he came to us and told us that he wanted to give the marriage a second chance. He had grown hot and lost his temper. He promised that it would not happen again. After hearing his story, we sided with him and supported a reconciliation but then she came to the house bruised and bleeding and we—if we didn't completely change our minds—certainly reconsidered things, and agreed at least that for now a separation stood in everyone's best interests. But after a few days she left our house, filed for a divorce herself, and departed from town. We still see Trevor from time to time. It's unavoidable since we go to the same church.

A few days after his conversation with her father, William approached Cindy about her husband and the beating he had given her. He proved such a caveman, she said, that she soon discovered that she could work him like a puppet. They didn't belong together. She had quickly realized that. So much smarter than he, she could not help but reach the conclusion that she should not remain hitched, tied, and bound to someone with such scant intelligence, that she should not waste her potentialities. The slap stood as a good excuse for her to go to her parents and put an end to a marriage which she should never have entered to begin with. Nonetheless she believed that he did in fact love her, for he whimpered like a sick child or a badly injured animal. Yes, despite his lower than normal intelligence, he did in his own way care for her, but, in the ardency of his desire to possess and cage her, he had grown obsessed to the point of mental illness. Her parents saw his pain, and Jesus had his claws into all three of them. He shared their religious prejudices and all the same hypocrisies. Why had she become mixed up with him in the first place? Well, he looked damned handsome at the time, she so susceptible and lonely because of Gil. She needed a man to share her life with. She had picked the wrong one, that was all. As soon as he realized that it had come to an end, the better for both of them, but her damn parents had to take his side, and she had no money. She needed their support, but they wouldn't budge. She found getting slugged a few times far less painful than putting up with a Christian marriage counselor for six or seven months, so she had, she confessed, set him up. She knew if she came home battered and bleeding that her parents would give in to her wishes and would cease to make any more serious objections. She had to move around and skirt the roadblock they had thrown up in front of her, the six months of Christian counseling she had agreed to enroll for. And Trevor proved so dumb, so easy to manipulate, that she easily tricked him into punching her in the face. He never realized that he had done exactly what she wanted him to do, and she made it sound even worse to her parents than it actually was. She cried a lot and put a real performance on in front of them. How did she manage to manipulate Trevor into striking her? By insulting his mother, she answered.

Bill's friend Rutger Poell, the successful Florida attorney, advised him to make Cindy Daughenbaugh sign a pre-nuptial agreement, and he offered to draw up such a document for him for free. "Don't take this wrong, Bill," he said. "Don't become angry with me." He spoke only as a friend now. He should protect himself. Sure he would gladly stand as his best man. That went without saying, but certain women—not Cindy per se—but quite a few females he felt reasonably certain—would have no qualms about stooping so low as to marry a wealthy man fully intending to ditch him in two or three years and then take him to the cleaners for all that he was worth. He, Rutger, wrote out such agreements all the time in his practice. And the beauty of such a document he had to confess lay in the fact that if the couple divorced due to circumstances not the wife's fault the man still remained fully protected. Look at Donald Trump's foresight. I know, Bill, I know. You say that you have fully committed to the girl. I hear you. But what about two or three years down the line, not to mention eight or nine years? People change. They fall in and out of love all the time. Over half of American marriages end in divorce. No, no, no. I only offer you a sound tip, some free professional advice. A lawyer's guidance, that's all.

The more he thought about it, Billy Steiglitz realized the wisdom of his friend's words, but he couldn't summon the courage to ask Cindy to sign a pre-nup. She held all the cards, possessed greater control and command than he. Her allure and his continuing fascination restrained and inhibited him. He didn't want to rock the apple cart, to do anything to upset her or make her angry with him, and he could see her becoming very upset with him if he asked her to put her signature to such an agreement. Goddam Rutger anyway.

His friend did not plant seeds of doubt about Cindy in his head. They already lay lodged and deposited, but Rutger's remarks did momentarily unblinker him. His self-imposed blinders removed, his previous reservations once again surfaced. Did she truly love him, or did she agree to marry him merely because he had money? Once more jealously gripped him, dug in its claws until he bled. His misgivings about the exact nature of her relationship with Kurt Kovacs again arose and they tore him up. He realized that we "act" to some degree in all our relationships, present ourselves differently to different people. Yes, we always put on and take off masks. Exchange them whenever it seems convenient. You could never absolutely know who someone was.

His internal debate went on for days. Did she purposely allow herself to become pregnant in order to trap him into proposing to her? Did she realize that having a baby would insure her success? Did Kurt on the sidelines encourage her to set him up? Did she believe that she could just as easily deceive and dupe him as she had brazenly admitted and declared that she had done her first husband Trevor? Was the baby even his? Could Kurt have fathered it? He looked devilishly handsome and probably broke records in the bedroom, but he remained penniless, not marriage material. But that wouldn't stop her from still seeing him for sex, and that all the time, even after she had become involved with Billy. No, stop, he told himself peremptorily, for he had determined to close his eyes to all her possible offenses and transgressions. He wanted, needed, had to have her, and after all those offences and misdeeds might not really exist. They might remain products of his own sick and overly fertile imagination, something he invented. *But, stupid, what if your doubts do prove true? They easily might, and in that case you allowed the wool to be pulled over your eyes and have no one to blame but yourself.* He could envision the good-looking Kurt pushing and egging her on. She'd do anything to please him. Maybe when she first detected her pregnancy she thought that she had better have another abortion because she didn't know which of the two had fathered her child, but Kurt urged her to have the baby anyway and to then reel in her mark. It stood doubtful whether he would demand a paternity test. He probably wouldn't, Kurt argued, and then at least on the books the state would list the child as his, and since at least officially she had borne him a son or daughter, she could demand an even bigger settlement when the divorce finally came, and, by golly, he would have to pay child support, too.

Billy Steiglitz considered himself fortunate and blessed in that he had the ability to tell himself to put certain thoughts out of his mind, and that then, through an act of Teutonic willpower, he could follow his own directives and obey himself. Once more he vowed to squash his suspicions. Maybe President Bush had the same ability. Surely he did not believe his own propaganda, but maybe he almost could. If you tell yourself something so long perhaps you really start to believe it. Bill intuited that his and Cindy's relationship would reach a crisis point. He feared that something would happen to spoil his happiness, but he successfully drove those thoughts from his mind, and, as the weeks sped by and their wedding date neared, he again began to think his fears unwarranted and his suspicions unjust, that no hammer stood poised to strike him, that he had either successfully skirted the danger or that it had never really been present in the first place—that he had only invented it. Da would have said that he had let down his guard and allowed himself to be gulled. Nonetheless especially during their last weeks together as the date they had selected to exchange their vows rapidly approached, everything conspired to expel all doubt and trepidation. Bill felt happy, happier than he had felt ever before during the course of his whole sorry life. He had also convinced himself that he would continue feeling happy for the foreseeable future. All vestiges of uncertainty evaporated for him. During the final week, he and Cindy spent but a few precious hours together, but, removed from her presence, Bill continued to dream and fantasize and to let his imagination run riot. In his mind's eye, he saw he and Cindy spending a lifetime together. That featureless phantom and construct of his, the ideal wife had suddenly come to life and now wore Cindy's features, and as he didn't have daily dealings with the real Cindy at this time, nothing dispelled his illusion. He did not have to foist and force the mask onto her features. It fit snugly and slipped on easily.

Despite the fuss and all the preparations then underway, they managed to steal half of one day to deliciously fritter away in each other's company at her father's hunting camp at the state park. The hours passed without incident. They made love passionately several times. Running his hands through her hair as he stared into the mirrors of her eyes in which he saw his face reflected in each of her pupils, he told his love that he adored her more than life itself. *Her image*, he thought, *is likewise reflected in each of mine. We have truly merged—become parts of each other. Our child will realize our union.*

They decided to hike in the woods, to follow a trail that passed a series of hunting cabins and eventually led down to a trout spring. The sun shone brightly and the woods seemed especially attractive. They saw no eyesores, no broken glass or other litter, no—he had read his Tolkien as a boy—orc droppings. However, it remained early in the season. Unlike the robins, the orcs had not yet arrived, or maybe this place stood far enough off the beaten path that it had never been orc infested at all. The air remained crisp and resinous: pine scented. He inhaled deeply one or two times and pronounced the woodland scene magnificent and breathtaking. Cindy and he had stumbled on paradise. Da's blackness didn't extend here. This place, he remembered thinking, has to be immune from it, but then they saw the three-legged deer. Actually they didn't make it out right away, for at least two-dozen deer grazed in the meadow beyond the trout stream. Another cabin stood in the middle of the field. Its owner had attracted the deer there with two or three salt licks and a large corn feeder. Before they noticed the doe's handicap, they saw other deer running at her and chasing her back from the corn trough. Then they saw how she hobbled on three legs. The fourth was halt and didn't support any weight but hung crooked and broken, the hoof suspended in the air, not touching the ground.

The previous winter and the last several before it had remained quite mild. Perhaps that and the presence of the corn trough explained her survival, but now the other deer, sensing her weakness, her impaired condition, determined to keep her away, at least until they ate their fill. But Bill put on his blinders again, wouldn't let the sight spoil his day. Come, he said, and he and Cindy continued their walk. At the close of the afternoon, he drove her to her parents and then headed back to Slippery Rock. Rutger and Roger would arrive in short order, and he and Cindy would still have the opportunity to chat on the phone several more times before the big day.

How MacNeil had learned that her parents would be out when he arrived at 1:30 that afternoon, the first of the two times he would force his presence upon her that day, would forever remain a mystery. But Billy did find out what he had said—the request he had made of her—for she told her parents what had occurred as soon as they walked in the door later that afternoon, the same door she had showed MacNeil earlier. God, if only he would have been there, he would have gladly handed him the sum. He asked her for a loan, a paltry amount, two or three grand, something to tide him over. He had hit the skids. Due to the recession, his construction business had for all intents and purposes gone belly up. He had no work—at least for the time being—and found himself behind on his vehicle, his rent, and his utility payments. Could she possibly float him the cash. No. After all he put her through, why would she want to help him? What gall, what cheek, to ask her—her of all people. What hope could he have possibly had of success?

Leave, she told him. Right now. He had seen, he said, the wedding announcement in the church bulletin and heard all about her fiancé Billy Steiglitz. They say he never left his house for years and years, but suddenly one day he comes out of his self-imposed exile like Superman out of his fortress of solitude and everybody in the town of Slippery Rock sees him spending money like it grew on trees. She could float him some cash if she wanted. He knew it. Highlight, she answered, if she wanted. She didn't. "I could care less about your troubles. Now go. Get out. Before I call the cops." What went through his mind, Billy wondered. Why didn't he come directly to me? I gave him a couple of fifties that other time, even though she didn't want me to, and got very angry when I did. Certainly MacNeil found his current situation horribly unjust. He had risked life and limb for his nation when they activated his reserve unit, but, now a year after the war, the economy had collapsed. Everything had sunk to such a sad state that he couldn't even make a decent living. Then his ex-wife, who always held her snoot high in the air and thought herself better than anyone else, announces her engagement to some bozo loaded with money and stupid enough to fall for her. Someone who she thinks *is* good enough. And what did this man ever do for his country? Not one damn thing. He sat out Vietnam. He had a college professor for a father, so naturally he became a student and received a deferment. Of all the people in the world, she chooses some good-for-nothing shit, some milk toast, like that. At least Kovacs had his good looks but when the time came she traded up and dropped him like a hot potato. You needed dough, lots and lots of it, to make the grade with Cindy. This Steiglitz fellow had only one thing to recommend him and that was gelt. Plenty of it. A person's integrity, his personal devotion and fidelity, his dedication and his service to his country didn't mean a hill of beans, a damn thing, to Cindy. Well, if she married for money, he hoped that hubby number two would make her earn every damn cent of it. Billy didn't know—could never know—the entire truth. He would conjecture and guess at Trevor MacNeil's thoughts that day for the rest of his life, but they would remain veiled and hidden to him. He could not even know for certain what MacNeil said to Cindy the first time he confronted her. He had it at third hand. What Cindy's parents told him remained hearsay: what they remembered Cindy telling them. Maybe Cindy had lied or not told the entire truth. She received a phone call from her maid of honor at around 4:00, and, when she left home within a few minutes of hanging up, she told her parents that she was headed to Bev's and that she would see them later. She never arrived at her friend's. At seven, Bev telephoned to see what kept her. Where exactly MacNeil waylaid her, no one could say with any degree of certainty. The detective guessed that he had ambushed her at a stoplight. Perhaps he hadn't even planned on doing it, that she had the bad fortune to drive up to a street corner where he just happened to stand, and he saw his chance. Perhaps he had left his apartment with no intention of ending anyone's life though the fact that he carried his gun seemed to speak otherwise. Here again things weren't so clear as the police would have liked, for MacNeil had a concealed weapons permit and regularly showed up at the local shooting range for target practice Thursday afternoons and the murder took place on a Thursday. As the sportsman's club sat only several blocks from MacNeil's apartment, he often walked to it carrying his piece with him. Perhaps he had spotted Cindy while en route there. The police asked the public for their help, but no witnesses to the car jacking ever came forth. If anyone saw him get in her car they did not report it or at the time they did not perceive his hostile intent and assumed that a friend had spotted and hailed someone he knew, had asked for a ride and had received permission to enter the vehicle. Evidently she hadn't locked her passenger door. MacNeil got in, they conjectured, and only then pulled out his thirty-eight, and ordered her to drive somewhere. If he had staked out the Daughenbaugh house surely one of the neighbors would have seen him. If he had waited for her outside and had come out of the bushes to aim the gun behind her ear as she unlocked the car or, if hours before, right after she showed him out of the house, he had gotten into her car immediately, seeing maybe that one of its two doors was unlocked and sat there all afternoon not knowing if she would or would not come out, or even if he went home for the gun first and came back later after Mr. and Mrs. Daughenbaugh had returned home and, turning his head back and forth, looking all round to see if anyone was watching him, got in and sat and laid in wait, someone would have surely detected his presence and witnessed one or another of his actions. Afterwards the detectives interviewed everyone on the block. They learned that MacNeil had initially driven to her parents' home. Something Cindy had neglected to tell her parents. A neighbor had seen his black Mustang in the Daughenbaugh driveway between 1:30 and 2:00 and a few minutes after the hour heard MacNeil screeching his tires and gunning his engine. As children played on the street, the man stepped outside to shout out at the driver to slow down and caught a glimpse of the Mustang as it sped down a side street. After that, no one had seen MacNeil anywhere near the Daughenbaugh premises. The police found Cindy's Corvette in a downtown parking garage the next day; the attendant testified he didn't notice who had parked it the previous afternoon or evening. No ticket stub was found in the vehicle or elsewhere so the exact time Trevor drove the car into the garage could not be determined. By the time the police found the car, however, hikers at the state park had already come upon her body in a clearing off one of the numerous trailheads. She had been shot in the head at close range. The body remained fully clothed, but tests later determined that she had been sexually assaulted, the semen positively identified as Trevor MacNeil's. He had been life-flighted to a Pittsburgh hospital at 9:30 p.m. the previous night. Numerous witnesses saw him lift the revolver to his head then pull the trigger, for he did it, sitting in his car in the middle of a town intersection. He had shut off the motor but left the keys in the ignition. He had tried to extort money from her earlier in the day, had failed to persuade her to take pity on him, and then had abducted her sometime after 4:00 p.m. The police determined the time of her death to be between 6:30 and 7:00 p.m. He had forced her to drive to some as of yet undiscovered but probably outdoor location—no doubt a secluded spot—where he had raped her then had let her redress or had made her do so. Then he had shot her and had hidden her body in her car trunk. Before shooting himself, he had driven up the dirt access road and dumped the body at the trailhead. Afterwards he drove her car to the parking garage, but why, if he planned on killing himself, the detective wondered, didn't he do it right there at the murder scene after he had offed her? He must have thought, for awhile at least, that he could get away with it. For he drove her car into town and parked it in the garage, then went home and got behind the wheel of his own vehicle. By then maybe he realized that his plight was hopeless and that the police would shortly apprehend him, or perhaps he began experiencing remorse and guilt. After driving back into town, he at any rate shot himself. If he didn't die, if he recovered from his self-inflicted wound, the police might get a fuller account from him. Perhaps when he abducted her he hadn't made the decision to kill her, maybe he only set out to work on her again for money. William Steiglitz would have paid a king's ransom for her life, but MacNeil had brains enough to realize that kidnapping her wouldn't work since she could identify him. He had to make her give him the money which she wouldn't do. He thought the cash his due and right, so he shot her. Maybe she taunted him, said that she didn't believe that he would do it and tried to leave, they just didn't know.

MacNeil lived, but unfortunately he could not provide any answers. Blind, paralyzed on the left side, incontinent, he responded to their questions like a retarded child. He had obviously regressed to a very pitiable extent, did not remember what he had done, and would not understand a court proceeding. The court judged him mentally incompetent to stand trial and placed him in his parents' custody in Altoona. They in turn admitted him to Harmony Heights Nursing Home and Convalescent Center—the facility formerly known as Colonial Court Manor—where he continued to live on in the same diminished state. For how long Billy Steiglitz would never know.

X

The war finally came home to its television spectator. He answered his telephone. From the opposite end came the choked-up, cracking, voice of a distraught, unbelieving Sam Daughenbaugh. Trevor MacNeil had shot and murdered Cindy. Sam's voice became William's scud missile: the one with his number, his name, written on it. It shot through his ear and into his brain across all that distance via miles and miles of telephone wire. He sat in the third floor tower round room of his Steamboat Gothic mansion, an exercise in excess, in superfluous adornment, detailing and embellishment with its dripping bargeboards and vergeboard trim; its steep pitch roof and scalloped shingles; its exaggerated cross gables and elongated finials and its pointed arch, bay, and oriel windows; its wrought-iron balustrades; its overdone gingerbread awnings, its pillared galleries, and its elaborate wraparound porches on the first and second stories with their ornamental spindles and brackets and their motif of beehives and honey dippers. Fluted pilasters flanked the wide wooden double-hung front door and supported the monumental entablature above it which all the lintels of the tall windows on the first floor duplicated in miniature. For God's sake, there existed ornamentation even in the ornamentation, level upon level of it. All the stylistic decoration, all the baroque frills and flourishes concealed and made you forget the structure's simplicity, its barn-like spaciousness. A bull's-eye window with glazed fan lights and trimmed with wooden voussoirs at quarter points in the circle pierced each of the four cross gables, and sunburst spires capped all the attic's dormers, but far and away the house's most elaborate and fancy woodwork had to be the lacy gingerbread scrollwork of the partitions, screens, and dividers on each of the four ornate galleries—one for each of the house's four sides. They all had patterns and designs woven into them like basket or wickerwork: labyrinthine, filigreed trim which featured designs within designs. The profusely adorned house looked oriental and pagoda-like to William especially when he placed wreaths and candles in all the windows at Christmas, each candle crowned with a bright red bulb.

He did not shatter. He did not lock himself in, but often, two or three times a day, went out of his house. However he refused to read the papers or watch the newscasts on TV. He would use his set only to play videotapes and later DVDs. For years and years he tried to keep his resolution, but he could not totally blind himself from all that happened in the outside world. He learned of international affairs by osmosis if nothing else, and many years later he happened to step into a Circuit City store the morning the two airliners hit the twin towers and he saw the second plane collide with its target then both towers collapse on half-a-dozen floor models simultaneously. A second Bush had succeeded to the White House, and, because of the terrorist attack in the big apple, the son determined to put paid to the father's old adversary and triggered another war with Iraq and William felt caught in a time loop as the past once again became present and the second Bush claimed that Saddam had procured a secret arsenal of weapons of mass destruction and the American people once again allowed their President to pull the wool over their eyes but those events, at the time of his fiancée's murder, stood nine years in the future. Bill certainly did not foresee them. In the weeks that followed Cindy's death, he ventured outside almost every day. However, he resolved that he would never again allow himself to draw close to anyone. He already saw himself as half a ghost. While he didn't shut himself into a bunker and hide as he had done after his father's death, he remained cold and aloof—this nothing more than a simple defense mechanism. He vowed from thenceforward not to ever again develop loving and affectionate feelings for people. He spurned emotional involvement with anyone alive. So to pass the time he began having conversations with his dead wife. In his own house, he began acting as if she had never died, as if he had never witnessed the workmen lowering her coffin into the ground. He entered into—never to depart—a fantasy life in which MacNeil had never shot Cindy in the head.

Before he found the faith and power in himself to fully believe in his dispensation, he had decided to follow the monastic path his father had once advocated, if only in jest. But then he started dreaming during the day as well as during the night. Cindy talked to him and he determined not to disregard what she said.

Their boy Roy, he and she, lived in the dream house, the Steamboat Gothic mansion. The new baby made four mouths that he had to feed, but he had always wanted a large family, and he joked with Cindy that she would find herself barefoot and pregnant for the foreseeable future. He also allowed his Civil War ancestors, the Cerls, as well as Perse McCalmont and Jacob Kemper, to trouble and haunt him. He talked aloud or held inner debate with them daily.

As he metamorphosed into a ghost himself, he did not find it strange that they spoke to him on a more frequent basis. Determined to communicate to his own kind, he entered into a trance-like state. Part of his mind realized what he was doing—how he conned and deluded himself. Deep down he knew that Cindy had died, but he also knew that by not accepting the truth and believing fervently in his fata morgana that he could hoodwink himself. His sufferings put him on a par with Job. Like Adolf Hitler, who in his last days dreamed about overblown stadia and monstrous edifices which he'd erect in the future, or else about wielding forces, legions, he no longer possessed, Bill could delude himself that his life with Cindy had never been interrupted.

He began to think that only voyeurs studied history. He understood why we dug up the past and why despite all its beastliness we glorified it. Why we scrutinized the battles in which our ancestors fought and why we romanticized and doted on those battles until we grew almost fond of them. The question inevitably arose if we still had to wage wars why couldn't our current conflicts resemble those remedial enterprises undertaken with such zeal and enthusiasm by our ancestors, those just and glorious crusades where we sided with the Angels and fought for some shining and righteous cause. If truth were told, we all conspired to clean up and sanitize the past and winked at each other the while.

William Corl's quick death in battle remained superior to William Steiglitz's slow, lingering, living one. But he blanked that judgment out, told himself he led as wonderful a life as Jimmy Stewart's in that stupid movie, that celluloid Capra corn. He vowed never again to write himself off, to dismiss his life as worthless, and also pledged to never refer to himself as Billy any more, but only to use his full name William Steiglitz. After all, he had had the power within himself to dismiss all his doubts and concerns about Cindy and had married her without qualm or misgiving. And, yes, she lived! Those doubts had arisen from his paranoia: the residuum of his father's doctrine that everyone stood at war with you.

For the last several years, they had led the existence of your average young American couple. He couldn't ask for any better wife now, could he? He wouldn't give the time of day to other people; if someone accosted him, he became rude, loud and obnoxious. Chin and chest out, he rebuffed every advance and would lunge out menacingly at whoever dared disturb his isolation. And why not? He wanted everyone to simply leave him alone. He did not wish to be bothered by the likes of them. So any person who approached him he treated insufferably. He swore not to put on pounds. He continued his daily regimen at the local YMCA and swam and lifted weights. At home in his he had now begun to think overly ostentatious Victorian domicile, he did sit ups and push ups while watching educational videos on the VCR or before his two small black stereo speakers listening to classical music.

He daily stood in the proximity of great minds through what he read. The stinking body would rot and go the way of all flesh, but a person could leave behind his headbirths, his books, and William would rather meet and hold converse with an author through his creations, the words into which he refined himself, than accost him in the flesh with his human warts and blemishes. A horrible human being might create a thing of beauty, produce sentences, containers of consciousness, on which the eye dotingly dwells and which the ear rapturously hears. In laying his words end to end, the author shed his physical body like a snake its skin, threw off all the dross and scum. One confronted pure mind—ideal beauty—and now William preferred to give up the insensate things of the world in favor of the words which said them.

He didn't need to treat with people on the outside, his house a time capsule, a museum, in which he had ready access to recordings of works by all the masters of classical music and to hundreds and hundreds of reproductions of works of art and architecture in his father's many reference books. He had access to volumes and volumes of recognized classics of world literature. He had a lifetime of study ahead of him. If he didn't eat out, he had his meals at home in the Steamboat, catered. Only the finest, highest-quality cuisine, four-star fare, went into his gullet. He allowed himself to lead in some respects at least, a soft and pampered sort of existence. He felt entitled to his comforts and luxuries, but he did not allow himself to again grow fat. He enjoyed and relished the human being's lifelong contest with death, the process of fighting back at age and attrition through exercise and diet in order to win for oneself extra years to joy in. He realized that he did not enjoy the prerogative and privilege of special election, that he would leave his father down, that he would not make his mark–his scratch–on the face of anonymity. Nor did it seem–he tried to repress the thought at the moment of its conception, but it struck him full force and temporarily at least he could not banish it–that he would now have children. Yes, it appeared that he would be the last Steiglitz, his days above ground the last gasp, the final experience of life in the skin for a number of his ancestors. Some, of course, were fortunate enough to have other animate and flesh-garbed descendants. The farther back they stood in the bloodline the more likely that such would be the case. Nonetheless he remained the last resting place for many a poor ghost. So he vowed to take care of himself in order to extend the grace period of those who needs must rely solely on him. For their sake, he would stay in his body, the house in which he presently lodged and couldn't escape from until death at last released him.

Unlike his brother Miles, he would not take the coward's way out. He would not hang himself or otherwise expedite that release. Instead he would strive to reach the ripe age of one hundred, just as Jacob Kemper had desired to do, though gravity had cut short Kemper's time when the mine roof collapsed and the falling rock and coal crushed him. Da had written that Kemper had wanted to live for a century, and William had no doubt that a soldier who had survived the war would want to die an old man in bed, having cheated the grim angel on the battlefield. But neither Da nor he had any way of truly knowing what Kemper had really thought. *Or did William?* In writing down his version of the story, Da had made some shrewd guesswork, but somewhere inside himself, William might actually know the truth, for Jacob Kemper's blood coursed through his veins whereas it hadn't run in his father's. The residue of Kemper in him–the part of Kemper living, still entombed, caught in the vital, living flesh, in the blood and skin, might tell him, if he could commune with it. When the dark angel bade William Corl come forward, his ancestor's younger brother had only just reached adulthood and Jacob Kemper's three sons Herman Joshua, Felix, and Edmund had received their summons as little more than boys and adolescents. He had already put more skin time in than all of them. Why soon he would turn forty. True, he hadn't yet lived as long as Jacob Kemper had done before fate finally struck him down or as lengthy, dragging, and prolonged a life as Perse McCalmont. But he felt that he could truly come to know these persons not because of his father's writings but because they lived on somehow in him. His father had been incredibly prescient. He had guessed many of the particulars and had made (as it turned out) many accurate conjectures, but he had no way no way of ascertaining where he deduced correctly and where he erred. Once Da had posed the question how could anyone know the dead and understand their motivations in life when we couldn't even truly comprehend the living, those whom we saw and spoke with every day, with all their myriad complexities and complications? All William's doubts again resurfaced. Did he ever know Cindy? Did she really know Trevor? The tears welled up in his eyes, and again he fought to repress the truth. None of it happened. He only dreamt that Trevor had shot his wife. She lay right now in his bed. William imagined that after arising from his slumbers and finding himself grown old and decrepit and stranded in a brave new world that Rip van Winkle would have wanted to return to his green knoll covered with mountain herbage from which he could overlook the low country for many a mile of rich woodland and view, far below him, the lordly Hudson moving on its silent and majestic course, once more recline on the grass and begin sipping liquor from his flagon until his eyes again swam and his head once more declined and he fell into a deep sleep. His dreams would have seemed more comfortable and less fantastic than the world to which he had awoken. Did he in fact only imagine that he had slept for twenty years? Could he distinguish the true reality from the false dream one or did he mistake the one for the other and mix them up?

He wrote his resolution—his promise to his father—down in his lined yellow tablet. He would start summoning his forebears and calling them up. His brain would become the organ that they would pass into and they would remain content to abide there, he their only doorway back into life: into the world outside which he viewed whenever he opened his eyes. He would find out if his father had related accurate accounts of their lives.

William loved the film *Amadeus*. He understood Salieri's rage against the deity because God had elected someone far less deserving than himself on whom to bestow so prodigious and lavish a gift. Nonetheless William would have counted himself fortunate to have possessed Salieri's by no means meager talents and considered himself "loved by God" to have enjoyed, say, Joseph Haydn's. Some might disparage Haydn's music as perfunctory, clockwork, and powdery, but they would be wrong. His achievement remained towering, perhaps greater than Mozart's. Haydn had paved the way for Mozart and he too recognized the younger man's greater gift but the father of the symphony and the string quartet celebrated and proclaimed that gift and did not grow jealous and angry with God. In awe, he beheld how Mozart took the musical forms that he himself invented and advanced them, and after Mozart's premature death, having in turn learned from the younger man to whom he had originally pointed the way, continued to perfect his art and in his final symphonies and quartets outstripped the infant prodigy. But a lucky star had not presided over William's birth; he could only hope to acquire more and more intelligence and at last to become one of the cognoscenti. He would not give anything back, create something new and fresh out of the work of others and advance the state of the art. He knew that he would not make any great leap forward in science or give birth out of himself to any electrifying and novel work of art. Intermixed with the blood of all the other forebears who had joined and fused together to make him—the new entity—the literary lady's blood had become diluted and watered down. He could not raise and summon Magda Markwort. Nor would he match his father's literary efforts. At least he knew his boundaries and limitations, the extent of his capacities. And he did not curse the deity. Nonetheless William Steiglitz would succeed in growing smarter. He would keep expanding his intelligence and adding to it, as long as his life lasted. Inevitably all his memories would be snuffed out with him, but he accepted his fate and did not let his limitations sap his vitality. Even though he couldn't create works of art, he still would be called on to perform daunting feats, for he discerned that everyone else had been brainwashed into believing that his Cindy had died, that her ex MacNeil had indeed murdered her, but he knew that this was not the case, yet he could never let on that he knew. He had to act as if he believed like everyone else. At least to their faces. At least in front of them. He could never slip up and accidentally give himself away. *I must never hint at my skeleton in the cupboard to anyone. I must keep my dispensation secret.*

It became a kind of game. He pitted himself against them all and won. He had to remain constantly on his guard. He had to rein himself in tightly in all situations in which he presented himself in public. He nodded and winked at the pink piglets in order to show them that he believed and thought as they did. He had to keep under his hat all the things they wouldn't understand or comprehend.

A secret war existed between him and the wider world. He fought to the full extent of his capabilities and strove to always appear normal in the eyes of all others. At most they might find him a little cold and indifferent or else a bit eccentric. However, he had all the love, warmth and nurturing he needed in his fictive life. Cindy awaited him at home and no matter where he went or what he did, in the end, he always found himself hurrying to get back home to her. No one knew how in the dark, under the covers, at night, he took her constantly, again and again. Almost every year she bore him a son or daughter.

With the exception of the first boy Roy, he gave them all names out of the Old Testament.

He found it easy to keep himself in control when he went out alone, but in later years, his sons and daughters began (much to his wife's chagrin) tagging along after him, and then he would have to remain extra cautious and not ever let their bad behavior divert him. He could never call out and reprimand them. *Yes, he could foresee what those with him would say, what their reaction would be.* No one else saw their monkeyshines, their antics, but him. He would have to wait until they returned to the Steamboat, before he could scold them and give them their comeuppance, send them to bed without their suppers, maybe even spank the younger ones. Every night after they'd fallen off into their own dreams, he stealthily opened the door to their mother's bedroom and snuck inside to make them more brothers and sisters.

Large chunks of time went by without William Steiglitz having any visitors, though four people continued to take an active interest in his life. Nor did he do anything to rebuff, to discourage and dissuade Rutger Poell, his aging Uncle Roger, or his still grieving in-laws Sam and Ellen. The Daughenbaughs tested his resolve to keep silent. He so badly wanted to tell them that their daughter had not died, that she had been married to him for years and that they had given the Daughenbaughs numerous grandchildren, but he understood that he could not persuade Sam and Ellen and win them over. Something warned him not to tell. Like in a fairy tale, if he revealed his secret, he would lose access to the fairy kingdom. Cindy and the children would evaporate right before his very eyes. Sam kept telling him he ought to find someone new, that he should stop living in the past, when right opposite him on the couch sat the very daughter he urged William to betray and break faith with. Her eyes shone daggers. How she glowered and scowled. But Sam did not see her, did not detect her presence. Only William could. She appeared glad when her parents went out the door. Then she walked over to him and put her arms around his shoulders, squeezed him tight against her, and offered, gave, him all the consolation he had ever wanted.

He continued using his credit cards to buy things—not for himself, but for Cindy and the kids. He had his purchases shipped to his address either through the mail or by UPS. He prepared a room in his house for each of the children Cindy gave him to call his own. He decorated the room to fit the child's personality. The toys, games, books, stereos, and televisions he furnished the rooms with always came from the top shelf, the best the mail-order catalogs had to offer. Mahalalel and Jared, the two eldest boys after Roy, both had a knack for the fine arts, Mahalalel music, Jared painting, so he bought the first boy nine or ten instruments and beginners' instruction books and sat down to teach him or rather learn alongside him. They'd do it together, and William Steiglitz actually became pretty adept at playing both the trumpet and trombone. Likewise he purchased Jared easels and paints. He spent an hour sketching with him each morning. Sarah and Ruth, his next two, gave him no end of trouble. The first remained entirely too timid and stuck in her shell. She would become interested in some new activity like dance or drama but then after only a few weeks would grow bored with the activity and would abruptly drop it. She would only ever get through the first several chapters of any book she would pick up. William found himself always lecturing her that she grew up with all sorts of advantages other little girls didn't have, but due to the perverseness of her character didn't make the most of them. Ruth, on the other hand, did exploit all the boons and blessings of her home environment. Her trouble lay in her totally uncooperative attitude. She became brassy and obstinate. He couldn't do anything, it seemed, to rid these two of their bad habits and wanton ways. But then the girls remained Cindy's province mainly, not his. The responsibility of their upbringing devolved primarily to her. William succeeded in cultivating a love of history in his fourth son Issachar. He handed over to him his own father's stories about the Civil War ancestors. William would read to his son nightly an hour before the boy's bedtime, Franz's writings but also historical accounts of famous Civil War battles. Maybe a chapter from Stephen Crane or one of the stories from Ambrose Bierce's *Tales of Soldiers and Civilians*, or a poem or story from one of the slick magazine scribblers such as John P. Marquand or Robert Edmond Alter. While he acknowledged another Billywilliam a colossus of American letters, Steiglitz found the author too subtle and persuasive a propagandist, too biased in favor of the South, to introduce him to Issachar just yet. Margaret Mitchell also showed her partisan colors, but he found her acceptable because she remained a full blown romantic, and he found her work easier to poke holes in, to label as poison, nothing but distortion and lies. Besides the boy having seen the Hollywood film on DVD so badly wanted to read the novel William did not like to discourage and disappoint him. He had not asked to read Céline after all.

On Issachar's seventh birthday, he let him meet the ghosts of the three Corls, Jacob Kemper, and the lame and elderly Percy McCalmont. The boy did not see them as they piled together into his room until William held his hand. As soon as his skin touched his son's, the scales fell from the boy's eyes and he saw the ghosts in their blue uniforms, only Peter Corl's not U. S. army issue. He wore a policeman's shield on his coat. His face lean and long, Peter sported curly black hair and a full beard. His strawberry blond no brunette brother Prosper looked much more handsome (his face slightly resembled General Custer's) than either Peter or his other brother the broad and squat William or, for that matter, either the bald and bearded Kemper with his sourpuss and his high-pitched voice or the Irish ancestor old man McCalmont. The latter had a lined and wizened face and a noticeable, oh-so-noticeable limp. They heard his cane thump on the hardwood floor as he limped into the room after the other ghosts. Steiglitz made his son promise not to tell his brothers or sisters about the presence of the ancestors—his ability to see them. They won't believe you anyway. You have a special gift—a second sight—which you inherited from me. But no one else must know of your special ability, else you will face terrible persecution.

He and Cindy's youngest child, the darling little Zilpah, remained too immature yet to have any special interests, but she behaved so politely and stood so ready to do anything you asked of her that he loved her most of all. Most nights she would wake up in the dark in her room quite scared from her dreams and run down the hall into his and Cindy's room and jump in bed with them.

His wife maintained that the family that plays together, stays together. Of course, Cindy remained perfectly content to wait at home inside the Steamboat. She realized that she and the kids would put William at risk if they went outside; that, if they accompanied him, in a moment of forgetfulness, he might call out or speak to them, and this simply wouldn't do, for someone might notice, think William's behavior strange, and report him to the authorities. She never asked to go on vacations, though William kept on urging her to accompany him on a trip to Europe. Circumstances had prevented their taking their honeymoon trip. He wanted to make that up to her now. He would plan the expedition down to the smallest detail, he promised. No, let's wait a few years, she answered. The kids will appreciate it more then.

In fact, William often had to sneak the boys and girls out with him when he left the house on errands. Cindy would try to stop him if she happened to see. It's not healthy to keep the children indoors, he argued. They need to play outside in the sun. We can always pull back the curtains and throw open the windows, she responded. He just shook his head. It was no use arguing with her. She stood her ground and remained adamant on the issue. He couldn't move her not even when he said: "Please, darling, I don't want any of them to develop complexes, to become agoraphobic like I was those eighteen years I spent snug as a bug in a rug in my parents' home." She wouldn't let him finish. "None of us are going to put you at risk. No Siree. Case closed." She raised her voice. "And that's the last thing I'm going to say on the subject."

But indoors, she expected him to spend lots and lots of quality time with the kids, and he, of course, complied gladly. Most of all she liked the entire family to do things all together. The activity didn't matter, she left it to him, so he would sit all the children down in front of the TV set to watch an opera on laser disc, or a movie or famous play on video tape. Unfortunately Sarah would often become insufferable ("I'm bored; I don't want to watch"), and he would have to punish the willful little brat.

Then one year out of the blue Sam Daughenbaugh fell dead of a heart attack, and William and his wife finally had a fight. He thought it only proper that she and the children should go to the funeral with him, but even on this occasion she felt it better for her and the youngsters to remain at home. He threatened not to go unless she at least accompanied him. Still her answer was no. She wouldn't leave the house. "Well, I can't very well not go," he sighed. "What would your mother think? I can keep my guard up," he pleaded. "Please come. I didn't slip up ever when the in-laws came to visit us, I mean me, here...." "But you had plenty of close calls. You so badly wanted to tell them that I hadn't died, even though you knew that, if you had, the children and I would have disappeared from your life as if we had never been, and furthermore you still will have to be very careful that you don't betray our secret at Dad's funeral. No matter how much you want to comfort my mother. Besides I know something you don't."

William Steiglitz hated funerals. The tears streamed down his face and he sat quite inconsolable, almost as bad as his mother-in-law Ellen, at Cindy's father's. They had to lead him out of the parlor by the arms at his own Da's. He had tried to destroy the place, overturned chairs, knocked down the lectern and several of the floral arrangements and cried out that he hated God, and took his name in vain, and said f. u. to the funeral director. They sedated him and got him home and in bed, where he stayed for the next several weeks, crying bitterly each day. He hated life and he feared the outside world. He vowed never to venture beyond the front door again.

Somehow though, he got through Mr. Daughenbaugh's.

But then when he returned home to Slippery Rock, he found Sam waiting there for him with the rest of his family. "He has decided to move in with us," Cindy said after William Steiglitz came in the door and did a double take when he saw her father sitting on the sofa, riding Zilpah on his knee as if it were a horse, she shrieking delightedly. "I hope that it's all right with you." "Why, of course, it is," he stammered. "Hi, son," Sam called out to him. "I can see them now," he said. "I couldn't before, but I can now." William Steiglitz turned to his wife and said, "I guess this is the something I didn't know. Am I right?" She nodded then ran over to him as he opened his arms to embrace her.

William's other dead started to appear in the course of the next several weeks. Up to Sam's arrival, he had thought his dispensation had only extended to Cindy and to his forebears who had fought in the Civil War. He now realized that it proved more embracing than that. First Miles and Carol Steiglitz appeared, then Ben and Libby Corl. His brother had forgotten that he had ever wanted to take his life. Furthermore he now succeeded at anything he put his hands to. His mother's health had never deteriorated. She had never lost any hair and didn't need to wear a wig. Plump and rosy-cheeked, the woman looked like she had never been sick a day in her life. Cancer had never wasted her body, so she had no reason now to welcome death. His grandfather, on the day he arrived, pulled the dinosaur tooth from his shirt pocket and gave it once again to a dazzled, overwhelmed William. He in turn gave it to Issachar, telling him not to lose it—to guard it most carefully.

He assigned his guests to their permanent rooms in the Steamboat mansion. He gave his brother Miles one of the round tower chambers; he put his mother Carol and his grandparents Ben and Libby in separate suites on the second floor. Sam occupied an apartment on the first, and he, Cindy and the kids remained quartered on the third. In William Steiglitz's house there were many mansions. He would prepare a place for his Uncle Roger's future occupation, and of course, he'd also make his mother-in-law Ellen welcome when her time came. He set about furnishing his loved-ones' new rooms right away. He consulted them on their likes and dislikes, and tried to make everything as comfortable as he possibly could.

One person, however, remained conspicuous by his absence.

Several months after the arrival of his family and also of course of his wife's father, while standing in front of a full length oval mirror in his and Cindy's master bedroom, it startled William to see that the scars on his back had vanished. If they were gone, it must mean....

It must mean that he was here too! William began searching through each and every room of the Steamboat. He looked through the whole house from top to bottom. He could not find Da. He frantically sought him out and checked every room in his house a second time but to no avail. Then several days later, he surprised Da in his hiding place or rather rescued him from his prison. When the answer came to him, William blushed at his previous obtuseness. The solution was so simple that he felt deathly mortified and humiliated. Da resided inside himself. William had internalized him. Why had it taken him so long to puzzle out something so simple? He had known the answer all along. He had heard his father's voice speak to him often, but still the scales remained on his eyes. He must have blocked and repressed the answer. A part of him must have wanted to forestall their reunion. Years ago, his father must have thrown his hands up in despair and, resigned to his state, given up all hope. So William would now catch him off guard and completely unprepared. He would have to prostrate himself before Da and apologize for being such a stupid mortal. For he realized now that all he had to do was summon his father as he had previously summoned his Civil War ancestors and that Da would appear. Lying down on the sofa, William simply exhaled—blew all the air out of his lungs. And from out of William's breath the form of his father began to condense and take shape. William had seen medieval paintings depicting the soul at death departing from a human body. He imagined that an onlooker would have seen something similar.

His father appeared different, older, the age he would have been if he had not been killed in the helicopter crash.

"*Mein Sohn*," he shouted, "I thought you would never find me. I thought you would never discover how to release me and that I would remain corked inside you forever. Forgive me William. I was so very, very wrong. You have proven me mistaken by the life you lead in this utopia. You remain relaxed and nonchalant. You certainly don't act like the world is at war with you, and because you don't take any precautions and *aren't* struck down but instead thrive, I have to conclude, I'm forced to determine, that my hypothesis was incorrect, completely erroneous. You are right to raise your children as you do. I see that you have developed in all of them a sense of their own worth and their total uniqueness. In my lessons with you, I should not have overemphasized life's Darwinian aspects, but I swear I didn't want to harm or hinder you, and you feel much more keenly than I ever did that to struggle is inherently noble. You want your children to make something out of their lives. Well, so did I. I hope you haven't set the goal posts too high, but then I know in my heart that you would never repeat my mistakes. Also I feel that at least one of your children will add something to the sum total of creation and make renowned the name of Steiglitz. The pain we have both suffered will then have become worth bearing. I see that you follow the advice of Voltaire to cultivate your own garden and to forget about the misfortunes and the travails of the larger world. You are really a marvelous son, and I am quite proud of you. I tried to toughen you up so that you would learn to fend for yourself and to protect and care for your own, for life can be quite ruthless. But here in your own home you have created a paradise." William Steiglitz had never been happier in his entire life than at this moment. He embraced his father and felt at peace.

The Mozart Machine

Table of Contents

Love in the twinckling of your eylids daunceth,
Love daunceth in your pulses and your vaines,
Love, when you sow your needles poynt advaunceth,
And makes it daunce a thousand curious straines
Of winding rounds, whereof the forme remaines,
To shew that your fair hands can daunce the Hey,
Which your fine feet would learne as wel as they.

Sir John Davies

One

Chapter One
Their First Disordered Combatting

I

They had been there at the same time. Elissa Hexfore had studied history and philosophy at Cannoshockton University when Michael Bolanger lived with his parents and sister in Hedgewood Village, a residential area just outside of town in adjacent Coburn Township, and his father worked as a professor at the university. At that time, Michael had just turned twelve and Elissa had reached the age of eighteen. He discovered the coincidence several days after they met at the Nexus of Nuance writers' circle, four months before they made love for the first time—more accurately, he for the first, she for the nth time—on a warm June night in 1981. Both had enrolled as students at Herneshopple University. Michael was now nineteen.

She attracted him immediately. While the circle's other writers were, to use Aldous Huxley's terminology, Betas and Gammas, Elissa remained the group's one true Alpha, her face long and narrow, the chin pointed just to the degree needed to suggest resolution and pluck, but not arrogance or snobbery. As she read, Elissa stood at attention. The upturned collar of her blouse covered most of her neck. Below the collar, at a diagonal from the thyroid notch to a bit below her underarm, ran four generous buttons whose transverse line suggested a cadet holding his rifle at "port arms" even though she stood at attention. Prominent nipples, contoured forward in the downward recess of her blouse, accentuated small round breasts. She looked Michael full in the face. He averted his glance but then immediately looked back up at her.

Her nipples saluted him. Both had stiffened. Each stood at attention.

Ideally centered eyes. Clear and blue and direct. They seem sympathetic and compassionate, as if in communication with her inward male anima. Elissa Hexfore returned to her seat; her appearance altered. Michael noticed that her narrow lips, though straight, did not suggest coldness or frigidity, that her eyebrows spanned most of the width of a rather high but delicately boned forehead, and that the two sides of her face did not appear quite proportionate. The right side had a wisp of hair hanging downward almost over her eyebrows, while she had brushed forcefully backward the hair on the left side.

Female. Female through and through.

Michael stood and walked to the podium. His eyes glanced a line ahead when he cleared his throat and began:

Eyesores become eyesores only on sunless days. Ahead Tom could see the barbwire fence that marked the end of his grandfather's property, and beyond that the dirt road that led to the top of the hill. The absence of sunlight made all the difference. The sun made the hill beautiful and attractive, lent it a special aura and magnetism, made it a thing which could engross a mind. But it made everything—broken coke bottles, rain-rusted beer cans, worn-down tenement buildings— appear that way. The right touch of sun will always bring out colors and make things captivating.

He continued to read from his story, an imagistic work which modulated through a variety of keys and dealt with an adolescent who felt he could become a writer because he had the first name of Thomas Mann, Thomas Hardy, and Thomas Wolfe. No one except Elissa Hexfore seemed to pay attention. One woman appeared particularly bored and unimpressed. At first she smiled and shook her head. Then she stared Michael directly in the face, offering him an exasperated and fatigued glance, as if to say, "When does this dreadful thing end?" She looked as if she hadn't had a bowel movement in days. Elissa focused on Michael's lips. They looked large and fleshy; one might have even called them voluptuous had it not been for the two white scars which ran across them, the souvenir of some childhood scuffle. He's beautiful. I wonder if he realizes that the anguish of my thoughts in verse stand as reflections of me? My God, I know where the white hairs run through my hair, where two wrinkles cross my forehead. And he appears flawless. A creamy, spiced dream in his green corduroy jacket.

Michael read last. The constipated woman served refreshments. Elissa introduced herself to Michael and told him her address. They ate cranberry-walnut bread and drank cider. Several weeks later, after Michael visited her at home a few times, Elissa would write about the night she met him. In 1983, when she mailed him several volumes of her diary, he discovered what she had written:

> March 10, 1981
>
> When he walked into Ormond Building that first night for the writers' group, he wore a green corduroy blazer, like M. K. used to wear. I thought him a beautiful fool—in only a corduroy jacket! It snowed hard that evening. He followed Renee up the steps. He knew only her. I dressed like a boy that night, with a perfectly flat chest underneath my blouse. Relaxed and confident, I read a few poems and feasted on him.

Michael didn't remember if it had snowed on the night of the Nexus of Nuance meeting. He did remember snow on the night he first visited Elissa's apartment. As he stepped out of the dorm lobby, the snow fell so hard that he couldn't see the stadium—that huge battleship lifted from the ocean to the meadow behind Whitman Hall. His roommate, Michael Douglas, slept peacefully. Douglas went to bed promptly at nine-thirty; Bolanger never turned in until after four a.m. He started across campus. The plows had already scraped the roads twice. Often one of his legs sank in the snow up to his knee. He wanted to see if Dr. Murcelli had posted the exam scores, but when he got to Demery Building he found the doors locked. He swore and turned back the way he had come. The high back of a bench emerged in front of him from underneath the snow. No, he'd go. He'd go tonight.

He trod through the snow until he reached Ackerman Avenue, then hurried down Beaver, past the bars, the all-night restaurants, and the video-game arcades. A woman of about sixty-five stood in front of the town library. She wore a fur coat (she had placed a pink flower in one of its buttonholes) and wielded a thin stick in her left hand as if she held a foil. He had run into her twice before—once at the Pine Grove Diner (then, too, a flower had protruded from her coat), and once at the Book Nook. She held long, loud conversations with imaginary people. "You, boy, you." She pointed her stick at him. "You know I own this library?" "Aren't you lucky," Michael said. "Gee, have you read all those books?" On he went, past the U-Mart, the pet store, the obstetrician's. Several cars sped down the street, the beams of their headlights cutting through the veil of falling snow. The Saloon belched four obstreperous drunks onto the street as a patrol car cruised slowly past.

Michael lit a cigarette and waited for the light to change. As usual, Otis and his dog spent the night in the laundromat, where it remained warm. A week ago Michael had come inside to buy a candy bar. Otis asked him if he had a match. He didn't. "Do you know," Otis then said, "behind that wall stand stacks and stacks of pornography, if only somehow we could get to them?" "As you can see," Michael said, "I've got plenty to read." He had several books with him that night.

He arrived at Elissa's at 10:35. She lived in a house that a Pennsylvania Governor once resided in and then many years later a famous architect; however, when the architect's family moved to a residential area in 1960, a realtor bought the place and converted it into the apartments. He learned this years later on a walking tour of Victorian domiciles in Herneshopple sponsored by the county historical society. It felt strange coming back to the place, the scene of such a signal event in his young life, and he experienced a queasy sensation in his gut. College students lived in the apartments—just as they had done when Elissa had lived there

Michael stepped off the sidewalk and under the portico. Opening the outer door and stepping into the foyer, he found and then pushed Elissa's doorbell. "Come up," he heard a voice call out. He opened the door, stepped across the threshold, and started up a wooden staircase. "Oh, it's you." She peeked over the banister clad in a black T-shirt and a pair of brown slacks. Her hair hung wild. In her left hand she held a wine glass between thumb and index finger. "How have you been?" she said. "Come up, I'll give you the grand tour." Her apartment seemed huge to him. His dorm room could fit in her kitchen! Well kept, very neat, too clean perhaps, it had a strange and unfamiliar flavor. She had pinned puppets and art prints to the walls. Plants peeped out of every corner. In the living room a small wooden crate—"her little coffin, her little box of death"—stood upright in a corner. She had fastened animal bones to its insides. Elissa sat down in a plain cane chair. Bolanger knelt on the *faux* art-nouveau carpet with its design reminiscent of a stained glass window, where he could better observe the crate and its contents. From where he sat he could view Elissa's bedroom. A number of her own paintings hung on the walls. A king-size mattress lay on the floor.

Elissa poured herself another glass of wine. "No thank you," Michael said. He had come to ask her if she would like to submit any of her poems to the literary magazine he and several of his friends were starting, or perhaps to join its staff. "Yes, I'll join," she said. "I worked on both the competing literary journals *Nosegays For Captives* and *Subject To Change* when a student at C. U. P." "You lived in Cannoshockton?" "From '73 to '75." "I grew up there." "Do you happen to know the Hedgepeths?" "I know a Sam Hedgepeth." "So do I. The last time I saw him he had only just turned ten though." She had started, she said, as a Greek major, but switched to history after two unrewarding terms with the "Idiot" and the "Oddity," two of Cannoshockton's Greek instructors. But now she had to go to the bathroom.

He looked through her record collection as he waited. Strange. She had everything from Stiff Little Fingers and Rachmaninoff to Leadbelly and Debussy. "Have you visited Big Red?" Michael turned his head. "No, I haven't." A ramshackle clapboard structure in West Pike, Cannoshockton, Big Red had stood a second home (and in some cases a first home) to perhaps a hundred college students. Elissa had lived there in 1975. Michael tried to think which house. He had to have driven past it when he attended District Orchestra rehearsals at Eisenhower School. In sixth and seventh grade the director appointed him solo clarinetist.

"Can you trust Cannoshockton men?" she asked suddenly.

His eyebrows drooped. "Trust them how? Sexually, morally, intellectually?"

"A motorcyclist named Bones lived in Big Red when I did. Once we went to a bar together. He stuck his hand down my pants." As she spoke she thrust her own hand underneath her pants and into her pelvic hollow. Michael's penis stiffened.

"That's Margaret now."

"What?" he said. Someone walked up the steps. A woman in blue coat with fur trim. "She's come to study with me," Elissa said. "We have a calculus exam on Wednesday." The woman stepped into the living room. The oh-so-carefully cultivated look of her hair impressed Michael. A good four or five inches longer than her shoulders, it hung down on either side of them. The strands of hair turned in and out in wide swirls up, down, and to the sides. Her ears, the upper halves covered by a sweep of hair over either ear, stood slender and long, the thin lobes pierced by small pearl earrings. Buttery yellow-green eyes softened an otherwise sour physiognomy.

"Margaret Bromion, Michael Bolanger."

My initials. "We scheduled the first magazine meeting next week," he said.

When Michael realized that it had stopped snowing he had walked nearly two blocks from Elissa's. He tested his vision by making out both horse and rider–Mizar and Alcor–while looking at ζ-*Ursa Majoris*. In the distance he glimpsed the Elk Ridge water tower with its pulsing red light. To save time he cut through Debs-Watson Park and, even though it remained very cold, he couldn't resist stopping for a short swing. He had pictures of his father and grandfather pushing him on these swings at three years old. His father had received his Ph.D. from Herneshopple University. She's interested in both my magazine and in me. I'll make her female flesh open of its own volition for my male, he thought. Oh yes I will.

I'll manage it somehow.

II

She took charge of things. Scabrous self-assurance. And supplanted Michael as the literary magazine's leader. In one month she did what he had failed to do in five: she got the necessary funding from the university, charmed the Faculty Senate out of three thousand dollars and obtained an additional five hundred from the Board of Student Grants and Stipends, set up an editorial board, advertised positions, drew up a contract with a Herneshopple printer, and got herself elected editor. Ben Cantwell ran her campaign: "She stands an expert at negotiation. She's got the experience, the knowledge and the know-how, business and managerial abilities, a heck of a lot of common sense—all the skills needed to run a magazine like *Thoth*." Bolanger felt happy for her. It didn't matter that he had lost out. Besides, women kept things running smoothly. They stood practical, down to earth, worldly. Their souls remained content within their bodies, that expulsion of fertile blood something extra to bind them to fleshly existence. After all, Frau Mann and Mrs. Huxley noticed the hundreds of condoms strewn on the beach or thrown into the water and somewhat impishly had to point them out to their hubbies—Tommy and Aldy—who had engaged and lost themselves in vague philosophical discussion.

Elissa's resignation took Michael by surprise. She said that soon she would leave town for two months (she and a friend had decided to go to Spain, her father would foot her bill), that the university had already returned her tuition fees, but not to worry, she would return summer term and get in touch with him then. He had not expected this. They had seen one another quite frequently, attending concerts together at Armsby Auditorium or art exhibitions at the Palmer Gallery. One night he had managed to unbutton her shirt, but she would not let him unzip her trousers. He didn't understand. Why did she boast about the motorcyclist? Perhaps she stood a virgin like himself. He didn't want her to go. But she'll be back, he told himself. Don't grow selfish.

Elissa left town in April, *Thoth* came out in May, and Bolanger moved out of the dorms in May, renting an apartment near Ben Cantwell's home.

Cantwell laughed, a cachinnation loud, buoyant, fruity. "You don't like it?" He could see plainly that Michael did not. "Well, what do you think of this?" With surprising agility (his fingers such big, bulbous monstrosities), Cantwell thumbed through the diminutive notebook, found the page he looked for, tore it out, and handed it to his friend.

Bolanger glanced listlessly at the page, dumped Cantwell's cat, Dr. Arbuthnot, out of his lap, stood up, stretched, and handed the poem back. "I'll read it to you," Cantwell said, "if you refuse to read it yourself." He cleared his throat, then declaimed:

> I was out with Doctor Johnson
> In the wilds of Wisconsin
> When we spied a handsome Swedish maid
> Selling Swiss cheese.
>
> And I said to Doctor Johnson
> 'Well, Sir, do you want some?'
> And he turned with a wink, saying
> 'If you please.'

Bolanger pretended to cringe. "Ben, how can you continually perpetrate such monstrosities?" Cantwell laughed; spit flew from his mouth. "Don't soft-soap me," he said, gagging on his saliva. "You're a sycophant, a bootlicker. I can tell when you're panegyrizing." He had to force the word out. "Your praise, it passeth all understanding." Bolanger grinned. Cantwell grabbed Arbuthnot by the scruff of his neck and lifted him into the air. "I find cats exceedingly perverse creatures, Michael. Have you ever seen one of them drowned?" Bolanger made a face. "Not even for a joke," he said. The two of them sat in lawn chairs beside the Cantwell pool, Ben in red swimming trunks and an ungirdled bathrobe, a pair of sunglasses dangling off his freckled nose, a cowboy hat on his head, and a box of cigars at his feet.

"Would you like one?" he asked. Bolanger nodded. "No, I'll hand it to you!" Cantwell shouted. "I know where you have put your hands." Bolanger grinned sheepishly. "So you have seen her?" "Yes," Cantwell said, lighting Bolanger's cigar. "Only yesterday. She's cooking you din-din tonight, isn't she? The two of you will probably fall in love and lie groveling at each other's private sewage plants. Children are an awful lot like urine, though, aren't they?" "Shut up, Ben," Bolanger said. "All right, all right. I'll shut up. I'm going to take a swim. Oh yes, someone left a letter for you." He stepped into the house, came back out, handed Bolanger the letter, then, after disrobing, jumped into the pool. Bolanger opened the envelope and began to read. It didn't take him long to realize Cantwell had written it:

> Please don't even guess who I am. I'm only writing this because B— C— is such a good friend of mine, and I don't want anyone else to find out. I used to be a Lesbian. B— tells me you want to know what it's like. I'm going to tell you, but only because I don't want you to make the same mistake I did. Believe me, I'm telling the truth.
>
> I first heard about the Lesbians in high school. I didn't know a lot about them, but some of the girls in school wore these jackets with a big "L" on them. I didn't know any of them very well, but they seemed

pretty nice, even if some of them did smoke. It wasn't until my senior year that I got really interested. I had just broken up with my boyfriend and I needed something to do—I come from a really boring town. There was this girl I sort of knew in history class who was a Lesbian, and I asked her about it. She told me they would be having initiations in a few weeks. I went. There were some girls there who were going to be initiated. I'd never met any of them before. We were alone in this building we'd been told to go to. Suddenly some doors opened and a whole bunch of Lesbians walked in. They all wore plaid. "What makes you think you can be Lesbians?" one of them said, sort of half shouting and half whispering. None of us could give a really good answer, since we didn't really know what the Lesbians did, but they didn't seem to mind. They just went on with the initiation. I won't tell you everything that happened, because it's still embarrassing, but just to give you an idea, first they made you sit in a dark room and talk about sports. Then they made you stuff your mouth with cigars and sing songs about animals. It was awful, but I figured it was worth it. But I can tell you now—if you still think it's worth it, you're wrong.

Anyway, it took a few weeks for the jacket to come. Everything seemed fine. I'd go to the Lesbian meeting every two weeks, but all they'd do was sit around and play cards. And some of them smoked. It got really bad. But one of the promises you had to make was that you would go to every meeting. Another was that you had to wear the jacket all the time. But the thing was, if I were wearing the jacket no guys would go out with me. I guess it was because the jackets looked like they came from the guys at Lafayette High, which was the other high school in town (I can't tell you what town, or you might look me up).

This went on for the rest of the year and then even when I went to college. You see, I made a mistake and said I was a Lesbian on this form I had to fill out at registration. The local chapter called me up. I had trouble saying no, so I told them I would be glad to join. I kept it up for two years before I had the nerve to quit. I just took my jacket to the cleaners and never picked it up.

How can I tell you what a terrible mistake you're making? You'll regret every minute of it. Or maybe not. Some people seem to like it. But it's a terrible life.

Please don't try to find me,
A friend.

"Ben," Bolanger said, "when did I ever take an interest in lesbians?" Cantwell heaved himself out of the water and onto the deck. "I don't know. I thought it might amuse you. My parents made me join Demolay."

Bolanger left Cantwell (his hair sodden and waterlogged, his cheeks pasty and blood-less) at the edge of the pool. Turning at the gate with a well-turned, well-hurled last Cantwellian salvo, Bolanger saw the son-of-a-bitch hurl himself off the diving board, the crack of his backside showing above the line of his bathing trunks. He heard the splash.

He mounted Vinegar Hill, trudged past the alternately fine and pretentious houses of medical doctors and college professors then on through Debs-Watson Park, down Camberson Way under the overhang of elm branches to his apartment, 144 N. Sigerson Street. He spent the afternoon reading to the sound of his electric fan from the volumes of Lautréamont, Mahfouz, Broch, and Musil stacked on his kitchen table. When he emerged with a bottle of wine under his arm and his grandfather's silver pocket watch in his left hip pocket, the sky was already purpling, the sun only a vague approximation. He found it much cooler and nicer out. Earlier in the day he had sweated profusely as he made his way across campus and walked the streets of the town. But he had showered and daubed himself all over with cologne. He enjoyed inhaling the crisp evening air, found it more invigorating strolling about now than in the humid afternoon. He walked with his head bent downward, his eyes fastened on the pair of blue tennis shoes he wore. He stopped for a second to look at a pool of oil on the road. In it the colors of the rainbow greasily refracted.

The chicken had already begun to sizzle. The tangy, orange-peel aroma of the ci-lantro-lime glaze overwhelmed and intoxicated Michael. He strained to recall the odor of ham or broiling beef, but couldn't with the biting, citrusy smell pricking his nostrils. Wearing a pink top and a denim skirt, Elissa Hexfore sat beside the park grill under-neath the tree. She smiled as Michael sat down beside her and handed him a dish of cucumber segments flavored with lemon-pepper. Michael began licking the segments clean before biting into them, enjoying both the piquancy and granular texture of the lemon-pepper. He dislodged the cork from the lip of the bottle, gulped a mouthful, then thrust the bottle at her. She took a long swig, smiled, wiped her lips with the back of her hand, and set the bottle down. With a wooden spoon she stirred raisins, dates, and walnuts into a bowl of vanilla yogurt, while he shoved carrot stick after carrot stick into his mouth. A large gray cat, creeping out of the shrubbery, darted at a blue jay. The bird squawked and beat its wings before gaining momentum and arcing upwards. Michael tossed a stone near—not at—the cat.

"Your marinade smells so good," Michael said, "But I'm at a loss as to how to de-scribe its peculiar scent. Fragrant and sweet, almost sickly sweet? Like fresh raspberries, but I swear it also has a slight numbing quality. A mixture of cumin, sage and caraway perhaps? But that is also inaccurate." "Not like bedbugs, soap or chemicals, I hope. You either love or hate cilantro. Some call the spice coriander, which derives from the Greek word *koris*, which means bedbug. I'm glad to see you are not a cilantrophobe, for I love the seasoning, consider it magic. The ancient Egyptians mention it in the Epers Papyrus and it remains one of the bitter herbs in the Passover tradition. I've heard that in the Middle

Ages enchantresses used it as an ingredient in their love potions. And, oh yes, *The Tales of the Arabian Nights* also classifies it as an aphrodisiac."

Elissa took the chicken off the grill and, after waiting for it to cool, the two of them began to eat. "Exceptionally flavorful," said Michael, tasting his chicken. "Green, clean and distinct." Elissa began to chatter. At first she seemed uncomfortable, but every sip of wine lifted her determination and her confidence and soon she spoke coherently. She talked about Spain, the erection of the Escorial Palace, the solid craftsmanship of José de Churiguera and Juan Gomez de Mora, and Diego Velasquez's inverted perspectives. She spoke of the bullfights, how she appreciated them better stoned than straight, how she found it far more interesting to note the truculent faces of the people watching (the gleeful expression on the face of a one-eyed woman wearing men's shoes, for instance) than to watch the fight itself.

She shifted topics frequently. She mentioned how she had taught beginning dance lessons at the Cannoshockton YMCA, how strange she felt switching academic areas, earning a degree now in Agronomy, how she dreamed about her father's strawberry-blond hair, his blue-veined forearms and the red pickup truck he drove on the tobacco farm. She laughed and told Michael how, when she was little, he used to sweep the kitchen floor with her hair, catching her by her ankles and pretending he held a broom, and how on Friday nights he'd always make potato pancakes but allow her to stand on a chair and fry her own quarter-sized "baby" cakes which she preferred to the regular-sized ones.

It surprised Michael that she would reveal so much. She talked on and on. She told him that in third grade she had a boyfriend named Herbie who played kickball with her and how one day when she taunted him with choice five-cent jawbreakers (she wouldn't give him one even though he begged her to) he offered to pull down his pants and, having no brothers at home, she took him up on the offer.

She started asking Michael questions, mostly about his family, about his mother and his sister Beth. He gave short, concise answers. They finished their meal, threw out their paper plates and plastic forks, packed what remained of the food into Elissa's knapsack, and headed back toward her apartment. At her door Michael reminded her that she had asked him to hypnotize her, having heard that he knew how. She smiled and said that she would still like him to try but not tonight. She had to study, in a few days her parents would arrive for the Herneshopple Arts Festival, and she needed to get a lot of work done before then. He sighed as she went inside. Then he crossed the street and headed downtown. He stopped at The Saloon for a few beers.

It began raining when he came out, and walking home past Boswick Building he noticed how the clock face glistened in the rain. He found everything immeasurably beautiful, the sky purple-pink, the illuminated face china-white and blazing bright, the buildings gray and stark, water dropping off the branches of the trees. He walked into the U-Mart and bought a Hershey-with-Almonds. Outside he sat down on a very cold and wet stone bench, the gift of the class of 1954, again recalling all the times he had eaten that brand of candy bar. When he took swimming lessons (he was six or seven) he'd always buy one and a can of Coke out of the vending machines afterwards; and later, when he took piano lessons, his father would shop at the A&P and always purchase a box of six with the order and he would greedily tear into it and eat two—his father would eat two also—and there would remain one apiece for Beth and Mom.

Don't stain your dress, he told his sister in his grandfather's car on the way to his father's funeral. She ate a candy bar then too.

Elissa also loved chocolate.

He recalled her teasing him with a chunk at Easter. She held it out to him, then quickly pulled her hand back.

Yes you Lissa.

Daring him to take it. To wrest the piece of chocolate from her.

Why did she speak about bedbugs and aphrodisiacs? For what other possible reason? And I had to act like a gentleman at her door. I did not try to accompany her in, did not follow through, and, with eyes always on the prize, pursue the chase to its inevitable conclusion.

She already told him on numerous occasions that he talked too much. Did his lengthy disquisitions about how attractive he found her bore Elissa? The signals she sent him remained mixed and contradictory. He felt, despite all her liberal and nonconformist poses, that she wanted him to adhere to the established practice handed down through countless generations of males and females and take on the role of the intrepid assailant. The passionate, pursuing male. How did her father court and win her mother? From all he had heard, he did not lack force or character, and she certainly loved her daddy. He swept the kitchen floor with her hair and drove a pickup truck, not a weak personality, not a milk-and-water man, not at all. Michael would have to initiate the liaison, make the decisive move, press the issue, cross the line of no return. Up to now he held back. She said no, *but she really meant yes!* Despite or because of her tenderness and tolerance, she wanted to submit to her man or rather wanted her man to break her resistance and bring her to submission. Deep down, even if she could not consciously admit it, she wanted to subordinate herself to her lover. He thought he had her on the brink many times. And she had told him that she had dated a lot of men. "I am seven years older than you after all." She confessed everything to him. Today in the park, she spoke about Herbie and the jawbreaker. Evidently she started teasing boys with candy at a very early age. During the several months of their acquaintance, he saw that she had many male admirers, that she enjoyed flirting with a wide array of men. But whenever he tried to bring matters to a head, she always withdrew and would never allow him to proceed beyond a certain point and always at the last possible moment … the critical juncture. Yes, she gave him contradictory signals. But when they embraced, she responded so strongly to him that he felt like he would explode and afterward when she pushed him away, his stomach clenched and he experienced severe, searing, stone ache. Was she just a tease? Why won't she give in? Why won't she just let me do it? He scratched his jaw. He didn't want to flub things up irretrievably, to proceed too quickly, anger Elissa, and thereby ruin all future opportunity with her. He had been very careful, maybe too careful and cautious, about going to her too soon. But God damn it.

He threw the candy wrapper down on the sidewalk, stood.

How do they taste? Baby cakes, tatoe cakes.

Pursued by chimeras of experience he had not yet relished and savored, he walked slowly, took his time retracing his steps back through campus to the little parklet where they had eaten their evening meal. He sat on one of the swings and absentmindedly started kicking his legs out into the air. He jumped off the seat and started running, heading in the direction of the old Victorian house converted years ago into student apartments.

Yes, why not? She wants you. Still a way to go. So pick up the pace. Come on Mike, march forward, double-quick. Her lights shone. He could see them from all the way down the street. But he had become winded now, so he slowed his pace and at last came to a standstill. He pictured in his mind what he wanted to happen ... Elissa looking up at him and half smiling. Come, she'd say, pulling him toward her and he would bend to kiss her relieved. She'd light a candle. He would sit down on the floor by her king-size mattress and undo his shoes. She would take out her barrettes. Off would come her blouse, skirt and slip. Hooking his finger on her lower lip. Kissing her eyelid. Pulled her down on top of him ....

Walking now heel having no trouble toe going down on her no trouble whatsoever he envisioned an entirely different scenario. Her reaction one of disgust. In his ears he heard her angrily shouting at him to leave. He took deep breaths and once again saw what he wanted and desired. Elissa kneeling down before him *performing throat thrusts*. Giving him plenty of tongue. He pictured himself on the swings only a few moments before, kicking his legs out harder and faster, faster and harder. He didn't know what would in fact happen. But he could no longer turn back now. A scene from a farce, a comic opera, played itself out before his mind's eye. Elissa throwing one chair then another in his path, keeping the table in-between them all the time. He had already undone his fly.

We should not I repeat we should not be having this conversation around the furniture.

No no no it remained still too early yet, too soon for him to play for broke, to let everything ride on a single roll of the dice. He should turn back. *You coward.* Move, I say. You're almost at her place. Just a half block away. Yes, there's no escaping now. He knew what he would do when she answered her door. He would brush her cheek with his fingertips and kiss her forehead.

She would smile and ask "Your first time? Come." Taking his hand, she would lead him into the foyer and they would mount the staircase. He pictured himself standing before her bed, where agreeable to anything she already lay. Come.

His tongue could touch her, make her come.

Dresden china plates from below pull down her zipper with my teeth it sounded like. What *did* she say? Dresden china plates.

Her head bouncing over your shaft. Feast. Gorge on it, it's *and feeling all of himself gather at no place inside himself* kosher *he became dizzy, faint.* Suck on that recessed pearl, drink that mucus *and for a moment he was gone, completely gone.*

Move I say.

Her lights?

Still on.

Go ahead. Press her bell

Look right in her eyes and tell her.

You're going to be my first

Footsteps. The door. "Michael!" Time will tell. One.

Pleasurable, yes; soul-satisfying, no. Seen upside down, her face grew manlike, as it had on the night they met. The throaty flavor of her lips and tongue tinged his mouth. Was she asleep? He felt like Icarus, plunging small and pale and unnoticed. He shut and opened his eyes. Turquoise spots gamboled on his retina, then dwindled and died.

He was almost there. He was. He was finally there.

III

They arrived at the bar early and ordered hot drinks. Unspeaking, they listened to the band and watched the people dancing under the strobe light. Lifting her cup by the rim, Elissa slowly raised it to her lips without using the handle and watched the flame flicker in the clear-glass brandy snifter beside her.

Tracers—red green yellow—move in such secure definedness: pulses, distances measured even in dreams. And yet, as if in a Dali painting, she sat transfixed by a multitude of candle flames in one squint. His reverie prompted her to think thoughts about reflections on reflections. Could anyone perceive what someone else thought? Perhaps one should remain satisfied with fantasy perceptions, faulty as they are: feel, sense, and leave it at that. But how had she come to sit across from him? Why had he chosen her? Michael Koremann always wore a corduroy jacket, too. He'd write poems, she'd read them, then draw illustrations for them. It felt as if someone played a queer trick on her. Two Mikes. One fair, one dark. One short stories, one poetry. But Herneshopple, Pa., differed completely from South Street, Philly. Days and nights they had bicycled with silver-heart balloons tied to their handlebars. Looking for jazz, discovering the bizarre old bookstores and exploring the new galleries. There had been moments of awkwardness, especially in the mornings, but the days had gone on—reading Delmore Schwartz's poetry, constructing Ready-mades for their walls, discussing Rossetti and Duchamp. The Demonic had to have a hand in it!

Here, she had gone to bed with a virgin who just happened to come from Cannoshockton. Something for the writers of the *fin de siècle*: a supreme example of *l'esprit decadent*. Certainly Michael had to have visited Brown's Woods. Wayne had taken her there a chaste girl who came back with her panties bloodied. She thought in the dark that they must have blood on them, but later, when she looked, they remained only soiled with dirt. Turnabout stood fair play. It was only fair that she set Michael on the path to Hell. Wayne had said that it would feel good, to trust him. Her palms felt wet, as they had in high school when boys asked her to dances. But, unlike Wayne, Michael did care for her. She found his distraction peaceful and calming. Before she met him, her life had already run the edge of recklessness: crash parties till dawn at her art friends' or Margaret's, mornings searching for her contact lenses and finding them stored in shot glasses, racking her brain trying to remember where and to what she chained her bicycle, attending Dr. Banter's lectures with a hangover—yet she always arrived on time and ended up with an A. Michael had settled her some, and she stirred his blood, even though he was younger.

Michael spoke.

"What did you say?"

"That I'm tired," he replied. "I haven't been able to rest for two nights in a row."

"Why can't you sleep?" she said. "By the end of the day I'm exhausted—empty, craving my dreams."

"I don't know—a mental constipation. School bores me. I thought I would be able to write this summer and enjoy myself, too. But I'm so nervous, so damn tense."

"Well, relax. Have some coffee. Listen to the band. You brood too much." Michael, saying nothing, merely looked out the window, watched the people pass, huddled couples, groups of proud, laughing college men searching for women as intently as their fathers, grandfathers, and uncles had stalked buck—a constant flux, a film of Walk-Don't Walk played by strangers. Elissa sat guessing who was going where. Hawaiian shirts: headed for the disco. Thursday night, ladies' night. Even the girls would be blasted at The Bitter End. Bolanger jerked his chair toward the table. "Have you ever noticed how so many musicians perform under the red and blue lights? White lights are uncomfortably hot. The colored ones are much cooler." He paused. "Would you like to leave?"

That evening Elissa jotted a quick paragraph down in her diary before she went to bed. Of all the entries he would later read, it remained Michael Bolanger's favorite.

August 28, 1981

We left with few words spoken, but they were enough. I wanted the silence. So many people irk me by burdening silence, force-feeding it with impotent words. Words that painfully drill into me. Thank God Mike allows silence. It was before two. The streets were still full. Music leaked from the bars along with a steady drone of laughter and odd howls. We slipped our arms around each other's waists. I was glad he was there and squeezed him slightly. After passing the last streetlight, the stars appeared, as if waiting until stillness and darkness set them off as they deserved. Michael stopped to point out Auriga and Cassiopeia. He knew all the constellations and the myths behind them. As he held me and told me about optical doubles and pulsars, I wished to be nowhere else. We walked on the last four blocks. He sat on the front porch step, patted his knee, and smiled up at me—waiting. We sat there, I on his lap, listening to the night hum, the crickets and cicadas beckoning to one another.

Chapter Two

Albumblatt

Michael had seen Elissa's photo albums before, but always in her presence; she would crouch beside him, pointing out important details and answering his questions. She had left for work Saturday morning when, reaching up from the mattress, Michael tumbled her albums from the shelf. From where he lay, he could see the tips of his toes and, pinned to the door of Elissa's closet, a New York Graphic Society reproduction of Edouard Manet's *Gare Saint Lazare*. Depending which of the two his eye zeroed in on, the other blurred. He lit a cigarette and, ogling his toes, kicked the covers from the mattress, booting Elissa's toy horse, Sheddy, off as well. He tossed it back onto the bed. Careful not to let the ash fall on the page, he opened an album. Pictures of Elissa at eight or nine, Grandma Hisfield's butter churn, a Hexfore family reunion, a dog. He shut it and opened another. A twenty-year-old Elissa sitting on the hood of her Volkswagen Beetle (its carburetor butterflied now, and the floor had recently rusted through, but she rejected any notion of selling it). Another of Elissa, in front of ... no, it still remained the Cannoshockton courthouse, not yet bought from the county by the Commonwealth Bank of Hanover to house outdated fiscal reports, old credit files, and crates of cellophane-wrapped lollipops for the kiddies. A double exposure: Elissa slaloming down Wayne Hedgepeth's nose. Sam's older brother. A snapshot of Wayne, straight-faced as usual, simulating copulation with a department-store dummy. Wearing his favorite clothes, khakis from Marty's Army-Navy and a yellow fedora, he courted the camera, pretending to ignore it. According to Elissa, he had a "cavalier poet appearance" which belied a "basically bourgeois get-ahead-of-everyone attitude." He married a fat but (naturally) wealthy socialite from Schenectady. Piss elegance, Bolanger thought. His one virtue. He put his cigarette out in the brass ashtray poised on Elissa's dresser.

He knew more than he ought to about them. He wished he had never learned that the photos existed, that she had kept him in the dark, resisted the pressure he had put on her to come clean.

When she first caught him looking at one of the albums a month earlier, she grabbed it from him. He asked her what was the matter. He had no right to without her permission, she said.

What could she possibly be that ashamed about? *The past times of illicit Elissa.* Not anything, she said. Did she think their love couldn't survive a full disclosure?

They had slept perhaps five miles apart, a distance both very near and impossibly far, but surely they had been closer than that. Both of them swam, almost certainly at the same place, the Memorial Fieldhouse. Had the splashes from his jackknifes and cannonballs attracted her attention, elicited a smile from her? In a town so small, their routes must have crisscrossed, synchronized, at some spot at least once. A church, shopping mall, county fair? Once, substituting for a friend, she had torn tickets at Laxallt Hall for some concert. She couldn't remember which one. He had been to many: the Pittsburgh Symphony, Lili Kraus, the Leipzig Philharmonic. A mother and her twelve-year-old son hand the anonymous girl their tickets. She couldn't have known, but what would she have thought? He turned the page: faces he didn't recognize, probably those of her uncles, aunts, and second cousins; the chapel at Camp Kiviok, where Elissa worked as a lifeguard; the "Fool's Bauble," a coffeehouse with a halcyon mounted on its roof as a weather-vane. He knew who came next. Draw, you rogues. Come, come. I'll carbonado all your shanks.

The first was Chet: a thick, aristocratically hooked nose, a prominent chin, slightly cleft; a domed, balding crown. With tasty irresponsibility, they had "sublet" a van and, in easy stages (along with Chet's two sons), journeyed from Disney World to Disney Land one summer—halting at all the backwoods bars along the way, brewing peppermint and Russian Georgian teas over open fires, toasting clams scraped up at the shore for the kids, purloining produce and gobbling it down in the store as they shopped. Standoffish Dorn, Elissa's third love, an anthropology student at West Chester State Teachers' College, could identify just about any opera after hearing the opening bars played on the piano but he could just as readily quote the complete lyrics of any Beatles' tune. He simply loved the Fab Four! He kept, Elissa said, a dozen liturgical books under his bed in a cardboard box, had large stumpy hands and had been born with a sixth toe. Elissa had a plethora of photographs of him, taken from all angles, postures, and positions. She even had one of him standing beside the deeply sensual, rarely aroused Michael Koremann, her last beau before Bolanger. Two were missing from her album but weren't missed: Guy, the exchange student from Holland who was better endowed than any of the others (she found that out one evening in 1976 in the tulip gardens of Hershey Park), and Robbie, the Jamaican tour guide who gave her a bottle of Wray & Nephew Appleton Estate Special after their morning swim off his pastel-blue littoral.

More?

He took a bowl from the cupboard and poured cornflakes, milk, and sugar into it. Looking down through laced white curtains, he saw the rooftops of two cars sparkle by. He crossed the hall and entered the living room. Elissa's box of death lay face down on a card table. She had been pasting photographs from newspapers and magazines to its backs and sides, a collage of stiff, brittle bodies and frozen, torpid faces. He recognized the glass-encased cadavers of Lenin and Mao, then the death masks of the serenely departed Haydn and Keats. Covered by an insubstantial layer of cracking skin,

Ramses' skull leered vacantly, his half-eaten ears as deaf now as they remained to Moses. A black-and-white from the *Post* of a Mafia boss and his most lovely coquette, gunned down in a clam bar, his Cuban cigar still smoking. Holbein's *Leichnam Cristi* juxtaposed against John Lennon's profiled corpse (an exclusive of the *Enquirer*), and Hermann Goering's dunghill of a body, noticeably discolored (a light green tint, the caption further specified) by the potassium cyanide he had taken. To the left of Goering's, two other photographs snapped by the official U.S. photographer at Nuremberg, the bodies of Jodl and Keitel, the noose still draped around Jodl's neck, his face that of a sleeping grandfather, blood seeping from Keitel's nose and eyes. Michael placed the cornflakes on the floor, staring at the faces until he could no longer hold them in focus. He blinked. Goering's open eye had affixed itself, cyclops-like, to Haydn's forehead.

When Elissa stopped to pick him up at 8 o'clock Sunday morning, Michael did not mention the box or the albums. He tossed his Minespot, flashlight, and phosphorescent chalk into her car and climbed into the front passenger seat. She embraced him with affection but, as all inamoratas publicly embrace, without zeal or real passion, a casual, secretive acknowledgment of previous evenings. Out of Herneshopple, they turned onto Interstate 61. He forgot about Wayne, Chet, and M.K. They stopped at the Marronsburg Hotel for breakfast and asked if they could eat at the bar. The waitress, unnerved by their dungarees and red flannel shirts, paused a moment and hastily agreed. They had been here before at night and knew that the management kept chess sets at the bar. As they ate scrapple, bacon, and toast, they played a quick game, which Michael slowly won.

They got back into the car, Michael finishing his toast, Elissa complaining that they would be late. The streets bustled with people: a miner helmet in hand heading for the strippings, a red-haired lady in a faded print dress walking her chihuahua, a long line of Pentecostals filing into their chapel bus. "Behold the Full Gospelites, the Assembly of Do-gooders. Or is it Dog-Goders?" Michael asked pointing out his window. "They look like a healthy bunch."

Yes, all their organs functioned, perhaps with flaws, but functioned nonetheless. They didn't drink or smoke. He'd have to say that for them. And if something did go wrong, they believed so fervently in Jesus' healing power, just like his grandfather did, that the pastor would simply place his hands on the affected area and they would stand cured. Mind over matter. Elissa passed the chapel bus and drove down the street to a little parklet adjacent to the junkyard and quarry.

At the same time, both Michael and she saw the oily brown curls and pencil-line eyebrows of Brent Cobin, Michael's Marronsburg friend and fellow caver, who sat underneath an old and gnarled oak tree beside several garbage cans. He jumped up, opened the car door, sat down on Michael's knees, and told Elissa to go straight at the light and then to pull into the dirt road leading into the junkyard. "Well," Michael said, "this at least allays your fear that he'd be lost by the time we found him." Cobin giggled, his long, rather aquiline face becoming broader at its nether point. Parking in front of the junkyard office, Elissa opened her door and slid out. Cobin led them toward the quarry, weaving a path through an interminable showroom of hollowed-out cars, rusting stoves, and punctured or slit tires, pointing to three large silos twenty feet in front of them.

Stopping at the silos, Cobin retrieved a bottle of whiskey from the bushes, where he had secreted it on a previous expedition. Unscrewing the lid, he lapped down the equivalent of three shots and passed the nearly drained bottle to Bolanger, who, after offering it to Elissa, who shook her head disdainfully, drank what remained. Through the trees, Michael saw the quarry wall, a gray-red shimmer. For a moment everything melted together: the alcohol stinging his teeth, tongue, and gums; a cracked crystal vase with diamond-shaped lid; glinting glass; a discarded diaphragm. Turning onto a maroon-black path, Michael worked his way downwards over loose, cascading rock. A wide, oval pool of yellow-green water abutted the cliff wall, which rose for one hundred twenty-five feet from the base to the extreme summit. For a moment, the pool stared back at Michael, a female eye resolutely taking them in. Cobin kicked the head off a discarded Bugs Bunny doll and then leapt over a rotting box spring, his unbuttoned purple shirt fanning out behind him.

It took them a moderately difficult five minutes to scale the thirty feet of cliff. Feet first, Cobin shimmied into the cave through the viaduct installed by the Herneshopple Grotto Society. Tossing the empty bottle down, Michael followed him in, then, grabbing her legs, helped Elissa through.

For three hours after entering the initial downward-sloping crawlway, they squeezed through interconnecting passageways, kicked unstable breakdown into pits, climbed over boulders the size of tricycles, and chimneyed down breakdown-choked fissures. Other cavers had broken many of the larger stalagmitic formations and had chalked or spray-painted an assortment of navigational marks—arrows (most of which conflicted), initials, and Greek fraternity letters—on the cave's bentonite walls. Every ten feet, Bolanger added his own directional mark, two parallel lines with a dot between. Cobin, interested only in the exercise, paused only when he had to, while Elissa seemed to want to stop at every interesting pebble. Bolanger was caught between grabbing Cobin's arm to hold him back and grabbing Elissa's to drag her forward.

They moved forward on hands and knees through a keyhole-shaped crawlway. The passage gradually opened. Cobin knew where he was going. A dome room with forty-foot ceiling.

"Almost there?" Elissa asked.

Cobin puffed.

"How long have we been underground?" Elissa said. "I can't tell." Michael lit several paraffin candles, the ends of which he had pressed into a large purplish chunk of flowstone known as the Wedding Cake. Cobin switched off his Minespot. The flickering flames, the play of Michael's and her flashlights on the ceiling and walls, the formation itself, reminded Elissa of some enchanted grotto, the pit's smell of an unbearably huge lime kiln. She bit into an apple. As they rested, Brent devoured a Twinkie, then lit a cigarette. He reached for the Minespot, stood, and walked on ahead warbling palliative nonsense. "Hare Krishna. Beau Regarde." Michael snuffed out the candles, helped Elissa up. "Nanki poo." He turned his head. "Trollops moo." Saw Cobin disappear between two breakdown blocks. Elissa dropped into the extremely tight crawlway next, followed by Michael, who later dubbed it the Birth Canal. It meandered a short distance to a dead end. Wrong turn. Elissa didn't want to go any farther. Greatly disappointed, Brent argued for some time, but after uttering what he thought to be the appropriate number of obscenities and imprecations, acquiesced.

Turning back, they found (as always) that it took far less time to retrace their way out of a cave than it took to trace it in. Pulling themselves up through Morris' Despair, a hole in the ceiling in which Ben Cantwell once had been inextricably wedged, they made their way to the viaduct.

Muddy and tired (except for Cobin, who was all for going in again), they crossed the junkyard and headed for Elissa's car. She unlocked the door, opened the glove compartment, and reached for her camera.

Michael Bolanger and Brent Cobin, smiling broadly, waited, their arms locked together, for Elissa to take their picture. Michael, impatient, looked away for a moment, and it was then that Elissa pushed the button.

At the intersection of Jefferson and Byron Streets, Marronsburg PA, a decrepit Volkswagen Beetle halts at an outsize red light, an invalid fleeing from the place it should be interred in, the light a final checkpoint, a last hurdle. Beyond it freedom. The passenger doors open, and two tatterdemalions scramble out from the front and back. The first turns onto Jefferson and walks twenty feet before—swallowed up by the hoi polloi streaming out of the Marronsburg Presbyterian Church: a large cruciform structure with exterior construction of Colonial red brick in a range of varying hues—he disappears. The second straps himself into the vacant but still warm seat of the first. He just manages to slam shut the door. The car lurches through the intersection.

Passenger

(Pretending to count the whorls on his index finger)

Although I acknowledge the possibility that a human specimen culled from any crowd on the planet, might turn out to be J.W. von G.'s superior entelechy, I can say with some certainty that the Superior E. won't call himself a native son or herself a native daughter of Marronsburg. No, the Übermensch won't hail from Brent Cobinville. I like him well enough, but he can become really, I mean really, disagreeable. How he swore when you wanted to leave. And what makes it worse, he's equipped as well as any one else, but his machinery is unused, he lets it rust.

Driver

Michael, stop.

Passenger

No, dammit, I'm not saying that a superior entelechy should have the usufruct of machinery belonging to other entelechies. Oh no. I do point out though that he exerts complete control over his own machine vroom vroom it truckles to him.

Driver

I've heard this. You're not sounding very novel or original, Michael.

Passenger

Well, what can I say?

Driver

Preferably nothing. I really don't like your attitude. This tired and silly pose of yours.

Passenger

(at the top of his lungs)

Well, dammit. Most people bore me. They're vapid and vaporous.

Driver

The Führer screams. Anyway.

Passenger

You're the exception. I'd classify—

Driver

Don't. It's unflattering and silly. However talented you are, someone always performs better than you. At my table, I will serve you nothing but humble pie, my dear. You had better get used to it right now at the start. And don't you dare call me superior entelechy, Mozartina, Alpha Double Plus or any other of your silly sobriquets. Call me cunt, bitch, whore. As nasty as I find those words, I'd much prefer you calling me one of them.

The Mozart Machine Reconsidered Commentary by M. Prime for the 20th Anniversary Chicxulub Press edition

(The reader may wish to skip over this section to continue reading the novella as originally written. He may find it more profitable to return to it after finishing the comic, clockwork third movement—the present Mozartian minuet—of our current opus, or ideally, he will only switch on and attend to this special commentary track his second time through our five-chambered cavern. The conductor taps his baton on the music stand and shouts da capo. Dare we hope that you reader will recommence our sin-phony again from the beginning?)

With some trepidation, M. Prime picked up and started reading the manuscript of his first novella late in 2007. Two decades had elapsed since he had completed the prentice work and earned his MFA from his second university, and the woman on whom he partially modeled the character of Elissa had miraculously and quite wonderfully come back into his life at a time when he reached an emotional ebb and suffered from the second of his two great life wounds. While he had not committed his manuscripts to the fireplace, he had not looked at them for years, not even *Final Drafts*, his one published and well received effort. Furthermore, he had written nothing new for half a decade. His great personal grief, poor health, and the unfolding of world events had all contributed to his despair and impotence. The only time he experienced comparable pain and desperation—when he had come close to dying himself in his early twenties. Rejection in love had nearly put paid to him then. His grandfather's deep and ardent affection for him, however, managed to pull him through. All these years later, "Elissa's" healing hands proved equally efficacious, and she had effectively returned him to life. He knew that he would have to tell the story of his miraculous resurrection even though he realized what such a telling cost and entailed. He understood and grasped Bradford Morrow's "metaphor of surviving the open wound that is being in the midst of making a novel, of keeping the inside open to the outside for the duration," and like Morrow he also did not find it specious or romantic. She had recently reread the book and told him that she now loved it nearly as much as other novellas and that it vividly brought back to her their student days at Pig Skin U., the campus of Giles Goat-Boy and Theodore Roethke, where they had served as founding editors of the campus literary magazine *Kalliope* and one of their fellow board members MD, unbeknownst to anyone, began his career as a serial bank robber. When he first sent her the manuscript in 1989, it occasioned a vastly different reaction. Although he had finished the novella and Wash U. had awarded his Master's degree two years earlier, he had procrastinated and delayed in sending the manuscript to her. He only dropped it in the mail after he began working as a social worker in a nursing home in his hometown. He vividly remembered the day he mailed it, as the police arrested a male nurse from the home that same day for stealing narcotics from the medicine cabinet, and he saw the police lead him out to their vehicle, his hands handcuffed behind his back, as, on his lunch hour, M. Prime returned from the post office after mailing his package to the now married "E." Prime. Naturally he found the sight a bad omen, and as he feared he received no response back from her. She stopped writing him for a period of five years, and, like the peripatetic and eponymous hero of his Revolutionary War novel *Henry Boulanger of Mushannon Town*, he came to the conclusion that the Beloved would not return. Whatever the novella's merits, he took liberties with the truth. Bill admitted that he wrote to get even—for the purpose of revenge. Playing God stood part of the joy of writing. One could change and reshape things, make it all turn out differently. Hemingway also joyously proclaimed that he made his bread and butter by telling fibs—in other words penning his stories. M. Prime knew in advance that certain passages would unsettle her and make her wince. As so many incidents came directly from his life, people would label the book autobiographical. He on the other hand thought of the novella as an auto-fiction or "faction." Its stimulus or occasion he knew profoundly at first hand. He, however, had changed and altered much. Still, even those who knew him well would find it difficult to separate the true from the made-up and concocted. With his entire soul, he celebrated the creative imagination, but he knew that the words of authors could sting and hurt. By intention but also unintentionally. Often the authors and storytellers in M. Prime's fictions infuriated those they loved with their tales—M. Prime's Henry James angered his brother William with his novel *Confidence* and felt enormous guilt for having betrayed Constance Fenimore Woolson by writing "The Aspern Papers" and "The Beast in The Jungle"—or else the stories they told had precisely the opposite effect than the one the storyteller had intended and therefore had deleterious consequences for the very person the storyteller wanted to help. The father in *Steiglitz's Folly*, for example, wrote his Civil War stories to toughen his son and prepare him for the slings and arrows which life would hurl at him. Instead the stories caused the son to retreat inwards and bar the door on the outside world. With time, "Elissa" warmed to the book, but in 2007 M. Prime feared that, upon rereading *Mozart* for the first time in over a decade, he would find it full of flaws and infelicities and would want to extirpate what he now considered a botched job. He remembered how his mentor the great PW repudiated his own first novel and wanted to buy up and burn all copies of it. Failing that, he struck its title from the lists of his publications in all his later books. M. Prime felt that he might experience a similar reaction to his own work. *The Mozart Machine* now seemed very cold and distant to him. True, the first two chapters which had served as his undergraduate dissertation had received a prestigious reward from his first university, and, later in St. Louis, Bill had told him that the novella showcased a considerable talent. PW had also praised it. What's more, M. Prime felt he saw aspects of *The Mozart Machine* reflected in his teacher's 1996 novella

Sporting with Amaryllis, an account of John Milton's sexual initiation at age seventeen at the hands of an otherworldly being—a dark-eyed, nutmeg-brown-skinned woman, seemingly Ethiopian, who nods to Milton on a London street then provocatively beckons him to follow her with an uplifted long-nailed finger. She leads the young Cambridge student, a virgin, intoxicated by the powers of language and myth, to her dwelling hung with dripping animal skins, proclaims her identity as the muse Kalliope, sexually initiates and later abandons Milton and thus precipitates his fall into language. When she disappears, a cold bolus sits in the pit of Milton's stomach and makes him heave! On account of this, M. Prime felt his novella had historical significance and that he should preserve it. Ironically PW had saved M. Prime's freshman effort from the flames. Too, despite all that happened to him at Pig Skin U., M. Prime looked back on his years there with a great deal of affection. It had been a time of learning and discovery in which he had burned with all a young man's ambition and simply read his eyes out. Not only did he study the works of the modernist masters, he sampled fiction and poetry from every era as well as discovered—thanks to PW—many contemporary world authors who would come to influence him. He began reading *The Avignon Quintet* by Lawrence Durrell, a writer with whom he shared the same birthday. Durrell's Eastern notion that all great books remain one book and act as palimpsests for each other fascinated him. Not only did an author break down and divide himself into all the separate characters appearing in a single book, those characters would transmigrate to his other books and assume different identities. Hanno Buddenbrook would evolve into Adrian Leverkühn. One could rightfully characterize him as an embryonic Leverkühn. Durrell, however, meant something even more momentous and weighty. He felt all great writers were merely copies and images of a single, eternal, ultimate writer and that those copies and images could change and transform into each other, as they all stood variations on a single theme. Even though he wrote about his own raw experience—subject matter that might seem trivial, inconsequential, or piddling to an older, more experienced person— M. Prime had grand aspirations for his *Mozart*. He envisioned a book where texts would constantly invade other texts and the characters would all reflect and mirror each other. With some relief he read the first two chapters. They seemed to stand up, but he felt particularly nervous as he sat down to read Chapter Three. An intrusive voice stood poised to invade his text. He needed his innocent fool Michael to encounter a father surrogate, a bluff and hearty Gurnemanz, to warn him of his danger. In his early fictions, M. Prime constantly wrote about orphans and half-orphans. Unlike his stand-in Michael Bolanger, M. Prime had a father, one whose knowledge of literature, music, and languages he stood in absolute awe of. At this early period of his career, he could not write about their relationship, so he ruthlessly killed off James Bolanger in *The Mozart Machine*. M. Prime knew how it felt to live in the shadow of a powerful personality and thus could empathize with George W. Bush and Klaus Mann, who likewise stood their fathers' sons and had their beds made for them. Above all else his father loved the operas of Richard Wagner, so M. Prime made Delone Frailey a Wagnerite as well. What a preposterous composite creature, a true Frankenstein monster. M. Prime had him earn his livelihood as an insurance agent like his beloved grandfather but also portrayed him as a hypocrite of the Sinclair Lewis stripe. In the late seventies and early eighties, M. Prime watched a lot of Vietnam war flicks and saw *Apocalypse Now* multiple times. He wanted his surrogate father figure to have experienced his own fiery rite of passage as a youth, so he made him a Vietnam vet. Samuel Beckett often treated his creatures in cruel fashion. M. Prime thought of *Company* and how the relentless Godlike puppet-master voice gave commands to his creature, a man lying on his back in the darkness of an enclosed room, and manipulated and tortured him as it invented past events in the creature's life and made him constantly change his position on the floor, telling him at last that words would come to an end and that the idea of "one with you in the dark" was nothing but a fable. M. Prime had put his own marionette—poor, frail Delone—through his paces in Chapter Three. He started reading the text with trepidation.

Chapter Three
Delone Frailey

I

An auspicious, happy day, thought Delone Frailey as he straightened his tie and slipped his glasses over the bridge of his nose (he had not, as yet, put on his pants). He had every reason to feel happy. He felt less like a lowly grunt—less like the bottom man on the totem pole—today than he had for a long time. He hadn't felt so up since the day he flew home from Vietnam and certainly not since he joined Firefighters' Union and Casualty. After all, today symbolized another year lived through (Mr. Frailey always found birthdays perfectly delectable); moreover, receiving the greatest honor in one's life should have some sort of therapeutic effect. But, as he looked in the small, oval mirror which when traveling he always took along (in this instance, a totally superfluous action, for the Company provided him with first-rate hotel accommodations; three mirrors hung on the walls of his suite), he saw nothing but the effects of atavism, Grandma's face—the loose pimply jowls, rosebud lips, and spatulate nose. Even her eyes' tergiversation. His wife never saw it, thought him crazy. But she had never seen "Mama" face to face, only her photographs.

The royal treatment surprised Mr. Frailey (and, although he was only thirty-three, one felt very comfortable calling him that). They did owe him. He had sold more new policies in one year than any other Firefighters' agent in North-Central Pennsylvania had in the last three, even more than Bill Umbower, the Herneshopple man, did in '78. Of course, he realized that (like the Baptist's head to Salome) it had been handed to him on a salver, that he himself had little or nothing to do with it. Perhaps his guardian angel (he believed firmly that people did have them), acting in a tutelary capacity, made sure the deal between George Hurd and the Germans went through. At any rate, he profited by it, as did all of Villa Nova; the opening of the automobile plant created hundreds of new jobs, and new jobs brought in new people, most of whom needed some sort of insurance. If, however, Delone Frailey realized that he had been merely "the right man in the right place" (and if he knew also that for all his efforts, he would receive only a plaque, not a perquisite), it in no way abridged his sense of accomplishment. He would hang the plaque on his office wall—it had a significance for him tantamount to that of a diploma to a doctor. Even the *Villa Nova Gazette* planned to do a story on him.

Delone Frailey's stay in Herneshopple would last for three days. The first company seminar (and the presentation of his award) would occur tonight at 7:30, the second, two days from now, on Thursday morning. He planned to spend his free time doing numerous things but foremost in his mind stood his plans to purchase the newly-recorded Karajan *Parsifal* (he considered himself a Wagnerian of the first order and spent his two weeks of vacation every summer in Seattle where he attended the annual German and English Ring cycles) and to visit a certain "shop" recommended to him by a friend with whom he shared a peccadillo.

After finishing his attire and breakfasting in the Carriage Room, where he feasted on ham-and-cheese omelets, home fries, and blueberry waffles, Frailey decided to take a morning stroll (he had not got out of bed until 10:30, an unusually late time for him), and, as it looked like rain, he carried his umbrella. As he wandered down Ackerman Avenue, the size of the Herneshopple Campus startled him, a much larger institution than his university. But he would recommend West Chester State to anyone. You got more individual attention at small schools than at big places like Herneshopple, Temple, or Penn State, and you met more people, made life-long friends. He smiled as he recalled the hours spent at the Rathskeller with Tom, Beatty, Schultzie, and Dorn. Friends one could count on, cut off an arm to do you a favor, yet mischievous, always on the lookout for fun, too. Tom and his cure for mid-term blues: dropping apples, oranges, Foster Tubes, down dormitory stairwells and, if they hit bottom, pretending that I**ntercontinental** B**ridgett** M**issiles**, named after the floor's janitress, took off, or Schultz with his eyewash about panty raids he'd never carry out or a rabble of dorm denizens "tubbing" Lubhold the linebacker and if he fought back and resisted conveying him to the commode and giving him a swirly. And, of course, Dorn, his best friend and roommate back then, who had introduced him to the world of opera, specifically to Wagner's *Lohengrin*. They went to a bar to have fun, but here what do they do? According to the *Gazette*, throw Liquid Plumber in each other's faces. Frailey's reverie ended when a plangent-eyed fiftyish man (a scrawny collie, hackles perpetually risen, leashed to his arm) buttonholed him for a buck. A bad risk, according to actuarial tables. "Sorry." He moved away and continued to follow more or less the same route Bolanger had on his first visit to Elissa's, occasionally asking people if they knew the location of Fraiser's Laundromat. If he would have known that Otis not only knew where the laundromat sat but also about the "shop," he certainly would have given him a couple of bucks.

Since he couldn't find it, perhaps wouldn't find it, he decided to see what the local newsstands had to offer. He visited two. Nothing to get excited about. Just *Playboys* and *Penthouses*. Outside one, he helped a young girl, about the same age as his daughter Jill, up from the pavement. Across the street he saw FRAISER'S LAUNDROMAT. Shit now that he'd found it he'd have to go in. But didn't he want something to eat first?

You freaking pussy.

The store specialized, among other things, in magazines of the type that had "no holes barred." Mr. Frailey had patronized similar establishments before but, upon entering them, experienced a slight embarrassment coupled with extreme nervousness.

He always remained conscious of the possibility of someone seeing him. Such places, naturally, did not have windows. Inside he could breathe more easily. If he encountered anyone he knew, well, they would face the same predicament as he. They'd probably both laugh it off. Not that this happened often. But when it did it always proved interesting. In Philadelphia, he met someone he knew from, of all places, the World Council of Churches—an Episcopalian minister from Hopedale. It fit. He had a theory. In fact, Doctor Gogarty had told him about the Herneshopple shop.

If the chance of encountering someone who shared his vice did not faze Mr. Frailey, the possibility of a person who didn't understand discovering it frightened him to no end. Certain individuals would classify him as a paranoiac, and in certain moods—ones in which he could calm down and view things in an objective manner—he agreed with that diagnosis. Still he constantly thought that loved ones, friends, and customers had found him out. The way his wife looked at him. He knew she knew.

He came dangerously close to confessing. Often (fearing that the person already caught him and found him out), Frailey hinted at his vice to someone who had the least reason to suspect it. After frequenting a shop, he chided himself for weeks. The Lord understood and forgave, Frailey knew that. On the sly, out of His great benignity, the Creator of everything (including voyeurism) would probably pat him on the back. *No one else'd think that. Certainly not the other parishioners.* If fact he had managed to keep out of the shops for several months, but today was his birthday, and he wished to purchase himself a gift no one else would think of getting him.

His hands. Clammy. He faced a combat situation. His spider sense tingled. He'd simply have to steel himself, then make a break for it, walk right in. In you go, Delone.

The (to Frailey's mind) not excessively large shop (which one entered after traversing a narrow corridor) carried three types of merchandise: magazines, Doc Johnson products (no relation to the lexicographer) and 16- millimeter movies for sale or rent. Booths where one could, for fifty cents, view five-minute stag films lined the back wall. A blue-gold, *papier-mâché* Chinese lantern provided the only light. A single clerk stood at the counter, two perusers at the specialty rack, flipping through magazines of men, for men.

Twice Frailey almost left. He did not like the looks of the clerk, a young, burly fellow with green eyes. Frailey liked shops with clerks his own age. One could never trust the young fellows. They likely stood Iscariots and would assuredly betray one. The youth of the Herneshopple clerk tempted him to leave immediately. He realized, however, that the clerk probably saw hundreds, thousands, of customers daily and probably remained too stupid to remember any one face, so he took his place at the rack and tried to determine the best magazines by price and cover. Again he felt like leaving when several adolescent college boys entered and he distinctly heard one of them say, in reference to him, "Pops likes to get his rocks off too," and another giggle. He watched them enter a booth, over which hung a placard, bearing in big, block letters, the film's title: "Nascent Girls Lose It." The clerk flew back and told them that only one could go in at a time. He grinned. They'd never be admitted to the best places, the homes of dealers who sold their products directly from their living rooms. Photographs of them....

Not at their present age but ten or fifteen years younger.

The air circulating through the ventilation system had a distinct smell, one Frailey recognized but couldn't pin down. It came to him in a few minutes—the Episcopal Home in Lancaster, where his father resided. He couldn't believe it: nonsectarian ventilators! For such a small place, Frailey thought the store had a remarkably large selection, being well stocked with magazines treating on bondage, bisexualism, transsexuals and shem-ales. He didn't go in for such exotic stuff. He skimmed over more titles. *Beef Chunks in Gravy.* That belongs in the other rack: for the fag boys. He just liked seeing men and woman doing it but "with no holes barred." It took him some time to make up his mind, but finally he settled on two magazines, took them to the counter and paid the clerk $17.50 in exact change.

Catching the two "inverts" in the corner of his eye, he remembered his Bible. Sod-omites, beware the wrath of God. It will descend on you. Get out. Now. Before this laundromat goes up in flames. He darted out the door.

The clouds vanish. Poof. Feel those flickering, prickering flames. Hell tingling deep down inside you. Disappear in the crowd. Slope on 'em dink style. Hide in plain sight but enjoy the tingle in your dangler! See, you didn't need that fucking umbrella after all.

Just blend in. Keep walking down the street. No one will ever know that you went inside.

The trip to the record store later in the afternoon proved a much more pleasurable experience, though not without a major disappointment. The angle and incidence of light, the polished floors and tidy aisles, the friendly and helpful clerks, the sheer number of as yet unlistened to, unscratched, albums could not help but cheer Mr. Frailey. Who said that no unexplored places remained—here he could find the recordings of the works of composers whose names he had heard (Stockhausen, Berg, Nemerowsky, Milhaud), but not their music. If like some people, he had inherited huge sums of money and had all the time in the world at his disposal, he could see himself doing nothing but charting these unknown territories, filling in the gaps in his knowledge of what he affectionately termed the not always straight-line, but often indirect and roundabout, course and pro-gression of musical development.

Among all the albums in the store, however, he could not find the Karajan rendition of *Parsifal*, his favorite Wagner opera. Its sublime music touched him in ways altogether different than the better-known strains of Handel's *The Messiah* with all its endless, boring hallelujahs. Checking a series of Schwann catalogs, the clerks told him that the record-ing had not, as yet, come out, that its release day still stood a month away. Though they said he could, Delone Frailey did not bother ordering it. He could get it cheaper mail order from New York. But as he stood in an especially good mood, he felt like purchasing something. He had no qualms about spending money. Today marked the acme of his career with Firefighters' Union and Casualty, and he could afford to act the part of the spendthrift and compulsive shopper. Every day he treated himself to a fifteen-dollar lunch and additional postprandial drink at Villa Nova's best restaurant. He chose a Grand Prix Du Disque winner, Karajan's "Brahms: Symphonie Nr. 3–Haydn Variationen" first, then two Mozart symphonies he had never heard before, and finally, to his great delight, Bruno Walter's famous *Die Walküre: Act One*. He already owned a copy of this album but had lent it once to his twelve-year-old, Jill (before the family trip to Seattle), who returned it in less than pristine condition.

He wasn't sure that after all these years he had caught sight of Elissa, so he increased his pace until he stood right behind them, her arm around the waist of …why she's robbing the cradle … but nothing's wrong with that … the girl who had dealt his best friend Dorn such a bad blow but who had always treated him in such a kind and friendly way, Elissa.

When the couple suddenly parted, Delone listened for many hours to Dorn's account of the breakup, a four-handkerchief sob story, and tried to commiserate with him but nothing seemed to help. Dorn didn't understand why she left him. She just did, boo-hoo-hoo. But was it really she? The young man, whose waist she held, spoke heatedly.

"You went to Spain after all. I don't see why I should give up my opportunity to study for a term in Cambridge and pay my homage to John Bull."

Shit. It's she.

Interrupt. "Miss Hexfore!"

"Delone …. Well it's nice to see you. You've taken care of yourself, I see."

"Oh, I've done all right. What about you? Still in school? You really are the professional student."

"This is my friend Michael."

"Nice to meet you."

"Wednesday, if you're here."

"Elissa!" The boy seemed surprised at the invite, Frailey thought. A little peeved and angered.

"Pardon me," she said to Delone. She turned her head. He couldn't make out what she said to the boy. She shook her head and smiled before readdressing him. "As I said Wednesday some of our friends, if you can."

Frailey apologized. He didn't have time to chat. He had a pending business engagement.

Elissa managed to commit him to her for Wednesday night, however, in the short interval before they continued in their separate directions.

II

In his relations with other people, Delone Frailey had always desired, one, to make his word as good as his bond and, two, to lend a helping hand wherever and whenever he could. While he did not trust hunches or intuitive flashes in matters such as the issuing of debentures, relying strictly on empirical data, he nevertheless believed in giving a person a "fair shake." If ever he could provide any sort of service to someone, they only had to ask, and, in most instances, he'd put all his energy into fulfilling and discharging their request. He took special pride in what he did for those who could not do for themselves, the checks he sent to Episcopalian benevolences, Indian reservations, the Pearl Buck Foundation, at Christmas time. Despite his eagerness to help, occasionally he felt as if he shortchanged someone. Three individuals in particular he believed he could have helped simply by disabusing them of false impressions—a vilely-mistreated clergyman, a comrade-in-arms, and an embryonic novelist. Of the three, he tried unsuccessfully to block out all thoughts of Todd Pettiman. He wished himself capable of completely forgetting memories which remained a burden and still traumatized him all these years later. If he could, he would erase all such recollections from the heads of a few others as well. Chuck Olsen, the on-duty attendants at Coatesville Veterans' Hospital, and even and especially Pettiman's wife Sally. They all deserved to have a clean slate and a fresh start. Todd should simply go away. If Delone could snap his fingers and expunge him from human history, he would not hesitate to do so. After all, if Private Pettiman had never drawn a breath—if no one had ever held and loved him—who would grieve for him, care? It didn't seem "right" to Frailey that a dead man could still stroll through a living woman's mind in a state of dishabille and get her heart pumping and her juices flowing, so much so that she couldn't even look at anyone else, or that the memory of him could suddenly resurface at inopportune times, when you were talking to a claims adjustor, for instance, causing you to wince and start (from the adjustor's point of view) inexplicably.

The mission had been simple: to build a culvert under a road to reduce the chance of the road becoming flooded during the monsoons. At dawn, acting in his ex officio role as the "man," Olsen—the company medic—passed out the water pipes and the daily ration of opiated hash to the men in their tents, and Private Frailey, as usual, turned his portion over to Private Pettiman, who smoked it down along with his own, as Bob Dylan's "Rainy Day Woman" honky-tonked (courtesy of Radio Saigon) over the Asian airwaves. He still remembered what he had said to Pettiman in reference to the song, how he had intended the phrase "pipe dream" to stand as the opening of a diatribe against getting stoned on duty, that Dylan was wrong, that the majority of the world's population didn't touch the stuff and never would, and above all, it wouldn't (as Pettiman thought) get you through your year of duty alive—no, the very opposite. But Pettiman misunderstood, thought that he had cracked a great joke, laughed and agreed that Dylan had meant a "pipe-produced" dream.

The then nineteen-year-old Frailey knew that if anyone could bridge the topic of drug misuse with Pettiman and not encounter, on a good day, a front of casuistry and gasconade or, on a bad, receive a black eye, if anyone could ameliorate the situation, he—Pettiman's friend, tentmate, fellow grunt and whorehouse cohabitant—could. And (though not an Episcopalian, but a Baptist) Pettiman might, might, just listen. The others—no—they'd laugh or even worse, to show their animus, threaten him with injuries known to produce aphasia. But he had sized Pettiman up, understood that a person annealed by an upbringing in the church, any church (Frailey remained ecumenical), could, would—had—to respond to an admonition from a fellow Christian. He had waited for weeks then the right moment had come, Bob Dylan's "Everybody Must Get Stoned" came over the air waves and experiencing something akin to divine afflatus Delone felt that he could refute the drugged-out and defiant rock star, that jackanape babyface punk in Cuban-heel boots with his bull frog voice and nasal sneer, but Pettiman had misunderstood, and, later in the day as Delone and the other men installed the culvert and dug an arroyo, along with two other G.I.s (all three stoned out of their minds) Pettiman—loud, boisterous, not giving a damn—went out on a search-and-destroy and got hit by mortar fire. The two corporals came back looking like sieves. Todd Pettiman's wounds necessitated the amputation of both his legs at the knees. After Frailey's tour of duty ended, he made a point of visiting Pettiman at Coatesville. Pettiman seemed happy enough, asking Frailey if he could smuggle in lefthanders as he found it difficult scoring smoke in the hospital. "Sorry pal, can't help you in that department," Delone said. The two shook hands as Frailey took his leave. Two weeks later, Todd Pettiman boarded the service elevator to the hospital's roof, rolled his wheelchair over the brink, and fell like a dive-bomber in a tailspin. They mopped up his blood from the sidewalk. His pal had died an unrepentant sinner but had slipped his shackles and no longer lay in cold irons bound.

In Rev. J. Tierton-Altimus' case, Delone Frailey did not realize fully, until years later (at the time, he was only a small boy of eight), how much a simple childhood gesture might have meant to the acerbic minister. The Villa Nova Episcopalian Church (the one he regularly attended for thirty-three years except, of course, when away in Vietnam and West Chester) had hardly changed since his boyhood. Every week, the walls' varying shades of green, blue green and tan, the ceiling's cream color, the light-putty gradations of the window draperies and curtains, the large sanctuary windows themselves (tinted ten different shades for the desired effect) continued to impress him. Only the globes, providing artificial light from pewter-furnished fixtures, changed. Strain as he might, he could not recall the color of Altimus' eyes, the shape of his nose, ears, or lips. He did not remember a face but a fleshy blur, a crown (more like an aureole) of short, neatly groomed, gray hair, a loud, deep-throated, slightly reverberating voice—"And if I ever choose to come back to Villa Nova to visit, would I be welcome, would a single one of you open your door to me?"

Few people cared for Rev. Altimus' loud, sarcastic delivery. His preaching style scared and frightened the eight-year-old Delone. Every Sunday sitting beside Mama in their pew, he cringed whenever Altimus raised his voice and glancing at the chancel at the rope which supported the adjustable sounding-board canopy equipped with acoustions connected to the various pews for the hard of hearing over the pulpit and the pastor, wished that the rope would snap and that the sounding-board canopy would come crashing down on the pastor's head, like the hand of God brought down on a noisome mosquito.

But on the day of Altimus' final sermon, Delone felt only pity. Collectively the congregation had decided to remove him, and C. J. Viddy, Firefighters' Union & Casualty's "captive" Villa Nova agent (he issued only Firefighters' policies, sold insurance for just the one company) who upon his retirement many years later would turn over all his former clients to Frailey after having first helped him study for then pass the licensing exam, had the political power at conference (not only did he stand a church lay leader, he had the additional distinction of hosting his own Saturday morning religious program on the radio) to effect the removal. During the sermon, with top-notch theatricalism, the orotund voice rebuked the congregation—just as the Pharisees and Sadducees had betrayed Jesus, so had the congregation betrayed Rev. Altimus. Was there not one true Christian there, one person who could see through the black conspiracy and recognize the hypocrisy and inherent injustice? The voice had such a lachrymose quality that Delone felt that he had to, in some little way, placate it. He'd raise his hand, as if he wanted a schoolteacher to call upon him. He felt sure that it was the right thing to do but looked hastily into his grandmother's eyes for approval and found in them only their wonted tergiversation. His hands remained in his lap.

Concerning Michael Bolanger, Frailey realized that he should inform him, man-to-man, that Elissa's affections could—indeed stood apt to—change very quickly. He had witnessed it before. Of course he could tell right away that the two of them slept together. Elissa kept sliding her hand in and out of his hip pocket. Delone had always liked her. He remembered with particular affection an afternoon when she and Dorn had visited him and brought live, blue-legged Maryland crabs for dinner, how she watched Jill, then seven (his wife worked and he had the licensing exams to study for), and held crab races for her on the red-tiled kitchen floor. No, he would not make a moral judgment—merely apprise Michael of the facts. As he dressed for the Company seminar, Delone Frailey made up his mind to definitely attend the Wednesday meeting of the writers' group and to set the boy straight.

III

Delone Frailey had hoped that Michael would arrive early. He wanted to speak to him straight away and have done with it—frightened that, if he didn't, he would temporize and end up saying nothing. Also, of course, he wished to impart his cautionary advice sub rosa. He hoped to corner the boy before the crazy poetry slam got started. Afterwards (the chip removed from his shoulder), he could, with a free conscience, make small talk and socialize. Contrary to Mr. Frailey's hopes, however, a number of the other writers— both current undergraduates and eccentric Herneshopple townies who came here as students years ago but had never left— arrived before Bolanger.

Dmitri Smeltanowski, a twenty-eight-year-old Polish exchange student with sallow complexion, sacerdotal face and poems chock-full of solecisms, showed up first (Frailey had arrived before any of the regulars). Entering the living room, removing the rimless gold glasses from his nose and slipping them into their case, he immediately engaged Frailey in a conversation about the inevitable (soon-to-be actuated) proletarianization of Art. "Like stealing an altar cloth—a desecrating, profane act, right? When an author becomes pedantic and opaque he breaks the most sacred, inviolable bonds—what do you say—ah yes—obligations of his trade union. In the first place, no sapient person would disagree that art should be—ah—real. Real with a capital R." Whenever Smeltanowski started preaching, Michael could not check his laughter. Frailey listened politely, occasionally looking over his shoulder to see if Bolanger had snuck by.

Soon after Smeltanowski, an orange-haired giant (a pair of sunglasses dangling off his freckled nose, a cowboy hat on his head) sauntered in, sat down in one of the two plush armchairs (Smeltanowski and Frailey had chosen high-backed wooden ones), and, after not listening to the exchange student, said: "Dmitri, spare us that party-line drivel. I'm in no mood to be misled by shibboleths just now." The two began to loudly exchange insults. Cantwell feigned a thick, foreign accent, playfully stuck out his tongue, and every couple of minutes resumed speaking normally in order to say, "Yes, yes. Spit it out." The noise they made forced Elissa to leave the kitchen where she stood arranging carrots and celery sticks on a tray and ask Smeltanowski if he would assist her. He stood, said, "Yes, certainly" and followed her out of the room. "The recipe must call for a *soupçon* of vitriol," Cantwell said, then winked at Frailey.

He knows. One of those smart alecks from the porn shop.

" … I tell you, that Pole collects dried dog dirt. He displays a box of it—yes, dog dung: black, red and all shades of brown from low-saturation graham flour to coffee-grain color—in his apartment, real art, you know." Delone Frailey stared Cantwell in the eye—a display of sang-froid—and hastily changed his seat. Within a few minutes, the others arrive: the constipated woman with twenty new poems about cute little kitty cats, the joys small girls feel when Mommy reads them their Dr. Seuss, and the expression of platonic love through bowling; Margaret Bromion, the hundreds of spangles on her dress glinting (she didn't write poetry, but she did wear dresses; after Renee Cantelo graduated, she joined the circle at Elissa's invitation; the girls needed another woman, Elissa had said, so the group wouldn't develop too masculine a point of view); pompous but untalented Terry (Bolanger couldn't remember his last name), who wrote under a pseudonym, seasoned his speech with phrases such as the "totality of the poetic event" and had not, for his numerous stupidities, received his full comeuppance; Michael himself, wearing his green corduroy jacket; and finally the near blind Walter Warnock, Nexus of Nuance's mandatory sci-fi-fanboy-fanfiction-practitioner-geek. Behind the lenses of his glasses, his immense goggling peepers rolled from side to side, darted back and forth, up and down, like guppies in a fish bowl. Michael called him cyprinodont. Slip on those straighteners and the words and letters would begin to weave and bob, to blend, blur, and flip their places for you, too.

Frailey sighed. He certainly could not chat confidentially with Bolanger now. How he hated dawdling! Elissa joined her guests and, as she was one chair short, sat down at the feet of the constipated woman, who had settled her considerable weight into the second Morris chair. The writers (except for Michael, who had not brought anything) began to pass out Xerox-copies of their work. Warnock volunteered to read first, the latest installment of his massive, never-ending, tripped-out space opera:

On arriving at Betio Green, Cynwulf Arpad put up at the Busche House, the planetoid's best hotel. Wishing to show his independence, he refused the stipend the Agency of Facts offered him. In fact, he cut all ties with government firms, listening now only to Felix Sieben's instructions to direct out of himself, through the pupil's aperture, the particle of consciousness which would dissolve gastropodically into the astral vault then reanimate itself—fulfillment at last—in the body of a sub-crustacean . . . .

Bolanger shut out the harsh, self-assertive voice. He had no desire to listen to derivative Hermann Hesse/L. Ron Hubbard. He knew, of course, that no one offered substantial criticism at one of these meetings, that nothing productive occurred at a Nexus of Nuance session, that the meetings only provided a cheap excuse for a lot of mutual hand clapping. Everyone found a nice word to say about everyone else's work, and no one went away (as Elissa would term it) "hurt," or, in other words, with the startling new *aperçu* that, for the most part his or her work could be accurately labeled tepid and generic, that is if it didn't stink to high heaven! Actually, the Wednesday nights fulfilled a social need more than anything else and Elissa had unfortunately taken on a role similar to that of Madame Verdurin. At first, Michael had participated in the charade and, when asked to give his opinion of a given poem or prose passage, would comment, "Well, yes, it's nice in its own way." He had always been terse. Of late, he said nothing at all, his only reason for attending the meetings, to please Elissa. The wallpaper's floral design interested him more than Warnock's twaddle. Glancing at the familiar objects in the room, her carpet, mahogany bookshelf, stereo speakers, the box of death, he tried to superimpose upon the familiarity the initial strangeness the same objects had possessed when, eight months earlier, he had first visited the apartment, so that both rooms—the familiar and the unfamiliar—would coexist in the same space, but, try as he might, could not make the rooms appear as weird and wonderful as they once had, so he gave up the attempt and began daydreaming about the places he wanted to visit in England: Ann Hathaway's cottage, Windsor Castle, the Lake District, and Stonehenge. Cantwell's voice disturbed him.

He read doggerel lines on an interesting photograph that Michael had shown him of Erika Mann and W. H. Auden shortly after their marriage. Both of them wore gray flannel suits, Tom's daughter (an authoress in her own right) looking more like a man than her husband:

> Mr. and Mrs. Auden out
> awalking in the garden, agreed
> that their suit supply would
> not suffice.

Said Mr. A, 'My dear,
Since our tastes stand very near,
why, one could shop for two and save us
half the price!'

Michael refused to look at him. "Notice the three consecutive stressed syllables," someone said mock-professorially. Elissa offered Cantwell the dish of radishes, carrots and celery sticks.

Aside from Elissa's work, M.B. found the poems of only one Nexus of Nuance member at all interesting, Mitya Smeltanowski's. He saw potential in Cantwell, who could write better than his doggerel would suggest. He had a knack for alliterative formulas and pastiche and what for today passed as an exceptional metrical ability. He also had what appeared to be a prodigious knowledge of prosody. When Michael put him to the test, he correctly identified an abba abba cde cde sonnet as Wordsworthian. He didn't as yet have anything substantial to write about—a paucity of experience. The same, of course, could be said about almost all of the young authors. Smeltanowski displayed no such technical competence. But despite his flagrant grammatical errors, the surfeit of lackluster language and the tendentiousness of his work—everything he wrote remained propaganda of one sort or another—there would always appear, somewhere within it, an evocation of the sensual, a few good lines, that made the familiar pungent and gave to his material an interesting perspective. He could somehow capture in a few lines about heavy drinking, for example, the sense of simultaneous diminishment and enhancement as one lost one's inhibitions and one's mouth and genitals became hypersensitized and took control. When he heard the Pole read, Michael felt that he listened to a recording of a very fine string quartet played, for most of the performance, at the wrong speed, but occasionally, for very brief intervals, at the right one. Too, the incidental or peripheral in Smeltanowski resembled the basic in Elissa. Never rationalistic or matter-of-fact, her poems stood all color, taste, touch, sound, displays of feminine pulchritude, glass permeable to light. Michael read over and over again his copy of the one poem she had brought to the meeting, a rushed second draft:

Camouflage

Camouflage green, a silent army
camped around us. No.
These colors weren't uniform,
though all shone green.
Nature, you said, camouflaging itself.
Even you appeared greenish
in that green light,
your veins, under wrist and forehead,
darker than your skin. I felt your pulse,
weak.

> Twenty feet far away, the highway—
> The cars, you said, became an intrusion,
> engines rushing through the bushes.
> But air-conditioned, isolated,
> they never saw what they passed,
> even later, when their headlights, searchlights,
> dashed, dappled, over your back.
> In the dark, scrambling to the shoulder,
> I couldn't see if your skin
> changed color with the light.

He realized that, like much of Elissa's recent work, this poem dealt with one of their mutual experiences. After hiking in Calumet State Park one Saturday, they had sat down for several hours in a glade near Interstate 61 and tried to count all the shades of green they could within a twenty-foot radius. He found seventeen, she thirty-four. He didn't understand what she had meant by extending the "greenness" metaphor to him. Was she only referring to the green jacket he had worn (the one he wore now) or—and this seemed more likely—to his inexperience, what she pedantically termed his "amatory esculence." What exactly did this greenness hide? His ability, perhaps? Naturally, the poem interested him more than anything else. In fact, it remained the only thing that evening that actually did.

Uncomfortable and completely out of his depth, Delone Frailey nonetheless commented favorably about everything he heard. He could make no sense whatsoever of Warnock's work, but he enjoyed listening to him anyway. After all, one did not need to know a single word of German to appreciate *Die Meistersinger*, one only had to experience the leitmotifs, the joy of uprooting one, excising a single strand from the orchestral tapestry and following its path through the whole opera or, as if looking into the face of God, listen to them all together, experience the Wagnerian panmixis. Every human voice was like a fingerprint, something rare and relishable. Warnock's voice intrigued Mr. Frailey. Together with the billions of other voices on the planet, each warbling its own unique motif, it had a part, albeit a small one, in the penultimate Wagnerian chorus. So did Cantwell's, for that matter, but Frailey listened to that voice with apprehension which after a time cooled into relief. A smart aleck, yes, but not one of the miscreants at the laundromat. He liked the constipated woman's poems most of all: ebullient, funny, full of hearth and home. He enjoyed the *esprit de corps* when Elissa and Margaret Bromion went to the kitchen to get the refreshments (Michael Bolanger followed them) and the other writers chatted about this year's football team, certain teachers, politics (predictably, the counter culture cretins in their spiral tye dyes all loathed Ronald Reagan), and the crisis in the Falklands. Within a few minutes, Elissa returned with the food: doughnuts, celery sticks, crackers, chips. They could have coffee, grape juice, white wine. "Michael's left," she said. "He said he has an earache." Cantwell giggled and then, seized by "an overmastering inspiration," whispered mock-impromptu:

I'll be surrounded by my peers
And all the books that they have written.
I'll bash those books against their ears
And they will fall so heavily smitten
That they will kneel, abruptly humble,
And like their pages curl and crumble.

Several of the writers laughed.

Always punctilious, Mr. Frailey would never have left the Nexus of Nuance meeting early (such an impolite action could rightfully be considered an affront) had not his mission in coming been to speak to Michael Bolanger. As soon as Elissa had said that Michael had left, he thought it politic to follow. He muttered what he realized stood lame excuses—his hotel stood some distance away, he felt tired and had to get up early the next morning to attend a second seminar—and waited impatiently for Elissa to bring him his coat and, just before he left, unable to resist, purloined a doughnut. He had to run to catch up to Michael, who had outdistanced him by about a block. Bolanger turned around at the clacking of the fast-approaching footsteps. Surprised to see Frailey, he congratulated him on his escape from the nexus, and the insurance agent responded by asking him about his ear. "No, it doesn't hurt, though I'll say all the burgeoning young writers have much abused it this evening." Frailey remembered a caricature depicting a two-inch tall Wagner, hammer in hand, bursting an eardrum, the nail for his hammer the symbol for a musical note. "These people need strictures, not kind words," Michael added. Frailey asked him if he was hungry and suggested they have their meal together, his treat. Michael shrugged his shoulders and said that the Old College Diner stood across the street. He ordered a hamburger, but Frailey told him to get something more substantial instead, so he selected the chicken dinner. Frailey had the same.

The insurance agent found it difficult, when it came down to it, to broach his subject, so he spoke to Michael about the music of Richard Wagner. Yes, Michael replied he knew a little bit about the German composer, primarily his enormous impact on world literature in both the nineteenth and twentieth centuries. Fascinated by Wagner's ideas, Baudelaire and the other French symbolists strove to create absolute poetry and turn words into music. The Irishmen George Moore and George Bernard Shaw remained devoted Wagnerphiles and Edouard Dujardin, the originator of the stream-of-consciousness technique, said that he found his inspiration in Wagner, and, of course, Thomas Mann, Michael's favorite author, worshipped the composer's music. Bolanger's knowledge surprised Frailey and although he had not, aside from G.B. Shaw, read any of the authors Michael mentioned, he found it refreshing to speak with someone who knew more about Wagner than most of the uninitiated to whom he mentioned the composer's name, who, if they knew anything about Wagner's influence, knew only that Adolf Hitler and the Nazis had adulated the man and his music. He urged Michael to listen to the operas and experience their magical bewitchment at first hand. Then abruptly changing the subject, he remarked: "Elissa's quite special, isn't she?" Michael nodded his head. "You know, of course, that you're not her first—" He had meant this to sound fatherly. It hadn't. He shut his eyes, but Michael only smiled. "We're happy together," he said. "Opposites attract, but not for long. Intelligence needs intelligence." Frailey flinched. Here, this Brünnhilde sat in front of him (he felt like Waltraute) insisting upon Siegfried's fidelity when at this very moment some Hunding or Gunther might be administering the fateful draught which would make the hero forget his love and grow captivated with another. Jesus, he thought. You've got to keep them under lock and key, boy. No one ever tell you that? "Don't you think her former boyfriends might have felt that way, too?" Michael looked pensively at his coffee cup. He shrugged his shoulders. "I doubt it."

Delone Frailey bit into his drumstick.

The next day, after the second seminar, a sales and coverage instruction session, ended and Frailey, having packed his scrupulously taken notes into his portfolio, prepared to check out of the hotel, the insurance agent decided to telephone Bolanger from a booth in the Carriage Room. He found the number in the directory. Last night, Michael had remained so unreasonable and inflexible, an egotist and cherisher of false illusions, that Frailey did not think he could unblinker his eyes, but he liked the kid because he treated Wagner seriously and admitted his cultural importance, even saying that he looked forward to someday exploring the German's music.

She left Dorn, he would say. A very smart person. A lot like you. The phone rang six or seven times before Frailey hung up. He wasn't home. Well, Frailey had tried. If Michael was as smart as he seemed, he'd see the wisdom, the warning, in last night's conversation and remain wary and on his guard when it came to Elissa.

TWO

Chapter Four
The Sin That Sleeps Too Long

Every clear day in October, for two or three hours in the afternoon, Margaret Bromion bicycled portions of backroad that eventually led, from various locations in the county, to Marronsburg or Herneshopple. The Mail Pouch barns, scattered mobile homes, fenced-in pastures sped toward her, and after twenty minutes, when she got her second wind, the fields, trailers, trees appeared, in fact, to be in motion. If was she, not they, who stood, or, in her case, sat, stationary. Everything swirled past her. She had perceived this illusion before, most sweepingly when she and Elissa Hexfore had crossed the Pyrenees by funicular railway, but until recently had fought against it, repeating to herself, "It is I who am moving—or rather we." However, clichéd as the conceit might seem, she had come to see life itself as a play, a moving picture, a novel—she didn't know which—that each day unfurled a new scene or spread out another chapter. One could not help becoming engrossed, one had only to examine the minute, fine-grained detail: wars in the Falklands, E=MC2, stop-gap animation, libraries full of books, green sunsets in the Antarctic—a treasure-trove of the supplementary that made life so real, so authentic. And, if one thought of existence as a movie, a fiction, while one could still cry (as Margaret did every time she played her video cassettes of Greta Garbo's *Camille* or *Anna Karenina*), one would remain far less unhappy. Life, in fact, would entertain you. Just as when bicycling you felt caught up in a moving landscape, by existing, you found yourself ensnared in a super movie, acting out a pre-written part. But you didn't know what would happen next.

Margaret Bromion decided that she had remained unhappy for too long. She had everything she ever wanted materially—cars, jewelry, clothes, vacations anywhere. Her father, Dirk Bromion, President of Atelier Scientific, Inc., had always seen that all her needs were met. Greatly disappointed by his daughter's numerous deficiencies, he had tried for many years to bribe her with what to him seemed mere lagniappes, no matter how excessive the largesse appeared to others. "Margaret, you're my daughter. Miss Stoor tells me you're not working up to your potential. If you can manage to make better marks next grading period, all B's, let's say, I'll take you to Europe over Christmas vacation." Margaret disappointed her father not only by being an atrocious student (which she remained from grade school onwards) but also by not inheriting her mother's good looks and, finally, by being impossibly, painfully shy. By his daughter's eighth birthday, Dirk Bromion had come to the conclusion that she would never live up to his expectations.

Stoically resigned to this, when put upon he withheld nothing from her and quite ironically began to refer to her as his "beauty queen" or his "little savant." Margaret had naturally remained much closer to her mother, who died shortly after Margaret's tenth birthday. She remembered vividly how, as each and every holiday approached, like everyone else they hung cardboard cutouts—cupids; Tom Turkeys; rubicund, twinkling-eyes Santa Clauses—in the windows, but by secret agreement no holiday figure ever on his appointed day: Santa Claus adorned their windows on St. Patrick's day, Tom Turkey on February Fourteenth. When unhappy, Margaret would also call to mind her mother's daily floral compositions of black-eyed susans, daisies and other wild flowers in the clear hourglass vase on the kitchen table; the white coffee cups, saucers, tablecloth, chairs; the green field and blue mountain seen through the kitchen window, the sound of the forsythia branches tip-tapping against it. They cut one breast off, then the other, but finally the cancer settled, inoperably, in the liver. The doctors could only administer morphine. Her mother held on for months, speechless, probably unconscious, her belly hard and distended, tears streaming down her face when her husband, mother, or daughter spoke to her. Simply a nervous reaction, the doctor explained. She looked much better in the casket than on the hospital pallet. Unfortunately, her funeral stood not so much a respectful memorial service as a lavish social occasion. Everyone turned up, all her father's business associates and the majority of his employees. Her father hired a caterer to provide the dinner and to serve cocktails. Each time her father married, they of course moved into a different house. Margaret did not much like Mrs. Bromion II (a cruise director half her father's age, later divorced by him when he found her unfaithful), Mrs. Bromion III, or, for that matter, any of the Mrs. Bromions *in praesenti*. They kept their distance, avoided all but the most superficial contacts, and Margaret gladly did the same.

Aside from bicycling, Margaret enjoyed two things: tennis and parties (as long as they remained her parties, not her father's; her friends, not his). Not nearly so shy as her father had at one time supposed, Margaret cultivated an endless number of "close friendships" at Brown (Dick Bromion had pulled all sorts of strings to get her in, only for Margaret to fail out) and then at Herneshopple. The parties thrown there by Margaret and her two cousins cropped up with disturbing regularity, only very slim intervals between them. Weekly, twice-weekly, thrice-weekly, the various purveyors in the town would receive huge orders from 57 E. Ackerman which they would fill most obligingly. The parties occurred even more frequently after the university placed Margaret on academic probation (she failed calculus) and when—her father thought she needed a break from the campus milieu—she returned from Spain. Ultimately, Mr. Bromion paid for these soirees, but, though he lived only two miles away, he never knew they took place.

They began early and of course ended late. On a typical night forty to sixty people came, most primarily for the alcohol and food, of which there stood plenty. Someone had nicknamed the girls' townhouse "Golconda." The name stuck. Margaret, Judy, or Ann met you at the front door (Margaret wearing the most fashionable dresses from Gucci, the other two clad in outfits from Ralph Lauren: their fathers remained, after all, only Atelier Scientific vice-presidents) and led you, their scintillant yellow-green eyes beaming with pride or glossy with drink—you couldn't tell which—into the front room, took your coat, answered your questions—where the bathroom or the beer sat, if Jim Owens had come yet—and then left you to mingle into the crowd on your own. The guests gorged themselves with all sorts of goodies: Pinoche or Divinity, Nut Loaf candy, Raisin turnovers, Roquefort or Pimento cheese, Lobster Wiggle. Often Margaret ordered a side of beef. Judging by the line in front of the bathroom door, no one suffered from dysuria. The guests quickly consumed then voided large quantities of champagne, beer, and bourbon. By the next morning, their house stood a complete wreck. Someone had damaged several very fine pieces of furniture … a girl tripped on the hall carpet, dropped a pitcher of Club-of-Ten punch, incarnadined twelve people, a davenport, and a love seat. Margaret and her two cousins grew accustomed to such devastation, expected it, as they expected some object—a ring, book, candlestick, record—to be missing the next morning. You had to anticipate such things. They happened all the time. You didn't worry or stress about them. The cousins often engaged local bands—Shenanigans, Wallace Carnaby, Johnny Hart and the Cyclones. As the musicians swung into "Crosstown Traffic" or "The Guns of Brixton" couples swung onto the floor and danced. After downing a few more drinks, they would begin to disappear. When Elissa's life "ran the edge of recklessness," she had reveled frequently at Golconda. Occasionally, she had left with a man, once with Margaret's mixed-doubles partner, Tim. Unlike Elissa, her cousin Judy, practically everyone else, Margaret, when propositioned, never did.

In her twenty-four years of life, Margaret Bromion had flown to Europe five times and Hawaii twice; three stars—each for an astronomical sum—bore her name; she had owned four cars and, at one time, twelve parakeets, but in all that time she had only ever taken two lovers. Two "ungainly obsessions" had, by all means, stood enough. Margaret had met Rick Waldo, a philosophy student at Herneshopple, who did yard work for her father shortly after she turned seventeen, during her spring vacation from Kanesatakee Prep. He immediately attracted her, and it did not take him long to discover Margaret's infatuation. He sneered at it—not on the job where he dissembled and tried to remain polite, but at home, school; in short, any place other than Bromion's. Waldo hated the rich, hated them even more for being such an obvious thing to hate. His aversion justified itself once again when he found a slightly soiled but otherwise undamaged shirt of Mr. Bromion's among the refuse thrown into a garbage can into which he dumped raked leaves. Not only did Mr. Bromion have the effrontery to bedizen himself with such vulgar finery, he had the gall to discard a shirt worn, at the most, three or four times when other people—Waldo's father, for instance—owned three "good" shirts, the rest of their wardrobes consisting of mere—Bromion would say it in such a sneering way—"functional attire." But then the rich never felt compunction for those plagued by insufficient funds or monthly amortizations. Oh, Mr. Bromion maintained a spirit of good will toward his employees, invited all the boys, the hardhats who drilled his oil, Rick Waldo, to a summer bash at his camp near Mushannon, where, sitting around the campfire, they'd look up at the stars and drink enough Wild Turkey that they experienced the trees' fluctuations and the curlicue and wave of the flame, so that, when they heard Bromion's voice babbling from somewhere—everything had blackened around them except the fire—that he had bought for blankety-blank-blank dollars the privilege of naming a star—actually three stars, but from earth they appeared to coalesce into one—after his daughter, a gift to the girl's mother on Margaret's third birthday, all they could do was laugh, the whole bulging span of pleasurable sensation condensed and alternately focused on their eyelashes, prepuces, and kneecaps. Mr. Bromion remained just the kind of person who'd buy a shirt in order to dirty and ruin it while drinking with the boys, Waldo thought, confident that he had guessed right.

Bumptious and pontifical, Waldo stood the paradigm of a slogan-spouting "New Causer," that angry activist always replenishing his stock of new Evils That Must Be Protested, forever willing to descant upon the country's, the world's, the Universe's problems and to subject those who disagreed with his analysis to hour-long philippics. He demonstrated against nuclear power, for instance, long before Jane Fonda. His friends found him at once bullheaded and sensitive, a would-be leader of the people, whose company and contumacy they scrupulously avoided. Margaret, however, remained unaware of these salient dispositions. Her attraction remained purely physical—a hungry and devoted admiration for the factotum's infrequent but toothy smile, his well-formed Myrmidon pectorals (she had managed to plow through *The Iliad* at Kanesatakee), his short, neatly groomed hair, tapered threadlike lips, and roguish black-susan eyes. By the summer, she had incarnated the amorphous bundle of odd desires and strange compulsions that somehow constituted for her an image—albeit featureless—of the ideal man, a phantom with whom she stood very much in love, into the body of Rick Waldo, and the word indeed became flesh. If she met him on the street she would wave, gesture, shout. He would nod his head, not bothering to wave, his hands thrust deep in the roots of his pants pockets, then try to move out of her direction as fast as he could. If, at this time, Waldo had asked Margaret to marry him, she would have accepted the proposal immediately, and, as a friend in the campus branch of "Freedom for South Africa" told him, not only would he have been set up for life, he'd have the rare opportunity to personally redistribute some wealth. Needless to say, Waldo remained intrigued, but his aversion for the rich and a strong sense of personal dignity—he saw himself as no prostitute—prevented him from becoming the fawning suitor.

However, Margaret's attraction to him did trigger certain fantasies. He envisioned the joy and satisfaction he would experience tossing her onto her bed (in his mind as vulgarly ornate as the Imperial bedstead at Versailles) and beating—to use a favorite expression of his father's—the living daylights out of her. Of course, when the chance presented itself, he did not realize this *fata morgana*, but what occurred still remained highly unpleasant for Margaret Bromion. The July Tuesday (Margaret forgot the date, remembering only that it was a Tuesday) had been highly unpleasant for Waldo. He awoke to the sound of crying. His landlady, the seventy something widow of some long-dead biology teacher, found her cat, a yellow-gray tabby named Sam, murdered on the sidewalk. Waldo gently coaxed her to hand him the rock-hard corpse, tried to say something comforting, winced at the pellet wounds in the cat's belly and neck, and buried the animal in his landlady's flower garden. Then, later in the day, while lunching at Owens' cafeteria, he found out that a friend had just lost his work-study job as a projectionist. Without the job, the friend, a student with a grade point average of 3.0, could not afford to remain in school. Naturally Waldo got drunk with him. He remained intoxicated at four, when he arrived at Bromion's to mow. Dirk Bromion had left home—he and Mrs. Bromion IV honeymooned in Barbados.

Waldo maneuvered the Lawn Chief through the maze of untrimmed evergreens and the tall, heavy elms that shaded Bromion's lawn, through pine-needle loam and over dozens of hard green apples that had fallen prematurely. He steered recklessly—overconfidently—hoping to finish in an hour, and enjoyed the sensation, almost like tobogganing, of the ground rising and falling underneath him. He knew that the two elms at the base of the hill were coming, but instantaneously they stood right in front of him. To avoid the nearest tree, he swerved to the right, toward the second elm. It fluttered, seemed to swish and throb, then suddenly grew bigger. He yanked the wheel again but this time with too much force and the miniature lunar land-rover—the tractor resembled one at least to him—rolled to its side, throwing him from the seat like a rider from a horse shot at full gallop. He felt a delicious, dazzled sensation ripple through his entire body as he lay on the ground and looked up at the sun, a seething orange bulb, watched a lone squirrel scamper up the trunk of one of the two trees, felt the warmth of the sun's rays on his face, and listened to the monotonous churnings of the still spinning cutting blades.

Margaret found him spread-eagled on the thick living-room carpet pouring himself a glass of her father's best cognac. Immediately she wanted to drive him to the hospital, or at the very least to call a doctor, the police, someone. She blenched at an unsightly contusion on his forehead and ran to get some ice, which he refused to apply. "Karma's a bitch," he said. "Where's your bedroom? I feel like lying down."

Waldo shut the door behind them and began to take off his shirt. "You do want it, don't you?" She hesitated, balking at his broad brown chest, the tone of his voice. "It's the only thing I can think of," he continued, "that would make *me* happy just now." She didn't know what to do. She had not envisioned this at all. If only I grew up an Indian princess, she thought. A lovely Indian—

Waldo gripped her shoulders and pushed her downwards.

Margaret suffered through her second ungainly obsession at Brown. It was not the person but the nature of the relationship itself that some considered ungainly. This second obsession caused Margaret much more pain than the first. After the twenty minutes of humiliation Waldo inflicted ended, Margaret never saw him again. However, when her relationship with Adrienne Sims—an involved and protracted one—came to its abrupt and irrevocable conclusion, Adrienne's dying in a perfectly absurd automobile accident. She grieved for months, indeed experienced the smarting, unendurable loss of a Patroclus. How insipid all earlier heartache seemed.

The two met at a revival house at a Rita Hayworth renascence and retrospective. At the time Margaret felt very low. Despite inordinate exertions on her part to court friendships with the sisters of several Brown sororities, they had all given her peremptory

NOs. Her hopes dashed, she resented her father's offer to fund a new sorority chapter at Brown, "where she could act the part of prima donna." She wanted a sorority to accept her on her own merits, not her father's, so she feigned that acceptance or non-acceptance stood unimportant to her and thus dissuaded him from purchasing yet another nosh, as he called it, by the adoption of a smugly indifferent air.

Of course, she could not truthfully shrug off the rejection or (as she had done in other instances) sublimate it. Her life stood replete with failures. Each additional one recalled the others, and the abrogation of these past setbacks came to depend on the success or failure of whatever endeavor she at the time pursued. To join a sorority had once meant everything to her, but the sisters had not accepted her. Once again she felt crushed beneath the wheel, thrown into the furnace, reduced to nothing. She desperately needed a shoulder to cry upon, and Adrienne, so kind and understanding on their first meeting, provided that shoulder.

At first Margaret did not realize her new friend's sexual preference, and imagined for a long time that she had an entire cortege of male admirers ready to usher her to films, restaurants, the theater, anywhere she wanted. For what man would not be attracted to those hard blue eyes, that enigmatic smile, malleable figure, and, of course, those long blonde tresses which—Margaret would later say—rivaled even Rapunzel's in length. Adrienne's first overtures, launched perhaps at too subliminal a level for the intended quarry, passed over Margaret's head, and when the older girl finally began her attack, so to speak, Margaret scarcely knew what was taking place. She thought that her friend was pulling her leg then wanted to say no but didn't know how (Adrienne became importunate but Margaret felt for her and believed her in great pain) so she said nothing—and continued to listen to her friend inveigle, solicit, and try to entice. The stream of words, unchecked, began to act like a powerful and unexpected stimulus touching off something Margaret could not control. Too, because this particular script stood a proscribed one, the prospect of acting in it became all the more attractive. It happened quickly; she said yes, and almost without realizing it she found herself lying with her friend in bed and actually *doing* all those things she could never imagine doing. Afterwards, she felt awful and for several days actually experienced physical discomfort—a Samson-like force inside her, pushing outwards, stretching her into something awkwardly, even grotesquely, big. But the urge returned with a concomitant desire to placate it. Society had wrongly prejudiced her, Adrienne explained. Anyone who expressed another view spoke—as her friend put it and Margaret now believed—"Tommyrot, blarney, and blather." Soon she found Adrienne's bed a comfortable place, and felt happier than she had for months.

Also a sort of success came attached to the new-found happiness. The year before, Margaret's first in college, had stood a disaster—she had barely gotten by. But now with Adrienne's help she maintained a solid B- in her field, consumer services (only later did she try to tackle math), and, at least, made passing grades in the rest of her subjects. Socially, at Brown at least, Margaret made no attempt to conceal the nature of her relations with Adrienne. On the steps of the library, in the restaurants, theater restrooms, people saw them kissing and caressing almost ceaselessly. Someone said—perhaps truthfully—that their eyes could radiate nothing but appetites and desires. At any rate, Margaret Bromion had fallen in love. Later she would claim that the most fulfilling experiences in her life occurred during the twelve months she spent with Adrienne.

But just before the fall semester of Margaret's junior year commenced, Adrienne died. A silly, perfectly senseless automobile accident! To avoid hitting a dog—a stupid, unimportant dog—she had swerved onto the wrong side of the road and into another car. The other driver sustained serious injuries—even after three operations he could not twist his neck from one side to the other without feeling his vertebrae crunch, pinch, and grind—but Adrienne had died, her car (nicknamed cognito, so she could say she drove in cognito) igniting in an exploding immolation.

Of course, during the months that followed, Margaret experienced the frustration, anger, and grief natural to one in her position. Everything that had ever interested her now seemed insipid and unsatisfying, her life hopelessly unfair. At the funeral, the director had to help her from the chapel—to the bewilderment of Adrienne's parents—before the service had ended. Twice, after arriving at Brown, she planned to commit suicide, unable to extricate herself from the emotional and moral abyss into which Adrienne's death had thrust her. She neglected her course work and did not attend classes, spending her days chiefly in bed, burying her face in her pillow, cursing and crying. When she recovered to the point where she again could open a text without shutting it just as quickly, salvaging the fall term already stood an impossibility. "Flunking out," however, meant next to nothing to her. She vowed that her intimacy with Adrienne would remain the last renascence of passion in her life—one put oneself in too vulnerable a position. Even afterwards, when she came to see and accepted existence as a movie, she kept to her decision: for a time. True, loving someone stood an illusion—you fell in love with a self-created and projected image, not an actual person—but an illusion that could trick you very easily into believing it, potentially the most dangerous scenario in a film that had—despite its treasure-trove of stranger than strange details—some pretty sleazy special effects. As usual, Margaret flew home at the end of the term in the family Lear jet (which landed on Bromion's private airstrip at the Herneshopple field twenty-five minutes after taking off in Providence), but this year without having passed her semester finals.

After several vain attempts to induce his daughter to re-enroll in a college or a university by labeling her a slacker and a drone, Bromion obtained Margaret a sinecure at Atelier Scientific, where she worked for four routine years. At first, still saddened by Adrienne's death, she remained aloof. Only after some time had elapsed did she begin to form a few friendships, which later blossomed into many. Before this, however (later Margaret looked back at what she had done with some shame), she often pretended to befriend someone, only to abruptly turn on him, a game she very much enjoyed. She felt like the leader of an army, impersonally negotiating treaties, then reconnoitering and launching surprise attacks. But this phase in her life only lasted for a short time.

After several years, Margaret grew tired and dissatisfied with her position at Atelier Scientific. She believed that, like the heroine of any good film, she had a destiny, some sort of important and satisfactory role to enact. Since her earliest childhood, she had realized that her life held some special significance. From her early teens onwards, for instance, she recorded her dreams, not so she could remember them, but because they remained her dreams and she ought, for that reason, to keep a record of them. Only one of them, she later concluded, actually merited preservation, a dream she had at age fifteen, her trip to the "New Mine" store:

Oct. 14, 1973

Weird, strange, and scary dream last night. Was in room reading a Bibel, everything seemed alright about it except it was not black, silver instead, and old, very old. Wasn't mine but the name of the person scratched out. I couldn't make it. Suddenly I stood shopping in the New Mine store with mother. You came in with one body and went out in another. The workers there gave you any kind of body you wanted to wear. I slipped in and out a couple of times but can't recall the bodies. Once had on an old tulle like one grandma showed me, also a black slip with a lot of lace. Was trying to meet some boy, but he kept going in as I went out all the time so didn't get to.

The dream, of course, remained much more vivid and detailed than Margaret's entry would suggest. Even now, nine years later, she desired to have it again, and often would concentrate on images from it before going to bed in the hopes of stimulating some mental process into reproducing it during the night. A dream, after all, stood as a kind of movie, too.

Margaret's sense of self-importance did not diminish because of her poor perfor-mance in school, even though every defeat crushed her. She resented the praise that her teachers bestowed on certain of the brighter students at Kanesatakee—the Sally Kellems and Elizabeth Anne Geists—who could execute their lessons in English, Geometry, and French without encountering any of the difficulties that she did. At the same time, she both envied and despised them. In ninth grade, nothing caused her more pain than watching Sally Kellem complete an Algebra exam in twenty minutes, half the given time, when she knew that even with an additional hour to work, she would only answer half of the questions correctly. But even though the learning aptitudes of the majority of her peers seemed, on average, higher than her own, she took comfort in the fact that no one could take anything she had learned away from her. She'd work hard, constantly try to improve, and her efforts would pay off. It took more time for her to master something, but she'd work with the handicap, and eventually catch up with the Kellems and the Geists, even surpass them. Her destiny did not alter. It only stood delayed. She would do something of significance; they would not.

For a long time Margaret believed that she would distinguish herself on the tennis court. She actually developed into a very good player, but she had not started to swing a racket at a young enough age to mature into anything more than one of the better players on the local league. At eighteen she finally realized this. Still, on the evenings when she did not host a party at Golconda, one would inevitably find her on the courts, playing several sets, perhaps a match, either with her mixed-doubles partner, the bearded and angular Tim, or Howard, a prominent Herneshopple businessman and friend of her father who'd call all questionable shots out and provoke her into shouting, several times at least, "Right on the line, Howie. Right on the line."

When she decided, at twenty-three, to again become a student, she had no idea what to major in, so she chose math. If she could succeed at something she had no talent for, perhaps then her time would come. Every morning, even when she drank heavily the night before, she rose early in order to scan the sky and on a clear day watch the ascension of the gypsy red sun. Perhaps the dawn marked the arrival of that new time when her promise would finally come to fruition.

Chapter Five

Road Trip

Apartment 2, 144 N. Sigerson Street, with its low ceilings, sparse furniture, dull gray carpet and constantly malfunctioning toilet, had become Michael Bolanger's office. Here, he tutored the illiterate freshmen assigned to him by Cal Keimers, the current head of work-study, wrote papers on commission for other more proficient but lazier students, read—he had so many books, including most of his father's, that he had to convert his kitchen cupboards into makeshift shelves in order to store them all—smoked an occasional cheap cigar with Ben Cantwell, and planned his editorial strategy for upcoming *Thoth* staff meetings. Usually one could not find him at his apartment unless one knew his office hours beforehand. Three or four times, a week or more went by before his landlord finally found him in order to collect a power bill Michael owed.

He unlocked the door, dropped a week's worth of mail onto the "parlor" floor, stepped into the kitchen with one long stride, and opened the refrigerator. With a handful of reddish-orange chips clutched in his right fist and an unpeeled banana curving out of his breast pocket, he walked gingerly into his unlighted bedroom, hoping to avoid stumbling over the chair, wastebasket, and record player and waking Tom and Maryjane, his neighbors on the other side of the wall. Switching on the light, he saw for the first time the four towels that Brent Cobin had nailed into the bedroom wall so they covered his rectangular mirror. Cobin had done this Tuesday night but had only told Bolanger about it that day. Michael came from Cobin's. He had wakened Brent in order to borrow a ratchet set. As well as hearing about the towels, he also had to listen to Cobin quote himself on the Russian armed forces: "They don't have guilt trips brought on by a cowardly apathetic public and a traitorous and vindictive press." A year later and he still stood enamored with his debut article in *The National Conservative Weekly*. "S. B. Cobin is a Pennsylvania-based free-lance journalist."

With his free hand, Michael loosened the nails—Cobin had not pounded them in very far—and tossed the towels onto his bed. Two months ago, he had stripped the mattress of all its sheets. Eyeing the mirror and his reflection, he mumbled, "I'll begin calling him 'Before Christ.'" Cobin called him "Gentile." He knew, of course, why Cobin had covered the mirror. In conversation, if he could glance at something in which he could see his reflection, Michael would. He enjoyed watching himself participate in the conversation—observing (as if from a distance) his reflection interacting with other reflections, listening to, touching, perhaps even punching them. But Cobin had put the towels up more to irritate Michael than to stop him.

The nose bulbed and the septum had deviated: such an awful turn of events for the beautiful one- two- three- four- and five-year-olds he had once been. But deformities, after all, proved individualizing agents. Cobin did enjoy irritating him: Hitler mustaches penciled-in on his three prints of Holbein portraits and Kaiser Wilhelm mustache and muttonchops on a book-jacket photograph of Romain Rolland, Michael's copy of *Jean Christophe*. But Cobin didn't know Freud was Jewish until Michael told him. Perhaps Elissa urged him on, his Henry VIII-Hitlers springing from her Haydn-Goerings. But Michael had expressly come early (he and his neighbor Tom Rathner would give Elissa's car the once-over at 9:30) in order to find a clipping about the five-year-old Michael Bolanger that Elissa did not believe existed.

For her twelve-college U.S. campus concert tour in the summer of 1966, Anna von Kurstenbach chose a program that would display her prodigious technical prowess but also included pieces that illustrated "genuine simplicity and affection." She scrupulously avoided old chestnuts but also the most obviously show-offish and pretentious compositions. Of course, the performance began with Beethoven (not the complete Sonata 12 as in the programme, only its *Andante Con Variazioni*). This she followed with an intermezzo of Brahms, two short Schubert selections, Robert Schumann's *Waldscenen*, and three of her personal Chopin favorites including the *Berceuse Op. 57* and the *Grand Valse Brillante*. She finished the first half with Liszt's *Consolation no. 5*, a little piece (certainly not a number from Liszt's "Teaching Abnormally Large Fingers to Play" album) but with its own difficulties nonetheless. After the Intermission came Claude Debussy—not *Claire de Lune* but the equally prepossessing if less known "Nocturne in E flat"—Emmanuel Chaprier, and Maurice Ravel. The concert ended with *Danza Negra*, the most highly regarded piano composition of the contemporary Cuban, Ernesto Lecuona. As an encore, she prepared Bibi Saccellaphylaccas' *Le Hibou*.

Frau von Kurstenbach did not alter her program from one university to the next but each audience reacted the same way. They greeted her, as their programme notes instructed and encouraged, "with rapt silence and thunderous applause." Executing a technically flawless performance, however, stood a matter of course for Anna von Kurstenbach: an ordinary event. Not the least bit novel or unexpected. Nonetheless, Madame Kurstenbach knew that two distinct breeds of perfect performance existed, not the simple Rubinstein/Horowitz split that the layman knew, for no matter how brilliant the effect, liberty-taking remained liberty-taking and thus Rubinstein disqualified himself. So if not in the interestingly flawed performance full of Romantic feeling, then certainly in the technically correct one, the pianist held the printed note sacrosanct. Yet she could distinguish mere virtuosity from higher inspiration. Technical precision accompanied by, yes, feeling.

During her career Frau von Kurstenbach had often experienced the thrill of going beyond herself and beyond the printed note, but, during her current tour, she did not strive to do so. At Laxallt Hall, Cannoshockton, Pennsylvania, however, something special occurred. For some reason, the houselights malfunctioned, and the auditorium remained lit. They could not correct the problem. They apologized. When she stepped on stage the sight of the audience irritated but did not unnerve her. However, it disturbed her that no one had lifted the lid of the grand piano. The audience, not expecting her appearance until the stagehands dimmed the lights, continued in pre-concert conversations, did not, for a moment, recognize that she had come on stage.

"Amerikaners." She threw the lid open herself, indignantly glanced inside at the taut steel wires and the felt-tipped hammers poised to strike them, put up the prop, and turned away from the piano to look, for a moment, at the audience. In the very first row, she saw a four or five-year-old child—yes, a young child—sitting between its mother and father. Anna von Kurstenbach doubted if American children behaved like their European counterparts. She sighed, sat down, thought how different things would stand recording live with the Philips engineers and sound technicians in New York City the following month, and commenced playing. She performed flawlessly and with formal elegance, but she certainly did not strive to push things to their utmost limits and pass into the beyond—that she reserved for the recording studio and a few select venues. As she played, every so often she glanced out at the crowd. Her fingers knew where the keys lay and the notes followed each other effortlessly and in proper sequence. She looked directly at the boy, waited apprehensively for his mouth to open into a giggle, yawn, or scream. The constant coughing in the audience, on the other hand, did not annoy her. Long ago she had become inured to it.

To her surprise, he remained quiet. Suddenly he seemed both precocious and intelligent. His eyes blinked almost metronomically and drew her into a Beethovenesque *quasi una Fantasia.* She felt his small brain listening to, grappling with, trying to assimilate music, felt the life inside it pulsing upwards through the bone, the white skin of the forehead, from under the shortly cropped blond hair. She looked at him and noticed that his blue eyes looked at her. After a time, his lids drooped shut in *Kinderscenen* ecstasy but then opened with wide-eyed concentration. He pulled her towards him, those eyes dug in. It became almost too painful. Anna von Kurstenbach found herself performing in a more inspired manner than she had expected. She did not glide fully from the one type of performance into the other until the second half of the concert began. She noticed immediately that the boy and his parents had gone and for a second more than a second, she experienced inner paralysis. Yet her hands energetically ranged over three octaves. The *Bouree Fantasque*: her fingers obeyed: *cantabile una cordo,* ppp, *Molto moderato e quasi misurato.* She played with mechanical precision but her personality entered the precision and tinged it. She detected something present in the music transcending all the salient points of its formal construction and directly attributable to the absent child or, at least, her perception of him. She frankly admitted this to the interviewer from the *Cannoshockton Chronicle*: "Madame Kurstenbach believes her rendition last night of the *Bouree* as well as her performance of Ravel's *Jeux d'eau* and Lecuona's *Danza Negra* ranked among the best in her career. She said that she had noticed a young boy in the audience very interested, quiet, and well behaved. After the Intermission, she saw his empty seat. She felt sudden regret and longing." Michael Bolanger still had the clipping. His father and mother knew right away who the young boy had been. He had told Elissa, but she did not believe him.

While he folded the brittle column along its old edge (he had taken it "pressed" from a manila folder in the top drawer of his dresser) and as he slipped it into his patent leather wallet, Michael anticipated the reaction that he hoped exposure to the truth would produce: saw Elissa's face wrinkle into a laugh, a happier, other kind of, disbelief brought on, in this instance, by—what should he say—further enlightenment. He planned a series of further revelations for today. Elissa would have a chance to go through his albums, so to speak. At least, some of them. He smiled, switched off the brighter ceiling light and turned on the lamp above his bed. He still had an hour of spare time before Tom would wake and they would begin the weekly probe underneath 'Lissa's hood, Michael limning her present difficulties, Tom trying, as always, to efficiently and quickly correct them. The checkup stood especially important this week as Elissa had recently had a new carburetor installed, the car had stalled a lot afterward, and Michael and Elissa planned to drive to Rallingsburg to visit Michael's grandfather later in the afternoon. But in the meantime, Michael felt like reading Alberto Moravia. He had read ten pages, also taken a shower, eaten a soft-boiled egg, changed his clothes, and stood brushing his teeth when the bell rang. Spitting out the water, he turned off the faucet, put his cup in its place, ran to the front door—the toothbrush still in his hand—and opened it, but not before Rathner had pressed the bell another four times in rapid succession. A cigarette in the mouth's left corner set; shoulder-length red hair dangling uncombed, unbrushed, but just washed; insouciant bloodshot eyes, blue-red button pinned on the army coat: "beatnik picnic." Rathner's entire appearance, as usual, seemed to say (or so Michael thought), I am a comatose ramshackle, but I hope I can still remain of some avail to you. Michael invited him inside and asked if he would like a cup of coffee. He did not but would wait until Michael had his.

Michael walked back into the kitchen, tossed the toothbrush onto the table, reached for a tall juice glass from the cupboard above the sink (nicknamed the "*anima naturaliter illiteraria*" by Elissa), spooned instant coffee crystals into the glass, and filled it finally with cold water (a Bolanger eccentricity dating back to high school), shut off the tap, and, as a brilliant afterthought, added "two" shots of Amaretto—to warm his cockles. Rathner, of course, needed a strong caffeine dose more than Michael did. But here again (Michael thought) the superior E. asserts a superior usufruct. He won't get a second invite. "Prosit," Michael toasted the distorted face reflected in the chrome of the toaster. He picked up the borrowed ratchet set from where he had laid it, walked back into the parlor, put on his coat, and asked Tom for a cigarette. Rathner gave him one, then said that, contrary to what Michael believed, 'Lissa was wrong: they really wouldn't need a ratchet set. Outside, Michael leading, they crossed the front porch, cut through the six feet of "back yard," and made for their landlord's parking lot. Tom asked the proverbial and unassailable questions he asked every week: had Michael seen how Super Destroyer pinned Count Nexco after only two rounds and then how Bonecrusher Brody stomped on his tag team partner's head? The distributor's had just opened and already three of their landlord's trucks drove off the property to make deliveries. "All my problems would end," Rathner said, "if I owned Herneshopple Bev. Even Maryjane's father would be happy." Having opened the hood, Rathner looked down at Elissa's engine. "It's been stalling when she snaps back from wide open to idle, right?" "But for what reason—you're the mechanic nonpareil." "Yeah. Well, that new carburetor needs adjusted, that's all." Rathner opened his toolbox and reached for a Phillips screwdriver. Strange, Michael thought, the first screw mill in the United States was built in Rallingsburg, where we're going today. He watched nervously as Rathner removed the idle speed adjusting screw from off the fast-idle cam, then opened the mixture-control screw one turn. After all, Michael knew next to nothing about cars. He hoped that Rathner could solve the problem. Before Tom had always done nothing, either passed the car or unequivocally stated that Elissa needed to take it in for servicing, but today he made the repair himself. He had Michael start up the engine as he tightened the first screw and adjusted the second to its highest setting, then signaled for him to switch the engine off. "There," he said. "She shouldn't have no more difficulties." Michael smiled. He was no mendicant schnorrer. Instead of asking people he told them and, surprisingly, they usually did. Once, in junior high, he told a younger friend to charge the enemy barricade during an apple battle, and despite the danger of running directly into the enemy line of fire, Andy did. "Usufruct," Michael said as he watched Rathner shut the toolbox and walk back toward the house. "I'm constantly saved by it. Yet how crass and ungrateful I can be." With hunched back and long strides, Rathner crossed the lawn. "No wonder Cantwell calls him anthropoid."

Having first returned to Elissa's apartment to pick up the picnic lunch he helped her make that morning at six, then stopping at the State Store for a bottle of Chartreuse (practically everyone in his and Elissa's generation was some sort of junkie—after all, a seven-year age difference was not an inordinately big one when looked at properly—so what the hell, *macht nichts*), Michael Bolanger arrived at Whitzel Hall eleven to fifteen minutes late (his grandfather's silver pocket watch was always three to seven minutes off). As Elissa got into the car, before she could complain, Michael handed her the bottle. She smiled and turned on the radio; he pulled out of the parking lot and onto West 324. The road described a wide half-circle around a protruding peninsula of golf course with a view of mountains parti-colored with fall foliage, then straightened and, bypassing the two granite obelisks pointing the turn-off from the interstate to the Herneshopple stadium, curved downwards toward the Herneshopple Highlander, the university-operated restaurant and hotel, painted white, disguised as a Hollywood set: "The Southern Mansion *Façade*."

As they spoke about their days, Rathner and the carburetor adjustment, the new cyclotron the department began training Elissa to operate, Bolanger ran over the many interesting things he would tell her later in the day concerning Rallingsburg and past generations of Bolangers—how the Revolutionary War veteran, his great-great-great-great grandfather, built the town's first house of hewn logs in 1797, opened the first drinking establishment, the Seven Stars Tavern, the next year, and how the drunken Indian, to prove his strength, broke Mrs. Boulanger's cast-iron pot. Or he could tell the story that had often frightened him of how his grandfather found the bodies of the two Polish immigrants—lovers though the man had a wife in Europe—in the cow pasture, a double suicide. They had shot each other. Or how Aunt Lenora went with her father and her two brothers (his father and Uncle Fred) deep into the mine, and the brothers would not go beyond a certain point, but showing no fear, she continued on and kept in step with her father. Or how when his grandfather was nine and had what was at that time a very dangerous operation on his lower intestine, *his* grandfather brought him the two things he most desired, toilet paper and Welch's grape juice.

Not until they had rounded the top of the hill, periodically halting behind a line of coal and gas trucks and Michael finally saw (cigarette resolutely set in her lipglossed mouth's left corner) the female construction worker, orange sign—STOP on one side, SLOW on the other—balanced on her surprisingly massive left shoulder and walkie-talkie clutched in her right fist, did he realize that an accident had not, as he thought, occurred on the incipient stretch of 341 West where the highway dropped in a steep slant to the Port Esmerelda valley and the ground, as you descended, seemed to palpitate and reach up for you.

"You're right," he said as the construction worker turned the sign to SLOW and the two trucks in front of them went by. "An accident hasn't taken place. But in the past, the dead life" (he could not help smiling at the pretentiousness of the lover he had chosen, but what he said was true, that part of his life was over, as dead as the grandmother who sat beside him on those splendid shopping trips that always ended in ice cream at the Herneshopple Creamery) "car wrecks have held me up here four or five times at least." He reached for the bottle, now opened and gripped between Elissa's thighs. "Actually, I had my first grammar lessons here." He explained that during the summer before third grade (Michael's great-grandmother had died that summer, the university had just conferred James Bolanger's Ph.D.), his father had often driven him back and forth from Rallingsburg to Herneshopple, giving him much personal instruction on the way. "One dinosaur is in the back yard. Two dinosaurs are in the back yard. Now, Michael, if there is a Brontosaurus, a Triceratops and an Allosaurus in the back yard—three dinosaurs, in other words—do you say 'is' or 'are?' " He remembered the moment of terror when his father asked such questions, the unanswerable anger waiting for the question wrongly answered. Then he recalled his bilingual edition of selected Hemingway short stories from which he taught himself German. Even though the Bolanger family came from France, Michael's father had always stood a great Germanophile—a Goethe and Schiller and Hölderlin enthusiast.

After swallowing a few mouthfuls of Chartreuse, Michael, following the lead of the coal trucks, accelerated. The road cut through a thicket of hemlock which gave way to a large meadow and then rose upwards. Elissa wanted to stop to photograph Michael and the parti-colored hillside, but he told her that he would take her to a better spot, the Fontefield State Park fire tower. A half-mile later he turned onto the park road, tripled his speed—he had often driven here before—drank more Chartreuse and passed the bottle to Elissa. Initially he planned to drive directly to the tower, but then decided to show Elissa the Sherman tank in the parklet surrounded by summer cottages at Stillwell Dam. How ironic, Michael mused. I don't think they even rent canoes here.

"I think I can hypnotize you today," he said.

Elissa laughed. "You thought so every other time, too. You know I won't truckle under."

"This is my tank. I've crawled inside innumerable times. We're cats and you're in my territory. Come on." Michael got out of the car and Elissa followed. In a minute he had already climbed the tank, but she stopped to pick a plant with orange-red flower-heads, the five-toothed rays overlapping in several series. "*Hieracium aurantiacum*," he said. "Tawny Hawkweed." *The Mayor of Casterbridge*, Michael thought. One of the rustics. "See how the peduncles end in a terminal cluster?" She reached up to present him with the plant. He took it and helped her onto the tank. As he pulled her up, his face perspiring, Michael stared at Elissa's suddenly too broad chin, her face now wholly in the light, and her long auburn ringlets like sprung copper coils. Without speaking, Michael lowered himself through the hatch.

Since he attended Summer Happenings—a program for gifted junior-high children jointly sponsored by Cannoshockton University and the Hedgewood Intermediate Unit—and had seen his first hypnotist, Bolanger had become fascinated with somnambulism. He had himself been hypnotized over a hundred times—recently, in fact, by Elissa, his maneuver to gain her confidence—had learned how to induce a trance, make a subject susceptible to catalepsy, and succeeded several times in taking someone to the ninth degree, where hypnotic and post-hypnotic hallucinations were inducible. He had seen somnambules play the violin, converse on the telephone with a friend (and in some instances an enemy), write poetry, and letters to Santa Claus. He had seen the most unwilling and resistant subjects lulled into a trance, induction attempts that succeeded, surprising everyone. Of those he tried to hypnotize personally, however, he found Elissa the most obstinate, had no success with her at all, even though she had it with him. He had given up using his grandfather's silver pocket watch long ago.

Now in the cramped and quite dark tank, Elissa sitting in the commander's seat, Michael on his haunches in front of her, he would try another technique, but first he kicked the trash in front of him towards his left. Over the years, so much had accumulated that Michael could envision a time when he would open the hatch only to find a full garbage can.

Elissa's resistance perplexed him—did she fear surrendering her will to his authority or did she look on hypnosis as a test of her capacity to perform? Did a fear of disappointing him prevent her from going under? Today, he would try to utilize her resistance in order to hypnotize her, the induction procedure he would use hypnosis by means of hand levitation. He had used this method successfully on other subjects. He told Elissa to relax, to place her hands on her thighs and concentrate on the sensations in her hands. He asked what these sensations were. She said she felt the texture of her pants, the pressure that her hands exerted, a slight tingling in her fingers. He repeated what she said, an attempt to get her to associate her descriptions with the sensations, so later on, when he again repeated her replies he would evoke the same motor responses. Finally, he told her the more she resisted, the more difficult it would become to resist.

"You say that it's not conceivable, that it can't happen, but very slowly, the chinks between your fingers will widen. They will spread apart."

"But I'm not—"

"That doesn't matter. Just do what I say."

He had her spread her fingers and told her that they would soon want to "arch upwards;" that her arm had become twine, her fist a helium balloon. Michael smiled. Elissa had lifted her arm several inches above her thigh.

"Watch it as it rises. The peaceful sen—"

"No." She let the arm drop: a sobering, moderately loud smack.

Like taking off a sweater but deciding at the last possible moment ….

"We'll try again. Chink by piece, the armor will come—"

"No." She touched her forehead with her index finger, looked straight at him, said, "Stop trying." He would never succeed—at least not with her. She flung back the hatch.

"But I consider it my usufruct!"

He followed her through, then jumped to the ground. She had stopped to pick *foetid camomiles* or—as her grandmother called the flowers—pigsty daisies.

"You look dissatisfied," she said. "That grimace—pure *moue*."

After leaving the State Park (Elissa had first, of course, climbed the fire tower and taken her photographs)—before driving into Rallingsburg—they stopped twice: first at a Texaco Full-Service Island (fortunately only for gas and cigarettes; Rathner had not failed him) and then at the cemetery (just on the outskirts of town) where Michael's father lay buried. Michael always stopped. Elissa put on the emergency brake—Michael forgot—and followed him. He stood for a few seconds in front of the granite marker: James F. Bolanger 1933-1970. Elissa put her left hand in his. She held the chartreuse bottle with her right. Glancing across the highway, then upwards through chartaceous yellow leaves, Elissa tried to think of a Michael description—chartaceous yellow leaves?—for what she had just seen and followed him (he still held her hand even though it remained awkward) round a squat, rectangular stone. He knew himself of course; presumably also her. But he didn't know M.K., yet he knew how to begin: "Because of the many 'reincarnations' in one's own life—those familiar repeated occurrences following a pattern slightly changed in each 'incarnation.' " Michael tightened his grip—why didn't he let go—and pointed to a Greek Orthodox memorial: a photograph of the deceased, encased in glass, stood embedded in the marker above the stone's lettering. Elissa smiled to please him (not because she was interested). Dorn loved wordplay. He said: "*Frieda Leider singt Lieden leider und besser als Fraulein Schneider.*" She wouldn't tell Michael. He'd steal it for a story too.

The naturally given smile pleased him. He knew that she'd find the stone interesting. He had so many things yet to show her. The clipping? He'd wait until his grandfather's.

Gustave Clair Bolanger lived in a row house on North Fourth Street, one block from the Presquisle Avenue intersection and the center of town. He had resided in Lynwood Estates (Rallingsburg's one residential area) until Michael's grandmother's death in 1975. A coronary. She had sat at the breakfast table smoking. She coughed, exhaled, and died. The paramedics could not revive her when they arrived ten minutes too late. G. Clair sold their split-level and moved to Fourth Street within two weeks. He and Mrs. Bolanger had lived in the row house until the birth of Michael's father four years after their 1929 marriage. G.C. had then divided the house into two apartments. Over the years, he had rented them to a series of elderly tenants who always took care of the place that, they probably knew, stood destined to be their last. Michael's father, too, had died of a heart attack. He and Uncle Fred had spent the day celebrating the conferring of Fred's Ph.D. when Michael's father complained of light chest pains. Aunt Leonora said that he went to bed early that evening. He didn't come down for breakfast the next day.

Michael and Elissa parked on a side road a block from the house. From the outside, nothing distinguished it. He remembered his grandfather saying the taxman looks at the outside only. Of the two apartments, his grandfather had chosen the larger upper one: the second and third floors of the building. Michael realized that his grandfather was not at home when, after entering the hallway and climbing the nineteen steps to his grandfather's door, he found it locked. He knew where his grandfather scotch-taped the key under the banister. The first thing he noticed, unlocking the door and stepping inside, the portrait of his sister Beth proudly displayed on his grandfather's baby grand piano. Every year, his mother had sent his grandfather prints of his and Beth's school photographs. Five years ago, his had stopped coming. Beth had just turned sixteen. As they passed through the kitchen, Elissa stopped at the table and picked up the saltshaker: a black nanny. Her husband, Pepper, wore a white chef's hat. "They're very old," Michael said. "Come, I'll take you to the third floor and to the best room in the entire house, my grandfather's museum." Elissa followed him across the plush red carpet of the parlor. "The first color television sold in Rallingsburg," he said, perhaps in jest, pointing to his grandfather's Magnavox console: a copy of Warner Sallsman's *Head of Christ* stood on the cabinet's top. The room's furniture belonged in a showroom. His grandfather had taken very good care of it. The quality of the workmanship stood very high—a few of the chairs were actually upholstered in silk. Built into a partition on the room's left side, Gustave Bolanger's one bookcase showcased novels by Zane Grey, Selma Lagerlof, Sax Rohmer, Thyra Ferre Bjorn and Robert Louis Stevenson: various other books such as *A Treasury of the Familiar* and *The Methodist Hymnal*; the favorite volume of Michael's childhood: a very inaccurate *Natural History of Sea and Land Creatures* published in 1870, to which the author appended a "description of the cannibals and Wild Races of the world, their customs, habits, ferocity, and curious ways;" and a fifties edition of the New American Encyclopedia. Underneath a large oil of a snowbound riverbank hanging on the facing wall, three small pillows stuffed and embroidered by Michael's grandmother rested on the posh green cushions of a Mediterranean-style sofa. Elissa picked up one to examine the stitchwork. Putting it back, she noticed, to her left, a corner cupboard filled with china and porcelain figurines and reached to open it. Michael stopped her. "There're older, more interesting, dishes upstairs."

She turned and followed him through a doorway and up a flight of stairs. Fingerpaintings Michael had done in Kindergarten hung on the paneled walls of a close hallway. Bolanger opened another door, and they stepped into the "museum." Shelves and cabinets lined the walls and exhibited family memorabilia, worn and frayed antiques. More heirlooms lay face down on a card table. Debris washed up on shore, she thought. "My heritage," he said. The tavern sign from the Seven Stars Inn, kept in the family for eight generations, hung on the wall, as did a steel-engraved portrait of George Washington, after the painting by Gilbert Stuart; in an old-fashioned oak frame, the front page of an 1829 edition of Philadelphia's *Saturday Bulletin* containing the obituary of Michael's ancestor, the Revolutionary War veteran; a daguerreotype of Michael's great-great-grandfather, Rallingsburg Mayor Francis Xavier Bolanger, who once traded a dying horse for a blind one and (Michael's grandfather said) felt cheated; and a photograph of Gustave Bolanger—at age three—wearing a brand-new sailor's suit. The hide of a wildcat shot by Michael's great-grandfather, Joseph Ray Bolanger, hung on the scotch-pine door. Michael pointed to a miniature photograph of the hunting party and the day's kill—the cat, two deer, and sixteen rabbits—on one of the shelves. The men wore Stetsons, deerstalkers and bowlers. They stacked their guns like a tepee.

He decided to show her the clipping from the *Cannoshockton Chronicle* but first would allow her to examine the antiques. He told her the history of some of the items, repeated what he always said taking someone through the room. The role of tour guide, by no means, stood unfamiliar, but he never perfunctorily performed the part. Respect, perhaps even veneration, always remained evident in what Michael said. He pointed to dishes, vases, and other glassware that had belonged to his great-grandmother, wood squares, planers, a leather punch and a bootjack, a celluloid collar box, a kerosene lamp, a box of whale-bone dominoes, and a United Fireman's insurance marker. From one of the cabinets, he carefully removed a wooden police whistle and a riot rattle, a Savage R.F.A. horse pistol, a box of percussion caps, and a Civil War belt buckle. One by one, he handed them to Elissa. As she looked at them, he placed on her head an 1887 Hope Fire Co. helmet with visor of black patent leather, two inches wide, with rounded corners on which the company insignia was painted in red and shadowed in gold. "I love these things. Every time I visited, an inventory was taken. They allowed me to play with these things . . . of course under their supervision."

Examining the antiques on the card table, Elissa discovered—to her great delight—a stack of turn-of-the-century postcards (drawings, not photographs) and began to look through them. On one of the more interesting cards—actually a packet of medicine—a young boy sat on a chamber pot grimacing, the caption underneath what the boy uttered: "Mama! I need a Cascaret!" On the reverse side, the same scene, a few minutes later, after Mother had administered the cathartic. Through a cellophane-like substance—after the packet was turned over—one saw the purgative contained in the card slide into the pot. The boy now smiled. "Mama! I feel much better now."

"Victorians could be crude, too," Michael observed. Elissa smiled and nodded her head in agreement.

Other cards advertised dry goods, millinery and clothing. One was a Sunday school "Reward of Merit;" another from the "Suffragette Series No. 9" ridiculed a "District Leaderess." It depicted the "Queen of the Polls" plastering her candidates' flyers on a telephone pole:

> Vote for Susie Peach for Alderwoman 5th Ward.
> Vote for Miss Spinster Justice Children's Court.
> Vote for Bill Sykes for Keeper of the Zoo.
> Ladies prove you are men.

"Horrid," Elissa said. After she put down the card, Michael showed her the oldest pieces in the collection (the tour's climax): a dagger that belonged to the Revolutionary War veteran (another descendant got the sword), and a book he had owned, a French version of *Robinson Crusoe* published in 1789. But before he could give her the clipping, she walked up to the oak frame to read the obituary:

> The decease of Henri Boulanger, a soldier of the Revolution, occurred in this city about ten days ago. In the year 1780, he enlisted in France as a private, and served as a Dragoon in Capt. deBert's corps of the First Troop of Light Dragoons, Free Legion, under the command of Col. Armand. He arrived at Boston, and proceeded thence with his Troop to Yorktown in Virginia, at which memorable siege he was present, and assisted in the capture of it by the united forces of America and France. He was wounded in the forehead and eye by a sabre and retained the scar until his death. He remained in the service until regularly discharged immediately after the surrender of Yorktown. On the termination of the war, he married and settled in Philadelphia, where he remained for about fifteen years. In 1793, he lost his wife by the yellow-fever; he then married a second time in 1797 and removed to Rallingsburg in Rallings County Pa., a perfect wilderness at the time. He built the first house in the place and where he resided until he lost his second wife, in the year 1822. In the year 1825, he again removed to Philadelphia with his only son, where he resided until his death.

"It's amazing," Elissa said. "You're very fortunate that you can trace your family genealogy that far."

"Grandpa's gone even further. He's secured information from the National Archives and the Office of War Records. Henri Boulanger came from a family of shoemakers in Paris, merchants who sold sealing-wax emollient and brilliant. His grandfather, we discovered, bore my name Michael. Yes, Michael! He earned his livelihood as a baker and wine gardener. In a deed for his Bordeaux properties, Henri Bolanger included an account of his progenitor's death. Michael and two farmers had transported barrel staves across the Seine. As they neared the wharf, a barrel fell, rolled, struck him while he had the poles in his hands. He fell backwards over the stern into the water and drowned . . . . But here, I've got something else for you to read." He took the clipping from his wallet and handed it to her.

So it was true.

"Surprise," he said. (The effect he strove for: Michael Bolanger *affettuoso*).

Two white snake fangs—thin, very thin. Tiny scars but so visible when you look for them. I wish they'd go, so they weren't on his lip. They don't belong. Elissa lifted her arm, her hand imponderable, the *Chronicle* clipping caught in the tight-purse clamp of her fourth finger and pinky. No, I won't give him the satisfaction. "That's nice," she said. "Here, take it back." He caught its edge after the two outstretched fingers stopped shaking the clipping like a dirty rug in front of his face, and he pulled it from between them. "I honestly didn't believe you. My father once told me his favorite smell came from the hot nib of a freshly sharpened pencil. I couldn't believe him, either."

"But do you believe us now?" (*appassionato molto*)

"If it's a retraction you want, you'll remain disappointed." He shook the clipping in imitation of her dirty rug. "But I am surprised."

(*Affettuoso*) "I should hope so."

Gustave Clair Bolanger stood surprised when he found Michael and Elissa waiting for him in the kitchen on his return home from the Comet Supermarket a half hour later. Stout, rosy-faced, blue-eyed—"hazel" according to his driver's license—he smiled when introduced to Elissa, complimented her on the prettiness of her dress and then invited them to dinner. They declined. After helping him put away the groceries, Michael asked if he would play the piano. He had told Elissa how, at a younger age, he had gone to bed and had often heard his grandfather practicing at night. What a wonderful way to go to sleep, she had said. Slightly embarrassed, Gustave Bolanger nonetheless complied. He played several pieces, including his wife's favorite, a popular composition from the twenties: "The Robin's Return," a Scott Joplin rag, and finally a Cesar Franck etude. Out of nervousness, because—Michael later said—he performed before a stranger—Mr. Bolanger made several mistakes. Elissa thought—an uncomfortable feeling—that Michael showed him off, too—treating him like a museum relic! And for her benefit. But perhaps she misjudged. After Gustave Bolanger finished the etude, they sat down in the living room to talk and drink coffee. Surely they wouldn't refuse coffee! Mr. Bolanger obviously enjoyed their company. Naturally, Elissa had heard all about Michael's grandfather. But everything Michael said was true. One could not help liking him.

Elissa seemed—or so Michael felt—a little too interested in the finances of Trinity United Methodist Church, the subject to which the ever-shifting conversation had just turned. His grandfather then asked, pleasantly enough, if she had ever read Michael's short story, "A Family Tradition."

And I took her to Stillwell Dam.

"I've read a lot of Michael's work. But not that particular piece."

She hadn't even heard of it.

"Well," Michael's grandfather said, "I'm glad you haven't. But if you ever do, don't believe a single word of it. It's an out and out lie."

Now, of course, Elissa would have to read it.

Chapter Six
"Blood Will Tell"

As Michael expected, Gustave Bolanger's exhortation not to believe a single word of "A Family Tradition" aroused Elissa's curiosity. She suspected, quite rightly, that the propriety of writing such a story remained a bone of contention between Michael and his grandfather and, of course, wondered why. On the drive home, she asked what his grandfather found so unseemly. Michael explained that his grandfather had thought that Michael had made defamatory, injurious, and libelous statements about his mother and sister, that he had slurred and slandered them. Michael, however, had not meant the family in his story to be viewed as a fictional treatment of his own. Nor had he intended to asperse and vilify Ruth and Beth. His grandfather's indignation remained highly understandable because of the parallel circumstances and the analogous situations between the real household and the fictive one. When looked at objectively, however, one could boil the similarities down to a single sentence: the two families each consisted of father, mother, son, and daughter and that the English professor father—a celebrated scholar and author—had in both cases met an early and untimely death. Michael had borrowed certain facts and details from his own life for the story but the characters he created remained almost entirely imaginary, so at first he did not understand his grandfather's hostility and outrage and felt shaken by it. His mother and sister need not feel naked and exposed because they did not even superficially resemble Trisha and Mrs. Beiden. The conformity ended with those few particulars which he had just enumerated. Anyone who knew his mother and sister would certainly realize this. Mrs. Beiden had more in common with the fantastic and improbable Mrs. Reilly of John Kennedy Toole's "A Confederacy of Dunces" or with one of Flannery O'Connor's exaggerated and flamboyant heroines such as the insensitive and manipulative grandmother of "A Good Man is Hard to Find" or the naïve and accommodating Mrs. Hopewell of "Good Country People" than Ruth Bolanger. He believed, though he might be mistaken, that he had stolen the phrase "little whore school for unwed mothers" from somewhere in O'Connor. When he wrote the piece, his sister had just turned twelve and she stood a virgin to this day. She had never become pregnant nor had Michael ever lost a scholarship because of her. The characters in "A Family Tradition" remained cartoonish caricatures. Only a very malicious and spiteful person would contend that Michael had exposed any secret truths about his family. The story should prove embarrassing to no one except its immature and prudish author. Certainly one could characterize it as cynical and misogynic and it spoke volumes about how—at the time of its conception—Michael had perceived the threat of female sexuality. He felt guilty now about writing it, and he had come to understand his grandfather's wrath. He should have disguised and camouflaged anything that appeared even remotely autobiographical. His protagonist Martin felt umbrage at his mother's lies, so he could understand his family's ire at his uncharitable and thoughtless distortions. Michael had qualms about the story also, apart from his grandfather's. He found the prose flat and pedestrian, the denouement hopelessly melodramatic. Nonetheless, he had managed to insert a few subtleties into a very unsubtle story, and he still stood proud of them. The word Depot, inverted (as Martin Beiden saw it), looked a little like "to bed," but he had not drawn the reader's attention to this as he should have. Also, he made an obvious if also artful and apropos allusion to the wife of Bath, another literary forebear of the mother in his story, herself the weaver of a whimsical and antic tale.

After Michael finished speaking, Elissa asked if he had any objection to her reading it. He said that he did not and that he would give her a copy of the manuscript that night. He had not shown it to anyone in Herneshopple except Ben Cantwell, who, after reading it, scratched out Michael's title and substituted in its place "Blood Will Tell."

Martin Beiden glanced through the glass partition, his view partially blocked by the large, red, painted words "Depot Restaurant." A long line of people filed out of the bus which had just put into the Millbridge Terminal. His mother, a skinny woman with big bloodshot eyes and wide gaps between her teeth, debarked. She grabbed the driver's hand and stepped carefully down to the sidewalk, only to disappear behind the "t" in "Depot." Martin's sister, Trisha, stood next in line. She, too, accepted the driver's hand, taking it the same way Mrs. Beiden had. She, too, vanished, but then reappeared in the clear spot circumscribed by the letter "o."

She looked much fatter now—no more hiding it!—than two months ago. Just before she left for Ardmore. If his father had still lived, nothing like this would have happened.

They crossed the street to the restaurant. He plucked the check off the counter with his left hand, brought out his wallet, lifted out a five-dollar bill, transferred the check to his right hand, and, flicking his wrist, flung the bill and the check under the table. Half-walking, half-running, Martin rushed to the other exit. As he attempted to leave, a curly blond man entered. As Martin and the man tried to move around each other, Martin's mother first and his sister second stepped inside and ran up to him. His mother began the kissing and the hugging. Martin stood motionless as mother and daughter dug their hands into him just as he had done to the man blocking his escape. He could not get out of it now; he'd have to stay with them.

"Martin, I'm so glad you decided to come," said his mother.

"Me, too," said his sister.

His mother didn't share his sister's good looks but they both acted the same way in any situation and exhibited, it seemed to him, all the same qualities. Neither of them thought good grades or training in the arts important, as his father had. They thought all a person should do was enjoy himself and have a "good time." In fact, his mother allowed his sister to discontinue her piano lessons and go to those damn hedonistic dances.

"Happy family," the blond man remarked to the closest waitress, as he sat down at a single table and ordered a bowl of oyster stew.

"We've had our share of troubles though," picked up Martin's mother, as she and her daughter likewise now seated themselves across the aisle. "Poor Trisha's husband died only four months ago."

Standing at the side of the table, Martin glanced angrily at his mother.

Silly lies. Trisha didn't even know who the father was. Everyone must know that she didn't live with them; she didn't, even when they first moved here. They all must know about Ardmore."

"He died so tragically such a short time ago. Just before we moved here. It broke poor Trisha's heart. She has never taken her rings off since then, not even at night. And I've told her how bad that is for the circulation."

Martin turned his head away.

His mother thought the engagement and wedding rings she bought (using money from his college fund) would convince just about everyone. But her elegiac tales—like the one she now prepared to tell—of the "poor husband's" demise, all differed substantially. Thus the subterfuge of the rings never quite succeeded. Monday, he died in an auto accident; Tuesday, of burns received from pulling a child out of a flaming car; Thursday, of congenital heart disease. Even the name of the husband changed regularly. Once he heard her call him both Mark and Bill in the same conversation. He often wondered why his father had married such a stupid woman. No matter how ridiculous the stories seemed or how they changed from one telling to the next, one thing remained consistent about them—they were all grandiloquently told. Story-telling remained his mother's one talent.

"What happened to the young fellow?" asked the blond man, looking for his oyster stew.

Quickly, Martin again tossed his head in the direction of his mother, wondering what new variation to the story she would now cook up. His mother's blue eyes, the outstanding feature of a pudgy face with a recessive chin, fell on him. A faint giggle escaped from her lips, and Martin felt sure he saw a saliva bubble form between them.

"Bill died, saving Trisha's brother, Martin here, from drowning. We went sailing on Stillwell Dam, four months ago."

His father would not have tolerated this. How could his mother distort the facts? As if he caused his family's unhappiness, as if he caused his sister's sorrow.

It stood the other way around. Because of his sister that they left Charlestown—to preserve her reputation—so no one there would learn of her condition. Because of her pregnancy, he could not finish his schooling there and, subsequently, lost the four-year scholarship he would have certainly received had he remained his senior year.

The community bestowed it to the top graduating student each year, and he had always stood first in his high school class.

"It was a clear evening when we decided to go sailing and when we pushed off . . . it takes a strong man to push off. Martin could never do that; he's like his father, more the intellectual type."

"Marty always performed poorly in gym. Everyone laughed at him," said Trisha.

His sister deserved what she got. She did. His sister and mother acted like everyone else; just like those motorheads at Millbridge High who laughed at him because he didn't know the parts of an engine, because of his love of classical music, because his work didn't shine in woodshop or he didn't win accolades on the gym floor. He didn't deserve such insults from them. He was better than they were. Why did his mother insist on portraying him as the one who brought pain to the family?

"Just like his father, all Martin ever does is read books, and at all hours of the night, running up the electric bill." She paused for a moment and continued wistfully, "I had always fallen asleep when Edward finally came to bed. I lie down and go out like a light. When I got up in the morning, he had left the house—gone off to teach his students or to work on his thesis at his office. I would always see the impression of his body on the sheets, move my feet from under my covers over to his side and feel his warmth, see his pillow on the floor. It's strange, but he never used one, always put his head down right on the mattress."

His mother stopped speaking for a moment. Her eyes became watery, and then she suddenly blurted out, "Excuse me. It hurts too much. I just can't go on."

The curly blond man didn't reply, his attention now drawn to the lissome second waitress poised to take orders from Trisha and Martin's mother. He still waited for his oyster stew.

"Good evening, ma'am, would you like to order anything?"

"No, I'm not hungry right now," his mother replied as she wiped her eyes with a handkerchief. "Well, maybe a cup of coffee and a slice of apple pie. Would you like anything, Trish?" His sister ordered a chocolate malt. When it was brought to her, she sucked loudly and incessantly on her striped straw.

His mother sickened him. She gave quite a performance; she played the part of the grief-stricken widow very well. But how could have love ever existed between so very different people? All his mother's actions seemed trivial and false.

On the other hand, his father had meant something. His colleagues respected him in Charlestown. He had a Ph.D. and a reputation as a scholar, and, after his death, the university named a building in his honor.

Martin remembered his father's den at their old house, all the strange books with their strange colored bindings staring out at him, tempting him to open them up and find out what lay within. He saw many names on the shelves, many strange resonant names: Thucydides, Homer, Hawthorne, Dostoevski, and Tolstoy. However, one book there had a very familiar name on its spine—Martin's own surname. He'd always slide that book out of the shelf very, very carefully, its binding black, like the Bible's. He turned to the first page and began to read:

Sublimated and Implied Sexuality in the Fiction of Henry James
beneath which in black ink his father had written in his firm hand:

> Dear Son,
>
> This original copy of my dissertation, I would like to pass on to you. All men have done things that they have regretted. I'm certainly no exception, but to alter Mark Anthony's phrase, "It is the good things that men do which they are remembered by." I firmly believe this. I want you to remember me by my book, Martin, and I want you to know that you mean a very great deal to me and that I love you very much. The good is not interred with the bones.
>
> Dad

For years, Martin hadn't known who Henry James was. One year at Charlestown a Hank James ran for county commissioner, so he imagined that his father must have written about him.

As he grew older, Martin realized with whom and what the dissertation dealt and that the book had received good notices in the academic world. Several years after his father's death, Martin began to read James and his father's commentary on the works simultaneously. He admired James' art, and enjoyed discovering the subtle inferences and suggestions in *The Turn of the Screw* and *The Ambassadors*. He thought the clever innuendoes made the books great. Implying such relationships in fiction stood far more difficult than writing candid sexual passages. Henry enjoyed and delighted in catching those not usually caught.

His father had received his doctorate in English and Philosophy shortly after Martin turned three. The following year saw the publication of the dissertation. His father's editor insisted on a pithier title and his father had come up with *James' Fiction: The Art of Discretion*. The Charlestown University Bookstore displayed copies of the book in its windows and had a shelf full of them inside. His father had told him that libraries all over the country had purchased the work, and he began to receive lucrative job offers from other universities, offers he knew he could not now accept.

At the dedication of the hall, everyone told Martin what an honor it was to have known his father. But Martin became truly aware of the book's distinction when in a shabby black army trunk in his father's den, he found, along with papers describing the death of Kennedy, obituaries of famous authors and reel-to-reel tapes of Caruso singing, copies of prestigious periodicals that had given the dissertation good reviews.

In the trunk, he also found his father's will. Reading it, he discovered that his father had set up a fund for his college education and had left him all his papers, all his classical phonograph records and tapes, all that he held most dear to his heart, hoping that Martin would pursue an academic career. The first Beiden to achieve recognition for his scholarship, he had started a tradition. Martin would stand his only worthy heir.

For several moments he had stood conscious of people conversing, and several phrases filtered into his thoughts: "scared," "didn't want to get in," "much coaxing." He listened more intently. "... convinced Martin it was safe, and all clambered into the boat."

His mother had been speaking, again addressing the blond man, again inventing.

"Trish and I positioned ourselves at the front, Martin at the left side, Bill at the back. It remained a cool, cold evening. We dressed warmly in white wool sweaters. Irish sweaters with special designs woven on them. Irish sailors wear them so if they drown, when their bodies wash up people can tell where they lived. Martin also wore his deer-stalker cap—Sherlock Holmes style, you know. He loved that cap, wore it all the time, his favorite article of clothing."

Martin had never owned a deer-stalker cap, though he had seen pictures of his father wearing one.

"Martin, for some reason I still can't figure out, decided to dip his legs in the water. It was October and not even daylight; the water must have been ice cold."

To add emphasis to her description of the cold water, his mother crossed her arms, placed each hand on the opposite shoulder, twisted her midsection, shook her head, and spun her lips to make a "brrring" sound.

"He rolled his pants up and started to swing his leg into the water, but he didn't only swing his leg in. He swung his whole body in. Martin never could swim so I knew he'd go under. Bill jumped in the water, grabbed hold of him and lifted him up onto the boat. And Martin didn't even say thank you, just asked Bill to find his stupid hat. It floated away from the boat, so Bill swam out to it. But the current became just too strong and he had swum smack dab into an undertow. A strong man, he fought the water valiantly, but he went under. We tried to steer the boat in his direction, but we just didn't reach him in time.

"If only Martin hadn't fallen in, if he had greater coordination, Bill would be alive today, and he'd still be alive if Martin hadn't asked him to find that stupid hat of his. His father wore one just like it." Martin clamped his lips tightly together and raised his eyebrows as far as they could go. He felt the blood rushing to his head.

How dare she. How dare she.

"One couldn't blame the poor dear too much, though. He didn't know how treacherous the water was."

What right does she have to insult me? I who will graduate Magna Cum Laude.

"Always such a nice little boy. Whenever we asked him to do something he'd do it."

She hasn't even read Dad's dissertation.

"As a small boy, he always wanted to hold his sister in his lap. We took quite a few pictures of the two of them."

Martin, still standing, turned away from his mother, dug his fingers into the back of an empty chair, pulled it out from under the table, took two steps backward, holding the chair in the air, and collided with the first waitress returning with the blond man's oyster stew.

All the muscles in his face contracted; he quickly sucked in air through his teeth and bit his tongue, thrust his chest out and took several steps forward, letting go of the chair.

He felt the scalded skin peel off; saw that the man now stared at him; felt the liquid run down his back and legs; and heard "I'm sorry," and "Are you all right?"

"To this day, Martin remains terribly uncoordinated."

He knew that he was clumsy. His mother was right. He never did very well in gym class. But he had never killed anyone. Damn the waitress for being there. Everyone would believe his mother; believe that he did kill a man and that he stood responsible for all his family's problems, not Trisha.

"Lies, lies, lies. Everything that comes out of her mouth is a goddam lie. Ardmore, that's where Trisha lives, at the little whore school for unwed mothers. She never had a husband; she just had a good time with every teenage male in Charlestown. Bill never existed, so how could I have killed him." His sister held her hands to her face and began to weep and wail. The waitress ran up to him and told him not to make a scene or cause any trouble, but he continued any way, "She's mixed our blood with that of some stupid Slovak jock's or worse. Who knows, maybe Negro or Chinese blood will flow in the veins of her little bastard."

"Hush, Martin, hush!"

Martin fell silent. His sister ran out the front door and into the street, running toward their new house. His mother chased her to the door, calling out for her to come back and that Martin would apologize.

He didn't believe he had said what he said, or, at least, how he said it. Goddam his mother. Her cock-and bull story had caused him to explode. He wished he had spoken in a more subtle, more Jamesian, manner, that he had not stated the facts so bluntly. He should have alluded to his sister's affairs artfully; he wished that in an indirect and roundabout way he had only implied her lovers.

His mother quickly paid her check, then turned and faced him.

"Come here this instant. I have something to tell you, child. Come outside with me this instant."

Martin smiled. Did she call him a child? He would graduate from high school in a matter of months and even though he stood her junior, he remained a hundred times smarter than she. He never told unbelievable lies and expected people to take him seriously. He would go with her, though; he wanted to leave the restaurant, as he stood ashamed of himself and embarrassed by his coarse behavior. His mother clutched him with her fingernails and urged him on to the back door. Martin quietly followed her; he wanted to leave the restaurant.

He saw the first waitress apologizing to the two or three people in the restaurant, calling him a spoiled brat, he imagined. He saw the blond man trying to conceal his mirth. He raised a fist to his mouth to hide the fact that he smiled and chuckled. They had provided him first-rate entertainment today.

"Martin," his mother said slowly and righteously, when they stood outside alone, "You had no right to do that. No right whatsoever. Hasn't Trisha suffered enough? She has more than enough problems without you adding to them. You knew that for months and months I have tried to keep everything hush-hush, but you had to spill the beans and tell everyone in that restaurant that your mother fibbed."

"You made me look like a coward. You blamed me for everything in there. You even said I killed someone!"

"I'm sorry, Martin, I'm really sorry, but—"

"Dad wouldn't lie about me."

"Maybe he wouldn't, but I could tell you some things about your father. You hardly even knew him."

"You're lying! You always lie! Dad wouldn't do anything mean. He loved me. He would remain honest. He certainly would never lie about me. I wish he was the one alive."

"If you knew the truth, you wouldn't treat me like this. If you only knew."

"What don't I know? You're making this up like everything else. You're lying."

"I'm not," she said, losing her calm for a moment.

"Then tell me what he did wrong."

"All right, I'll tell you," she said, calm again. "It might make you a little less arrogant. Trish wasn't the first unwed mother in the family. There's a tradition. Your father didn't want to marry me. I was five months pregnant with you."

"Do you expect me to believe that?"

"It's true. He married me after I became pregnant with you. I thought he wasn't going to. It's terrible not to have a husband, to be an unwed mother. Do you realize that? Do you?"

Trisha seduced and came on to all her lovers. But Dad differed from those scum.

"He didn't want a wife and son. He didn't care that I had to drop out of college. It only mattered to him that he got his Ph.D."

This couldn't be true. This wasn't true.

"Maybe I shouldn't tell you this . . ."

"I told you to shut up and I meant it."

He shoved her against the wall and ran down the street away from her and the restaurant.

"Remember what I told you before you criticize Trisha and when you think of your father," she called, massaging her shoulder.

He didn't stop until he reached their house. The door remained locked. Apparently his sister had not come home yet. She'll be home later, when she calms down, he thought, as he unlocked the door.

Would his father have done such a thing? Or did his mother tell him yet another one of her lies? Probably. She always told lies. But this time she spoke only to him and not in front of any audience. To protect her reputation he assumed. She had acted discreetly and didn't go off on any tangents or into minute details. She spoke very straightforwardly and to the point. Did she tell the truth? Or did she purposely move away from the people to make this lie seem more believable to him. First off, she wasn't subtle or clever enough to think of changing her style, and secondly, she would never create or manufacture a derogatory untruth about herself. She would never demean herself in the eyes of her son not even to make him more sympathetic towards his sister. In this instance, his mother was not lying. His father had gotten her pregnant five months before he married her!

He ran upstairs to his bedroom and threw himself into a chair, facing his bookshelf. He put his head down, looked at the floor, and began to count the number of tiles. Holding back tears, he slowly glanced upward. Immediately he saw the black binding of his father's dissertation. He walked to the bookcase and pulled the black book from the shelf. He opened the book to the front page and again read the inscription his father had written there. His father knew all along that he'd find out about his conception, that he'd discover that at one time his father had not wanted him. His father had learned to love him but that didn't change the fact that originally he didn't want a wife and son. He couldn't destroy all the copies of his father's book, but he could destroy the original manuscript with its hypocritical, fulsome dedication.

Yet his father had done the proper thing, at least. He did marry her, and she must have seduced him. But it didn't matter at all if he did the proper thing afterwards. Being discreet and proper didn't change anything; he still did what he did. When James dealt with human sexuality, he treated on the same topic as the most lewd, pornographic novel. It didn't matter that he dealt with it only through implication. The subject remained the same. It didn't matter that his father amended the black book's title. The text still stood the same. Trisha didn't have a husband, whether she wore rings or not. The fact that she didn't have one didn't alter when they moved away from Charlestown; his mother couldn't change that fact, try as she might. His father got a little whore pregnant. It didn't matter whether he married her or not. Getting her pregnant stood crime enough.

Martin ran downstairs and plucked a pack of matches out of a dish in the kitchen cupboard. He ran outside. His hands shook violently. He dropped the matches then snatched them up. Then his legs began to tremble—they had quaked this way only once before, when he boarded a roller coaster that his mother insisted he ride with her. His hands felt moist and clammy; sweat trickled down his face.

He lit a match. It went out. He lit another and then another; they all went out. Finally, cupping his hand around one, he got the first page to light. The page smoldered, but no further pages caught fire from it. He burned several more one by one. He would have to burn the book section by section, and he knew it would remain a difficult and tedious task, one he would not complete this evening even if he wanted to.

Some of the flaws Michael perceived and, more noticeably, the grounds for Gustave Bolanger's resentment and low opinion of the story stood apparent to Elissa as she read "A Family Tradition." She had met Ruth and Beth Bolanger only once: ironically at the Old College Diner. They had come to visit Michael two days before the Fall Term had commenced, and Michael had arranged for the four of them to lunch together. She found his mother and his sister very personable and surprisingly natural and friendly.

Although they had chatted aimlessly (Elissa could not, in fact, remember what they had talked about), the meeting remained pleasant and not the tedious occasion she had expected. Mrs. Bolanger did not put up—to Elissa's relief—that deferential, polite, but unmistakably false front that parents of one's lovers almost invariably wear when introduced to you for the first few times. For this reason, Elissa considered the day of their meeting one of favorable omen, what the Romans called a *dies faustus*. A red—no—she smiled at her pun—a *scarlet-letter* day.

She could not believe that Michael would have intentionally maligned his sister and mother. More likely, he had unconsciously sifted autobiographical details into the work, realizing the unpleasant implications only afterward. Nonetheless, the urge arose in her, even though she found it wicked and wrong, to find out the date of Dr. and Mrs. Bolanger's marriage in order to calculate the time between it and Michael's birth.

She disagreed, moreover, with Michael's appraisal of the story. She found it powerful and compelling—yes, a bit over the top, but part of the power derived from its melodramatic character. She thought it merited a reworking. After all, he had written it when only sixteen. But what did the book burning mean? Had Martin Beiden become the requisite blond-haired, blue-eyed automaton or did the book burning stand for his liberation, a symbolic breaking away from all that bound him and held him down, an acceptance of the sensual and of his mother and sister?

Either interpretation seemed valid.

Chapter Seven
This Far Outstripped the Other

It irked Michael that Elissa refused to take up fencing, even after an old man recently widowed had given her, after seeing them traipsing with Michael's foils across his lawn on Vinegar Hill just after sunrise, his wife's equipment, ca. 1928, slightly tarnished but by no means antiquated. Michael squirreled the foil grudgingly away, along with his two (one pistol-grip, the other in the French style, both mail-ordered from Costello's of New York, "where the blades stand stockpiled"), in the crock containing peacock feathers and umbrellas in the back left-hand corner of Elissa's walk-in bedroom closet. The masks became bookends. Her black wire-mesh, uninsulated and thus unsuited for use in electronically scored bouts, and his white insulated anchored an esoteric row of her books featuring fluid morphology texts beside Martin Heidegger's *Being and Time* and Louisa May Alcott's *Little Women*. When he suggested politely that they joust, she either refused outright or offered some insubstantial excuse. Once he brought out two of the peacock feathers and offered to teach her with them, but still she refused. In their only bout, Michael remained so merciless that Elissa, realizing that this event would always remain unwinnable, had lost interest in competing. She flailed instead of parrying, letting him, for her lack of an adequate defense and his lessons at the Cannoshockton YMCA (where she had taught ballet) score innumerable touches on her chest.

At chess, Michael sacrificed pieces purposefully, to build her confidence and to orchestrate, methodically and Germanically, his preplanned *coup de main*. She knew this, of course, but played anyway, knowing that here, unlike in their fencing, she might somehow win. He once managed to capture all her pawns, and she accused him, holding one of them against her own capacious heart, of crimes against humanity, of slaughtering little babies—little black babies—without the least remorse. Knowing that for once he held the moral high ground—Elissa, from ages nine to twelve, had raised a pig for the county and once for the state farm show, each year a new little Chuckles, knowing quite well, even at that age, that Chuckles, after she had won with him, would die at the slaughter-house—Michael answered with a cruel non sequitur (meanwhile pulling a knight out of the way of her sole remaining dangerous piece, a bishop): "You're posing. I know you're not a full-fledged cow." Sometimes she did beat him, and the next time he took greater care and stood more cautious while toying with her.

At swimming, Michael thought, they might stand more even and his victories might have more meaning. They had both swum competitively at the community level, and as its captain Elissa had always led her high school team. Both had worked as lifeguards—Michael, in fact, still remained certified until May 30, 1982, the month he returned from England. But after Elissa won everything but the breast stroke—where she insisted that they had tied and he that she had disqualified herself by not touching the slop channel with both hands when she pushed off on the turn—they swam like persons of leisure, only the appropriate number of laps, or floated on their backs, or stood still, talking, in a shallow corner, or swam beneath each other's spread legs, or glided together, suit fronts discreetly touching. Afterwards she led him on her bicycle, he on foot, to the supermarket. Precisely at 3:00, just before Brent Cobin got off work, they stood in his check-out lane, taking advantage of his special rates—rock-bottom, build-your-church-on, Before Christ bargains.

Elissa divided her six-days-a-week run into three parts; from her apartment to Michael's, from there across the Herneshopple Beverage parking lot, and finally onto the golf course where the majority of jogging Herneshopplers did so; unlike the others, she ran only part of the green's circumference. She paused for a second time just before where, when she re-commenced, she would diverge from the mainstream and onto a path to the left, after crossing the railed wooden bridge (below a dirt road stretching out into the blue) on which someone had spraypainted blue and red and gold swastikas. She ran to the edge of the meadow, then followed the path as it turned and cut through a cornfield to Durkam Road. From there she would walk home. Sometimes, if Michael held office hours, she would stop to see if he wanted to run the remainder of the course with her. When he did, the same thing usually happened. He would keep up with her for a mile, but then, before crossing the bridge or turning onto the dirt path, he would begin to lag behind and eventually stop, a stitch in his right side.

He walked for a while, resumed running, gave up, and began to walk a second time. She would wait for him at the edge of the cornfield. Occasionally, he could keep up with her, usually on a day when he had not eaten a large breakfast. When this happened, at the terminus (both of them very sweaty), she allowed him to kiss her salty forehead and wide-open, perfumed mouth. She stood giddy from the exercise. The reward remained an incentive to try for the tie, but the stitch in his side became stronger. Once or twice he exerted himself in spite of the stitch and continued to run, which caused him to throw up and to catch up with Elissa even later. She would sit down, no longer breathing heavily, when he reached her, picking flowers and searching for catnip for Michael to give to Ben Cantwell for his cats (Bezaleel would roll obscenely in the driveway, coming up covered with gravel and brown leaves and looking like a hedgehog or King Lear. Dr. Arbuthnot, more the cultured aesthete, would accept the offering politely, with an enthusiasm discreetly concealed). Before he reached her, she would stand up again, a poem tucked in her skirt (the only one on the golf course), and take off, before he could reach her. At Durkham road, she would stop again to read him the poem (one she read him concerned a Mama Bird's convulsions as her Sweet Papa alighted from their mating), but for now she ran with reverted face, keeping him in sight but unable to let him catch up.

Afterwards, she would fondly recall, even become sentimental about, running with Michael. To her, their runs would come to exemplify the pleasant aspects of their short-lived—she adopted the commonplace term–relationship. The letters Michael received early in 1982 always contained, he thought, looking back at them, wistful reminiscences about their runs. Yes, he concluded. She missed him, and if he remained just one charm among many on Elissa's burgeoning bracelet, he stood, at least, a little tin elephant among a herd of even tinier horses. Or maybe he only prancked like a peacock and appeared nothing more that a puny?:

> I've just come from a run. I've yet to develop a "three-part" trail, I do have a first and last leg to my runs–down Samuel St. past beautiful large homes from the 18th century–past where the scaffold stood from which they hung John Brown. I've found and become friends with an old woman who owns a seventy-four acre farm on the outskirts of town. Here I find my refuge, where the second leg begins.
>
> I miss running with you. Now I always run alone–no one to show a striped violet to or pick catnip for. I'm frequently harassed by men– whistles, yelling, beeping horns, slowing cars, arms grabbing out of cars, and always stares. And I don't run in my skirt. I don't feel safe. It's dreadful to have to stand defensive. But not only do I encounter hooters and troublemaking men every day, rabid animals also abound in the country.

Later, conjuring up memories of their runs helped to conciliate Michael to the new arrangement because he remembered that, when they ran, he literally had to follow in her footsteps, and, though this perplexed him (an obvious symbol, when found, should be discarded), he could not help regarding it as an analogy for their lives. She had experienced so many things that he had not but would. She was he, six to seven years in advance. If entelechy survived after its entrapment in matter, could not one soul divide itself at the same time into two separate suits of clothing, detached from one another by a gap of time, as well as by a curtain of flesh and mucous membrane? He stood drawn to himself. There remained too many coincidences, events could not possibly have concatenated as they had of their own accord. A more satisfactory explanation had to exist. He was what she had once been, but she had become what Wayne Hedgepeth must have been. It would depress him to continue to know his future. He felt glad that their paths, which had first crossed at Cannoshockton, later at Herneshopple, had again diverged. To meet again? He did not know, but he was content, no longer trying to catch up, to let her run forward, not starting again till she had turned safely out of sight. The coincidents, the repetitions, fascinated him, even though he knew coincidences could, if looked for, always be found. His mother, for example, thought it significant that she had to take

Michael to the hospital for weekly x-ray treatments when he was eight (he had plantar warts on his feet and refused to have them burnt or cut off), the same age she had been when her mother took her weekly to the optometrist's to undo the damage of falling off a horse—to uncross her left eye.

On days when nothing else would do, Michael and Elissa diverted themselves with a game invented by Michael and John Salmos, a Cannoshockton friend of his that she had not yet met, the object of which was to ask your opponent a question he didn't know the answer to. If somehow he did, he scored. The first to score four points won. They drew their questions primarily from their own seldom-overlapping academic shticks. Depending on their mood, the questions asked could either be (as they most often were) frivolous and petty or, if they felt particularly self-important that day, the wherewithal for missionary work: teaching something the other didn't know but should. Even asking something frivolous, such as who wrote *The Orrmulum* (Orrm, of course), Michael—perhaps out of spite—would always add an additional fact for her edification. "He employed double consonants to indicate short vowels." When asked by a friend to explain the game to a friend, Elissa chose as a metaphor the conjunction of two cells, an exchange of genetic information. Playing the game, she learned that, as an astronomical term, the word conjunction meant the meeting or passing of two or more celestial bodies in the same degree of the Zodiac. She already knew, however, what a conjunctive or copulative conjunction was, but she preferred simple sentences. She also discovered that "Honker" meant "Dinosaur" in *Turok son of Stone* comic books. Sometimes a question opened an interesting conversation.

"Can we show," she asked, "that a fourth dimension might exist? I don't mean Time."

Michael shrugged.

"Yes. You know how we diagram a cube in two dimensions? Well, by adding an additional orthogonal—in other words, perpendicular—lines, we draw a tesseract, project something fourth dimensional. This doesn't prove that a fourth dimension exists, only that it might. If it does, we couldn't detect it. Something fourth dimensional would appear in three dimensions here, just as a sphere appears as a circle in two dimensions."

"God, if he exists, would stand fourth dimensional."

"Interesting hypothesis." She adjusted imaginary glasses.

"On earth, he'd appear to us as a man—Jesus or the Buddha!"

"Not necessarily, Michael. If what you say is correct, he could appear as an icicle, a stalagmite, a tree, a dog, anything three-dimensional. One can draw orthogonal lines forever. Theoretically, an infinite number of dimensions could exist."

"Not as a dog. An altogether different spirit inhabits dog's flesh. See Part One of Goethe's *Faust*."

They usually exchanged at least fifty questions before one of them—to the relief of them both—finally won.

Chapter Eight
In the Valleys of Corrosion

I

The day already had demanded a great deal of her and she felt terribly depressed. Despite Dr. Blanchard's last-ditch efforts, her stepmother's fourteen-year-old golden retriever had died of kidney failure—because of Margaret's forgetfulness. For two years Gretel had suffered from nephritis and nephrosclerosis, but because the dog meant so much to Mrs. Bromion, Margaret's father—to the initial shock and incomprehension of the Herneshopple vet, then later his abounding gratitude (for Bromion involved Dr. Blanchard fully in the project, and he made a name for himself and his clinic)—had a dialysis machine built exclusively for dogs. Doctor and patient had received national exposure late in 1980 when *60 Minutes* did a segment on the clinic and, as Morley Safer put it, "the new—to most of us, extravagant—veterinary procedure." Whether Margaret heeded some subliminal desire stemming from her general dislike of dogs and stepmothers or, with the double pressure of her finals and the *Thoth* elections, simply forgot, she neglected to take Gretel to the vet's for her weekly treatment (in fact, instead of keeping the dog at Golconda, as she had promised, she had put it into the Marronsburg Kennel for the two weeks that Dirk and Mrs. Bromion would attend the oil and natural gas convention in California where new products—including Bromion's own line of straight flute and single twist drills—currently stood on copious display). When the dog did not arrive for its appointment, Dr. Blanchard, neglecting his other patients, immediately telephoned Bromion at home and, receiving no answer there, dialed his Atelier Scientific office. No one at the plant knew the dog's location, but the secretary informed him that the Bromions vacationed in California and gave him the number of their hotel. He did not succeed in reaching them until eleven p.m.—two a.m. eastern. Margaret remained awake at two, studying for her differential equations final.

Her head ached. She laid the book down and gazed at the bookmark, a postcard of Julia Margaret Cameron's "Rosebud Garden of Girls" (1868, foto folio reprint). A gift from Adrienne, mostly for the resemblance between Margaret's name and the photographer's. A woman and three girls, flowers and embroidered white gowns and hair healthily disarrayed. One girl, her eyes downcast, looked to Margaret like a Leonardo da Vinci Madonna. That stood a supposition on her part. She could have been thinking, for all she knew, of an El Greco or a Michelangelo or a Jackson Pollock Madonna. The other three, not quite so Madonna-like, wore vague, dulcet expressions. Margaret fished a comb from her purse (she couldn't find a brush) and combed her hair out rapidly, wildly, freely, letting it fall as thick and haphazardly as she could. Her head felt lighter, her face and scalp warmer. Almost feverish, caught in morning dreams she had never awoken from, she wondered if the girl's breasts had swelled and ached to the touch in exactly this way, if her cheeks, whose color had become and would remain black-and-white, had flushed as Margaret's did, and for the same reason (if that was the reason).

She stared again at the equation:

$$\int x\sqrt{x+3}\,dx \quad x = 4 \quad dv = (x+3)\frac{1}{2}dx$$

$$v = \int (x+3)\frac{1}{2}dx$$

$$= uv - \sqrt{v}\,du = \frac{2}{3}x(x+3) - \int (x+3)\frac{3}{2}dx = \frac{2}{3}(x+3)\frac{1}{2}dx$$

$$= \frac{2}{3}x(x+3)\frac{3}{2} - \frac{4}{18}(x+3)\frac{8}{2} + c$$

On and on, a fugue with endless variations. Cold bland coffee, a watch, a black turtleneck covering her and silence to lead her through this night like so many others. All her senses craved something which felt more like life.

The four phones at Golconda rang simultaneously. Margaret shuddered when her father's voice exploded in her ear. He did not rail at her very long. Dr. Blanchard had told him time was of the essence. After she hung up, she telephoned the vet, told him that she had absentmindedly put the dog in the Marronsburg Kennel and agreed to meet him there, and sped in her Camaro down Interstate 61. She arrived first and woke Mr. Bailey, the kennel's owner. Gretel lay on her side, tongue distended, teeth clenched, heart beating much too fast. Because of the already acute state of dehydration, Dr. Blanchard had Margaret hold the dog's jaws open while he inserted a ruler-length syringe into the animal's mouth and down its throat. The dog shook her head free and bared her teeth. Mr. Bailey had to help hold her while Dr. Blanchard reinserted the syringe. Near death, like a Greek hero, she seemed to find new reserves of strength. Blanchard managed to force the water down, but he feared that if the dog lived until they reached the clinic, the sedation he would have to administer before putting her onto the machine would, because of Gretel's weakened condition, prove fatal. His misgivings proved superfluous. The dog died en route. The episode had started in exciting fashion. What an adrenalin surge. An angry phone call, driving at maniacal speed through a snow squall late at night, a medical emergency. But had ended unhappily. Margaret did not return to Golconda fearing a second phone call from her father.

At 9:30 she took the final but did not know how she did. After the exam she ate, attended her two afternoon classes (ceramics and European History), and then went home to sleep for a few hours. Before lying down, she disconnected the phones. That evening she practiced reciting her platform for the *Thoth* elections in an empty classroom in Ormond Building, and, still nervous, stopped for several drinks at The Bitter End. She glanced at her watch, her face fuzzily reflected in the scratched crystal. Two hours, then a thirty-minute meeting, and it would finish one way or another. Her hopes hinged on a constitutional ambiguity, Elissa convincing the other editorial board members to allow the publicity, business, and general staffs to participate in the election. If Bolanger prevailed and the board did not amend the constitution, Cantwell would certainly win. According to Elissa, he had more supporters on the editorial board than Margaret. Only if the other staffs participated would she have a chance.

And the other staffs should.

The jukebox selections stood exclusively top 40: no Golden Palominos, no Stiff Little Fingers. Running her hand through the wide swirls of her hair, Margaret checked a second time, making sure she hadn't inadvertently missed a track. Still nothing interested her. Admittedly, her tastes ran toward the avant-garde, but The Bitter End, on certain nights, catered to those tastes. Twice a month, the management imported unknown icon-oclastic Philadelphia or New York based bands: New Wavers, Rastafarians, punks. Chris Ukase, the bar's owner, took money from anybody. The Bitter End welcomed customers of all bents, but usually in homogeneous groups. Like everyone else in Herneshopple, Margaret knew what night what crowd converged there according to (Bolanger's phrase) "a mutual sharing policy of separate groups separate nights, seldom infringed on." Thursday night stood Ladies' night, the girls' turn. Forthrightly seeking kisses, women slid dollar bills into the G-strings of the male strippers, their faces and the strippers' skin garish under red lights. Sundays under flashing, swerving purple, green, and yel-low lights, the disco throng overcrowded the dance floor. On Wednesdays female mud wrestlers performed before forty-eight-year-old celibates, sleepy frat boys, and teenagers using fake IDs, until one night a fight broke out (someone threw Liquid Plumber into the face of a nineteen-year-old), the police arrived, showing their ID at the door, and the Pennsylvania Liquor Control Board shut the bar down for two weeks (fortunately for Ukase not during football season). Margaret also knew who came on Mondays, though she never went. Elissa, who went with Michael, described the men with rouged faces and gold earrings, the women slow-dancing together with thighs pressed, hands in their partner's hip pockets. At her first *Thoth* meeting, Margaret heard Michael say that he was a Mannophile. She didn't know for sure what he meant until Elissa informed her afterwards of the German writer named Mann. Elissa explained that she liked to go to The Bitter End on Mondays because, among that crowd, she felt less ill at ease when she "danced dirty." Michael, she added, went to be with her and to flaunt the unwritten segregation policy. Although Margaret never went, she would always glance, when she waited in line in the lobby waiting to show her ID, at the "Monday Night Newsletter" pinned to the bar bulletin board and read the verse from the Song of Solomon printed on a file card and tacked beside the Newsletter:

> I come into my garden, my sister, my spouse: Eat, friends, drink, yea, drink abundantly, O beloved. I sleep, but my heart waketh, it is the voice

of my beloved that knocketh, saying, Open to me my sister, my love, my
dove, my undefiled.

Waiting in line for so long, she could not help looking, but if her thoughts later reverted to the Newsletter and to what went on Monday nights, she blotted them out with
memories of a closed casket ceremony, the chalky taste of a mouth half full of aspirin.
She couldn't swallow, couldn't breathe when she tried to swallow, and chose breathing.
No, she would not stand duped again.

Sitting on a stool, downing her fourth shot, enjoying the aftertaste as she waved
to the bartender for another and slid a dollar to the counter's edge, Margaret tried to
remember Humphrey Bogart's line about drinking gin in *The African Queen* or from *They
Drive by Night*, she couldn't be sure which. Maybe it wasn't even Humphrey Bogart? She
looked at her watch. If Bogart said it, she'd win; if not, Ben Cantwell would. She would
remain glad to do the busy work as editor no one else would enjoy. Cantwell would still
have his say on the board. And she would finally succeed at something.

The bartender put the napkin down, then set the shot glass on it. Lifting it to her
lips, Margaret tilted her stool in order to see around the man who had just sat down two
seats away and watch the people dancing under the strobe light.

II

Michael heard footsteps, someone whistling, the scrape of the door and click of
the light switch. Two seconds later a nine-pound hammer hit the tabletop above him.
The plywood underside didn't crack. Solid oak face. He stared at the soft, unprotected
belly of the dragon. Turning his head, he saw flared pant tips, brown loafers, navy blue
socks. Who dared to bring light into his sepulcher? The whistling stopped, replaced by
a wobbly baritone Michael knew all too well: "Fun's the one thing that money can't buy.
Something inside, always denied."

Couldn't surgeons implant a sphincter to contract the impulse that made him do
that?

Prolonged crimpling. A tab. He saw it fall to the beige carpet. As the newcomer popping his top pulled the tab off and discarded it, Michael recognized a tell-tale fizz, like a
lit and hissing whirligig. Spume. The window screeched and cool air surged in. Michael
rolled from beneath the table where he had lain for the last half hour and stood up as
Roger Leland, lips attached to the rim of a 16 oz. can of Rolling Rock, climbed out
to the snow-covered ledge. Michael deduced correctly. He had heard a six-pack thump,
not a hammer fall. The tab on the floor and the telltale fizz provided the answer. He
reached into the bag and pulled out a can. Why did Roger drop them? Now the foam
would jet up like a geyser, and you'd lose half. Michael set the beer down and glanced at
his watch. Eight o'clock. Already they had begun arriving—an hour prior to the meeting's
scheduled start time. He tapped on the lid gently with his right forefinger to settle the
foam inside.

The English seminar room could fit in Elissa's kitchen, but her kitchen had only
table and chairs, not the seminar room's brown paneling or its two chalkboards (one

black and part of the wall, the other green and on rollers). Two slightly sagging posters marginally prettified the room, making the paneling less monotonous: a still of Anthony Hopkins in blackface (distributed by the local PBS station to advertise the third season of the Shakespeare plays, hung in the classroom by a stuffed-shirt secretary or a blue-nosed professor with a predilection for the obvious) and a reprint of a famous Ringling Bros. and Barnum & Bailey placard selected by someone with more brio: "Captain Barry's Famous Educated Equines." In full harness but without riders, wearing little felt hats, eight anthropomorphically drawn Lippizaners pranced on their hind legs in front of the illustrious Captain Barry, who wore his hallmark red coat, white trousers, and knee-high black boots and looked like a conductor, arms outspread, a baton-like whip in his left hand. Michael believed that the person who chose the poster had done so to make a statement about either sycophantic students or the education process generally. A locked door on the room's left side opened into a small closet where the English Department kept its copies of the theses written from 1930 on by its graduate students. Cantwell called it the bathroom. Inside Michael could find copies of his father's Master's and Ph.D. theses.

Like Luther, we students should compile a list of grievances, gripes, and grumbles and nail it to the door, Michael thought and hiccoughed.

Unaware that anyone else had entered the room, shifting his weight from buttock to buttock, Leland began to shout, between sips, choice lines from the worst poems that year. Still shouting, he crushed the green can, dropped it into the shrubs thirty feet below and lit his last cigarette. They had received on the whole mostly dreadful submissions, and Michael maintained that the most "outstanding" of the dregs deserved publication. Leland promised that if he came up with any surplus cash (he would know in several days; the galleys had just gone to the printer, who had not yet tabulated the total cost), he would do a mock-up and have nine copies, one for each editorial-board member, printed of fifteen of the worst poems and the worst short story, an anthology they would call simply *Thoth Outtakes*. It would include four poems written, Michael felt sure, by the constipated woman (the board judged everything anonymously, but he recognized her "style" from Nexus of Nuance); three of the thirteen John Lennon elegies they had received; two plodding, overbearingly local jingles, unsurpassedly banal and written—Michael peeked at the list—by a former Rallingsburg miner back in school earning a degree in nursing now that the deep mines had closed and the owners had flooded the old passageways and dynamited the entrances: "A Chocolate Bar for my Stepdaughter," "A Chainsaw for my Neighbor" (the staff planned to print them either interlinearly or with the gifts transposed); and, of course, "Loretta My Wife," with its all too audible refrain, an acoustic effect repeated eight dreadful times, "But I luv you most, babe, when you lick, suck, and kiss my twisted black dick." A number of other poems deserved a spot in *Thoth Outtakes*, but only the poems that every editorial board member had given a rating of four or less to on a scale of ten stood eligible. Several poems that Michael had given ratings to in the negative numbers would not go in. He wondered if as editor he would bend the rules and insist Leland include them anyway. If the outtakes found their way into print, he would receive his copy of that as well as the magazine in England. Of all the editorial board members, only Ben Cantwell disliked the idea of *Thoth Outtakes*. He felt it more sad than funny that so many people could compose such bad verse in such copious quantities.

If only on a surface level, *Thoth* would change for the better that year: the cover shiny and slick, the type now professionally composed. Leland, the magazine's copy editor and business manager, had stood more enterprising than even Elissa and had wrested more money than anyone had expected from the Board of Student Grants and Stipends. Michael went with Leland to the last of eight budget hearings. Seven of the twelve students on the executive panel majored in Agricultural Science. Four brought spittoons. Michael didn't see how the budget would pass without drastic cuts. But Leland told him to say nothing, so he sat taciturn and assertively defiant, smoking an exceptionally malodorous cigar in the manner of Bertolt Brecht before the House Committee on Un-American Activities. The budget, however, passed intact. The committee allowed the increase of four thousand dollars over the previous year. Leland's miracle would bring about a better-looking magazine, but the contents would still remain the measure of the magazine.

The weakest of the poems stood facile or facetious enough to make them, at most, only mildly offensive to a refined sensibility. The best featured a mind interestingly at work, but generally without a broad command of poetic forms and situations. They remained derivative, limited in scope, and sometimes elusively private. Forty years later, board members would probably still remember "Loretta My Wife" and "A Chainsaw for my Daughter," but would have long forgotten the poems chosen for publication. The magazine wouldn't win any accolades for its poetry (except perhaps for Elissa's submission, "Camouflage"); its short stories would distinguish it, though no single reader would likely admire all three. Unfortunately, those who would take most satisfaction in "A Country Encounter," particularly two faculty members, little ants who thought themselves giants, both strong advocates of Raymond Carver minimalism, would in all likelihood dislike "Between the Ties," an imagistic work which ironically dealt with an adolescent who felt he would become a writer because he had the first name of Thomas Mann, Thomas Hardy, and Thomas Wolfe. With his immediate, playfully meditative reactions, as he ran along an old railroad in pursuit of his chimera, to a mosaic of evenly spaced ties, deep oil stains, and wheel-burnished rails. Nor would they care for "A Clear Case of Demon Possession," a parable in the style of "The Grand Inquisitor," in which, seeking the salvation of his soul, a mob burns a twelfth-century multiple personality at the stake—a medieval cure for a twentieth-century malady, clearly a rebuke to the excesses of a psychology-ridden age. The two professors would call the former ostentatious, purple and opaque, the later extremely tendentious. To their mind, only one tree in fiction's forest stood worth cultivating, and cultivate it they did, stressing "accessibility" and "true-to-lifeness" in the classroom, discouraging anything remotely speculative or "experimental." What remained insipid about much of the work they praised was not its true-to-lifeness but its banality in conception, execution, and every other criterion except subject matter (which, of course, never in itself stands banal). Seeing this, those who knew differently—Dr. Murcelli most emphatically, biting down on his ubiquitous Cigarillo—thrashed out by taking exactly the opposite view: extirpate their tree from our forest but don't use their old saws. Precisely for this reason, Murcelli would unfairly dismiss "A Country Encounter" as pretty predictable, as lending itself all too easily to concise capsulation: amid Syrian plums and Spanish olives, after meeting at a bazaar, a fast-talking CIA agent with an optic-fiber magic wand seduces a two hundred fifty pound radiologist. Another tale of Virginity Lost, he would say, overlooking how well, the author, in this instance, had executed the formulaic and the familiar.

No democrat himself, Michael hectored board members who displayed inordinate bad taste by liking something he considered vapid. He tried, often successfully, to humiliate them. Feigning astonishment, he asked, his voice rising in an almost operatic crescendo, how anyone could admire a poem which averaged two clichés per line or a story so abysmally dilettantish, so perfectly devoid of merit that it possessed all the grace and subtlety of a Ben Cantwell belly flop. "Milk-fed kitsch," he said and, disdainfully rolling his eyes, continued to make his pronouncement, "Treacle, twaddle," sustaining his final word like a high C: "Tripe!" His legs twitched in anticipation of a fight as he looked one at a time at the faces of the other editors sitting around the table. The more disputatious his opponents had become, the more high-handed and vicious he grew. In short, he stood the self-appointed conscience of the magazine, a role he had appropriated for himself the previous year even though he had not yet become editor-in-chief. Two board members had resigned because of him then. This year, one of his allies, a girl who agreed with him in virtually every instance, even had a dream in which he chased her, knife in hand, through the library stacks. Not even a good, gory slasher, she told Margaret, just a low-budget celluloid reject. Michael's judgment, however, stood mostly sound, although he occasionally preferred ambitious failures to better but less grandiose submissions. In fact, he had shoved "A Clear Case of Demon Possession" into the magazine despite nearly everyone on the staff's disliking it, disregarded magazine policy by sending it back to its author, Dmitri Smeltanowski, for revisions—twice (it came back the second time remarkably similar stylistically to "Between the Ties"). But if a majority of the board hadn't approved of his methods, they approved of the results of their application. Michael became much more interesting to listen to when battles broke out, when, as he put it—for he saw himself not only as the conscience but as the will of the magazine, "an obstruction had to be expunged and consensus kept from shifting in the wrong direction." He had in his hands the means of applying pressure. If verbal abuse didn't tip the scales, he'd try another strategy, simply press a different button. If the opposition remained intransigent, before calling for a vote, he'd shift his attention to those who blew hot and cold and passionately and eloquently exhort them to vote his way. Usually he would sway them. Because of these persuasive skills—"Michael's magnetism," Elissa said, "his ability to galvanize"—Ben Cantwell had, at first, thought him more personality than writer and, for that reason and for the multiplicity of her talents, nominated Elissa for editor-in-chief in 1981. Elissa dubbed *this* Michael "the hypnotist." In contrast to him, another much duller "self" emerged when meetings ran smoothly and a consensus did not need forged: a pedantic Michael who unintentionally flattened and ground up poems and stories by overanalyzing them and who bored almost everyone. At an editing session in October, he had explicated "Camouflage" thus. Wearing his corduroy jacket. Self-involved.

"It examines the resolving powers of two pairs of eyes, each set's ability to distinguish different shades of the same color. For the man at a certain distance all greens blend into a single monotone, gradations dissolve into the whole. The female's resolving power stands superior. For her the greens don't remain uniform. . . ."

Harried, B— C— read the poem a second time. Not varying. In other words, homogeneous. Suddenly triumphant, he smiled broadly and made an aside to the person on his left, "Uniforms. You know—liveries, regimentals, team colors." He looked up and saw that he had made the comment to Margaret Bromion. His eyes positively beamed, as he smiled at his unintended drollness. He had hit the bull's-eye blindfolded, but he had just enough presence of mind not to burst into a fruity cachinnation. He had heard from M, who had heard from E. *High-school Lettermen's jackets. He-he.*

Her reverie disturbed—she stopped listening long ago—Margaret looked to see who had spoken to her and quickly regained her bearings. A good four or five inches longer than her shoulders, her hair descended downwards on either side of them. The strands turned in and out to the sides. The upper halves covered by a sweep of hair on either side, her ears stood slender and long, their thin lobes pierced by small pearl earrings. She looked her analogue directly in the face, offering him an exasperated and fatigued glance from yellow green eyes.

M. B. ♂

(The weaker of two transmissions
broadcast at the same frequency)
The implication stands. What differentiates also makes the same.

M. B. ♀

(A side and voice over)

What tommyrot! What possible relevancy does it have to anything? It doesn't apply to my life or me. How he hogs center-stage—won't give anyone else a chance. I'd run things very differently. No speechifying. None of this highminded, highfalutin stuff—it's dishonest and misleading. Counterfeit. Let us make up our own minds! What does Elissa find so attractive? I wouldn't want to stand in her shoes when the credits roll.

Throughout the conversation, Elissa remained equally insufferable. She said, "Michael's remarks are *in propria persona* but remain inappropriate. The man in the poem is 'green in the green light' because he won't reveal himself to the woman. He keeps things back, conceals. The poem concerns why he does this: his paranoia." (By then, Elissa had visited Michael's grandfather's home and knew more than the persona in the poem did.) Then, in defending his interpretation, Michael had tried to take Elissa's poem away from her. Each, as they debated, adopted mannerisms and phrases of the other (later, meeting a stray cat or dog, Michael even found himself greeting it in French in the same coy manner and with the exact same words Elissa had always used: *qu'est-ce que c'est?*). If Michael had definitive "selves," so did she. Most of the time, Elissa proved anything but insufferable. *Thoth* brought out the worst in both of them. Cantwell found it unbearable. "Enough!" he shouted, and brought both his cumbrous fists crashing down on the table.

The editing staff had met twice-weekly in September, October, and November, three times a week or more in December. The other staffs met biweekly. Of course, they faced the usual quota of snafus—lost manuscripts, last-minute cancellations of meetings with not enough time to contact all the staff, a misunderstanding with the printer resulting in his ordering the wrong paper and cover, missed deadlines, a typo found the day after Leland had turned in the final proof. Michael was glad that his year as editor-in-chief stood almost over.

"Roger," he said, "if you recite one more line, I'll push you to your death." Leland twisted part of an arm through the window and motioned for Bolanger to join him on the ledge. Michael reached for his down coat under the table (he had used it for a pillow) and, putting it on, plucked the can of Rolling Rock from the table, gripped Leland's arm, climbed out, and sat down, the contour of his bottom imprinting itself in the wet snow. "Don't spoil my fun," Leland said, drawing on his cigarette, his lips curving into a smile, his crosswise, cater-cornered brows yanking together in a huge, momentary scowl. Roger's short-cropped hair—he attended Herneshopple on an ROTC scholarship—had already begun to recede. His cheeks, as always, stood freshly shaved.

As his bottom dampened, Michael pulled the tab and hastily brought the spurting can to his lips. He swallowed furiously, wiped his mouth on his sleeve and glanced upwards. Boar-tusked icicles dangled from the rooftop's cornices and quarter round, fillet and fascia moldings. The convex limbs of the moon stood barely discernible. The sky shone hazy and slate-colored, brim-full. Across the quad, fifty yellow rectangles blazed at different angles and stories from Kastner Building, a dodecahedral high-rise. The tallest building on campus, everyone referred to it by its nickname "the bacteriophage." Behind it, barely visible, the floodlit clockface of Boswick Building. "How long have you stood eavesdropping?" Leland asked, swishing his legs.

"Ten minutes," Michael said but decided to elaborate further. His Classics exam began, he said, six hours after they finished their final in "Chaucer's Children." "It let out" (Michael double-checked his watch) "only an hour and seven minutes ago." Gowered at nine a.m., then Infernoed from five to seven, he didn't feel like walking home when he finished the second bluebook just as the proctor called time. Two finals side by side on the same day was bad enough, but after one early in the morning, and one late in the afternoon you felt like a condemned man facing two executions, or a mother giving birth to the same child twice. After the second test Michael felt played out, too tired to tramp the ten blocks to Sigerson. He had to return to the campus to preside over the election anyway. Besides, he told Leland, his alarm clock sat at Elissa's. He did not explain how it got there. If he had gone home, he'd not only have risked sleeping through the election—meaning that the torch might pass to the wrong hand—he'd also have jeopardized the excursion to K-7. If he missed the meeting and if they couldn't find him after crowning the new king or queen, as the case might be, they'd have lost access to K-7. Only he had the key to the viaduct. So, instead of home, he went directly to the seminar room and lay on the floor under the table and dozed. He heard a bang. The first thing he caught sight of: the vulnerable plywood belly of a Trojan-horse dragon. He found himself caught inside. No, pinned underneath. Leland grunted.

Because of the cold (both his face and hands lay exposed), Michael remained still conscious, but his brain, he realized, had switched off. Spent and burnt, he clammed up. Realizing then how tired Bolanger must be, Leland, holding a cigarette between his teeth, pulled a No-Doz bottle from his coat, twisted off the cap, and offered Michael a pill. "This will keep you up for a bit. You'll lead out in the cave." Taking the diminutive white tablet speckled with blue crystals from Leland's palm, Michael swallowed the purported caffeine along with a little snow he removed from the ledge, like icing from a cake, with a swift stroke of his index and third fingers. Leland said it would take at least an hour before the pill took effect.

Roger remained affable, Michael assumed, for a reason—probably he wanted to discuss their final. But Michael did not care to speculate on how well or poorly they had done. Though tired, he still remembered his priorities, and—avoiding all possible digressions to the survey course he had called "Chaucer's Children"—he wanted to last-minute-check-again that Leland still planned to vote for Cantwell.

So keep that lid on its gate, sucker.

Bolanger coughed. Leland stopped whistling again. Then, trying to look like the top-drawer officer everyone said he'd evolve into, he straightened his shoulders and, without being bid (Michael, helpless to stop him, frowned at his coat's upturned collar and genuine brass buttons), Roger Leland addressed his CO and point-blank offered his solution to what he defined as their problem: "Instead of an editor we could have co-editors next year. Everything'd stand peaceably resolved. And who knows? Being co-editor could become, well, like a sort of growing experience for Margaret. Cantwell wouldn't mind palming off part of the workload either. And we'd reach the cave a lot sooner."

Cheeky of Roger. Michael crushed his can and dropped it into the bushes. He would have stood more irritated had he felt less tired. He had done Elissa a favor by permitting Margaret to sit on the editorial board. She sat, precious little else. "We have to adhere to the constitution," Michael said, affecting mock-sanctity. "And it stipulates one-man editorship." His bottom frozen numb, Michael cut Leland's protest short and pulled himself through the window to the inside. If Leland could vote for only one of the two candidates, Michael felt sure that he would choose Ben. As he slid in, hands reaching for the floor, he knocked over a chair but blocked its fall with his left arm. Leland asked for a beer. After untangling himself, Michael handed him one. Leland snuffed out his stub and pulled the tab, letting loose an upspurting lava-flow of Rolling Rock. Looking at his drenched pants, he caught sight of Ben Cantwell and Bradley Scott crossing the quad and shouted to them. Walking very slowly heel to toe, toe to heel, Cantwell heard him and looked up, a lit cigar clenched in his teeth. He raised a gloved fist. His stomach continued gurgling. Bluefish curry, ice cream, and El Productos didn't mix, or so he found out. He had already found out that he shared the same name with someone else, a major-league baseball player; his stomach hurt, and over the last few years he had grown overweight. But he remained urbane. He didn't jam himself into clothes like Michael did. Ben Can't-well indeed, in name too, he would genuinely like for his peers to elect him editor. He knew (how couldn't he?) that he was best for the job and that he would enjoy running those meetings. But nothing in the world could appear more trivial than the outcome of this election or, for that matter, than *Thoth*, that three-toed moribund beast. That's what he told Scott—and to everyone. If they fiddle-faddled about selecting him, he would withdraw his name from consideration. *Thoth* stood doomed. If not this year, the next, or the one following that: sooner or later the magazine would fold, or worse, rot away. Just a matter of time. He tossed his cigar into the snow. Michael's hopes for *Thoth*'s future stood hugely inflated, untenable really. This was no *Hound and Horn*! But if Bolanger could secure his victory without too big a fuss, he'd hold off the sounding of the death-knell at least another year. Future editors would still have something to work with in '84. Thwarting Elissa would also have its recompenses. After he got her elected, she returned his favor by supporting—of all people—Margaret Bromion instead of him.

He'd eat a roll of antacids, drink a quart of Pepto-Bismol, have his stomach pumped. Anything. Right now he should lie flat on his back, and not stand light poised on his toes while *they* talked. Maybe he had a bug. Then he'd have a legitimate excuse for skipping K-7. *Get me out of this cave*, Ben thinks. *Bring a saw, bring dynamite, bring a corkscrew to twist down my throat.*

From his perch Leland asked if they'd do him a favor. Bradley Scott said sure. Leland didn't have smokes. Cantwell and Scott didn't have change. "Catch then," Leland said and began tossing them quarters to feed into the machine on the ground floor. He paid for three packs before they scooped up enough change from the snow for one. Cantwell went in for the pack. Scott stepped back several feet, stooped down, stood up again, and lobbed a snowball at the cadet, forcing Roger to retreat inside. When Scott ran into the room, he dodged the eraser Leland flung at him from behind the chalkboard-with-rollers and, skirting the table as Leland dropped to his knees and tried to crawl under it, opened fire. Michael jumped for the closet. Leland and Scott joined forces against him. Michael tugged on the doorknob—locked—then reached out the window for ammunition. "Look to your backside," he shouted. Scott and Leland turned. The unsuspecting Cantwell, stepping into the room, cigarettes in hand, became a large, easy target.

Bradley Scott had brought a pint of vodka, a shot glass, and a copy of the *Herne-shopple Examiner*. After the battle he retrieved them from the hall. Reviving a bit, Michael drank. Cantwell declined (sick stomach) and read the newspaper while the other three played "quarters." Scott hit a streak and plunked his coin into the shot glass seven times, making Leland take four of the drinks, Michael three. Spilled vodka swam on the table. Michael asked for a cigarette. "Roger, Bolanger," Leland laughed and pulled two from the pack. He lit both and handed Michael one. Scott meanwhile lit his meerschaum. Suddenly Cantwell became excited. He handed Michael a section of newspaper and pointed to a column. Michael didn't see how it stood of interest and said so, but kept reading anyway:

DONATIONS SOUGHT FOR CHAPEL REPAIRS

The Union Chapel, built in 1859 as an Episcopalian Church, stands as a landmark in the area that needs donations to keep it under roof. Lightning damage to the bell tower and ceiling of the chapel as well as a need for roof repairs have prompted the Union Chapel Memorial Cemetery Committee to undertake a letter campaign seeking $2,500 in donations to put a new roof on the chapel, according to Delone Frailey of Villa Nova, secretary. Interested parties should submit donations by Jan. 25, Mr. Frailey said.

Michael kept reading but also gave ear to the cantwelling spew that either—the anatomically sound account—issued from Ben's lips, its component sounds produced primarily in the structure of muscle and cartilage at the upper end of the trachea when air from cantwellowing lungs caused the lower (true) membranous cords or folds to vibrate, or—humoral whimsy—originated in the lower parts of the alimentary canal from a he-heeing jejunejejunum which obstructed then suddenly released the current of air passing through it. "Banished from our thoughts and hearts," Cantwell poetasted, "our Mr. Frailey . . . ah . . . farts?" Michael looked up. "A swing and a miss," he said, "Strike one," then raised the paper and crossed his legs. Not the baseball Ben, Cantwell decided. Michael wouldn't know about his *Doppelgänger*. The other Ben Cantwell. So he must mean me. No reactions from the other two, but they never had the pleasure of meeting Mr. Frailey. So back to the only appreciative audience, Bolanger. Cantwell tugged the paper so Michael's face stood partially revealed. Batting his lashes and mock-apprehensively quivering, he said, the rumble from the jejunejejunum again, "Delone, baloney?"

Prime-sausage kisser. Fey smile. Michael glowered at his hand-picked successor, his Taft. Cantwell's lashes continued twittering. *As peacock his painted plumes doth prancke.* But his aren't rainbow colored, Michael thought. They're white. He's an albino. A pee cock.

Turning to Scott, Ben said, "I never," but interrupted himself. Seized by an overmastering inspiration, he brought his right hand to his brow and clutched a carrot-colored forelock, motioning to them to remain silent with his other arm.

Well? Michael thought.

Then he stared even harder at Cantwell: a first-rate magician pretending to have forgotten the spell, strategically suspending the moment before he effects the rematerialization of the peroxide-blonde assistant in purple and ruby sequins. Well? thinks his audience.

First Cantwell stamped his foot, then, drolly imitating Frailey's polite and almost inaudible speaking style, took his third and final swing: Drum roll please: "D. F. Deaf. At least when it comes to judging poetry." Then in a louder voice: "resurfaces, of all places, on the printed page!" He ceremoniously raised his arm. "Ta-da!"

This conclusion to that wind-up? Michael thought. Why, Frailey should have jumped out of the closet-watercloset brandishing James Bolanger's *Pater's Art: A Starting Point for New Creations* like a minister swinging a Bible. Boulang. Gism.

Michael began expressing his scorn for Cantwell's antics: "Low, worthless, beneath contempt." He abruptly lurched forward, and the two front legs of his chair—he had tipped its back against the wall—hit the floor. He stared at the buttons on Cantwell's shirt, then again at his face. Cantwell was smiling. His lips and teeth ta-daing. Then (bababadalghahtakamminaronnkonnbronntonnerronntuonthunntovarrhounawnskawntoohoothurnuk!) an unexpected swoosh of exhilaration as the involuted meshwork of peripheral sympathetic nerves, that crisscrossed the structure in which he resided like house-wire, snapped and crackled as surplus norepinephrine poured into his blood and nerve impulses began transmitting at the synapses from sinuate nerve cell to sinuate nerve cell. Turquoise dots gamboled on his retinas, then dwindled, died. He glanced at the poster of Captain Barry; the Famous Educated Equines shimmered, pulsed, wriggled and pranced. Captain Barry's knee-high black boots shone a nacreous purple, his hallmark red coat an illicit orange. Dripping with sweat, heart thumping, he or "where-he-resided" sat nearest the draft and rose to shut the window. Already out of his seat, Roger Leland ran for the door and then for the head (the thesis closet stood locked, and he wasn't boorish or drunk enough to climb out onto the ledge and go from there). In a battle situation, he could order men to their deaths without flinching. He could give Michael a weight-reduction tablet without telling him what it was. He always stole several for finals week. They wouldn't test his urine for that and he had a reason, of course—Bolanger had to stay alert to lead them through K-7. But though Roger Leland could do a lot of things, he could not control his own pituitary and curb the inhibition of anti-diuretic hormone and the resultant interference inhibiting the reabsorption of H_2O. He had to make water. Michael wiped his brow and took Leland's seat. He looked up at the ceiling and, engrossed with what he saw, sat there lost. Bradley Scott looked at him then at Ben Cantwell then at Michael again. "Who's Delone Frailey?" he finally asked, running his hand through his yellow hair and nervously smiling.

Elissa, Margaret, and Keylee (the girl who dreamed about Michael moving through the library stacks, stalking her with a knife) arrived. Leland returned. Other staff members arrived. Michael came back (he had lost himself in the fissures, gaps, chinks and cracks of the ceiling). He sat stargazing, looking at the surface of the moon through a telescope, again experiencing that same sensation of awe he once felt as a little boy when he saw for the first time the huge—alas devitalized—skeleton of some four-legged reptile of the Mesozoic Era. Then the great flesh eater Tyrannosaurus rex held up by cables, its hind legs shaky and unreliable as an old man's. Teetering Michael felt all of himself gather at no point inside of himself .... First he realized that he existed in time and space but not who he was. Then a personality emerged, dazzled, deliciously dazed. The ceiling remained just the ceiling. He felt as if he had dozed and just waked. He saw Margaret and Elissa. First unthinking acceptance (Margaret and Elissa) then startled surprise (when did they arrive?) *But then you shatter into yous*, he thinks. *But strangely you still remain whole, one.* You talk to Cantwell but "you" don't talk. You observe yourself, as if from a perspective outside of me, where neither of us belongs. The self we observe (where you belong) talks, not us. The words that crowd into its mind and out its mouth. Where do they come from? We don't know. "The particular and general," we hear ourself say, "can interchange, keep in mind."

Elissa had circles under her eyes. Scars of an austerity recently carried out to win academic kudos, or perhaps merely to get by, to earn an honest, anemic C. She wore a blue blouse and gay, spangled, diamond-patterned tights of many colors. The expression on her face suggested resolution and pluck. But what more? A militant, knee-jerk resolve? Her capacious sense of duty? Her grit, backbone and single-mindedness? Her moral ire?

Drrum, brrum. She stands ready to fight!

Margaret looked at the Formica tabletop (Elissa saw her doing this) as intently as Michael formerly had looked up at the ceiling. Why? she wondered. Too little sleep or because she feels self-conscious? (Margaret didn't like looking at the large red letters, Barnum & Bailey, a mocking reminder of Mr. Bailey's kennel, Gretel's death, her absent-mindedness.) *She's swimming*, Elissa thinks. *She's tight.* But charity without expectation of return at the proper time and place and to a worthwhile person (such as Margaret) remains entirely praiseworthy.

Elissa warmed. A veteran of the *Thoth* wars, as well as similar frays when she served on the boards of the two literary magazines *Subject To Change* and *Nosegays For Captives* at Cannoshockton, she determined to stand up not only for her rights but everyone else's too and to make sure that no one shouted down opposing voices, that everyone had a chance to provide their input and have their say. She understood his pose, his snobbism, his call, his *playdoyer*, for the resumption of serious literature, the dueling cap he put on, and how to parry him. She stood for civil rights, women's rights, as well as art and culture, and felt it her duty to protect people against arbitrary or discriminatory treatment. Besides she saw such lambent sorrow in Marge's green eyes.

She had stood with the protestors in Philly, D.C., and Baltimore. An activist, she had fought for her causes. Her generation had put an end to L.B.J. and Tricky Dick's war and had vowed that their beloved nation would never again become mired in another Vietnam. Later, a mathematician-historian-philosopher-agronomist, she put herself on the front line in Harrisburg when everyone awaited the explosion and the resulting dispersal of radioactivity. She actively demonstrated again. And the Federal Government restructured the NRC.

Someone should take a hammer and . . . but he won't know the reason why. She made a sound with her lips. Michael glowered at her. *A vexed whore's curettage*, he thinks. *Certainly not courage.* He tried to look through her as if she didn't sit across from him. Just to annoy her, he would pretend that she did not exist, that anything she said stood beneath contempt, not worthy of his comment or refutation.

She wanted a round table of equality. Michael found it architectonically boring in comparison with his irregular polyhedrons and inverted hexagons. Elissa had thought that Sir Roger Leland in mightie armes and silver shielde would gallop to Margaret's and her aid in the manner of Sir Perceval, Sir Galahad, or Sir Lancelot. After what he's done for *Thoth*, he and only he could unhorse Michael. At our moment of need, he will appear like a star of splendor in the sky. A shrilling trumpet will sownd on hye. We need no more dread. With greedy force the two will each other assayle and Sir Roger will impresse deep dinted furrows in Saracen Michael's already battered mayle. Roger understood her point of view, that a vote for Margaret stood tantamount to a vote for a large private donation from Atelier Scientific Inc. He called the rest soupy sentimentalizing. "Needs a chance?" Roger Leland had said. "Poor little rich girl? Ha." Fun *was* something money could buy.

Waiting for the three absent board members to arrive, Margaret stared at Michael. *My day will dawn.* Soon her long night would finally reach its end. She imagined herself standing on a hill brow, the top of a rock, an overlook. She views from high above a seemly, symmetrical town surrounded by hills, woods, and fields and makes out two tree clumps in one of the fields as the sun spreads on the eastern sky fingers of pink light. She finds herself situated at an ideal altitude for her crossover to that new dawn when her promise can come to its fruition. She only needs to continue looking and not avert her glance to behold the clear ascension of the dawn!

Walter Warnock arrived. Margaret continued watching Michael.

He didn't mind committing violence on other bodies to prove his puissance in battle. The steel could bite the tender flesh and streams of blood could flow down red and purple. If only she had someone to hold her just now. She looked at the tabletop. Touch her. Champion her.

Why couldn't God have blessed her with *his* abilities and skills? If she could only somehow steal and make her own his intellect, his composure, all that would make her a more acceptable person in her father's eyes. But she wouldn't take only from Michael, she'd steal attributes she envied from all sorts of people, and Margaret the succubus would incorporate what she stole into herself and effect her transformation. She would compact everything she lacked into herself and shape herself anew, as if sculpting herself out of snow.

People died. She'd die. She accepted this, but it didn't frighten or faze her, because even if her life ran by swiftly and if, before she knew it, the sand had all drained from her hourglass, what she experienced at any given moment always preoccupied and diverted her. Gretel's death, say. Or her period starting. Or all the events that would unroll and happen tonight. She put aside all reflections on her mortality. Her former and current life experiences overpowered and overwhelmed her. She recalled Adrienne's nightly explorations and experiments and felt wonderfully and completely alive. Would Michael unbutton her blouse in the same way? She had incorporated Adrienne into herself and made her one with herself. Her ghost lived along with Margaret's in one flesh, Margaret's flesh. Michael? If she could command a series of zeroes, taken from the burgeoning supply chest of his talent, in front of them she could place her magical numeral one.

She'd stand more complete if she had his ghost inside her. If she could integrate him too.

Thoth didn't matter. She knew this as well as Cantwell. But if she won then it would matter. Because she, Margaret, won.

An accidental encounter would give her something to chew on. But would it pull her from night to dawn or would it crush her completely?

She still looked at Michael. Once taken in, she would not find him easy to discharge. Too much of Michael might indeed prove fatal. But the right amount would make her flower, bloom. *Rain, Sun*, she thinks. *Tamped-down damp. A seed deposited in it.* She wanted to savor each and every pleasure. To know it better, to experience it more fully. She wanted to see the sun. *Absorb*, she thinks. *Incorporate, digest.*

Michael Bolanger stopped watching Elissa watching Margaret watching him. He recalls Dante's line: *Fix your mind on what your eyes see and make them mirrors to the figure which will appear to you in this mirror* and smiles. Mitya and pompous, untalented Terry arrive. Michael, seeing that everyone stood present, clears his throat and coughs. His eyes briefly widen.

"We meet tonight to select next year's editor. But first we must resolve a procedural question. We must determine who should vote."

He goes on and on, elaborating his qualifications for editor-in-chief. Elissa finds him tiresome and coy.

Stop treating us like shit. You rattle on so. Don't dismiss her. You shouldn't write off any of us. Even Marge.

Boulanger: "Do I adhere to the policy of my namesake? Is that what you ask? You know. The French General Georges Ernest Jean Marie Boulanger. The political movement Boulangism adopted his name and aims. He demanded revenge on Germany. The deputy of the department of the Seine—the river in which the other Michael Boulanger drowned. Oh, these chance connections! He might have seized dictatorial powers He could have effected the usurpation of France. Do I make a case for . . ."

B– C–: "The first coherent thing he's said tonight."

Boulanger: ". . . a sort of Boulangism here? I look at you, so many mirrors on which to break myself and remain one. In Dante and the *Bhagavad-Gita*, the stars all reflect the sempiternal sun. They return His light back to Him."

He continued rambling, lecturing and adding additional facts. The vexed whore seethed.

"No. No. No." She shook her head. "*Thoth* stands as the result of our desire to establish a permanent outlet for the many and varied skills of this university. We unite these skills into a common effort. Everyone should vote to select the next board. Not just certain people, as Michael says. The other staffs will gather in the mailroom in a few minutes. Who'll tell them they can't vote? We don't need personality cults. We need a collective leadership. Everyone chooses, not just Michael."

She narrowed her lips against his reply. She couldn't say what pushed her over the edge, but the sense stood strong and constant for her that she would like to strike Michael. Slap him hard across his face. She didn't allow him to interrupt her—afforded him no opportunity to speak.

"We pile up words and waste time. I think the editorial board should determine right now if only they will participate in the election, or if the business, art and general staffs can vote too."

Bull: "We should treat the other staffs like camels in war." He resolutely put his Camel out.

"Michael and I view this differently. You decide."

Anger: "Go ahead, recite the program that'll make the magazine second rate. Ruin *Thoth*."

He looked from board member's face to board member's face.

Witless driplets, he thinks. Mirror me, he challenged. By now he also had to make water.

He washed his hands, glanced into the mirror at his reflected phiz and smiled.

Flowers offered on an altar, he thinks.

He smelled then tasted words and grinned once again. The ones running through his head just now—the denouement of *Between the Ties*, Thomas Englehardt's orgasm, he their only audience:

> Thomas would do what he had to do tonight. Tomorrow he would see the sun. And he would not have to be meek or diffident and, without qualms, he could sit down and sup with his brothers. They would be his brothers, wouldn't they! And he would shine so resplendently, prevaricate so well, that his brothers might even throw him into a well. Would his brothers do that? Yes, they might. They remained his brothers and he stood a son of the sun. The next Amun. Hardy, Mann, Wolfe. Hardy, Mann, Englehardt! Suns!

Michael saw a Frankenstein-assemblage-of-faces in his own face. He strutted over to the throne, flushed, and then went back to the mirror. Did he experience attraction, revulsion, or narcissism? These faces constituted the organic tissue of the museum room, and he stood the latest avatar. Could he possibly transcend these dualities of love and hate? He looked in the mirror. The eyes reflected back didn't seem his. They were his father's eyes transposed from the dust-jacket photograph on the Walter Pater book. He stuck out his tongue, watched himself do so. Lifting his chin, screwing up his face, he could make himself look a little like his other grandfather, "Pop" Sower. Mom's dad. The deal closer. His nose resembled Beth's in shape and size and in deviated septum. He had seen photographs of "Dad" O'Keefe, his mother's grandfather on her mom's side. He had the same (as his mother put it) "height of brow." He saw it now in the mirror. The other Michael Bolanger wouldn't have looked like him. But he remained one of many, many people who had lived, died, but had joined together to form the new Michael. His roots stretched deep into the well of the past—until he lost sight of them, could not follow them further. But they still stretched back. At birth he came sleepwalking out of this past and into consciousness. He could make himself sick by thinking of all those many, myriad, people. He had seen the ferrotypes, photographs taken directly as a positive print on a sensitized plate of enameled iron, from Gustave Bolanger's grandmother's album. Her relatives, their names now forgotten, variations on a single theme. His theme. He turned from the mirror. This tedious election . . . now that he washed his face and felt refreshed would he speak coherently and quickly make his point when he went back?

Elissa exhaled. Good for Ben. Things would stand fairer this way. Margaret would have a fighting chance. Whatever happens happens. They would make their pitches and proposals and recite their platforms, and then the whole staff would take a majority vote and choose a winner. They'll pick you Margaret, if you let them know you'll listen to them and remain open to all they say, Elissa wanted to tell her. As for Michael. She still rankled. He could have used more gentlemanly tactics. He dropped too much into character, the stance fit too snugly, smugly. On another occasion his persistent posing had angered her to the point where she started throwing magazines from a stacked pile at him. He wouldn't force anything on her against her will. She had twinges when he privately revealed his multiple personalities. But when he did his laundry in public, she grew furious with him.

Would Roger still vote for Margaret?

Cantwell told Michael he didn't care which staffs voted. Just that this ended. Now. So he told the board that he didn't care who voted.

"Behind my back while I took a piss." Michael threw a pencil at the floor. He wanted it to ricochet and hit Elissa or Cantwell. "All these tones, shadings, idiosyncrasies," he mumbled, suddenly dizzy. Ghosts joining together to form him. Each one trying to take control. He threw up his hands. "Do whatever you want," he said. "Trade Wow for Yeech," and he stormed from the room. Leland followed.

He came back after making Michael promise not to leave them without a guide to K-7. Michael had started the first of the ten blocks to Sigerson. If they still wanted him to go, drive to his apartment, he said, and pick him up there. He had the Minespots and maps. Leland rejoined the other board members in the mailroom, where the art, general, publicity, and business staffs had in the meantime also assembled. Elissa informed them of the board's decision. Cantwell walked to the podium first.

"I would like to remind you first off that I am the only one of *Thoth*'s founding members still with us not to be editor yet. Maybe that's all right. Ben Franklin was never president, but the French ladies didn't seem to mind. The past two years I've neglected my duties as secretary and as treasurer to give my attention to the editorial board, and I think it's safe to say that as editor I don't intend to neglect my duties as such to go count the money. You might question my leadership, but when has leadership ever accomplished anything? I believe—and you can have this in writing—that leadership is the most overrated quality, next to liver pate, ever foisted on this world. Now some of you may think I'm the candidate of the trusts. Big Oil. Big Wallpaper . . . ."

M. B. ♀ (On the spot, her legs shaky, an appealing smile on her face. Very earnestly): ". . . I have ideas. This magazine has such options open to it. Such a great number of people we could appeal to. And we need to reach out to these people. These people—I just know it—want this magazine to reach out to them, to feature poems, stories, and pictures that speak to their own lives. They're here. This magazine's for them. For everyone who truly wants it. My point is, and it's my real reason for running, that there are more of those people than you think. There are probably even more than I think. Elect me as editor and we'll find out how many there are."

Elissa collects the strips of paper. Bradley Scott and Roger Leland will count them. At the door, Cantwell taps Bradley Scott's shoulder. Scott turns. "Three-toed Thoth," Cantwell says.

Elissa smiles at Margaret.

The beam from the Minespot lanced over the formation up to the dozen, dripping soda straws on the ceiling. Michael pointed them out to Bradley Scott. They (Michael, Ben, Roger, Elissa, Margaret, Dmitri Smeltanowski, three people from the publicity staff, and Tim Cassill, Margaret's mixed-doubles partner) had reached the massive breakdown blocks and now stood at the kidney-shaped hole, the entrance to a crawlway which sloped downward for sixty feet, straightened, then rose up through flowstone and more breakdown to a formation climb and flowstone overhang. Cantwell had tried to jam his body through the tight squeeze once before, never again. "So this is Morris' Despair. The subject of your nightmares," Roger Leland said. "You can fit through." "I won't become the sword in the stone again," Cantwell said. "I doubt if any of you could pull me out." His grandparents hadn't earned their livings as miners. He didn't look like a miner. "Besides," Cantwell said to Michael (Michael did look like a miner) "that mole, that weasel Cobin said there's a second, a wider way." "But he isn't here," Michael said. "And Brad and Roger want to reach the Dome." "You go, then," Cantwell said. "Why did you come then?" Leland barked. "You knew where we wanted to go."

Michael had gone home, changed. Scott had picked him up. He, Cantwell, and Leland went in Brad's Plymouth. Elissa, Margaret, and Tim drove in Margaret's Camaro. Walter Warnock also drove. They parked in the junkyard.

If Ben had to squeeze through Morris' Despair to get there, he would not proceed one step farther. Michael flipped his beam eight feet to the right of where Cantwell stood to an arched entrance to, he said, "a not-so-elliptical conduit." A passage with a fifteen-foot high ceiling. It led, he told them, to a fairly large chamber decorated with broken stalactites and chipped stalagmites and with clear calcite crystals, the Hanging Forest Room. Those who wished to avoid the three-dimensional maze, straddling the breakdown-choked fissure or crawling on hands and knees through the tongue-and-groove passage, could go there. Two parties formed. They would meet again in approximately an hour at Morris' Despair. Cantwell led his group—Mitya Smeltanowski, Walter Warnock and two of the publicity people (all inexperienced cavers) into the conduit. "Exploring the upper level will remain enough for the Editor-elect and his flunkies," Leland said. In Brent Cobin's absence, Michael led the others on hands and knees and lowered himself into the crawlway. He listened to, counted his heartbeats. One by one the others followed him through the kidney. He crawled till the passage ended, pulling his body through breakdown blocks and flowstone till he came out on a ledge below the flowstone overhang. It wound its way above the breakdown-choked fissure and led to a t-shaped junction, the entrance to the maze. The others executed the various maneuvers, sometimes in pairs, but Michael kept outdistancing them more and more. If Cobin and he caved together tonight, they'd traverse the cave in record time, racing from the Birth Canal to the Dome to the Wedding Cake Room and out via the cakewalk to, then through, the vexing zigzag honeycomb, the 3-D maze, to this passage, catch up with B– C– in the Hanging Forest Room, then climb up the initial breakdown and out of K-7. He and B.C. Maybe they would explore the rooms he hadn't previously reached: Mud Rooms One and Two and the Ship Prow Room, which had a crystalline floor (step carefully) and stood chock full of speleotherms and chockstone. One got to these places through a high-balconied, high-arched room with popcorn draperies at one end of the Intestine. One entered the other end, its mouth, somewhere in the maze. From the high-arched room one could also reach the Dome by an alternative route. One could reach that room from the Dome, too, of course, after getting there the normal way through the Wedding Cake Room. Cobin avoided the Intestine not so much because of the mud but because the other route took less time. "I don't give a shit about the mud shit. I just want to get there."

Leland, who successfully kept up with Michael, complained that his pace remained too fast for the others, and told him to stop. So they waited, halting at the cross-shaped junction. Then Leland waited alone. Michael entered the labyrinth. But he returned shortly. The others had caught up. Michael said something to Elissa before re-entering the maze, but she wouldn't speak to him. They followed as he led with the Minespot. She talked to Tim and Margaret, he to Roger. They followed blue arrows to the east, halted in a square room with a breakdown pile and clay floor because Michael couldn't find the next arrow and had to either go ahead and continue looking or backtrack. Tim and Scott each lit a pipe. Michael spoke to Elissa again. She still felt angry but finally said, "I saw that stalactite myself. I'm not blind." Margaret struck her shin on a rock. The smooth-spoken Cassill said he'd take a look. His voice seemed oddly nasal and high-pitched. He chewed continuously on the stem of his pipe. Margaret had informed him about the staff trip to K-7 at the courts and asked if he could come. Elissa also knew him. They had gone ballroom dancing once or twice. Michael stood aware of this and that he taught History and Geography at the Herneshopple Junior High and in the summer worked as a carpenter and a house painter. In fact Cindy, the publicity staff member who had stayed with them, had been a former student of his. Before she met Michael, Elissa had once slept with him. Michael did not know that.

He tried to find their present location on the map. Margaret sat down, resting her back against a breakdown block. Michael told Tim to stay with her. He, Leland and Elissa would look for the next blue arrow. Bradley Scott and Cindy could look too, but in the opposite direction. "No, I'm staying with them," Elissa said. Cassill turned off both his and Elissa's flashlights, leaving only Margaret's burn.

Michael didn't find any arrows and prepared to turn back when he saw his own mark, two parallel lines with a dot between them, and decided to follow in the direction it pointed. He knew that they had taken the wrong turn, Bradley Scott and Cindy the right one. The passage Scott took would branch like a Y. If Scott continued straight ahead, he would reach the Ice Cream Cone, a flowstone formation rising up from a wide pit. Another formation, broken at its base and up where they would emerge, seemed on the verge of falling into the pit. A number of holes opened in the floor. A blue arrow marked the one that led down to the pit. Through the hole you negotiated your way down to the tapering V of the flowstone cone. The walls of the pit stood splotched with spraypaint. At its further end lay the cakewalk, the only passage in K-7 that didn't intersect with any others. After you passed the intricate purple mound with paraffin candles pressed into it, you reached a hole which you crawled into feet first, then slid down breakdown to a ledge to downclimb a flowstone wall into a canyon passage. The ceiling rose over fifty feet high. A dozen stalactites glittered like organ pipes. You had reached the Dome. If Scott, however, took the passage branching south at the Y, he would walk for twenty feet then reach a medium-sized, low-ceilinged room with more soda straws: a dead end.

He didn't tell Leland that they had taken the wrong passage. He had gone the other way so many times that he had become tired of it. He didn't feel like acting as a tour guide; he felt like exploring. Let Elissa sulk, he thought. He didn't mind losing his bearings. He'd find the way out. He wondered when he had passed here and made the marks which they now followed. According to the Grotto's March Bulletin, three known routes to the Dome existed and perhaps others awaited discovery by the patient explorer. He wanted to take an alternative route. He had never crawled through the Intestine and gone that way. He had never seen the Ship Prow. At the northern end of an obscure breakdown room—the Dome Room would stand to their north—an arrow pointed to a crawlway so tight they were forced to belly-crawl. It led to a passage branching out offshoots into all directions. His made an entirely arbitrary choice when he selected one of many narrow zigzag walking passages to the north. Only the slimiest of cavers have squeezed through here, he thought. The passage continued to narrow.

Could he ever successfully write about this cave, minutely describe these passageways without becoming monotonous, without all the details lying about like gravel?

Michael felt sure that he had never entered this passage before. Others had taken it. He saw their footprints on the floor as he looked at his own mud-caked shoes. Undoubtedly someone had previously trod all these countless, dead-ending paths. Every passage in K-7. But no one, not even Brent Cobin, who had explored more of the cave than anyone else Michael knew of, had visited on his own each and every single passage, all these infuriating infinite passages that always ended (at least mainly ended) in rooms with unstable breakdown. The passage they followed terminated in breakdown and stood waterfilled up to their shins, but at the same time the ceiling opened, rose from seven feet to fifteen feet to twenty-five feet. Where would it debouch? Michael kept plodding on. Leland followed, each of his footfalls splattering water on Michael's back. The passage continued to twist to the north. They climbed out of the water and up a breakdown pile into another complex of rooms and passages but also found a series of arrows chalked on the wall which they found easy to follow. Ahead they heard the lick and lap of water.

The red spraypaint blotch at the entrance to a muddy crawlway, six feet wide and four feet high, resembled a water buffalo. Michael and Leland entered it. They crawled on hands and knees and eventually had to belly-crawl. Leland complained that the passage became too narrow and muddy, said something about little kids getting stuck in drain pipes and drowning, how his mother always warned him not to crawl into them. The crawlway went right, swerved left, then zigzagged again. If it dead-ended, they wouldn't have room to turn around and would find themselves trapped, Leland said. Michael told him that he knew the passage. He didn't. He had a suspicion though: this crawlway ran for a greater distance than any other Michael had previously inched and edged through in K-7. It pinched in places like the Birth Canal.

It just keeps going on, Leland thought. Like Michael explicating a poem. His body contacted the water. He swore. They'd stand covered with mud when they came out. "This crawlway calls for ingenious contorting," Michael said. "I'm going to bleeding kill you if I ever get out of here," Leland said. They crawled for seventy-five more feet before Michael reached the other end and plopped out of the Intestine. *He had been right.* The room rose fifteen feet high. The popcorn kernels, muddy and purplish, looked like fish eggs. Intestines normally end in rectums—Michael could remember how they were described in the Grotto Glossary. This room wasn't that constricted. Two walking passages led out of it and also another crawlway. He saw the initials B.C. chalked at the entrances of both passages. "I told you, I knew our location," Michael said. "From this pocket one can get to both the Ship Prow and the Dome Room. The problem is, I don't know which path leads where."

The crawlway led to the Mud Rooms and the Ship Prow. But Michael ruled it out because he knew that Cobin had reached those rooms and thought that he'd have marked the way to them as well as the alternate path that led to the Dome. They agreed to each take a path and meet each other back here in fifteen minutes. Leland took the one which meandered to the north and (Michael thought) most likely led to the Dome. He, on the other hand, forged forward on the other B.C. trail. But not, as he imagined, to the Ship Prow.

Tim Cassill put down his pipe and took a bag and bowl out of his jeans-jacket pocket after unfastening its snap. He took off the jacket; under it he wore a heavy red plaid flannel shirt, its cuffs worn to a fray. He sat with his legs crossed on the flat clay floor and loaded the bowl. "Want a hit?" he asked, addressing Margaret and Elissa, whichever of the two responded or both of them. He fumbled a lighter from a pocket and lit the pipe.

After blowing out his smoke, he said, "Come on, girls." Then: "Certainly, at this blessed epoch of the equality of mediocrity, of rectangular abomination, as Edgar Allen Poe says—at this delightful period, when everybody dreams of resembling everybody else, so that it has become impossible to tell the President of the United States from a waiter—in these days which are the forerunners of that promising, blissful day, when everything in this world will be of a dull, neutral uniformity, certainly at such an epoch, one has a right, or rather it is one's duty, to be stoned." Elissa reached for the bowl, offered it to Margaret (she shook her head), then put it in her mouth, took three quick puffs. Holding her breath, she watched the minute hand on her watch. As she exhaled, she took strawberry, sandalwood and rose-scented votive candles from out of an inside coat pocket and handed them to Tim to light. He switched off Margaret's torch. She yawned, laid her cheek on and wrapped her arms and hands around her pulled-up knees, closed her eyes, then opened them. Tim emptied the bowl and reloaded it. Margaret watched the candles flicker. Elissa's eyes watered. She wiped them with her wrist, then smiled, giggled, until, after several attempts to curb herself without success, she finally stopped, only to start again. Tim laughed and coughed. They both laughed, stared blankly at one another and at Margaret and their own ballooning shadows, as well as the ones the breakdown cast on the cave's bentonite walls. He handed her the bowl and lighter; she began to chatter. She spoke with confidence—nonchalantly—about a soil-judging contest she had recently participated in, the Arts Festival, a Jazz band in town that she liked. He stretched out his legs (he wore green chinos like Wayne Hedgepeth did) and, not knowing what to talk about, said whatever came into his mind—spoke effortlessly. Margaret asked Tim how he thought his girls would do at regionals (he coached Girls' Tennis at Herneshopple High). He said the Highlanders had a first-rate team this year. They stopped talking. She watched the curve of his lip as the fire points flickered. They heard footsteps, voices, then saw the beam from the Minespot. Bradley Scott came through the passage into the room. Cindy followed. Brad angled his head to avoid hitting the ceiling and shone his light in Tim Cassill's face. Pausing, he sniffed. Cassill turned his head (he had already pulled up his knees), picked up the bowl, and, stretching out his hand, offered it to Scott, who shook his head. "I don't do it," he said. An outright refusal. Gee, Cassill thought. They found the blue arrow, Scott said. But he thought they'd better wait for Michael. It surprised him that he hadn't returned by now.

Roger Leland followed the passage as it sloped gently over more loose rock. Side passages, small tunnels jutted off everywhere. Sometimes the hard clay floor, strewn now with trash, cigarette butts and broken glass, would open in pits and pockets which he would step over and shine his light into. This was fun and easy now. He followed the B.C.s. ABCs, he thought. A long, narrow slab of rock jutted out in front of him and looked like a long-snouted dragon. Complete with glaring eyes and forked tongue. Leland paused, blinked. It didn't disappear. He climbed over the dragon's back instead of crawling under its belly. Paths veered to the left and to the right, but the B.C.s pointed straight ahead. The ceiling kept rising. The passage enlarged into a room. Thank god he didn't have to fit through any more tight holes. He saw the end of the corridor. He didn't pause to look at the shapely stalactites and stalagmites or the interesting rocks on the floor. He had seen too many rocks, too many formations. He rushed forward. The temperature dropped. The corridor opened on a window, a ledge, twenty feet above the Dome Room's floor. He had crossed a rainbow bridge. All the sections, segments of cave he and Michael previously negotiated stood in no way suggestive of this, what he now saw. He looked up at the ceiling—the dream Dome—cathedral-like, what a mosque must look like from the inside, or one of the tombs Schliemann excavated at Mycenae. He looked at the organ pipes, icicles as thick as saplings hanging from the roof and sides of the cavern, at the stalagmites formed on the floor of the cave by the drip of calcareous water. Some curved in like the one or two heavy, upright horns on the snout of a rhinoceros. He yelled to hear his voice echo. Across the gulf he saw the flowstone slope on the opposite side, rocks cascading down to that slope from a hole higher up in the vault which led into another room. He saw the Wedding Cake, small and diminutive from where he stood, in that room. On his side, the wall did not look free-climbable. He'd need a rope to get down. He would double back. One of the leftward-sloping passages might connect into the room. Then he could look up at the Dome and at his current position from the floor. Entering the cathedral, he could almost hear *Toccata and Fugue* resounding from the pipes.

Ben Cantwell, Mitya Smeltanowski, Walter Warnock, and the two members of the publicity staff had reached the Hanging Forest Room and had backtracked to Morris' Despair. After seeing the upper levels, Warnock now wanted the others to explore the lower passages. Cantwell began protesting. "Ah Ben," Walter Warnock whines, "Don't be such a crybaby. You remind me of a little girl."

Michael completed another turn and stood at a pit three feet across, fifteen feet deep. A fissure with a vertical extent of fifty feet bisected the wall on the other side. The arrow pointed into the fissure, which meant Michael would have to step across. He wiped his forehead on his coat sleeve, then, clinging to a rock that jutted out over the drop with his hands, he stretched one leg across. After finding a toe-hold, he groped for another hand-hold with his right hand while still clutching the protruding rock with his left, and, finding it, pulled himself into the fissure. Inside, he stood on a shelf that jutted from the wall. He wondered what to do now. Downclimb the fissure to a small room at the bottom fifty feet below—he saw a stream of water run through it, through the gap between his feet. He crossed up high near the ceiling, a leg and arm on either side. The shelves formed as the stream cut its way down through the limestone at varying rates. Above and below each other they stretched across the fissure; to downclimb it, he would have to drop from shelf to shelf until he reached the bottom—or should he cross it horizontally, arms braced, to, it appeared, a room on its other side? With the Minespot, he searched for arrows or B.C.s to guide him. He found two small arrows which pointed forward, so he continued crossing the fissure lengthwise, as if he walked down a hallway on the fourth floor of an apartment building, the shelves below him the third, second, and first floors. The stream bisected the building's basement. To think it once flowed where he stood. He looked up. Through the gap the stream had cut in a fifth floor above him he could make out a bat hanging from the ceiling. He looked once more at the "floors" below him, at the shelves jutting out from either side, the gap between his feet. Finally he reached the small room on the other side and entered a walking passage that tapered to a crawlway. Dry it rose upward and led into yet another room. As Michael pulled himself up through the breakdown blocks into the room, he thought he had arrived at the Ship Prow. The room appeared large and had a twenty-foot-high ceiling.

He had never seen it before quite from that perspective. For half a minute he thought he had reached a new room. Then he saw the keyhole. He was at the entrance! He recognized the breakdown pile as he turned his head. He had come full circle, only two hundred feet from where Elissa and Margaret would be if they still waited for him where he told them. He saw the first blue arrow, the one pointing to the initial downward slope. From his present spot he could reach Morris' Despair in a matter of minutes. He had found the second, wider way that Brent Cobin had told Ben Cantwell about. It led to the Intestinal pocket which in turn led to the Ship Prow and the Dome. The crawlway in that pocket must lead to one of those two places, the passage Leland took to the other. What should he do now? Go back the way he had come and find Leland or go straight ahead and find Margaret, Brad, Cindy and Elissa? They could take the cakewalk to the Dome and meet Leland there. But what if Roger had taken the path to the Ship Prow? Or gone back to find him? (Michael didn't know how to get to the Intestine from the Dome). He couldn't make up his mind. Tired of breathing cave air, he closed his eyes, listened to his heart beat. He'd decide outside. He clambered through the keyhole into the viaduct. He saw the swung-open gate, pulled himself through it to the niche in the quarry wall. He looked up at the stars and the top of the quarry where the rock, generally unstable, could fall at any time, then down at the base of the cliff, where the pond, iced over now, abutted the wall. The cage of a shopping cart was frozen in the pond; its legs and wheels rose above the surface. Michael picked up a rock and threw it at the cart. He missed. The stone bounced and skidded on the ice. He looked across the junkyard at the silos, three giants standing against the night glare.

The valley of corrosion, he thought. He shifted his weight as he sat, pushed the sweat from his forehead. The ice and snow would make the climb down difficult. More snow had recently fallen. He heard voices from inside the cave but could not make out the words. He heard Warnock's shrill tenor. His words rang clear and unmistakable. "Ah, Ben, don't be such a crybaby." Tomorrow, Michael would probably have a bad head cold. He should go back in. But not yet.

As he sat, the photographs from Elissa's album—Chet, Dorn, M.K.—and the cutouts trimmed from magazines and newspapers pasted to the back and sides of her Death Box flicked before Michael's eyes. He suddenly felt fatigued. The dead die in a thousand ways, he thought. But death resolves them into one like the man in her poem does the different shades of green. He yawned. Could the same be said of him as one of Elissa's lovers? That that which differentiates also makes the same? He wondered.

Another green leaf in her album.

Chapter Nine
In the Valleys of Corrosion (conclusion)

III

He didn't know if it actually happened. Michael sat bolt upright in bed: awake. He remembered or imagined he remembered his mother touching his arm and saying that *The Sewanee Review* had accepted one of his stories, one that she and his sister Beth had sent out. The letter had just come in this morning's mail. He recalled how miserable he had felt when his mother had briefly roused him at 10:30 a.m. The postman came early in Cannoshockton. He looked at the Westclock alarm on his dresser and saw the current time: 3:15 p.m. At first he thought that waking him his mother took revenge for his making so much noise when he had stumbled into the house at four a.m. that morning that he awoke both her and Beth. "Where did you say you placed it?" he asked, blinking his eyes and feeling full force his big head. His mother beamed and repeated herself: "*The Sewanee Review.*" "Which story?" "*Eight and Nine.*" "Don't kid me, Mom. They took that?" Had he not had a splitting headache, he would have either leapt out of bed and danced at the good news—*The Sewanee Review* had bought his story, the goddamnedsewaneefuck-ingreview!—or else miffed, enraged, that his mother had sent something out without his permission, said something nasty, given his mother a severe and rigorous dressing down. She had to leave for work. "We'll talk later," she said. Michael smiled at her—tried to show some emotion—before she went out his door, then rolled over and pulled his covers over his head. He had drunk so much the night before, he thought, before he fell asleep again, that he'd probably have to run to the toilet to blow oats.

He never stood satisfied with *Eight and Nine*, a story about two young boys aged eight and nine, inexperienced and innocent, who found a decapitated and rotting human head floating in a farmer's well behind the one boy's house. Too *Grand Guignol* and obvious, he felt. But there sat the acceptance letter along with something else from—he looked at the manila envelope under the one with *The Sewanee Review* letterhead—his Aunt Lenora. He took them off his dresser, where they lay beside the Westclock and his King Arthur battery-run radio—an eight-inch knight in silver armor with a golden visor stood atop the small walnut receiving set, a sword/letter opener thrust between his joined hands—a Christmas present from all four of his grandparents twelve Christmases ago—and went into the living room. Lying on the carpet, their aged dachshund wagged its tail and rolled over onto its back. She started doing this as a puppy after the vet had spayed her because his mother kept turning her over to clean the incision and later he and his sister would constantly pet her "poor little tummy." The Siamese cat sat in the bay window in front of the drape like a piece of statuary. Michael looked at the Christmas cards on the mantel and the ornaments on the tree. He went into the kitchen. The dog followed. He reached for the dog biscuits on the counter and threw her one. He laid the letters on the snack bar, and, as he got a coffee cup out of the cupboard, it struck him all over again. *The Sewanee Review* had accepted his story. He couldn't believe it, *The Sewanee Review!* Whom could he call in Cannoshockton to celebrate with? John Salmos, Andy Raoul, Freddie Fregno? He stared again at the acceptance letter as he sipped coffee and orange juice and ate donuts and Christmas cookies from the freezer. He took the letter into the living room (Ginger followed him) and read it through a second time. He turned on the T.V. Whom could he call? Elissa. He got up from the sofa, bit off, and spit onto the carpet, a chunk of donut for the dog and went back into the kitchen, stood in front of the wall phone, lifted the handset off the hook and dialed both her Herneshopple and Lancaster numbers on the fingerwheel but didn't receive an answer at either place. He hung up. In the living room, he sat down at the piano and laid the letter down beside him on the bench. He knew that he had a singular destiny and that he would achieve something special in this life. Others had received intimations of his fate or had detected his specialness. His mother had often told him how her beloved maternal grandfather the ever-jolly Dad O'Keefe had returned to her from the dead in a dream after she had become pregnant with Michael and had smilingly informed her that she would have a baby boy and that he would make a name for himself in the world. The famous pianist Anna von Kurstenbach saw that little boy and detected his Cain-mark, the signet graven upon his brow, his badge, his emblem, and the sight of him inspired her and occasioned one of her finest performances. She spoke about the child in a newspaper interview and admitted the powerful impression that he had on her. Whom could he tell? His eyes trailed across the living room bookshelf. He looked for his father's study *Pater's Art: A Starting Point for New Creations.*

It wasn't until Beth came home and until she started their supper that he opened what Aunt Leonora sent him—more family research, it turned out, information on the bloodline of Francis Xavier Bolanger's wife, on her atavus, Henry van Poole, specifically. She continued to excavate on the family's peripheries, spending hours culling through records at county seats, sending out letters, requests for archival information, working on the project Gustave Bolanger had started, his hobby for over forty years: the compiling of the Bolanger family tree. Michael browsed through eight or ten Xeroxes of newspaper clippings, court records from Franklin, Rallings, and Centre Counties. He didn't understand it or try to understand it. He unfolded his aunt's letter. She wrote that she had solved a mystery that for years had plagued Gustave and then her.

Michael's great-great-grandfather, Francis Xavier Bolanger, mayor of Rallingsburg (he once traded a dying horse for a blind one and felt cheated) married Mary Catherine Barbary of Armstrong Co. Her mother Elizabeth Jean's maiden name was van Poole or von Puhl or Pole or Poole (people spelt the name differently on different records— "the vagaries of English orthography!" his aunt wrote. And to make matters worse, the documents she consulted claimed the Pooles' ancestry variously as Dutch, German, and French). Elizabeth wed John Barbary of Kittanning, Pa. Gustave Bolanger attempted to find the names and birth dates of her parents during the course of his researches and for a long time believed that he had succeeded, but Aunt Leonora had found new information. Gustave Clair's conclusion proved wrong. Rummaging through the files in the Rallings Co. prothonotary's office on one of his weekly visits, G.C. discovered that Christian van Poole—"the durable Dutchman of Rallings Co, Pa"—had a daughter named Elizabeth Jean. He assumed that he had found John Barbary's wife.

Christian Poole earned his livelihood by farming and for most of his life resided in Halfmoon Township. He died Oct. 20, 1866 at the age of one hundred and twelve. He had stood six-feet two-inches tall and as a young man had taken an Indian bride. "Except for some rheumatism," he said on his one hundred and eleventh birthday, "I'm as good a man as I was at sixty-five or seventy." Or some such platitude. He remained the oldest man ever to have lived in Rallings County, so both Gustave and Lenora had found many written references about him. He appeared in all the local histories. He still harvested grain in his one hundred and eleventh year, a cradle, a five-pronged reaping tool, slung over his shoulder. "His cradle," Aunt Leonora wrote, "may have kept him from his grave." He sold produce in Philadelphia during the Revolutionary War, saw colonial soldiers walk the street and once glimpsed Lafayette. However, it turned out that Christian Poole had a sister named Elizabeth Jean, and his brother Jacob Poole also had a daughter named Elizabeth Jean. Christian and Jacob Poole also had another brother, William Poole, and two more sisters, Nancy and Susan. Their parents bore the Christian names of Henry and Susan, and Henry Poole served as a Quartermaster in the Revolutionary War. Lenora had discovered all this and that of the three Elizabeths, the daughter of Jacob and Mary Poole (or so her records indicated) had married John Barbary of Kittanning, Pa. But Gustave claimed that his father Joseph Ray had always said that his mother Mary Catherine, who had died before Gustave's birth (the youngest of her fourteen children, Joseph, unlike all his brothers and sisters, lived in Rallingsburg his entire life and thus received most of the family heirlooms but not Henri Boulanger's sword), had been part Indian. But she wouldn't have been if her father were Jacob Poole instead of Christian.

Like his brother Jacob Puhl had built a homestead and farmed the land, but he also operated a tannery. He and his sons together dug the pits and built the vats. Oak forests and pine plantations covered the many tracts of land which he owned. He had an inexhaustible supply of bark. Fording the Juniata River, he fell off his horse—at age ninety-eight—and drowned. He had married Mary Saltsgiver-Olivet, and they had a daughter named Elizabeth. According to Aunt Lenora, she married John Barbary. Their daughter, Mary Catherine, wed Francis Xavier Bolanger, Mayor of Rallingsburg and grandson of Henri Boulanger. The daughter of Christian Poole married a man named Beamer. But how did she find this out? By discovering a reservoir of new information on the Pooles. Something fantastic and Faulknerian! At the little town museum in Kittanning, she found an article about the Pooles in an 1895 *Raftsman's Journal*. She had arbitrarily chosen the '95 binder.

Heirs to a Vast Fortune

Some months ago, John Clawson Sr. of Kittanning, Pennsylvania, an old man eighty years old, was in this place with his lawyer Thomas Rogers, and his son John Clawson, a conductor on the Beech Creek Railroad in reference to his claim against the Government of the United States for fabulously valuable property located in the heart of Washington D.C. on which now stand the Washington Monument, the United States Engraving Building and the Natural Museum of History. Clawson claims this property by right of inheritance; at the time of the consultation, the parties decided to go over the old grants in the National Archives, Revolutionary Department, in the left wing of the Capitol. Clawson found a copy of the grant among his family's possessions. "In a dusty corner," Rogers states, "we discovered a land grant signed by George Washington, first president of the United States, in which he bequeathed property in Washington to one Henry Poole, Quartermaster in the continental army, to him and his heirs forever." The value of the property now stands at over a million dollars. A Frenchman who immigrated to America, Poole fought bravely in the Revolutionary War. In 1792, he moved to Washington, and beside the land grants, Poole bought large tracts of land. Suddenly dying, he moved to Nittany Valley, Centre County, of this state. Poole's family remained uneducated people and did not realize the immense value of the property which stood rightfully theirs.

John Clawson's mother had been a Poole on her father's side, her only surviving descendants John Clawson Sr. and his family. A Raftsman's correspondent interviewed Clawson yesterday. Clawson stated that he had retained attorneys and that they are currently working on the case now in Washington. They have informed Clawson that his claim will be presented to the next congress and that he will obtain a settlement that will give his family wealth beyond the dreams of avarice.

The mother of John Clawson Sr., Catherine Poole, descended from William Poole, the brother of Christian and Jacob. With news of the claim, the other descendants of Henry Poole materialized. The Xeroxes contained a complete list of the heirs of Henry and Susan Poole up to that time which the *Raftsman's Journal* published later in 1895; their sons and daughters, William, Jacob, Christian, Nancy, Susan, and Elizabeth Poole; their children and their children's children and even their children. The *Journal* continued to report on the progress of the claim. Four months after his attorneys filed the lawsuit, Clawson Sr. reported that his copy of the land grant had been destroyed in a house fire. The copy of the grant in the National Archives also mysteriously disappeared and shortly thereafter the civil authorities accused Clawson of trying to defraud the government. A *Raftsman's* reporter wrote to the Bureau of Pensions, the Department of the

Interior, to see if there stood a record of the settlement there. The reply he received was also published in the *Journal*:

> In answer to your letter relative to William Poole, who was a Teamster in the War of the Revolution from Pennsylvania, and also to examine the Quartermaster roll for the settlement of Henry Poole also of the same state and send you a copy.
>
> You are advised that the army employed such a large a number of civilians as Teamsters that it makes it doubtful when a person is specified as such whether he stood an enlisted man or not. No accounts or rolls of the Quartermasters' department are on file in this bureau and neither of the above-named persons has been found on any record of this office.

Lenora wanted to know if John Clawson had lied and, if he had, why he had bothered to file the claim. Did some document actually exist? Would the lawyers have taken the case without seeing it? So many unanswered questions. A big scandal apparently ensued, but prior to its breaking, lawyers in the case had compiled a half-a-dozen lists of the heirs of Henry and Susan Poole, and she had found the documents and had discovered that there had existed three Elizabeth Pooles and had determined which one had married John Barbary. Probably. Could the heirs and lawyers have made a mistake and confused the Elizabeth Pooles?

Another scandal? Michael thought. He doubted it. Three women in the same family all happen to bear the same name, not that unlikely of a coincidence. He again looked at the list of heirs. What he saw arrested him. He blinked in disbelief:

> The following claimant Nancy Hexfour, wife of John Hexfour
> Their heirs: Emanul Hexfour, John Hexfour, Maggie Gearheart

What? Could he and Elissa, like Franklin and Eleanor Roosevelt, share the same bloodline and, unbeknownst to either, stand cousins many times removed? Probably not. A remote possibility. He looked to see how the Hexfours stood related to the Pooles. The first Elizabeth Poole, the daughter of Henry and Susan Poole, married John Kroster and their daughter Nancy married a John Hexfour from Pleasantville, Pa. Michael again read the names of the couple's children: John, Emanul, and Maggie. He saw that these people spelled their surname Hexfour instead of Hexfore, but he remembered what his aunt wrote about the vagaries of English orthography, how many different ways Poole was spelt. He and Elissa probably did not share a common ancestor. He knew that a number of "Hexfours" resided in the Pleasantville-Rallingsburg-Herneshopple area. One owned a well-known contracting business. He and Elissa had often seen his trucks on the interstates near Herneshopple. People were forever asking Elissa if she was related to that Hexfour. She always replied that her family spelt the surname differently, and that she came from Lancaster and not Herneshopple. Michael probably stood very distantly related to those other Hexfours but not to Elissa's family. But if he and Elissa were not related, he still found it a remarkable coincidence that he could claim kinship, no matter how distantly, to anyone bearing a surname so similar to hers. What further cards would the demoniac deal him? Their paths had crossed at Cannoshockton, again at Herneshopple. He remembered how Elissa explained Einstein's theory of time: that time was a dimension, the passage of time the most persistent of illusions. A living entity exists in time as it exists in space. It fills a portion of it. Humans and all other life forms stood four-dimensional space-time worms. Seen truly we'd look like a worm, one end of which would be a fetus, the other end a skeleton, both existing simultaneously in an un-time in which all times resolved into one. Fetus and skeleton and everything in between would abide contemporaneously, he thought. Yet the illusion of time passing remained very persistent. Perhaps E. had got it wrong. He and Elissa would surely keep bumping into each other at odd intervals. Their life-lines would continue to reintersect at curious, felicitous angles.

Such coincidences could not always be found. Things like this didn't happen to everybody. Were he and Elissa re-repeating something that had already occurred? Had he found another reintersection? Another reinterpenetration? History always repeated itself. Elizabeth Poole and Elizabeth Poole and Elizabeth Poole. Elissa Beth Jean Poole, he thought. Elizabeth Jean Poole.

Ruth Leah Bolanger drove into the driveway, parked the car, and got out. Ginger started barking at the other side of the door as Michael's mother opened it, but stopped when she stepped inside and put down the bag with her bathing suit and shampoo. After work she swam everyday at the YMCA. As Mrs. Bolanger walked into the kitchen, before following her the dog shook its head, flapped its ears and barked once for no reason. Beth had made lasagna and had set the table. Michael poured the ice tea. He turned to look at his mother. She had a small round face with small round features. Her two front teeth appeared slightly crooked and she wore special glasses so her right eye wouldn't overcompensate for her weak, formerly crossed left one. She worked as a physical therapist at the Cannoshockton Area Hospital and volunteered on Sundays in the baby fold of the Methodist church. Michael knew how she would have replied if he would have actually had the gall to take her to task and condemn her for sending out his story without first asking his permission. "Because I'm your mother," she would say. Or "You don't have any initiative, Michael," or "But you left it here, hon." Yes, in my desk, mom. He said nothing. *The Sewanee Review* had accepted it. She had made the right decision. He owed her an immense debt of gratitude. Beth walked to the stove and served herself. She wore sweat pants and a Cannoshockton University, C.U.P., T-shirt. She had strawberry blonde hair and wore red eye shadow and salmon-colored makeup. A sweet virginal girl, Michael thought. Not at all like the sister in his story. Beth had never read it, and he hoped that she never would. It would no doubt deeply hurt her feelings. Perhaps he should commit all copies of it to the fire. Once again he felt contrite and penitent. He had never intended that people would identify his sister with his fictional creation. She had only been twelve years old when he wrote the damn thing, but folks always jumped to wrong conclusions and wanted to see everything a writer wrote as somehow autobiographical. No doubts tongues had wagged, as he had showed the piece to a half-a-dozen of his high school teachers. Ironically his two victims had sent out another one of his stories and would stand responsible for his first major publication. Michael wiped his eye as his mother filled their plates and the three of them all sat down to eat. The dog reared on its hind legs and sat up and begged. After finishing his second helping, Michael walked into the living room, as his mother stood loading the dishwasher. The phone rang, and Beth answered it. Michael wondered if Elissa's parents had caller ID and if she returned his call but as Beth continued talking, he concluded that his sister spoke to one of her girl friends. After she hung up, Beth asked their mother if she could use the car. His mother gave her permission and, after she left, asked Michael if he wanted to come with her and walk the dog around Hedgewood Village's outer circle to see the Christmas lights and the decorations in the neighbors' windows. He put on coat, gloves, scarf and cap and watched as she put the dog sweater on the dog and then her own gloves and coat with hood. He wanted to say something especially nice to her but couldn't find the right words as they strolled through the neighborhood and she told him the latest news, the most recent gossip. She never made up outrageous, incredible stories or behaved in brazen, imbecilic fashion as the mother in his story did. Again Michael felt ashamed as his mother, as the sun set, looked up at the snow-covered trees and pointed to a red cardinal perched in the crisscrossing branches of a maple. She saw a first star pulsing in the sky and called Michael's attention to it, then gave the dog chain a quick but gentle jerk, so that Ginger would keep moving along. They passed Mr. and Mrs. Laaks. Mrs. Laaks said hello. They rounded the circle and went in. He drank a cup of cocoa and chatted with his mother a while longer. She exhorted him to take care of himself and to remain careful and alert overseas. Perhaps Elissa had tried to call him while they had taken their walk. He again dialed her two numbers but still did not reach her. He tapped his fingers on the counter and waited for someone to pick up the receiver. No one did. He told his mother he was going out. "Over to John's," he said.

He hadn't written to John Salmos or replied to his letters and wanted to see him during Christmas break before leaving for England. They'd take an hour-long hike through the woods or have a three-hour conversation, or perhaps play one or two games of chess. Maybe they'd toss a football or shoot one of John's guns, his H.K. They would certainly hike. Six years older than Michael, Salmos had always acted the part of his surrogate older brother. John had gotten married over a year ago (Michael had just met Elissa), but his wife divorced him in only six months' time. Michael should have written and consoled his friend, but he could never find the time.

Prior to Michael's acceptance at Herneshopple, they would disappear into the woods for hours and they knew all the streams, caves, hills, and trails in Brown Township and near Hedgewood, the residential area where they had both then resided. They hunted together, using bow and arrows, and they sharpened and hurled throwing stars, carrying out "military operations" against imaginary enemies: the trees. Their friendship remained intellectually reciprocal. They exchanged books. Michael lent Salmos Nortons from his father's den. For someone bent on a practical education, he stood very much interested in the humanities. He read all of Michael's novice work, but Michael also learned from him. When Michael attended high school and John still lived with his parents in Hedgewood, Michael proofread Salmos' college term papers, learned about methane gas detection in coal mines, the storage of radioactive wastes in salt beds, and the conversion of mechanical energy into direct current electricity by electromagnetic induction; once he visited a deep mine that had hired Salmos as a safety consultant. John continually introduced him to people. Michael thought that, as Salmos was the same age as Elissa, he must have, some time or other, gone to a party at Big Red or perhaps even knew Wayne Hedgepeth or Bones Reddle. He remembered the threadbare Cannoshockton apartment to which Salmos moved during Michael's senior year in high school, a Jim Morrison poster on the wall, a kerosene burner on the floor, grids, compasses, red and blue pencils strewn on the tabletop, a silver motorcycle helmet hanging from a hook in the wall, and a mangled much abused copy of *The Brothers Karamazov*, a birthday present from Michael, tossed in a corner. He would always stumble over John's tennis balls, six or seven of which always lay on the floor. Michael had not gone to his wedding or bothered to correspond with him after his divorce, so he adjudged it high time to make his amends. Michael asked his mother if Elissa called to take a message and to tell her that he would ring her back. He told her to commit him to anything Elissa wanted if Elissa needed an immediate answer or even if it merely seemed like she pressed for one.

He tramped toward the woods that separated Hedgewood Village from the trailer court where John now resided with (John's mother told him) Andy Raoul, who had just come out of the navy. Years earlier, Michael told Andy to charge the enemy barricade during an apple battle, and, despite the danger of running directly into the enemy line of fire, Andy did. Shod with Elissa (Michael tonight wore the Street Cars she told him to buy which had high arch supports and proved excellent for hiking and climbing over massive breakdown), he cut across the road, slogged through the snow between the hemlock and pine trees, looked up through the skeletal, crisscrossing maple branches, at the stars. He saw the lights of the trailer court in the distance and heard several dogs barking. A branch cracked under his foot. He kicked the snow. It phosphoresced. He saw John's truck with its fish, bear, and deer decals parked in front of a trailer. Michael knocked. Salmos opened his door, a can of Budweiser in his hand. He had olive-colored skin and his hair looked like black fuse wire. A moustache concealed his upper lip. He had gained weight since Michael had seen him last. Salmos stared long and hard at Bolanger, his eyes a hard yellow, before letting him in. He handed Michael the beer can and, without speaking a single word, walked down the hallway and into one of the adjoining rooms. Michael waited in the kitchen by the sink. After a minute or two, he called his friend's name. Salmos stepped out of the hall brandishing a shotgun. He cocked it and pointed both barrels at Michael Bolanger's chest. Michael winced. "Just who the hell do you think you are to come banging on my door and barging into my house?" Salmos demanded. Michael stood bewildered and at a loss for words. Salmos continued pointing the gun at him: a Mexican stand-off. Finally becoming irritated, Michael shouted,

"Knock it off John. I know the damn thing isn't loaded." The flexible medium of their friendship. How things could bend, twist, metamorphose. Salmos lowered the barrels and, stooping over, tilted the gun against the wall. He spun to face Michael. "Just tell me one thing, Mick," he shouted, wagging his forefinger. "Answer me this." Michael didn't lower his guard and replied in a spiteful, catty manner: "If you insist, John." Then, receiving no response, he added: "Shoot." "How's the wife," Salmos said. "I know you haven't pledged your troth yet but you might as well have, you henpecked Bolanger."

Michael remembered what Salmos had always said about women. His philosophy of how to deal with them. He didn't lack principles. He had a code of morality which stood very well defined: find, fondle, and forget her. "Why don't you just leave," Salmos said. "And don't let the door hit you on the way out." Michael tried to justify himself but quickly became incoherent. "I don't want to hear it." Michael threw up his hands, spilling beer from the can, then made as if he would go. "No, stay," Salmos said. Michael turned around. John Salmos seized the Budweiser from his outstretched hand and glared at him. "Bonehead," he said. Michael followed him into the living room and they both sat down. Salmos didn't speak. Michael decided to start one of their games by asking John a question he wouldn't know the answer to. "Who wrote the *Tartarin of Tarascon*?" "You know," Salmos said, "I don't care." "Alphonse Daudet," Michael answered. "You always retreat," Salmos exploded, "between the covers of some book. You think you're already a great writer, but you sit in an ivory tower creating," he jeered, "what—aesthetically pleasing shit for a small group of people—immune, blind to the tragedies that surround you." "John, you know that's—" "You really want to have it out, college boy?" Salmos asked. Michael nodded. "So you find a wife," Salmos said, "and what do you do? Disappear. Pull up stakes. Don't bother to say goodbye—screw John." Bewildered, Michael raised his hands and once again began stammering incoherently. John Salmos threw a pillow at him and stood up. "Just remember who your real friends are, motherfucker."

Salmos walked back into the room, hoisting a cooler with both hands and handed Michael a beer. A bottle of scotch sat on the T.V. stand. Well, once again he would return home in the wee hours. After downing four or five beers, Michael told Salmos that *The Sewanee Review* had accepted and what's more paid him for one of his stories! He looked at the black velvet murals of a tiger and an eagle and a cobra on the wall, at the Halloween cutout of a green skull above the door. Its orange eyes sparkled. He wondered if Elissa still planned to come to Cannoshockton to drive him to the Pittsburgh airport. Why hadn't she called? She had promised that she would. John Salmos got his chessboard out of its box and set up the pieces. Michael took too much time between moves. "Go!" Salmos shouted. Michael did. "Are you sure you want to do that?" Salmos asked, then: "Do you want that move back?" Michael saw and said yes. "Tough." Salmos took Michael's queen with one of his rooks. "In life you don't get the chance to do things over." At some time (Michael didn't know precisely when), Andy Raoul arrived home and started drinking with them. Salmos went back to his bedroom and brought out the H.K.—his semi-automatic rifle. They decided to go out for a drive. They took the H.K. with them. Andy took the wheel, and they drove deep into the heart of the county, past the power plant, through a cemetery onto the RDs, the rural routes, swerving by barns, woods, an occasional filling station. They stopped at some field and tumbled out of the car, watched their shadows waver across the phosphorescing snow and looked up at the pear-shaped bowl of the sky. They stood reduced and diminished to hypersensitized mouths and genitals. Salmos brought the scotch. They drank. They stumbled, fell, and got up and shot off several rounds. Andy wanted to go deeper into the wood to spot deer, to shoot a deer with the H.K. if they saw one, take it home, clean it, and have a freezer full of meat. Before he finished talking, Andy started to keck in the snow. Watching him, Michael thought he had friends that Elissa wouldn't let sit at her Round Table of Equity—they howled at the stars. Two days later, Michael again stood in Salmos' trailer. His mother telephoned and told him that Elissa had just pulled in the driveway. She had called the day before. Michael knew that she would arrive sometime that day but had no idea when. He bolted out of the trailer, forgetting to shut the door, buttoning his coat and putting on his gloves outside. He heard John Salmos say to Andy Raoul, "the wife," as he crossed the road in front of the trailer and headed for Hedgewood Village through the gusting snow.

He told Elissa about *The Sewanee Review* and about the van Pooles and the Hexfours. She said that, as her father's family only arrived in America in 1897, they couldn't possibly claim kinship. Later that night he read Tennyson and Dylan Thomas poems to her beside the fireplace. She got along excellently with both his mother and sister. His mother served cake and cookies on her best china. The next morning, they drove into Cannoshockton and stood in front of the Courthouse (now the offices of the Commonwealth Bank of Hanover), walked on campus to Laxallt Hall and the Memorial Fieldhouse and then back into town to where Marty's Army & Navy used to stand. They went to a movie at Cinema Four. Developers had built the Regency Mall only after she had graduated. They hiked through Brown's Woods. Michael asked a barrage of questions. Why hadn't she called? He had become nervous and worried. As they walked through town, he asked her about the various locations where she had lived while a student at Cannoshockton. He already knew about West Pike and Big Red, so she escorted him to a white house with a large portico on School Street. She had rented a beautiful apartment on the second floor. "Two doors down," Michael said, "stands the Methodist parsonage." Her landlady—an elderly woman—made her and the other three tenants sign in and out on the chalkboard by the stove. Once she got locked out and stayed overnight at a fraternity. She had switched majors and felt very low as Wayne had announced his plans to marry the fat girl from Schenectady. She would in short order move to Big Red but she didn't yet know Bones, the drug-dealing biker, who at home strutted about in only black underwear. She pointed to houses where certain (to Michael almost mythical) people had lived. Michael began pointing to places central to him. He put his arm around her waist and they kissed. She wore a red scarf and purple mittens.

Two days after Elissa arrived, Michael packed, got his tickets and passport together. The next morning they loaded his things into her Beetle. She had purchased the vehicle from a Mennonite who would only drive in a car painted black. She had to install the radio. The back seat lay crammed with her stuff: Sheddy, peacock feathers, rice paper, paints and her camera. She waited as he stepped inside to kiss his mother and sister goodbye. The dog waddled up to him and licked his hand. Elissa honked the horn as they pulled out of the driveway. They drove around the Outer Circle (Michael looking one last time at the split-level and ranch-style houses, the snow-covered lawns and the crisscrossing branches of the trees) and out of Hedgewood Village. Michael had borrowed the key to Freddie Fregno's apartment in Shadyside. Fred had come home for the holidays. He and Elissa would have the place all to themselves. Michael mustn't forget to change the sheets and to mail the key back to Fred before boarding the 747 the next morning.

Elissa stood nude in front of the bathroom mirror, piled her hair on top of her head, then let it fall over her shoulders. In the living room, Michael put on an album that he purchased earlier in the day—orchestral highlights from *Das Rheingold*. Several months ago he had followed Delone Frailey's advice and as he began work on his honors thesis had started listening to the favorite composer of both Thomas Mann and Adolf Hitler. The record dropped and the tone arm lowered. The stereo blared, and Elissa called out for him to turn down the volume. She couldn't believe that he had grown captivated with the same operatic music that Dorn had always loved and, playing it so frequently, nearly driven her crazy with. He walked out of the bedroom, kicked off his shoes and socks, stepped into the adjoining bath. He kissed the nape of Elissa's neck. She turned her head, offered him her mouth. From behind her, he touched her breasts, her small aureoles, her pricked nipples. His hand worked downward as his penis began to stiffen. He cupped her pelvic hollow. She took his tongue into her mouth as he rubbed her vulva. Still standing behind her, he brushed the front of his trousers against her backside. She turned around and flung her arms around his head. They stumbled into the room and fell on the bed. Michael looked at the blue throw rug on his side. He took off his shirt, his trousers, kicked them to the floor. She pressed him to her breasts. She had a tuft of brown hair that rose to her navel. A zebra stripe? Horse's mane? Rat's tail? He nuzzled her stomach with his face, rubbed his cheek against her hair. She straddled his stomach then slid to his face, lowered her damp flesh onto it, and began swaying her hips back and forth. Afterward, tonguing his lips, she arched her body backward, willing, waiting for him to impale her. He shifted positions, rolling on top. She parted her legs. He entered her, butted her loins, pinning her wrists to the bed with his hands. He bucked, rolled, tightened. She kissed his face, held his head in her hands after he let her wrists go. He kept up the pace, and she began to breathe more rapidly. She tightened her legs around his back. He felt her tensing. *The distance*, he thought. *Worlds apart.*

In the other room, ignoring the wails of the Rheinmaidens, one by one, the gods slowly crossed the rainbow bridge to Wahlhall, diving back into the font of music droning out of the speakers into the room. Michael turned on his side during the crescendo. Let them go, he thought. If we offend their "sensibilities," let them sniff their spiritual noses. I prefer these valleys. Closing his eyes, he touched her breasts with his cheek. The tone arm clicked, rested once again on the pick-up clip. Elissa was still panting. Michael opened his eyes, got up, and went into the bathroom.

The next morning they dressed each other. She changed the sheets, and he went out to look for a mailbox in which to drop Fred's key. They hurried through breakfast and out of the apartment, arriving at the airport just as his flight began to board. He gave her the album. "To England," he said. "To cricket, sculling, the Rock of Gibraltar, Edmund Spenser and Dunhill cigarettes." He ran his hand through her long auburn ringlets like sprung copper coils. He looked into her face.

When Michael received Elissa's diaries late in 1983, much of what she wrote about him surprised him. Such as:

He lies with soft lips and thoughts that penetrate.

Time passes or perhaps does not. Instead it rolls into itself and becomes space. He received her letters. He sent her post cards and wrote her letters, mostly about where he goes and what he sees and does. He took bus trips to Salisbury, Coventry, London, Stonehenge, Liverpool, and Wales. He read books, planned a new short story, and handed in his weekly essays. It stood only appropriate—he wrote her—that he led a monastic lifestyle during his final semester in one of our modern monasteries. Today universities preserved knowledge that would otherwise stand lost, as monasteries had done in the Middle Ages. Although our technologies continue to expand, we have already entered a new Dark Age. Elissa had already finished her course work Winter Term. In May, she had accepted a university-sponsored internship at Herneshopple's agricultural research station in Charles Town, West Virginia. She would return to Herneshopple later that summer. So would Michael. Bradley Scott had arranged for him to work as a bartender at The Saloon. Elissa wrote Michael back and asked him to continue sending postcards. He complied and chose cards of Windsor Castle, Big Ben, various locations in the Lake District, Westminster Abbey, where Handel lay buried, and of the medieval clock at Salisbury Cathedral. He sent her a pamphlet about the Salisbury clock: "The oldest clock in England and almost certainly the earliest remaining mechanical clock in virtually complete and working condition in the world, the Salisbury clock had been constructed entirely of hand-wrought iron and was controlled originally by a verge escapement and foliot balance, but, to increase its accuracy, a pendulum escapement was added at a later date. It has been calculated that this six-hundred-year-old clock has ticked more than five hundred million times, a great tribute to the workmanship of those who built it."

THREE

Chapter Ten

Who Maketh Now to Thee His Compliments?

I

Rain again. A chameleonic day. Sun clouds. Brooding sun. Sun storm. She smelled the still warm, folded blouse before putting it away in her dresser. Hot steamed cotton, she thought. The delightful scent it gave when you lifted it to your nose. She had taken her bath. Earlier she transplanted marigolds and zinnias to the garden. Perhaps her uncle would plant tobacco today if the fields remained dry enough, she thought, as she sat down and took up the lavender pillowcase she had just begun to embroider.

Her family had a cow missing. She had crawled under the fence by the creek and had remained on the loose for five days. They knew of numerous sightings of her by other farmers, but no one could catch her. The worst of the matter was that she had started calving. Two days ago, someone observed her in partial delivery, the legs of her calf sticking out. The next day someone else sighted her in the same condition. She had to be in terrible pain. Elissa's sister went out on her bike and with the dog, their mother informed her (she had telephoned that morning), to look for her. She roamed somewhere near Spragg's woods.

Elissa had stopped reading Proust. She sat down to today's *Washington Post*. Today marked her return to her Herneshopple apartment. She had been away for an extended period of time, an interval during which she had felt both sweet and wretched.

Too little, she thought. *Too much*. For her internship in West Virginia she had worked in the field and in the laboratory testing soil. Her hours stood rich with mallards and their ducklings; with the fragrance of spearmint tea, the spearmint gathered from a farmer's meadow where she worked, dug her samples; with fallow fields of nodding daisies, buttercups, and fleabane. And with Tim Cassill. They had said their goodbyes, parted in Herneshopple. Perhaps it would have remained a week-long thing had the Herneshopple School District not gone on strike and he hadn't showed up one morning on her front step in Charles Town. She didn't want him to stay at first. But she caved in to his entreaties. She had done this to herself. Now she'd have to tell Michael about Tim. And Tim about Michael? He had rushed off to Trenton, where his father had underwent emergency surgery for gallstones.

[Photos came of my visit with you and your family. I can't part with them. I day-dreamed over them, forgetting time and place. I'm sending you one of my poems. The title reflects back to you. You see, I'm an alloy now, a blend. I dearly miss the blending of our senses.]

Michael didn't realize that anything had changed. She never wrote him a "Dear Michael" letter.

[The painting on the front doesn't quite resemble the scene out my windows, but what I've got suits me fine. Big trees, a large yard, a tire swing, a barn shed, a cemetery and a part of the town: large old homes. I find it positively Dutchy. It reminds me so much of home. I have endured a very hard week. My parents came down with me to help me move in. We got a guided tour of the Research Facility. I was impressed. My parents stayed to settle things with my new landlord and see a bit of the area. Since the kiss mother gave me goodbye, I've felt unwell and it has lasted all week. A cold, the flu—whatever. I just wanted to close my eyes and sleep. What a first impression I must have made. Everyday work proves challenging, the equipment I use the best $ can buy. Everything's computerized from soil analyzers to "field notebooks" you don't need a pencil for. I have my own office, desk, bookcase, and file cabinets. This weekend I took home a little work. The instruction manual for the Perkin-Elmer Model 4000 Atomic Absorption Spectrophotometer (only 300+ pages) and another book on instrumental methods to help me understand the former.

I finished *Mantissa* Friday. I loved it, my one blessing this week. Fowles, coffee and pills each day and ten hours of sleep each night. I stood in a bad way. It's been a long while since I've been so sick. But now I feel back on the road to health. Friends invited me to a New England Dance last evening. I declined, planning to go out to hear blue-grass music tonight. However, our rains waited until concert time approached. I had about forty miles to drive, so I said forget it. I just got your card as I left my apartment to explore more of the town, so I went with fresh eyes. When I first came here, the town frightened me. Why? At first I thought it due to the stares men gave me and, when I'm alone, penetrating stares do make me start and shy. That's why I didn't wish to move to this town. However, I've asked about twelve young women and they all say it's safe and pleasant. So perhaps my fears will prove ungrounded.]

But the Particular had dissolved into the Usual. Though the Particular—at least for M. Boulanger—still seemed—how *would* Proust put it—"ineffably pungent?"

[Today I went downtown to explore and run errands. I saw dogs prancing, crossing the street, big dogs used to their freedom. As I progressed, I saw almost as many dogs as people. I think everyone just lets their dogs roam. I only saw one cat, a gray one who watched me but hid behind a car tire, stared at me but wouldn't come out despite my wooing.]

Her hex.

[So I left her and found a friendly Irish Setter on the next block. The town. Few on the street. Not predominated by any one age group. Poor people, many poor. Few stores, mostly Five & Dime Dollar stores. Yet despite the small size of the town, we have two Western Shops (bridle & tack & Western ware) and two old hardware stores with wooden floors and barrels of grass seed. And lots of beauty and barber shops with lots of people inside them. The town has a single arcade with about seven electronic games in it. A large room. I walked past to see a few black kids around the machines. No one else. We have a little town library. So any books you think I should read, just let me know. They seem well supplied w/ current lit. too. I had two keys made in one of the hardware stores. But only one works.]

[I spent this evening hiking around the Shenandoah River at Harper's Ferry. The river ran green. Yellowed where it shallowed from protruding rocks. Along its bank, the remnants of a mill. 3' solid stone walls. Beautifully arched conduits. It could have lasted for centuries had the Civil War not raged here. What destructive force to blast this wonderful building apart. And why? Oh enemy of stone, it seemed to breathe. As I looked across the Potomac River, I saw smoke rings rising, sometimes campfires on the mountainside. The last stand of John Brown occurred near here, his frantic effort to use violence (just a little then) to free slaves. But the army caught, convicted, and hanged him in my town. And as I wandered—more smoke over the Blue Ridge Mountains—I looked for its source and saw a forest fire. Then I remembered the man I saw leaving his campfire in that area. I had thought he would come back, but didn't stay to see.]

Even in the future, Michael would read her letters with interest, whatever she did—wherever she currently lived.

[I executed a prize *faux pas* this evening. My cheeks burn and I laugh repeatedly in recalling it. Last Friday, while shopping at Bon Ton, I ran into a familiar customer from the Hu-Nam in the dressing room. We exchanged a few words and passed on our way. Well, tonight a familiar couple sat down along my route in the restaurant. I stopped to say hello. I said to the woman, "Well, it's nice to see you with your clothes on again." And she and her husband looked at each other to determine to whom exactly I spoke. It became apparent to me that I had confused my couples. My oh me, gee, my face flushed I grew so embarrassed. The boys in the kitchen laughed and laughed when I told them. Wait till I tell the real lady. She'll love it. She and her husband love jokes anyway. I have them clearly in mind now and won't confuse them with anyone else again.]

[I had my first taste of dealing with a sick baby this past week. I stood ready to hand in my mother's badge and go look for an easier job . . . like high-rise steel construction or Intensive Care Nursing. Eii jii jii, he says. I yi yi? Eye yih yih? I, I, I? Being a stable, well-adjusted woman, I'm brought to wonder how most children survive childhood. What a trial. He's back to his healthy, happy self. And my tolerance for his brief periods of crankiness has increased immeasurably.]

Michael phoned. She had written that she would be back in Herneshopple today. He wanted to stop over—have lunch. Tomorrow, she said. She was busy. She had to unpack, clean the apartment. Could he stop tonight then? No, she said. He had better not. Why? She'd talk to him tomorrow, she said. She was tired, far too tired to talk. *She'd tell him tomorrow.* All day, into the night, Elissa's unresponsiveness gnawed at him. She wrote that she didn't have a telephone in Charles Town, but he called directory assistance and found out that she had. After last call at The Saloon, walking home, he decided on an early-morning visit. Her lights were out. Michael looked up at the stars, stepped off the sidewalk and under the portico. Unlocking the outer door and stepping into the foyer, he put his key into Elissa's door, opened it, stepped across the threshold, shut the door, and tiptoed up the wooden staircase. He walked into her bedroom, did not switch on the overhead, walked forward in the dark. He looked at the dark blotches on the wall: her paintings and prints. Although he could not see them with the light off, he knew each one, from the large New York Graphic Society reproduction of Edouard Manet's *Gare Saint Lazare* to the tiny Holbein *Leichnam Christi*. Her own canvasses affected Gauguin-like colors with interpenetrations of light and dark, calculated geometric designs, and purposely flattened two-dimensional forms. He turned on the tiny lamp on her dresser and dropped to his knees beside the king-size mattress. She had rolled to her side. Her head pressed to the pillow, she curled like a child in her blankets.

See, she's alone.

He touched her shoulder; she arched her back, murmured something that sounded like "Charles Town's Bovine Ovaries." Michael's forehead wrinkled. Such nonsense. It gushes out of her like a toy doll's squeak at the application of your thumb to its belly. He patted her shoulder again. Dresden china plates. Charles Town's Bovine Ovaries. Charles Bovary? His name was Bolanger. She started, saw but perhaps didn't recognize him, and pulled her sheet to her chin like some affronted medieval landgravess. Sleeping Beauty after the kiss? "Hello," he said.

"Michael!"

She got out of bed, walked barefoot to the kitchen, turned on the light. Puppets and art prints stood pinned to her wall. She had taped post cards, including some he had sent her, to her kitchen cupboards. He looked at the cabbageleaf-green sugar bowl on the wooden table then at the high ceiling—his dorm room, the English Seminar room could *both* fit in her kitchen—and out the window at the white apple blossoms. The impervious beam from the spotlight outside spread through the branches. She opened a cupboard, shut it without taking anything out. Michael pulled a chair from the table. Before he could sit down, she turned to face him—he stood in a nebular corner.

"I've begun seeing someone," she said softly, ". . . That will affect things between us."

Her lips twitched. In the reflected and fluttering light, her face—a palette of pale tans shading into browns, its two sides congealing in a Braque-like Double Image. Two profiles, not a frontal view. "I can understand" (she paused) "you might not remain inclined to" (she spoke so softly he couldn't hear her; she sighed) "— after what I've done. And yes I still care for you. Part of me—"

"Elissa!" he interrupted, pleaded, the muscles in his face tightening. He felt as if they spoke across a void because of an inflexible-sharp-free-floating what? Obduracy? that emanated from her. Palpable, inflexible, it pushed outward, put pressure on his chest forcing him back as it stretched and expanded like a balloon on a canister nipple slowly filling with gas. "Part of me," she said, "will never—"

He said, "sure."

He closed his eyes then opened them. The balloon didn't pop. She looked at him. "I *do* care. But I love Tim." Pin prick—he thought—now! *Right* now. But I love Tim—Tim who? Cassill? He saw the apple blossoms through the reflection of his face.

He stares through You outside. You stare back at him. Between your eyes and his I's, form disintegrates, and object and subject disappear. She speaks but you aren't listening. *You look at two barriers more impenetrable than adamant—at his corneas as he looks through You. They appear as transparent as glass. His image floods through the keyhole is dissected chopped up but the building blocks put themselves together again to form the picture he sees but You can't pierce through the curtain plunge through the viaduct through his pupils. You look up as he flings the stone at the shopping cart but just as the other rocks had previously done it skims across the ice—across Your cornea. It begins to rain much harder but it isn't a spring or summer rain a rain that would bring life out of the soil it is an icy rain a freezing rain ice from the sky falls on the cataracted oval eye that stares up at him. You see its reflection reflected in his and as You watch he begins to turn his head away. The other shade walks toward him crosses into Your peripheral vision but as though weighed down as if a crevice a chink opened up between two seconds and Time's what? molecular motion? slowed down its molecules solidifying in your Ice. The reflections waver fade as he turns his eyes from Yours hurtling you towards Absolute Zero. Falling you glance darkly at your shadowselves reflections. At MB The Final Abstractionist. As they darken all goes black.*

She spoke but he didn't listen. He looked through his reflection out the window. She once said she didn't "feel burdened by the injunctions of any Jewish god." He thought of the ferrotypes. One by one they flicked behind his eyes. The faces stood blurred, irretrievable, but he recalled that the women clutched Bibles. A source of strength? Charles' Ovaries, he thought. Someone had usufructed his. He had become Rodolphe Boulanger. Cassill-Leon had taken his—

He fell further and further into himself, disappeared entirely behind that curtain of flesh and mucous membrane and gray matter.

Couldn't he stop, jam the signals, halt the flow of words, excretions from a brain perpetually filibustering.

He wanted to hit himself and hit himself and hit himself. He seemed seely as a surd. The square root of three. A voiceless speech sound. Absurd as a surd. M.B., he thought. Me.

But the words just came—a defense mechanism?—interposed themselves—another gulf—between him and the real, her, piercing him with pain. *Ecce homo*, he thought, looking at his reflection in the window. Behold the man. He turned his glance as she walked toward him. She touched his hand.

"I hope we will remain friends," she said. He looked at the bright potholders and stack of black-and-white photographs on the tabletop. He had two impulses. He could turn without saying a word, walk out of her apartment, continue under the street lamps and stars to Debs-Watson Park and the swings (he glimpsed the pulsing red light through the window) or upset the table, smash the sugar bowl, pick it up and throw it at the refrigerator or at her. He looked at her eyes. As always they gleamed clear, blue, and direct. She opened her mouth. "You bitch," he said. "You contemptible bitch." He walked out of the kitchen into the hall, looking at the posters and prints on the wooden walls, feeling that the walls of her apartment had suddenly become the sides of the box of Death, that he lay in the crate with the other Bones. She followed him. "Michael, I hoped—"

Not bothering to look over his shoulder, he started down the stairs. How dare she? he thought. He stumbled on a step. *As you rebalance yourself Tim Cassill walks through the door and up the steps a pained and haughty expression on his face. What's going on? he asks. What's wrong? I heard shouting. You try to force your way through but he won't let you pass you knee him in the groin then with a flurry of lefts and rights you pommel his face until he falls you pull the handgun from the holster Elissa hears the shots screaming she runs down the steps you aim the gun at her face fire.* He opened the outer door and stumbled off the portico onto the sidewalk. He looked up at the duplex, at the yellow hostile squares of light. Her windows. They went black. *Fuck her fuck her fuck her.* He turned, crossed the street, didn't look back. Cursing, he slowed to a walk under the trees lining Sigerson Street, kicking the stones on the sidewalk and the weeds growing up through the cracks. *Alyssum and Boulangerite*, he thinks, scattering them. *Stop.* He hit his head twice with his fist. *Enough.* He'd rip through the curtain, tear it down. He unlocked the door, flicked on the light switch, walked to his bedroom, took a throwing star from out of one of his drawers, and flung it at the wall. He walked to the wall and pulled the star out. He turned, threw it at the facing wall, then slumped to the floor, held his head in his hands, and cried.

II

Your eye opens every time he looks at You. You appear on every sort of surface. He sees You in his pupils' reflection when he presses his nose and lips to the glass. You watch him. He watches You. Between Your eyes and his, form disintegrates and subject and object disappear. He remains the curtain of flesh bone heart lung mucous gray matter *et al* that covers You. He watches himself watching himself watch himself. You can see through him or his image can transfix You. Depending which of the two the I zeroed in on, the other blurred. He had the power to mesmerize You. Why not her? You know what he thinks, what he feels—You believe that he is You. What follows hard on jealousy and bull-anger? You know. Answer quickly. Not self-evaluation. Instead he will take stock. Indeed he already takes stock of the dream-weapons in his dream-arsenal and how best to use them. You know what means he'll adopt. He will delude himself that he spins a web and creates a mythos, that he shapes and sculpts sun-drenched form. How? *By continuing to be Michael Bolanger*, by not creating, shaping or sculpting anything at all. But the glory, renown, praise for being himself—was *that* what stood essential to him? Wasn't what he did under its auspices more important than it itself? Weren't You/he striving to heighten perception or did You prevaricate yet again and tell another lie, eye? You want to smolder constantly somewhere in her mind or if that remains too much to hope for, if she refuses to stand dazzled by Your coat of many colors and resists and fights against its mesmerizing powers, he'll make something so gripping and compelling so as to force her to look and think upon it. And once she beheld that reflector of *his* shifting Kaleidoscope. Of *Your* Kaleidocoat. It would fasten her attention, snare, catch and entangle her. Yes. Something—what?—fleeting yet all-encompassing—that would make her palms damp with sweat—that would haunt her and the hers to follow—the twenty-nine, thirty-four, and forty-five year-old Elissas. *Yes*—she would incorporate Your reflection into hers and she would find it difficult if not impossible to exorcise it. She would sink back into the drove, the herd-pack but not he. Your gift would serve as a memory of the height she attained but fell from. Yes, You would proudly wear the Kaleidocoat, the I-Ilusion. It stood tailor made. You only had to lift Your arms. It would descend over Your shoulders, molding itself to the contours of Your desire. Becoming them. Outside and inside of her, the posited-You would rise upward like a helium balloon while she plummeted and watched him rise. And she could never, whatever she did, live up to the him, the You, in her—the complement You made her, the deficiency You supplied. And no one could cut away Your coat—cut away him—strip by strip to reveal a nakedness that he could not understand or fathom or find a word for: You.

He sat on the dull gray carpet in his "parlor," chain smoking. You do not choose to look through him and remain entranced by the contours of your desire. *Do You have left-right symmetry? Do You remain unaltered by mirror reflection?* You watch, Your reflection's task to blend his reflection into hers, imbed it in hers like the throwing star wedged in his wall. To charm her with Your coat, to prancke Your rainbow-colored and Argus-eyed plumes since he stood her beau no longer. Yes, in response to her choosing a new lover, an albino peacock with pallid ashen skin and glazed pink pupils—even the spots, eyes, on his loosely webbed tail coverts looked yellowish and off-white—Your reflection would shine so resplendently, so refract all the colors of the spectrum, that its/his brilliance would blind her and she would again desire You. But she'd resemble a girl looking at a rainbow dress through a shop window. Each time she reached for the dress, she would find that she could not plunge her hand through the barrier transparent as glass but only see her reflection on the surface of the keyhole as her image floods through it. He would take her then fling her aside, give her the boot like some mangy cur. Fool me once shame on you. Fool me twice shame on me. But perhaps she thought one man stood as good as another. Because everyone died. Because a periodic dislodging of comets from the Oort cloud by the yet undiscovered planet X or a red star circling the sun in an elliptical orbit—comets which would bombard and crater the planets—could extinguish all life on earth and leave mankind as extinct as the dinosaurs, rendering all his myriad accomplishments null and void. Because human endeavor would not stand the test of time, that even the plays of Shakespeare and the pyramids of Egypt could not claim immortality and thus all endeavor and accomplishment stood reduced to absurdity? From a planet orbiting Mizar or Alcor could ? test its vision, he wondered, by looking at a yellow star eye and making out a second star while staring at it, a pulsing red diacritical mark, the dot on the i, displaying iridescent golden and green colors? More than half the stars in the sky stood binaries. He saw pairs of stars—optical doubles—staring at each other. Since some-day our sun, the entire universe, would explode … she thought sets of walking molecules stood interchangeable? Equal? So because we all remained walking humus, she could blithely ditch a mann for only a man? He wondered. Would she—a poet-painter-agrono-mist-mathematician—make light of his ambitions by saying—if he asked her—that, looked at objectively, from a cosmic point of view, little or no difference separated Batman and Robin from Pierre Bezukhov and Rodolphe Boulanger? That *War and Peace* and *Madame Bovary* stood merely comic books on a grand scale? That (as everything remained relative) compared to the art works higher beings produced on some heavenly planet circling some other sun, they would appear as comic books appeared to them here? She might even say that everyone thought they wore Kaleidocoats, that a pig wallowing in the mud wouldn't change his mud for the comforts of Nymphenburg Palace. But You know that there exist machines and, yes, mozartmachines. Entelechies and Superior Entelechies. How very, very long You desired the coat. You don't wish to remove it. But does he, could he, wish to? The two models stood subject to the same nuisances—eating, sleeping, voiding, desirenvying—and to the very same ending, endlessly repeated: to switch off and come stuttering to a stop. But the latter model surely remained more desirable than the former. There had to stand a hierarchy of coats. Some remained more fashionable than others. Perhaps they misunderstood this hierarchy and ranked lower coats higher that they actually merited. Margaret Bromion believed her life had cosmic significance. She had three stars named after her. God. Perhaps everyone dreams the same dream. Perhaps everyone wears the same green corduroy jacket. But despite that, You made Your choice. You chose the coat or the coat chose You. He You. You he. It made no difference. If the coat could not demonstrate its merit—its quotidian otherness?—in any tangible or concrete way, for focusing purposes, she could view the image it formed in a mirror of the coat's making—in notational and relational characters on a white page.

Instead of him?

Tim Cassill?

Did he and Elissa re-repeat something that had already taken place? Would further repetitions occur—an encounter later in life in Weimar where she would stand Lotte Kestner to his Goethe? Or perhaps she would need to borrow cash from him? He would say currently all his capital stood tied up in investments, that he couldn't touch it, and—knowing the final occurrence, the issue, the outcome in advance—he would not frankly give a damn if she swallowed arsenic like Emma Bovary. No. But now the coat—the notational character—he/You must bend back her hex upon itself but also set the posited You securely and deeply inside her.

Your eye opens every time he looks at You. The only way he can view himself from where-he-resides, from within, is to stare at You. He recognizes himself in his own image, his characteristics revealed as mere form, as a glassy play of lines. You stare back at him, though often he does not detect or forgets that he has detected Your presence. But there You are looking up at him from a pool of oil on the road in which the colors of the rainbow greasily refract; in the tinted windows, in the headlights and bumpers of cars as they rush by, never seeing what they pass; in pewter-furnished fixtures; in the juice glass he drinks out of; in the chrome of the toaster; in coffee urns; in beveled, polished wood—everywhere. You even look down at him from the black sky covered with ocellate spots, eyes, displaying iridescent gold and green colors. He looks at them. Do they look at him? And even when he becomes too absorbed to notice You watching him watch himself or when he looks through You, does not see his image doubled, Your eye remains open. You look at him when he looks through You at her standing on his porch and says, "What could you possibly want?"

"To still remain friends."

It hurt, but he made the necessary effort. "If you want," he said.

"I'm torn, split, Michael. Only time will tell how things will work out."

And You watch him when, a few days later, she stops again and lets slip that tomorrow she plans to leave for Trenton to be with Tim and how he swears, screams and after she leaves how he goes back to his bedroom and (the pun comes right then) masterstrokes. You watch him buy cases at Herneshopple Beverage and show up drunk for work, and after not seeing or speaking to her for a month, You watch as he telephones her one June night and, receiving no answer, continues telephoning every thirty minutes, stays up all night doing this, and the next day, when Tim Cassill picks up the receiver, You see him slam his on the hook. You watch as he pounds on her door three days after that. He knew that she was home. He saw her walking from window to window before he stepped onto the front porch and into the foyer. He banged on her door with both fists, but she would not come down the steps. He took out his key, tried to insert and turn it, and discovered she had changed her locks. Nightly he would walk past her apartment building. Some nights more than once. No matter how far away from the building his day would take him, as if he stood a comet caught in its gravitational pull, he would inevitably—at dusk before he was "on" at The Saloon or, if not then, certainly on his way home after last call—be drawn back to it at night.

Why Tim Cassill? he would ask himself as he went by. Why such a mediocrity? Did she have to stand the more dominant, the better endowed of the two "partners" (he now used the commonplace terms) in a "relationship?"

He looked up at the duplex. "Slut," he heard himself say. But oh, those coincidences. He continued on past the next building. A coincidence, perhaps retrospectively not that unlikely a one, had first attracted him to her—that she had lived in Cannoshockton in 1973. But what about the others? What about the name on his family tree? Elizabeth Pool? They seemed—all those symmetries he saw, erected—to indicate that it stood demonically preordained that they be bound together. He could not leave go, even though he considered her a full-fledged cow. A *vache*.

You watch as one evening he walks past her apartment on the side of the street opposite to it. He hears someone yell his name. He turns. Tim Cassill runs across the street toward him as a gray cat scuttles up a tree in the next yard.

"Let's talk," Cassill said.

Michael ignores him and continues walking. Cassill catches up, walks beside him.

"Elissa tells me that you've got some sort of" (he paused, then spit out) "obsessive infatuation for her which *isn't* reciprocated. A kind of puppy love, I guess. Although she considers you a good friend."

Michael froze. He turned again to look at Cassill.

"Is that what she told you?"

"No secrets stand between us."

"She's kept things back. We were once close."

"Close! I can go up there and *be* with her right now. That's what I call close. And yes, I believe what Elissa tells me. The three of us need to sit down together and thrash this out."

"Talk to her yourself," Michael said. He started to walk away. *Never before had he felt so humiliated.*

"You stop bothering her," Cassill shouted. "You hear me. You stop bothering her."

He held his hands behind his back, his head bent downwards, his eyes fastened to his shoes.

He sat on the swing.

He watched three boys play "Around the World" on the blacktop.

He killed a mosquito, flicked it off his palm, then wiped his hand on his pant leg.

He swung.

A particolored Kaleidocoat?

Ha.

III

Too little becomes too much. The paucity of what each offered gradually became, as she grew accustomed to the many shadings of his personality—how he left her missing this or desiring that—the paucity of what he offered (no matter how complex or multi-dimensional he stood) became—well—overfulfilling, smothering. She got tired of it as she would a kind of food eaten repeatedly. She sat drinking her coffee at her kitchen table and watched a blue jay flit from branch to branch of the apple tree. If only she could divide in two, like a cell split longitudinally into hers. And those hers would keep on dividing *ad infinitum*. But somehow her hers would still all stand connected. By nerve cells? Telephone cables? So each would simultaneously experience what the others experienced, so she could simultaneously lay in the arms of Tim, Michael, M.K., Dorn, and even Wayne, so she—a poet—historian-mathematician-philosopher could pursue every one of her disciplines. It took a lifetime to fully master one, no matter how narrow the specialty. The smallest doors opened on wider doors which, in turn, led to doors that no one could force. *O amazement of things—even the least particle.* Leptons and Tauons. Neutrinos and color-charged Quarks—red green blue. So again she thought too little always too much.

Chapter Eleven
Chewing the Chewed

In March '82 things started shaping up for Brent Cobin. He hated working as a cashier at Shop and Save. He read the want ads. Nothing interested him. He couldn't imagine himself at any of those "McJobs" for more than two days. He wanted to move up a corporate ladder, make a stack of greenbacks. He had given up on journalism. Almost. He wouldn't toil on any backwoods paper recounting what went on at boring Borough Council meetings and (yawn, ho-hum) sleep-inducing Kiwanis picnics. He had seen too many James Bond movies to stand satisfied with that. He wanted excitement—glitter, razzmatazz. He dreamed about achieving rock star status and owning Porches and Ferraris. In Journalism that meant you had to reach the cutting edge—the front line. He fantasized about going to work as a war or foreign correspondent and in his wildest dreams he envisioned himself a presidential press secretary, a talk show host like Geraldo, or even a network anchor like Dan "the man" Rather. Despite his conservative bent and bias, in his heart of hearts, he would have preferred to write for *Rolling Stone* than for *The National Review*. He saw himself going gonzo and emulating Hunter S. Thompson or the lunatic Lee K. Abbott. No, you didn't start at the top, but you took every damn short cut you could—like his friend Billy Harkleroad. They graduated from H.U. in '80 and right out of school Billy lands a job working for the State Department because his dad, some sort of judge, knew Al Haig's press secretary. So poof, just like that, Billy disappears behind the Teflon curtain.

Brent Cobin didn't have such illustrious connections. He kept trying to form them. Job-hunting in D.C., he knocked on George Will's front door to see if he would read his stuff. He didn't even have to ask Billy to go through channels for the address. He found George's number listed in the D.C. directory. But Mr. Will was not at home. He sought out Will because if his copy seemed a bit (Michael's word) blowzed, it stood ideologically true to color—red, white, and blue. Sure, his heroes did not all come from the right. He admired Abbie Hoffman, Jerry Rubin, Country Joe and above all Hunter S., but their day had come and gone, and *you had to go with the flow*. Adaptability stood the key to success. *Call it time-serving*. He had to make it in the eighties—in the age of Reagan. He sent videotapes of mock broadcasts to network affiliates on both coasts but not the Midwest. He tried writing television scripts, even found an agent for his *Magnum* episodes, though she didn't sell them. But in March, persistence paid off, kind of. An ABC affiliate in York gave him an interview. They needed a new sportscaster for the fall and wanted someone young. He'd start at the bottom, at a Podunk local affiliate in Palookaville, but at least he would have his foot in the door—that is if he got the job. A big if. The day after he went for an interview, he crashed a party at Golconda. He heard music as he walked by outside, saw people dancing through the windows and walked in. Brent met Margaret. He stood by the keg helping himself to a mussel, a cheese ball, and a marinated mushroom, at the same time asking a dumpy redhead if she wanted to dance, when someone touched his shoulder. He spun round to face the person, and, his fingers still to his mouth, swallowed the mushroom whole. "Hi Brent. How are—" (Elissa turned her head. His cologne floored her) "—you?" She withdrew two steps and recovering said, "I didn't know you knew the Bromions?" "I don't." *The name did sound familiar.* Bobbing back and forth, he threatened to come closer. "The friend I came with does." Elissa glanced over her shoulder and around a few people and saw Margaret, still smiling and still nursing her scotch and soda. "Marge," she called. The girl looked up. "I'd like you to meet someone." She sidled toward them, repeatedly bumping into people and saying excuse me. He turned around. The redhead's freckles had disappeared. So had she.

Elissa looked at the back of Brent's head. She'd use Margaret as a shield and then make her getaway. "Brent," Elissa said when Margaret finally got there, "I'd like to introduce you to your host—" Again he spun like a weather vane. "—ess." "Margaret, meet Brent." "Hi," he said, looking her over. She wore nice clothes (a striped jersey and denim culottes). Her hair looked pretty. Black curls tossed backward. Not bad, he thought. Better than the redhead. Elissa reached for the marinated mushrooms then said she had to make her way back to someone in the other room. Sure you do, Brent thought. And if you lift your nose any higher a fly will buzz up it. He wouldn't want to scoop her even if she weren't his best friend's girl. Margaret's breath smelled sour. She looked tight. He also had caught a buzz. Why the hell not? he thought.

He did not find it difficult getting her upstairs. After a few minutes of small talk, he had grown bored. He made a show of listening, thinking *Come on, girl, make your move,* when Margaret told him that she had just purchased a book on the *Cinématique Française.* He asked if he could see it. She said she'd have to go to her room to get it. He watched her mount the stairs, then knowing that he should seize the opportunity (*now or never,* he thought, shrugging his shoulders) snuck up behind her and followed her into her room Looking for the book under her bed, she knelt on her hands and knees.

"So what should we do now?" he asked "Do you have any suggestions, babe?"

Margaret Bromion withdrew her head from under the bed and stood up. Her cheeks flushed. Before she could say anything, he stood beside her. She could feel his nearness, hear his breathing. She inhaled—drowned in—Patchouli. Was this inevitable? Could she bring it off? she asked herself. She saw her chance, but could she take the leap? Abandon her resolve? She looked at his brown eyes, at his pencil-line eyebrows, his white teeth, his broad temples, at the gold chains around his neck. Her nipples hardened in her jersey. "I can't," she murmured to her shoulder. Token resistance, he thought. With his left hand, he lifted her skirt. He didn't know the difference between a skirt and culottes. That the latter—a petty distinction—while giving the appearance of a skirt, divided and stood seamed like trousers. She started breathing heavily. "Please don't," she said between gasps. "Stop." Her inhaling and exhaling, the way she shivered when he touched her, her pricked nipples contradicted what she said, but, knowing that the authorities could if he proceeded make an issue of his behavior and say that it did not observe or conform to the law, he took a step back and stared at her. *Your move.* She looked down at her toes. *Time's up.* He turned around. Maybe freckles still loitered in a corner somewhere downstairs. "No," she said. *Be brave.* Her thighs dripped. It hurt, but she made the necessary effort: "Stay." She quivered, as he shut her door with the sole of his sneaker and sat down on the edge of her bed. "Please be gentle," she begged, when he touched her shoulder with his palm and rubbed his leg against hers.

He didn't see her again for two weeks and didn't plan on ever seeing her again. But then, in a Marronsburg bar, his ears pricked as he overheard a hardhat telling a goober— appearances didn't deceive; the goober looked like Jim Nabors—that the board of regents in "College"—the locals way of referring to Herneshopple in M-Burg—had elected Dirk Bromion—his boss at Atelier Scientific—as a trustee and that Bromion had amassed more gelt than everyone else in the county put together. As the goober replied, "That so? I wish I had all that money," Brent slapped himself on the forehead. Cobin had driven through Herneshopple's Industrial Park, seen the plants and the smokestacks, but didn't know that much about the companies that had established themselves there, though he remembered the person with him saying Atelier Scientific remained the largest and the most lucrative. He wondered if Margaret stood related to the hardhat's boss (everything in that house, come to think of it, seemed upper-upper class), so he phoned Elissa and asked her about Margaret's father, if the board of regents had recently appointed him a trustee of the University? Elissa replied that she hadn't known about Mr. Bromion's appointment, but yes, he was Margaret's father.

He had the opportunity to take some of that money. Why hadn't he known this sooner! Take it off her. If he hadn't already blown it. Fourteen days had lapsed since he had seen her last. She might slam the door in his face. But he had to try anyway. He couldn't pass up such a life-changing opportunity. He recognized his big chance. He would have to contact her ASAP.

"The early bird catches the worm," he would later boast to all his friends.

He rang the bell four or five times in rapid succession. But no one came to the door. He tried again two hours later. A blonde girl wearing a tapered T-shirt, Property Of The Steelers, answered. "Is Margaret home?" Cobin asked. The girl said she'd check and see. "Guess not," she said when she came back a few seconds later. He asked her to tell her that Brent Cobin stopped and gave her a business card *S. B. Cobin Freelance Journalist* with his telephone number. He waited. For two days no response. He'd try catching her at home again, he decided. Circumstances spared him that embarrassment. The next morning, after he had soloed in K-7 and had started walking home (he lived with his mother in Marronsburg), he saw Margaret bicycling up Byron Street and shouted to her. She braked and he ran until he caught up to her. "Margaret," he panted. "Hi. Glad to see you. You must have a busy schedule. I've tried and tried to get in touch."

"That night," she said, "didn't mean anything, right?" "Maybe not to you," Cobin replied, still panting, "but it did to me." "You're all dirty," she said. "Yeah," he gasped, " I've just come from caving. But Margaret. You're a really special person. Unique—" "K-7?" she asked. Disconcerted, he licked his lips, shaded his eyes with his hand, "Yeah." "I've spelunked there." "Great. You can go with me sometime." "Brent," she said, "do you know what a vulnerable position both you and I—" "You saw that I came prepared. I always carry pro—" He cut himself short. "We'd take the necessary precautions." "I don't mean *that*," she said, then mumbled something about special effects in movies and similar movie magic in real life: "It has hurt and caused me pain before now," she said. He didn't know what she meant. That life resembles a bad movie? he thought. That old cliché. The oldest in the book. She needed someone to treat her real nice, to spoil and baby her. He'd start doing that right now. "Margaret," he said, "Nothing comes free. In life, you gotta take risks." She needed more convincing. "Don't let me down," he said. She agreed to meet him the next day for lunch.

He needed to find out everything he could about Margaret's family. He would follow every lead, check with all his sources, and hit pay dirt.

He stopped in to see his dad down at Union Federal and asked if Dirk Bromion had an account there. His father said the bank did some business with Atelier Scientific. Why did he want to know? Brent replied that he had become friends with one of his daughters. He only has one? Then it was she. Bromion. He had heard that name in connection with something else. Strain as he might, he couldn't think what. "Saul," his dad said, "if that T.V. thing doesn't work out, you can always start working here." "Yeah, yeah," he said.

He called his Great Aunt Rose, a charter member of the Herneshopple Country Club, and asked her what she knew about the Bromions. Did they belong? Yes, his Aunt said, all three Bromion boys joined in '52. During the Thirties, their father, Sam T. Bromion, owner of Bromion Coal and Land, acquired the coal, gas, and mineral rights for most of the county from the bankrupt Carsten Coal Company. They struck gas outside Rallingsburg, oil in Marronsburg. The Country Club had catered all four of Dirk Bromion's weddings. "Hmm," Brent said, after hanging up. His life paralleled hers. His mother, too, had married four times. She had wed his father, a loan officer; then the chairman of the Drama department at H.U.; then a rabbi; and finally the funeral director who supervised the rabbi's funeral, whose slogan "we tailor our services to your personal needs" fit his mother's case in ways it wasn't meant to. One for the money, he thought. Two for the show, three to get ready, and four to go.

Every time he saw her, he decided, he would give her a present. Before meeting for lunch, he bought a rose at Village Florist FTD on his way out of M-burg. Driving toward Herneshopple—things often popped into his head while he drove—he finally remembered—click—where he had heard the name Bromion before and felt stupid as shit. Of course! Doggy dialysis. In February he had seen Morley Safer's follow up about the dog dying, too. Boy he felt dumb. "Owned by breeder *Dirk Bromion* of Herneshopple, Pennsylvania." He shook his head and rolled his eyes then swerved back to his side of the road. He always forgot things. For two days once, he couldn't remember that people called lima beans and corn when served together succotash! They must have lots of money to throw it away like that, he thought, down yonder in the papaw patch—as he looked in his rear-view mirror at the black pickup barreling down the road that he had only just missed sideswiping. They ate lunch at the Highlander. Fish. But all through it she kept saying that she had second thoughts—that she didn't feel safe getting close to anybody, and did he understand? "Well let's stay friends," he said, handing her the rose. He got her to agree to that. Wooing her would prove more difficult than he thought. Twice weekly, thrice weekly, he would show up on her doorstep to ask her out. More often than not, she went. They'd see a movie and have a few drinks afterward—whatever *she* wanted to do. Or he'd ask a favor. "How 'bout helping me pick out some new threads. You know I don't know diddley about clothes." And of course, Margaret always invited him whenever she and her cousins gave parties, and he would always come. On one such occasion late in March, he saw Elissa dancing with Tim Cassill; Margaret told him that Elissa and Tim had known each other for years and, when they later saw them leave together, that he probably would just drive her home. "She's leaving town in a couple of months," Margaret said. "She has accepted an internship in Charles Town, West Virginia." "Oh," Brent said, quickly losing interest.

In April Brent Cobin made a serious mistake. He came on to her again, too fast. He asked her if she wanted to go caving. She said she'd like to. He said he'd take her, and, in the Dome Room, he tried to. "There you go, getting hot and heavy," she said, "like you promised not to." They sat on the ledge outside of the viaduct. They had reached a most critical juncture. "Margaret," he said, "I only did what any other normal hot-blooded male would do if he found himself alone with you in a dark cave." "Really?" For a second, her face brightened. Then she became forbidding, hard. "Remember your promise, Brent," she said, looking him straight in the face. "I'll try," he said. "Believe me, I'll try." So he took things slowly, seeing her as often as he could, always trying to show interest in everything she said and did. At times this proved difficult, especially when she got together with her cousins Judy and Anne, the girl with the Steelers T-shirt, and their friends. He grew bored stiff listening to them squawk like sixteen-year-olds about a third-rate rock star (such a hunk!), what happened last week on General Hospital, or whosis finally getting engaged and what a nice wedding they'd have. Her real name should be Margaret Bromide, he thought. He preferred when they went out alone. As the weeks passed, he took her water-skiing, to a Phillies game at Veterans' Stadium (he stopped in York on the way down—the secretary could only say the station had not as yet selected a candidate for the job) and to a REO Speedwagon concert in Pittsburgh. They played tennis regularly at the Country Club. He didn't mind losing. For her part, Margaret enjoyed being with him. She relished their little adventures. They went hiking and had a cookout at Calumet State Park and then went caving again, and, on their way home, his Chevy Impala broke down and they had to hitchhike; it was after midnight and, closer to Herneshopple than Marronsburg, they tramped down Interstate 61; no one picked them up until they reached the State Penitentiary and Brent stopped in his tracks and put out his thumb; they stood covered with mud, looked like convicts who had just tunneled out! "No one will stop," he said, "I want to watch 'em accelerate and speed by." But someone did, a farm boy driving an old red pickup. "What a goober," Brent said, after he dropped them off.

She liked that he'd make even mundane things suspenseful—exciting. After he had his car fixed, he stopped one day and said I bet you have never driven through the choing-choings. The what? The choing-choings. That's all he'd say, so she got in the car and shut the door; they pulled onto West 324 from Ackerman Avenue and took the turn-off from the interstate to the Herneshopple Stadium and drove between the two granite obelisks. The stadium looked like an aircraft carrier; they drove toward it and when they got to the gate, Cobin said, "Here we go," and turned onto a walkway that curved in a wide half circle under the stands. The exits, she saw, opened out on it. He put his foot down hard on the accelerator. As they sped under the seats, she looked up at the iron and steel latticework. She heard a "choing" every half second as they passed between sets of evenly spaced steel girders. The car sped out from under the stadium, careened over a small hill and rolled into a parking lot. That night Margaret had a dream that began with a moose chasing her through the woods trying to nip her and ended with her and Brent XXXXXXXX-OOOOOing on the fifty yard line as the Highland-ers scored a field goal.

Something unexpected occurred for Cobin. As the weeks went by, he began liking her more and more (though he still considered her Margaret Bromide when he found her in the company of her cousins) because, except for one thing, she would do anything he wanted. She never carped or criticized. No, she didn't even bitch—like so many girls would have done—when his car broke down. It could only stand to his advantage to like her. He knew that he struck a chord with her too. When he put his arm around her when they went to see *Raiders of the Lost Ark*, she let him keep it there. Things had begun to look up.

Chapter Twelve

Bloomsday

Bradley Scott walked up to Michael and said, "Hurry up please, it's time," and Michael yelled, "Last call!" Bloat asked for a Busch, Lush for a screwdriver and gin-and-tonic, Rummy for (what else) a rum-and-coke and barfly for her fifth lime daiquiri. He reached for the various hollow glass vessels with narrow necks or wide mouths, with and without handles. He plugged in the blender for the daiquiri, threw out the twist-off cap, poured, mixed, and served the other drinks, seized either crumpled or brand-new bills, rang up the drinks on the cash register and made change, thinking (from six to one he didn't think at all, only performed mechanically, a dumb waiter, large tracks of his brain having been consumed or in the process of being consumed in a bourbon bath—to cleanse the surface of the castings. Perhaps he thought—as *he* thought—even *his* thinking's mechanical. Yours?): canned, potted, pie-eyed, tight, tipsy, bacchic. beery, stimulated, mellow, fuddled, befuddled, blind drunk, dead drunk, hung over, crapulous, crapulent. Then: *adjective-diseased and mega-coloned*. Pushing the sweat from behind his ears into his hair, he shouted, "That's it," and turned off the switch behind the register. He watched as they stumbled off their stools, put a dime or a quarter on the bar for a tip and began to file out. Brad locked the door and took off his black bow tie and brown vest as Michael dropped the glasses into the sink under the counter and the empty bottles and cans into the trash can. Scott walked behind the bar and turned on the T.V. Michael had just switched off, as Bolanger wiped the counter with a red washcloth, his profile and Michael's back reflected in the mirror behind the bar. Scott took the bottle of Jack Daniel's from the rack and a clean mug from under the counter and drew a draught to make a boilermaker. "How 'bout a mitigative?" he asked Michael, adopting his word. Michael asked for Vodka and Triple Sec. "Banzai," he said as he put the glass to his lips. "Beer and skittles," Scott said, lifting his mug. Up close Michael looked terrible, his face ashen and pasty—even his hair looked pale, its shine, its gloss gone. A heavy drinker according to his complexion—and all because of her? Lubricious Lissa, he had said, just like lubricious Liz—all of them. Having a smooth surface, he continued. Slippery. What could Scott say? He could understand and commiserate with Michael. He remembered what he went through when Liz ditched him, but at least he kept quiet about it. We bit into the apple core, Michael said. Swallowed the damn seeds. I'm not a misogynist, he added, I'm a misologist (what *could* Scott say?) and I suffer from logorrhea.

Either long-winded and diffuse.

Or tight-lipped like tonight.

But why have they puffed up? Scott thought, looking at Michael's lips, which had swollen like tubers.

Music leaked from the bars along with a steady drone of laughter and odd howls. She sauntered down Beaver past the bookstores, the all-night restaurants, the video game arcades, the U-mart, and the pet store. As she went by, The Bitter End disgorged its patrons onto the street. Frightened that gypsy-moth caterpillars would fall into her hair (the devastation this year was horrible), she tried not to walk under the branches of the trees jutting above the sidewalk. Her fear of bats, snakes, rodents, gypsy-moth caterpillars *et al.* increased in direct proportion to the number of drinks in her. Tonight she had four glasses of sherry at Tim's. Scale four fear, she thought as she walked by Roy Roger's. She hadn't seen Michael in weeks, but he returned her Christmas gift, *Thirteen Stories*, by Eudora Welty. She found it wedged in her mail slot. She'd like to explain to him that it wasn't a fault of hers, that her lot stood fixed; she remained subject to a force, a susceptibility that drew her compellingly along Cupid's bow. She couldn't resist. *Ultra vires*. She trembled where she stood. The line of his lips had fascinated her. She tottered forward, swung her head back, looked up at the streetlight. Ultra virus, Michael would say. They were both alike. He pressed her after confronting Michael. They stood face to face, and she said, yes, she and Michael had been physical. Once. He raged, ranted, but apologized the next day.

rant (rant), v.i. [Middle Dutch, *ranten*, *randen*, to dote, to be enraged]

Several cars sped by as she neared The Saloon. A spontaneous inclination propelled her to the window. She saw Michael and Bradley Scott standing at the bar, then turned and walked away.

Staggering home from The Saloon, Michael encountered Delone Frailey for a third and final time. Through the windshield of his Catalina, Frailey saw Michael on the sidewalk (later, doing a writing exercise, Michael would imagine Frailey thinking *Isn't that that cherry boy Elissa snatched out of his mother's cradle* as he caught sight of the twenty-one-year-old Bolanger) and swerved his car over to the side. The automobile rolled to a stop, but Bolanger continued walking. The driver followed at a snail's pace. Michael cursed. He feared some faggot cruised him and regretted, and not for the first time, that he had allowed Elissa to persuade him to squire her to The Bitter End on Monday nights. Flaunting the establishment's unwritten segregation policy had unpleasant consequences. The driver beeped. Michael clenched his fists and swung round ready to shout, "go to hell" if the window lowered and a man from the disco propositioned him. The last time a driver cut him off on the street it had turned out a Monday night regular who proceeded to ask him if he wanted a ride and then, before Michael could decline, said, "I thought you might want to mess around."

The window did come down, but Michael did not see a face that he recognized from Chris Ukase's bar, but rather that of the insurance agent who attended the Nexus of Nuance meeting the previous fall. "Sorry, but I frickin' forget your name," Frailey said before taking a long drag on his lit cigarette. Later Michael imagined him thinking: *Ho-Chi-Minh? Wile E. Coyote?* Michael had recently reread Edouard Dujardin's *We'll to the Woods No More*, and he remembered that he had told Frailey that Dujardin had found his inspiration in Wagner, so, after their glorious drinking spree that June night, he tried his hand at writing an interior monologue recounting all that had occurred from the moment Frailey caught sight of him while driving his car until they left The Saloon at 5:00 a.m. the next morning from Frailey's point of view. Michael knew that there existed churning cataracts and mighty streams but also mere trickles. From Frailey's slopped-up, ploughed condition (though later in the night, roused and stimulated by Michael's conversation, he spoke not only coherently but even eloquently on a whole range of subjects), Michael knew that this stream would have to begin as a trickle. "It's Michael," Bolanger replied.

From the sidewalk, he could smell the alcohol on the older man's breath. From his previous acquaintance with Frailey, Michael would never have guessed that the insurance agent ever indulged in drink, he seemed such a straight-laced company man, a Ronald Reagan republican. Michael recalled the newspaper clipping about the chapel repairs and Delone's devotion to the old church and thought *bell tower and lightning!* Frailey had seemed a small town country bumpkin, a latter-day George Babbitt and a card-carrying member of the Moral Majority, yet he spoke in such an impassioned and fervent way about the operas of Richard Wagner, that he defied easy classification. Had he not confessed his love for Wagner, Michael would have guessed that he played hickerbilly music on the jukebox or that if he listened to any "long hair" music it would be Strauss waltzes or Sousa marches. After their meeting, Michael had himself become enthralled with the music of the German composer and written his University Scholars' Honors Thesis on Wagnerian influences upon Thomas Mann's four Joseph novels. "Good to see you, Michael, " Frailey said, "How's Elissa?"

Don't tell him a thing. Michael thought. He tried to warn you but don't give him the satisfaction of knowing he guessed right. Leave him in the dark.

"Say, do you know where I can get a drink?"

"It's after two. The bars are closed." Frailey took another long puff and once again blew out the smoke through his nostrils dragon fashion. Michael smiled. "But I know where you can wet your whistle and still bend an elbow. We'll have to go back where I work."

"Then, hell, what are you waiting for? Get in."

Michael unlocked The Saloon door, and he and Frailey entered the closed bar. The following day after he awoke in the late afternoon, Michael could only remember fragments and pieces of last night's conversation. Frailey had admitted that he acted un-characteristically. He said that by drinking himself into a stupor and risking a D.U. I., he staged his own protest—a protest against the ultimatum his wife made him about having only two children. She would see that he meant business! They already had one daughter Jill, and his wife had just gotten pregnant again. Delone wanted to have a son—Delone Jr.—but she insisted that boy or girl she would have a tubal afterwards: if I'm gonna have one at all, it's squawk squawk squawk my last. They had a big fight, and he told her he was going out on a bar tour. He drank hardly at all any more, but he knew his wife hated it when he fell off the wagon and went on a binge. He determined to put her on pins and needles—and take a walk on the wild side. No, he wasn't acting like himself. He usually espoused sobriety and argued that you should treat your body like a temple, like the Bible says. He really didn't like to drink and smoke, he said, as he stubbed out his cigarette. He had acted in Spartan fashion as a soldier, for he respected and did not want to disgrace the colors. But when he and the old lady fought, he fought to win, not with his arm tied behind his back like in Vietnam. He bet Elissa fought to win, too, he said, and looked significantly at Michael. Michael could not remember if he took the bait or not. He knew that he saw red and felt that he might have let something slip, but, if he had, Frailey did not commiserate with him or say I told you so. He continued talking about his own problems with his wife. Maybe she would have a boy, and he wouldn't have had to stage this—ha, ha—domestic protest of his, but, since the baby's sex remained un-certain, he felt he should forcibly impress his feelings on his wife now, even if she stood emotional, barefoot and pregnant, and he knew no better way than this. He would have his way. Once she gave him a son, she could have her tubal but not until then.

Michael spoke about his own family's reverence for the military and how he had an ancestor, who fought in the Revolutionary War. He also told Delone that his father had served. A private with two Master's degrees, Michael's dad had studied Russian for military purposes in Germany during the Suez conflict and the uprising in Hungary. Michael recalled his father telling him how, during the tense weeks when it seemed that the U.S. might become involved in either Egypt or Hungary or both, he had feared that he might not perform well under fire. This touched a chord with Frailey. He said that he was not proud of everything he did over there and that he saw several buddies die. Later while attending classes at West Chester, he confronted some of his fellow students. He found it a real kick in the groin seeing a Hanoi flag flapping in the breeze in front of the Ox House on fraternity row. Yet on another occasion when he watched a student protest from the sidelines, an older cop mistook him for one of the activists—a Vietnam Veteran Against the War—and shouted that Nam vets were nothing but drug addicts, degenerates, and closet commies, the wrong thing to say to Delone. He had already done his tour and had taken part in a hell of a lot of firefights. The two of them ended up macing each other. Combat scared him shitless. As a boy he loved his country and wanted to do his duty, but no one knows in advance how he will react under fire.

Michael commented how different college campuses must have been in the sixties and early seventies. Frailey smiled and said that he had forgotten about Michael's youth.

He asked him to pour them both another one. He started reminiscing about elementary school field trips he had taken to Gettysburg and Antietam. All the boys wore crew cuts, and their old warhorse of a sixth-grade teacher Miss Nisewonger kept strict discipline as they waited in line. They had beautiful weather, and he felt eager and excited to tour the battlefield. Miss Nisewonger told them to show respect for they trod on sacred ground. If she caught anyone littering, she would make them pay for it. They built majestic monuments for the Civil War dead. Not an ugly black scar like the memorial they'd begun to construct for Delone's fallen comrades. He told Michael that if the call came, Michael's father would have stood tall and done his duty. Delone hated war and feared combat, but he never turned tail. He fought at age nineteen and went through one hell of an initiation, one hell of a rite of passage, but he faced his dragon down and conquered his fear. He accomplished something hard and demanding. You can't call yourself a man until you undergo such a test. Once you experience the maelstrom and pass through to the other side you are no longer a cherry boy. For Frailey, the test had come in Vietnam, but the test did not need to be military combat. People had different dragons to face and slay. But sooner or later everyone would lose their innocence, their cherry so to speak. "No, Michael," Frailey said, "You can't imagine combat until you really see it. It's not what you imagine on that tour bus in sixth grade. I love my veteran brothers. People don't know what we had to face on a daily basis. I saw people pushed out of helicopters. I knew a guy who after his first taste of poontang slit the girl's throat. We suspected she was V.C. We had crossed into Cambodia. She submitted to Arkansas, thinking that he would spare her life. But damn man we couldn't let her go. They had underground tunnels in that jungle everywhere. He knifed her because Charlie might hear a shot. He crouched somewhere in that jungle listening."

They moved on to other topics, and Michael kept plying Frailey with drinks until he became more convivial. Michael could recall little of their subsequent conversation, except that once again they treated on the subject of Richard Wagner. Michael spoke about his honors essay, told Frailey how Mann had admitted in the preface to the 1948 one-volume English edition of *Joseph and his Brothers* that Wagner's great tetralogy of pre-Christian German mythology *Der Ring des Nibelungen* was constantly with him as a guide and inspiration in his working out of his vast undertaking of Jewish and Egyptian myth. In his essay, Michael pointed out that Mann's novel had many elements that related to two other major Wagner works *Tristan und Isolde* and *Parsifal*. It especially interested Frailey that Mann felt that the Biblical storytellers consciously used a leitmotival technique roughly the same as Wagner's operatic one, two to three millennia later. Frailey commented that Wagner had a lot of both Parsifal, devout man of God and servant of guild and grail, and of Tristan, celebrator of physical love between man and woman and shameless adulterer, intermixed in his own enigmatic character. Michael said an artist's biography held no interest for him. Wagner's technique of composition the leitmotif and his use of mythology intrigued him far more than the facts of his life. He had even revised some of his Tom Englehardt stories to include Wagnerian elements. Frailey asked Michael—probably out of politeness—to send him copies of the essay and stories and scribbled his address on a bar coaster. They talked and drank on. Frailey again babbled something about his wife.

But Michael wasn't listening. He closed his eyes. No one would believe him if he said that his experiences as a young man stood every bit as traumatic as Delone Frailey's. He felt that just like the insurance agent he had gone though one hell of an initiation, one hell of a rite of passage. He knew that his experiences would prove life changing. He wanted to put those experiences into words and turn his abject life into something beautiful. Never had his vocation to write burned so fiercely within him. He wanted to write a whole series and slew of books. New ideas came to him constantly. He vowed that he would serve lady language all his days, the fall of man the fall into language. He wanted to write a book about a soldier for his father James and for his grandfather Gustave. He would not write about poor Delone's war, however. If he could complete such a book, accomplish something so hard and demanding, if he passed through the maelstrom to the other side, he would no longer consider himself a cherry boy. He could call himself a man.

Think back, far back. "Be very careful when you handle one of my books. Make sure your hands are clean. You always want to read about Yorktown. That's a very old and valuable book. I don't want you pawing it all the time. All right. All right. I'll get it." Actually his father stood pleased that his son was interested in the American War for Independence. Two of his ancestors served in the continental army, Henri Boulanger at Yorktown. The book? *A View of the Heroic Adventures, Battles, Naval Engagements, Remarkable Incidents and Glorious Achievements in the Cause of Freedom from the French and Indian Wars to the Close of the Mexican War Enlivened by a Variety of the Most Interesting Anecdotes and Embellished by Engravings.* By Jacob K. Neff, Lancaster PA. John Pearsol. 1856.

Michael read out loud. His father held the book and corrected his pronunciation.

> The two advanced redoubts below the fort of the enemy, of which we have already spoken, interfering with the completion of the besieger's second parallel, by their incessant and galling fire, Washington resolved to take them by storm. One of the redoubts is on the high bank of the river, the other a few hundred yards from it. In order to excite a spirit of emulation (for they could see each other) Washington ordered Lafayette, at the head of the American light infantry, to storm the redoubt next the river, and Baron Viomesnil, at the head of some French grenadiers, to take the other. Relying entirely upon their bayonets, the Americans with unloaded guns rushed forward with extreme impetuosity. Col. Hamilton leading the van drove some of the enemy headlong over a precipice one hundred feet high, killed a few and took all the remainder prisoners. The French, with a little more fighting, carried the other redoubt at point of bayonet.
>
> "Round the pent foe approaching breastworks rise,
> And bombs, like meteors, vault the flaming skies."

Chapter Thirteen

An Idyll

Cantwell whipped the towel across his shoulder blade, then straightened his goggles. He looked down at his feet, both planted firmly on the fourth step, his knees below the surface of the water. He crushed the towel into a ball and threw it over his shoulder onto the deck, then kicked his left leg out in a quarter goosestep to touch bottom, and plunged waist deep into the water. His skin goose-fleshed. He wheeled around, snatched the rail and climbed up the steps. Settling his mass into the lawn chair, he took off his goggles and, still shivering, with one hand jerked his red trunks on high (stuffing his fat purse) and with his other felt for the damp, pulpy novel on the stand behind him, as Dr. Arbuthnot darted from under the stand into the sunlight. The first paragraph left him cold. The lines of his face drew in, and his nose wrinkled as he puckered his lips and assumed the expression of a peevish child in capricious ill humor. He pitched the book at the deck and lifted his bulk out of the chair. Dr. Arbuthnot shot between his legs as he opened the screen door and stepped inside. He walked through the kitchen into an unbelievably cluttered living room. Five years worth of *New Yorkers* and *Sports Il-lustrateds* and *New York Times* lay on the floor, on the furniture; plates, knives and forks lay under and on top of them, as well as paper cups, empty Fritos and Doritos bags, cans of Dr. Pepper, inside-out shirts, socks, pants and underwear and white cardboard boxes with *Gilbey's Gin* or *Trophy Cantaloupes* stamped on the sides. Pieces of a chess set made to resemble African sculpture stood on the mantel of the fireplace, on the two windowsills and on the bench and the lid of an upright piano. A guitar lay under the bench, its neck out. Cantwell stepped over it and stopped at the bookcase that stood between the piano and the door leading to the front hall. Ever since his father retired and his parents moved to Florida and Ben rented three rooms upstairs, the house had been a mess. He scanned the titles. Again a petulant look crossed his face. Even if he hadn't read them all, he knew what they all were, and had grown tired of the choices. He settled on *The Return of Tarzan*, one of his grandmother's books, a first edition, he thought, and pulled it from the shelf. As he opened it and flattened the title page, a tiny piece of paper flitted out and fell to the hardwood floor, landing just beyond the rim of the puddle he was making. He bent over and picked it up and, carrying the book under his arm, walked to the couch and leaned back on the newspapers. She must have trimmed it from the *Inquirer*, he thought, looking down at the yellowed clipping in the hollow of his massive hand:

The second and third innings stood placid at both ends, but in the fourth, Ruth lifted the highest and longest homer ever seen at Shibe Park. The ball hit John Peacock's asphalt on Twentieth Street and then took a majestic bound to the window of a dwelling where a boy on the second floor tried to spear it but missed.

He heard someone on the porch open the front door, step into the hallway and swing the door shut, but, thinking it one of the three tenants, didn't budge until he saw the handle on his door turn down. Dammit, he thought, sitting up. They know this room's off limits. They can get to the kitchen through the others. The door swung open and Brent Cobin stepped in. Seeing Ben Cantwell sprawled on a sofa, wearing only a swimsuit, looking first at his sullen, frowning face, then at his Sidney Greenstreet dugs and belly, Cobin thought, slugabed. Interlacing his fingers and stretching out his arms, he said, "Come alive. We're outta here." Cantwell said nothing, his eyes still daggers. You torpid blob, Cobin thought. "We have to cheer up Michael," he said, "He's down because of that other guy." Bolanger lived, Cantwell realized long ago, in as many different worlds as possible, but how he ever lit on this person, under what rock in what riverbed on what planet, and how he could tolerate him for more than two hours without wishing to put a few parsecs between them stood beyond his comprehension. When Michael introduced them, Cobin bounced up to him, convulsing with laughter. He had burnt a cigarette through a Styrofoam cup filled with beer so he "could smoke and drink at the same time." The ashes fell in the beer, but Cobin didn't mind, or even notice. "Well," Cobin said. "What have you got planned?" Cantwell asked and, before Cobin could open his mouth, added, "No caving. Not with you two." "A drive," Cobin answered, shrugging his shoulders. Cantwell stepped into a pair of pants from the floor and hunted for a shirt. "All right," he said, "let me find my socks."

Bradley Scott had told him about Tim Cassill and that Michael had grown dispirited–he showed up for work boiled. Dispirited? (Cantwell smiled.) Nah. He remained attached to Bolanger by esteem, respect, affection and *sport*. Boola-boola Ben. He'd cheer him up, even if it meant spending the day with Cobin. Who told him? As he buttoned his shirt, Cantwell saw a reddish brown blur with black ears tipped with silver hairs spring from a corner. Dr. A– darted across the floor towards the kitchen. Ben turned his head, saw that Bezaleel had come into the room from there. Territorial infringement. Bezaleel hissed, bared his single rotten tooth as his tail distended into a giant exclamation mark. Arbuthnot swiped first, caught Bezaleel behind the ear, then again on the nose. Bez swatted back but, declawed, stood no match. Cantwell swooped down, grabbed each cat by the scruff of the neck, and lifted them into the air. *Ha-ha*. "Want one?" he asked, looking at the cats, then at Cobin's obscenely gleeful face. A bettor shouting, Fly at him Red–knock his eye out–at fighting gamecocks heeled with metal spurs. Cantwell dropped Arbuthnot onto the couch (he sprang off it and ran into the front hall) and took Bez into the kitchen, his long gray hair (he was half Persian) so matted that Ben could never comb it out. Besides, it stank. Cantwell tossed him through the cellar door. Bezaleel thought litter boxes existed for rolling in.

They stepped out on the porch and Cantwell sat down on the swing to tie his shoe. As he crossed one string over the other, a yellow jacket flew out of the cushion—buzzing. Cantwell got away from the swing, sat down on the sill, tied the knot and made the bow. "Come on," Cobin shouted, already across the street, opening his car door. "Sit in the back," he said, when Cantwell, puffing, stared at him through the front passenger window, waiting for him to unlock the door. Brent reached over the seat and pulled up the other knob. "Michael rides shotgun," he said. Before getting in, Cantwell looked over the hood splotched with bird droppings, at the peaked, shingled roof of the house set back from the street like a witch's cottage, behind two huge firs. Slamming the door, he put both his legs up on the seat and pressed the back of his head against the window as Cobin put the key in the ignition. Twelve cars blipped by before Cobin could pull out. As they waited, Cantwell stared at the yellow foam bulging from a tear in the vinyl (Cobin had patched and repaired a number of other tears with green duct tape) and at Cobin's brown curls. He closed the ashtray on the armrest. A butt fell to the seat and rolled off. Reaching for the butt, Cantwell saw a pair of laced white panties under the seat, *a trophy of a long-waged battle that ended with a wedding proposal,* but thought it only an old cloth until he picked it up. Cobin had decided to launch a major offensive to break the impasse. On a dirt access road in a State Forest late at night. Ben moaned and tossed the panties onto the front seat. "Shit," Cobin said. He cracked the door and dropped the panties on the road, then seeing the way clear, pulled out.

A strange, wonderful outpouring came from his lips when, looking at him, she said, "Why did you stop?" He pled, he went on, for one moment out of all the future. Her assurance started evaporating. It began happening again: again she came in contact with that magical catalytic agent (what precisely was it?) that opened her emotional sluice. Re-exposed her. She felt the old turbulence begin to roll. She could not resist or fight it.

The expression on her face did not change, but she felt wholly altered. Only momentarily? she wondered. No. Everything jumbled and mixed up. Everything turned inside out and upside down. Everything changed in this magical crucible on four wheels. She shuffled off her coil and emerged a snake in new skin: she loved him. She felt sure of it. Her plans shot, her calculations collapsing, she said, still outwardly calm, "You talk too much." One moment out of all the future.

Michael saw the long, tapered olive body of the Squid roll to a complete stop. He sat on the front porch, his feet on the railing, and stared at the Film Lab across the street. *The view from a camouflaged Sigerson's perch. From Sherlock's Home.* The life story of the driver stood known to him, so he didn't have to employ Holmes' methods to deduce it. The light changed. The Squid made a left, shot up Sigerson, u-turned, glided down the street, and pulled to the side. As Cobin parked, Michael got up and walked to the far side of the porch. Cobin rolled down the window. "Come be a gadabout," he said, his elbow jutting out. An olive-green door flew open and Ben Cantwell heaved himself out onto the sidewalk.

In cases of acute exacerbations, Michael thought, healers administer diuretics or employ blood-letting. Well, boys, make me well.

If he had followed Salmos' advice to find-fondle-forget, he wouldn't need to search for an anti-dote now. Can't-well tried a few one-liners. Sure-fire jokes. Michael smiled at one or two. As Ben spoke, Bolanger looked up at the treetops, thinking (oh, how he hated them. He would *never* be duped again): *on the margins—bristles and on the insides sensitive triggers which when touched cause the two leaves to hinge together, close. Or better yet, the other plant, the bladderwort. A sticky membranous sac with flask-shaped, lubricious sides— slides—and water at the bottom. Cunt macerated the fly. Cunt digested and dissolved the ant. The bed-bug. Gypsy moth eaten the cunt. Green's gone.* "What?" he asked Cantwell, climbing over the railing.

"Never mind," Ben said, waving his hand and getting back in. Michael jumped down, also got in. Slammed the door. Three cars blipped by, then Cobin turned the key and pulled out. "Remember last winter," he said, hitting his brakes at the light, "when I tied a rope to the Squid's fender and had you pull me on my downhills up Siger-son and those two drunken goobers ran out and wanted me to let them try." "You're a goober, Brent," Michael said. He didn't laugh, seemed a little cross and testy even. Switching tactics, Brent reached into a bag and pulled a beer off the six-pack ring and handed it to Michael, then pulled off another one for himself. He had bought two six-packs at Sudsy's on the way to Ben's. The car behind them beeped, and Cobin, see-ing that the light had changed, took a left turn at Camberson. "You're not drinking?" Cantwell said, seeing them both chug simultaneously. "Come on," he shouted. "Sure we are," Cobin replied with mock Hunter Thompson breeze. "I always drive better af-ter a few. I'll watch for cops." "Stop being such a cunt," Michael said, playing the part of the big bad brother, John Salmos. "You sure do cunt well." Cantwell threw up his arms.

From Camberson, Cobin turned onto West 324. The road described a wide half-cir-cle around a protruding peninsula of golf course with a view of mountains with trees minus their leaves, as if, despite the heat, it still remained winter, or, for some reason, the trees had not renewed their foliage in the spring. The caterpillars had ravaged acres of land—the insecticides had proved ineffective—and there stood no natural predators—the birds could not digest them because of their fuzz.

The crisscrossing branches reminded Michael of the vein system of the body. He thought of blood returning to the heart, of the overlapping series of transparencies found in anatomy texts, one of the organs, the next of veins and arteries, the third and fourth of the nervous system and muscles, that one could pull off the two dimensional skeleton layer by layer like onion skin and thought: *If I flip the transparency over the leaves would return to their proper place.*

"Hey Mike," Cobin shouted, "Name three ways you can tell Jesus was Jewish?" Bo-langer shrugged his shoulders. "One, he lived with his parents until he was thirty. Two, he went into his father's business. And three, his mother thought he was god." Again Michael didn't laugh. A Jesus joke, Ben Cantwell thought. I can do better than that. You want Buck Mulligan. Here. Take him. It was easy, sailor to saviour. He started descant-ing. Each line three times, with the refrain *ur-lye in the morning*:

> (3) What shall we do with the drunken Saviour?
> Nail him to the cross until he's sober
> Throw him in the tomb when he starts snoring

'Way, hey, and up he rises
With a headache just like thorns have pierced it
Soldiers sleeping right beside him
Takes their bottle and keeps on walking
Finds his friends still sad and weeping
Says, Happy Easter, have a swallow
'Way, hey, and up he rises
What shall we do with a drunken Saviour?

"Save your souls and drink right with him," Cobin cut in and still singing: "And no we won't stop, and I'm ready for another." That doesn't scan at all, thought Cantwell. Cobin broke off, tossing his can on the seat. "How 'bout you, Mick."

Speeding up the first hill, then coasting down it and up the next one, Cobin made a hard right turn where the highway dropped in a steep slant, the landscape fast-forwarded and the ground reached up and tried to pull you down. They drove up the Port Esmerelda Valley but not through the town (the port?) as they would if driving to Rallingsburg. Cantwell saw a glider's nose, then its wings, their shadow, through the rear window as he looked at the barren peaks on either side of the road, cocoons in the tree limbs. Michael and Cobin looked out at the fields, a small white church, the sign that said *Grange*, a cluster of firs, hemlocks blue in the distance, the barbwire fence and Holsteins swishing their tails and chewing, standing or lying down in the field. Accelerating through the hemlocks, Cobin steered to the left as he shot out of the trees into the meadow and onto the narrow, paved but peeling rural route. Michael crumpled his can, still held it. Cobin threw his out the window. Cables, stretched across towers dotting the hills, cast shadows across the slopes and into the pines above as well as onto the road. Cobin punched the accelerator, swerving left. Cantwell saw the truss bridge across the depression: horizontal girders bound together by a vertical web. They had mastery over life and death, he thought. And Michael won't make him stop!

The top of Cantwell's head hit the inside lining. He fell back into the seat. Michael and Cobin's bodies, strapped in, bounced but the belts kept them in their seats when the front and then the back wheels slapped down on the pavement across the span.

As they hurtled onto another road, a dirt one upwards into the pine wood, Cantwell saw himself as the highest and longest homer ever seen in Shibe Park—crashing into Peacock's asphalt. He saw a white disk roll onto the floor. He reached for it and snapped it back over the light. He looked out the window at the redtop, trailing stems and purplish flowers, bordering the road. "Not every day you jump a bridge," Cobin said. "Want a beer now, Ben? Hand him one." He nudged Michael with his elbow: "Give him a beer!" Then seeing Michael's pursed lips, the sweat dripping from his nose: "It was just a bump, not a volt bolt to the privates. Gee." Gripping the wheel with his left, Cobin reached into the bag and handed Cantwell a beer with his right. They drove into the woods over the rocks and rubble. "Let's roll some more hills," Cobin said. "Say something, Mike. Like I'm okay."

Ben pulled his tab, took two sips: shock absorbers. The car rattled and popped over the stones up a steep slope. "I did a video tape—special interest segment, you know—on Carl," Cobin said. "The Jane Goodall of Rallings County. One of the things I sent WJAT. Those bastards kept me waiting for four months before they sent their regrets." Ben looked down at the valley as they rose up from it—at the hundreds of deciduous trees without green outgrowth. No foliage leaf with midrib and veins and epidermis of flattened cells. Bent over the dash, looking out the windshield, Michael saw—from that panther perspective—rose-colored knapweed flowers at the road's edge then, lifting his head over his hunched shoulders, perennial green: Scotch pine, spruce, evergreen, fir— Norwegian wood.

A white rock road to the left led to a hunter's cabin. Cobin went by it deeper into the woods. The car bounced and wobbled over rocks, then into a pickup's tracks, splashing mud up on the fenders. Cobin steered from one dirt road to another to another. Finally one led upwards to a peak well back from the interstate and everything else. Cobin rolled to a stop at a chained driveway that dipped back over a hillock (you couldn't see the cabin) with Smokey the Bear forest-fire posters tacked to two pines beside the chain posts. "You two will feel like you've landed on the backside of the moon or descended in a diving bell to the bottom of the ocean. As if the grays have abducted you and dropped you off in some sort of space aquarium," he said as he got out of the car, slinging the second six-pack under his arm. "Whatever you do, don't act like you're scared. Walk straight to the cabin, follow me. You'll be surprised by what you see." That did scan, thought Cantwell. Michael stepped to the side, reached out and touched the thick, flaky bark of a pine tree. Stepping under its branches, he felt the dark green bristles and small spiny-tipped cones. He walked into the tall grass, continued forward to the next tree. "No," Cobin called, "stay on the road." Michael bent over and picked up a twig from the loam at its base and jabbed at the trunk. He walked back to the bend in the drive where Cobin and Cantwell stood, holding the twig in his hand, the caterpillar's head speared and paraded on the twig point like an overthrown tyrant's. Green ooze spurted on the tree. A punctured toothpaste tube, the caterpillar fell to the ground. He flattened the piece of blue fuzz with a stamp of his foot. More green ooze. After they saw it, he tossed the twig in the grass. The driveway sloped downwards, turned sharply to the left. They saw a part-wood, part-tarpaper cabin and a four-wheel-drive truck parked in front of it. From the lawn, four peaks stood visible of what would have remained dense wood had it not been for the devastation and what looked like a corn feeder in a shaded area on the far side of the yard further down the slope and below the cabin. "None are out," Cobin said. "When I did the video, fourteen grazed, including Max. The biggest." They crossed through the grass toward the cabin, Cobin leading. "There's one," he said, pointing to the porch steps, "with Carl." Michael turned his head away from row upon row of naked beech and maple on the far hillsides, to see first Cantwell in shock, then what shocked him: a gaunt thirtyish man, wearing a red cap, feeding a black bear marshmallows out of a plastic bag. "Howdy, Brent," the man called out, seeing him in the field. Ben stood stock still in the grass, astonished, as Cobin sprinted down to the house and hopped midway up the steps to where the man and bear sat. "Come on up," Carl Penny shouted, cupping his lips with both hands. "It's all right. Take the other steps." Michael shrugged his shoulders and started down the slope. After laying down the half-filled can, Cantwell tramped up behind him. They mounted the wood steps and used the wooden rail on the far side, came up onto the porch and crossed it to where the other steps and banister started. There, Cobin supported himself against the cabin wall on the top step. Peering down over the man's shoulder, they watched the massive, short-limbed, short-tailed and jet-black animal lick and tongue white goo into its mouth out of the man's left palm, never attempting to stick its snout into the bag on the man's lap but waiting patiently for the man to take out the marshmallows to feed it. Slobbering, it swayed back and forth, never menacing the man with its claws or teeth, ignoring the newcomers, Cobin, Cantwell, and Bolanger.

The ball cracked on the bat—flew out of the park. B.C. took a majestic bound up from the pavement. But going out with Brent and Michael always had uncomfortable consequences for Ben. Stuck in Morris' Despair—that kidney-shaped hole—or found mauled with his neck broken, his face disfigured by claw marks. Yet with them, he felt alive and giddy. What they did remained exciting, new. Everything he did that week seemed like sleep or repose in comparison. The man touched the bear's neck. "All gone," he said twice, then stood up and stretched out his arm to shake Cantwell's hand. "Hi, I'm Carl Penny." "Here comes another one," Cobin said. Penny turned around. A second bear waddled up to the steps. "Stay down, Jane," Penny said. The bear kept coming. "Get back now!" Penny stuck out his sunken chest. "Now!" The bear flopped down into the grass, licked its lips. "You had yours." Carl scooped up the plastic bag with a scrawny arm. "Come in, guys," he said and pushed down the latch. Last, Cobin pulled the door shut. "Do you need a brew, Carl?" he asked. "Mine are in there," Penny replied, pointing to the white Frigidaire by the window. Cobin walked over to it, swung the door open, and unloaded his cans beside Carl's Strohs. Cantwell and Michael stepped up three two-by-fours to a higher level, following Carl deeper into the cabin's single room. Lumber steps led to a balcony with bed in the rafters where one could step outside on a ledge over the front porch. Below, they sat on a couch further in. A long glass table, magazines strewn on it, a white ottoman, three or four other chairs, a Panasonic sound system, a coal stove, and a television hooked to an aerial antenna filled out the cabin. On the varnished wood walls, framed photographs of Carl Penny feeding and wrestling with different bears, playing with the cubs. He wore a khaki flak jacket and polyester pants like those he wore now.

Penny picked up a pipe from the table, lit it, and said, "I only had one accident. A buddy of mine started baiting Max. I jumped in. So it wasn't too bad. Thirteen stitches on his arm. I got fo'teen." He pointed his pipe at Ben. "How do you know Brent?" he asked. "Old acquaintance," Ben said, looking at the walls, the coal stove, the magazines, the metal cage on the ottoman, and at the ceiling through the rafters. "Fourteen stitches?" he asked. "No," Carl said, "fo'teen bear." Penny's bristling eyebrows looked purposeful, energetic. He had no belly to speak of and only thin, spindly legs. His face stood brightly colored with metallic hues from the sound system. "I don't live at the edge of the woods anymore. Caterpillars. Four of them have turned up so far. Hell. The rest must have never stopped hibernating." Cobin bounced up the two-by-fours with four beers and handed them out. He took a seat and began searching through the magazine pile. Finding a *Hustler* and flicking it open, he skimmed through it, then put it down and opened another. They heard a bang on the door then a second, louder detonation. They looked over their shoulders—except Michael. He stared straight ahead at the solid aluminum cage perforated with air holes on top of the ottoman. "I taught her how to hit the latch," he heard Penny say. "Look, Michael," Brent said, touching Bolanger's arm. Michael turned his head and saw the upright bear swaying on its hind legs—inside the cabin. Penny got up. "Here, Jane," he said, then shouted "sit!" Jane flopped down at the foot of the three steps. Carl grabbed the bag of marshmallows from the tabletop. He sat on the top step, the bear's snout between his legs, his feet on the first step. "Here girl," he said, taking one marshmallow out at a time and putting his fingers in front of the bear's nose.

Ben Cantwell pressed his shoulders into the cushion's folds, his hands gripping the arm rest as an expression of pure glee took hold of his features, shaped his face. He couldn't hold back his laughter. He wanted to pound the floor with his heels. Carl fed the bear five marshmallows before the second beast lumbered into the cabin. She got too close to Jane. "That's her mother," Carl said. Jane responded by turning her head and flapping her jowls. Like my teeth chattering through an amplifier, Ben thought. The second bear mirrored its mother. A stand-off. Carl took the bag of marshmallows back outside and scattered its contents into the grass. The younger bear followed him out into the yard.

Because Michael said that he didn't feel well, that the room was too close, Cobin led him up into the rafters and outside on the ledge. They looked down at Carl and the bear and out at the barren peaks and the aquamarine sky—the sun inching down. Cobin shouted to Carl. Michael felt a sudden jab in his side. Intense pain gone before it started (as if he had been touched by a cattle prod). He stumbled in and sat on the cot. To his left, he saw a pneumatic doll with pneumatic chest in the rafters. He has no wife to hassle his life, he thought. He felt like he would throw up; he leaned over, and put his head between his knees. Carl turned when the bear put its nose in the grass, hurried up the steps back inside and shut the door. "She can't hit the latch with her front paw," he said.

Jane and Cantwell sat frozen in the exact same positions as when he left the room. He sat down beside Ben. "That friend of yours sick?" he asked. "Unsettled," Ben said, gripping the armrest. "Not because of the bear?" Carl asked, craning his neck to look down at Jane. "Some hikers a couple years back. Just before bear season. A lot of hunters going to be out. Well, maybe it was a good idea, maybe not. None of my bears got shot. I spraypainted their heads. Red and orange like a hunting cap. Well, these three teenagers see Max in the woods and—" Cobin bounded down the steps. "Your friend okay," Carl asked him, "he looks as white as a ghost." "He's just a bit dizzy," Cobin said. "He'll be down in a sec." Parsec, Cantwell thought. Brent started doing toe touches and leg stretches. This gymnast journalist, Ben Cantwell thought. This weasel with my initials. And now this second nut. How did Michael find these people? Bears, for God's sake. Live bears. He started laughing hard and couldn't stop and spilled beer on his pant leg. I would like to discover which of us two BCs is made of matter and which of anti-matter, he thought. I won't forgive Michael for introducing us unless, by some exceptional lack in taste, I start liking this. He looked at Jane. Something to store away with various odd fragments in the lives of the poets. Michael slowly descended from the rafters, his feet clunking metronomically on each step. Cantwell's face lit up. Two bears fighting over the marshmallows. Just like one of the cats finding the other at its dinner dish.

"Ben, you look effervescent," Michael said. "Why, he's fizzing up and over," Cobin interjected before sitting down on the ottoman beside the cage. "What have you got in here?" Carl told him to lift it up by the handle and bring it to him. As he lifted it up and the cage swayed in the air, an alarm clock went off inside it. "The horny interlocking joints at the end of his tail did that," Carl said and grinned. "He's got a sluggish disposition. Don't hatta give him much fo' feed." Carl spat. Cobin laid the cage with the rattler on the floor. "Well," he said, "I just wanted to show these two your bears." Cantwell and Michael stood up, picking up their beers. Carl Penny shook their hands. He led them around Jane to the door, told them to wait, stepped over to the refrigerator and got out their three remaining beers, then opened a cupboard and brought them each a bag of assorted nuts. "I'm a distributor," he said. They stepped out on the porch. Penny waved to them as they started up the driveway.

Chapter Fourteen

Intussusception

After the operation. Before he came to, as he came to, he started screaming for something to still the pain. After monitoring his vitals, the nurse whose face he could only half see, scrambled for the needle. He still hadn't fully come to when he felt the jab in his arm.

Back in his room. His mother sat in the green chair. Tomorrow, they'll sit you up in a chair, she said. The appendix had perforated and grown gangrenous. An abscess developed and walled in the poison, masking Michael's true condition. His peritoneum had become infected. But you'll heal just fine, his mother said. Antibiotics trickled through his IV into his arm.

Michael had "recovered" six days after the emergency room physician had admitted him for observation. He did not experience the typical right-sided pain. It diffused over his entire abdomen. The evening before they planned to release him, he ate solid food for the first time in ten days and immediately threw up the meat loaf, mashed potatoes, jello and juice. The spasm struck suddenly, the tenderness located in the pit of his stomach. But he experienced another kind of pain—sharper and more severe—after the surgery. Not until the appendix had burst and the infection had reached the overlying peritoneum did they wheel him in for the exploratory that up to then they had been loath to perform.

His doctor milked his insurance for all he could, Michael later concluded. He had come into the hospital with all the signs and symptoms of appendicitis (except that the pain had not localized on his right side). His appendix did not rest in the typical position, but doctors know that often stands the case. He had a moderately elevated WBC of 15,000/mm³. His temperature had risen to 102. So why the need for all the unnecessary tests, the lower GI series? They stuck a tube up his rectum to examine his colon. They sent him down to x-ray at least twenty times. They gave him barium enemas and sent him to ultrasound. "Ultrasonic radiation," he would later read, "stands injurious to secondary tissues because of its thermal effects when absorbed by living matter, but in controlled doses physicians use it therapeutically as a diagnostic by visually displaying echoes received from irradiated tissues." They examined him with a fluoroscope, "a device used for examining deep structures by means of roentgen rays. It consists of a screen (fluorescent screen) covered with crystals of calcium tungstate on which the technician projects the shadows of X-rays passing through the body placed between the screen and the source of the irradiation." He saw his insides displayed on the screen as he lay there. He could see through the organs, see the barium flow into them. He turned his head away. Then on the sixth day, his pain stopped. His doctor said he had appendicitis, but that it had healed by itself. But in the first medical book he opened, he read: "Sudden cessation of pain indicates perforation or infarction of the appendix."

For four days after the operation, the pain persisted. Demerol deadened it. The incision ran six inches, twice the normal length of an appendectomy scar.

The first forty-eight hours, he really suffered. He nearly fainted when they put him up in the chair. The IV needle infiltrated in his arm. It puffed up so the nurse had to transfer the IV to his other arm. When Peg, his day nurse, helped him walk into the hall, he felt so weak and stiff, he thought he would collapse on the floor. On the fifth day, the pain subsided. They gave him Tylox orally. Twelve days after the operation, his doctor signed his release. The doctor thought he remained too weak to travel to Cannoshockton, so his mother stayed with him at his Herneshopple apartment. They would leave for Cannoshockton as soon as he felt up to it.

Cobin drove him to the hospital. Of course, the boys' day (night) out had not finished with the road trip. Penny's cabin stood only the first stop. The three friends attended a party at the Briarwood Apartments. Michael ended up walking home, drunk. Cantwell and Cobin left him to mingle on his own and mingled themselves. His stomach remained upset. The beer made him sleepy. If he'd only have come to me and said let's go, we'd have gone, Cobin later said. Michael crossed the golf course to reach Sigerson Street. Coming out from behind the trees onto his landlord the distributor's parking lot, he nearly ran into an old woman. He saw and recognized the pink lady. She didn't have her stick nor did she say, "Hey, boy. You. Do you know I own this distributorship?" Her eyes just bulged. Her lips parted. Gaining her balance, she stamped her foot and huffed. He heard her mumble something to herself after he had turned the corner. He unlocked his door, shut it, and sat down on the couch. His buzz did not stand proportionate to the number of beers he had drunk. He felt more inebriated than he should have. He got up and stepped into the kitchen and pulled a book out of one of his cupboards. He staggered back into the living room, the book he had randomly selected Henry P. Johnston's *The Yorktown Companion*. His grandfather had bought it for him at Harper's Ferry when the two had vacationed in Virginia shortly after Michael's eighth birthday. As a boy, he had often daydreamed over the illustrations and about his illustrious ancestor Henri Boulanger, the Revolutionary War hero who had fought at Yorktown and received the blow from the British major's sword that blinded him in one eye and scarred his forehead for life. Henri killed the officer by twisting a bayonet into his bowels. He took the man's sword which bore his coat of arms on both the blade and the bell guard. Alexander Hamilton had led the assault on redoubt ten, where Private Yankee Doodle silenced the British guns in only ten minutes. French grenadiers and chasseurs simultaneously took bastion redoubt nine, but the French dragoons of the Partisan Legion accompanied the Americans. With the capture of the two redoubts, Washington's siege stood complete. The French navy had entered the Chesapeake and Cornwallis found himself caught between the bay on one side and the French and American forces on the other. Michael read:

The work to be stormed was a square redoubt, "Number 10," somewhat smaller than the one captured by the French, standing within twenty feet of the river-bank and held by the British Major Campbell and about seventy men. It was upon the site of this work—the "Rock Redoubt," as it was afterwards called—that the triumphal arch was erected in honor of Lafayette, upon the occasion of his visit to Yorktown in 1824, and under which he paid a feeling tribute to the worth and valor of his "dear light infantry of 1781."

At the given signal—six shells—Hamilton and his column advanced rapidly, with unloaded muskets, Laurens having first been detached to take the redoubt in reverse, and prevent the escape of the garrison. Under the almost perfect discipline of the troops, every order was executed with precision. As they neared the work, they rushed to charge without waiting for the sappers to remove the abatis. Climbing over or breaking through the obstructions, they reached the parapet, made the capture within ten minutes after the start. The American loss in the affair was nine killed and twenty-five wounded.

He put the book down on his table. Of all places, he thought, he bought it at Harper's Ferry—where she wrote me from and where the Federals took John Brown into custody. They hanged him in Charles Town, where she betrayed me. He picked up a copy of Joseph Conrad's *Victory* from off the table but couldn't read. Again he felt depressed and bitter. Bitch, he thought, as he started crying. Contemptible, heartless bitch. He threw the book down, got up, switched on the T.V., and pulled a lime-colored sleeping bag out of the closet. He lay down on the couch and covered himself with it. He did not get up from the couch except to use the toilet for the next three days. At first, he thought that he had come down with the flu. He drank half a bottle of Pepto-Bismol. Cobin stopped by the third day. "We're going to the hospital," he said. He helped Michael up from the couch. Michael took his copy of *Victory* with him. Conrad would remain at his bedside during both his stays in the hospital. The nurses remarked what a sight it was seeing him reading with all those tubes and wires attached to him. After Michael's release, Cobin would visit him at the apartment. He had just gotten married to, of all people, Margaret Bromion. "Well, I hope you'll be happy," an astonished Michael stuttered, all that he could manage to say. Cantwell also visited. Michael spoke about other injuries to the body that he had sustained and convalesced from—cataloged his scars and deformities. Oh, go peddle your relics elsewhere, Cantwell thought.

At the age of eight, he broke two fingers on his right hand when a pickup rear-ended his mother's parked car. A year later, he needed seven stitches when he struck his head on the kitchen snack bar. He lost his balance while running, slipped, and fell. He tore a ligament in his right leg in gym during his senior year in high school.

Please go peddle your relics elsewhere.

As for deformities, he had come into this world with two: the deviated septum and an extra tarsal in his right foot. He was flatfooted; both his feet pronated. For many years, he wore orthotics, but they so badly callused his feet that he discontinued using them. During her pregnancy, his mother had started reading *Of Human Bondage.* After their marriage, his father had given her a reading list, so he wouldn't find it embarrassing to take her to faculty cocktail parties. And he was born with an extra tarsal in his foot. Figure that one out. He didn't remember now his age when he had his tonsils out. He had not yet reached his teens, but he could ask his mother to make sure. That's all right, Ben said. And, oh yes, he forgot about the two scars on his lip, the souvenir of some childhood scuffle.

Salmos phoned regularly, said he would visit him as soon as Michael came home to Cannoshockton. Even Elissa dropped by to see him. She stayed only a short while. Michael hadn't told his mother that they had stopped seeing each other, didn't tell her now. He wanted to cry. He had to go through this ordeal, this horrible operation, in order for her to visit him. Maybe she felt guilty—responsible. Illness did have its recompenses. If he had a relapse perhaps . . . .

The next few days, he hoped that she would stop again. The day before his readmission to the hospital, she did and told him that she had accepted a permanent job in Charles Town and would leave Herneshopple at the end of the summer.

After the second operation. "The intussusceptem," the surgeon explained to his mother in the waiting room, "is the portion of the intestine that has invaginated within another section, the intussuscipiens the part into which the intussusceptem has invaginated. After the invagination occurred, peristalsis propelled the intussusceptem along the bowel, pulling more bowel along with it into the receiving portion. This produced hemorrhage from venous engorgement, edema, and the obstruction." In other words, one intestine had swallowed a portion of the other.

Not until he fully recovered would he try to comprehend what had happened. A long period of forgetting, rejuvenating, and slowly gaining back weight, came first. Only when he had healed in all ways could he look back. One of his mother's nursing books provided the initial information. He thumbed through *Gastrointestinal Disorders* and found it: "Intussusception: a telescoping of the bowel into an adjacent distal portion. Intussusception may prove fatal, especially if treatment is delayed for more than twenty-four hours. During surgery, the surgeon first attempts manual reduction. After compressing the bowel above the intussusception, the doctor endeavors to milk the intussusception back through the bowel. However, if manual reduction fails or if the bowel has become gangrenous or strangulated, the doctor will perform a resection of the affected segment."

Elissa stopped at the apartment a little after noon. That night Michael had intermittent attacks of colicky pain. He clutched his right side and drew his legs up to his abdomen. Mrs. Bolanger immediately telephoned his doctor. He instructed her to have Michael soak in warm water and assured her that he experienced normal postoperative pain. After sitting in the tub for twenty minutes, Michael got out and lay back down.

He had no more attacks that night, but by morning, he had turned pale and diaphoretic and again experienced colicky abdominal pain. His mother rushed him to the emergency room. He begged for a shot. The attendants put him on a pushcart and wheeled him into an examination room. A nurse checked his blood pressure then took a blood sample. Other people went in and out. He again asked for something for the pain. They had to wait, someone explained, until the doctor examined him. A half hour went by before the surgeon entered the room. He asked Michael several questions, then pressed his stomach with his hand, asking Michael if it hurt. He pressed in several places. Michael's pain had localized in the lower right quadrant. He ordered an IV and the injection. He said they would keep him overnight and run some tests the following morning. He had to leave town for the rest of the day. His daughter participated in a regional basketball tournament in of all places Cannoshockton.

His mother stayed at his side all day. His grandfather relieved her at nine p.m. and would stay in his room all night. The Demerol eased his pain. A nurse administered it every four hours, but late that night it ceased working effectively, and Michael began to moan. Gustave Bolanger thought that he lay dying. He ran out to the nurses' station and asked if a doctor stood on call. This boy needs attention. The nurse said no, and he added that a hospital that size should have a doctor there at night in case of an emergency—could she please get someone. She said she'd have the supervising nurse check on him. If she felt they should call his doctor at home, she would. "Hurry," he pleaded, "Please, please hurry." It stood a family curse; Michael was not the first Bolanger to be struck by it. At the age of nine, Gustave had an intestinal obstruction, a partial blockage of the lumen in the small bowel, and had to have what at the time remained a very dangerous operation. His grandfather brought toilet paper and Welch's grape juice to the sanitarium for him. His father Joseph Ray became the second victim in 1943. He became ill on a Wednesday and Friday evening underwent an operation for perforation of the bowels. He died that night at the Rallingsburg State Hospital. G.C. worried about his children Fred, Lenora, and James, fearing that congenital bowel deformities ran in the family. Bless Jesus; the Lord spared all his children. His brother Harry's son John Henry, however, had appendicitis at age ten. He survived the surgery. The doctors said that the ether had killed him. Such a nice little fella. His poor parents went through so much. Johnny swallowed lye water at the age of three and almost died then. For years, his father and mother had to take him to Philadelphia every three weeks for special treatments, then the boy died anyway. Now Michael stood ill with the same thing. Please don't take him, Lord.

He sat down in the chair beside the bed, took Michael's hand in his. "Don't let it master you," he said. "I can't stand it. Why won't they give me another shot?" "It's not time yet." "Tell me about someone." Gustave knew what he meant. Michael had often asked him to describe someone in the family he had never met but never under conditions like these. Gustave spoke about his Aunt Sally. "I remember her cracker box. It was wooden and always contained a round soda cracker the size of a silver half dollar. A visit to it was always worth the trip through the field to Aunt Sally's. She stood fond of the flowery growth around the home. She had numerous flowerbeds and flowery shrubs. I recall she and I going to the tulip beds in the front yard …." He paused. *Why isn't she here? What's taking her so long?* Then continued. The rapidity of his speech betrayed his nervousness. "Her back porch was ornamented with such a vine that brought forth a bluebell flower. I can't recall its name, but I do remember that I loved to look at the small bellflower in the vine. To the right of the back porch, there stood a huge horse chestnut tree and under it on a bracket hung a very large cast-iron kettle, the country size. You still see these large kettles on farms. Their service remains varied. Making apple butter. Harvest time use. And the cooking of pork meats. Aunt Sally used the kettle to make soap. I watched her do so any number of times. One time I saw her use a sword to cut the soap into squares. Whose sword did she use? None other than the one captured by Henry Bolanger on the battlefield of Yorktown." *Please Lord, don't take him.* The two nurses entered the room. The supervising nurse decided to telephone the surgeon. The doctor directed her to increase the dosage of the painkiller. Fifteen minutes after the nurse rubbed alcohol on his buttock and pricked him with the needle, Michael slept. In the morning, they sent him down to x-ray. As the technician sat him upright for abdominal X-rays, Michael vomited black bile. The technician had an orderly hold him up while he took the X-rays. Michael later learned that they would have shown a soft-tissue mass and signs of complete obstruction, with dilated loops of bile. His latest WBC was 22,000/mm^3. An hour after the orderly brought him up from x-ray, the doctor stepped into his room with the consent forms for the second surgery. An orderly came into the room and prepared the surgical field by washing the skin and painting it with antiseptic. Several orderlies and nurses lifted Michael from the bed onto the pushcart and wheeled him to the elevator. Music played in the OR. Michael saw the scalpels, clamps, and wads of cotton. A nurse attached electrodes to his chest. The anesthetist told him to count to ten. The bowel resection took five and a half hours to perform. The long wait weighed heavily on his mother and grandfather. Gustave Bolanger had not been at the hospital when the doctors performed the first surgery. He had sat at his piano and played for two hours without making a single mistake, thinking that if he didn't strike a wrong note, through some kind of sympathetic magic the surgeon would not make any mistakes either. The success of Michael's surgery would rest on his shoulders. Sitting in the waiting room, he silently repeated *Ezekiel* 16, verse 6, substituting Michael for thee, as the old practice dictated. Otherwise the charm would not stand effective. And when I passed by Michael and saw Michael polluted in his own blood, I said unto Michael when thou was in thy blood, Live; yea, I said unto Michael when thou was in thy blood, Live.

He awoke in Intensive Care. A nurse stood at his side irrigating his tubes. He lay surrounded by machines. Three drains went into the incision. After the surgery, while he remained unconscious, the physician had inserted a nasogastric tube through his left nostril and down into his digestive tract to decompress the intestine and minimize vomiting. Broad-spectrum antibiotics dripped through his IV. His doctor had catheterized him because of possible urinary retention due to bladder compression by the distended intestine and had ordered him fed by hyperalimentation. He had already lost a great

deal of weight from the first surgery and now suffered from a protein deficit. Any movement he'd make would cause the hyperal to beep, and a nurse would have to adjust the
flow of the lipid-protein solution into his subclavian. He would still lose more weight,
digest more of himself. But hadn't he done that his entire life—each time he stared into a
mirror?

His nurses continued injecting him with Demerol every four hours. Before giving
him the shot, they turned him on his side, had him splint the incision with his free arm,
and asked him to cough. He needed the injection afterwards.

When the nurse changed the bandage for the first time, Michael looked at the incision. They had cut him in half! The six-inch scar now stood thirteen inches long.

After three days they moved him from Intensive Care to the adult ward. Even though
his doctor had inserted a nasogastric tube, Michael still continued to vomit fecal material. The pain became overwhelming. The doctor began administering morphine intra-
venously and within minutes Michael would fall asleep. He'd waken and see different
faces looking down at him: Beth's, Grandmother Sower's, Ben's, Elissa's. She came every
day and often brought flowers. It comforted Michael that she visited him so regularly.
He'd ask to hold her hand and she'd give it to him. She wiped his face when he vomited
and ran the lemon-flavored swab round the corners of his mouth, over his tongue, and
across his dry, cracked lips. Michael stopped throwing up a week after the operation.
The doctor pulled out the drains two days later. However, bowel sounds and peristalsis
did not return for fifteen days. When Michael drank his first thimble of Gatorade two
days after peristalsis resumed, his stomach had shrunken to the size of a quarter. He ate
his first solid food five days later. He also felt a surge of new life awake in his loins, and
for the first time since he had been admitted to the hospital he took his faltering tulip
between his fingers and daydreaming of Elissa kneaded it until he brought himself to a
climax so thunderous he thought he burst his stitches. Thoughts of her helped restore
him to life.

She still visited him regularly. A week before his release, she told him that the next
day she would leave for Charles Town.

She promised to visit him at home. *Don't have a relapse, please. Don't you dare. I'm angry
with you getting this sick over me.*

Maybe, just maybe, she did love him.

Chapter Fifteen
Blue Littorals

Self-absorption became Margaret's refuge. But it stood harder now to fold into her-self. The familiar yet—yes—strange stretch of beach kept her attention, ate into her con-sciousness—constantly drew her out of herself. The white walls of white-roofed houses sparkled down the entire length of tide line as far as the eye could see. The sun stained them a pinkish red as it sank into the ocean. Margaret, half expecting to hear (greatly amplified) the hiss a sparkler makes touching water, looked directly into the face of the sun, shut her eyes and watched bright orange spots dance on the screen of her lids, then opening her eyes blinked and saw the same spots appear on the sky where they would quickly evaporate, then reappear only to dissolve again. She turned her head and looked down the opposite stretch of beach and, still seeing spots and still squinting, made out the lighthouse—a slender white pencil—on the headland's far tip. Her father had taken her there just after she turned eight. She remembered the purple morning glories grow-ing around the lighthouse's base. She shifted her weight to her left side on the rock on which they now sat.

He (her husband) realized that they would actually really go only ten days before they left, five days after their visit to the j.p. when she presented him with the airline tick-ets. She had talked about making the trip, but blew both hot and cold, and said she had so much to do furnishing their new house that they had best postpone a month or two. Then she suddenly decided the hell with the decorating. She wanted to make the trip after all. After arriving in the islands, she continued making snap decisions. He learned only two days before that they would spend the last few days of their honeymoon on Abaco when, as he entered their hotel in Nassau after spending the day on the beach, the clerk informed him that the hotel staff had forwarded his baggage there and his wife had gone on ahead of him. Margaret pointed to the lighthouse. "I want to go there," she said. "Not now," he said, watching her fold her fingers into a fist and press it into her palm, "I feel too tired and too weary." He helped her to her feet, then squeezed her close to him. After a few seconds, he looked over his shoulder and above the shell-gray rocks at the low hills and dunes, his eyes searching for the cottage (shack?) they had rented. Margaret's kept shifting from the pink strand to the turquoise sky dotted with orange spots dancing between, and superimposed upon, towering cumulus shapes. Two mulat-toes returning from a swim eyed them curiously.

As he stood beside her, his thoughts drifted back to Nassau–to the great time he had been having there. He noticed the gaping swimmers. They reminded him again of what the clerk said about the poverty of the island–that it stood doubtful if he could find a glass-bottom boat in operation much less rent scuba equipment there, and he thought again of the scintillating red-white, pink-orange coral he had seen diving in the sinks and canyons off New Providence, of the waving purple sea fans. And the fish! Watching the workings of a whole other universe through his facemask, he had seen so many: fish as blindingly bright colored as the reef itself. At least he had a mask and snorkel here and a rod, reel, and spin tackle. He could still float above the grotto world–watch amber-jacks and yellowtails cruise the reef, and only yesterday he had caught a something hoo. It ended in "hoo." He couldn't recall its full name (but it would come to him shortly) even though he had heard the fishermen on New Providence say it daily and it had only two syllables. But on the sandy beaches he discovered an altogether different kind of aquarium, one which kept his eyes glued. The girls' variegated bikinis outdazzled even the most tropical fish and those finless beauties most certainly did not stand behind glass. Brent smiled wickedly. Sadly this aquarium did not have a counterpart on Abaco. Yes, dammit anyway, he had every right to be angry. Was it because of his girl watching that she came here even if he only looked and didn't touch? Opening his mouth to say something, he saw that she stood preoccupied. He trained his eyes on the lighthouse then, too. But while her eyes remained locked there, his wandered up the beaten stretch of sand until he again caught sight of the mulattoes. Their children still played on the beach but without pails and shovels.

Why, he thought, does she have this constant need for exotic backdrops? Why out of the blue did they come here? He answered himself (he now understood the workings of her mind): she's going to spring something. But how many takes will it take her? Two? Three? Fifty? One hundred? "We'll go there tomorrow," she said, pointing to the light-house. Not bothering to look at him, she turned the corner around the rock and headed inland in the swimmers' wake.

Margaret's current trip stood very different from her last trip. For one thing, she had switched roles. Then Elissa had acted the part of tour guide and she the tourist. Now, playing the Elissa role, Margaret answered the best she could her husband's endless questions. They irritated her the way she now realized hers must have irritated Elissa. She didn't know the answers to many of them. But she had come here twice before, he said. It didn't stand unreasonable that he expected her to know the place. Never mind her two previous trips, she answered. They took place so long ago that she had forgotten every-thing. And, unlike Elissa, she had not read the travel brochures beforehand, so she did not know everything about where they traveled before they got there. But the comparison between her role and Elissa's didn't seem exactly fair. Elissa had many more things to remember in Spain that she did here. Train schedules, hotel reservations, the list went on and on. She only had to book their flight and make one hotel reservation in advance (the staff at the Hamilton made all the necessary arrangements when she decided to spend their last four days in the Bahamas on Greater Abaco instead of in Nassau). At the age of fifteen, she had stayed at the Hamilton during her second trip to the Bahamas while her father and the Mrs. Bromion *in praesenti* honeymooned on Abaco. Business had taken Dirk Bromion there for the first time in 1966 a month or two after Margaret's eighth birthday. A geological survey indicated that large oil deposits lay beneath the ground. Bromion came to sniff out a potential site with his wife and daughter in tow, their entertainment for the trip's two week duration: watching the locals dive from a platform midway up the lighthouse as the tide came in each morning. And although Bromion decided not to drill for oil there, he fell in love with the island. Except for Abaco, he considered the Bahamas one big tourist trap. Upon arriving there, Margaret looked for, and felt reasonably sure that she had found, the cottage he had headquartered himself in 1966. Tomorrow she would again visit the lighthouse.

Apart from the fact that she took charge of this trip, it differed from the previous one in that then she had remained chaste while now she stood anything but. In a small pension in the Pyrenees, the room which she shared with Elissa had only one bed. This proved awkward. Elissa knew about Adrienne, and, while Margaret knew that Elissa wasn't gay or bi (at least she thought she wasn't), she felt tempted to initiate something (a liaison?) because of the way her friend acted: not so much as if she regarded her sexuality as unfixed (she considered herself heterosexual) but as if she remained curious and a little tipsy from the wine she had sipped that evening at least once in her life felt the urge and inclination to experiment. Margaret did not proceed because, one, then she had stood quite determined to stick to her resolve, and, two, she felt that Elissa playacted. Because they shared a bed, conditions stood right for it. Margaret realized that nothing real or lasting would come from it. This trip, however, things stood very real from the day of their arrival. Every day at five, they shut themselves into their hotel room and did the wild thing (as Brent called it) repeatedly, for hours on end. They became very inventive, tried everything once. Only once before had she ever experienced such ecstasy. New Providence truly proved a new Providence. She had wanted to move outdoors but feared someone would spot them. Now that they had come to Greater Abaco, it would remain far less risky. Perhaps tomorrow morning after she had done what she had made up her mind to do at the lighthouse, she would ask him to take a swim with her and—if they could contort their bodies the proper way—and that remained a big if—they could try a position Elissa had once described to her. One taught to her by a certain Jamaican tour guide.

Margaret had to prod him out of bed after she pushed in the button on the alarm clock. "Why on earth did you set it so early for?" he asked after rolling over to check the time: a quarter past five. "Let's go back—" "The tide," Margaret answered. "What?" "The tide. You know, the rising and falling of the surf." "I know all about it. You still haven't told—" "I want to see the divers." And not only that, she thought to herself. "Shit," he said. Rubbing his eyes, he sat up in bed. Already up, Margaret had put on her robe. "How about making some coffee?" The sun rose as they left the cottage, and the luxuriant, fragrant flowers of the night-blooming cereus began drooping as the sky turned a brownish yellow, but the red, pink, and yellow flowers of the hibiscus shrubs lining the path to the beach began unfolding. *In order for something to bloom,* Margaret thought, observing the one flower close and the other open, *another thing must fade. It's the world's it's nature's way.* He sneezed. It amazed her that so much life could crowd itself onto the coast. Glassy-leafed trees had rooted themselves to the tidal flats; bamboo put down shoots everywhere; huge ferns with five-foot stalks rose out of the marshes, and creepers clothed the blasted stones. Everything stood in competition with everything else. Vines strangled trees which crowded out the light. Thinking of her hometown in the low Pennsylvania valley (the barren ridges of which, whenever she recalled them, prompted a desire in her to prolong her trip) and again feeling blue about their incipient departure, she sighed, slipped her arm around her husband's waist and squeezed him slightly. Already she could hear the waves breaking into foam against the shore. They passed the last cottage. Maidenhair fern grew on its walls. A single rubber tree graced the lawn. Gypsy moths couldn't chew through its leaves, she thought. The beach remained deserted except for several fishermen. Everything stood in a haze as the sun rose above the horizon (with all the accompanying atmospheric effects).

It took them twenty minutes to reach the lighthouse. Built a hundred years earlier to warn approaching vessels of the reef, it had been virtually out of operation since the date of its construction as the principal port rested on the other side of the island. Only when a storm blew up and there stood a chance that a ship might drift off course did someone bother to snap a circuit breaker. From the observation deck eighty feet above the ground, one had a bird's-eye view of the island. The wooden platform from which the islanders dove girdled the tower's waist, forty feet below the observation deck, forty feet above the morning-glory-bedecked base. After climbing halfway up the spiral staircase, the diver pulled himself onto the scaffold through a window on the side of the lighthouse facing away from the ocean. Below him rocks reared and there rose no rail to block his fall. Not looking down, moving either to his right or left and keeping both hands on the lighthouse for support, the diver slowly moved to the other side. There, straightening his shoulders and standing erect, he took three to four steps forward, bent his knees and locked his toes around the platform's edge, then pushed off, either tucking into a somersault or launching into a swan dive but invariably hitting the water seven to eight seconds later. Only one diver stood on the platform when Margaret and her husband reached the lighthouse. They watched him plunge into the waves. "Is that all?" her husband asked. Margaret shook her head. "No, we're—correction—I'm going to jump from that platform." He raised a pencil-line eyebrow. "You show more spunk now that you're married to me." He paused a second. "Let's go."

She had made a similar statement to her father in 1966. The tide had already ebbed when she said it. She remembered that no one dove at that time, that the lighthouse stood deserted. Why she and her father had gone there and why her mother had not accompanied them, she did not remember. Had her mother stood by their side, her father never would have done it. Had he been drinking that day? She could not recall. At any rate, something inside him snapped. "So you want to jump from there. The girl who takes a half hour to decide whether or not she wants to jump into the pool back home, who has to stick her big toe in the water first because she's frightened that it will remain too cold for her—she's so delicate. She can swim better than any of the other boys and girls but no one would know it because she remains standing on the deck when they've already swum for fifteen goddamned minutes. Yes you'll jump. I'll help you." She remembered that he had taken her inside the lighthouse and that she had screamed over and over again that she hadn't meant what she said. She didn't remember when they turned back, only that they did. Probably they hadn't even started up the stairs, and after Adrienne's death she once had a dream in which she committed suicide by leaping from a lighthouse during low tide. She awoke to find out that her life had not come to an abrupt and irreversible conclusion.

But now, before Margaret knew it, they had crept out the window and stood on the platform. *A breeze buffets her warm, wet forehead and whips her shirtsleeves.* She looks down, shudders and can't move. Her foot must be sure. Each step she takes challenges fate. He eggs her on, tells her to stop looking down, and somehow she makes it to the other side. The hard part's over she tells herself. Her back to the lighthouse, she looks down at her feet, then at the water below. "I can't do it," she says. "You've got to." "No I—" "Sure you can." She looks at him. He smiles. His chin becomes broader at its nether point. "It's easy." He takes two steps forward. She says no, but it's too late. He has already sprung off the platform into a perfect gainer, and she stands there alone. His head pops up from beneath the waves, and she can hear him call to her to follow him. Jump, he says. Jump. She steels herself, takes a step forward, but even if she does jump, even if she can force herself to do it, it would not stand the same. She had to jump first. He had done what she should have done, done it for her, in her place. She steps forward again. No, it would not be the same. He had taken one more thing away from her.

Chapter Sixteen
Of Lines Both Parallel and Skew

He had come home three weeks ago. After he had lain on his back for fifty days, it stood intolerable to him that his recuperation confined him to his bedroom and to the living room and dining room of his mother's house. After his release from the hospital, Salmos once snuck him out to see a movie. His mother awaited them when they exited the theater. She had pressured his sister into telling her where they had gone. She made a scene, and Michael got into her car as quickly as possible.

He weighed forty-two pounds less than when he went into the hospital. Despite the IVs the doctor had administered and the hyperal which pumped a lipid-protein solution into his subclavian, he had digested that much of himself. Each morning when his mother changed his bandage, he looked at the thirteen-inch long purple-pink exclamation mark running across his belly, the dot marking where his surgeon had inserted the largest of the three drains into his side. He always turned his head away after a few seconds. Had they even bothered to make sure the two sides lay flush when they stapled the incision shut? He didn't think so. A finger could fit snugly inside that crevice.

He remained in bed, on average, fourteen to sixteen hours each day. Never before in his life had he slept for such long intervals or so deeply as he did now. Because of his inactivity, the muscles in his back, neck, arms and legs or what had remained of those muscles knotted every day and his incision smarted and throbbed constantly. Some days he doubled his prescribed dosage of Tylox on account of it. Two days after arriving in Cannoshockton, he threw a plate of food at the living room wall. He lay on the sofa under an afghan knitted by his Grandmother Sower and stared at television. He lifted his fork, took a bite. It tasted all right, but he had no inclination to eat, saw bile forcing its way back up the digestive tract and out his mouth. His hand shook. He didn't want food. He needed an injection. He flung the tray into the air. The plate smashed into two pieces. Food smeared on the wall, and dropped onto the carpet. He started crying and continued for at least a half hour. He felt that rattled. No, Tylox did not put him at ease the way Demerol or morphine could.

It took him two weeks to build up enough strength in order to walk around the Outer Circle. He worked up to it, each day lengthening the distance he walked. He determined to push himself. He felt he needed to hatch out of his present confinement, and despite his mother's injunction not to overtax and exhaust himself, strive to work his body back into shape. He would double, triple the distance he usually walked, climb up the hill behind Hedgewood Village. What he could have accomplished easily two months ago would overwhelm him now. His mother would disapprove, say that he tried to do too much too soon. He would cross the trailer court behind Hedgewood, take a path cutting through the farmer's meadow to a dirt road that led to the top of the hill. He would attempt this before his mother returned home from work. Only his sister knew. He promised his mother that if he went outside, at most he'd walk round the outer and inner circles of Hedgewood Village. He put a sandwich in his coat pocket before stepping out the door.

He had even tried to do some writing. He did not push himself too hard. Having crossed through the former cornfields, he could see the woods and hill ahead of him. He frequently sat down, as he often felt winded. He had managed to begin, had managed to do the hardest thing, and he stood pleased, genuinely pleased with what he had done. But carrying through became increasingly difficult. TM characterized the process correctly when he called it a descent into hell in the prelude to the quadripartite work, the beautiful god invention of Joseph and His Brothers. What intellection. What massive erudition. And the ultimate humanism of his cosmogony, a soul light man creating the universe; god—albeit a sympathetic, understanding god—only helping, Mann's explanation wise and winsome of how the mythic past merges with a prophetic future to form an eternal present. A feast of life and death in which two conflicting principles, those of the Spirit and the Soul, so contend with each other that it remained inconclusive which principle stood as the death principle. But calling Adam Qadmon's creation of earth a descent into hell, calling his own god invention the same thing, meaning both a descent into the subconscious, the collective unconscious—and the struggle with stubborn, refractory matter—the form becoming more important than the idea—there TM came across an eternal truth. Would Tom Englehardt make the sacrifice? Down, down into the depths, he'd go. He saw it as his duty. If it be possible, Father, do not let this cup pass from me. TM said that his artist's sensibility resulted from the exotic mixture of his blood. No Portuguese—South American Indian blood coursed through his veins, but a little North American Sioux did, and, with a name like Englehardt, a lot of German burgher blood ran in him too. Maybe even some of the same blood. Then the two of them would have something more in common than just their first names. Perhaps future, past, and present could fuse together in a single moment of time. A name stands all important. Tommy M. said so in the god invention, where the Egyptian kings all took the name Amun-is-satisfied and all stood as sons of the son and rulers of the earth.

He reached the woods, and oaks, maples, and elms surrounded him. Ahead he could see the barbed wire fence that marked the beginning of the farmer's property and beyond it the dirt road that led to the top of the hill. Minus the u, he had the same name as his great-great-great-great-great-great-grandfather: *Michael*. He reached the fence, lifted up the lowest rung of the barbed wire in order to crawl under it, and cut the third finger of his right hand on a barb. Immediately, as hard as he could he pressed the bleeding finger into his palm.

Direct pressure. Use direct pressure.

He had bled too much already. Must stop it. Got to. Everything depends on stopping it . . . still bleeding? He let go of the finger. Still bleeding. Press harder. Harder. Still not stopping . . . . Taking the sandwich from his coat pocket, he rolled a bread slice around his finger, ringing the fingers of his other hand around the bread slice. The bleeding stopped.

You're an idiot, he thought. A fool. He tossed what remained of the bread into the dirt. Body and Blood of Our Lord, he thought. But no hundred-handed or one-eyed monsters sprang up from it, but then again the blood had not come from his genitals. No one had snipped off his genitals and thrown them into the sea, nor did a starry-eyed Phallus Goddess arise from the waves. Disregarding the no-trespassing sign, he crawled under the fence and began to walk up the dirt road. Ten minutes later, he sat down in the shade, hyperventilating. Needles churned into the muscles in his arms. For a quarter of a mile, he had supported his weight on a stick that he had picked up from off the ground. He didn't have the strength to reach the top. Like a hand thrust in and out of a pocket, the sun came out from underneath then darted behind a cloud. The atmosphere completely altered. He wished the sun would reappear. 'Metheus embark on thy sacred journey. Bring us, thy subjects, fire. The hill itself didn't seem especially pleasing to look at now. Sunlight made all the difference in the world. It made the hill beautiful and attractive; it made all things captivating. Cruel deceptive sun! Deceptive lying sun! But without its magic life-giving light, nothing could be beautiful, nothing at all. Nothing could be born. Nothing could die. Without the daily golden shower of the sun's rays (Ancrisius shut Danae up in a brazen underground chamber, but Zeus came to her in the form of a shower of gold and lay with her) no plant could sprout out of the earth, nor any animal rise from out of the sea. Cold perpetual night. Sunlight! Sunlight! Needed, necessary for life: $6CO_2 + 12H_2O + light \xrightarrow{c-h-l-o-r-o-p-h-y-l-l} 6O_2 + C_6H_{12}O_6 + 6H_2O$. And did not the sun, out of itself, give birth to the planets?

He rested his head on the trunk of the tree. A particolored Kaleidocoat?

"No," he said out loud.

He stood just like all the others.

They all resembled one another.

Green, green, green. They reflected him as much as he reflected them, Elissa, Margaret, Ben, Brent, John, Roger, Brad, Freddie Fregno, and Andy Raoul: nine definitions for the color green. He supplied a tenth.

He felt sure that he would find it difficult to stand up, so he didn't try—he just sat under the tree and waited for his body to shift into a higher gear of its own volition. For many minutes, he did not attempt to rise. Someone had cleared this land the previous spring but had not planted any crops in it. Already nature had begun to reclaim it. Timothy, ragweed and Queen Anne's lace again abundantly grew here. The final half-mile to the hill's top would tax Michael greatly. He felt so weak that he didn't even raise his head to look at the microwave dish on the hilltop. He just continued to gaze ahead of him.

In Elissa, he had thought he had found the perfect mirror in which to view himself—someone the same shade of green as he. Another self. One he could touch, embrace, and hold in his arms. Why should he go on living if he couldn't possess even that? Just that. Of all the molecules in the universe, why couldn't he lay claim to hers as partial recompense for all that he would give back, the great books he would write? He felt a stab in his side once again.

Despite the sharp, shooting pain, his life impulse did not extinguish. Indeed it remained quite strong. He could still enjoy this simultaneous feast of life and death. One by one he saw the faces of all his friends. Like him, they all stood beginning players in this game—even his seventy-seven-year-old grandfather. Looking into their faces, he saw his own. He saw himself in the leaves of the trees, in the drake swooping down on the duck, in the owl swallowing the squirrel. Eating, sleeping, mating, defending, and seeking shelter—that's all nature, everything living in the universe—himselves—ever did. All variation stood built on *that*. Any other face would have reflected his as well. Even Margaret's. The coarser Brent and Margaret succeed whereas the much more cultivated Elissa and the equally fine-grained Michael—despite his swaggering peacock manner—fail.

Once more the sun brightened. He opened his eyes. He had almost fallen asleep. M M M.

Michael mirrors Margaret.

Now about that name. Margaret—Latin, "a pearl." Dante called the moon the great Margherita. It became the name of a flower when Saint Margherita of Italy took the humble daisy as her symbol, which the French named the *marguerite*, the English "may-weed." Goethe made Gretchen the beloved name of Germany, and in England it became Meta, Margery, Margo, Peggy, Greta, and—yes—Daisy (who, in the U.S., rode a bicycle built for two). A diminutive for Candace as well, Daisy meant "the day's eye" in Anglo Saxon.

He wiped his forehead on his coat sleeve. The son of the sun naturally took the name Amun, so it made perfect sense that her name meant the moon. But it also denoted sun. So whose light reflected whose?

Michael struggled to stand and slowly pulled himself to his feet. He supported himself on the stick. He kept moving. He dared not stop now that he had his second wind. The stick made things easier. He fixed his eyes on the microwave dish. He wouldn't stop until he reached it.

Yes, he would always remain a little distance ahead of her, and he would never run with reverted face. Let her try to catch up. He would put on the next new body before she relinquished hers. He would keep on going in as she went out.

She'd never again meet that boy.

Chapter Seventeen

Delone Frailey: reprise

Mr. Delone Frailey of Villa Nova heard Bob Dylan's "Clean Cut Kid" from the just released album *Empire Burlesque* on his newly installed Kenwood car stereo while cruising the back roads between Herneshopple and his hometown in his '78 four-door beige Catalina. It started raining as he drove home from the annual sales and coverage seminar in Herneshopple.

He had grown up as a clean-cut kid. Ask his teachers, his neighbors, the ministers he knew as a boy. And he stayed clean-cut and respectable—despite Uncle Sam sending him to the napalm health spa—as Dylan so sarcastically put it—to shape up.

He could have sold insurance for the rest of his life.

He did fucking sell it. Did they—the public, that is—really expect every vet's mind to short circuit because of delayed stress? For each and everyone of them to up and take

A dive one day off the Golden Gate Bridge into China Bay.

Delone didn't like the song—just another clichéd depiction of the crazed Vietnam vet. But Dylan had found Jesus. The rock star reached a turning point in life, a fork in the road. Accepting the Lord as his Saviour, he entered the fold. He could preach the good news and proclaim himself saved. God would forgive all his sins and no longer hold Todd Pettiman's death against him.

But Delone had exorcised all his personal demons. He had put the war behind him. It didn't have that kind of power over him—not still. He had passed through the maelstrom to the other side and had survived. "I'm over it," he said out loud. He made this definitive pronouncement, as he watched his wipers slice through the rain splashing down on the windshield. He "rolled" the hill. The car flew up the yellow line and around the curve. He sped up to seventy on the open stretch of forested road, braking to sixty-five as he swung into the next turn, then, around it, again floored the accelerator. A few minutes ago, he listened to Stravinsky's *Firebird* on WQED, but another station began to bleed through. He twirled the tuning knob and heard Dylan's drawn-out nasal sneer. He stopped fiddling with the dial, but, before Dylan finished, vintage 1985 ghettoblasterbreakdancesoulfunk announced (spliffsplaffsplunked) its ascendancy over the PA airwaves, bomp-bomp-bomp, and drowned out Dylan's voice. Strains of Stravinsky once more began to pierce, seep, and for a moment gloriously thunder through but they faded and he again heard nothing but the bomp-bomp-bomp. Disgusted with hair-line tuning and the option of choices, Frailey switched the radio off and popped a Lauritz

Melchior tape that he had made into the Kenwood. The farther away he drove from Herneshopple the poorer the reception for the PBS affiliate became, and the local power rock stations didn't play anything that he wouldn't immediately want to switch off, nothing but current Jiggerboo music or vintage acid rock, those same sixties and seventies songs that bomp-bomp-bomped in the jungle and made it hop and boogie.

He spent several nights in the same tent with a Jig who later spent time as a POW. Corporal Harbaugh (but Chicken or Lips to his friends) had a wife in D.C., the sister of a sergeant who graduated from Theodore Roosevelt High School four years before Chicken did and spent his first tour of duty in Nam in '64 building airstrips, then reupped as a chopper pilot. Dwight stepped on a booby trap. Chicken said that Uncle Sam called up twenty-two young graduates of Theodore Roosevelt High, all inner city kids—Uncle Sam's sambos, Chicken said derisively, Whitey's cannon fodder—who up to then had lived their entire lives in the concrete canyons—he started humming Elvis Presley's *In The Ghetto*—only rarely getting the chance to glimpse the rolling green hills beyond the city. The day he and Delone met, Chicken—"Kentucky fried" as usual—wanted to do some serious killing and maiming and to make those gooks pay for Dwight but also for a more recent debt: Leroy, Earl, and the Roach.

Delone could not find his location on the map. He should have reached the village by now. Separated from his platoon, he had fended for himself for over a week. A LURP had his dog. But Delone wandered all alone. He looked through his binoculars. Completely out of place, if anything stood out of place in these jungles (he swore that once he saw an angel—downy wings, white robes, piercing blue eyes and golden hair—suddenly materialize on an LZ and smile at him; other grunts he knew claimed to see flying saucers zoom off into the night), a Saigon Midas (Delone later found out—what he saw: someone out here in the mud wearing an expensive linen big city suit) emerge out of the brush and into the clearing. Through the glasses, Delone saw the old man run his fingers through his short white hair. His face had the smug and contented look of the well-fed and happy-idle coupled with the arrogance and the superiority of an especially well-heeled banker. He walked whistling song snippets and, oblivious to his surroundings, displayed total nonchalance, as if he believed himself bulletproof. The businessman stopped, then flung his hands in the air. He made a loud cry, a look of happy befuddlement on his face, and began waving his short-fingered hands. He shouted the boy's name a second time as if his life depended on it. The girl with the basket stepped from behind the trees, stopping on a dime when she saw him. The boy smiled at the man as if his days revolved around chance encounters of precisely this kind. The man again raised his arms and shook his head in disbelief, as if in his wildest dreams he couldn't have foreseen this, and then both children started toward him. Walking across the clearing, the boy reached him first. A huge sigh escaped from the man's lips. The girl raised her hand, and Delone glimpsed the pistol. She put three slugs into Moneybags. Immediately bullets whirred to her right and over her shoulder. Four black G.I.s sprang into the clearing. One blew her chest open with a 357 magnum—sent from back home with affection from one of "the chicken's" home boys, a T.R. graduate lucky enough to win a basketball scholarship to

Temple. Crouching behind the dead man, the boy pulled the pin from a grenade. From his position in the tree line thirty yards away, Frailey aimed and fired. The boy heaved the grenade as Delone's bullet pierced his chest. Before the explosion lifted him off his feet and threw him backward, one of the blacks opened fire with his 16 and spun in Frailey's direction. Dumb fucking cherry boy, Frailey thought, flinging himself on the ground. He looked up after the blast. He expected to see only dead bodies but he heard shrieks and moans, piteous and heart-rending. What he saw through the glasses caused Delone Frailey to throw up. Three men lay crumpled on the ground. Only one screamed. He thrashed from side to side and shouted, "Kill me Chicken. Shoot me now." During this latest patrol Delone had seen the worst action of his tour. The fucking second lieutenant. He'd frag him himself for sending them out to play army when he knew things were this hot. The men had separated during the ambush. Delone had managed to cross the river. Hiding in the reeds, he saw three of his buddies machine-gunned by the enemy. He stayed put for hours before venturing from his hiding place. He spent the last several days walking in circles, lost. He watched the black come out of the bush and kneel down by his wounded pal. The latter stopped shouting, and a minute or so later, Chicken closed the man's lids with the palm of his hand and began wailing like a child. Relieved, Frailey shouted, "American. On your right." Chicken immediately dropped to the ground. Frailey had to show himself first. When he saw it was a pink boy, Chicken sprang up. Once again Chicken glanced down at the mangled bodies of Leroy, Earl, and the Roach. Once again he started bawling and blubbering. Frailey said they had best beat feet. Only after they had some distance between them and the six corpses, did Chicken open up: "They send a motha-fuckin' brain-dead old dink like that up here and order us to watch him and help him…." He coughed. Suddenly it dawned on him. Delone could see the light bulb come on above his head. "They set him up. They fuckin' set him up. He lost his gran'childrens four years ago then all a sudden they sighted way up here? Damn glad Earl made him walk point through that thicket" "Nothing here makes any sense," Delone said, glad that he had found another G.I. and no longer would have to make his way through the jungle alone. Chicken said that the village stood but a short distance away but that they had seen no Americans or ARVNS or other gooks V.C. or friendly in the vicinity until the old man spotted the two kids. The dumb fuck had thought all the children they came across during the last two weeks were his. It stood the same goddamn story in every village they visited.

Frailey took the hairpin and elbow curves at sixty-five. He had lived in Villa Nova all his life and had memorized every twist and turn of the road–knew how to take each curve. He listened to Melchior sing *Nothung! Nothung! Neidliches Schwert!* Wagner did not write his roles for the run-of-the-mill tenor. The work of the future demanded more. Frailey could not detect the least sign of weakness in Melchior's voice. Moreover Melchior performed live. Frailey listened to an old Metropolitan opera radio broadcast from the golden age of American Wagnerian performances in the 1930s and 1940s. The current crop of Siegfrieds recorded in the studio, where they could stop after every few bars and rest their vocal cords. Their artificially contrived recordings sounded much more impressive than any of their live performances. Melchior's voice, however, never gave out. A golden intonation! A legato of such consistency! Delone felt like a medium summoning up the dead whenever he popped a cassette featuring opera singers from the 30s and 40s into the player. The words of the Dylan song, however, still continued to haunt and upset him.

They took a clean cut kid and made a killer out of him that's what they did.

He didn't need to take a swim in China Bay. The local YMCA would suffice. He swam thirty-five laps with Mrs. F. during his lunch hours weekdays from twelve to one and along with Delone Jr. they attended the "water babies" class on Tuesday nights. All the infants including young Delone seemed to take to the water without any difficulty or problem. But maybe he should start lifting, make an all-out effort to take off some of that artistic fat. He did not sell the most new policies in North-Central Pennsylvania this year and thus did not receive the company award at the sales and coverage seminar in Herneshopple. That happened only once, the year the Volkswagen plant opened in '81. But he did all right. His money market certificates earned over twelve percent.

Yesterday the company presented the award to–no surprise–the Herneshopple agent Emily Selden. She had opened up some new territory, and had sold a few liability insurance policies in neighboring municipalities, but she made her money the same way her predecessor Bill Umbower did: because of her Herneshopple location. Each year new businesses opened in the college town and new construction projects took place on campus as well as in the downtown Herneshopple business district, hotels, convention centers, high-rise apartments. Every few years they added on a thousand more seats to the football stadium. Herneshopple experienced a perpetual boom, the only community in Rallings County so lucky. The Herneshopple agent usually always stood first in sales. Bill had retired only a year before. Emily Selden had bought him out. She had taught grade school but resigned. Scuttlebutt had it she could not maintain discipline in the classroom, that some boy placed her ukulele on her chair, and not noticing that the kid had done so, the badly overweight woman sat down on it, smashing it to smithereens and badly splintering her hind end. She must weigh over three hundred pounds, Delone thought. She looked as fat as his Italian grandmother, Mama Catalano, who despite her Catholic prejudices attended Episcopalian church services with Delone as a boy, as her daughter had converted when she wed Delone's father. Mama had been a very practical woman. She told the girl that the Lord would understand, that State Senator Frailey stood too good of a catch to forego because of religious differences. Delone's dad remained a stalwart and fierce Episcopalian. After her daughter died giving birth to Delone (whom they named after Mama's father), she did not regret or feel penitent about her advice to Mary. Her God remained a loving God. She did not believe that He struck Mary down in punishment for leaving the one true church, especially as she had not done so in her heart of hearts but for form's sake only to please her husband. After all the Bible said wives should submit and obey. Yes, Delone's grandmother practically raised him as a child as his father spent most of his time in Harrisburg. She took her ward to his dad's church each and every Sunday. Kids today don't know how to behave.

If he had played such a trick on Miss Nisewonger, she would have reddened his behind with a belt as would have Mama when he got home. Speaking of splinters. As a child whenever Delone got one, Mama always took a sewing needle from her kit, held it over the flame, and sterilized it. He remembered at a very young age he once became so scared that he ran outside and climbed to the top of an apple tree. She said it wouldn't hurt and pleaded for him to climb back down. Now. This second. But Davey Abrams said. She didn't care what Davey said. He cried and screamed that he did not want his blood to become infected. Something else, young man, your fanny, will become infected if you don't come down this minute. Both Emily and his grandmother had the builds, the looks, of circa 1940 beer-barrel Brünnhildes, and they both wore the same staid dresses. Wagner envisioned his heroines as paragons of beauty but usually the sopranos who sang the roles hardly ever looked the parts, the more beautiful and lush the voice, the heavier the singer. But fat girls needed loving too. It made one laugh to think of some fat boy heldentenor like Melchior trying to mount one of his equally massive and rotund Isoldes. They certainly did not look like the idealized lovers in the drawings. Why the slats of the bed would break. Despite their weight, neither his grandmother nor Miss Emily Seldon had especially attractive or powerful singing voices. Not all fat ladies could sing. Emily smoked and sounded raspy and hoarse. Whose voice could he draw it from the compact disc or the Shamrock or Memorex reel-to-reel tape would he transfer into Emily Seldon's throat? Which ghost's spectral voice singing? Flagstad's? Traubel's? Nilsson's? Gertrude Grob-Prandl's? Helen Traubel's, Delone concluded. She remained his favorite Wagnerian soprano. She had her critics, including Irving Kolodin, who wrote that despite her many great strengths as a singer her performances would remain forever flawed because of the notes missing from her upper register. She did not sing her high Cs and B-flats. He wanted to write to the Metropolitan Opera Guild and urge them to release more historic broadcasts, especially those of Traubel and Melchior, but he feared that he might write so sloppily that they might regard him as a red-neck hick, a Penciltawky (Pennsyltucky?) hickerbilly. If only he could run into that young writer Michael. He never did send him that essay. Pierced by Dorn's thorn, he looked so pale the night he encountered him on the street and they went to the bar after hours. Probably graduated and long gone by now. It did not surprise Delone that night when he barked that he and Elissa had parted ways. He said plenty of fish swam in the sea or something to that effect and went on to speak, if Delone recalled correctly, about *Tristan* and *Parsifal*. Funny that he brought up those two operas, for that night Delone felt that Michael resembled both the suffering Tristan of Act Three of *Tristan und Isolde* and the equally tormented Amfortas of *Parsifal*, who wounded by the spear that pierced Christ's side by Klingsor the sorcerer while the witch Kundry held him in her arms, thereafter suffered from an incurable bleeding gash in his side. Delone saw that the boy tried to put on a brave front but felt that he had received a wound as painful and devastating as his friend Dorn. Michael said that he was over and done with Elissa and quickly changed the subject, but the boy, so it at least seemed to Frailey, protested too much. Just like Dorn, he would have opened his arms wide for Elissa if she would have returned to his side as Isolde came running back to the dying Tristan. But didn't Delone recently read that in an interesting new production, the director staged Isolde's arrival as only the fantasy of the dying Tristan? In reality, she did not come back to try to cure him. *Mein Irisch Kind wo weilest du?*

Delone remembered that night he explained to Michael that Wagner's spiritual and sensual sides often came in conflict and how the German struggled to align his Pagan and Judeo-Christian impulses in order to find a solution to his impasse so that he once more could stand whole and unified. Wagner expressed the division and bifurcation of his soul in the mighty prelude to his opera *Tannhäuser*; each of his two opposing personalities, the dual sides of man's nature, had its own music. They played as if in opposition yet at the same time counterpointed and balanced each other beautifully. The ear "tunes in" one of the two opposing motifs: either the Venusberg music (the sensual) or that of the pilgrims' train (the pious and profound). Whichever one the ear fixes on drowns out and overwhelms the other. Both forces whirled continuously inside Wagner as they did inside Delone Frailey. One power might master him, compel him to satisfy certain appetites and push him in a certain direction only for the other to yank him back, for the two forces contested continually within his breast, and, one moment, one force would have the upper hand, and the next the other would suddenly gain the ascendancy. But the division remained a false one. Frailey remembered reading in one of his many liner notes that Wagner said, "I often turn my eyes toward the land Nirvana. Yet Nirvana always becomes *Tristan* again." Wagner knew about the Buddhist theory concerning the origin of the world, that the merest breath troubles the heavenly clarity, yet he understood that God made us all *Sturm und Drang* creatures and that He made us in His own image. The Pope might not forgive Tannhäuser, but Tannhäuser's staff shoots forth green buds. God pardons his affiliation with Venus. His *amour* is understood. Another Faust, Michael commented and smiled. Yes, Frailey thought, as he coasted around the curve by the new economic development center and rolled down the hill into town, the Volkswagen plant for a few minutes coming into view on his right side then again nothing but open fields and woods, both Tannhäuser and Bob Dylan can celebrate human nature and lust yet still proclaim themselves saved. Our sexual and creative drives come directly from God: his greatest gift. On both sides of the road mountain laurel and rhododendrons bloomed. The new Dylan song still irked the hell out of him. Its damn words continued repeating themselves in his head.

He had a steady job, he joined the choir, he never did plan to walk the high wire. They took the trail back into the jungle. Without backup, Delone felt they should not enter the village. They made shift for three days and pitched Chicken's canvas tent in a suitably camouflaged spot. Delone had lost his beeper over a week ago. Chicken and the dead Jigs carried neither beepers nor radio so their only chance of rescue stood if they ran into an American patrol or an ARVN unit in the area. By the third day, they had drained the water in their canteens. Despite Delone's protests, Chicken headed back to the village. I know what they call me, he said, but I'm not yellow. In the clearing where the bodies of Leroy, Earl, and Roach lay, he saw two green berets beating and thumping the holy hell out of a dink. The slope lay on the ground, his hands tied behind his back. The two men kicked him again and again in the ribs. "He's V.C.," the captain explained after Chicken saluted. "We found sharpened punji sticks in the village. Except for his ass it stood completely empty. Charlie's moved on." Chicken told the two berets about Delone then stared down at the V.C. The small-boned man looked thin and malnourished. The green berets had ripped the shirt from his back. He wore black pajama bottoms. "Army intelligence in Bien Hoa wants to question him," the captain said, "but we thought we'd have our fun first. Get your buddy. We'll be coptering our asses out of here pronto." As the one man resumed roughing up the prisoner and the other radioed for transport, Chicken ran back for Delone.

Reaching the clearing, they heard the whir of the bird's blades as it came down through the trees. The green berets pushed the V.C. through the hatch first, then pulled themselves in. Then Delone and Chicken also climbed aboard. They rose up above the trees, river, and swamp. Looking down after taking off his helmet to sit on it, Delone was glad to see the jungle recede behind them. He had his ticket out of there. The V.C. managed to free his hands. He lunged at Chicken. "Try to shove me out. You're the one without the chute," Chicken said, and out the dink went, head over heels and down.

Chapter Eighteen
The Rewards of Continence

I

Ted Muntz looked at John Salmos.

"Just who were those guys Mike spoke about?"

"Old hippies," Salmos said, referring to Blue Dew, Bones Reddle, and Wayne P. Hedgepeth. "Reddle ODed." *Back then I wore my hair below my shoulders and had just fallen in love with Eileen Rugby.* Ted Muntz had started to hang out with John a couple of months ago and had only just met Michael. Salmos robbed the cradle for friends. His sidekick had just turned sixteen. Salmos could have been his father

Almost. Who did I date at fourteen? Corinne. If I had knocked her up the kid would be twelve or thirteen now.

In September 1983, Michael Bolanger received two volumes of Elissa's voluminous diary. Both volumes had black bindings. They contained sketches and poems as well as her diary entries. One volume covered the years 1973-74, the other 1981. The package bore the Charles Town postmark. *Wish Fulfillment No. 1.*

The Continental Trailways Scenicruiser always arrived late. It stopped at every flyspeck, butt-fuck-Egypt town between Herneshopple and Cannoshockton. After twenty minutes, Michael grew tired of waiting; after thirty, the bus finally pulled into the depot. Michael watched the people file out of it from inside the station. Cantwell stood last in line.

"I think that aerobics instructor," Salmos said, "will do him a lot of good. I try to turn Freddie Fregno onto a girl, but he just blows every opportunity that comes his way and refuses to take advantage of an opening. But Michael—it didn't take him long to get over on Debbie after I introduced them. He's my buddy. I like seeing him, and she'll attract him to town, I hope."

"But you're not sure?" Muntz interjected.

Salmos shook his head. "With Michael, one never knows."

August 20, 1973

The developer wouldn't even send back the negatives. The one photograph I got didn't show my breasts. Just my head and hair. I set the timer and took half-a-dozen shots of myself. I opened the last tube

of Body Paint for Lovers Wayne gave me and smeared green, red, and
yellow streaks on my stomach, legs, and thighs . . . .

Cantwell threw his suitcase onto the back seat, slammed the door shut, and buckled
his belt. Michael pulled out of the lot. Tonight at the high school field, the Cannoshockton Cougars took on the Herneshopple Highlanders. The game would start in
twenty minutes, so they'd have to hurry. As Michael suspected, the high school parking
lot stood filled to capacity, so he parked on a side street nearby, and they walked back
to the playing field just as the parking lot lights turned on. "How much do you want to
wager?" Michael queried. Cantwell had made this trip expressly to see their alma maters
face off.

Salmos stepped into, then out of, Coney Island. Ted Muntz waited outside the bar,
his back against the wall. Salmos and he crossed Philadelphia Street. Traffic remained
unusually heavy. They turned down the first alley, and Salmos handed him a beer from
under his jacket.

"Any action?" Muntz asked.

"I've told you, shithead, a bar's the worst possible place in the world to meet women.
You'll have better luck in a grocery store or even out here on the street. Just smile and act
natural. Eventually one'll bite. Even if she's ugly, she'll have friends—sisters. You've just
got to invest a little time. That's all there is to it. Like they say every night on the lottery.
If you don't play, you can't win"

December 1, 1973

My parents wouldn't give Wayne a chance. We took up their
invitation to stay at the farm over Thanksgiving, but their attitude to
him from the time we got there remained stiff, unnatural, and cold. I
confessed to mother, so I guess it's my fault—confessed it to her in the
same sisterly spirit that I've told her everything else of importance that's
ever happened to me. She must have told Daddy. He didn't care much
for the counter culture child who broke his little girl's hymen. From the
moment we got there, he seemed a storm just on the verge of breaking.

Aunt Sara made her oyster stuffing for the turkey just like any other
year. Mother arranged her dishes artfully on the table. As we sat down,
two worlds came together in violent collision.

"Ah, Bernie don't blow it," Michael said. "He's so predictable. They should have
promoted J.J. to head coach twenty years ago." "Retire O' Fallon," he shouted then once
again turned to Cantwell. "He won't let his quarterback pass. He loses for the same
reason every year."

Cantwell watched the Herneshopple cheerleaders perform their routine. Their orange megaphones thrust outwards, they howled and whooped rowdily.

John's chin rose above the bar for the twenty-first time. He wanted to do four more,
but couldn't, so he dropped to his feet. Running the rest of the paracourse would remain

exercise enough. Muntz did a few more sit-ups but got up when he saw that Salmos stood ready to run. He always had trouble keeping up with him.

John looked at his watch. He would still have time to shave and shower before meeting Michael at the bar (Coney again) at nine.

July 2, 1973

The four of us had a great time today. Cathy and Blue Dew, and Wayne and I. We did everything from making breakfast and pulling onions in the garden, to trimming Wayne's and Blue Dew's beards to sitting in the living room listening to music and twisting up a spliff or two and just chatting with one another.

Cathy impresses me as a woman who's really got her act together. She chose someone young, hard working, and smart. Dew's got great charm and beauty and a most winning style (especially with that British accent). He has soft, fawnlike features.

Michael pulled in a Hedgewood Village driveway then turned off the headlights. "I'm dropping you off at a friend's for the night. Listen, it's so I can see Debra. Mom doesn't know I'm in town yet, and I'll get a heck of a lot more satisfaction out of this trip, guaranteed. So don't protest or give me any grief. Anyway you'll like the Fregnos."

Cantwell watched him hop onto the porch. He didn't even bother to knock. He just walked in and shut the door behind him. A few minutes later, he and a tall, spindly person Cantwell had never met came out. They walked up to the car window. "Fred said you could bunk in his basement tonight."

You bastard, Cantwell thought.

"Get out," Michael ordered. "Now," said Fred (*fils*).

Sipping beer from a mug and watching an old oater on the tube, Fregno (*père*) reclined in his Lazyboy in the rec room, his slippered feet crossed on the chair's footrest. Several Blatz longnecks sat empty on the stand beside him, dead soldiers Michael said. Mrs. Fregno had gone to bed early as usual. Michael called her an angel and told Cantwell that she mothered and took care of the entire Fregno clan, family and boarders. Having quarreled with John Salmos over his treatment of Fred's sister Susan, Andy Raoul now rented one of the extra rooms upstairs. Michael said that he knew these people all his life. When Freddy and Michael were boys, Mr. Fregno would have poker parties every weekend. Michael tasted alcohol for the first time at one of those card games. Then Freddie liked two things: building models and playing army, but he always had to fight on the American side. Once Freddie blew pins with aluminum foil wrapped around the heads through a soda straw at his older sister Susan and her friend, Michael's former babysitter, Marcella Waters while they sat watching T.V. in the basement. They had an old black and white at the time. Freddie stuck his head out under the wood banister, his feet braced on the wooden steps, and blew on the straw. Another time Susan chased him down those same steps with a baseball bat when he shot her with his pellet gun. Fred always raced down the stairs, taking two or three at a time. Michael went slower, clutching the handrail tightly as he descended. At age eight or nine, Freddie and he would take turns spinning inside the Maytag dryer. One would climb inside. The other would push the button to start him tumbling. They left the dryer door open. Inside the rider braced his knees, arms, and head, and around and around he went. Once he and Fred had seen a Halloween mask floating in a farmer's well and at first thought they happened on a severed human head.

Ben would sleep on Susan's cot. She stayed in the basement when home, as Andy Raoul now rented her old room. She and two of her friends shared a townhouse in Poets' Village. She had finally discovered that there was life after John.

Fred kept his weight set on his side of the basement. Susan had painted a red line across the concrete floor. They had divided the area in two and if both happened to be present they kept pretty much to their own sides. Beside Fred's weights sat a brand new stereo system. Fred had a slightly older set in his bedroom. He had also installed stereos and new speakers in all three of the Fregnos' cars. He had to have his music playing all the time, but if Susan happened to be home, she made him use earphones as she couldn't stand his acid rock and heavy metal. Next to the weight set and the sound system, a brand-new color T.V. sat in front of an old sofa. A dartboard hung on the wall. Michael pointed to the bathroom. It sat just across the line on Susan's side. Beyond it, Cantwell saw a workbench with circular saw, an old refrigerator, Susan's cot, a washer, dryer, sink and ping-pong table. A sump pump operated in the far corner. An old brown carpet lay in front of the cot and the decapitated head of a Raggedy Anne doll sat on top of a nearby dehumidifier.

Suddenly the basement door opened, and they heard someone come down the stairs. Michael turned and said, "Hi, Susan." The two exchanged pleasantries and made small talk. Michael asked how he looked and questioned the young woman about his hair. Ben's lips twitched contemptuously. "You said that she had her own place and wouldn't be here—that I wouldn't be putting anyone out." "It's okay," Susan replied. She would sleep on the sofa in the living room upstairs. "Susan," Michael interrupted, "does my hair really look all right?" "It could use trimming." "Would you?" "Sure." He turned to Ben "I'll be back before seven." By then Mrs. Fregno would have just about finished cooking the family breakfast. They'd say that he slept downstairs with Ben. He'd come in the basement from the backyard through the cellarway, down the steps to the screen door beside the workbench on which sat one of Freddie's prize possessions, a lamp, the shade a vintage tortoise-shell helmet, the base, a World War I shell.

"Make yourself comfortable, Ben. I'm abandoning you. You've been stuck in worse places. Far scarier caves." Once again he addressed Susan. "Where do you want to cut my hair?" "In the kitchen," she whispered. "After you're done, I'll leave," Michael said in just as low a voice. "Thanks." He had already used the bathroom to shave and clean up.

April 1, 1974

Though it is with great sorrow that I see Wayne go, leave my life, I still wish him well because, despite his marrying A—, I still love him— expect to see him involved in great things, and, if I live until I'm ninety, I'll always treasure our time together and will remember the shade, texture, and colour of his caresses.

M.B. looked down at what he had written.

Blah. Honk Honk Honk! He needed to make her earthier. Less ethereal. He scratched out the last line and wrote in its place: He showed me such a good time, I'll never forget it. Even if I live to be one hundred!

Michael and John walked inside the Coney—Cannoshockton's busiest oasis—to watch the local yuppies gathering there, Michael "return of the native-ing," seeing people he used to know in high school, most of whose names he had now forgotten. He found a booth by a window. He asked Salmos to purchase him a Bud draft. At the same time, John would order another coke. Working his way through the crowd, Salmos came face to face with Ted Muntz. "I didn't get carded," Muntz whispered. Salmos and his new protégé came back and sat with Michael, Ted eyeing every well-dressed girl standing at the bar or sitting opposite them in the tables and booths.

"Did you have any trouble stashing fuck face?" Salmos asked. A badass jive Blues guitarist, Michael decided. He had spent the last several minutes struggling to find just the right simile—just the right trope—to suggest his friend's cocky demeanor and attitude.

"I tossed him down a mine shaft."

"He whine?"

"Yes." *Show him malice.* "I left him with a wild, nymphomaniac Sicilian defloweress."

"Susan Fregno?"

Michael nodded.

"You're evil."

"Through and through."

"You son of a—. I can't fucking believe you."

"What's the matter, John? You can't be jealous, can you? Remember you already f, f, and f'd her."

"Screw you," Salmos said. " Anyway, she'd tear him apart. Or maybe not. She's certainly porked out since she stopped seeing me . . . . So how's Debra?"

"Showing her true colors at last. In-outing with some guy who plays hacky sac."

"No. You care?"

"Not really. But after she gets off work, I'll still go over and visit and try to prevail upon her to change her mind. But if not, who cares?"

"You're so fucking bad!"

"Yes, I know. Hey, there's Andy Raoul. I've got to say hello. Later." *Arrange a little surprise for B.C.*

"Don't bring him back here. He and I aren't exactly getting along. He thinks I screwed Fred and betrayed his friendship by nailing his sister." Salmos again addressed himself to Ted Muntz. "I guess he and Deb have called it quits. Oh well, he needs to play the field for awhile after spending all that time with that whacked-out Elissa chick."

"Ted's caved in K-7 before," he commented to Bolanger when the latter returned from speaking with Raoul. "I just told him about that first time you and I spelunked in Bear Cave in Blairsville."

"That treacherous rat hole," Michael interrupted. "Intent on having a good time, we were stupid enough not to mark our route in."

"That's because your friend from Pitt Alvin came along with us and led in and we trusted him. He said that he knew the place like the back of his hand. Remember how your flashlight went out?"

Turning to Ted, John continued: "After getting lost in a cave once, you'll never make that mistake a second time. I say that from personal experience."

E. had told Michael about her friend's suicide. "Jeff" had sent her one of those letters/envelopes too.

February 2, 1974

Cathy said she made the worst mistake in her life getting involved with a married man. Poor Jeff. Cathy and Dew had an open relationship and enjoyed threesomes, foursomes, the whole free-love, sexual-revolution, swingers' scene. She told Jeff he would find swinging both liberating and empowering, but his wife didn't understand. She freaked out and, possessive bitch that she was, immediately filed for a divorce.

Jeff Strunk painted beautiful pictures, but no one appreciated his work or his shoulder-length Thor hair. He really disturbed the clerks at the post office. Every envelope in which he mailed a letter had scores of very thin black lines intersecting each other and forming complex geometrical patterns drawn across it on both sides, the only blank space where he wrote the address.

The envelope looked the same as the others, but when Cathy opened the letter inside, she unfolded a black sheet of construction paper. Jeff hanged himself. Losing his wife tore him up. He had become so emotionally dependent on her.

Six a.m.

Andy Raoul pulled back the charging handle on the A.R., pointing the gun at the sleeping Cantwell's cheek, then let go of the handle. As the bolt shot back into place, Cantwell awoke. The sound brought him out of his sleep. His eyes widen. He makes out the concrete floor, vaguely a toy racer on the floor, hears the sump pump pumping. He looks up and sees the barrel of the automatic rifle.

The person holding the gun sported a red robe and wore flip-flops. He had hairy legs. Cantwell tilted his head further back and saw a squat, anthropoid face.

"You commie sympathizer. What you doin' in the home of true blue real red-blooded 'Mericans? If you're some college boy spouting propaganda for the Sand-inistas or asking fair play for Castro and Cuba, you'd best say your prayers." Raoul couldn't control himself and started laughing. "Prepare to meet your maker, mother fucker."

Ben saw Michael sitting on the workbench, swishing his legs and laughing and knew it was a joke.

Of course, the diary entries in his book would differ markedly from her actual ones, but they would have to have the same flavor as the originals in order for him to achieve the effect wanted (certainly not Michael Bolanger *affettuoso*). She had shown him her diaries numerous times as well as the journals in which she jotted down her dreams of two decades. She would often read him a passage or perhaps a poem penned on a stray page of her diary. "I was your age now when I wrote that," she would remark.

He knew Sam Hedgepeth. 'Peth played trombone in his high school orchestra. His dad taught History at Cannoshockton U.

He put together bits and pieces of information related to him at different times and by different people and worked out how the pieces of the puzzle fit in order to recreate what had happened—what must have happened—to her. He felt intense satisfaction con-structing a timeline for her years in Cannoshockton.

Once in a fit of depression, she had lined the pillboxes out of her medicine cabinet up domino fashion on her kitchen table. She had planned to swallow every single pill (she had hoarded several months' worth) but at the last minute couldn't go through with it. But Dido, Dido, your namesake did it with a knife. Shouldn't you follow suit? Would Wayne-Aeneas feel any remorse or regret? Or would everyone forget her just as they had forgotten about Jeff Strunk? She said that she wore only black the year after Wayne mar-ried the girl from Schenectady when she had behaved so promiscuously and had seen the two psychologists from Cannoshockton University of Pennsylvania's Mental Health Services. *What else*, he thought. *Think.*

After they left Fregnos that morning, Michael said he'd give Ben the grand tour and really show him Cannoshockton. Neither Ben's undisguised boredom, nor his pent-up anger built up from last night and pitching over this morning when he awoke to find the A.R. thrust in his face, fazed Michael. Despite the fact his blood boiled, Ben held the semi-automatic weapon and marveled how streamlined and light it was. Now sitting in the car, staring out the window, he sulked. In Herneshopple, Michael had met an elderly woman—a former babysitter of Ben's. She said that he had always been an obstreperous and cranky baby and that he positively refused to eat his boiled rice, that he spit every spoonful back out at her. No, he hasn't changed a bit, Michael thought. They stopped at the new Courthouse to see the statue of Cannoshockton's most renowned, celebrated citizen, the famous but now aged and long retired Hollywood movie star. They stopped in front of the old courthouse (now office space for the Commonwealth Bank of

Hanover). They drove to several places where Elissa had lived. They parked at the paddle tennis courts near Brown's woods, where through a cut in the tree line, they could view the town, see the crocus-yellow dome of the old courthouse, the steeples of the churches in the distance as well as Horace Mann Elementary School, and much nearer in a state of crumbling desuetude a turn-of-the-century factory. They hiked one of the numerous nature trails, and Ben began to warm up and become a little friendlier as Michael plied him with a bunch of questions about last night at the Fregnos. Ben said that he had a pretty good time, that he, Fred and Susan watched a little T.V. and had traded stories about him. He liked them. "But you shouldn't have just dumped me, a total stranger, off there. I don't know these people. They don't—"

"Hey Ben," Michael interrupted, "Pound in the nails, why don't you. I've already got the wound in the side."

When interrogated about spending the night with the "new one" (Debra), Bolanger, of course, concocted a fantastic, peacock lie. Then he said, "This morning before we left, Susan told me she liked you and asked me to invite you back. If you asked her out, I bet she would say yes." He saw that Ben looked at him very attentively now. *Wouldn't John be pissed?* "In fact I know she would." *You are evil.*

They followed the path to Brown's mausoleum, the builder one of Cannoshockton's more infamous personalities, a fabulously wealthy bootlegger who had beat a murder rap in a celebrated murder trail in 1920s. When Mr. Brown's heirs sold the property to the township several decades after his death, they removed his body from the mausoleum and interred it in Greenwood Cemetery. The supervisors had plans to tear the structure down but never carried them out. As boys Michael and his friends camped at the old crypt and told ghost stories. One Christmas, they had tried to find the new grave but gave over their search when they came across wrapped gifts stacked in front of the stone of a school fellow of theirs who had died the previous year. They ran away as fast as their feet would carry them, much more afraid than when they spent the night in the empty crypt the previous summer. Tommy's parents had probably left the wrapped presents, but one of the boys had suggested that they had come from old man Brown, that he had set them out for them. Michael stepped through the door. *Here. In the most gothic of styles. During a rainstorm. Wayne, dressed in khakis from Marty's Army Navy and wearing his yellow fedora, at last takes her, the words chasing one another right off the page like the frenzied notes in a virtuoso cadenza played by Ignace Pederewski.* He would make the reader's palms sweat as he or she turned the pages with greater and greater speed.

They hiked back to the car. Michael had more to show Cantwell. As he unlocked the passenger door to let Cantwell in, he said, "This is the way to the musey-room. Mind your hat going in." Ben had had enough. He had begun to find this endless tour boring and tiresome. He tried to put it diplomatically, but Michael did not pay him the least attention. They had to see the old Army Navy store, the Memorial Fieldhouse, and Big Red. They drove to West Pike and stopped in front of the house.

Yes, this is where Bones Reddle lived. After moving out, Blue Dew and Cathy rented a trailer on Eighth Street. Bones wore only black underwear. He's totally caught up in this, Ben thought. They got out of the car, stepped onto the porch. A For Sale sign hung in the window. "Which room did she stay in, I wonder?" *Oh, go peddle your relics elsewhere.*

"Michael," Ben finally said, "Fred, and Susan said they'd like to do something with us today. We should get back. Let's not blow them off."

And Elissa said to him letting fall the armor of the ego, "I have let men come in my mouth, through my hair, on my face."

"What are you doing now?" John Salmos asked.

"Providing the enemy with cannonballs," Michael said. *Für Elise.*

"So *how* will I get home tomorrow?" Ben asked.

"Fred'll drive you as a favor to me," Michael said. You thought Cobin was bad. Wait until three hours go by with Freddie Fregno behind the wheel. He'll have a case of beer inside him to start. And you'll just love listening to him blast his stereo while playing Yngwie Malmsteen, Johnny Winter, the Beastie Boys, and the Angry Samoans. Fred will hot rod the mother, too. Yeah, he drives like Yngwie plays the guitar. But you need rattling.

He could see it now. Fred would march down the steps and come flying out the front door.

He would have on his shades and racing gloves.

Michael smiled at Cantwell.

Usufruct. I'm always saved by it.

II

Michael opened the envelope, took out the creased letter, unfolded it and read:

Out Out *Brief* Candle

It's me again. I'm writing to you because it's only fair that you learn this first. So I've decided to give you the dope before anyone else hears and sits in judgment. They don't want the details to leak out—before the first of kin has been notified and before the cops and coroner can confer. No one knows yet, but B— C—'s dead. The chain of circumstances leading to his death begins with you mineshafting him at your friends the Fregnos. You were so involved in other, hotter pursuits that you forgot about him. The next morning you didn't perceive what happened the night before. You still don't realize what happened, so that is why I am writing you now.

After switching off the T.V. and after F— F— and S— F— said good night and went upstairs to go to bed and B— C— retired to the cellar and got in Susan's cot, his stomach started growling. He opened the refrigerator beside the ping-pong table. He found all the shelves stuffed with Hostess cupcakes. B— C— had to have coffee with his cupcakes, so he crept up into the kitchen to make some. When he came back, he switched on the lights. There, naked on her cot, lay S—. He clutched his chest with one hand and toppled over onto his backside. Sue had to revive him. It was his first time. But, as you know, he didn't die then. The sight of a nude S— didn't slay him on the spot. F— F— drove him home. He survived that, too. But he couldn't accept the fact that she didn't want to see him again. It put him in a most depressed mood, so he came to visit me.

Since leaving my jacket at the cleaners, I've begun working out. See, I made this resolution to lose weight and to sculpt my body. All that tension, all that energy that builds up in me every day, I channel out of myself through exercise. As B— C—'s friend, I advised him to engage in physical activities of the toughest, roughest kind in order to beef himself up. "B— you sure do need to shape up and start working out," I said.

When I got initiated, aside from the many unspeakable things they made me do to others and had others do to me, the gals with the brazen Ls on their jackets forced me to take on the dirtiest man's job I could think of, so I became a plumber.

So I tell B— to spend a few hours declogging clotted toilets.

I knew these people in my home town who had been looking for a plumber for months to flush the sewer lines underneath this church and to unclog the piping inside it, so I gave him the address of the church along with my old gear.

Now if toilet paper and human waste has clogged up a toilet and Liquid Plumber won't dissolve the obstruction, a plumber takes a metal coil known as a snake and sticks it down the toilet bowl and inside the pipe and keeps pushing it in until it pokes through the obstruction. Well, B— rolled up his shirtsleeves, and pushed and pushed. With all his strength, he rammed it through, huffing and puffing the while. Well, his heart stopped beating a second time. They found him several hours later. So the next time you invite a friend to Cannoshockton don't—I repeat don't—leave him all alone with sweet Susie.

Please don't try to contact me. I won't be attending the memorial service.

Your former friend

III

He withdrew to his grandfather's row house in Rallingsburg to write. He started *The Translator* after abandoning (for the third or fourth time) his work on Elissa's college days in Cannoshockton, *First Time*.

Thomas Porschinger first visited America in 1927. There, the Central European writer met for the first time the loyal English translator of his works, Stacey Lowell-Keaton. She thought that only an old man long experienced in the ways of the world could have written his first novel. It greatly surprised her therefore when, after Edgar (Porschinger's American publisher) asked her to guess Porschinger's age, she discovered that her author had only reached his twenty-fourth year.

She would translate all but one of his early fictional works as well as the novels of his middle and late periods except for the final three. Porschinger completed them after her death, and no one had yet dared to step forward to take her place. Her final translation came out several months prior to his seventy-fifth birthday. He lived a little over ninety-two. An extraordinary span of time in which he produced an extraordinary body of work.

She didn't always appreciate his heavy irony, but nonetheless she prostrated herself and knelt at the altar of her acknowledged master. At a young age, she demonstrated great skill at languages, and she stood quite adept at what she did to earn her livelihood. She had two little girls. Both blonde, pink and blue ribbons in their hair. Her husband Donald always appeared deferential and unassuming yet he stood an expert in his chosen field, the author of several important (if unread) essays on early archaeological excavations in Mexico. He remained the one man in her life, but Porschinger would not have told a lie if he claimed to match him and say he stood the other. She realized his importance to world literature and believed it her duty to somehow render his rich, complex (and very long) sentences into English.

A very difficult task. It took over her life. She channeled all her energies into her translation. Edgar paid her for her efforts, of course, but, nevertheless, her work caused her to make great sacrifices. Even in old age, Porschinger remained prolific. She always had to stand at his disposal.

They met in 1927. He had come to their summer home. Donald, she and her children had taken a drive that day in the country. Mabel their maid had ushered him into their library. The shelves offered sparse pickings, the sweepings from their other home. She of course felt embarrassed. He had found one of her husband's publications and amused himself with it until they finally at long last stepped into the library. She had seen his photographs. He had always appeared so formal and stiff. In person he looked much more unassuming. She drove him into Washington for his lecture series—and all across Maryland sightseeing. He posed, postured, and playacted a lot. She received the impression that he wanted to have relations with her.

Fidelity to an author's intentions remains the hallmark of a good translator. A good wife, of course, will stand faithful to her husband. She had to make him realize that she would never submit to having relations with him. Thankfully, he never broached the subject with her again in after years. However, she found the final novel she translated by him such a masterpiece, so beautiful, complex and Central European as to make it almost untranslatable into English. She succeeded in rendering it into another language, but she thought that no one would judge her sentences beautiful. She wrote a translator's note, expressing her opinion that the average reader might find the book—an undeniable masterpiece—hard going. She had translated it faithfully. She regretted that her sentences could not compare in beauty to his. Thomas asked Edgar not to publish the note, but he thought it charming and included it in spite of Porschinger's objections.

Of course, Michael wrote his novella in as ironic a style as one of Thomas Porschinger's own.

Michael would always write in the mornings, rise at five, go downstairs to the second floor of the upper second and third floor apartment and make coffee, careful not to wake his sleeping grandfather. He'd strike matches from matchbooks older than he (stolen from a kitchen drawer) and advertising a General Hardware store his grandfather had briefly owned to light a candle on his desk (a ritual he performed each morning prior to starting to write).

Whenever he tired of *The Translator* or suffered a block working on it, he switched back to his book about Elissa's early days in Cannoshockton, *First Time*.

It took him three years to complete *The Translator*. When not at his grandfather's (he commuted to Herneshopple from Rallingsburg to take classes—did his turn in grad school for two years; the year after receiving his M.A. he continued living at his grandfather's because G.C. needed a hip replacement and would have to have someone around the house while he recuperated), he spent his spare time on R&R in Cannoshockton. Usually with Salmos.

John would visit him in Rallingsburg too and sometimes bring along his current girlfriend. Privately, he'd admit that he pressed another loaded revolver to his head. But he'd keep on going back, he said, because the girl meant for him had to exist out there somewhere.

"You know what will happen," Michael would say. "I'm done. As long as I have Rosy Palm to take care of me, I will forswear all Kundrys and Mut-em-enets."

"Yeah. Yeah. But you can't say it's bad to want companionship and true, deep devotion from a woman."

"But celibacy's so much simpler. Look at the time they take up, time which could be devoted to other, worthier pursuits."

"Maybe Virginia will be the one," Salmos said.

And while not writing, he would do all sorts of things with his grandfather. They'd attend church and Kiwanis together, drive across the county stopping at the seat or a town museum to sift through more documents, continuing work on Gustave's research project of forty years. Michael would videotape his and his grandfather's conversations. G.C. knew so much; his stories about the early settlers of the town fascinated Michael. He wanted a permanent record of this—his—oral tradition. It couldn't be lost.

After three years of work, he finished *The Translator* one day at the end of an eight-hour session. He walked into the museum room and stared at the relics. Exhausted, he didn't want to reread what he had written. He put the manuscript down on a chair in the room, walked out and closed the door. He would retrieve it another day when he would feel physically more capable of doing the editing and revising he knew he still had to do. He went downstairs. His grandfather sat in the window reading *The Upper Room*. He turned the corner, opened the other door and went out into the yard.

He remembered the heavy black bricks he used to swim to the bottom of the tank to retrieve, bring back to the surface, at the Memorial Fieldhouse as a child. It had taken him three years to bring up this brick.

He thought of the Herneshopple golf course. In his mind, he jogged Elissa's three-part run by himself. He recalled everything on both sides of the path, the swasti-kas spraypainted on the bridge. A wide-open, perfumed mouth.

He did not think he followed in her footsteps any longer.

She had written him often and although he always read her letters with interest—wherever she lived, whatever she did—he had not written her back for over a year.

> Dear Michael,
>
> How are you? I have written several times and have yet to hear from you. Have you finished your Master's program? I live out in the country (eighteen miles from Lansing). I walk at dusk when I can often spot deer, and sometimes in midday I run with Tasha, the neighbor's dog who sits beside me now.
>
> Last night, I rode on my bike for two miles on the lake path. It was dark, windy, and drizzling. As I pedaled, I looked at the moonlit whitecaps and thought about you.
>
> As I write, I look out my window, spy killdeer, jays, and warblers. The peonies' red-fingering leaves have emerged. The woods stand full of Dutchman's Breeches. Tasha chews on a deer skull she recovered this morning—the lawn strewn with her little treasures: rotting moles, steer bones, a deer leg from a road kill, miscellaneous dead animals rotted past recognition.
>
> Variety remains the spice of life.
>
> She likes her variety.

Lying in the grass, looking up at the sky, Michael started writing Elissa a letter in his head.

Elis. Words still percolate through me. It remains inexcusable of me not to have written before now, but I've been and still stand preoccupied with finishing the novel. More about that later. Also I have little to relate. Nothing of much account has happened in my personal life. I enjoy the rewards of continence and write everyday. I'm sure you live your life to the fullest—heaping experience on top of experience. I spend my days polishing my sentences. My life stands uneventful. But don't feel too sorry for me. If composing "winding rounds of which the forme remains" has taken over my life, if I'm only navel gazing when I look at those sentences, my gasps of joy and surprise when I read what I've put down on the page compensate me for whatever loss I have sustained.

He had, after all, finished *The Translator*. And in the future, they would want to come into his *Boulangerie*. Their mouths would moisten at the thought of one of his pies, even if now they contemptuously called them "crusts made of dough paste."

But in the future his icing would not consist of sugar combined with water, milk, and egg white. The patrons would find all kinds of baked goods for sale in his shop. Hard rolls. Base bread. But also innumerable delicacies. All similar but none the same.

This first loaf?

He was young and had been infatuated with a *Boulangera* at the time when he first started to actually—if the expression didn't sound too queer (*cuire?*)—*boulange*. The yeast had made the dough rise. It stood finished. He had baked his loaf.

A bowlegged Bolunger's ballestra lunge.

FIN

Addendum by M. Prime for the 20th Anniversary Chicxulub Press edition

Out of the blue one day in 1995, M. Prime received a post card from "Elissa." She had telephoned his parents and Prime's mother had told her that he had lived for many years with her father Jacob in her and her husband's old hometown. Over the next eight years, he would receive a veritable avalanche of letters from her. He wrote to her less frequently. From time to time he would telephone her at work. He sent her all his subsequent unpublished novels. He finished several of them during the years they had remained out of touch. So she received three or four bulky manuscripts the week after she contacted him. He would send her his subsequent works as he finished them. One day early on, he received a notecard from the Metropolitan Museum of Art. It had a reproduction of the tempera on wood "Portrait of a Man and Woman at a Casement" by the Florentine painter Fra Filippo Lippi on its front. Inside she told him how central to her life he had become. Alas she remained married and had young sons. After seeing no one for a period of seven years, M. Prime had dated any number of women, but no one seriously. He never found anyone whom he loved on so many levels as he had "Elissa" as a young man, but he enjoyed casually going out as long as his female acquaintances did not become too earnest or ardent. If a woman grew too romantically attached to him, he would end the relationship. Despite the fact that she lived four states away from him and that they could not see each other, he felt great joy that she had come back into his life. He would love her in whatever manner he could and stand satisfied. In 2000, he sent her a copy of his first major publication, his five hundred-page study of famous literary suicides, *Final Drafts*. Within four or five months of his book's appearance, his ailing grandfather died at the age of ninety-three, and M. Prime's world crumbled. He could not read. He could not write. Within a year of his grandfather's passing, he had his own health scare. He remembered that when his love rejected him as a young man he wished himself ill and had almost died of an intussusception. He had chronicled those events in his first novella *The Mozart Machine* but in a self-serving way. His grandfather Jacob for whom he felt a very strong attachment since early childhood had helped him through his crisis then. Now M. Prime believed that a part of him had died with Jacob. Did he again will himself ill? Jacob had peed red. Shortly after his death, blood began to pour copiously from M. Prime's nose. Fortunately the tumor in his sinus turned out benign. M. Prime nonetheless underwent a series of painful operations. Then on 9/11 the planes hit the twin towers. Once again the nation found itself embroiled in war, and M. Prime's depression deepened. Other matters—including a car accident which paralyzed his agent's only son— troubled and upset him greatly. A long fallow period of five or six years' duration followed. Eventually he began reading again, but he suffered from writer's block and his production all but ceased. A vital part of him, it appeared, had died with Jacob. During this same time frame, "Elissa's" marriage deteriorated, and she went through a protracted and vexing divorce. M. Prime tried to comfort her as best he could, but her woe only added to his. Then she wrote that she would shortly pay him a visit as her parents were planning to move out of state and she would be coming home to help them pack. One summer day, the beloved did in fact return. After her visit, he began writing her weekly letters. They both attempted to describe in their own voices the events of that magical day. He felt like he walked on broken legs but the miracle indeed happened. He started writing again. She also began to gush words. One day he received a packet containing her latest poems.

[I have stolen some time to write to you. Ted always wants to know when I will be home—I am already late even at this letter's beginning. It was wonderful—your call—you wanting to hear my voice. I too have such longings. Again and again it becomes so apparent to me how much of my essence's cravings lean to the subjective world. Last night I dreamed of living with the de' Medici's—a completely different land and time full of roasted garlic and yellow pepper and fennel sauces served over the meal. In the darkness of my room in the massive, labyrinthine stone home—I recollect melding fragments from all my days. I have been pondering you and us. Ted told me a dozen days ago he cares not for the dreams of the night and has no interest in the inner world which constitutes so much of me. He has no patience or interest there (I knew this from the start) and thus I feel the most important part of my being exists in a vacuum. My inmost cravings of soul and spirit need somehow to be nourished, or I shall perish. And so I will and do and will forever reach out to you.]

[They have mountain bikes here, so I ride the trails of the Chequamegon-Nicolet National Forest which we are within. Some trails go back to sphagnum bogs so dark— like the pupils of one's eyes—you can see nothing through their depths—surrounded by mossy green tamaracks and black spruce trees covered with lichens, the understory dotted with beautiful shades of reds, greens, and yellows, a Bonsai Japanese garden with sphagnums, blue bead lilies, wild iris, Labrador tea plants, sundews, pitcher plants, so beautiful, so rich and diverse, so alien and almost frightening. I go here everyday just before sunset. We also have canoes for the lake, where the loons let you come within as close as ten feet from them. Beavers have built huts on the far end, their dams surrounded by rushes, cattails, reeds, and more lilies. Beyond the lake woods and a few desolate cottages. I went canoeing one day right after dinner and then went at night for the last two nights with another woman to canoe by starlight, then just float and watch the heavens as we drifted … into the Milky Way—no structure to our movement or time—we picked out a few constellations, saw many satellites and shooting stars and heard owls call and green frogs croak. I write you from my tent. My colleagues have gone to a local bar to watch a Green Bay Packers' preseason game. I opted out, preferring some solitude. Today we found freshwater sponges. I didn't know WI had any. I always associated them with Key West and oceans. I'll send you a bit of it, Labrador tea, and sphagnum moss. I think of you daily and tenderly. Know I am with you. P.S. Sending no sponge as it might ruin the photos.]

[The boys had their last day of school yesterday, so summer is theirs. I found them both in bed with me (I like to dream into the morning) and soon was protecting myself in a pillow fight. They were tussling all day. I made them forts with sheets and chairs. I read to them and went to the library as we always do on Fridays, sat down to decide meals and activities so we would all be happy and have time to look forward to Folklore Village for a potluck supper and English contra dancing, Mineral Point's carnival, an auction in a nearby small town, Friends' Meeting, a browsing-only visit to the toy store, a hike on Saturday, "our nature-trails day," and some time at home to enjoy and relax. I am rambling, I am hopeful and look forward to the trip to Pa and Friday when at last our paths will cross again. Am I in dangerous, uncharted waters? I do not know. All I know is that I cannot give up my deep affection for you. It is rooted into my very heart and soul and is bound by joy. It would destroy my being to part from you. I do not speak in hyperbole. Goodnight my beloved. I look forward with great joy to seeing you again.]

[How I loved your letter and blushed as you revealed "a secret compartment in your Victorian dresser." I too think our protagonists should have their night of bliss (but more on our story later). I hope you can make out my handwriting. I've chosen a new coffee shop to steal away to write to you and planned for this time last week when I had my pieces together for you. I loved your description of Cold Stream but held myself from reading it until I had written and twice edited my Cold Stream narrative for you because I wanted it from my vantage point and not colored by yours, so it and the poems "Preparing Our Food" and "In Search of Love" came before I even glanced at your wonderful description. What fun to see the same events from two points of view. I have been gushing with words lately and send you a few more poems (about one half) of what I've written in the last month. I've also drafted a series of sketches on my Lancaster visit—and the whole trip which so moved my heart. My heart hangs here ripe and sweet. You have brought it into the sunlight where it has been nurtured my dearest. I hope you enjoy the poems. I must confess I was nervous when typing "In Search of Love" on my home computer. My hands became damp as I worked on it. A few of my poems I had to hide in my own secret compartment.]

In Search of Love

Across the rise to the walnut grove
Nod the queens in lacy gowns.
Their slender legs dance through wild weeds
Wet with dew and the spider's net.
I wander here in search of love,
Amid the fragrance of the fields.

A startled fish darts into dark
Within a stream of flowing cress
Bedecked by jewel and pye-eyed weeds
Where damsels light upon their thrones.
Springs babble up their liquid pearls
Filling with freshness the midday air.
I wander here in search of love,
Amid the flickerings of the stream.

And here upon this spongy earth
Softly I tread among the nests
Of marsh wrens woven fine with grass
And lined with down of mother's breasts.
The frogs and toads take comfort here
Singing the longings of this world.
The sweetness of this watery green
Ooze through my toes and blackened feet.
I wander here in search of love,
Amid the softness of the marsh.

M. Prime read her poems with great joy. He also felt hopeful and rejuvenated though he did not know what the future would portend. Only time would tell. He did realize, however, that the wellsprings of his art had been renewed and that he would have to tell both the story of his time in the slough of despond but also that of his miraculous resurrection. He felt impregnated. A new novel began taking shape inside of him. He would eventually give his characters different identities and histories, but, as he felt intimidated and scared when he first sat down in front of his machine, he decided that he would use the familiar and comfortable names of Michael Bolanger, Elissa Hexfore and Gustave Bolanger—at least for the present. He decided to ease himself slowly into his task, his first order of business to lovingly resurrect his grandfather in words. He would begin with a happy recollection:

Many of Gus' favorite stories were fire stories. Ushering visitors through the Rallingsburg museum, in his role of curator, he would never fail to stop in front of the firefighters' exhibit where with one hand he would reach for one of the leather helmets and jam it on his head. At the same time, with the other, he would be lifting the ornate silver megaphone, the Chief's trumpet, to his lips and bellowing a stout "Let's go, boys!" Then bestowing a triumphant grin on his dumbstruck visitors, the Rallingsburg Historical Foundation curator would say, "That's the way the Hope Fire Company Chief did it before there were loudspeakers. I bet they could hear him in Horse Hollow, don't you?

Rallingsburg had two competing fire companies, the Hope and the Reliance, which had engaged in spirited contest since their organization in the 1880s. They would compete at the First District Fire Association of Pennsylvania picnic every year. Each company had relay teams of which they felt proud and they would contend in the following races: the two hundred fifty yard hose race, the two hundred twenty yard hub race, the one hundred yard foot race, and the plugman's potato sack race. They would also try to carry off the honors of having the best band and being the best-uniformed company in the district. Michael wished that he had listened to Gus more attentively. He seemed to recall him saying that the first fire company in town—the Rallingsburg Fire Company—had organized around 1877 but only lasted a few years before it disbanded and the fire apparatus, hose, etc., fell to the care of borough officials as the people's property. A few years later it reformed and took the name of Reliance. By mid-decade the company owned a Class Four steam engine, three hose trucks, one thousand feet of cotton hose and one village hook-and-ladder truck and occupied its own building on Second Street. Late in the 1880s, people started calling for a second fire company. Michael's memory became fuzzy here. He vaguely recalled his grandfather talking about a barn burning on the far (Pleasant Hill/ Stumptown) side of the Mushannon creek and the Reliance boys not responding on time and not wanting to take their new third class La France rotary steam fire engine across the water.

Earlier in the year, during a fire at one of the town's commercial hotels, the top flue of the engine boiler of the old Class Four Silsby had received so much damage that the company had to retire it and after due deliberation as to the merits of the La France and Silsby engines (the Ford and Chevy of their day, Michael laughed), they chose Mr. La France's new model. Everyone agreed that she stood a perfect beauty and with great fanfare the men brought her to Rallingsburg from Altoona by night express. The boys took especial pride in her and paraded her all through town but did not relish the prospect of running her through the muddy ruts of the old log road across the creek in Stumptown. The ensuing uproar resulted in townsfolk taking up a subscription for a second fire company and, if Michael remembered correctly, Francis Xavier Bolanger the elder, a friend of the farmer whose barn had burned, had vociferously clamored for the creation of the second fire company—if we can't rely any more on Reliance, we will still never give up hope—and later served as the Hope Fire Company's first assistant engineer. The two fire companies worked mischief against each other, damaged their rival's equipment and even engaged in fisticuffs at fires. Whichever company got to the scene first claimed dibs on dousing the blaze. The owner's preference did not matter, and it remained best for him to stand neutral, unless he belonged to one or the other of the two companies. In that case, his property would burn to the ground if his own boys did not attend to it. The men of the rival company would stand aside and cheer, but at a nonaligned, uncommitted house or a municipal or commercial building, the rival firemen literally beat back the competition. Not until the late 1890s did the two companies at last begin to cooperate and coordinate their efforts. F. X. Bolanger II had a hand in effecting that. As Burgess ("F. X. will fix it" became his campaign slogan), he ordered, with the concurrence of council, that the two fire companies then in service and those which thereafter might be organized and recognized by the borough, shall together form the Greater Fire Department of Rallingsburg, Pennsylvania, each company recognized by the borough to be furnished a certificate from council, signed by the Chief Burgess and the Secretary of Council and sealed with the borough seal to be framed by each company and hung up in the company's regular meeting room.

The following day M. Prime looked over what he had written and adjudged it a false start. Possibly he could use some of the material later in the book. He decided that today he would confront his demon head on. For several months, he had read nothing but Tudor and Stewart plays and felt in a very Elizabethan mood. He chose a pertinent motto for his first chapter from Cyril Tourneur's *The Revenger's Tragedy*:

For since my worthy father's funeral,
My life's unnaturally to me, e'en compelled;
As if I lived now, when I should be dead.

He wrote hurriedly and heedlessly as if trying his hand at automatic writing:

Before crashing and burning, Michael Bolanger had his short, sweet flight, his small triumph, but then his life turned to ash. What he had worked for single-mindedly and obsessively for more than a decade had finally happened—he had at long last published a book—but the deity had vouchsafed precious little time for him to bask in his glory, to wallow and luxuriate in his success. His revels abruptly ended when once more circumstance brought home to him that he remained a terrestrial creature, a denizen of the sublunary world and thus subject to mutability—a target for the irrational and the demonic. For immediately following his jubilation and triumph, the Goddess Fortuna yanked her cord. The great wheel took a sudden, sharp turn. It whirled on its hinge, revolved with such great speed that it underwent combustion—ignited in bright flame—and he, who stood at the apex staring at moon and stars, spun underneath. The blaze seared his flesh, scorching and charring him as he rolled below until at last the full weight of the wheel bore down upon him and crushed him, a caitiff churl who had refused to plead and thus underwent slow execution in the press yard of old Newgate.

The year Gustave fell ill and Michael's book came out, although he did not realize it at the time, for a while, he fell and ascended simultaneously. For the moment, he perceived only the whoosh of elevation. Wildly rejoicing, jumping up in the air, the brass ring in reach, he did not realize that the elevator, the aluminum box, he stood in was not going up but plunging in free fall and that he actually plummeted downward. *Your legs won't break if you jump and are in mid-leap when the elevator hits bottom.* He did not know. Damn it, he did not know. He remained highly distracted as he sat on the launch pad strapped into the capsule of his Apollo rocket awaiting lift off. He was there. He was. He was finally there.

In the first flush of his triumph, Michael pictured that his still favorite author, the worryingly, excessively meticulous TM arose from the dead like Hamlet's father in order to present his disciple the blue Frederick Cross, *Pour le Merite*, for staying the course and in an age of publishers of no taste producing and yes selling a book of caliber and distinction. He had written seven novels beside the newly published work, a nonfiction study devoted to the literary suicides of the late nineteenth and twentieth centuries, and, in his heart of hearts, would have preferred to have sold one of them, for he felt fiction his true calling. Michael dubbed and cynically referred to his study as *Last Writes: The artful and awful quietuses of the whole sick crew of sad sacks and literary losers.* He had, of course, incurred a karmic debt. He had written his study purely for personal gain, to advance or rather to jump start, his stalled career as novelist. He saw the need for such a book as no group portrait seriously exploring the frustrations, agonies, and deaths of the many important authors who had decided to end their own lives from the late nineteenth century onwards, had at that time as yet been written, and Michael realized if he could execute the thing with aplomb and professionalism it would not only attract a publisher (college libraries would certainly order copies) but also (he fervently hoped, prayed, and crossed his fingers, toes, and gonads) that it would open a path for his other books. Despite his mock title, the morbid had never fascinated him, and he had not written his study for the morbidly curious. No, his was not a lurid or gossipacious book but a highly serious endeavor, and he felt not only sympathy but also a deep affection for most of his subjects. He also experienced a complex and unusually strong subjective response toward their deaths, especially those of authors whose *felos-de-se* had been heroic acts of resistance against a world gone wrong, for whom the past century, with its global wars and crises and profound societal changes, had proved too violent and dehumanizing an age, but also and even more so, those who had striven to make their last act a work of art in itself, a quietus of strange beauty and appropriateness, a fitting capstone in some odd but felicitous way to their career. He was no ghoul gnawing on bloody bones, no cold-blooded autopsist dissecting his corpses for the enjoyment of sadistic voyeurs, his target audience those perverse and cruel individuals who delighted in watching grainy footage of executions, say, or of mass graves recently uncovered. He had no secret sympathy with the abyss. Surely a sapient reader would see that he stood squarely on the side of life. Yet he had to admit that certain persons probably should not read his book. There stood something eerily attractive about self slaughter, and, although he himself dismissed the Romantic ideal that genius was inextricably intertwined with suffering and death, although he never felt the slightest inclination to blaze brightly for a moment then load his sparkless ashes into an unlamented urn or to extend so much as his little finger toward the Savage God, he realized that others were more susceptible than he and that his book might fascinate those already half in love with easeful death. You do not, however, utilize and showcase the suffering of others for your own promotion. Of course it came back to bite him. If he had not plumbed the depths of human wretchedness prior to writing *His Quietus Make*, he would afterward.

From the high parapet of his at long last achieving publication (just as the field marshal-visaged Mann, ever attentive to punctilios, in precise observance of the formalities, clicked his heels, or so it seemed afterwards), Michael Bolanger fell downward into the pit, the grave, and found himself encased in aluminum and commencing his dirt nap with Grandpap. After the brief magical elevation came the plummet. Death had snatched away from him the person whom he loved most. What matter his laurels? What for years had terrified him in prospect—many times during the decade he had lived with his grandfather, Michael had awoken in a sweat having dreamt that Gustave had passed away. He so feared one morning finding him dead in bed that several times a night and certainly when he stirred from one of his all-too-frequent nightmares, he would race down the attic steps form his third-floor apartment to check upon the sleeping Gustave on the second floor and upon hearing his regular breathing, would again retire, reassured and thanking his lucky stars. What had terrified him had finally happened and only a few short months after the appearance of *His Quietus Make* (at least his grandfather had seen the book published). For although Gustave did not have to endure intense pain, although his death came several years after his ninetieth birthday and although during his final half decade he did not experience or undergo any diminution of his mental powers and aside from growing a little hard of hearing and suffering from perpetual arthritis, know any great physical debility, the process of dying, the death life finally dealt Gustave, seemed pathetic and protracted if not all that painful, and Michael's own decline began with his grandfather's falling ill—he could see this now in retrospect—and that Gustave's death , more than anything else, had poleaxed him.

For a series of reversals followed his grandfather's passing. Michael suffered through four years of sadness and disappointment, and, when for the second time in his life, his own mortality came home to him, he knew both dread and shame. His grandfather had stood fearless, but Michael could not compare to his grandfather. Nor did he have his faith, the faith of a little child. Never had he experienced such fear, agitation and anxiety, as when he learned that he would again have to go under the knife twenty years after the Herneshopple physicians had butchered him as a youthful college student. Gustave's cystostomy also remained fresh in his mind, and he remembered how his grandfather had emphatically stated that he didn't want a second operation—fortunately he died and did not have to face a second surgery—when a week or so of his release from the hospital he again began to pee bright red and then began expelling from his urethra, like lengths of rope, stringy mucousy blood clots. "Clair," Michael said, using his grandfather's middle name, the one everyone in Gustave's immediate family had used when speaking to G.C. or when talking about him to others, for he had been named after his mother's father and to distinguish between the two, the family had called him Clair or less frequently Gus, and throughout his life most of his friends had called him by his middle name and Gustave himself whenever he'd write his signature would invariably pen *G. Clair Bolanger* (Michael treasured a tie clasp which Clair's fellow office workers had given him upon his retirement and which bore his signature engraved in metal; how they transferred it there, traced from his John Hancock on some stray piece of paper—Michael did not know—his grandfather did not remember signing anything unusual or out of the ordinary—but Michael treasured it and kept it with the other family memorabilia passed down by previous generations of Bolangers which Gustave had willed to him: "Clair, if you have to, you have to. What do the Kiwanians sing: No one has endurance like the man who sells insurance. And you are as tough as an Indian." During the entire length of Michael's campaign to convince Grandpap to live forever, from its inception when Michael again moved into Gus' duplex in October 1989—he had lived there for several years in the mid eighties while earning his graduate degree at Hermeshopple but upon graduating had taken a job as managing editor of *Liver Dye*, a triannual literary journal published by Haverford College which stopped publishing after a sixteen-year run, private and public funding having all but evaporated, two years after Michael had joined its staff—during the entire length of the campaign, from its inception until Gustave's death eleven years later in July, 2000, Michael had taken on the part, the role, of boss (as a boy, Michael had called his grandfather that), and Michael strongarmed his grandfather into taking whatever measures he deemed necessary to insure the continuance of his good health. Assuming the role of caretaker proved a burdensome task, a supreme test of loyalty, for Gustave proved a troublesome and often uncooperative, even belligerent patient. Therefore, when dealing with his grandfather, Michael had to act in a positively Prussian fashion. He had to drag him to the doctors and hector him into taking his blood pressure pills. Michael had diagnosed his hypertension and had gotten him onto medication to begin with, and he afterward monitored his grandfather's vitals when his meds changed or when his doctors added an additional prescription. Toward the end of his life, Gustave took both beta and calcium blockers as well as a diuretic and an ace inhibitor. Every Sunday Michael counted out twenty-eight pills—seven from each of the four bottles—then placed the daily cocktail of four pills in each of the seven compartments, one for each day of the week, of the clear-plastic ruler-length pill organizer that sat in front of Gustave's seat at the kitchen table. Finally he made sure that he got up each morning to see Gustave ingest the medication at breakfast. He had to monitor him closely, for Gustave had a strong bias against taking drugs. According to him, doctors over prescribed, pushed, pills, and too much medicine, he averred, stood hard on the system. A healthy person did not need "dope." He required nothing but nourishing food and drink, especially ample draughts of Rallingsburg's Clear Stream water. It will freeze your teeth and give your tongue a sleigh ride. Numerous times Michael had caught his grandfather cutting his pills in two and ingesting only a half dose. Gustave had always been a frugal person (until his last year he still maintained a 1950s refrigerator which he had to defrost every week), and, as Gustave's income exceeded the cutoff for medical assistance and he had to pay the entire cost of his prescriptions himself, Michael felt that his grandfather cut his dose in order to penny pinch. He tried to explain calmly the dangers involved in not taking the proper dosage. Your blood pressure readings will stand inaccurate. They'll shoot up, and your doctor, assuming that you take your medication properly, may again change your current med for something stronger because he thinks it has become ineffective or that you have developed a tolerance to it, and then you'll find yourself in real trouble. You may precipitate the very stroke or heart attack you're trying to avoid or, cutting your nose off to spite your face, cause your doctor to increase your dosage when he doesn't need to and cause your blood pressure to drop drastically or your heart to slow down or even stop. The look of blank incomprehension that Gustave would give him or his rough reply of "Get off your high horse, sonny" would unnerve and exasperate Michael. He would have to increase his vigilance and make doubly sure at the breakfast table that he watched G. C. take the proper amount of each of his medications. When he reflected that his grandfather had refused all pain shots when he had his hip replacement surgeries in the early eighties when his insurance paid for everything, Michael realized that stretching the money he paid out monthly for his blood pressure medications was probably not the determinative factor behind Gustave's actions but that Gus truly believed that taking too much medicine was bad for one. He also recollected that at the age of eighty-eight his grandfather had downed Tylenol-3s like candy when he developed shingles. They must hurt like hell, Michael thought. Gustave had come down with chicken pox at the age of eight, and the virus had lain latent in his blood for eight decades. Michael hoped that he had an equally strong immune system because he also had caught the pox as a boy. He remembered how he had itched all over and how he had scratched himself even after his mother had daubed him with Calamine lotion. Gustave's mother Sally Belle had probably inculcated in him the belief that taking too much medicine could harm one. Gustave had adhered to her precepts his entire life and in turn preached them to

Michael. Always act like a gentleman. Never turn discourteous. Strive to be polite and deferential, especially toward the ladies. Always take note of your appearance. Look respectable—like you are somebody. Don't gamble, drink, or smoke. The money you save will pay for a nice vacation each year for you and your family ….

In his role of boss and caretaker, the hardest thing Michael had to do was to decide what operations Gustave would and would not have and where and when he would have them. No matter how burdensome Michael found his other duties as caretaker—taking his grandfather for a hearing test and seeing him fitted with a proper hearing aid or marching him to the clinic for his annual flu shot or persuading him to have the single pneumonia shot, or even the onerous task of constantly monitoring his blood pressure and making him take his pills correctly—those other duties all stood easy in comparison. Yes, having to determine on an operation, having to weigh surgical risk versus potential health benefit and possible betterment in quality of life, having to harangue and hector someone else into having an operation, having to sting someone into having surgery by becoming an interminable gadfly repeating over and over again, "You must do this," greatly strained and taxed Michael, the victim of botched surgery himself. Michael would have fought and resisted far more than Gus had ever done. They would have had to drag him to execution, and he would have screamed and fought the whole way. Again and again over the years, Michael insisted that Gus have needed surgeries while he completely disregarded his own breathing problems. After he realized that he had a surgically correctable condition, he procrastinated and stalled, could not make up his mind whether to have the operation or not. He knew that he had a deviated septum since his teens. Staring at his reflection, he could tell. But then he had no difficulty breathing through his nose aside from when he had a cold and became congested or during those few weeks each spring when he became bleary eyed and starting sneezing because of the pollen. Some springs he suffered hardly any symptoms. Other years he could not venture outdoors. Otherwise his nose functioned normally and continued to do so throughout his twenties and early thirties. He ascribed his increased difficulties to the natural aging process. The deviated septum finally began making itself felt. In summer and fall he would be fine, but, during the winter, he began having difficulties breathing indoors as well as outdoors in the spring. His right nostril would swell shut. He had no trouble inhaling through his left. Nonetheless he remained continually conscious of his inability to sniff on the right side and he had trouble sleeping. He felt that his balance was more than subtly influenced, if not entirely thrown off … a bit like a cat with the whiskers on one side of its face snipped.

He swore that if the right side stood open instead of the left he could have endured it. He would have felt less askew somehow. Right-handed, right-eyed (staring at any object at a distance with both eyes, if he shut his left and kept open the stronger right, the object would remain stationary, but it would appear to jump—move in space—if he switched eyes, shut the right and unclosed the left), he would invariably also thrust his right leg into his trousers before he did his left. Instead of having his septum surgically corrected he took other measures. He used Vicks Inhalers and constantly smeared his face with vapor rub. He drunk bottles of Dimetapp and popped Sudafed tablets every three hours. His nose might open up for a short while but would soon shut again. In the end only nasal spray would bring him lasting relief.

Michael took comfort from all the right choices he had made for Gus, all the successful operations. The hips to start with. That gave Gus twenty extra years of mobility. He would have been in a wheelchair otherwise. And Michael had caught the skin cancer in time. He did not hem and haw but gave the okay to have the growth whacked off right away. No wavering or hesitation there. The cataract operations worked wonderfully too. They had been harder to insist upon. Michael could understand Gustave's reluctance, his fear of irreparable damage to his organs of sight, but the cards went their way once again. The mention of the possible eventual need for a pacemaker at a doctor's appointment concerning his grandfather's once again elevated blood pressure shortly after Gustave's ninety-second birthday worried Michael and made him uneasy. Alerted, he began to prepare himself for the eventuality, but then the red pee and the blood clots began. Were Gus' kidneys going also? Would there be a race between heart and kidneys as to which would fail first? The urologist noted the raised creatinine levels. He warned of kidney shutdown in the not too distant future. But as for the immediate problem, he suspected a small kidney stone in the right ureter. A cystostomy was discussed, and Michael insisted that his grandfather go under the knife yet again. The decision would in short order come to torture him. He felt almost as guilty about cutting all salt from Gus' diet during his last months. He felt like a rat bastard doing it and went on a salt-free diet himself to set a good example and not lead his grandfather into needless temptation: "If I can give it up so can you." Yet Gustave was dead and in the ground within six months anyway. In retrospect, Michael felt wretched about serving Gus flavorless food and depriving him of one of life's simple pleasures. The cystostomy proved a very painful but seemingly successful surgery. But several weeks after his grandfather's discharge from the hospital and his limping up the staircase to the second floor apartment, the bleeding from the penis started all over again. Gus did not live long enough to undergo a second procedure. To the last, the very end, Gustave set an example. He taught Michael a final lesson. He showed him how one should die. He displayed dignity and quiet humble acceptance of the inevitable. Even in the hospital, his mission of passing on history never wavered. When not watching Pirate baseball games on the little T.V. above his hospital bed, he amazed the local aides and nurses with his encyclopedic knowledge of their extended families and spoke to them intimately about their grandparents and great-grandparents.

In furtherance of his campaign to make Gustave Clair immortal, Michael knew better than to simply scold or goad. He used the carrot as well as the stick and was always encouraging his grandfather to look forward to some future event. "Pap, you know that you simply have to live until Rallingsburg's bicentennial. You're Mr. Rallingsburg after all, the town's biggest booster, its leading historian." "Michael, you know because I've told you that our hamlet took the name of Casanova from 1882 until 1885 to honor its then mayor for building the power plant and erecting and turning on the street lights. We changed back to Rallingsburg after Squire McGonigal and Commodore Hassinger caught J.P. with his hand in the till. He stood a very enterprising man—quite the innovator—and bringing electricity to the town was his brainchild. His first experiment occurred in eighteen hundred and seventy-six when he used a waterwheel to power a dynamo imported from Cuba—the country of his nativity—to provide electric light for a small farm outside of town. Successful in the small venture and newly elected mayor, he and the officers of the Light, Gas, and Power Heating Company met with the directors of the water company and persuaded them to provide the necessary water power for the venture at a cost of six hundred dollars a year. He had already raised eight thousand in capital stock—he must have been an extraordinary salesman—by inducing our wealthier citizens to purchase a goodly number of company shares. He used the capital to build a new forebay and penstock on the Clear Stream Mill, where a large waterwheel or rather turbine would generate the electric current. Eight arc lights, having two thousand candlelight power each, would replace the town's small and dangerous coal oil lamps and the town's Episcopal church would stand the first church in the world to be lighted by electricity. The streets first illumined one memorable evening in October of 1882, the same year that Edison, the creator of the electric industry, perfected the incandescent light. On the night J.P. pulled the switch to turn on the power, hundreds of strangers who were attending the horse races at the driving park, waited and watched for the first faint touch of twilight. Townspeople and strangers both expressed fears and doubts and questioned whether the new fangled lamps would work. If the lights did work, the crowd expected they would be quite dim. At half past six, those nearest to the lamps heard a faint sputtering, and a second after, the success of the enterprise was proven beyond all dispute, for every lamp blazed forth in splendor and the former fears of the expectant watchers turned to admiration. The following day at the meeting of the borough council, one of the city fathers made the proposal to change the town's name to honor its enterprising mayor J.P. Casanova. Within a couple years, as I said, we would switch back to Rallingsburg. The original settlers called their settlement Mushannontown. It's only our town's bicentennial if we discount those first years and the three years we went by Casanova. I don't like when I read in the newspaper **TOWNSFOLK BEGIN TO PREPARE FOR RALLINGSBURG'S 200th ANNIVERSARY. FORM BICENTENNIAL COMMITTEE.** I'm a stickler for accuracy, see. Our town has been called Rallingsburg for at most one hundred and ninety-four years. I thing we should have a big two hundredth birthday party, don't get me wrong, but we must preserve our history scrupulously and not make misstatements in print. The headline should read **RALLINGS COUNTY COMMUNITY BEGINS PREPARATIONS** and then in the first paragraph of the article the author should note that, during its history, the town has gone by three names." "That is precisely what I mean Pap. Only you would insist on such accuracy." Michael told his grandfather that he must live to eighty, then eighty-five, and then ninety. He told him that he must reach the turn of the century which was also the beginning of the new millennium. Then in 2000 he told him that he must live to see his suicide study published. After he handed him the first copy of the book, he said that he now had to live to be one hundred and see him complete his fictional account of the life of Henry Boulanger, Mercier's Migration. You must not die, Michael thought, because I need you and could not imagine living on without you.

Gustave looked at him sadly, then shook his head. "Even the best of friends must part," he said.

The miracle had happened. After a hiatus of many years, M. Prime was again writing.

Elissa had healed his wound.

Intrusive Voices

Closer inspection ... would reveal a multiplicity of personalities inflicted on the ... document and some prevision of virtual crime or crimes might be made by anyone unwary enough before any suitable occasion for it or them had so far managed to happen along. In fact, under the closed eyes of the inspectors the traits featuring the *chiaroscuro* coalesce, their contrarieties eliminated, in one stable somebody

Almost might I say of myself, while keeping out of crime ... I was veribally complussed ... to isolate i from my multiple Mes

James Joyce,
Finnegans Wake

Table of Contents

FIRST PERSONALITY

That place was full of banks ....

Saturated. Sight sound scent, Alvin Roy Arretto took in the world about him—swallowing him up. Birds in flight. A Shaker barn octagonal and bright red. The damp, musky, smell of the pinewoods. Dazzling crimson, orange, and yellow leaves on both sides of the road and on the hilltops. A duck pond in the middle of a field. Sheep grazing on a grassy knoll. Two distant barking dogs. A waxing crescent moon barely discernible high up in the pure clear blue....

How he enjoyed bicycling! Breaking loose he never felt more alive. Building up speed while coasting downhill, he'd glide part way up the next slope before having to stand up and pedal hard. He always had an eye for bikes since his first purple Schwinn. Rainbow-colored streamers had trailed from out of its plastic handgrips. They fluttered in the breeze as he flew down the big hill behind his parents' home not hitting the brakes even once. He had first seen the Schwinn in the display window at Sears and had pointed it out each week to his old man. When Daddy finally brought it home one day in a brand-new Olds ("Both of us needed new mounts," Daddy said), Alvin had told him not to bother putting on the training wheels. If he wrecked, he did. You either leapt forward, you got on and rode, or you remained right where you stood.

He downshifted. The Japanese ten-speed he currently sat on had an alloy frame. Pity that he would have to leave it. But he would steal another. Bicycles had been parked on either side of this one. But he knew immediately which he would take. Between four and five a.m., his dingy rusted car (a black Mercury) parked several blocks away, he approached the house on foot. Six or seven students lived there. It had no garage. They chained their bikes to the porch. He simply snapped the lock with his bolt cutter, carried the super light bicycle down the steps, jumped onto it, and pedaled up the street to his car. Then, he lashed the stolen ten-speed to his roof rack, covered it with a tarpaulin, got in the car and drove away. At a very slow speed.

He would just walk in. Afterwards he would just walk out.

He had done it so often, forty-seven times in fact. But first he transformed himself by squashing his ego. Alertness, concentration, not personality, would see him through. The army had taught him the art of identity suppression. As a warrant officer stationed in Panama City, he became all spit, polish, and brisk salutes. Dressed in his uniform, he ceased to be himself. Just like he did back then, he would execute his own private rite, an elaborate ceremony he performed in an established, prescribed manner, exactly the same each time he carried it through to completion, and would begin to strip his identity away piece by piece so as no longer to remain Alvin Roy Arretto. It began by putting on his costume. He did not have to think, he told himself. Calm comes to the grunt before the battle breaks. He knows that he can rely on his reflexes, and it's almost as if he's not there when the shells start exploding. An executioner pressing the button does so without contrition. Without sadistic glee. He tells himself he's just flicking a light switch or pulling a lever, believes it. A concentration camp or gulag guard probably underwent a similar process, developed and performed an insane little ritual to lose all sense of self as Hans or Ivan, to banish the tenuous ego where birds sit silent in the dark. He would open and close his eyes three times. The third time he'd have the shades, wig, and Yankees' cap on. And Al wouldn't be there any more. In his disguise no one would discern his receding hairline or ears without lobes. The wig covered them. They would remember facial hair causing him to look not bardic, just seedy. Had he not worn Blublocker sunglasses they would have certainly noticed his brown irises with yellow-green flecks. For most people one feature predominates. His mother always said people would remember his eyes. They keep in mind only it. You must choose that feature for them: disguise it completely—exaggerate it to the point of absurdity. The wig. Those kinky perm curls. That they would remember. You had to camouflage anything that would give you away.

A shirtsleeve always covered the tattoo of a marijuana leaf on his left shoulder. Something he did, drunk, right after his release from prison, afterwards regretting it.

As the monster hidden inside your trousers expands and grows, you come alive.

When the band cranks up again and with her writhing against you, all else shrinks before the supremacy of the one thing asserting itself. Try not to smile too wickedly. He knew how to throw off the yoke of personality, to sample being nakedly—without any interfering ego. Fornicating and getting high stood two easy, readily obtainable, methods of escape, and the army taught him yet another way to get away from himself, to join in with the rest of the gun-toting automata—to sieg heil and goosestep, to goosestep and sieg heil. But long before his enlistment, he had mastered a suppression technique. Part of him as if from a distance would watch as he performed the disagreeable, potentially embarrassing or dangerous task with cold icy indifference. He would complete whatever he started doing without fear or any sort of emotion. He found it refreshing to experience this shrinkage and diminishment—to become an unreflecting machine. Yes, he could hide and fit in easily—nothing differentiating him from anyone else. He would disappear into the herd and perform acts of anonymity—now as then. He remembered that, in his early teens, only he had enough courage to purchase the *Playboy*. His two friends Swayback-tubby-pot and Slimypus waited outside the store. When he removed the magazine from the rack and tossed it down on the counter, he no longer remained Al Arretto. And he wasn't Al Arretto now. He could resume that identity immediately—rebecome himself just as he had when he walked out of that newsstand with a brown bag under his arm. Or years later exiting the convenience store where he bought his dope papers. But most of all he hated purchasing Annie's Encare ovals and Maxi-pads. Or his condoms. He felt less like Alvin buying them than at any other time.

He always said please and thank you. He worked quickly. After he ditched the bicycle and spotted Harlan's car and got in and Harlan turned the key and they started to put time and space between themselves and the bank, he gradually grew more secure. Soon he would return home, resume his age-old front and no one would suspect anything, but he would now have a whole pile of money to blow. To his friends and neighbors he would remain the same old Al. He'd water their plants when they went on vacation or take care of their cat or dog. They could depend on him. For sure, he would say with a wink and a smile.

Compared to what he would do later today, ripping off someone's bike stood as nothing. But he could pull it off even though he knew it far more dangerous. After all the risk rose in ratio to the gain, and he had ample time to reduce himself to such a total complete blank, and, for the moment, for the next forty-five minutes yet, he would remain nothing more than a bicyclist out for a spin on the back roads. *Don't think about it. For now you can still be yourself. And you don't have to go through with it.* He had turned tail before when something hadn't felt right. He had just ridden on past the target and rendezvoused with Harlan as planned. The perfect accomplice.

A dead head, Har partied with everyone. He also thought that everybody would always remain up front and truthful with him. "Everything's cool," they all said, and Harlan Houser took them at their word—gullible idiot. The first time Al met Harlan, they both got high together in the trailer of their mutual friend—a big time dealer—with a bunch of other people. Then Al hooked up the TVs of the tenants moving into Harlan's building to the pay-for-view movie channels such as Showtime and Cinemax, connecting them all for Harlan too. Eighteen months earlier, Al had received his second Master's degree. He had earned his first in his home state of Wisconsin. The second had been conferred by the University of Pittsburgh. Stu, the friend who got Al the job with the Altoona/Tyrone cable company, happened to rent from Houser. Al scored coke for him. Soon he became Harlan's connection as well. As they got better acquainted, he let the teenager know that he could always find weed or blow. Professors, who made it a point to keep in touch with their former grad students, kept in touch with him for one reason, and he kept them well supplied. Harlan at first also cultivated his friendship solely for that reason. He liked to talk a lot about himself and the problems he had with his parents. A rich kid. Must be nice to live off one's folks like that. Free to remain a total failure. But from what he said about mom and dad what other result could you have possibly expected?

Blinded in one eye one July 3rd when a paper cylinder containing an explosive and a fuse discharged just as he lit it, Dr. Harold Houser, the great surgeon, could no longer operate, carve people up with a scalpel, so he became even more of a drunk, and bedded a candy striper. Ma was a real winner too. After the divorce, she abandoned Harlan completely, letting him live off his father's child support. She takes the house and lets Har have the former office building in town. She got both in the divorce settlement. Meanwhile she continued her job as a social worker at Tyrone Hospital all the while looking for another MD. Other kids Harlan's age (he had just turned nineteen, whereas Al, at thirty-six, stood seventeen years his senior) would have died to have had a pad handed over to them and wouldn't have minded keeping out of mom and dad's way at all. Sure all that money could buy them off.

They must have spoiled him rotten as a youngster. Let him get away with anything. No wonder he became nothing but a freeloader and a sponge, a party animal and dopehead.

Alvin's mom died when he was seven. His dad kicked him out of the house when he turned seventeen. He went to the local recruiting office and enlisted.

Yes, Harlan took him at his word. Believed everything he said. No matter how fantastic or outrageous.

The core being around which Alvin fashioned his other identities had to snicker and smirk: candy from a baby. In the past, with others, he had to become much more duplicitous to convince and sway them. With Harlan, he merely bent his finger and motioned for him. And Harlan came forward. He got him to drive the getaway car by telling him their take would go toward the purchase of one hundred-percent pure flake and that both of them would make money. He showed Har how to freebase right there and then, telling him that he had never pulled a bank job before, that they were both virgins. But as long as they got in and out quickly the cops wouldn't apprehend them.

For any person he let get close, Alvin Arretto assumed an identity different from all the others, one congenial to, made to order for, the individual he wooed. For Alice, his ex-wife in Wisconsin, he became a land developer, always taking business trips to other states. He met Alice in '75, spoke to her in a grocery store in Phlox. Duane and Wayne and he had shaken hands earlier in the day.

He had just served out his four-year sentence at the University of 'Consin at Oshkosh consecutive to a three-year stint in a Florida federal penitentiary for an armed robbery he had committed in 1968, two years after his general not honorable discharge from the army. Gone for all that time, out of the blue one day, he turned up in Phlox, his home town in Langlade County, where his father had earned his living as a door-to-door salesman, and where, within the space of three years, a silent partner in Duane and Wayne's construction company (later he told Harlan that if he ever got into the construction racket his firm would have a ready-made slogan: "Be housed by a pro. Live in a Houser house"), *he* achieved the sort of affluence his father always wanted. Al made money. The company served as a front and cover for a drug distribution network. He had grown up with his two partners. They came from monied families which ran Phlox. They provided respectability, concealment and protection, whereas Al knew the right people, could always arrange deals. He married Alice, a beauty to be sure but extremely straight-laced. She did see his tattoo. He could only show her one of his many sides. That part of his life had ended, he explained. Once he had a problem. Years ago when he served in the army but he had put all that behind him now. He no longer used drugs. A tattoo didn't just wash off. He took her in and duped her. Their relationship remained staunch and unwavering for two years. But in the end she saw through his lies. Eventually it dawned on her why he took all those flights to Texas, and she threw a fit and tore open his suitcase when they came home from the airport. A half-kilo of white powder spilled out onto the tile floor. She could have pulled the rug out from under him then, but he played upon her sympathies and she never did betray or bust him even though their marriage disintegrated on the spot. He also had no trouble deceiving gullible Gail, a nineteen-year-old sophomore at Oshkosh. They shared an apartment for two and a half years. He moved in a month before he and his wife signed the divorce papers.

When he told Duane and Wayne what had happened, his business partners grew jittery and nervous. They twitched and shook and perspired. If only he stood at risk, fine. But it wouldn't be just him; the authorities would doubtlessly investigate them also and that they found unacceptable. The bitch died unless he guaranteed she wouldn't talk. He said maybe he had better just disappear. That would take the heat off them and convince Alice that no conspiracy existed, that only his hands were dirty. They'd feign just as much surprise at his disappearance as she. School remained a safe haven. Al always excelled as a student. He had graduated cum laude from the University after all, his at least partially plagiarized papers having impressed enough of his teachers. Surely some must have known or guessed that he cut corners and fudged or forgot his documentation. So again he put on the student mask, returned to University of Wisconsin at Oshkosh, but also resumed the identity of bank robber. Shrewder, older, and more cunning this time round, he succeeded beyond all expectation. Gail knew he had to support his habit somehow but would never have guessed that he robbed banks, and one day he exited her life for good. The university had just conferred his MA in History and Literature.

While in grad school, he had successfully robbed thirty-eight banks in seven states, most of them in the final year after he finished his course work. No, he wasn't paranoid. By now he had to be hot. He felt a change of scenery in order and had gotten into Pitt, been accepted in the Ph.D. program. He never told Gail that he applied or that he had been accepted. He would never complete the doctorate, would settle for a second Master's degree—this time in Political Science—instead, then drop out of school completely. Gail had really loved him. Alvin believed that she still might take him back, even now, several years later, if he could come up with a plausible explanation for his mysteriously and suddenly leaving. However, at the time of his departure, Alvin refused to look over his shoulder, just proceeded onwards into new territory, never to return to 'Consin again. His failure to conceal his other life from Alice made him all the more determined that the second woman he married, Annie, would never learn about his past. He met her after dropping out of Pitt and never told her about his army or his college days. She knew nothing other than he worked for a cable TV company in sales and service and, consequently, had to travel a lot. He did travel but instead of installing cable he cased banks.

Alvin pulled off the berm, got off the bike, and reached for his cell-phone holster. He dialed Harlan's number to make sure that Harlan had arrived at the shopping mall on time and that he had parked his car at the spot they had previously agreed upon. After Harlan answered affirmatively, Al reholstered the cell phone. He had been issued one of these new gizmos, portable communicators right out of Star Trek, when he worked for the cable company. Later, after recruiting Houser as his partner, he purchased two, one for his accomplice and one for himself. Finished with his cell, he reached into his jacket pocket, pulled out a pipe with a screwed-on lid, and put it to his lips. A short time from now, he had to be all pumped up. He took a hit. Blast off, he thought. Crack killed Apple Jack. Stepped in, couldn't step back? No way, no suh, it fixed his head just right. He found it amusing, more than just a little bit ironic, that he would soon risk his life for paper, albeit paper currency, U.S. legal tender, good for all debts, public and private. That he would shortly pull a gun on someone and point it in his or her face and that the cops, should they arrive on the scene, would surely not harbor second thoughts about greasing him. All over little slips of paper, Uncle Sam's greenbacks. He, Alvin, certainly would never do something so foolish. But he wasn't there, remember. He had been repressed. Someone else had taken possession of his body, had displaced him. But not completely. He would observe his hand take the gun out of its holster in his coat once he stepped into the bank, a disinterested bystander. The ego so often overpowered, precisely because he put and held it in check so many times before, fought hard against further suppression—and some days would not be subdued or put in restraint. For a while, "Al" would gain the upper hand, overcome his dark opponent, and they would stay away from the banks.

But when he decided to go ahead, he made damn sure that he took all appropriate precautions. He mapped out everything in advance. He had a plan and counter plan for every possible contingency. He would visit the town numerous times. He knew where the crowds gathered on what days. He would decide on the bank and the rendezvous point with Harlan and then come to a determination as to the best time to walk in and walk out. He again hit on the pipe. The mental work finished, he merely had to put his plan in execution. It helped entering a zombified state. He took off the shades, tilted his head back and looked at the sun. Yellow burned into both his retinas. He closed his lids to save his sight, then opened them once again.

Suddenly everything shone a little bit brighter. He recalled rousing from sleep at the break of dawn earlier that day.

Again he woke up. Annie still lay asleep at his side. The monster began to stir in his trousers. Anew, once more, he threw off the sheet. Her sweet, firm, squeezable breasts cried out to be handled. To be kneaded, softly pinched and lingeringly caressed. He kissed, fondled and stroked them. She opened her eyes, wound her fingers in his hair as he traced a trail of kisses down her flat belly until he reached the pungent perfumed smell of delicate lingerie. He gave her several feathery licks (the intimate attention of the devoted underwear eater) then pulled down her panties to reveal her henna triangle. He raised her leg over his shoulder then buried his face between her thighs and began devouring the orange-bearded clam. She gasped when he found the little boy in the boat and began to violently rock her hips. His beard scratching hers, he pressed his tongue into her thatch. She started to moan. Then a moment of extreme passion. Taking the little nubbin in his mouth, he pushed his finger deep into her rectum....

His back arched against a tree, he sprang to his feet. He felt as if he had drunk a hundred cups of coffee. Ready, more than ready, he hopped back on the bicycle. He was about two miles from town. He'd soon reach the highway. He went over the escape route one more time. After exiting the bank, he would abandon his bicycle two hundred yards away in the Coronet Mall parking lot. He would walk through Sears, K-Mart, and Bon Ton; gun holstered: wig, hat and money stuffed inside his coat: and go out the exit by Pearl Vision and Hickory Farms where Houser sat waiting in the car. He'd tell Harlan where to drive (some ten or fifteen miles distant) then get out there and change vehicles—get back behind the wheel of his Mercury Cougar, and they would drive off in separate directions. He would not have to race, speed, or drive recklessly. He had learned from his past mistakes and would cruise like a bluehair, as slowly and cautiously as an eighty-year-old grandmother. In seven-to-eight weeks, he would contact Harlan by phone. By then he would have selected another target. Naturally it would require a great deal of preparation. That went without saying. But they could do it, just as Harlan could "do" any girl he wanted and, if he didn't discriminate and become too pick-and-choosy, a different one every night. The boy just wouldn't listen!

Al had no room to talk. But talk away, mock and chide, he did. He stood quite the authority in these matters despite the fact that he had had dry spells in the past. Committed anonymous acts during those periods of drought and famine and even after when he happened to be involved with or married to a woman that he would just as well shut his eyes upon. They made him envy the cat, the dog, the animal, that would thoroughly enjoy its rut then forget it ever took place. Only the partner who didn't know his name would remember, but his face would blur into all the others just as theirs did for him. Yet he retained the memory of the act itself. Sometimes he wanted to repress the memory, but sometimes he wanted to remember, usually when alone in bed. His partners could later fantasize too, if they wanted to, how horny and strung out, he let them go down on him now and again. He didn't reciprocate. Probably some of them had died by now, first victims of the gay cancer. It started in the joint. In the cities he went to the saunas and steam baths or made trips to their known stalking grounds in the parks. He simply stepped into the woods, unbuttoned his trousers and exposed the monster. And sure enough some faggot dropped to his knees just as his first cellmate had done. Everyone knew about Forest Park. Even people from as far north as he. He had followed the Mississippi south. With each subsequent job he drove greater and greater distances from his home base in Oshkosh, Wisconsin. Farther and farther away from Gail. Occasionally he would reach as south as St. Louis. He would drive till he got there. The greater the distance the better. He would go the extra mile. Besides he'd have quite a buzz on by the time he reached his bank. He would snort several more lines. Once he arrived, he'd go in then come right back out but first he'd stop at the park.

Women remained different. He fell in love with them. For four long lean years he worked solo—had no need of an accomplice. All of a sudden, due to circumstances beyond his control, a little over a year before, that need arose. Trashed, totaled, but still getting higher, and speeding as fast as his car would go on a little-traveled back road, he crossed the West Virginia state line from Ohio.

In his lifetime he had seen many dead animals lying splattered on the highway. If he ever ran over one—why should it remain any different, why should he feel any worse, if he hit a rabbit or slammed into a pet cat or dog than if a bee or kamikaze hummingbird flew into his windshield? Accidents, road kills, would continue happening as long as people traveled at such speeds. Nonetheless he'd honk the horn and slam on the brakes if something darted at his tires. He would much prefer to collide with a mailbox than hit some kid's collie.

Why did it have to be a little girl with pretty blonde braids on her bicycle? He turned the curve and saw her too late. He slammed on the brakes and jerked the wheel hard but he still hit her. She flew over the handlebars, bounced off his car, and landed on the macadam, where she flopped and writhed like a fish out of water. He had driven for years and had avoided collisions. Why now? Why her? He took one quick look then punched the accelerator. She didn't have a chance, or he would have stopped. No he wouldn't. Why lie? He had close to nine thou in his car, the murder weapon in his glovey. He'd get life or worse. He had no way of telling that the security guard would pull through. The girl died almost instantly—of that he stood certain. But he couldn't let his conscience eat away at him. Some things just happened. He could live with it. And that's why he took drugs. At least one reason. To blot out guilt, shame and regret. To become comfortably numb. He tried to expiate his sin and balance the karma by going out of his way to be nice to his neighbors' kids in Allison Park, buying his newspaper or magazine subscriptions from them or carving their jack-a-lanterns at Halloween, helping them to build snowmen in the winter. He dropped out of the Ph. D. program and began his search for a driver, and in Tyrone he found Harlan Houser. Until the Ohio job, he had never shot anyone. True, he pointed his Smith & Wesson at numerous faces but never had to pull the trigger until he said put all the money on the counter and then, working in unison like synchronized swimmers dissolving then suddenly recomposing some elaborate group figure to be beheld from the viewing stands above, the bank employees plunged and dove to the floor all at the same time after the security guard came out of the bathroom, saw that a robbery was in progress, and stretched out his hand and motioned for them to all drop together. Al wheeled around. A sole teller remained standing, the one he held the gun on a moment before. The guard had drawn his piece. Arretto fired twice, the first shot missing and the second hitting the rent-a-cop in the chest. His heart pounding, he demanded the teller's car keys, took them, determined the make by looking at a key (Ford Family Of Fine Cars) and asked where she parked and what model she drove. He steered the red Escort into a residential area, parked it in front of someone's front lawn, got out and started walking. He heard sirens. His Bonneville sat just around the corner.

After accidentally killing the girl, he experienced remorse perhaps for the only time in his life and cried, actually bawled, as he sped down the country road, fortunately for him not a car or a person in sight. He even thought about ending his life. About driving his car over an embankment or head on into a telephone pole. Finally reaching that destination that he all along knew he would arrive at. What all those hundred thousands of miles of driving had from the very beginning been leading up to: a crash. A smash-up. But his hands couldn't yank the wheel in the right direction at a suitable moment. He remained a coward. So the hell what. Self-preservation was the first law of nature. You had to remain strong to survive. Once before, in Panama City, he had thought of cashing in when waking up one more day seemed worse than never waking again.

But he had resisted then. And he would resist now.

That place was full of banks. A Latin Switzerland. The hoards and war chests of revolutionaries, drug traffickers, and dictators lay in the same bank vaults.

Everyone paid the banker.

Al served his country in the Canal Zone while simultaneously investing all his earnings, whatever capital he could put together, in the pack-your-nose export business. He met the right people through the offices of one Ferdinand Jesus Varga, a well connected *Guardia Nacionale* who frequented the bars along the Avenida Fourth of July and knew the local riff raff, all the street level black marketers, but also had access to the big houses on Ancon Hill and even into the formidable barricaded Presidential residence. The smugglers brought the cocaine across the Darien jungle from the safer hills of Columbia.

Nick Moon, the first officer of a merchant marine freighter, would pick up the shipment. He had given Al the cash six months earlier and Al had kept it in a safety deposit box in the *Banco de Occidente*. He selected it from the myriad others because it stood farthest from the base. Moon owed him another five upon delivery so he would have more than enough money to replace the two thousand that he blew on the hookers and prize fights. He'd have it in twenty-four hours. Moon's dust would be waiting on the dock for his ship to steam into the Canal Zone.

Vargas introduced him to Esteban at the Golden Key, one of the bars that lined the Avendia Fourth of July. They agreed to exchange an attaché case for a duffle bag at one of Panama City's many "pushbuttons," a building with a line of innocuous looking garage doors. You put money in a slot, pushed a button, the garage door opened and you drove in. When the garage door closed, you and the whore would get out of the car and enter a fully furnished bedroom. A perfect place for adultery and drug deals. You see no one. No one sees you.

He arrived twenty minutes late. Possibly the delay saved his life. Had he been there he might have shared Esteban's fate. He watched the man and woman drive up to the fifth garage door. It goes up, they drive inside and the door comes down like a curtain on a stage. He puts money in the appropriate slot and garage door number three rises. He drives the rented Mercedes two-seater inside; the door goes down. He turns the knob and enters the bedroom. Blood everywhere. Esteban had been shot at close range. In the head. He had been sitting on the john. Probably he heard the gun go off just as he finished his shit. He had toilet paper in his hand. Take more than that to clean him up now. No duffle bag. Godamit to hell. Vargas had set him up, signed his death warrant. He felt like removing the sidearm from its holster inside his linen suit, putting the muzzle in his mouth and squeezing the trigger. Esteban's people would think that he stole the merchandise and they would snuff his life out with professional efficiency. Maybe they would kidnap and torture him. Or even now the police might close in. Maybe El Presidenté wanted an international scandal. U.S. soldier busted. Panamanian Government produces evidence of U.S. military involvement with drug cartel. He would prefer death to rotting away in Leavenworth. Esteban's assassination would have ugly consequences for Sergeant Arretto no matter who did it. No matter which interpretation of the data proved correct. He got back in the car, pulled out of the garage and fled to the base. They couldn't hit him there. He might as well have dumped Nick Moon's seven thousand in a garbage can, but he arranged to have a friend (a sergeant like himself) redeposit it in Moon's name in the *Banco Nacionale de Panama*. His pal promised to meet Moon on the docks and give him the account number. Al didn't have time to worry about if he would or wouldn't. After his friend took the cash and agreed to straighten things out with Moon, Sergeant Alvin Roy Arretto went to Captain Sherman "Can do" Harrison's room. The Captain stood naked and dripping having just stepped out of the shower. They had almost come to blows once before, the matter of an unpaid two thousand dollar debt. Two weeks earlier, he turned over the money he owed. Now he proceeded to hit his superior officer in the face two times. He wanted a general discharge and that's exactly what he received, spared a court marshal in view of his past service to his country, his tour in Nam. He didn't merit the reprieve. A warrant officer attached to the general staff, he never left Saigon. The real reason the brass exempted him: because he could implicate other military personnel–higher-ups including the captain–in drug running. Al found himself stateside where he devoted his life to carnal and chemical pleasures. He first did time on a possession charge in Houston. Then he got popped attempting to rob a bank in Tallahassee. After being paroled to his home state from the Florida penitentiary, he entered the University of Wisconsin and earned a Bachelor's degree in American History with a minor in Political Science, a university scholar and honors student. After graduation, he and several friends started a construction business and he married the daughter of a minister: Alice White, who later became Alice Black, a real bitch and pain in the ass when she found out about his double life.

After the debacle of the shoot out with the bank guard in Ohio and then the hit-and-run accident the same day in West Virginia and not getting apprehended for either but feeling rash and self-destructive, he drove back to Allison Park and returned to his other life. He traded the Bonneville in for a Cougar, finished up his course work for his second graduate degree, his Masters at Pitt, got a job with the central Pennsylvania cable company the summer after his graduation (1982), quit after a couple months and moved back to Allison Park. Annie Rogers patronized the same bar he did. He had admired her before he left for the summer; now he decided to go for the kill. She worked at a travel agency. His immediate success with her–the attention she paid to his every word, her willingness to let something develop between them but nothing casual or cheap–surprised and startled him. He got to really liking her and then felt resentment when she did not spend all her free time with him, because she did not always come when he snapped his fingers. They often went out on drives, one and two-day excursions. His desire would wax and wane for her but she seemed a creature of such depth and penetration that there always stood the promise of something more, an inexhaustible profusion of red-haired Anne. Sure they got together. Why not? Nothing stood in their way to prevent them.

After their marriage, they relocated to a small rural town in Cambria County, where Anne found work as a secretary in a realtor's office. Even so, the banks drew him back. After all that's where they kept the money. He told his wife that he worked for the cable company.

As he got closer to downtown Marronsburg, the distance between houses grew less and less. Two flocks of southward flying birds—hundreds of individual dark dots—stretched across the sky. One flock passed behind the other so that the birds resembled a swarm of bees dividing in two, a new hive accompanied by its own queen, departing the parent stock to take up lodgings elsewhere. He saw a jet high up in the blue and once again glimpsed the crescent moon. But straight ahead, to the right and left, everywhere he looked: whirring autos, car sheen, the expressway with its mid-morning traffic. He turned onto the main road and, after the first barrage of cars whizzed by, crossed over to the right and pedaled a quarter mile uphill, then flew down a slope, a Volkswagen dealership on one side, a David Weiss store on his other, and then an intersection with a light stopping him dead. He turned right when he got the green. He could have gone straight ahead, followed the expressway straight to his destination, but he preferred to approach his target from behind. He peddled down the new road, an equally busy thoroughfare for about thirty feet, before making a hard left onto a side drive. Three or four houses with imposing gables and French windows and doors blipped by, next a row of brick and stucco condominiums, each one identical to all the others. A sign proclaiming Canterbury Commons waved in the wind. Another apartment complex sat across the street. But he turns left, sees the original expressway once again up ahead of him, approximately one hundred feet away. Where the street met the highway the Union Federal marquee rose like the golden arches. He approached the depository from the rear and could see the Coronet Mall across the freeway. When he reached his destination, he cut through the grass—the drive-through window sat on the opposite side of the brick building, the parking lot and sidewalk straight ahead—dismounted and put down the kickstand. He turned the corner and strode past the ornamental trees and shrubs toward the pillared entrance, ready to push open the glass door but first pausing to look at his reflection. The wig, Blublocker glasses and baseball cap greeted him from the glass. In his shirt pocket he had his "suicide" note. He remembered from the movies that it had to be composed on his own typewriter. He laughed when he did it. It actually read like something someone might write about to take his own life intentionally. It told who he was, where he lived, and that his wife thought she was married to a cable TV serviceman. He paused only a moment then went through the door. He looked around him.

Turquoise carpet and curtains. Two thinly veined white marble counters meeting at a right angle and separated by a swing gate. Five lines formed in front of the one he faced. He glanced to his right at the other counter. Three lines formed in front of it. Four to six people stood waiting in each. Everyone open. No Next Window Please. He saw the backs of heads, every shade of hair color, dyed and natural. The teller nearest him—a thin woman with girlish face, brown braids, braces, and a red dress—in addition to the people in her line also serviced customers doing their banking at the drive-up window. He spun his head again to the right. Behind the counter, a stately tall, rawboned, blonde woman dressed in a burgundy blouse and wearing several necklaces sat at one table speaking to loan applicants. At an adjacent table sat two men in business suits, both middle-aged and the one quite large with shiny black hair and an acne-scarred, red-cheeked face. He wore a scarlet tie with his black sport coat. Looked like he played on a high school football team that had an undefeated season—say his junior year. CA 1951. The other man with dark brown eyes and gray hair shot with black wore a blue three-piece suit. Behind them an attendant opened and ushered a woman into a room with safety deposit boxes. Arretto glimpsed row upon row of them like in a P.O. The three tellers looked like grandmas prim and imperious, the first had her iron-gray hair up in a bun, bags under her eyes and a triple chin; the second stout and slow with orange hair and a K-Mart taste in clothes; the third, a bird watcher or a lady librarian had a dour face and snub nose, glasses. He turned his head to again check out the four other tellers besides Braceface directly in front of him. Two looked matronly, but two appeared in their late twenties or early thirties. He saw a clock behind them on the wall. Short and flat chested, the first of the two younger tellers poured coins into a machine that swirled them around and separated them. A bouquet of flowers and an upright plaque with a gold disk in its center sat at her window. Two TV cameras came out of the wall above her. The last girl's ginger brown hair hung down to her shoulders. She was tall and fine-featured. Her made-up face, red lips, and blue eye shadow coordinated nicely with her black-and-white checkered dress. She handed a boy a lollypop. She wore gloves. White ones up to her elbows. He got in her line, glad of the crowd. Soon they would forget whatever they now deliberated and fussed about; in a moment or two they would all be watching him. By then he would have achieved blankness and would think about nothing except the matter at hand. But in the meantime, he heard snippets of conversation—could sense all the thought in process around him. He heard voices inside his head other than his own, but they remained muffled. He couldn't make out anything they said. Don't tune in; you don't want to hear. Think where you stand. Don't be scared. Stop sweating. It just like you're in a checkout line buying rubbers. Don't be uneasy. Play it out smoothly, with finesse.

It'll go down as it always has. Pretend you're an actor in a movie. You know your lines. Just follow the script.

Stop trying to tune in the voices. Switch to autopilot.

Her feet hurt. A half hour and her shift would end. She wanted to just sit down. She earned her meager six-fifty an hour counting out money, making change. Thousands of dollars went through her hands. Today neither a bill nor cent of it profaned her on account of her gloves. She had a skin rash. If only a tenth of that money could somehow find its way into her pocketbook. But hers remained the only job in the world where you could be arrested for taking your work home with you. She smiled at all the customers, cashed their checks one after another. The better-looking men chose to stand in her line instead of being waited on by one of the crones. She already had her intended chosen though. He had a nice car and a new house, owned a bar and café and made a nice income. Tonight, after weeks of waiting, he would finally take her out for dinner and dancing. Then she'd invite him into her apartment afterwards and hope that against all odds he would fall in love with her and want to get married, have *her* bear his children.

So many people stood ahead of him in the line. When would he get his cash stream card so he could use the automatic teller and avoid wasting all this time?

That Mr. Cobin, what a perfect hypocrite. He knew all along that he wouldn't give me the loan. Sanctimonious ass. So solicitous. He hoped he might oblige but really his hands were tied.

They come to me. I show them the stern face of the law but also benevolence and mercy. I stand a judge like Samson or Solomon. I decide who gets what and how much. The first rule of thumb is to remain strictly professional. The clientele won't resent but respect you for it.

Can't they ever remember to endorse the backside of a check?

Never seen him before. Greasy hair. Red eyes. Best punch up the account number and see if he's got fifty dollars to his name. Since I got the award for most personable teller, I can return to being a bitch I guess. Just a moment, sir. Flash him a smile as you punch up his number.

He sat behind a desk, wore an expensive jacket—blended in perfectly. His tie accented his appearance. He did nothing but sit—never had cushier work. Thanks to the Gentleman Bandit. The FBI had developed a profile of him. Studied the kinds of banks he hit. When he surfaced in Western Pennsylvania, the bureau shared this information with area banks and encouraged them to hire off-duty and retired police officers like himself, armed and authorized to use deadly force, as security guards. He'd again tell Ernie that the bandit stood all the drinks, paid their whole tab, after the bank closed, and he stepped into Harrigan's for the obligatory beer and shot. If his kidneys could hold out till then. He had a couple of shooters on his lunch break.

May I have two tens please?

Horton, I have lived with you for so long I know all your tricks. You don't know I know where you hide the checkbook. You act so casual, make sure that I've gone into another room before you sneak into the parlor and put it behind your books. Volume Six of *The World's Greatest Literature.* I've asked you for two months now for some money for the yard. Today I just wrote out a check for what I needed.

The baby's stock keeps going up. I bought the kid one hundred shares and myself seven hundred. But I put the kid's in her name also. She cashed them. And she shows up at the company dinner with that goof. At least she could have spared me that. I'll pay her back though. Karma's a bitch. Even now I'm closing out both my savings and checking accounts. Women's lib's fine, but it's the man that always has to pay. Always. To see someone else is one thing, but to do it so openly, so brazenly. And only for one reason. To hurt me. To publicly humiliate me. Well, I'm divorced from the cow now.

If you would speak to Mr. Cobin, please. Mr. Samuel Cobin.

Someday I will walk off with several thousand. Unnoticed and scot-free.

He couldn't wait any longer. He had to pull out the iron monster.

He barged through the two people waiting in front of him straight up to her. He leveled the Smith & Wesson at her head but spoke to the other tellers as well: "Ladies, this is a robbery. Please put all your money up on the counter."

I was going to walk off with all the cash and now he comes and shoots me. And Matthew! I'll never have the chance to—

Move lady. A little to your left, and I'll have a clean shot. I'll drop the son of a bitch.

He fired, but just as the target moved.

Al heard the detonation of the gun and felt the bullet go through his left shoulder at the same time. He winced in pain. She had emptied her register. Always the gentleman, he had been about to tell her thank you.

Instead he squeezed on the trigger. Teeth and fillings flew out of the woman's mouth. Her face just opened up. Ladies screamed. Instantly he had a woman in the next line by the throat, the gun barrel in her ear. As if he stood in the middle of a busy intersection, cars coming at him from all directions, Al swung round, holding his hostage close, and trying to look all places at once. He took in the whole bank, but he couldn't pinpoint the gunman. *Can't see with all these people.* "Give it up," someone shouted. Al saw his mark. "Throw down your weapon. You can't get away." "Then I'll kill her," Arretto barked, staring at the gun in the chubby hand of the heavy-set man with the greased back hair, black sport coat and red tie. He came from under the desk, crawled round the counter, stood up, drew and fired. Now he had his pistol aimed at Arretto's head. But his hand shook. Badly. "You're under arrest. Please don't move." Behind his human shield, Al stretched out his arm, and pretended that he would drop the gun but fired instead. The big man crumpled, dropped the thirty-eight onto the turquoise carpet, and fell to the floor. His white shirt turned as red as his tie. He kicked a lot. Al's shoulder stabbed and stung. He felt blood trickling down his chest.

He started for the door.

The bastard, Cobin thought. *He'll die right here, won't get out of my bank.* He jumped onto the floor, stooped, and grabbed the weapon, then got up on his haunches. The thief darted like a deer, but he had shot many deer. He aimed and fired twice. Both bullets pierced Arretto. One went through his leg. The other lodged in his spleen.

Al dropped to his knees, then on his face. His entrails burned. The bank must have two rent-a-cops. The second had greased and put paid to him. He saw Annie's face contort in horror. She wouldn't believe a word of it. They told terrible lies. To her, Al would always remain a sweet, loving man. Why did they slander him so? *Damn you all*, he thought. He raised his arm and shot randomly. A boy screamed as blood spurted out of him. A woman fell. Did he hit her? Or did she faint? Someone again shot in his direction. He saw the gray-haired man in the blue three-piece suit. He aimed at his face, fired.

The bullet went through his forehead. Small hole. Al lay back. He bled badly. The note! He pulled it out of his shirt pocket, crumpled it in his hand, tore it with his teeth and swallowed. He heard wailing sirens. They grew louder. No, he decided not to tell them his identity. He took another bite then another until he ate the whole letter. They'd have to earn their pay. Figure it out for themselves. The sirens became deafening. Squad cars pulled into the parking lot. Al put the gun to his temple and fired the last round.

SECOND

Welcome to Colonial Court Manor ....
Harlan's Dream

A celebrated sword-cock-and-wordsman, a brigand who waylaid the rich to relieve the poor, an erstwhile captain of a band of outlaws who dismissed his men from service after the Duke of A— captured a confederate and broke him on the wheel, Craggio had already won the heart of the town, before his boot ever touched its soil. Everyone knew of his exploits. The sharp-witted adventurer had secured a widespread and illustrious reputation. True, he had practiced and perfected all three of his crafts—he could cut and thrust with his narrow, pointed two-edge, arrange words so as to win the Muse's crown of laurel with his quill, and delight his paramours and lady loves with his unscabbarded smallsword, but, if truth be told, many-tongued rumor like a blatant beast exaggerated his achievement while broadening his fame. For in the first instance, his name instilled more fear and more respect from the masses than his skill with épée and sabre actually warranted and in the second, while a troubadour who composed verse and who had captured the hearts of many marchese with his lyrics, he had never bedded one hundred noblewomen in a single night, a feat worthy of Hercules, a veritable thirteenth labor. For the townspeople circulated and readily believed the tale, such was the breadth and extent of their credulity. For the common folk he enjoyed an exalted status and had become a figure larger than life, a man distinguished for his exceptional courage and fortitude and for his great physical prowess who had fought many duels (the townspeople maintained with all the best swordplayers of Europe), and a poet-musician who had captivated an equal number of fair hearts. Craggio knew his limitations, his human, all-to-human failings. To the peasants of Northern Italy, to the poor townspeople of Santa Lucia, however, he had become a hero, a God.

The village nestled in the Italian Tyrol. Aside from the townspeople and peasants, the monks of the monastery of San Sebastian resided there, a strict and solemn order. From reputation alone, they thought Craggio a demon damned. Only Antoli considered the possibility that he might remain an ordinary sick soul deserving of love, commiseration and pity.

The monastery and the town both lay in the province of the aforesaid Duke of A— who resided in a grand castle at the ducal seat a half-day's ride distant. The old Prince had recently wed a young flower from Venice. The rich and powerful can have all the things they want. They have the means in their hands to purchase the favors of comely and beauteous women, to obtain their leave and gracious consent. Craggio had once paid court to the Duke of A—'s wife. It came into the adventurer's mind to liberate his lady love, to set her free from bondage and confinement, to release and extricate her from the sickly embraces of her decrepit and moribund husband, his present enemy. Foolishly he wrote to her of his intentions. The lady in question did not desire her freedom. If you stood virtually heiress to the province of A— would you wish to be carried off? In his missive, Craggio relayed how he planned to wend his way to her and how he would traverse a certain mountain pass near Santa Lucia. She promptly showed the letter to her husband. Troops lay in ambush at the pass. Struck with bullets, the wounded adventurer roamed the woods and found himself on the monastery grounds and at the door of the Abbot. Craggio made his departure from our stage.

Antoli's father remained a great personage, a prince of the realm, but illegitimate, the son of a chambermaid, Antoli could never succeed to the chair of the state, the throne on a dais with canopy. His father's steward at first raised him as his own son then later put his charge to the church. Educated in Milan by monks of his future order, the boy loved to search through the old parchments and illuminated manuscripts in the collection. The stories of the noble knights of times gone by stirred his very soul, and he wished that he had been born several centuries earlier in time so that he might have become a fair lady's champion and put on chain mail for chivalric combat. But as he grew older he relinquished such childish fancies. He determined that he would enter the institution which had raised him. A promising young novitiate, he spoke his prayers with devotion and fervor. Everyday he told his beads, rapt in prayerful union with his Saviour. His station improved and when he turned but thirty his order appointed him Abbot at the monastery of Santa Lucia. Everyone loved him and considered him the most pious of men. Sage and well informed persons predicted his further advancement. One day, they said, he would win a red hat.

Antoli heard the dying man's knock. He helped Craggio onto a pallet, undressed him and attempted to tend his wounds, but the adventurer expired within minutes of his arrival. Antoli knew and identified Craggio's costume. The great billowing black cape, the boots of the finest Spanish leather, the silk hat with purple plume and wide brim shading the wearer's face, the frilled frock coat and the dove-white gloves. Youth! How at times we wish to escape the seriousness of life and return to the fancies of youth. Antoli never wore the costume of a troubadour. He was sorely tempted and in the end gave in to his temptation and put on the dead man's romantic garb. Abbot Antoli. Sir Antoli!

An elderly and wizened monk came to ask the young Abbot a question. He saw and recognized Crantoli. Enraged, he ordered the adventurer off the sacred ground.

The old man had caught the young Abbot red-handed but did not make him out in his disguise, his countenance shaded by the brim of Craggio's great hat. What could Antoli do? If he removed his headgear and showed his face the monks would lose all their respect for him for certainly the old man, a former candidate himself for Abbot, would inform all the brothers of the young Abbot's depraved action of bedizening himself in the garb of the notorious adventurer and reprobate. So Antoli had no choice but to leave the holy ground. Later he would return and change his costume for monk's habit and an end would come to his foolish escapade, his momentary loss of reason. May the Lord God above permit such a conclusion, he murmured outside the monastery gate and crossed himself. So Cragtoli walked into the village of Santa Lucia. All the town recognized Cragtoli, and stood in awe, amazed that the great hero had stridden into their midst. A young buxom girl ran up and kissed the cape of the august Cragtoli. The mayor invited him to a banquet. He thought to himself that the people treated him with more honor and deference, respect and love than they would extend to even Pope or King. He had to eat and drink excessively. He could not act like a priest. He could not give himself away. The pressure on Crantoli remained immense. But Cragtoli always wanted to live the life of an adventurer. Craggoli thought it just a little leave and respite into another side of life. A hero came into the dull, lifeless town, and the town paid attention. More attention than to the most enlightened discourse of Antoli.

The town square and the Mayor's villa stood in the center of Santa Lucia. Outside the city wall lay green farmlands dotted with peasant shacks. Marked by squalor and wretched living conditions, the narrow and crooked streets remained thickly thronged and crowded day and night, perfect places for pickpockets to ply their trade. To reach the gate that opened on the road that wound up into the mountains, Antoli would have to go down them. Little did he know whom he might encounter . . . .

Before he got there eternities passed, and people passed into eternity. And every day as he made his way down his assigned hall, he would sense the presence of his ghosts. They must have felt as neglected—no—abandoned as ever they had when they pushed their call bells and waited for him, maybe wetting themselves or befouling their sheets and covers with BM because the bed pan did not arrive in time. Or they let go just as he got it under them and urine or liquid BM splashed onto his hands and shirtsleeves. Perhaps they died in the interim. They waited, tried to linger. But no one came in to grasp their hand. He dreaded going in and finding them dead most. As for the ghosts, he tried to ignore them.

Harlan's thin face closed in a recessive chin. He had a button nose, cobalt blue eyes and inky hair he always brushed to the left side. His small evenly spaced teeth never seemed to fill his mouth. When he smiled one always saw too much gum, too little tooth. He had very long legs but, small boned with a washboard stomach and no body fat at all on him, he also had no muscles in his stick arm. When he tried to make one, nobody could see or feel it. Elsewhere he knew himself better endowed thank the Lord. He had white tennis shoes on. Stood attired all in white. Welcome to Colonial Court Manor. A three hundred fifty-bed convalescent center certified by Medicare and Medicaid for skilled and intermediate nursing care located in El Dorado, Pennsylvania, a tiny town adjacent to the city of Altoona. To the three-to-eleven shift of an aide paid ten cents more than minimum wage. Screams, wailing, tears and depression greeted one at every door. One geri-chair-confined lady never spoke but would laugh as if privy to some secret of the dead that made us living, our goals, worries, and petty concerns, a source of constant amusement for her. Harlan hated the chronic ringers—straighten this, fix that—who wanted you back as soon as you left—most of all "Larry, Moe, and Shemp." The call bell could only be shut off at the nurses' station. Room 218 Blue Hall remained a perpetually wailing siren. He would shoot up the hall to the desk to see that it was 218 again. He silenced it. A red light outside the patients' room came on. He put off answering them as long as he could. But when he went into the room, he faced the same questions, gave the same answers. If he could only strangle the life right out of them—turn them off like the dagum bell. But Willie started in sure as shooting: "When can I go home?" Sam just as predictably sat up and begged: "How about that cigarette—I'll pay you back, so I will!" And Joe, the flyboy paralyzed on one side and in a wheelchair, whose spirit nonetheless still soared, started to bitch about and at the two crazies he had to live and put up with: "And the hollow-horned devil's got a two-inch prick," he sputtered, spit. "No, clit. And no balls. Instead of a greasy goat specker. No, horse cock." He coughed. "Sam old fart. Har ain't gonna swallow none of that pay back crap," he paused. "Since you're here anyway, Har be a buddy. Har bout emptying my urinal. Want a beer? I've already had two too many." "Sure," Harlan said and reached for what was proffered him, took the urinal from Joe's outstretched hand. He stepped backwards into the bathroom, emptied it out into the bowl, a bright yellow waterfall, then flushed the toilet with his foot. He would have to go to the maintenance department for the beer. At the end of his shift. They kept Joe's case back in the cage. The doctor allowed him two bottles daily.

No more. Joe still had a lot of fight in him. But the other two had reached the point of turning into ghosts but still lingered and stayed put in their skins. Yet there remained others—others he couldn't see.

Through their relics and the ambience of the rooms and environs, Harlan detected *their* aura. Yes certain days, when he stood off his guard, he would feel, say, Ida's presence in her old corner in two-oh-four. He heard the unmistakable voice, repeating the same words again and again—"I'm God and your days stand numbered." His former reaction would have been to look over his shoulder and tell her to sing "When Irish Eyes Are Smiling" or "Amazing Grace." She'd sing "My daddy my daddy no he's dead he's dead and gone to heaven" or "I'm God and your days stand numbered" to the tune he suggested. But he suddenly remembered and froze. All sense of her suddenly vanished. A phantom pain. And he could never help but feel Ruby's closeness whenever he chanced to enter room 213. One hundred two years old, she spent most of her life in Alabama. How she ever found her way north to end her days in this god-forsaken hole he would never know. She would just clap her hands and sing to herself. When someone white put a question to her, she'd answer yes sir or no sir, a fossil black who still bowed to the old white authority. Respected it. Yet all the aides knew that she bit. Once he had the privilege of removing foam from a rubber ball she had chewed from out of her mouth. Day after day, the more that you worked around her, you saw that she did in fact have lucid periods. Once some new cad from the activities department interviewed her, filled out some assessment form, did a chart audit, Har didn't know which, and she woke up. "Do you like music?" "Yes'm." "What kind—church music, hymns?" "Yes, sir, I like those." "Are you Protestant or Catholic?" "I believe that I am Baptist." She claps her rawhide nigger hands and hums. "Ruby, how far did you get in school?" No reply. "Can you wash your own face? What's today's date? Do you drink?" "No, sir. I don't drink no whiskey!" "Do you smoke?" She hadn't the seven years she resided there. "Yes, sir. Do you have one to spare?" The cad not knowing this (they had just hired him) diligently wrote down what she said. "How many a day?" he asked. "Just a couple. But I'll do real good," she added quickly to reassure him. "I'll clean your house good."

And one night he and Keefer came in to answer her roommate's bell and there Ruby sat in bed, her nightgown pulled off. A rosy palm under each black breast, she juggled her boobs. "These here for you, honey," she said to Keefer, who was also black. She liked to sass the Negroes employed at the Manor.

During the one-to-one when asked to identify the use of a wooden spoon, she couldn't tell them that you stirred sauce with it, but said she had one she used on the backs of her children when they richly deserved it.

Yes, Ruby lived on in him—a grace period before all memory of her faded away when those that knew her also passed on. Maybe he would be the last to remember her. She would live only in him. Then: utter extinction.

Various apparitions roamed the hallways of Colonial Court Manor at night. Many of them he didn't know—the home had operated for decades before he ever found work at it. The shadow of Melisandre Lange, the patient who strangled in her restraints two years earlier, in 1987, hung over everyone involved with the Manor, tormented and troubled and put the fear of God into more people than the other ghosts combined. She terrified all the employees, residents and family members as well as Mr. Falisec and the other owners. She garroted herself during the night shift. No one had checked on her for several hours. The aide and the charge nurse took her down (apparently she had attempted to get out of bed and had managed to climb over the guard rail), put her back under the covers, cleaned the BM off the floor, and tried to make it appear that she died from natural causes, not as a direct result of their neglect. They charted that they had made their rounds hourly. One corroborated the other. But the autopsy determined the time of death as 2:00 not 6:00 a.m. The Department of Health attempted to close the facility after this "unfortunate incident" and filed criminal charges against Falisec. The courts reinstated the nursing home license on appeal, however. Since then forcing Falisec out of the business remained high on the Department of Health's agenda. The State targeted the facility for immediate inspection. While the deficiencies lists did not disclose any deficiencies that posed a threat to the health and safety of the patients, nor impaired the home's ability to render acceptable nursing care, the Secretary of Health issued four provisional licenses one after another. By state law, the Department could not issue a fifth provisional license. When the fourth expired, the state could once again revoke Mr. Falisec's license to operate a nursing home. In addition, the Department of Health had placed an admission ban on the facility after the last state inspection. The census had dwindled since then to less than two hundred patients. Most of the remaining residents had only Medicaid coverage, so the home went further and further into the red. If the State and Falisec didn't reach a compromise soon, Falisec would be bankrupt, the residents homeless, the employees out of a job.

But two shades remained even more terrible from Harlan's point of view than Mrs. Lange's. They stood as his personal demons. His to exorcise. His alone. One a skin specter, the husk of his great-grandfather Anton Rausch, a corpse that breathed. Harlan had often thought of suffocating him with a pillow. The other, thirty-six but already dead, had come with Harlan to this place, had not entered the facility as a resident and seemed out of place due to his relative youth. A bearded, balding brown-eyed man with a nine-mm Smith & Wesson automatic handgun gripped in his fingers.

He knew that something had gone disastrously wrong. He had heard sirens, waited and waited, drummed his fingers on the steering wheel. Sweat began to pour out of him. He got out of his car and went into the stores as if to shop, saw through a display window the police cars and ambulance in the First Union Federal parking lot across the street. Two hours and forty minutes went by before he pulled out of the mall. He drove for four hours straight then stopped at a bar and began drinking beer after beer. It made all the papers the next day. But the dead bank robber remained unidentified.

Two weeks later, again in a bar—this time an Altoona bar—he saw the announcement on the local cable company's bulletin board/advertisement/headline channel that the authorities had finally identified Al as "the gentleman bandit"—his attention directed to the green letters flashing across the bottom of the TV screen by the man on the stool beside his just as the jukebox started to blare. Harlan had just sat down. The dude next door introduced himself: " Hi, I'm Michael." He didn't seem special in any way. Upon closer inspection though, he appeared to be in a state of total shock. "Glad to meet you," Harlan said. "You know I knew him." "Who?" The man pointed to the TV screen. "Al Arretto."

Harlan's heart skipped a beat. His blood turned to ice. But he kept on reading. "Wife had no idea what her husband did for a living. Arretto remains a suspect in more than forty unsolved bank robberies in a dozen states. His MO fits the FBI profile established four years ago in 1979...." The words vanished and another story began before Harlan read to the end. What's that about forty banks, he thought. We only took down five. Do you mean to tell me that bastard lied to me when he said he never pulled a bank job? Only now did Harlan realize the full extent of the danger he had placed himself in. So, everyone now knew about Alvin Roy Arretto's crimes, knew things that Harlan hadn't known or even had the faintest inkling of. Al never told him that he had married. How could this wife know anything when the wheelman, the partner, didn't? How could he have fallen for that line of crap? Never done this before. Nothing about an accessory. No one knew about Harlan's complicity in the last five of those bank robberies. In the future Harlan would tell only one person, his Pappy Rausch. He would confess to him on a regular basis. No one knew that he stood Al's accomplice, rather his stooge—no one except maybe him! Pigcop! What's he yammering about. "... took the same classes. Who would've thought he'd turn into a modern day Jessie James." Keep cool. Remain cool, Harlan thought. Chill. "Old Al must have functioned just as well in one world as another. A real two-timer with women I remember. He told me that years ago he had served in the armed forces. They say he installed cable TV when he wasn't robbing banks. How exciting those moments must have been when he escaped the ho-hum existence of hooking up HBO and Cinemax and became the new Dillinger. Hey, didn't g-men gun Dilly down coming out of a movie theater?" He rambled on, obviously very drunk. "I've become the tongue for all the mute mouths. I also knew the son of the man he shot." Harlan stood up, was on his way out the door. Five years had elapsed since then. It had all blown over. His secret remained safe. Al never stuck out. Nor did he. That remained the key.

Certainly Arretto's days couldn't have appeared any more ordinary and tedious than those of Harlan's life now. He got up every morning at five, stepped out on the back deck into the chill air. The three-year-old twins and the sixth-month-old baby slept quietly while Fat snored, sprawled out on their waterbed. He sat down on a lawn chair, glanced out at the trailer park across the road then up at the sky. Maybe he smoked a joint. He gave up coke but never did stop using pot. He hid his habit from the wife. Al married too. Twice Harlan learned from the papers. After roaching the doob, he pulled down his jamies and fondled himself while looking up at the Milky Way. Yes, Harlan did love Harlan. With his whole heart. Someone had to. At seven his wife would arise. She'd shower, dress and they'd eat. She'd leave and he would baby-sit the kids, watch cartoons and talk shows with them, until 2:30 when her workday ended and he went out the door to put eight hours in changing diapers and wiping asses (but not gratis like at home) at Colonial Court Manor. He did it for them, his wife and kids. He loved his children. Like little animals, they cherished and idolized anyone who bestowed affection on them. Al never had that kind of love, or he would never have put himself at such risk. Before they had ever associated with each other, Al had robbed banks. For his getaway, he would steal a car. He had hit the same kind of banks then—branch offices near shopping centers—as when they later worked together. He held up banks in Wisconsin, Minnesota, Iowa, Missouri, Kentucky, Indiana, and Ohio before he reached Pennsylvania. True, he spent little time in the bank and never became too greedy. He took what he could and then would disappear. But he grew too sure of himself. Harlan would have to admit that Al had totally fooled him. He let Al talk him into pulling that first job and believed him when he said that he had never robbed a bank, that they both stood virgins. He had not known that Al had done time in a federal penitentiary. Arretto had become as addicted to cocking a pistol and pointing it at someone's face as his customers had become to snorting, ingesting, and shooting the junk he pedaled. He just couldn't stop. What motivated him to keep it up? Harlan knew. Money for blow. The press estimated Arretto's total take at around a quarter million. Harlan vowed that he would never participate in another robbery attempt. Never again would he run such risks. His share from the five hold-ups—a meager six grand; Al cheated him out of a proper cut—he had safely stashed. He wouldn't put it up his nose like the money he had inherited from his dad. He wouldn't put his neck in a noose. But he kept living those moments over again and again in his head.

The following day, his shift at Colonial Court Manor started like so many others. He stepped in the door to be greeted by utter chaos. Today not because the aides stood understaffed due to call-offs or because of six in-house transfers that no one had been notified about until 1:00 p.m. that afternoon but because of a whim of the Administrator. She decided that the facility could more efficiently utilize its space. She could shut down several wings and consolidate the patients in fewer rooms. The DON had tried to dissuade her, but the Administrator wouldn't let an upstart half her age undermine her. "Your girls lollygag. Every single one of them. Nothing but a pack of draggletails." "That's not true and you know it, Charlotte."

"You don't pay the bills," the Administrator said, "Mr. Falisec does." She ordered all the patients moved ASAP.

The Activities Director threw up her hands when the Director of Nursing told her. "For months now, Dorothy, our goal has been to have these people find their rooms. All that work's shot because Charlotte suddenly decides to penny pinch." The charge nurse's voice came over the intercom. "Attention all aides. We are going to make room changes today. Report to your supervisors at the hall stations." Harlan did as they ordered. Today he worked Blue Hall, the Intermediate unit on the second floor. His usual assignment.

Occasionally, however, he would put in a double shift or fill in for a call-off, taking someone else's place on another floor. At one time or another, he had worked on every unit in the facility, except the fifth floor's Alzheimer's ward where they kept the problem cases sedated at all times. He headed towards the nurses' station. Other aides hurried down the hallway. The Social Worker Tommy Kean greeted him with a new dirty joke. "Harlan, do you know the difference between a nun and a whore?" He paused. "The one's got a soul full of hope while the other's got a hole full of soap." Tommy came out with crap like that all the time. One moment a best buddy to all the union guys, the two-face would dictate their letters of termination to the secretary "Miss Lardass" the same day. Harlan smiled to assure Kean that he didn't hold a grudge. The social worker turned and went into a patient's room. Harlan walked straight ahead until he got to the end of the hall, then he turned left. Keefer, Mother Mary, and two hundred pound Edna Gerber had all beaten him to the desk.

"Now that all the aides have arrived," the Health Service Supervisor said, "We can begin." Two LPNs also stood in attendance. Mary Ann continued: "We'll move the patients three to a room. That way we will free up a dozen or more rooms. Tomorrow we'll bring patients from the third floor to Blue Hall to occupy the open beds. The patients' families must be notified before we make the moves. We informed some families yesterday. Others we couldn't reach." She proceeded to pass out census sheets with certain of the residents' names starred. "We can start moving these patients. Their families have already been informed. You will find the patients' new room assignments on the second page." "Wait a moment," Keefer said. "You can't move Charlie in with Redenzio. He's always saying someone's stealing his stuff. He'll blame Charlie and they'll get into a fight and Charlie's no match for him." "These moves will call for some adjustments on the patients' parts. The Administrator, DON, and Social Worker make the decision on who is going where, Mr. Peoples, not you or me. Aides, you remain responsible for moving your regular patients to their new rooms—first several trips you take their personal belongings. Then you take them. We nurses will remain at the desk and continue contacting families by telephone." He and Keefer would have to move fifteen patients, the same fifteen assigned to them to push to the dining room every day at 5:00 o'clock. The nurses notified the families of the room changes. The aides had to notify the patients. Harlan hated this. Today he would have preferred working in a skilled unit or Alzheimer ward where the patients would either not realize what was happening or be too sick to care. The intermediate patients would grow sullen and discontented. They'd bawl and beg. They'd become hot under the collar, start screaming as loud as they could. They were still people, you see. The others weren't. As he and Keefer walked off together, his co-worker said: "You know what this means, don't you? After they bunch up the patients like this, they'll lay some of us aides off. Wait and see."

They would inform Ronald Orlofsky about the moves first. He shared his room at the end of the hall with no one. He had a colostomy bag that stank constantly—his roommates always complained and he grew very self-conscious. The staff had moved him a half-a-dozen times already. Finally someone promised him a private room.

But that was two administrators ago. Whoever made him that promise did not have the authority to do so, Harlan said. Besides he'd move in with understanding and kind guys. Did he like to play cards? Well so did Stanton and Harry. No, he'd gone through this all before. Everyone lied today. In his time a person's word stood as good as his bond. They had promised him his own room! His daughter would straighten things out. Could Harlan get him to a phone? "Ron," Harlan said, "She's already given her permission." The old man closed his eyes. Tears welled when he opened them again. "It's not right," he said with a sob. "Come on, let's get started," Keefer said. He began pulling the drawers out of the dresser. By the time they carried them to the new room and replaced the empty drawers in the dresser there with them and walked back to Mr. Orlofsky's room with the empties under their arms, all the residents knew what was up. They sat in their wheelchairs outside their rooms in the hallway. Some headed toward the elevator (the fire doors at the stairwells remained, as always, shut and locked). When they reached the lobby, they'd line up to use the public telephone, or perhaps they planned to barge into Charlotte Boggs' office and argue their case with her. Alice Reighard, champion each year in the wheelchair relay, propelled herself down the hallway at full speed. She determined to have it out with the nurses at the desk. Ron did not say anything as they carted off the rest of his belongings. He sat on his bed staring out the window at the municipal park, his trees. The nurses had assigned him bed A in his new room instead of bed C. He wouldn't have his window. Damn, Harlan thought. "I don't care if we get a new roommate as long as it ain't his great-granddaddy" Harlan heard a resident say as he and Keefer angled Mr. Orlofsky's TV through the doorway. For a split second, he thought that the man had referred to him and bristled, but he quickly recollected that Pappy Rausch was a Heavy Intermediate patient and that he stood in an Intermediate wing. Then he heard: "No, I'm not sharing my room with coloreds." He recognized the voice—Willard Hodge's—and turned his head. Mr. Hodge pointed his finger at Keefer Peoples. The day wore on. All the patients they moved put in their two-cents' worth. Howard Hempsen feared that someone would steal his personal belongings or that the aides would lose them in the shuffle. His wife Genevieve had entered the home as a resident at the same time as he, but she had Alzheimer's and her room sat on the fifth floor. He wanted to know if the staff would also move her. They didn't know. He started cataloging items of hers that had gone missing and that he presumed stolen: her wedding ring, a wool sweater, Genny's Christmas present from their daughter last year. Then he began listing his missing property ... a leg brace, a brand-new radio, several suits. His level of care kept changing from skilled to intermediate. He had had several slight strokes in the past year and suffered from diabetes mellitus. Sometimes his blood sugar level would soar. If they could skill him—even if it were only for several days to monitor his sugar levels—they would do so in order to receive the higher state reimbursement. He felt like a goddamn yo-yo.

The day wore on, grew even more chaotic. Edna Gerber's back went out lifting a patient, or so she said. She remained a clever, old pro. Three months would go by before she'd return to the floor. Her physician would say that she should not work and she would file her compensation claim. Falisec would try to fight it but would lose. The aides would remain one person short. Mother Mary, a frail sixtyish lady with arthritis, couldn't possibly transfer Mable and Ellen, two very large and wide ladies, alone. Keefer went to help her, and Harlan had to move both Wilhemina Diehl and Sadie Siegler and all their clothes, knickknacks and whatnots by himself. He started by removing their photographs, posters, and silver heart balloons from off their bulletin boards. Mrs. Diehl had trouble hearing. Harlan had a devil of a time communicating to her. Born in Germany, she arrived in America in 1910 and had settled in Conemaugh. Harlan had heard that once she had great facility with languages. Her family said that she had spoken fluent Czech, Slovak, Polish, Lithuanian, Italian, and Hungarian as well as German and English. She had served as a court interpreter for many years, but now suffered from a communication deficit. He had to resort to writing her a note. He made the letters huge. Her eyesight had also failed. One eye watered and she had a cataract in the other. He began moving her property out of her room. He almost dropped her heavy and bulky TV. The Health Service Supervisor happened to stand in the hall and saw him almost stumble. She called him a clumsy oaf and told him that it appeared that his job didn't mean that much to him. He apologized and said that he would take more care in the future. He wished that he would have herniated. He adjudged it high time to slip on a wet floor and break a leg. He could use a six-week paid vacation. No, Edna was no dummy. He had to work like a nigger and made little more than minimum wage. One day with Al remained far more lucrative. He could "make" a quarter's entire take-home pay in an hour. The first bank they robbed was located in Lemoyne. After Al left Altoona, he did not call Harlan until six months had passed. He moved back to Allison Park and married, never told Harlan he had taken a bride. Before he left the area, he had said that the time for the two of them to make a windfall would soon arrive. Initially Harlan had resisted the idea. "You're crazy, man?" he had said, "You spend five years in the can for armed robbery." "If you get caught," Arretto said. "We won't. Besides you'll remain an accessory—a driver sitting in his car in a supermarket parking lot. No one would notice you. After I hit the bank, I'll walk up to the car real slow like and get in and then we'll drive away. You'll park close to the freeway. The trick's to get in fast and get out fast. You can't carry off all the money, just a small portion of it. I have thought about this for a long time. Have everything worked out in my head. Maybe I don't have the stones to go through with it. But I think I do. Here, try some of this." He handed Harlan a waterpipe. "Have you smoked coke before? Well you're in for a treat then. Harlan I can get pounds of this shit. Just think of the bucks we could make." "Al," Harlan interrupted, "I can't get involved in anything like that." "Ok. Ok. I'm probably nuts in the head for suggesting it. Think about it though. There's no hurry, no rush. If we would do it—and I'm only speaking hypothetically now—it wouldn't happen for months. Hey, you need to fork over that money you owe me?"

Harlan had run up quite a tab. Suddenly he found himself cut off. Al kept showing up at his doorstep. You shouldn't spend what you don't have," he said. "We're going to have to come to some sort of arrangement." Harlan had felt the pressure for weeks and finally collapsed under it. In the end he acquiesced and agreed to drive for Arretto. I'll do it, he decided. Just this one time to square my debt. He'll have nothing to hold over my head and I'll crawl out from under. Please God, don't let me get popped. Just this one time. Al could tell right away how scared he had become. "Don't worry, Harlan," he said. "You're doing the right thing. This'll be a precision job. There'll be no fuck-ups. We—no—I have to find the bank first. That'll take a good two or three months. Just any bank won't do. I'm splitting town soon. Here, take this." He took a baggie out of his pocket. "Have an eightball on me," he said. "It's good toot, too." He brought out his wallet and counted out five one hundred dollar bills. He stuffed them in Harlan's pocket. "I have something else for you, what they call a cellular phone. They're just now coming on the market. I'll have one also. Yours will arrive in the mail soon. Harlan, from here on out, I own your ass. Sometime in the future, you'll receive a telephone call from me. I'm going to give you a date, time, and place. I'll expect you to show. You fuck me, and you forfeit your right to live. Understand? There's no turning back. We're gonna do this thing. You want out. Say so right now." The cell phone came by USPS within the week.

Harlan hoped that he would never receive Al's call. After four months went by, he thought himself off the hook, that the plan had fallen through or that Al had gotten cold feet. But eventually the phone did ring, and Al told him to meet him at a state park on such and such a date. From the park they drove to Lemoyne and Al showed him where to park his Mustang the following morning—in an Ames Plaza parking lot. Al told him to try to take the fourth or fifth space in row eight. A Landmark Savings Bank sat across the interstate. Harlan fidgeted in his car. Al telephoned him at 9:00 a.m. A half hour passed, and Harlan remained on edge. Why did he agree to do this? Was he born stupid? His heart thumped. He thought several times about just taking off. If he left now, he'd arrive home in about two hours. His teeth chattered as if he sat in a draft. His left leg started to shake. Pappy Rausch had Parkinson's. Did the disease appear this early in life? Was there such a thing as juvenile or early onset? He rather enjoyed the sensation of the leg tremor. It kind of tickled. He put his hand on his kneecap. He saw Al walking towards him in the distance. He opened the passenger's door, got in and told him where to drive. Harlan obeyed, turned left, then right, whichever way Al directed, a robot without a will of its own. Soon they sped on the interstate. "Let's party," Al said. "We earned it." He handed Harlan a joint. "You know some day someone's going to write a ballad about me. I walked in, brandished my gun, asked for the bread, took it, said thank you, and left. Slam, bam, thank you mam. This real old guy stopped me at the door, offered me what he had in his wallet. I stood as gallant as John Wesley Harding—just as much of a friend to the poor—and said, 'That's ok. I don't want your money. I want theirs.' It went without a hitch. It came off easy. I can see you're still nervous. It's written all over your face. Just think how I must feel? Well, we both can chill now. Remember when you did coke the first time? How apprehensive you acted? Then you tried it and afterwards you felt silly when you realized what a big pussy you had turned into."

Harlan thought of the score from that first hold-up, all the coke they had bought. They lived high on the hog for a good two months. When Al said let's do it again,

Harlan thought what the hell. They had to get the money up for more nose candy somehow. He remained calm and collected during jobs two, three, four, and five but his unease returned during Arretto's botched, final attempt. When Al didn't show, he again started to question his sanity and to wonder how he had let himself become entangled in such a mess.

After he finished moving Mrs. Siegler, Harlan took his half hour "lunch." He went into room 216 to visit Anna Hudak during his break. He tried to step in and see her every day. Thankful that the moves would not disturb the three ladies in 216, that they would stay put in their old room, he said hello to Anna's roommates first. Both Helen Loughner and Donna Turnbull appeared elated that they did not have to change quarters. The three ladies had lived together longer than Harlan had worked at the nursing home and remained inseparable. He tried to act as if he liked them all equally but Anna remained his favorite. She had lived now ninety-nine years. Her hundredth birthday stood only a month away. Sharp as a tack, she still liked to do her own laundry and nimbly got about with a walker. Harlan would carry her loads back to the laundry room for her, and she would talk his ear off. She told him how raised on a country farm with seven brothers and two sisters she had learned early on in life the meaning of work and the importance of collaboration. They grew and harvested crops and raised cattle and horses. She attended grade school in a one-room schoolhouse. She loved to describe her courtship by a neighbor boy, how he escorted her to many a Saturday-night square dance. They married just after her seventeenth birthday, and her man found work in grocery and coal company stores. They had a good life but she could not bear children, a bitter disappointment for Melvin and her. She still liked to crotchet and last winter had made Harlan a cap and a scarf. She told fortunes and interpreted character by reading palms. She often requested that he read her something from out of the Bible, as her sight now wasn't so good. But she could still see well enough to read palms.

Harlan admired her so much because she always appeared happy. She never pulled a long face and every day seemed perfectly contented. She still had the will to live. Harlan knew residents in their fifties who wouldn't even try to get out of their wheelchairs, who expected you to wait on them hand and foot. Anna walked, still did her own laundry and needed only minimal assistance with ADLs (Activities of Daily Living). One day it suddenly struck him that she would have turned fifty during the 1930s. She had character all right. You would never catch her in a wheelchair. Not at ninety-nine. Certainly not at age fifty. He hoped that she would go fast when her time came. It would crush him if she turned into another vegetable like Pappy. A year his senior, she stood in far better condition than he. If Harlan ever lived to such an advanced age (which he very much doubted) he hoped that he would possess all his faculties and remain as active and as in as good shape as she.

When Harlan came back out onto the floor, he saw Alice Reighard's son standing at the nursing station speaking heatedly with one of the LPNs. At least one family member didn't kowtow to the authorities. Harlan slunk by and didn't involve himself in it. Further down the hall, Mother Mary and another aide argued over which patient a coat belonged to. Next week would be hell. It would take at least that long to straighten everything out. Everyday they would look for some missing item. The families would continue breathing down everyone's neck. He passed room 218, saw that the red light was on, thought *just what I need but I better stop and check*, and went in. "At least they're not busting you guys up," he said. Stanton Smeltzer had stopped in to see Joe. Both men had fought in the World War. He answered Harlan: "And you had to put stinko Orlofsky in with Harry and me. Thanks a lot." Willie wanted to go to the toilet. "No, I don't have a cigarette Sam," Harlan said, as he helped Willie out of the wheelchair and held onto him as they walked at a snail's pace past Joe and Stanton. Willie had a very unsteady gait. In the bathroom, Harlan undid Willie's trousers and sat him on the commode. Mildly retarded, Willie sat and sat, groaned a couple of times, but couldn't go. Joe and Stanton started swapping war stories. Joe served as a bombardier and gunner on a B-24 liberator and flew twenty-eight missions over Europe including raids on Hamburg, Dresden, and Cologne. He bragged about his plane and how he manned the two fifty-caliber machine guns in the Emerson Turret located at the nose of the B-24 and faced both Messerschmidts and Focke-Wulfs. "Liberators," he said, living in the past, tears in his eyes, "could carry the largest loads higher, faster, and much greater distances than any other aircraft. We nicknamed ours Ford's folly and Consolidated Mess." Harlan looked at his watch. "Well, boys it's chow time," he said. He and the other aides spent the next half hour pushing people to the elevator and taking them down to the dining room. While the residents ate, the aides continued to move their belongings to their new rooms. One lady had ten plants. The women she moved in with also had a lot of flowers. There simply wasn't enough room in the window for all of them. One headache after another. Would it never end? And tomorrow they'd begin bringing patients down from the third floor. Harlan shuddered. He had the next two days off, thank God. He pitied the people who would have to work.

He and Keefer saved the worst move for last, introducing Charlie into Redenzio's room. Redenzio acted just as Keefer predicted he would. He sat in his wheelchair outside his door in the hallway, as far out of his room as he usually ever wheeled himself, and all afternoon had watched what went on with keen interest. "What's the idea," he said as Harlan stepped by him with the first load. "This is my room. Why are you bringing his stuff in? If someone asks me for something, I'll give it to him. I'm generous, see. I'm Italian. But if they take it, well then ...." He stopped speaking and drew his index finger across his throat. "You should be glad to get a roommate then," Harlan said. "You can't stay in your room all the time. Charlie can keep an eye on your things when you're not there." "Ok, boy," Redenzio said. "I guess that'll be all right then." He offered Harlan his hand. "Let's shake." Redenzio worked in the mines all his life and had a firm, strong grip. Harlan squeezed back. "You can't hurt that hand, boy," Redenzio said. It did not take very long to move Charlie's belongings. A Medical Assistance patient, he didn't have much. When they wheeled Charlie around the corner, however, Redenzio had tossed all his stuff out onto the hallway floor and had shut the door. Harlan opened it a little way. Redenzio had attempted to barricade himself in the room and had pushed the dresser up against the exit. "Redenzio," Harlan said, "I thought we had agreed—" "This is my room, not his. Let him stay in his own room." Charlie started to shake all over. "I'll take an ice pick and stick him in the chest if he comes in here. Where's my gun. Some bastard stole it." Still can't remember they made you leave it at home, Harlan thought. Wouldn't even let you keep a pocketknife. And for good reason. Keefer crossed the threshold and started to push the dresser into the center of the room. Redenzio attacked, swung at Keefer with his fist. Harlan ran to the nursing station. "Redenzio's having one of his fits again," he shouted. "We need help. He keeps getting worked up like this, one of these days he'll take a stroke." The nurse picked up the phone and paged Anthony Bolet, a male nurse on the fourth floor. They had a PRN Thorazine order for Redenzio but none of the nurses on the second floor could hold him down to give him the shot. A giant of a man in his mid-to-late fifties, Bolet looked like a professional wrestler. For a number of years, he had worked for Bethlehem Steel as variously a warehouse manager; forklift, bulldozer, payloader, and backhoe operator; gas and diesel mechanic; and a welder. But the factory had downsized and had laid him off. He qualified for job retraining and graduated in practical nursing from the area vocational technical school earning LPN certification after passing the state boards. He had started to work at the Manor two months ago. It took all three of them to hold Redenzio down. He flexed the muscles in his arms as Bolet tried to jab him with the needle. They got his pants down and gave him the injection in his right buttock, then lifted him back into his wheelchair. Within fifteen minutes, he sat calm as could be. Tommy Kean appeared on the scene and told Harlan to take Charlie back to his old room for tonight. "Damn," he said. "Salerno is an MA patient. The state pays us only $44.00 a day to care for him. He can't have a private room. We can't afford to give him one. But we're going to have to put someone in there who can fend for himself." He asked the nurse for a list of the patients from the third floor whom the staff would transfer to Blue Hall the following day. "We'll see what we can come up with," he said.

Harlan did not take his second break until the end of his shift. He usually took it at nine o'clock. He would ride up to the sixth floor on the elevator and would sit with his great-grandfather for fifteen minutes or until an aide would come into the room to put him to bed. A vegetable now thanks to two massive strokes, Pappy remained in the same condition as he had for over four years. Harlan would talk to him anyhow. So what if he couldn't hear or comprehend? Harlan pretended that he could. He needed someone to talk to. Really he had a conversation with himself. Perhaps Pappy stood as his conscience. Instead of something invisible—air—his morals and principles took on human shape, thus weight, reality. Before his father opened up his practice in Tyrone, Harlan and his parents resided in Houserville, PA, just outside State College, as did both his paternal grandparents and maternal grandfather. Harlan's dad descended from Jacob Houser, the founder of the town who bought three hundred seventy acres and allowances along Spring Creek in 1787. The following year he brought his wife, infant son, one horse and one cow to Spring Creek and erected a log cabin. The son of a redemptioner from Switzerland, Houser had served in the fourth battalion of the Lancaster County Militia in the War for Independence. He cleared fields and built a sawmill, his single sash saw pulled downward by a water wheel, to cut logs for houses and barns. A little town sprang up. Harlan learned about Jacob Houser not, as one might have expected from his father, but from his mother's father Otto and her grandfather Anton. Both men studied local history. Anton's grandfather on his father's side Casimir Rausch, a deserter from the Prussian Army—in civilian life a mining engineer, emigrated to America in 1872 with his twin brother Eberhard, an anglophile, Cambridge graduate, and Methodist convert who had for a time been a missionary in India. The twins settled in New York and subsequently in Houserville, Pennsylvania. Richard, their oldest brother, remained in Silesia and took over the family estate. Anton's mother was a Cronemiller. Her people had come to America much earlier and stood among the earliest settlers of Houserville. The blood of a number of the early settlers flowed in Anton's veins—he was part Etters, part Wertz, and part Halderman—but he didn't have any Houser in him. Anton had taught in the public schools, his son Otto a Penn State professor in American and European history. Anton and Otto shared a house. Otto died of cancer shortly after Harlan turned ten. Harlan remembered visiting nursing homes with Anton and Otto and his mother Grette when eight and nine. Otto and Anton planned to enter a nursing home together. They toured church facilities and the state Masonic home. Much nicer places than Colonial Court Manor where Anton would finally wind up. He decided not to give up his home after his son's death and lived in Houserville until his first stroke. As a young boy, Harlan often slept with his great-grandfather when he stayed over at his grandfather's house. Pappy often told him stories about Lewis and Connelly, two notorious Pennsylvania bandits of the early 1800s, on account of the boy's name being Houser and the fact that the Widow Connelly, the mother of the future outlaw, put a curse on Farmer Houser when he evicted her and the Widow Lewis from his land as squatters. Originally they had made an agreement by which Mrs. Lewis and Mrs. Connelly could stay in return for clearing a certain amount of land each year. But the women did not fell enough trees to suit Jacob Houser. As Houser's men evicted the Lewis and Connelly families, Mrs. Connelly screamed: "May a vexing, bothersome weed spread across your fields." To this day Harlan remembered his great-grandfather's stories about Robber Lewis, the highwayman who roamed the valleys of the Alleghenies and the ridges of the Seven Mountains and buried his ill-gotten treasure in Indian Caverns. A gentleman bandit, he never shot a man and gave his money to poor widows. He remembered lying in bed listening to his great-grandfather relate Lewis' exploits: "The young man never should have been in the wild country that late at night. He rode one horse and led another by the bridle. A man dropped out of a tree and landed in the saddle of the second horse. 'Shall you sell me this horse then?' he asked the young man. 'What do you think is a fair price?' The young man did not know what to do. He pulled a flask from his pocket and offered it to the stranger, who accepted it gladly. After he took a drink, he said, 'I don't think that it is very wise to travel these mountain roads alone. Especially at night. Who knows whom you might meet in the forest?' He pulled two pistols from under his coat. 'I say come prepared. Have you ever heard of David Lewis? He has a price on his head so I hear.' The young man trembled, but he tried to appear calm. 'I have heard that he is very brave,' the youth said. 'I would like to meet him.' 'Would you like to meet him in the mountains?' 'No I don't believe so, but if by chance I should I don't think that I would be imperiled. The man is magnanimous, I'm sure.' 'You would really like to see him then?' asked the stranger. 'Yes, sir,' said the youth, quaking. 'Well, behold him then. I am Lewis,' the stranger said, rising to his full height. 'I did intend to rob you of your valuables and take your good horse. But since you treated me like a gentleman, I will not take a cent from your pocket nor harm a hair on your head.' Lewis dismounted and permitted the young man to ride off, which he did at a moderate pace—until he lost sight of the high-wayman, that is, when both spirit and flesh moved him to spur his horses and travel as fast as he possibly could."

Before he punched out, Harlan rode up to the sixth floor anyway. He wanted to see if they had moved Pappy. They had not. He lay in bed asleep. No bedtime story tonight. Well, Pap, you'll have to wait to Thursday to hear another of the ongoing adventures of Harlan Houser and Alvin Roy Arretto.

When Harlan reported at the nurses' station Thursday afternoon, both the floor's RNs, Sara B. Oldenbusch, Orientation and In-service Director, whose major respon-sibility was administrative supervision of the staff and developing and implementing patient care plans (the aides and LPNs always ran to her in an emergency; fifty-two years old, and a retired army officer, she and only she would perform cardio-pulmonary resuscitation) and Mary Jane Milford who had the easier job of coordinating all health-related services, scheduling doctor's appointments, and patient trips to the hospital for urinalysis, electrocardiogram, or periodic lab work such as CBC and Chem 10 tests, and who would never insert an IV or perform a treatment (her children had grown up and she started working again, but boy, oh boy, how things had changed; she could only do the light stuff) notified him that a staff meeting would take place in the activity lounge in twenty minutes, one right after the other. Sara buttonholed him first, as he reported. Then as he took a seat at the desk, she came from behind it, turned the corner and unlocked the med-room and stepped inside. Mary Jane came out of her office. She hadn't overheard their conversation, so he got it all over again. The aides had transferred patients from the third floor to their new rooms. They came from another Intermedi-ate unit and from the home's Chronic Obstructive Pulmonary unit. Old miners for the most part. And a few three-pack-a-day smokers who paid privately. "We want to keep those coal miners alive for Mr. Falisec. They receive benefit checks they sign over to us, so today we'll give you aides a crash course on COPD," Mary Jane said, "We'll in-service you on how to operate a portable compression-driven nebulizer and teach you pursed lip and diaphragmatic breathing exercises so you can instruct the residents how to get trapped air out of their lungs. Bill will be up from PT to talk about percussion and vibration therapy and other treatments available to the residents." Harlan didn't exactly enjoy in-services but they ate up time, made the day seem to go by quicker. Everyone sat around a table and bullshitted. Maybe they watched a movie or saw a slide show with an accompanying audiocassette. A beep sounded to switch to the next slide after the narrator on the tape finished whatever he had to say. He had watched the same or very similar presentations in science and health classes in junior high and high school.

He remained at the desk looking busy until the in-service began. The 3-to-7 aides (all earning overtime as they stayed over) had stood waiting in the lounge for over an hour. They made themselves comfortable at the table and lit up. The girls passed glass trays back and forth to flick their ashes in. Most of the nurses smoked even though they knew smoking caused lung cancer and emphysema. "Doctors will light up and puff on a cig," they said in an attempt to justify their own weakness, "coming out of surgery after just cutting out the diseased part of a lung. Even though they have just seen the effects of smoking close up." Mrs. Oldenbusch took her seat. An LPN or two opened up a notebook. A slide projector sat at the head of the table. So did the nebulizer device. When she saw it was time for the in-service to begin (she glanced at her watch), Nurse Oldenbusch cleared her throat and began: "Our objective is to slow or arrest the progression of the disease, to protect the patient against complications and to keep him as active as his functional capacity permits. We administer drugs that open up constricted air passages through inhalants and nebulizers. Portable compression-driven models are a major improvement over the old hand-held devices. The compressor creates an aerosol of very fine mist from liquid and directs the flow of air through the mouthpiece. Expectorant drugs thin the sputum blocking the airways and make the mucus easier to raise and expel. We keep portable oxygen tanks in the rooms of patients with severe breathing stress. Depending on disease level, antibiotics, theophylline preparations and corticosteroids might be prescribed. Lungers remain tricky. They last a lot longer than most people would anticipate seeing them initially. Oxygen costs. That's why we have strict admission policies. Medical Assistance won't pay for oxygen. The home would have to supply it at a loss to patients on assistance. And, as you know, the Department of Health has bled this home dry. We can't do charity work for the community right now even if we wanted to. We remain glad to oblige the UMWA and take real good care of the coal worker pneumoconiosis patients though. Bill's going to show how to set up and use the nebulizer and show you some breathing exercises. I surrender the floor to him. Afterwards we'll watch the American Lung Association program on COPD."

Harlan yawned. Bill went through the motions, had an aide (Cindy Mehan, a 7-to-3 girl) act like a patient. He explained that gravity pulled the mucus toward the upper part of the lungs so that the patient could cough it out more easily. The patient had to stand. Cindy did. If he couldn't, they would strap him to a tilt table in the PT room. Next Bill demonstrated percussion and vibration therapies on Cindy's back. "We do this to loosen phlegm in the lungs," he said. "Of course only an LPT should attempt it."

Ho-hum. Harlan thought. But best attend. Better than changing diapers.

"But you aides and LPNs can make your lives easier by teaching your patients pursed lip and diaphragmatic breathing. Many of these miners have lost their minds, have Alzheimer's or OBS, so you have to constantly reorient them and watch to make sure that they follow through. I see that we're a bunch of smokers here. You'll have learned your lessons ahead of time so store them away for future use. They might come in handy." Here Nurse Oldenbusch interrupted him. "You all know we restrict smoking to designated areas in the building, but I don't so much as want to see a cigarette on the person of anyone working in the COPD unit." "We'll do these simple exercises ourselves first," Bill picked up. "What we know, we can teach. Anyone play the clarinet or sax? No? Well, a person who performs on either of those instruments knows about breathing from the diaphragm. A pursed-lipped breather slowly draws in air through pursed lips like sucking on a straw."

Harlan felt like he again attended kindergarten as all the aides sucked on the straw together. Seeing Cindy getting hooked up to the nebulizer didn't thrill him either, and the background music on the cassette accompanying the slide show from the American Lung Association sounded like the sugary melodies played in shopping malls or elevators. He twiddled his thumbs and closed his eyes. When Nurse Oldenbusch flicked the lights back on, Harlan exited his chair and went out the door. By day's end he had gotten round to see all of the new inmates. He would get to know them better as time went by. Kean did come up with a roommate for Redenzio Salerno—Tyson Hicks, a veteran of WW 2 and Korea who waited for permanent placement at the Van Zandt VA Medical Center. He had kidney failure and had to go to the hospital once a week for dialysis. One mean son of a bitch, he insulted the other residents, swore, and laughed at the Alzheimer's patients, and remained uncooperative, cranky and sexually suggestive with the nurses. The staff reprimanded him for verbally abusing or even striking other residents—again usually the infirm and doddering who got in his way. "He can fend for himself," Kean said. "Stand up to Salerno." Harlan knew that one of the miners Virgil Dobbs, had a reputation as a problem patient. Third-floor aides constantly complained about him. For years he had lived back in the mountains in a shack and made moonshine. He refused to shave and shower and used chewing tobacco, his chin streaked by it and his shirtfronts stained. He became belligerent and uncooperative when asked to bathe and wielded his quad cane as a weapon when upset and agitated. Also, it surprised Harlan to discover that he already knew one of the new wards. The man, a Paiute Indian the third-floor aides had nicknamed Crazyhorse, had worked as a janitor at his high school. Kean put him in with Willard Hodge over the latter's loud protests. The Social Services Director gave Kean quite a civics lecture. Colonial Court Manor does not discriminate. Thomas Kean did not make room assignments on the basis of race, religion or national origin. At least not for Medical Assistance patients, Harlan thought.

The day passed slowly. Harlan did manage to visit his great-grandfather on his break, and as usual commenced relating the further exploits of those modern-day Lewis-and-Connellys, Harlan and Al. He had just sat down on bed A. An aide had taken its normal occupant—a violent Alzheimer's patient subject to sudden mood swings—out of the room for a family visit. Up in a geri-chair, his great-grandfather sat between this patient's bed and his own. The thing in bed C never got up. They fed it through a gastrotomy tube. Someone had switched on a battery-run radio on the dresser at the foot of bed B. Harlan turned it off before sitting down.

Anton would either sit there mute or else groan. Aside from two small tufts behind each ear, he was totally bald. His blue eyes clouded and his mouth turned down. Deeply lined, scarred by the drives and compulsions of a lifetime, his face clearly showed the ravage of nine decades: its expression had a terrible simplicity, a horrid total complete vacancy. Weighed down with the heaviness of existence but unconscious of it, today Great Grandpap made no utterance. Leer at me. Go ahead, Harlan thought. I know you can't hear, but I'll tell you anyway. "Well, Pap," he started. "This is how we robbed the Drovers & Mechanics Bank in Lewisberry." Harlan felt free to take certain liberties with the truth in his tales—for one thing he took center stage, not a bit player, a stooge, any more but the star of the picture, whereas in reality he sat in the car, never entered a bank with guns blazing—yes he felt free to exaggerate, embellish and overstate, but *not* in the manner of the old story tellers who romanticized the career of Robber Lewis. Al might have envisioned himself as a future gentleman bandit. He told the old man, after all, that he wanted their money not his, a Robin Hood-like deed. But Harlan didn't see Al or himself as subjects fit for a tall tale. He did not want to make the ugly pretty, to sanitize it. In fact he aimed to do the very opposite. He had to show his great-grandfather just how hideous the world stood into which his mother bore him. Pap had held him in his arms, loved protected and comforted him, told him to remain moral and to never lie but had lied to him when he said that life was good and that everything had a meaning, that a merciful father existed in heaven. Yes Harlan's tales and stories resembled the truth very little. But if they remained fictions, they at least stood true to life, containing all the horrors which one sees each day in the headlines of every major newspaper.

"The bank doors swing open and we waltz in. I aim the sawed-off shotgun at the security guard and pull the trigger, blowing him away. His blood spurts on everyone and everything. All the women scream until Al shoots a round into the ceiling, and then they all shut up. 'I'm David Lewis and let me introduce my partner Philander Noble,' I say, now that they have all become quiet. 'We have come to clean you out.' 'You see,' Al chirps in. 'We want to make a reputation for ourselves as bogeymen.' 'Now empty your registers. Quickly.' Then I make them open the vault. 'All right move. You can all squeeze in.' 'You'll come back out on the judgment day,' Al says, as he slams the vault door. We took one hostage, a blonde bank clerk. We had our way with her, raped and sodomized her then shot her twice in the chest and threw her face down in a field."

This man's blood quivered in his veins. Partially responsible for Harlan's being here, he now had to hear his complaint, his moan. Life held such promise but remained fraught with bitter disappointment at every juncture. Harlan could never get ahead. Everyone stood against him. Look at the job he had, the only one he could get. His father had served the community as a doctor, but he worked as a stinking aide. His mom didn't care—she just forgot about him after she remarried. His dad at least took a passing interest in his life but when he discovered that the candy striper whom after the divorce he had married and fathered two children by had cheated on him all along, he gassed himself to death in his car in the garage. His wife had taken the children and left earlier that day. Harlan found him the next morning. Blue face resting on the steering wheel. A hose leading from the tailpipe to the back window. "And look how God treats you. You always called Him fair and just, but he gives you me as a great-grandson. Awfully decent of him, eh? And I have to see you like this, reduced to this. Do you wonder I went bad? I should hardly think so. I thrilled to your stories, always cheered on Lewis, Connelly, and Noble. I don't know why people regularly extend their loyalty to a Lewis, a Jesse James, a Dillinger instead of to the lawful authorities? Why did you make him so appealing in your stories? I'm sure in real life he became a holy terror, a monster like me. Yet you said he showed himself pleasant, agreeable, smart. I laughed at this wily escape artist who always outfoxed and outwitted his pursuers. Weren't you telling me that the criminal mind stood superior to that of the ordinary mortal when you related how Lewis would return each night from his thieving to a warm bed at his stepmother's and how he, appraised of the approach of the irate citizens from town when they came hunting for him, escaped? I could see him so agile and swift of foot as he sprang up out of bed and ran out the door, sparsely clad, for the posse from Bellefonte to chase him across Spring Creek and up Sugar Loaf Mountain. Yet he got away like he always did. And I remember when I turned ten or eleven how we went looking for stolen treasure at a point in the Allegheny Mountains known as Wolf Rocks along a stream known as Six-Mile Run and you said how in 1819 it grew exceedingly dangerous to travel in the mountains. We went into the forest that day, you and I, and I became scared when you said Robber Lewis might be waiting for us just around the bend, yet even then I began to envy the lives of those high-waymen who disappeared so completely out of sight, making their home in the wild."

Almost all the hamlets in Centre County had their own Lewis and Connelly legend. The stolen treasure—$62,000—reputedly buried at this location, but also at that, had never been found. Harlan remembered taking a tour through Indian Caverns with his grandfather Otto and how the guide had said that the notorious bandit David Lewis also known as Louis Lewis had quite probably hidden his treasure "in these very caverns." A newspaper article from 1893 which his great-grandfather had in his possession claimed that a hunter had found the treasure at Wolf Rocks near Philipsburg. The man had discovered a cave running back into the massive rock. It ran a great distance but the air became too foul to proceed. The article stated the treasure consisted of mostly bills, but they stood in such a bad state of decomposition that the man who uncovered them (one L. Ackerly of Scranton) could not count them. He found the cave at Wolf Rocks while stalking game. The newspaperman seemed more interested in the hunting expedition than the finding of the treasure, for he reported that Ackerly had killed one bear and twelve pair of pheasants and that his companions had killed sixty pair of pheasants, four bears, one having but three legs, and one wild cat. Perhaps the whole thing was a shaggy dog story, his great-grandfather had said. For neither Anton, nor Otto nor anyone else for that matter had ever located a cave at Wolf Rocks. Who exactly was this Lewis? A spy along with his friend Philander Norton Noble for both the United States of America and Great Britain during the war of 1812, he, Noble, and another man circulated spurious paper, printed bank notes intended to pass for currency which they produced at a camp in the mountains, where they pretended to work as a crew of surveyors. A jury found Lewis guilty of passing counterfeit money and sentenced him to six years in the penitentiary, but he escaped from the old Bedford jail. *His arms tapered from the shoulders to the ends of his fingers, his legs from the hips to the ends of his toes so that it remained impossible to keep manacles upon him.* Recaptured he served three-and-one-half years of the six years, then in 1819 Governor William Findlay pardoned him (an action which would cost Findlay the Governorship), and he and the friend of his boyhood John Connelly, their mothers together expelled from Spring Creek as squatters by Jacob Houser, promptly began their reign of terror in the mountains overtaking the weak and taking their goods such as suited them. Lewis had a fine figure and physique, the local lasses thought him an Adonis. His contemporaries said of him that had he pursued a different course he might have made a valuable citizen. Connelly, on the other hand, stood vicious, savage and vindictive. Lewis often constrained his companion from excesses and murder. They stole from the rich and gave the proceeds to the poor ....

Harlan repeated his great-grandfather's name several times. Occasionally he could get Anton to maintain eye contact for four or five seconds by touching his arm or by saying his name very loudly as if the old man had just dozed off and he wanted to awaken him. Today he stared straight ahead. Harlan fell on his knees and cried: "Absolve me father." Then he stood and kissed his great-grandfather Anton Rausch on the forehead, turned around, switched the radio on and strode out of the room.

Harlan and the other aides had to make additional room changes during the next couple of weeks due to patient incompatibility. Lillian Taylor, the seventy-six-year-old from the third floor who joined Wilhemina Diehl and Sadie Siegler in their new room, complained because both those ladies were hard of hearing and she wanted someone to talk to and as she paid privately her whims had to be coddled to, so she and Gladys Shipley, an MA patient who had come into the home not because anything ailed her but because her husband had become terminally ill (he had since died), traded rooms. Lillian much preferred the two fat ladies Mable and Ellen. They talked back and acted congenially and solicitously. Lillian applied rouge to her face each morning, still liked to dress up and to wear her jewelry. She had frequent shortness of breath and her legs mottled. She would cry on occasion. Her son lived out of state, and she missed him. She had reoccurring fainting spells, the reason she left the personal care home where she had resided for the two previous years. Ellen, who had one sister who visited fairly frequently, took sympathy on Lillian and became her friend. Soon she shared in the sister's visits as well. They brought her as much joy as they did Ellen. Meanwhile Mrs. Shipley's sole amusement remained her television.

The nine patients on the COPD unit just moved down a floor, quartered in rooms 201-204 where before they had resided in 301-304. Coal macules appeared in the lobes of the lungs of the two miners in 201, groups of cells attempting to wall off and surround the dust breathed in day after day, year after year, in the mines. These macules caused the alveoli to become over inflated and stretched. The smallest airways leading into the sacs began to collapse. Both men had focal emphysema, but they still remained active, one even had a car and had permission to leave the facility to attend church services or go fishing. Kean placed Charlie in the third bed, even though he didn't rightfully belong on this unit. To make room for him, he transferred Dobbs down to '03, put him in the same room as the sickest man on the unit, Carl Tibbons. He didn't like doing this. But he had to put Charlie somewhere if not in with Redenzio. All three men in '02 had lost their minds. They restrained them all day in geri-chairs. Kean should have put them on the fifth floor, but, because they had earned their livelihood as miners, he admitted them to the COPD unit.

Virgil Dobbs hardly ever coughed, but the building shook when his roommate Carl Tibbons did. "Functional impairment of the lungs with marked distortion of lung architecture." Dr. Laird, the staff physician, adjusted his glasses as he made the new diagnosis. Tibbons wheezed all the time and had a productive cough. A cough which sounded like a canon going off. A sudden noisy expulsion of the air from the lungs attended with expectoration from the bronchi. Green hockers that flew like cannonballs. When Kean had admitted him to the nursing home, Carl Tibbons had come to the convalescent center by private auto, his diagnosis degenerative joint disease, unstable angina, and progressive massive fibrosis, major physiological changes having taken place in his lungs, large patches and shadows appearing in the upper lobes which had themselves contracted. He needed round-the-clock care, or so they said. But he walked into the facility of his own accord and signed his own admission papers. He knew that he would soon die. But he faced it head on. He weighed eighty-nine pounds, and had lost one eye in an industrial accident many years before. Months went by, but he didn't "ctb," so he moved up from the first floor out of a skilled bed to the third floor and the COPD unit and now down to the second floor. He had oxygen at his bedside but often refused it. He could still ambulate short distances without assistance and would propel his own wheelchair in the hallways. He seemed always to be choking. And his eye prosthesis rolled about in the socket from side to side making him look cross-eyed. Two females, both heavy cigarette smokers in the past, and Alice Reighard shared the next room, '04. Having interceded on his mother's behalf, Alice's son at last got his way. Alice didn't want to leave her room with the view of the South Park and the distant Borough Building, a water fountain, benches, a stone soldier standing guard by the flagpole. She didn't mind parting company with her old roommates Olive and Winifred. She sat all day looking out her window, working puzzles or playing cards. She had stuffed animals and dolls galore: on her bed, under the card table, and on the windowsill. She had framed photos of her dead husband Alfred and her children and grandchildren hanging on the wall. She pulled her curtain and tried not to notice Hazel or Nannie, their loud coughing the price she paid to keep her window. Nannie remained periodically confused. She wore a Philadelphia collar at all times due to an old cervical fracture. Her breathing had become more and more difficult. She needed oxygen around the clock. Hazel still begged for cigarettes even though she had a chronic cough. If she stood up and walked ten feet, she became all tuckered out.

The flower problem solved itself. One lady died in her sleep, so there arose no need to share the precious windowsill and sunlight. The staff discarded the dead woman's plants. Room did not have to be made for them after all.

One terrible day two weeks after the moves, Ronald Orlofsky's daughter saw her father's shower robe and slippers on Willie as Harlan and Keefer took him to his weekly bath and all hell burst loose. "Listen lady," Peoples said, "I don't have time for this." Harlan nudged him in the ribs. Oldenbusch had just stepped out of an adjacent room and into the hallway. But Keefer paid him no heed and, angry, just came out with whatever came to him at the time. Tired and just getting over the flu, he didn't feel like being polite. Everything had been going wrong all day: "They're his anyway. He's had 'em for six months now." "Are you calling me a liar?" the woman screamed. "I guess I am." "No you're not," Mrs. Oldenbusch said, stamping her foot for emphasis, her face reddening at the same time. "Apologize to Mrs. Wiggens at once. This kind of behavior simply won't be tolerated." "But," Keefer interrupted. "They're Willie's." "We will establish to whom the slippers and coat belong." "I've spent a lot of money here and deserve to be treated with more respect," Mrs. Wiggens cried. "Right you are Mary. Mister Peoples report to the DON's office immediately." The DON told him to clean out his locker and punch out. Harlan had to finish out the shift alone. The following afternoon a nurse told him to report to Tommy Kean. He wondered if Kean would give him the ax too? The Social Worker's office stood behind the reception desk adjacent to that of the Nursing Home Administrator's. The Administrator's door opened a crack, and he saw Charlotte Boggs sitting at her desk talking on the telephone. He knocked on Kean's door. The man had it in for him though he couldn't possibly have known about his current girlfriend Kaleena Kirby's seduction of Harlan years and years ago when Harlan was only sixteen and both she and he worked as lifeguards at Whipple's Dam. He had driven to work in his dad's Mercedes. He had only one job, lifeguarding, until his mother interceded and got him hired as an aide seven years later. Kaleena had been twenty-two at the time and his boss. One look at his trim body and she decided to employ him. Since then she had gotten a physical education degree and had opened a dance studio in Tyrone. She advertised herself as the principal instructor. She and Kean had just begun seeing each other. They both belonged to the same health club. Kean worked out regularly. Could he have found out that he and Kaleena had once seen each other? But how could have he? She certainly would have never told him?

After Kean said come in, Harlan opened the door and crossed into the office. Kean looked up at him from his desk. "My cluttered mess," he said, then: "We had to let your buddy go. Sit down. Read this." He handed Harlan a yellow Progress Note. Harlan sank into the leather-cushioned armchair in front of Kean's desk like a family member about to sign everything away. They all met Kean first in his bright office with posters on the wall, brochures and piles of papers on the desk and sets of spare dentures in Tupperware containers on the file cabinet. Well maybe he wasn't gonna get fired. He glanced over the progress note. "Anton Karl Rausch, a ninety-eight-year-old white male, appears alert but remains disoriented to person, time, and place. He also at times looks as if semi-comatose. There are stretches when no type of stimulus will arouse him. The patient can't speak. Occasionally he will make a grunting type sound. He has wrist restraints ordered to prevent him from pulling or attempting to pull out his catheters. He has a cystostomy and has both suprapubic and Foley caths. He is incontinent of bowel. He has the following diagnosis. Old CVA with left hemiparesis, CHF, recurrent TIAs, chronic ulcer on left lower anterior shin and history of Parkinson's disease. Goal is to maintain Mr. Rausch at his present level of functioning. There is no potential for discharge due to mental regression and the patient requiring total care of ADLs as a result of old CVA. Mr. Rausch's grandson Harlan is employed at this facility and visits him on an almost daily basis." " Sum him up?" Kean asked. "Yes," Harlan replied. "But I'm his great-grandson." "Oh," Kean said, uncapped his pen and corrected his mistake, put in "great" with a caret. "We're having care plans this afternoon," Kean explained after a moment's pause. "Sign underneath my entry," he told Harlan and handed him his pen. "This will indicate that I have reviewed his plan of care with you. A new policy. We're inviting family members to participate in care planning." "Is that all you wanted to see me about?" Harlan stammered. Kean looked him hard in the face, very stern for a moment. "And," he resumed, "to say that I'm sorry about your buddy. I'll be sending out his letter of termination today. I couldn't do anything. They tied my hands. Oldenbusch wanted his head."

Thomas Kean remained a survivor. He had served under four Administrators and continued on as Social Worker coup after coup, administration after administration no matter who currently sat in the commander's seat. He spent hours lifting weights and ran four to six miles daily. True, he did not have a degree in social work but he did earn a BA in something else. Business administration. He had once stood as a union man when he had worked for a tire and rubber company, but the bosses had busted the union, and he had lost his job. He sided totally with management now. His loyalty to the Falisecs and the fact that he worked for only six dollars an hour explained why he remained a permanent fixture at the Manor. "What is it about the second floor anyway?" he asked Harlan who had just gotten up. "We moved patients on all six floors, but all the big problems occur on the second. We expect an inspection any week now, so I try hard to keep everyone happy. Why just this morning I had to yank Crazyhorse out of Hodge and Johnson's room. Why not call me Andrew Jackson? I sent at least one Injun on a trail of tears. I'm sure Willard brought this to pass. He told me he would never accept a colored for a roommate, and he found a sure-fire way to get rid of him. He calls the nurses into their room, and they see Crazyhorse has crawled into bed with Johnson. I just can't figure out how Hodge got him to do it. Johnson as you know has all sorts of psychosocial needs. He just had his first stroke and finds himself suddenly debilitated.

He cries a great deal. He has not accepted nursing home placement, feels that his second wife has betrayed him by having him admitted to Colonial Court. His children, all to the first Mrs. Johnson, agree. He can't bear and won't accept that his body won't do what he wants it to. Now he thinks his new roommate tried to assault him sexually. Of course I had to separate them. I sent Crazyhorse up to the fifth floor with the other crazies. As I said, I don't really believe that he wanted to poke Mr. Johnson, but he's slow, dimwitted and the nurses did see him in the wrong bed. And with an inspection just around the corner, I can't afford to take any chances. Just what we need right now. A cornhole incident."

Back on Blue Hall as he moved among the patients Harlan wondered which still fantasized about forbidden pleasures. Surely for most of them the sex urge had withered and died. It made him sick to his stomach to think of them desiring each other as they stood now. Who'd want to nuzzle up to shriveled decaying skin? But if they fantasized about their past when they were young, healthy? But surely most of them didn't think about such things anymore. He intuited that for many of the frowning men with cast-down eyes that their organ had stopped working or given out due to advancing age or an enlarged prostrate whereas the majority of these old sweet Christian ladies looked as if they had remained neuter pears their entire lives. Now Joe the flyboy still read his *Playboy*. Harlan could forgive him. It didn't seem so unnatural as it would have with the others. He seemed less dead. If he and Redenzio's new roommate who also seemed alive and not to belong in the home occasionally teased and propositioned the girls Harlan didn't see anything wrong with it. That's not to say that the girls didn't mind. But Tyson Hicks and Joe Crinsky remained sick and dying. They had to be forgiven. Harlan wouldn't mind taking a tumble in the hay with the aide to whom this very day the DON had coupled him and assigned him to work with—Keefer's replacement, the busty and vivacious Cindy Mehan. But he couldn't proposition her. A paid employee differs from a resident (they stood worlds and universes apart); therefore he couldn't make advances with impunity like them. "We're both in the same boat," he told Redenzio. "They've partnered me up with someone new too." "But she's pretty," Redenzio said. "And she doesn't steal." He thought about Cindy in the rest room but not exclusively. He remembered Kaleena Kirby pulling down his swim trunks and grabbing hold of him. He imagined what both Peggy the activity aide and Hanna the medical secretary would look like with their clothes off. He even remembered Al relating how a Panamanian prostitute fellated him for three snorts of cocaine. Sweat dripped off Arretto's face as his fingers razored the powder into thick furrows. Harlan could taste it already between his teeth. But Al put the blade down on the tray and set the tray on the floor. He reclined in his chair, put his arms behind his head and closed his eyes then started telling Harlan his story. "'You know baby I'll turn you on,' I said to the whore, 'but you got to do something for me. You can slide slow or fast,' I told her and undid the cord of my drawers and displayed a pillar as formidable and as large as a monster of legend." Har got a cockstand, as Al teased and tested him. But he saw Arretto had one also. "Up and down she went. Up and down and adding simultaneous sideways motions of her head." Al picked up the tray and did the lines himself. "I know boys who'd agree to do just about anything for me that I wanted them to if I would lay down more lines. Some for them. How bout it, Har?" Houser didn't show any willingness to comply. He wanted the turn-on, but he held himself in check. Al worked him all the time back then, always kept trying to talk him into driving the get-away car, Harlan's solution to throw a pillow at him to shut him up and tell him knock it off. Yeah he had grown addicted. So hooked he could almost have given in, said all right let's go. Al knew how vulnerable he could become. How four years after she dropped him, he still could not forget Kaleena Kirby or become involved with anyone else because he remained shy and retiring, because he could not talk to women. They went out together to bars. Arretto always so brave and so cocksure, would start up a conversation with anyone, talk to whichever girl caught his eye. Even if she had an escort! That guy in the bar called him a cheater, a real two-timer, too. Harlan could never act like that; he became terribly self-conscious and nervous. Kaleena had taken the role of aggressor, not him. After work she asked him to accompany her to the other side of the lake to a secluded spot where they went swimming. She reached into his trunks. She stood behind him in the water which rose up to their necks. Harlan moved his hand up and down. They swam to shore where lying in front of him she developed a pleasing rhythm, pumping fast and rough with both her hands. Then she brought her mouth down and caressed and enveloped him. He came as he thought about it. It devastated him when she gave him the heave-ho a couple of months later and started dating someone older. She took him like a man takes a woman or as a panther pounces on her prey. Genders seemed to switch. She wanted sex but no commitment. He told Al all about her. In his sixteenth and seventeenth years, he didn't suffer want, but four long years of famine followed that feast. Al teased him constantly about his inability to find a woman. "What's the matter with you? You're young, just twenty for Christ sake. You should put the bone to a new one each night. You're good looking, and got your own pad. Why can't you score?"

Harlan said that he would wait until he found the right person and finally he found her, or, more truthfully, Pat offered and gave herself to him. Al had died over a year before and so had his father. Arretto on October 1, 1983, his old man three-and-a-half weeks later. She helped him get his life back together and kick coke. You'll take the taste test and switch to Pepsi, she said. Call me Pepsi Pussy and I'll come. Although she had put on the pounds since he knew her in high school and had a plain Jane face, Patricia Fisher focused and concentrated all her love on Harlan, and he credited her for saving his life. In the Blue Hall john thoughts about their sex life never crossed his mind. He fantasized about screwing other people. But at home he always did his duty. No she did not super-excite him in bed. People said that he had married so as to find another mother, someone who would lay down the law, someone he could yield all authority to. Yet his welfare always stood her chief concern. Now Kaleena Kirby could definitely show him a much better time under the sheets in the sack, but she didn't care two winks about his welfare. She remained selfish and vain. Whereas Pat always put the needs of everyone else ahead of her own.

After his father's suicide, Harlan inherited a large sum of money. His six thousand dollar cut from the successful bank robberies, he earmarked for the purchase of more blow. But now he could put it aside as other funds had suddenly become available. He stood relieved for he learned several banks had taken down serial numbers or else at the request of the F.B.I. as a precaution discreetly and unobtrusively marked their larger bills upon learning that the Gentleman Bandit had surfaced in Pennsylvania. As a lark, he buried the bank money in a cave in imitation of Robber Lewis. Oddly enough Alvin Arretto also enjoyed spelunking. He had a friend at Pitt who had spent many hours underground. Al talked him into taking him along on an expedition to a popular cave in western Pennsylvania. His next outing there, however, turned him off the sport. He went back to the place with two other explorers but not his friend, the experienced caver. Al acted as their guide. He felt confident he would remember to make all the right turns but he and his friends got lost, didn't come out for five hours. One of their lights had gone completely dead; another's beam wavered, faded, went out, but then came back on—to their immeasurable relief—when Al vigorously shook it. In a second he would have thrown it to the ground and smashed it. Al had told him he felt more scared in the damn cave than he ever did in a bank. Yes, foolhardy Har stashed and hid away all his ill-gotten gains, but he blew ever bit of his inheritance on coke. He smoked six or seven grams a day, then, like Sherlock Holmes, he started using needles. Content to live off his dad's money, he had no ambition. He never enrolled in any college courses at the Altoona branch campus of Penn State even though his mother begged him to. He partied all the time. All his friends began calling him Highser instead of Houser. "Hi Highser," they would say. It didn't matter that Al had died. For a long time Harlan had dealt on a pretty exclusive basis with him, but he quickly found replacements. When it came to connections, Harlan believed in redundancy. It took only a year and a half for all Dad's money to run out. Fat Pat rented one of his apartments. He let her keep a dog, a white Samoyed named Belle. Everyone else said no children or pets. He had met her in high school, but he stood out of her league then. He had driven to school in his dad's Mercedes. Dr. Houser had willed it to him, but he had later sold it when desperate for cash. She confessed that she had wanted him even during those days, but she suffered from low esteem due to her weight though she carried it like a Goddess then in comparison to now, but, as shy as he, she did not have the gumption or nerve to act on her desires. Now she saw him hit bottom. She worked as an aide at the United Methodist Home in Tyrone and attended night school to become an LPN. She asked him once when he collected her rent if he felt lonely and if she could do something about that. He accepted her as he had once accepted Kaleena. If a woman initiated things, he did whatever she wanted, fell down at her feet. But he would never on his own volition have approached her. But once she broke the ice, he stood to attention ramrod straight. She told him he would have to quit poisoning himself. He had also gone through most of his cash. He could count only on the rent from the five tenants each month, but, if he and she decided to make babies, they would *both* have to stay clean. She got her LPN and stopped working at the nursing home after finding a cushier and better paying job in a doctor's office. Thanks to his mother's string pulling he then found gainful employment (you had to be in a most generous mood to call it that) at Colonial Court Manor. They had three children in four years, first twin daughters Stacey and Carrie, then a son. His wife named the boy Jethro after the lead singer of her favorite band. He had planned to check out like Harold Houser, to use his Mustang like his dad had the Mercedes, but first he would have one last party, the big blow-out and final send-off, and he would use her rent money to pay for it. The night before his mother stopped by to see him, and as usual they fought and put on a show. He screamed that he would blow his brains out. He hated life. Pat had heard the two of them arguing. When she opened the door to him when he came for the rent, she really opened the door. She said he looked down. They'd fix that. Did he want to stay the night here with her? He looked up surprised. Yes, he said. Afterwards she told him she'd love him if he'd love her. She'd take care of him, called him her baby. She came from a Catholic family, had eight brothers and sisters. Her parents never had time for her. If someone would make time, she would give him reason enough to live. He could clutch onto her like a life buoy. He needed someone to hold onto, to anchor his life. She stood as good as her word and stayed with him for the entire time he went through withdrawal. He felt safe when she lay by him and when he could curl in her arms like a child. He would put his head down on her lap, or they would just hug each other. He didn't need to have a cockstand every night. Having someone there to hold and clasp secure when he needed comforting actually meant more to him. And the children. He loved to cuddle them. They all shared Mommy's love. A little parrot, Stacey sat on his knee and repeated over and over again whatever he said to her. He started teaching her colors. She couldn't pronounce yellow, said wellow. He touched her nose and said nose. He touched her lips with his fingertip and said lip. Carrie screamed and ran over to his chair. "Daddy," she sobbed and held out both her arms. He had to embrace both girls. He could not favor one over the other. He clinched each one tight. He found within himself the capacity to love. In the end it would save him.

He loved babysitting, watching Stacey and Carrie play in the sandbox or ride around in circles on their tricycles in the front yard. He lived for them and for them alone.

After the aides completed all the moves and changes, management immediately cut their hours from forty to thirty-two hours a week. Because the patients were no longer spread out over as many rooms, the home could make do with fewer aides per shift. Everyone lost at least one day of work a week, but the owners laid no one off, and only Keefer Peoples had been fired. And for just cause. The union couldn't get him back. For a time, work remained trouble free and comfortably routine, the proverbial lull before the storm. With no new admissions, the aides naturally had less to do, and all the patients on Blue Hall appeared stable, the major medical event of May Stanton Smeltzer having his five remaining teeth extracted. Even Tyson Hicks and Redenzio Salerno had begun to tolerate each other, very begrudgingly and tentatively to be sure. Redenzio still threatened Hicks behind his back, but no one, not even Harlan, took him seriously. Hicks stood up to him, shouted him down, and put him in his place. Salerno cringed before the man who stood twenty years his junior or at least at the Sergeant's bark: his loud mouth that had cowed many and had always kept his men in line and on the *qui vive*. The voice of undisputed authority.

A few years back or even longer, someone or other in the health profession had dubbed May Older Americans' month. This year the country celebrated National Nursing Home Week the week of May 8-14. Bill Falisec flew to Pennsylvania from his winter home in Florida. "A retired county commissioner shouldn't have to put up with crap like this," he said and shook his head. He would launch an all-out media blitz: heartless State officials stand determined to shut down convalescent center and to deprive the elderly and for the most part indigent residents of their home. People owed Falisec. He had taken care of the county's elderly for over twenty years. He would give Miss Malmquist a fight. She thought she could just walk in and shut him down. Hell, he'd invite the press in, hold an open house. The director of nursing said Colonial Court Manor stood very fortunate to have so many dedicated employees. Falisec put the words in her mouth. He told her to applaud everyone for their commitment, diligence and sensitivity. Even the union would stand with him this time, as, if he went down in flames, they all stood to lose their jobs. Beth Ann Faust, the Activities Director, a short squat woman with curly orange hair, had put together and organized a number of nice programs this month. She had recruited all sorts of volunteers: girl scouts, junior high school and elementary students, barbershop quartets. A pet store owner brought in kittens and puppies for the delighted residents to hold and coo over. They brought animals in to certain bed-bound patients on the first floor. To a woman with osteoporosis who periodically signed herself into the home, coming in each time with a new fracture and a new cast. Transferring from chair to bed, she had put her weight on one foot and all the bones in it broke, bones as brittle as chalk. She remained the last patient admitted to the facility before the ban went into effect. They also brought newborn kittens for Annabelle Neibower to hold. She and her brother remained single all their lives, and both had taught at the Altoona high school, he analytic geometry, she the fine arts. In their old age and retirement, they had lived together for a time in a house on Kettle Street overrun by over fifty cats and stinking to high heaven. He died one day of a heart attack, and she called the police. Unable to take care of herself or her brother's many strays she quickly sank into a feeble and infirm state, and the authorities eventually placed her in Colonial Court Manor. Six months later the medical director diagnosed her as having colon-rectal cancer. The doctors opened her up, cut out the tumor and later sent her to chemo but within a short time detected further rapid and uncontrolled growth of the cancer, i.e. metastasis to other sites. Malignant cells had invaded neighboring tissues and had spread by way of the blood stream and lymph vessels to the lungs and liver. Dr. Laird pronounced her terminal and gave her three months at most. She cradled the baby felines in her arms all day.

Harlan learned that the scheduled events and programs of NNHW would culmi-
nate in the recital on the 18th by the Kaleena Kirby Dance Studio. Kean had obtained the
services of Kaleena and her students for Beth Ann. One morning early in the week, along
with Beth, a nurse, and Patrick a new guy from housekeeping—their driver for the occasion—Harlan accompanied Blue Hall residents Virgil Dobbs, Joe Crinsky, Alice Reighard
and Helen Loughner on a van trip to the Logan Valley Mall for an antique show. They
took a roundabout way back. Virgil Dobbs, who looked at every display case, didn't want
to leave and on the trip home requested that they drive through neighboring farmland
and woods. The patients didn't often get a chance to motor on the highway unless they
lay prone in an ambulance. So Patrick took a little detour in the country, and the boys
and girls glimpsed a deer darting across the road, then saw in a pasture cows huddled
together in a ring, a sure sign, Patrick, said, that a storm stood in the offing.

A certified activities director and department head, Mrs. Faust had developed over
the years her own views and opinions and ran Activities accordingly. Once she explained
her philosophy to Harlan. She favored what she called intergenerational programs with
give and take and mutual benefit on all sides. "What could be possibly more demeaning
than to view oneself as the object of charity? All persons have an innate need to both
give and receive. Everyone has some special skill or ability, something unique to contribute. Many intergenerational programs all too often center round doing things for the
elderly, not with them. Such programs remain one-sided. The elderly have little or no
input in them. No one affords them the opportunity to offer anything other than their
warm and heart-felt thanks to the young people devoting their time and talent to serve
them. Older people need opportunities to attain gratification through doing for others.
Age minimizes feelings of productivity and usefulness. People generally recall periods
in their lives when accomplishment stood at its peak. Elderly persons especially enjoy
reminiscing about past events. Remembering past satisfactions and triumphs often helps
older persons to cope more effectively with their current disappointments." Falisec had
given her the green light this year to pull out all the stops. She worked with area schools
since September and her pet projects now began paying off. Falisec would have Hawkins,
his friend from the *Altoona Mirror*, write complimentary articles. Cameras would click for
the paper's "Maybe You Were There" Friday feature. During the fall and early winter,
Mrs. Faust had Colonial Court residents, either individually or in groups, use a tape
recorder to record their memories. Her residents recalled as much as they could about
significant events such as prohibition, the great depression, World Wars One and Two.
Among others Stanton Smeltzer and Mable Hutchins participated. Later teachers in the
public schools played these tapes in elementary and junior high history classes. Certain
residents—those in better health—even attended such classes, where interaction between
the senior citizens and the pupils took place in the form of listening to and discussing
the tapes. The students learned about the past from the people who lived it. Now during
National Nursing Home week elementary students would perform a follow-up puppet
show before certain of the residents. The kids put on skits depicting historic events
and even of several of the residents' private, personal memories. All the skits incorporated taped-memory and discussion materials. Other elementary students and Colonial

Court Manor guests created easy-to-make hand puppets in a joint crafts activity which Mrs. Faust videotaped with the home's camcorder. She also planned to include a multi-media slide show in the entertainment, and Kaleena Kirby's dance studio pupils would later perform period dances such as the Charleston and Jitterbug. Anna Hudak's one-hundredth birthday party stood as yet another highlight of National Nursing Home week. "A great coincidence," Mr. Falisec said. "Milk it for all it's worth" President and First Lady George and Barbara Bush extended their best wishes to Mrs. Hudak as did Willard Scott, the Today Show weatherman. Director of Nursing Dorothy Yeazell and Acting Social Service Director Thomas Kean presented the letter from the White House to Harlan's favorite resident in a special ceremony May 9th. On her birthday three days later, the staff and family and guests of Mrs. Hudak celebrated. Silver-heart balloons tied to her walker, Anna made her way to the dining room accompanied by her nephew. The kitchen staff served cake and beverages to the residents. Peter DeJean strummed his guitar, and the residents sang. Indeed everyone strove to make the day a fitting and special occasion for Anna.

Thirty students from Kaleena's dance studio put on a show for the residents two days later. They executed ballet, pointe, tap, jazz, and baton routines before an enthusi-astic audience of over one hundred guests, friends and family. The dancers whose ages ranged from three to eighteen wore colorful tights, leotards and pink ballet shoes. They performed to music that ran the gamut from classical and jazz standards to the current pop hits. The residents had smiles on their faces, tapped their toes and clapped their hands to the music, and applauded all the dancers at the performance's close. Along with the other aides, Harlan had wheeled residents to the dining room for the special pro-gram. After bringing in the last of his assigned patients, he took a seat at one of the back tables. He wanted to see her—what she looked like after all these years. Mrs. Faust stood behind him. She had just plugged in the camcorder. At the recital's close the principal instructor came out to thank everyone. She had kept her figure. She looked tip top and as sexy as ever. He remembered her bright, mocking eyes more green than blue, and the masses of golden hair he used to pile on top of her head, and which now hung loosely to her shoulders. He hoped she wouldn't see or notice him in his current disgrace and think how far the mighty have fallen as he wheeled patients back to their rooms for the night. As the concert ended, everyone agreed that NNHW closed on a high note and on the whole stood a resounding success. They would all make a name for themselves with the intergenerational programs that the Activities Department had developed. The paper devoted a lot of space and copy to Beth Ann Faust. "My residents feel that they have passed on an essential heritage to the young people of this community." Hildegard McClelland, a local schoolteacher agreed. "The students," she said, "profited from inter-acting with the seniors. They had a chance to grow personally as they made new friends, developed new skills and gained new insights as they responded to real human needs."

Harlan worked the weekend. He had Monday through Wednesday off. Early Mon-day morning Harlan received a phone call from his mother. She called him from her office at the Tyrone Hospital. Through the grapevine, she had heard of new and breaking developments at the home. Mr. Falisec had announced a press conference for that afternoon. Perhaps he had succeeded at long last in selling the facility. Everyone would benefit if he had. Falisec turned up on the local news that night. He read a terse statement. He looked bloated and very tired, but his uncanny resemblance to Archibald Cox had never appeared more manifest with his red bow tie, horn-rimmed glasses and dark suit and his closely cropped graying ashblond head. A portrait of his father hung on the wall behind him. Old Mr. Falisec the wise Mason (gloves, hat, and cigar clutched in one hand, the other thrust jauntily into a coat pocket; a jutting jaw, crease under his lip, one above it, two vertical hatches on his forehead) had died at the Manor four years before. In 1960 he had bought the Filmore and, after thoroughly remodeling the building, a year later had opened the nursing home. The Falisec family had made their money in the coal business. A nursing home seemed like a good investment, and Colonial Court Manor had proven a gold mine until two years ago when the home's present difficulties began. A more detailed account of Falisec's press conference appeared in Tuesday's newspaper: "Mr. Falisec said that the owners in the past two years had advanced from personal funds in excess of $450,000 and could not afford to advance any further funds to continue operation of the home unless the State lifted the admission ban and new revenue began to flow into the facility." He thought the State unfairly singled Colonial Court out. They continued to persecute him over an unfortunate death that occurred two years before. But they did not only punish him, they also hurt the residents and their families. He hoped forced relocations would not ensue. Falisec timed his press conference for maximum impact. National Nursing Home week had drawn the community's attention to the elderly; they saw in the papers what excellent programs Colonial Court Manor had developed for its clientele. Falisec hoped the people would rally behind their old county commissioner. He knew his announcement would cause a panic, and that the families of the residents would rise up in arms, get up petitions, and ask local politicians to intercede. Family members scheduled an emergency meeting at the home. Candidates for public office, representatives of local church groups, and the news media also attended. Falisec spoke first, again told the public how the State had issued four provisional licenses to the facility. The deficiencies, he said, remained slight. The home suffered from documentation problems—poor note taking on the part of the staff. Nothing serious. Nothing that impaired the center's ability to render acceptable nursing care. Harlan attended the proceedings as his mother experienced a scheduling conflict and could not come. As a family member, he had a right to go, but of course he also acted as a mole for the union. He would report any new revelations to the other employees. Falisec had arranged for some family members pleased with the care their loved ones had received at the Manor to make declarations of solidarity. The wife of the superintendent of public schools spoke last. A small, fiftyish woman smartly dressed folded her hands on the lectern. She went off on the occasional tangent but knew how to work an audience and play up to people. She had her talking points, and she stuck to them. First she told everyone about her mother, her disease, and the family's anguish. Obviously a sympathy ploy staged and rehearsed. Harlan began to fidget; she droned on. Most of her audience, however, found her story sad but inspirational. Thus she built up to her peroration, rallying her troops to back Mr. Falisec tooth and nail:

"Much to my mother's chagrin, I could never memorize any of the piano pieces assigned by the piano teacher. I could sight-read, but I couldn't memorize. My mother's frustration stemmed from the fact that she, a much better player than I, seemed to have an almost photographic memory. She could successfully memorize a sonata or polonaise almost as fast as she learned to play it. One of the saddest moments of my life came one morning last year when I found her sitting at our old upright, the sheet music open in front of her, but she was no longer able to play even the opening bars of the 'Fantasy Impromptu.' A piece she had committed to memory a decade before I drew breath.

"Mom came to live with us after Dad died. Bill and the children adjusted quickly to having Grandma as a permanent fixture in our household. She contributed a lot to our lives, and I loved the fact that I had a live-in baby sitter. Mom never ran out of things to do. She continued active in the church and the DAR and did volunteer work in the community. She also taught little fingers to play. On my birthday when I came home from work, strains from the hymn 'Amazing Grace' greeted me at the door. To my surprise and, I must say, my great joy, my four-year-old daughter sat at the piano. 'Do you like my present, Mommy?' she asked. On the sly for over a month, Mom had given her lessons. Together they planned my birthday surprise.

"Everything seemed fine for a few years. But now as I look back I realize that I could trace the initial stage of Mother's illness to this time. Occasionally, Mom seemed disoriented, confused and clouded. She would forget to attend the meetings of her church circle. Often she grew fatigued and sometimes for no reason at all felt depressed. Well, Mom was getting on. I dismissed her occasional memory lapse as a sign of old age. But with time things started getting worse. Mom could no longer remember our names, and she began to do bizarre things. She would pace up and down the hall for hours at a time, and again and again she would rearrange the furniture. She began to employ nonsensical language when she talked. Then the wandering began. Mom would leave home to go shopping and would get lost on the way. She would end up on someone's front doorstep across town.

"The doctor informed us that Mother probably suffered from Alzheimer's disease. He said the illness had several distinct phases starting with limited confusion and ending in total physical and mental incapacity. He said that we should consider nursing home placement. I resisted making that decision and quit my job in order to devote all my time to seeing to Mom's needs. I had the best intentions in the world, but I continued to keep Mother at home past the point where it remained safe and prudent to do so.

"I see now that she needed constant monitoring and supervision. I felt guilty because I got angry at Mom when she would not cooperate with me, then grew more angry at myself because I realized she couldn't control her behavior and because I neglected my husband and children to provide Mom with the extra care she needed. I found it painful to look at her now because I remembered her old self. I had to stand guard twenty-four hours a day so that she wouldn't slip off. I slept on a cot in her bedroom in order to watch her during the night. She grew frightened after dark and said someone waited in her room wanting to do her harm. I became ill myself and suffered from physical exhaustion. I cried all day when I found her sitting at the piano no longer able to play. The crisis reached its climax two months later. I dozed off one afternoon in the living room, and when I awoke Mother had again run off. To my horror, I discovered that she had taken the car. I became frantic and called Bill at work. He told me to calm down and that he would phone the state police. They put out an APB on mom. I waited at home for the next few hours praying that everything would turn out all right. The telephone finally rang and I rose to answer it. Praise the Lord, the police had found her safe and sound. She had driven forty-five miles then steered our car into a ditch. I knew then that matters had reached a head and that I would now have to act.

"Once I realized that we needed outside assistance to care for mother and had decided to admit her to a convalescent center, I had to find the right facility. The doctor told me that I must remain levelheaded when making my decision and said that I should visit several homes to find the one best suited to our needs. He instructed me, when I paid a call on a facility, to look for buildings and grounds in good repair, conspicuous nurses and aides, and well-lighted patient rooms painted bright and large enough to insure that the patient had room to move about easily. He said to make sure the rooms and hallways stood clean and free of odor. I should notice how fast the staff would respond to patients' call bells. A good facility, he said, would have an activities department and would provide laundry service. Finally the doctor said to talk to the guests—I would learn more about conditions at the homes from them than from the administrators—and to look for a facility with an Alzheimer's disease Unit. He warned me that many long-term facilities had developed such units. Some facilities created such special wings to truly help the patient but others merely to look current and up-to-date. In a good facility the staff would have extensive training and would constantly update knowledge and ideas. On one hand there stood torchbearers and trailblazers and on the other minions and slavish followers.

"A good unit would provide reality orientation, remotivation and goal planning in their care for Alzheimer's patients and a physical environment that would strengthen feelings of security and structure for the resident. After visiting several homes, I decided on this one. Colonial Court offered the first specialized Alzheimer's care in our area directed at retarding the progress of the disease through attitude, communication, and physical therapy. It also provided around-the-clock supervision for its residents. The programs aimed at keeping the patients busy. The nurses encouraged exercise to maintain a patient's strength. They employed constant communication therapy because conversation increased socialization and independence. The personnel strategically placed memory boards with photos and objects linked to the patient's past in every room as well as large labels, calendars and other written reminders at appropriate locations. The staff seemed friendly and helpful and provided a number of suggestions as how to make mother's move easier and less traumatic. Mr. Kean from Social Services told me to bring her to visit the facility before we admitted her.

"I still stood stricken and experienced strong guilt feelings on the day we brought Mother for admission. She began to cry and said that she wanted to come home with us. Then she said Dad would come for her. I started to tear, as Dad had died six years ago. In the car on the way home, I wondered if I had done the right thing.

"I did not visit Mother for two weeks after I admitted her to the Manor. The hardest thing I ever had to do in my life, I think, but Mr. Kean advised me to keep away for awhile because Mom required this time to acclimatize to her new environment. To adjust it would take on the part of all of us, I felt, a feat of adaptation rivaling the lungfish. At first she became belligerent, the staff later told me. I thought constantly of her. So many things crowded into my head about Mom from when I was a little girl right up to the present time. How when I had my tonsils out, she stayed in a chair beside my bed all night in the hospital. How later she scrimped and saved to help put me through college. Her advice about men when I first needed that advice. How she taught Darla to play "Amazing Grace." You can bet that as soon as Mom accepted placement I became a frequent visitor to Colonial Court Manor.

"I have noticed everything about Mom's new environment her first year here. The diligent hard-working nurses. The learned Medical Director Wilson Laird. Tom Kean. The cheerful aides. The bright residential quarters and the nutritious meals served from the kitchen. And every aspect of her daily routine. Each week Mom attends a wide variety of activities that she finds both intellectually stimulating and just plain fun. Her mornings begin with a coffee klatch, current events hour. She then goes to exercise class which builds up her strength and keeps her fit and active. Even on days when Mother turns belligerent and combative, the staff treats her with dignity and respect. She attends weekly church services, movies with family participation and a residents' council where the guests of the home have an opportunity to air grievances and add their input to their care and service. The Alzheimer's staff has also designed special activities for Mother's ongoing and disease-specific needs. These include daily reality orientation and remotivation therapy. My guilt feelings began to dissipate. I became more comfortable with my decision to admit her. The realization that I could not care for her by myself and the fact that Mother's actions had endangered her life had determined my decision. Gradually she grew accustomed to the nursing home surroundings and began to feel more at home. Besides the family and I never kept very far way. We dropped in several times a week. Each time I saw someone or something new to praise. So many dedicated people work here.

"Darla and I stopped by recently late one afternoon. We didn't find Mom in her room. She attended a special Easter sing-along. Decorations hung in all the halls and in the dining room where the activity took place. A volunteer from a local church Peter De-Jean played hymns on an upright piano. I immediately distinguished Mother's voice from the others as they sang 'The Old Rugged Cross.' They all sat at the activity tables, some in their geri-chairs. A few didn't sing. But most did. Darla ran to the table where Mother sat. She stopped singing, put her arms around Darla and gave her a big hug. 'I love you, Nanny,' Darla said. 'Well, that goes for me, too sweetie,' Mom replied and laughed."

Harlan looked up to see that the woman was crying.

"Then she smiled at me. How dare the State say the patients here don't receive adequate care? I don't see those inspectors coming through the door every day like I do. I have visited other homes. Both county and church-run facilities. And it's my opinion that our loved ones can obtain no better care anywhere in Blair County than at Colonial Court Manor. We just experienced a fabulous National Nursing Home week and saw what wonderful activities the caring staff here arranged for our loved ones. Yes, splendid entertainments. Unlike the county home, Colonial Court provides air conditioning on every floor. The nurses have all had special training and in-services, and I for one applaud the dedication and sympathy that these skilled health-care professionals show on a regular if not a daily basis. I remain very satisfied with the care my mother receives here."

A woman in the midst of the assembly stood up and cried: "My mother calls them her angels of mercy." "I have never heard any complaints," someone else said. Suddenly everyone spoke, and the room whirred with separate discussions. The Superintendent's wife presided over her congregation. "Let me finish," she said. "Please." After quieting them down, she resumed her call to arms: "We must stand as the advocates of our loved ones. We all need to raise our voices to make sure that the powers that be hear us. We need to fire off letters and sign petitions. Every one of us needs to pick up the telephone and put a call into these people. All of us must support the Falisecs. We must present a united front and let Cynthia Malmquist know we're going to fight her to the bitter end if she tries to come here and close us." She stepped down and took her seat. People again started speaking among themselves. Some would stay and chatter a half-hour yet, but Harlan had heard enough. He walked out the door and headed as fast as he could for the exit.

Pat shoved him with her shoulder then handed him the phone. It was for him, Charlotte Boggs. He looked at the alarm clock and saw the time: 6:10. He wondered why the Administrator would call him this early. She didn't usually arrive at the facility herself until 9:30. They needed someone to fill in on Gold Hall. Could he possibly come in? They'd still need him in the afternoon on the second floor, so he'd have to pull a double. He would, he said, provided that he could find a baby sitter at such short notice. His wife, he explained, had to work that morning also. Could he dial her back? In five minutes, he returned her call and told her that he could come in, as his mother-in-law had agreed to take the kids.

Just as he pulled into the parking lot, he saw Boggs step into her Cadillac and drive off. Later he learned that she and Dorothy Yeazell had stayed the night to spy on and, if necessary, put the screws to the eleven-to-seven crew. The idea had been Bill Falisec's brainchild. "Who knew when the inspectors might walk in?" he had told them. Everyone had to be on their tiptoes. After all, the night shift had caused all the problems to begin with. Your eleven-to-seven employees have done you in, he remembered Mr. Campbell, the Administrator at the time of Mrs. Lange's death, saying when he reported the incident to him. If they would have come clean right away, called him at home, apprised him of what had occurred, asked for his instructions, but no, they took it on themselves to cover the death up. But they, of course, got caught and exposed and, as you know, from that time on the State's never let up on us, has constantly breathed down our neck. At night no one's there, he went on. The patients sleep in bed. Sure there remains less to do. That's why he needed someone looking over the night shift's shoulders. He mistrusted them still. So Dorothy and Charlotte had come in unannounced and scared the graveyard-shift girls to death when they surprised them in the employees' lounge playing cards. Well, they won't watch and evaluate me today, Harlan thought. They won't have me in their goddamn sights. One good thing.

Only rarely did he take someone's place on the first floor. Annabelle Neibower had died the day before. The news hadn't reached him on Blue Hall, and he found out only as he passed her room and saw the door open, her bed stripped and her personal effects gone. "When did it happen?" he asked one of the skilled unit's LPNs. "Only yesterday," the nurse said and told him about Annabelle's recent diversion: the kittens she had so delighted in during NNHW. Harlan felt glad that she had smiled and laughed so close to the end. He didn't know any of the other patients. He recalled Annabelle because the staff first admitted her to the facility as an intermediate patient and had assigned her to Blue Hall. He had planned to stop in and see her this morning, but she had passed. Most of the patients on Gold Hall lay comatose or else had terminal cancer. The aides had to bathe them and wiped their asses. Furthermore they had to weigh them periodically in the Hoyer Lift. Harlan found such work hard and taxing. Several patients weighed over two hundred pounds and it took two to three aides to raise them out of their wheelchairs. A great decubitus ulcer spread over both buttocks of one woman. She fought and screamed when they tried to sit her down on the scale. The nurses had also placed a number of patients in isolation due to staph infection, so the aides had to maintain secretion precautions. The youngest patient in the home belonged on this unit, a thirty-two-year-old quadriplegic who broke his back in an automobile accident, Dan Stiles. The saddest case of all. Harlan began his day all over again with the second shift. It pleased him, however, to leave the first floor and return to Blue Hall, where at least most of the patients talked to you and didn't just stare straight ahead. Yes, he had to admit he had grown bored and dissatisfied doing this kind of work. True, his minuscule pay remained constant and he needed every penny of it, but he saw no career advancement working at the Manor. He had to find a way out of this dead-end job.

That night he took Pat by both hands, feigned that they danced together and waltzed her into their dining room, made her sit down in a chair while he remained standing still holding her hands. Would she support him if he decided to go for the BS, the bull shit degree, that both she and his mother had always wanted him to get? They couldn't possibly survive off her current salary at Doc Kinter's office alone, but she could return to working at Epworth Manor, Tyrone's Methodist home. They wanted her back. And she always said they had Colonial Court beat. "That's heaping an awful onto my shoulders," she said. She didn't know if she could handle two jobs. She owed it to him to speak truthfully. But, he pleaded, if he could get a degree in something practical like Accounting, her sacrifice now would insure a brighter future for both of them. He could earn a lot as a C.P.A. "Honey," Pat said. "Maybe I should go back to school. In two years' time, I could become an RN. Did you ever consider that?" An impasse. "At least think about it," he said. She promised him that she would.

Because one of their aides took all the vacation and comp time coming to her and they stood one person short, Oldenbusch assigned Harlan to work the fifth floor—the Alzheimer's unit—during the last week of May and the first week of June. How could his job dissatisfaction not increase? The unit offered around-the-clock supervision and custodial care for its patients. Most of the personnel, including the majority of the aides permanently assigned to the unit, had taken special seminars in order to acquire the appropriate knowledge and familiarity in treating Alzheimer's patients at Altoona or Mercy hospitals. Harlan had no such training. However, the charge nurse paired him with an experienced aide and handed him a brochure on the disease to read in his spare time. "Not all the patients on this floor have Alzheimer's," she told him. "A number of other conditions produce similar symptoms. We admit patients with Organic Brain Syndrome and senile psychosis to this unit as well. Others have a history of mental illness."

Harlan heard a great deal of wailing on the hall. An evil spirit dwelled in one old man—or so one of the LPNs claimed. A practicing and observant if not strictly orthodox Jewess, she insisted that the patient didn't need a doctor but someone who could cast out a dybbuk. Whenever she touched Mr. Zanvl's hand or spoke his name, he broke out in hysterical laughter, rolled his head from side to side and, if he could, would unzipper his fly and bare his penis. Apparently these crazies still feel procreative urges, Harlan thought. Desire has not died and withered for them! Then he would try to grab her hand and place it on his sex organ. All the while he'd say over and over again, "He's gone away. I have driven him out. I have." Then he would laugh all the louder. His eyes would widen and he would stick out his tongue. She half expected his neck to snap in two the way he whipped it back and forth in such an exceedingly fierce manner. "I've had a change of skin," he would shout. "I've entered a body again." And the voice didn't sound like Mr. Zanvl's. She would swear so, for she had known him for years and years. They had attended the same synagogue. Harlan kept out of Zanvl's room. He remembered how Ida Klebbers had given him the willies when she said, "I'm God and your days stand numbered" and shuddered all over again. No, he didn't want to repeat that hair-raising experience. Several patients wore stockinettes over their hands and arms because they would otherwise scratch themselves constantly with their fingernails. The aides tied down one woman's hands because she would play with her stools and would throw excrement at the staff and at other residents. Another woman would always lift her skirt to reveal her hairy triangle and an expanse of withered thigh to the male aides. A blubbering former alcoholic, she would spit in the aides' faces if they tried to cover her. Crazyhorse resided here now also. On the third floor, he had ambulated up and down the hall looking for his room telling everyone he met he worked here and that he searched for his tool belt, his hammer and wrenches. He would even sweep the floor if someone from house-keeping offered him a broom. Here he sat in a geri-chair all day (as did all the other residents), and, when he grew agitated and started pounding on the tray with his fist, the nurses would give him Haldol injections. God help you if you took his lunch tray from him before he finished with it. He would swear or strike out at you. He had never acted this way before. His behavior started to become erratic and unpredictable when they started him on the medication. Many of the patients remained non-verbal. You could evoke no response. They would just stare at you. Or only gibberish would come out of their mouths. One woman would say nothing but "Little Jack Horner sat in a corner" and that only rarely. Most had developed contractures, and the aides would daily tug at their arms and legs to increase range of motion and improve circulation. They would help a few patients out of their chairs and walk them up and down the halls. One man remembered how to play paddycake. He liked to swat people and would hit them over and over again while singing, "Pit it and pat it and mark it with an end. Throw it in the oven for Mother and me."

During his second week on the fifth floor, Harlan attended a special in-service, an annual update on the latest research being done in the field. He learned how Alzheimer's caused the progressive impairment of memory, judgment, language and spatial relation-ships, robbing the victim of intellectual capacity and finally of life itself. He saw slides of brain cells. The ghost-like voice intoned: "Groups of nerve endings in the outer layer of the brain degenerate and disrupt the passage of electrochemical signals between the cells. There remain accumulations of twisted filaments and other abnormal structures within neurons. Only a biopsy can reveal such characteristic changes in the brain, so the diagnosis of Alzheimer's disease must remain conjectural during the patient's lifetime." Harlan hated working on the unit. He hoped that his two-week stint would fly by so that he could return to Blue Hall and not have to deal with the crazies. The time could not pass fast enough for him, for he looked forward to the twins' upcoming birthday—they would turn four on June 4th—the day after Oldenbusch scheduled him to return to Blue Hall. Yes, the time couldn't pass fast enough for him. Harlan had to wait until he turned seven until the date of his birth May 7 coincided with the number of years he had lived. His wife still had three years to go for her birthday fell on January 30th. The twins would have the experience too early, when it would have little meaning for them, yet he deter-mined to outdo himself and make them as happy and as exultant as he possibly could. To insure their high spirits, he bought them each four toys, two stuffed animals and two dolls apiece. He planned to take a bunch of snapshots. Each girl would have her own chocolate cake with four candles. His wife's sister's children would attend. So would the grandparents. He planned to purchase helium balloons, candy, and paper hats.

The party went off just as he planned. "Just two more years before you start school, girls," Harlan said. "I can hardly believe how old you're getting." He kissed each one on the forehead.

The day before, his last on the Alzheimer's unit, a woman he had to spoon-feed spat her jello in his face. "You disgusting old bitch," he growled as he wiped his cheek with his hand. Later when he took off her diaper he put it under her nose and held it there so she could smell the odor of her own waste.

He remained gruff and ungentle with the brain dead. He mimicked their speech patterns, spoke the same baby talk. If he had his say in the matter, he let it be known, he would put all the useless eaters to sleep. Several staff members including the Medical Director took note of his behavior and attitude. "Opposite impulses work in him," Dr. Laird remarked one day to Mrs. Oldenbusch. "He remains loving and respectful with the patients who are alert and oriented but becomes contemptuous and unfeeling to the senile residents except his great-grandfather whom he visits almost every day. Never assign him to work on the Alzheimer's unit again." For his part, Harlan felt relieved to again find himself on Blue Hall. The PT room sat on the ground floor. Bill Osbey, the home's L.P.T., worked as a private practitioner and independent contractor. He rented the room at Colonial Court Manor and supplied his own equipment such as tilt table, parallel bars, and whirlpools. He had similar contracts in three other convalescent centers in Blair County and soon would expand his services to include a facility in Clinton County. He hired two assistants Amy Beck, an LPN, and Cheryl Thorgood, an occupational therapist whose areas of expertise included sensory stimulation, feeding training, and upper extremity kinetics. She helped patients debilitated by amputation, stroke or elective surgery such as hip or knee replacement to readjust to daily life. Harlan wheeled Blue Hall patients down for their appointments. One man had recently tripped and fallen. Cheryl had his foot in a basin and applied ice to reduce swelling and pain. Meanwhile Bill melted paraffin over the arthritic hand of Wilhemina Diehl, providing warm, evenly contoured heat clear down to the bone. Next he would employ mobilization therapy, a manipulative type of treatment which involved stretching of the joints. Finally since she had both Medicare A and B and the government would reimburse him for his services, he would give her an electric galvanic treatment where he applied direct current DC voltage to her joints for pain control. Harlan pushed Johnson's wheelchair up to Bill's desk. Johnson didn't like therapy and would often scream or protest. He became terribly frightened before a manipulation treatment and often started to cry and say that he would welcome death. This therapy didn't help. Why bring him to this medieval torture chamber? He couldn't move either his arm or leg. He stood a hopeless cripple. He hated the shocks. Bill used transcutaneous electric nerve stimulation at acupuncture points to treat muscle fatigue and for muscle reeducation and also employed neurodevelopmental therapies in an attempt to reprogram the central nervous systems of stroke victims. As Bill completed Mrs. Diehl's treatment, Johnson became more and more apprehensive and misbehaved in a manner reminiscent of Harlan's twin daughters at the pediatrician's. Meanwhile on the other side of the room behind a curtain, Amy Beck lifted a very old lady's legs out of a stainless-steel whirlpool. I'll have her ready for you in just a moment, she called out to Harlan. The P.T. staff utilized the whirlpools for, among other things, the treatment of decubitus ulcers and to ease back spasms. He took charge of Mrs. Siegler, wheeled her to the elevator, rode up with her, and got someone else. As Harlan wheeled him forward to wait next in line, Hodge could hear a terrified Johnson howl and shriek as Bill began his manipulations.

Carl Tibbons' condition had progressively deteriorated over the two weeks Harlan had worked on the fifth floor. Two days after he came back, Carl went into a coma. They moved him out of Dobbs' room to the one directly across from the nurses' station. Oldenbusch sat with him. His respirations grew shallower. She put bags of ice on his feet. Kean notified the family; his brother and sister and their spouses arrived within the hour, sat with him throughout the rest of the day, and held his hand. His heart went on beating for seven hours. Harlan stood in line to punch out when he got tapped on the shoulder. Mr. Tibbons has finally passed away, Mary Jane Milford said. The family wanted to take some of his belongings. Could Harlan carry the television? The maintenance boys, she explained, had all gone home.

He always dreaded this most and steeled himself before entering the room. Inside, he looked down at the waxy husk of Carl. A nurse had lowered shut his eyes, having removed the prosthesis from the one socket and slipped a wad of cotton in its place under the lid. No color to the lips. The tip of the chin curved up, seemed to reach out to touch the tip of his nose and one side of his head looked slightly caved-in. Harlan lifted the TV up from off the shelf. Had he gotten any enjoyment out of it? he wondered. A nurse held the elevator door open for him, and he carried the TV out to the sister's car and put it in her trunk.

The following evening, taking his "lunch" in the employees' breakroom on the first floor and finding that no one had made coffee and moreover that the can beside the auto-drip maker stood empty, he took his cup and made his way into the main office where he knew another percolator sat. Walking past the reception desk, he heard someone crying behind Thomas Kean's half-open door. He assumed that a family member sat grieving in front of Kean's desk. Kean should have gone home for the day, but someone had died late in the afternoon (or so Harlan conjectured), and Tommy got stuck passing out Kleenex and saying "It's all for the best" or "There now." He could tell that a man sobbed. A husband? He craned his neck to look in. Kean sat at his desk crying, his face held in his hands. Several days later he found out the reason why. One of the LPNs told him that Kean had just broken up with his girl friend. She had dumped him to take up with a yuppie lawyer. Tom had sat down with Beth Ann and told her everything. Soon everyone in the building knew. Harlan had to smile. He knew this would happen all along. People just don't change.

One morning without warning and three weeks overdo—Bill Falisec had flown back to Florida as everyone felt that the state would now wait until after the Fourth of July holiday to inspect the facility—Cynthia Malmquist walked into the building a little after eight a.m., wearing an apricot jacket and skirt and a ruffled white blouse. A tall big-bosomed and heavily haunched woman, she had an oblong face with a square jaw, dilated nose and prismatic blue-green eyes. She liberally employed facial make-up and ruby-red lipstick and wore her silver-frosted hair high over her forehead and feathered back on both sides so that it sheathed her face like an aureole and looked like she had spent hours styling it with brush and blow dryer, then had applied large quantities of hair spray to hold it in place. Most certainly, it would remain brittle to the touch.

Two other surveyors Patricia Howell, an old pro with slightly graying hair and a foreshortened face, near retirement age and content to play second fiddle, and Cheryl Fliegel only twenty-four, a recent college graduate who, wet behind the ears and along strictly for the ride, accompanied her. The girl had frizzy red hair like Raggedy Ann. The lenses in her bifocals hugely magnified faulty, substandard eyes, and her nose looked like somebody had pressed up its tip, stretching out her nostrils so that they gaped like huge in-and out-bound tunnels.

The surveyors sauntered into the administrator's office, not with an air of professional impudence, but with kind smiles, a so-happy-to-see-you-again-look on their faces. Indeed all day, an aura of good will and helpfulness seemed to hang about them. They always had a friendly word for a resident, something reassuring to say to any relative who would accost them. But to the staff they remained absolutely mum. On one of their prior visits, a previous administrator, the stalwart Mrs. Dougherty (an old warhorse who had worked as an RN in the OR of Mercy Hospital and who for many years had served as the administrator of Crestwood Center, a successful home in Altoona which never had a negative survey, any problems with the State whatsoever) had laid out all manner of cookies and pastries, slices of her home-made carrot cake, in her office for the exit interview, but the surveyors, back then led by Cynthia Malmquist as well, had refused to touch them, wouldn't even accept a cup of coffee or freshly brewed tea. At the conclusion of an inspection, during their final half hour in the facility, after having stood stonily silent for three days or even longer, the surveyors always remained evasive. No one could really say how the facility fared until two weeks later they received written word. During the interval before the results arrived and on the basis of the exit interview, some people always found reason to be optimistic. And during Rita Dougherty's tenure as administrator, such expectations did not remain wholly unjustified. Falisec had hired her as administrator immediately after the Pennsylvania Superior Court had provisionally reinstated the home's license. Falisec had induced her out of retirement with a thirty-five-thousand-a-year salary worth every penny and more for her past unblemished record and high reputation redounding to Colonial Court. The seventy-one-year-old woman would arrive before nine a.m. often staying as late as ten or eleven at night. On top of that, she lived with her sister in Blandsburg, so her driving time added forty-five more minutes to her workday. Even though the home received its second provisional while she acted as administrator, the deficiency lists had considerably shortened, and Ms. Malmquist had publicly admitted that progress had been made. Before he found Rita, Falisec had hired and fired three other persons as administrator in just two-and-a-half years (one of the deficiencies stated that there existed poor continuity of care due to the high turnover rate of key personnel), but superior to all her predecessors, far and away the best administrator the place had ever had, she had overseen the operation of the home down to the minutest details. She told Mr. Falisec that she would have the home in shipshape by the time of next survey. She demanded absolute authority, and Bill gave it to her. She sacked a large number of bad employees—pruned away all the deadwood, she said—and instituted a number of reforms including implementing new infection control and evacuation policies. She also managed to keep Mr. Falisec firmly in the background, no mean task and perhaps the prime factor behind her partial success with the State. She had known all the surveyors for years and had no compunction about phoning their offices to speak confidentially with them and to find out if she and they could strike some sort of deal or satisfactory compromise. Similar attempts at shuttle diplomacy on the part of previous administrators had always ended in failure, but the State officials seemed to grant special dispensation to Mrs. Dougherty. They let her know what they wanted, and she strove to bring everything into compliance, but, due to her age, all the stress she worked under, or the incredibly long hours she spent at the facility, the task in the end proved too much for her. The gods thumbed their noses at the Falisecs yet again. One morning Rita Dougherty suffered a heart attack while speaking to Mr. Falisec on the telephone and paramedics rushed her to Altoona Hospital. Everyone dreaded the possibility that she might return to the facility as a paying guest for they as health-care workers all knew that people in their profession make the worst possible patients, much more demanding than anyone else. Everyone's fears proved unfounded. After a three-week stay in ICU, Rita recovered to the point where her doctors deemed her well enough to go home, but on no account would they let her resume working. Falisec brought in Charlotte Boggs.

The Department of Health granted a two-month extension to the license on June 15th, the date the fourth provisional stood due to expire, because the surveyors had not conducted an inspection by that time. And although surveyors never announced the dates for inspections, the granting of the extension suggested still further delay—so Falisec flew back home, and the entire staff felt secure. On Blue Hall, only Mrs. Oldenbusch remained apprehensive. "We're living on borrowed time," she said. Charlotte Boggs became apoplectic when she looked out of her office window and saw Ms. Malmquist pull into the home's parking lot in her white RX7. Tension had already reached an all-time high level when Harlan walked into the building at two o'clock. All day he fastidiously performed his duties, took more time to make doubly sure that he did everything right, by the book. Nervous, walking on eggs, he felt like someone constantly peered over his shoulder. All day he had the sensation of being watched. He couldn't tell if it was an inspector or just one of his ghosts.

The team stayed for the entire week instead of the usual three days. As Har executed his various tasks, he relied entirely on his reflexes, on pattern and routine. As he spoon-fed a resident or emptied a bedpan, his thoughts wandered, his past rewinding itself before his mind's eye like film through a projector, then stopping, freeze-framing, say, at a point six years earlier when he got off a train in Miami with Al.

They had taken a taxi to an inner-city address where Al had met his connection, and they had scored two kilo's worth of blow. Then they went back to the Amtrak station and booked double bunks in the sleeping car and left for home the same evening. Always the worrywart, Harlan prayed that their train wouldn't derail on the long return trip to

Pennsylvania. They spent some of their time in the lounge car quaffing beers but for the most part remained content to stay in their sleeping-car cubicle where they could snort lines and shoot up as they waited to pull into Pittsburgh and Altoona, their respective stops.

Everyday as he went through the daily grind, the same dull routine, the old memories rekindled in him. He thought about the robberies, the sums of money they had stolen, and the thrill he experienced breaking the law and getting away with it. He hated his job more than ever, and in a half-hearted and facetious manner flirted with the idea of holding up a bank on his own. How he longed for the security that having money brings. It seemed that fate now punished him for all the dough that he had let slip through his fingers—the money that had gone straight up his nose—by forcing him to work so hard and under such stressful conditions to earn only a measly pittance.

When would this damn inspection end? Would they ever finish?

Each day seemed an eternity. Finally late Friday, the surveyors walked into the DON's office for the exit interview, and the staff breathed a collective sigh of relief. All the department heads wore glum faces afterwards. "Well that's it," Veda Fletcher, the home's oldest housekeeper, said. "Our goose is cooked."

The first few days after the inspection went by uneventfully. At least two weeks would pass before they would receive the survey results. Then Redenzio died. During the last month, the aides had made steady progress with him. Two of the girls he had taken a shine to had even induced him to walk hand-in-hand with them down the hallway, to take more than a few steps outside his room. But late one afternoon, another shouting match erupted between him and Tyson Hicks. Redenzio's face reddered. "You fucking bastard. You know I'm Italian, what thatta means? Do I have to show you?" He locked his wheelchair, tore the blanket from off his knees, placed his palms on the armrests of his chair, and put all his weight on his hands. Fingers tightly gripped, knuckles turning white, he slowly raised himself, red cheeks puffing. But then he tottered and fell face forward. Hicks hit his buzzer. Two aides a couple of doors down responded. One ran for Oldenbusch. Salerno's heart had stopped beating before she arrived, and he was a No-code. His family had signed a paper that the staff should make no attempt at resuscitation in an emergency situation. On duty at the time, Harlan had to clean the body. He pulled the curtain the whole way round Redenzio's bed which two other aides had lifted him up onto as Oldenbusch wheeled Hicks out of the room.

As usual when one of his favorite patients died, after work, Harlan went to a bar—in this instance the Half-Moon Lounge in Tyrone—and got loaded. There he saw one of his old doper friends talking animatedly to a fellow boozer. The old desire returned, grew quite strong. He came up behind Larry Yetnikoff's barstool and clapped him on the back.

"Hey if it ain't Harlan Houser. How ya been?"

Harlan sat down beside him. "Not bad. You?" "I'm okay. Hey, I'll talk to ya in a sec," he said and resumed his conversation with his bar mate: "As I said, skunks have sprayed me many a time. Bathing in tomato juice takes away the smell. The only thing I know that does."

A life-long pothead, Larry always knew where to score a bag or pound and probably still did (the po-pos had busted Harlan's main man in a sweep several weeks beforehand, leaving him without a reliable connection, so he'd see if Lar could help him out). He asked the waitress to bring him another shooter and listened to his friend tell hunting stories to his neighbor. How after he let fly his last arrow and missed (the first pierced the lungs but not the heart of the daddy buck), the twelve-point turned and charged at him, and he had to resort to swinging his thirty-pound bow like a ball bat, but still the deer knocked him down. At least he rapped head and horns away and the buck did not gore him. The deer fell to the ground too. Did they know how mad a daddy buck got after someone cut its throat? He turned to Harlan, included him now in the conversation. An audience of two pleased him more than an audience of one. He knew, for that's exactly what he did after scrambling to his feet. All he had to say was one had best get out of the deer's way. Why? After its throat had been slit, the damn buck reared up on its hind legs and kicked him in the nuts. Those stories about throwing up after taking a shot to the stones proved all too true. He puked his guts out and hurt down there for weeks. But he had plenty to drink and smoke with him. Stuff to kill all that pain. "There you go," Harlan said. But after that experience, he continued, he had to say that he no longer found it exciting to kill deer with bow and arrow. To just wait up in a tree, after sprinkling scent all around its base, for the dumb critters to come right to him, then shoot them through the neck. This year he would switch to a bowie knife and jump down from his perch in the branches onto their backs and dispatch them with it. He looked forward to the challenge.

Here the other guy got up to go to the latrine; shaking his head, he said, "Yeah sure," then lifting his arms he observed that, "You only rent beer." As he stalked off, Harlan took the opportunity to ask Yetnikoff if he knew where to score. "Sure I do," he said. "Stop by tomorrow sometime. Hey, you don't know where I live now." Harlan took down the new address.

The next morning as soon as Pat stepped out the door, he packed his babies into his Mustang and drove to the trailer park where Larry had just moved. Afterwards he stopped at the state store for a bottle of tequila and at the Video Dome to rent a movie. He had a real buzz on by the time Pat came home. It had started raining, so he couldn't go out on the deck. He left the girls in front of the TV and locked himself in the master bedroom with Jethro. Afterwards he plugged in a fan and opened the windows, so the room would air out. The next night, as soon as his wife left with the kids (they planned to spend the weekend with her mother), he immediately sat down on the couch and twisted up another doobie. He lit it and inhaled deeply. Suddenly everything shone a little bit brighter, and he felt that his moment of truth stood at hand, that he had reached some pivotal turning point. Whenever he got stoned or liquored up, he began to bluster and to vow to knock over a bank himself and to again enjoy the good life. He always changed his mind by the next morning. Tonight he again swaggered and strutted. Perhaps the nine planets had lined up with each other. Or the moon stood full. He had seen omens and portents for weeks. Yes, he should make up his mind to go ahead and do it. Everything everywhere seemed brimful. He should seize the day and proceed because he couldn't keep living like this. He made up his mind to take a decisive step. He needed some of the old excitement injected back into his life. Otherwise it just got too damn boring. But did he have the courage to follow through? *Today is the first day of the rest of your life.* The stupid TV evangelist said this each week at the close of his Sunday broadcast. Harlan always caught the last couple of minutes when he tuned in to see "Superstars of Wrestling." Maybe he just didn't have the guts. But could he do it on his own, without Al? Perhaps not. But look how many times Al got away with it. And Harlan would know when to quit. While ahead, of course. The percentages had to go against you after so many stick-ups. With each one you pulled off, you stood that much closer to apprehension or else having to eat a bullet like poor old Al. He would know when he reached his limit. He would know when the odds stood ready to turn against him. And he'd stop. He would not attempt to pull one job too many.

He took another puff and recalled an old toy of his that his parents had bought him as a birthday gift when he turned seven or eight. Strange the connections you make when you're high. How things just pop into your head. He remembered the gadget transformed cubes into creatures and that Mattel—the toy king—manufactured it. At first glance, the device resembled a vaporizer. On top of a metal base, a glass chamber resembling a large overturned cup fastened over a mesh screen with wire rods under it that grew red hot like the coils in a toaster when you plugged the toy into the wall. A window in the chamber slid open and shut. You plunked a green, yellow or red dough square (bought separately of course) through it and switched the transformer on. The heat would cause the square to unbend and expand—to sprout legs and arms, a neck and head. You never knew what would pop through the pretend time machine/interdimensional gateway, a three-inch-high dinosaur or a two-headed insect man from some distant star. After the creature cooled, you could add it to your collection of creepy crawlies and plastic monsters, or you could place it in a second chamber, a long narrow rectangular slot, also behind glass, in the metal base. A square-shaped wedge operated by a crank extending out of the base moved down the chamber until it finally reached the opposite end like a wall closing in on screaming people in a B horror movie and crushed the creature once more into a cube. The directions said that you could put the cube back into the transporter again and again, and each time it would uncoil like a bud opening to the sun. In truth, the dinosaur would always come out malformed the second time through. After he recubed it, a tyrannosaur from the Upper Cretaceous period would return weighed down by a top-heavy head and neck. It would exhibit marked curvature of the spine and would have to revert from walking on its hind legs to inching along on all fours with its tail pointing up in the air like a beagle's. Even worse, the brontosaurus' legs would splay out to the sides or disappear altogether, and thereafter it would have to slither on its belly, just like the commonplace garden snake. Harlan felt that he had devolved in the same way his miniature dinosaurs had. He felt as if he had been "recubed" several times in his life, each time emerging as something less. First he shone as the fortunate upper-class son of a doctor and a social worker. But then his parents got divorced. But he had his independence, his autonomy, and he became the Robber Lewis of the 1980s—the accomplice of the Gentleman Bandit. But Al had made a dupe out of him and then had taken his own life in a robbery attempt. The walls closed in again. Next he became a half orphan. But as a result had money. Lots of it. But he managed to lose it too. Now he had sunk to working as a lowly aide wiping asses in a nursing home. If he held up a bank, he'd recube yet again. To emerge even worse off? He didn't know. But nothing could stand much worse than his current living hell.

That night, he decided it high time to relate Al's last stand (rather his expanded, mythologized, Harlan-centered version of it) to his Pap-pap Rausch. He had thought a lot about Lewis and Con lately, and now he remembered how they had met their end on the Sinnemahoning. The boys had experienced a hard spring back in 1820.

A wayfarer spotted three men shooting marks at Col. McKibben's farm on top of Muncy Mountain and assumed the men the same three who had committed the robbery of the Hammond-Page wagon train. He reported what he had seen to the local authorities who suspected that Lewis and his men had perpetrated the outrage. If Lewis had indeed made camp at McKibben's farm, they supposed that he would steer for Sinnemahoning, where his mother then lived. Patrols tramped the night away. One team included McGhee, the coroner of the county; John Hammond, part owner of the plundered wagon; Armer; Lebo; and Deisal. Later Walker, Carnel, Mannah, Kuhns, and Roder joined them. The first night McGhee's party lost its way, and the men encamped in the woods. The following morning the group struck Trout Run, which emptied into Bennet's Branch. Their guides started ahead to see if Lewis had made his appearance at his mother's and finding that he had not, they joined the rest of the squad that night and crossed over the Driftwood Branch opposite Shepard's Tavern, and upon inquiry found that two men answering the description of Lewis and Connelly had breakfasted there. The group proceeded up stream for about eight miles but uncertain whether they pursued the right men, turned back. Five miles down, they saw a man named Brooks engaged in gigging fish, who told them that Lewis and another man had passed that way. They returned with Brooks in their company, till they came within hearing of the robbers, who shot mark in a clearing. Brooks took them to a hillside which overlooked and commanded the proceedings, and McGhee demanded their surrender. One of the robbers shouted: "Shoot and be damned." The posse fired. Lewis fell at the first volley, hit in the arm. Connelly escaped to the bank of the river, where, struck by a ball which cut the rim of his abdomen and caused his entrails to protrude, he collapsed. In commandeered canoes, they took the wounded captives down the Sinnemahoning to Great Island, where Connelly gave up the ghost. David Lewis died of gangrene in a Bellefonte jail cell twelve days later. The inquest found the coroner and his posse had acted according to law.

That night, as, half asleep, Harlan lay under the blankets watching TV and drifted in and out of sleep, Lewis metamorphosed into Connelly and vice versa in his dreams. He nodded off somewhere toward the middle of the night owl movie, an Italian flick hideously dubbed into English, concerning an abbot in the 1600s who opposed a wicked nobleman and each night became the dago Scarlet Pimpernel. The swashbuckler seemed to also continue in his dream, but somehow the two gentlemen bandits also became involved in it. Then he dreamt only about them and not any wop caped crusader.

Connelly had blond hair hanging over red-veined, blue-black eyes, a red nose, the gaping smile of a mental defective. He wore a greasy sleeveless t-shirt. Lew the bullethead had a blackish swollen face, hollow orbits instead of eyes. Greenish skin peeled off the skull in strips revealing the warped cartilage of the nose. Both his lips and ears started to dissolve. Black fluid seeped through cracks in the skin.

Then suddenly Nellyloo changed into Conis. He crushed two creatures together into a single cube. Their molecules fused and their DNA combined. The bullethead now rode on the shoulders of the t-shirted body. Suddenly blue eyes appeared in the death's-head's hollow orbits. Then yellow hair began to sprout out all over the face. The two outlaws had become one.

The next day, two hours before his shift ended and he could punch out for the night, he took his break and rode the elevator up to the sixth floor. Alfonso Walker had taken Pappy out of his geri-chair, put him to bed, and turned down the lights, but Harlan stepped in anyway nodding to the diminutive sixth floor aide who just then stepped out of the room to put someone else to bed. He had worked at the Manor for four years, several months longer than Harlan. Negroes come in all tints and tones. Little Alfonso appeared coal-seam colored. A blacker-than-pitch pure blood. Frein, the loudmouth crazy, slept quietly in bed A. Harlan passed the foot of his bed careful not to wake him, and sat down in the chair beside bed B and whispered into the sleeping (?) ear: "I kept it up even after they got Al. We went out of state. Al had brought in this third guy who must have tipped off the Feds for they stood waiting in the bank for us. I carried a shotgun. Al had an Uzi, its corrugated barrel hidden under his coat, and Schumann held a 45 Mag in his hand. Al charged in first, and the Feds gut shot him, but he managed to empty his clip as he fell, before he hit the ground. Or I should say nearly empty it. For he experienced such pain, he turned the gun on himself and put a bullet in his brain. I put a hole as big as a barn door in Schumann's chest when he spun around and pointed his gun at me. Then I likewise did an abrupt about-face and sprang through the entrance out into the parking lot. They followed me, and one quickly lined me up in his sights. As I threw open the car door, he squeezed his trigger, and I got winged in the arm, but I toppled in, put the key in the ignition and tramped down on the gas, squealing my tires. A squad car came right up behind me, as I screeched out of the parking lot, so I flew through two red lights at ninety miles an hour then onto some back road. But he still followed on my heels, and I knew I would have to smoke him. I had a revolver in my glovey. The road forked up ahead. I did a one-eighty, faced the pig head on, floored the accelerator and ran him off the road and into a guardrail. I drove as fast as I could, kept taking turns onto other roads, and lost myself in the country. Al had said he would have a second car parked near the bank, but he didn't tell me where. I knew I had to change vehicles. I drove down a dirt farm road and finally saw a house. No neighbors. A car and station wagon in the driveway. Garage door down. I pulled up alongside the station wagon, took the gun out of the glove compartment, opened the car door and jumped out. I didn't knock or ring the doorbell but just went up and tried the knob. It was unlocked all right. I met an old woman, late seventies, I'd say, in the hallway. 'Where do you keep your keys,' I cried. I pointed my gun at her heart. She didn't seem to grasp what went on. 'Tell me,' I said. She pointed behind me. I quickly looked round, saw a big wooden key hanging on the wall beside the front door. Sets of keys dangled from little hooks in the wood. I shot her in the chest. She fell to the floor. I shot her two more times in the head, then someone came charging down the stairs with his hunting rifle, a twenty-two. An old man in his bathrobe and slippers. I shot him in the eye, then grabbed all three sets of keys from off the big wooden key, and stuffed them in my pocket. I locked the front door from inside, went through living and dining rooms then out the kitchen door into the garage. I lifted up the garage door, got back inside Al's car, drove it in, then pulled the door down. I drove away in the station wagon. Still lost I kept on taking winding roads. I heard a helicopter overhead but he went by. Finally one of the roads came out onto the highway. The cops set up three roadblocks. They waved me through each one. Believe me I perspired and shook. But like I said, I couldn't give it up. I started robbing banks on my own and you know something I've become very good at it. I work here as an aide. A great cover. No one suspects me. Only you and I know, and it remains our little secret."

Harlan broke off. He whispered into Pappy's ear, but he couldn't at first see very well in the dark. Then after a few minutes his vision started to adjust. He saw that Pappy lay awake and that his eyes stood open, their corners wet with tears. He got up from his chair, suddenly pale, and left the room.

Finally the inspection results came in. By letter dated July 14th, the Department of Health revoked Falisec's license to operate a nursing home. It further stated that, on the same day, the Department notified Health and Human Services that Colonial Court Manor no longer remained eligible to participate in the Medicare reimbursement program or receive any payment from the Department of Public Welfare. This action by the Department, in stopping the flow of all governmental funds to the nursing home, would effectively bankrupt Bill Falisec in several weeks' time and require the relocation of residents and the closing of the facility. In addition, Welfare still owed $300,000 to the home for care rendered to MA patients in 1987, but the courts had placed this money in escrow shortly after Mrs. Lange's death. For a year following her strangulation, Falisec had kept all the patients at his expense. He simply didn't have the resources to do so any longer.

State officials and attorneys representing the owners convened an emergency meeting the following day in Harrisburg and hammered out an arrangement to help facilitate the sale of the home. The State granted Colonial Court Manor a six-month stay so that the facility could remain open. For that time period, it would remain eligible to receive governmental funding; Bill Falisec agreed to find a buyer within the time frame, or, at the expiration of the six months, the State would order the doors padlocked. As a condition of the agreement, the State appointed a medical management company from Philly, Schuylkill Health Services, to run the day-to-day operations of the convalescent center during the interim period. The company received a temporary license to manage the Manor. Mr. Falisec would have no say at all in the administration of the facility. However, he would still fork out the money to keep the Manor in operation. Mr. Charles Francescatti, a Schuylkill Health Services employee, became "Master" of the nursing home. He would have the authority to make any and all decisions. To fire and hire. To spend Falisec's money however he saw fit. And by agreement, Bill would have to pay. Charlotte Boggs tendered her resignation. A ship can't have two captains, she said. The State granted Director of Nursing Dorothy Yeazell a Temporary Nursing Home Administrator's license, and she became the Acting Administrator of the facility.

Mr. Francescatti tried to ingratiate himself with everyone. At first he let Dorothy take charge and stayed in the background, only crossing the threshold of Colonial Court Manor at most once or twice a week, and, although Bill Falisec technically no longer had a say in the everyday oversight of the facility, he regularly kept in touch with Yeazell. He would also call Thomas Kean or Beth Ann Faust to see what transpired. He wanted the State to come in as soon as possible to reinspect the facility, as the Department of Health had only granted Schuylkill Health Services, Inc. a temporary license. He wanted the State to certify that the staff had corrected all the deficiencies and to issue the Manor a full license. They owed him that. He had budged after all—raised the white flag for Christ's sake. Folded his cards, agreed to get out of the damn business. They had him by the balls. So he would stop fighting, declare them winner. In recompense, they could at least reinstate the bloody license so that he could ask a fair price for the place, for who'd want to buy a nursing home with only a Temp? And an admission ban to boot? Who'd want to step into Bill Falisec's shoes? No one. Well someone would. But on the cheap. He'd have to sell at a huge loss. Furthermore, he spent money hand over foot as it was, keeping the place open when he could not admit any new patients, and the old people didn't stop dying. The census kept on dwindling right along, so the money that did come in from the State didn't pay the overhead. Not the half of it. Already he had lost a substantial part of his life savings. He even had to mortgage his pension fund. He wanted the place sold, taken off his hands ASAP. He didn't want to lose any more goddamn money!

Charles Francescatti told Dorothy Yeazell that he would invite the State back whenever she said that they stood ready.

In one month's time, following her employer Mr. Falisec's orders, his deadline, she gave the word. The four weeks she had sat in the commander's seat remained positively hellish for the employees. They worked their buns off. Attended fire, disaster, and evacuation drills and other mandatory in-services. The LPNs had to pass all the meds and do the treatments because the RNs occupied themselves exclusively with the paperwork. Besides doing the monthly billing, the office staff also worked on charts to make sure that the other employees had entered all the necessary information. Tom Kean, Beth Ann Faust, the medical secretary, the two receptionists—everyone—tore apart then put back together charts. The RNs at the various stations had taken the Nurses' Notes, Doctors'

Orders and Med Sheets off them for report in the employees' lounge. Several aides drove to various doctors' offices in Tyrone and Altoona to get needed signatures, for although Wilson Laird was Medical Director, not all the patients in the facility were his. Everyone had to catch up on their bookwork. Dorothy Yeazell determined to resolve all the documentation deficiencies. She sat sequestered in her office coming up with answers to all twenty-seven pages worth of deficiencies that had arrived with the letter revoking the license. Twice her plans of correction had come back from Cynthia Malmquist, twice she had revised what she had written, and twice Miss Lardass had typed her responses onto the State and Federal forms and made carbon copies to send to William Falisec.

Union reps from the American Federation of State, County, and Municipal Employees exhorted the aides and LPNs to work a little harder to show what good workers they all were, to impress possible new owners, for groups of investors started regularly touring the building during Yeazell's month-long tenure as Acting Administrator. The reps told them not to worry. They would not lose their jobs. Their contract stated that, if Falisec ever sold the facility, a condition of the sale agreement would be that the new owner would honor the union and the old contract. Even so the waiting, the tension in the building, began increasingly to affect Harlan. He started to snap at Blue Hall patients. The least little thing would set him off.

He felt trapped. He wanted desperately to quit his job. But for now it continued to provide for both his and his family's livelihood. It was asinine for him to fantasize about robbing a bank. But doing so got him through his day. He had worked here too long. For three-and-a-half years he had watched people die. He had given over his life to doing this shit and what did he have to show for it—a dime an hour raise.

If he could just get away. If only he had no wife or kids and stood unencumbered, he could just sit down behind the wheel of his car and drive to some new place and start over. He always wanted to see Arizona or California—go someplace faraway out west and experience the vastness of the plains and desert. Grandpap Otto would have called it wanderlust. But he never had the opportunity, the chance. But he could travel great distances sitting in his own living room. Every payday he visited Larry or some other dealer of his acquaintance. One day subbing on Blue Hall, Alfonso Walker caught him as he lost his temper and became rude with Willie, who had just urinated on the floor because no one had answered his buzzer. "Ten minutes ago I took you. Why didn't you go then?" "I didn't have to," Willie cried. "Why you little fuckwad. I ought to—"

"Belt him one Harlan," Joe Crinsky said.

"I should."

Walker walked in to answer the red light outside the room which Harlan hadn't yet switched off. "Do you see what this little bastard did?" Harlan asked.

"So what," Walker replied. "It's no big deal. Chill out brother."

Afterwards in the employees' lounge where they both stood feeding quarters into the vending machines, Alfonso said, "You gotta be more patient with these old folks, Har. Keefer Peoples goes and gets himself fired, so now you have to start acting just like him. That's real dumb, bro."

"I wish I could become more tolerant and accepting," Harlan said. "But they get on my nerves. What can I say?"

"I know the slow ones can make you mad. Like you get when you find yourself driving behind some idiot going twenty miles an hour when the speed limit's fifty-five and there's no room to pass. But if that idiot turns out to be one of them. One of them that is still on the outside and not in here. Why then you don't beep you horn, you just remain content to follow. You had best defer to anyone who's lived on this earth so many more years than you."

"Yeah I guess," Harlan said. *Nigger what the hell do you know?*

"You should have belted him," Joe Crinsky said.

"Sorry," Harlan replied. "Maybe next time."

I bet these nigs don't like having a white Master, he thought. *No sir.*

The return inspection was a fiasco. After the exit interview, Mr. Francescatti asked Dorothy Yeazell to remain in the office so that he might have a word with her. Before the interview, he had gone to lunch with Cynthia Malmquist and the other two survey-ors—ostensibly to speak to them privately. Cynthia Malmquist said that she had seen only marginal improvement and could not recommend that the State lift the admissions ban. "You said we were ready." Francescatti screamed. "Obviously we weren't. Do you know how bad you made me look? What are you? An incompetent boob?"

He fired her. "Well, all right," she said, "let me step down as Administrator but remain DON." No, he said. The State surveyors had tied his hands. Cynthia Malmquist had told him quite bluntly that she deemed her unqualified to work in any capacity in the building.

The true reason Francescatti fired her, of course, was because she stood a trusted and loyal employee of the Falisecs.

One by one, Francescatti let all the department heads go. Kean first, the same day as Yeazell. He did not have a degree in social work. The home needed an MSW—someone qualified. Francescatti himself became Acting Administrator. He found an MSW who came to work for fifteen dollars an hour, whereas Falisec paid Kean a mere six dollars to do the same job. Falisec blew up when Francescatti informed him of his decision over the phone. "You promised to maintain local people's jobs," Falisec complained. "The regs don't mandate a degree in social work, only having an MSW as a consultant. Kean did. Besides he's always done well by us. Moreover I can't afford that kind of salary." "I've done what I think best," Francescatti replied. Falisec seethed but could do nothing, as Francescatti continued to bring in new people to fill all the management positions. Interested buyers toured the facility almost every day. One by one all the non-union employees began receiving pink slips in their paychecks. Francescatti also laid off a few aides—the ones with the least seniority—due to the decreased census. Harlan began show-ing up for work drunk, hung over, or loaded.

Pat complained about him going out what seemed like every night, leaving her with the kids, then always coming home smashed. "Don't nag," Harlan said. "Stop acting like my mother." Then one day, she busted him smoking pot, came home early from

Bingo (he had put the kids to bed a half hour before) and surprised him with a lit joint. Of course, she started right in, screaming at him for what seemed like an hour. He got so mad he had to leave. When he came home he found the bedroom door locked, so he slept on the couch. His downswing continued the next morning. Walking into the Manor, he heard his name called over the p.a. The voice told him to report to the DON's office (Francescatti had promoted the Assistant Director of Nursing to DON). The new directress Miss Mathews charged him with verbally abusing several patients. She also stated that it had been brought to her attention, that he came to work intoxicated. He never found out who reported him, but assumed it had been Walker. That little nigger, he thought. I'll break his goddam neck. He filed a grievance with the union, but the labor board found that justifiable grounds existed for his dismissal. He applied for unemployment compensation, but, as the home had fired him for willful misconduct, he was not entitled to any benefits. Pat blew a gasket when he finally got up the courage to tell her. "What will we do now?" she asked. "We can't make ends meet on my salary alone. How will we take care of the kids? This all happened because you smoke that wacky weed. You go out of your head, get irrational, loud and abusive. My God Harlan I thought you had put that behind you."

Her voice rose higher and higher. He asked her to keep it down so the tenants in the other apartments wouldn't hear. "What do I care," she said, "if they do or don't?" "Screw you, then," he said and stormed out of the apartment and down the stairs and out the door of his father's former office building. He went to a sportsmen's bar a couple of blocks away and drank shots of JD, one right after the other. When he returned home several hours later, he received the blast from the second barrel of the shotgun. His mother lay in wait for him. Pat had telephoned her, and she had come straight over. "How could you, Harlan?" she asked. "My son verbally abuse a patient." People will talk about this. It won't only affect you. And what's this that Pat tells me about you taking drugs?" He glowered at his wife. "Why did you tell her?" he said. Then he faced his mother. "I've used them for years, Mom. You just never noticed, never took time to care." "How can you say that Harlan?" She held, hid, her face behind her hands and sat down, and Pat began abusing him. "How could you spend money which should have gone for the children on wacky weed? Tell me. I want to know how you can justify that." Tears began to well up in Harlan's eyes. "Maybe we should get him into some sort of treatment program," his mother volunteered. "Christ," Harlan shouted, tears running down his cheek. "I smoked a single joint. Don't crucify me." "Ah honey," his mother said. "We want to help you is all." Little Jethro started to cry in the back bedroom, awakened by their loud voices. Pat ran back to him. Meanwhile Harlan's mother had gotten up from off the couch to embrace her son. When she got close, she noticed the alcohol on his breath. "You've been drinking," she said. "So what," Harlan replied. "I've had a rough day. I just got fired. So why don't you just lay off and leave me alone." He jerked away from her, switched on the television and sat down on the couch. His mother just as quickly turned the TV off. "We haven't finished our conversation yet," she said. "Oh no?" Harlan replied. Springing to his feet, he strode out of the living room and into the hallway. There he met Pat on her way back from Jethro's bedroom. "Get out of my way," he said. She wouldn't let him pass. His mother came up from behind. "Harlan," she said. "We both feel very worried and concerned about you. If you've got a problem—"

Harlan cut her off. "All right already," he said, "I'll stop using. Now will the two of you just get off my case?"

"You had better," Pat said. "Because if you don't, it's all over between us."

Each week he went to the Office of Employment Security to see about jobs. But without a reference from his previous employer, they told him, he would find it quite difficult to find work. Finally, after about a month, he got a part-time job pumping gas for which he received minimum wage. He also decided to raise his tenants' rents, but this backfired for two of the tenants decided to move out, and he lost more than he gained. Bills accrued. Soon he had spent most of the money in both his savings and checking accounts. He began to understand now what William Falisec had gone through and to appreciate his dilemma. He didn't want to ask his mother or Pat's parents for money. He remembered the cash left over from the bank robberies that lay buried in Veiled Lady Cave and decided to retrieve it. He had hidden the attaché case behind some breakdown blocks at the far end of the main passage. After Al's death, he read in one of the newspapers that the banks had marked some of the money Al had stolen. He didn't know if they spent those bills in Miami, or if he still had some of them left in what remained of his cut. Back then he didn't care—he would have taken his chances and purchased more blow anyway had not his father died and he inherited all that cash. When his situation changed overnight so completely, he saw no reason for taking unnecessary risks. The statute of limitations would run out in seven years. He vowed not to spend the money till then. He didn't want to keep such incriminating evidence in his apartment. He had to get rid of it. In high school, a lot of his friends used to hang out at the cave, a favorite party spot. It had worked for Robber Lewis. Why not for him?

Now exactly six years later, his situation had modified once again. He needed the money and decided to take his chances. In just a year, he would have stood home free, but he had debts right now. They couldn't wait. As he drove to the cave, he thought about the night he had hidden the bills there and how he had entered the dark tubular conduit alone.

An ex-commercial cavern, Veiled Lady set about ten miles northeast of the town of Centre Hall on PA Route 192 near the old Hoy Schoolhouse and just west of a softball field, the entrance located in a sink at the base of a seventy-five-foot cliff near where a local stream, the Grenoble Run, disappeared underground. Guides had ushered tourists through the caves during the 1930s until a flood washed out most of the commercial improvements, all that remained of the old business venture old handrails and concrete steps inside the caverns. The entrance, Harlan remembered, rose about fifteen feet high. The property owners had boarded it up and nailed No Trespassing signs into the wooden planks. His friends, however, had loosened one of the lower boards, and they had been able to crawl in. Just inside the entrance sat the remains of a white dripstone deposit which quaintly resembled a seated woman who wore a veil over her face and which gave the cave its name. Harlan remembered a place early on, about fifty feet in, where the underground stream had washed out the cement walk and gushed like a waterfall over a ten-foot drop, then disappeared. He would have to take care for he wouldn't want to tumble over that precipice and into that hole. Short side corridors veered to the east and west at the top of the falls, but the main conduit gradually descended for four hundred more feet. Debris had fallen from the ceiling in large quantities. Then the cave became more complex, with the main tube becoming less straight and with one long branching passageway and several shorter ones appearing. Several pits and chimneys suggested higher passages still unexplored. Again there followed a number of deep drops in the cave floor below which one could hear running water. He would have to remain wary. The most varied section of cave stood at the far end. One went up a set of cement steps to two dome pits over seventy-feet high and to several chimneys. The cave ended five hundred fifty feet from the entrance over a pool of water, the so-called Hidden Lake. Here Harlan had concealed the attaché case.

But even this end section could not rival the splendor of the world-famous Indian Caverns in Spruce Creek which stone-age people had occupied as a winter shelter, council chamber, and burial grounds over four hundred years before. David Lewis and his highwaymen had later used these same chambers as their headquarters from 1816 to 1820. The commercial developers of the cave had unearthed skeletal remains as well as five hundred Indian relics including a tablet of picture writing. These remnants and vestiges of the past stood on display in a relic room inside the caverns. In one of the rooms known as the Grotto of the Wah Wah Taysee, the guide would shut off the electric lights and phosphorescent "stars" would appear on the cave's ceiling. The guide said the Indians imagined that deep in the cave they looked up at the night sky and characterized the phenomenon as a natural marvel not known to occur in any other commercial cave in the United States. Well, one had to suspend one's disbelief and remain fanciful. It didn't look much like the night sky to Harlan. In another room, a musical rock bewitched tourists with its bell-like tones which rang and reverberated through countless passageways. An immense sheet of flowstone higher than a two-story building, the Frozen Niagara also fascinated cave visitors. Harlan had taken the tour many times. The guide led you through nearly a mile of electrically illuminated splendor. He first went as a boy of seven with his grandfather Otto. A week after he found work at the gas station, he went back with his daughters Stacey and Carrie. They pitched pennies in the cave's wishing well and marveled at a large stalagmitic formation nicknamed the Devil's Bake Oven in the room known as David Lewis' hideout. Again he stood where the old highwayman had. People had changed very little during all those intervening years. The lure of easy money had tempted Lewis and his cohort Connelly just as it had him and Al. Perhaps circumstances had forced them into a corner too. Perhaps they had no other alternative but to steal? Now he had children to feed and clothe and bills forever coming due. His new job didn't compensate him well enough. He would have to come up with the needed cash somehow. There and then he made up his mind to retrieve the stolen banknotes, even though the statute of limitations had not yet expired. After their tour concluded, Harlan snapped photographs of his daughters standing beside the totem pole and in front of the tee-pee in the picnic area outside the cave.

Although he had taken the tour at Indian Caverns many times, he had not returned to the Veiled Lady since he had buried the money there in 1983. He hoped that he could still find the place where he had hidden the attaché case and that someone else had not come across it in the meantime. He drove through State College to Centre Hall then turned left on a farm lane at the decrepit brown-brick schoolhouse. He parked at the ball field and continued on foot until he reached the cliff–about one thousand feet from the highway and to the left of the private road. He looked down the mountain ridge but did not see the familiar boards and planks. Instead he saw rubble and boulders, the entrance dynamited shut. The owners, frightened because of possible law suits–of the Pennsylvania courts finding them liable for any injuries some foolhardy caver might sustain while trespassing on their property–had solved the problem once and for all by adopting the most drastic of possible measures. Harlan experienced a great sinking feeling. Everything on this earth conspired against him. Choking with impotent rage, angry enough to split someone's skull, he picked up a stick and swung it at a tree trunk. It snapped in two, and he shouted a whole string, a litany, of obscenities. Then he turned around, walked back to his car, and drove homewards.

As his wife worked more than he did–he got no more than fifteen hours a week at the gas station unless someone called in sick–he spent many hours at home watching the kids. He would occasionally leave the twins alone in front of the TV (Jethro slept in his crib) to sneak out on the deck to smoke. He had to remain extra careful, really watch his ps and qs, now that Pat had found him out and had made such a ruckus. He kept his stash in one of the unrented apartments and kept both keys in his possession at all times. He had smoked in front of the girls when they were younger, but now he had to make sure they didn't see. For Mommy had told them to tell her if Daddy ever smoked. Where before, as a teen, he had to hide his habit from his parents, now he had to keep it a secret from his kids.

He again daydreamed about hitting a bank. He remembered how carefully Al had planned the hold-ups he had taken part in. The bank had to sit near a mall or shopping center–somewhere where a lot of cars sat parked and a crowd of people had gathered. He knew such a spot. A Savings and Trust branch office sat catercorner to the Century Mall in Tipton. He would need a gun. He had one. His father's old Ruger. He would park his car nearby, put a ski mask over his face, walk through the double doors up to the counter and demand cash from the tellers. Al said one must work quickly. The faster you got out of there, the better your chances to get away. Maybe he should take down a convenience store–a 7-11 or Mini-mart first? No, the attendants never kept that much cash in the register. Why take such a big risk for small change. Besides a storeowner might just have a gun under his counter. Well, banks had security guards. A rent-a-cop shot Al. But not all banks had them. Maybe city ones did. But rural ones usually didn't. In Marronsburg, they hired one special because the Gentleman Bandit had knocked off a bunch of banks in PA. Moreover, Harlan had not once seen a security guard at the

Mid-State Bank in Tyrone where he kept his checking and saving accounts and where he formerly made three-or-more transactions a week. But as always, thoughts of what the wife and kids might have to face and endure should he be caught held him back. He thought about how hellish Anne Arretto's life must have become after the authorities had identified Al as the Gentleman Bandit. He found himself torn like a character in an animated cartoon. A little devil whispered wicked thoughts into one ear but a tiny angel counterbalanced him at the other, constantly admonished Harlan to resist temptation.

In October the Housers began to receive a miscellany of notices from the different utility companies concerning unpaid bills. Their telephone company disconnected their land line, and the gas, water, and electric companies all threatened to discontinue their services and not just to his unit but to the other apartments in the building as well. For Harlan had always taken care of his tenants' utilities—included them in the rent. In the past, he had always made his payments on time, but now he needed his entire check for his family's living expenses, so he had let the power bills slide for two months. His wife's salary paid for the groceries. But he also had to take Jethro to the pediatrician for booster shots, and then Stacey fell on the steps and needed stitches. His car insurance also came due, and his wife had to have new brakes installed in her Honda Civic. In addition, he had lost his Blue Shield/Blue Cross coverage when Colonial Court terminated him and had to take out private policies for his children and himself; he had bought a half bag of weed in August just before Miss Mathews fired him, and then purchased another one in September, an extra one hundred forty bucks down the drain. He also spent money on booze. But he had nothing to do but baby-sit. He had to have something to help him get through his day. Otherwise his life would remain a total bore. Finally the unpaid bills caught up to him, as he knew they would, and he found himself in a real bind. His tenants would move out then take him to small claims court for restitution if suddenly the utility companies shut off their water, gas, and electric power. Naturally Pat was furious about the phone. Harlan had to take a step he had up to then avoided making: he asked his mother for a loan. He drove over to her new house, the one she and her second husband had bought, a beautiful three story in one of the swankier residential sections across town. She and Dr. Ramon Tagolo, a Filipino orthopedic surgeon, had moved in over three years ago, but Harlan had never put in an appearance at their residence until now. He told her his troubles. Well, he had money in the bank, she said. A lot of money. "No, mom. I don't" He cringed as he spoke. He had wanted to keep this all from her, but he had realized before coming here that he would have to tell her the truth, admit to everything. Everything except the bank robberies, of course. She now learned how bad and out of control his drug problem had once been. He said he started doing coke after his father died because he had grown utterly and totally depressed. He couldn't come to her. He still harbored a lot of resentment because of the divorce. She said she had thought he had gotten in with the wrong crowd, that he had a bad attitude and no ambition, but she never realized that he had sunken so far. You'd written me off, and you know it, Mum, he wanted to say but didn't, realizing that to speak his mind now would go against his best interests. Naturally it mortified her that he had gone through his $100,000 dollar inheritance. He explained that he had a three hundred dollar-a-day habit, that he had become a junkie—an addict. Even now he still dreamed about cocaine and would wake up in a cold sweat afterward. And of course, fool that he was, he had stood very generous with his supposed friends. When the money ran out, he sold his dad's Mercedes. He had loved that car. She had presumed that he had gotten rid of it because his father had committed suicide in it, but he had done so for an altogether different reason. He told her how Pat had saved his life, how she had come through for him in his darkest hour. He deserved his plight. He had this coming to him. But she and the kids didn't. They were *her* grandchildren after all. And he might lose them if she didn't help him now. Of course she wrote out a check. He paid off all the bills and had the landline hooked up again. He deposited the rest of the money in his savings account. His mother had bought him some time.

Every morning, he opened up the paper to the obituary page to see if any of his Blue Hall residents had died. The first death notice he saw was that of Sadie Siegler. Then the grim reaper cut a swath through rooms 210, 212, and 213. Stanton Smeltzer, Mable Hutchins and Theodore Johnson all "ctbed" the same week. Harlan never understood that regulation, why the State prohibited them from saying that a patient died. They could only respond that he ceased to breathe. Nurses could not even write the d-word in a chart. They didn't have the authority to pronounce a person dead. Only a doctor did. Sometimes he learned what caused a patient to "ctb" from some statement in the obituary. For instance, Mable's said that in lieu of flower friends and relatives should make contributions to the American Heart Association. He assumed that Johnson had another stroke. But Smeltzer had always seemed so healthy. He hadn't a clue as to what got him. None of these deaths particularly saddened him. He had known the residents and liked them. Seeing their obituaries satisfied his curiosity, a need to know who among his patients had died, for although he no longer had any connection to the home, he still felt tied to the old people and wanted to see how their stories played out, to keep on top of all that happened to them. But seeing their names in boldface produced no great emotional response. Not so Anna Hudak's name. He cried no out loud, and, as he recalled her excited smiling face as she made her way with her walker into the dining room to celebrate her one hundredth birthday wearing a red corsage pinned to her dress and her hair just permed at the beauty shop, he started to tear up. It felt like losing a grandmother. He remembered the cap and mittens she had knitted him and her fortune telling. How she would give him one word commands and he'd at once drop everything to go do her bidding. All she had to say was "cold" and he'd run for her sweater or "kiss" and he'd bend down and give her a peck on the cheek. He hoped she had a peaceful, painless death. One day Anthony Bolet pulled into the Atlantic station where he worked, and Harlan, after inserting the nozzle into his tank, asked him if he knew of the particulars of Mrs. Hudak's death and Bolet told him that they had found her dead in bed one morning. Apparently she went gently in her sleep. Harlan stood grateful for this information.

One afternoon as he opened up the newspaper to turn to the obituary page, he saw the headline NURSING HOME SOLD in the State and Local section; he scanned the column and found out that a group of investors from Greensburg had bought Colonial Court Manor and renamed the facility Harmony Heights. Well, forced relocations would not occur now after all. He wondered if Falisec had gotten a fair price. He didn't care one way or the other really. A fair market price for Bill remained only a secondary consideration. It stood far more important that the residents would now no longer have to face the prospect of transfer to other homes. Social Services would have had a very difficult time placing the Medical Assistance patients. The county home had filled to capacity, and there stood long waiting lists at the church-run facilities, and they would only accept the MAs that belonged to their particular denominations; none of the privately owned facilities in the Altoona/El Dorado area took more than a few token MAs, usually only patients who remained alert and oriented and who did not yet have severe health problems. They wanted only private-pays. Had the State forced the home to close, Social Services would have ended up transferring most of the residents to other counties, perhaps even out of state. The moves would certainly have traumatized the patients. The residents wouldn't have wanted to leave. Colonial Court had become their home. Some of the guests had lived there for as long as nine or ten years. Many were life-long residents of the Altoona area. Their families or friends visited them on almost a daily basis. Suddenly weeks would go by in between visits. They would all have become quite depressed, and many would have died within a short period of time. At least they had escaped this and now stood out of danger. The sale would spare family members further heartache. The period of uncertainty had finally passed.

Shortly after reading the article, while shopping at Riverside Market (now that Patricia had become the sole breadwinner, he had to take on the role of Mr. Mom), Harlan ran into Edna Gerber, who had long ago come off compensation and returned to work. He queried her about what took place at the home and about the conditions of several patients. No one knew about the sale, she said, until the day it happened. Not even Mr. Francescatti. Of course rumors had gone around for weeks but she had learned to disregard them. If she had a dime for each time someone told her a sale was imminent, she would now be a rich woman. The new owners came in one morning and announced the sale over the p.a. system. They sent three or four of the housekeepers out to take down the old sign and put up the new one and asked Mr. Francescatti to leave the building without saying goodbye to anyone. Maybe now he knows how Dorothy felt when he handed her her walking papers. They also asked Dr. Laird to tender his resignation. One of the new owners, an Indian doctor named Shiva Singh, took over the duties of Medical Director. He and his wife had toured the facility a month before the sale. He had western clothes on, a three-piece suit, but she wore a traditional sari and had a red dot on her forehead. Already the aides found a nickname for him. They called him Ali Bubba. She hadn't formed an opinion about the Greensburg group. Not enough time had gone by yet. She would wait and see how things developed. Immediately after the sale, the State lifted the admission ban. One of the new patients, a Mr. Seilhammer had given them all quite a scare. He had a diagnosis of first-stage Alzheimer's but remained alert and oriented times three, so they put him on Blue Hall instead of the fifth floor. A former Penn State professor, he still took pride in his dress and every morning put on a tie and jacket. Three days after his admission, he walked right out of the building. The family members who saw him go out thought him a visitor because of the way he dressed. No one realized that he had slipped off until two hours later. The police found him six miles down the road. He said he headed home because someone was keeping him prisoner against his will. She asked Harlan if he knew that Mable Hutchins, Stanton Smeltzer, and Anna Hudak had all passed away, then told him that Howard Hempsen had also taken a turn for the worse. His wife Genevieve had died several weeks ago (since the Hempsens came from out of town, an obituary didn't appear in the *Altoona Mirror*), and they began having problems with him. He refused to eat or drink or to take his medication. His sugar level shot up, and just yesterday they sent him to the hospital. It looked like he might need to have one of his legs amputated below the knee now, due to his diabetes.

The next time he met Edna (two week later, again at the grocery store), she sang an altogether different tune, calling the new owners scalawags and carpetbaggers who snatched away local people's jobs, replacing Falisec employees with staff from their nursing home in Greensburg. Miss Mathews, the ADON Francescatti promoted to DON, had gotten the sack first. Worse (Harlan had already heard this from his mother) the new owners began shipping MAs to the hospital and then didn't accept them back. Only the private-pays remained safe after all. The families all thought their ordeal over but apparently their troubles had just begun and that's a rotten shame. "It sure is," Harlan said.

Soon Harlan didn't have time to worry about other people's problems. He faced a momentous crisis of his own—Pat left him, taking the kids with her. One of his wife's girlfriends had become engaged. She, of course, invited Patty to the bridal shower. There the bride-to-be introduced her to some of her other guests including Lucy McCann. Lucy patronized Harlan's main man. Harlan had run into her again and again when buying pot but didn't know that she also knew his wife's girlfriend. The party got pretty wild, and all the ladies drank. Someone lit and passed a joint, and Ms. McCann offered it to Patty. "I don't get high," she said. "You don't?" Lucy gave her a puzzled glance. "But your husband does all the time. Just last week, I—" Pat got up and left, said goodbye to her hostess, and drove straight home. She flew into their apartment like a fury, yelling as loud as she could: "You thought I'd never find out, did you? Well, I've just had a nice long talk with one of your doper friends. I now hear that you've bought reefer every month for the last two years and that you still continue to do so." "Who told you that? Whoever said so's lying." "Come on Harlan. You can't seriously expect me to—" But he didn't let her finish. He shouted just as loudly as she did: "What kind of wife would take someone else's word over her husband's?" "And what kind of husband," she answered, "would lie to his wife and take food from the mouths of his children? Does the name Lucy McCann ring a bell?" "Who?" "A selfish, lying prick. That's what you are. You don't care about the kids or me. Getting high remains the most important thing in your sorry life. Well, you can find someone else to share it with. I'm not raising my children in a home where their father exposes them to drugs and where they'll learn to think abusing them's okay. You promised me you'd quit. But you lied to me, Harlan. So I'm taking the kids and—" "The hell you will." "Do you want me to call the police? Well that's what I'll do if you don't get out of my way." "Patty calm down, listen to me—" "No, Harlan. I'm through listening." She shoved past him and entered the girls' room. He followed her in. Stacey sat in a corner crying. Carrie crawled under her bed and hid. "See what you did," he screamed. "Look how worked up and scared they are?" "Come on girls. Get your coats on," she said, pulling two jackets off hangers and tossing one down to Stacey, who continued sobbing hysterically, then broke out coughing. "You're not leaving. Get that out of your head right now." "Snap to it Stace. Get your coat on, I said." "You just won't listen, will you?" "Carrie get out from under there. Come get your coat."

She wanted a big scene, and Harlan let her play it out. He should have said nothing and walked away. If she had then carried her threat through and had left with the kids, she would have done it only to scare him. She would have returned in a couple of days, and he would have acted suitably repentant. But something inside him snapped, and he feared that maybe she wasn't bluffing, so he shrieked, "You won't steal my children. I'll kill you first, you filthy, fat bitch." He lunged for her and caught hold with both his hands, then began to shake and throttle her. Her head snapped back, and she lost her balance and toppled to the floor, and he came crashing down on top of her. He released his grip around her throat, sat upon her stomach, and started slapping her face with both his hands. Soon he clenched them into fists. "Daddy don't hurt her," Carrie shrieked, jumping up and down. He broke his wife's nose with one punch then cut his knuckles on her teeth. Still he didn't stop. His daughter ran up behind him and started pounding on his back with both her fists. He didn't even notice her. Pat's face became a bloody mess. He took a clump of her hair in either hand and began banging the back of her head onto the floor again and again. He realized that he had gone too far. He let go and rose to his feet. He needed air. His wife and daughters all bawled and sobbed as he left the room. Pat drew her knees up to her abdomen. She lay on the carpet moaning and convulsing. He had to get the hell out. He rushed outside, and walked in a daze. It took him a great deal of time to calm down. When he came back, they had already left. The next day, he tried calling Pat at her parents'. "You beast," Mrs. Fisher said, when she picked up the phone. "Patty ought to throw you in jail. God knows why she won't file charges. You broke her nose. Knocked out two of her teeth." Crying he said he was sorry and that he wanted to work things out. She hung up on him. He dialed the number again. He let it ring and ring, but nobody answered. Give her space, he told himself. She needs it. She'll come round. She just has to have time to sort things out's all. You can't expect her to come embrace you and say all is forgiven just because you say you're sorry. Yes, it'll take time, a lot of time. But then, then …. He knew that he was trying to delude and hoodwink himself, that they would never salvage their marriage now, that he had put paid to it. He stepped into the girls' bedroom, saw the stuffed animals he had bought them for their birthday lying on their beds. His stomach tightened. He felt nauseous and had to leave the room. After pouring himself a drink and gulping it down, he threw himself onto the living room couch and fell asleep. Several days later he called again. He asked to speak to Pat, but she wouldn't come to the phone. Once more, her mother served as go-between. He pleaded for another chance, promised that things would change and that he would never touch her again. He realized now that he did have a drug problem. He'd do everything in his power to quit if Pat would only come back to him. His mother had promised to fast track him into a treatment program. Pat's heard this all before, Mrs. Fisher said. She saw no point in continuing the conversation and asked him to please not call again. Again he heard the phone click. He tried two or three more times the following week, but as soon as he said "It's Harlan" or "Please talk to me," the person on the other end hung up. Finally he made the trip over to the Fishers'. Pat's mother answered the bell, but, after opening the door and seeing that Harlan stood on her front porch, she slammed it shut. He threw open the screen door and began to force his way in. He met resistance. Mrs. Fisher vainly trying to close the wooden barrier on him. But she had neither the energy nor the brawn to keep him out, and she hadn't had time to fasten the bolt behind her after she first shut the door before he started to come in. "Where are my kids?" he asked after thrusting his way through. "Where's Pat? I want to see them." "There're not here, Harlan," she replied. "Then where are they? Please tell me, May." "The children are perfectly safe. I can guarantee you of that." Before she could say anything else, her husband charged into the foyer from out of the nearby rec room. "You cowardly son of a bitch," he shouted. "Get the hell out of my house before I—" "Colin!" Mrs. Fisher raised her voice. "No." She put herself between them. "Please leave, Harlan," she urged him, her arms up in the air. "Right now." Mr. Fisher pushed his wife aside, followed Harlan out into the yard. "Hey tough guy," he said, "come at me, why don't you? So help me God I'll smash your face. Do you understand me? I'll smash in your fucking face." Harlan didn't turn around. He got into his car and pulled out of the driveway.

Several days later, he received a certified letter from a law firm notifying him that his wife had initiated divorce proceedings. It gave a phone number where Harlan's attorney, if he or she so desired, could contact hers. Harlan immediately dialed it. "I'll fight this," he said. "I'll sue for custody." "That Mr. Houser," the man on the other end said, "remains your prerogative. However, do you really think you've got a chance? No judge will award custody to a wife beater and drug addict. We're prepared to play hardball if we have to. It's your choice. If you can see reason, I don't think there'll be any problem about the court granting you some sort of supervised visitation rights. Say one weekend a month." "I'll have to talk this over with my lawyer." "By all means do. Good day." Harlan let the receiver drop. Again he listened—not anymore to the attorney, but to a voice from inside his head, but not his own, someone else's. It remained as unfamiliar to him as the attorney's. Why continue to go on living? it said. You should take Al's option, your father's option, and end it, a sure way of getting back at Pat. Killing yourself would make her feel real guilty, and in time she'd come to believe that she had pulled the trigger herself. What would she say when the kids asked her why Daddy did it? Mommy made him? How would she answer them, eh?

Harlan found merit in the voice's suggestion. Its arguments swayed him. All he had to do was follow through. He went to his and Pat's bedroom. He kept the Ruger and the shells in a locked drawer. He turned the key then took out the gun and loaded it.

Put it in your mouth, the voice said. Suck hard on it.

Harlan parted his lips, inserted the barrel.

Now slowly squeeze the trigger.

No don't listen.

Another, friendlier voice and not quite so unfamiliar.

Harlan took the gun out of his mouth and laid it on top of the dresser. I need to go over to Larry's, he thought.

Who did he see waiting in a Ford Fiesta in Larry's driveway?

None other than Keefer Peoples. He rapped on the window. "I didn't know you knew Larry," Harlan said. "I don't," Keefer replied, "I'm waiting on someone." "Come in with me. I'll vouch for you." "No," Keefer said, "I think I'd better sit here and wait." "Okay have it your way." Harlan skipped up the steps to the door of the trailer and knocked on it. "Who is it?" Larry shouted. "It's me. Harlan." "Hold on." The door opened, and Harlan stepped into the living room. Larry shut the door and shot the bolt back into the fastening bar. A heavy-set black man wearing a camel's hair coat, earrings, and Blublocker sunglasses reclined on the sofa. In front of him on the coffee table sat Larry's triple-beam scales. "Don't worry Sanford," Larry said, "He's cool." Then he asked Harlan what he could do for him. "I want a half bag," Harlan answered. Larry sat back down beside the black guy, reached under the sofa with his hand, first pulling out a tray and then a heavy-duty Ziploc freezer bag stuffed with grass. At least a quarter pound. Several numbers already lay rolled on the tray. He handed one to Sanford and said, "Torch her up." The black reached into his pocket for a butane lighter, put the spliff in his mouth, lit it, took several hits then passed it to Harlan, who in the meantime had taken his wallet out, counted out seventy dollars and laid the money on the table. Larry weighed out two bags, an ounce and a half ounce. Harlan traded the joint for the smaller of the two, and Larry tossed the larger one to the black man. The joint went around several more times before Sanford finally roached it. Then he asked Harlan if he would like to do a line. "I know Larry does."

Might as well. Nothing to hold me back now, he thought. In for a penny. In for a pound. "Why thanks," he said. "Hey," Larry said, "I thought you had sworn off the stuff." "Not any more," Harlan replied as Sanford reached into an inside coat pocket and brought out a vial. Larry again felt under the sofa, this time for an oval mirror which he handed to Sanford who had just unfastened a chain from around his neck on which a gold razor blade dangled. He twisted the lid off the vial then tapped it gently with his finger so the powder spilled out onto the glass. Larry opened a drawer in the coffee table and took out a straw and a pair of scissors. He cut the straw into three pieces, kept one and handed out the other two. Harlan's palms dampened as he watched

Sanford razor the powder into three lines. He watched the two bend over the mirror and each do a line, then, holding one nostril shut with his finger, he snorted his up through the straw. "Wow, what a rush," Larry said. "I told you. I could find pure flake which no one has stomped on," Sanford said and smiled. Harlan asked him if he could score more. Sanford looked at Larry. "You say he's cool, right?" "He wouldn't be sitting here if he wasn't." "Ask Keefer if you don't believe him. I saw him out in the car." "You know Keefer Peoples?" "Yeah we used to work together at Colonial Court Manor." "Well if you know both Larry and Keefer, I guess you must be all right. I can cop an eighth for two hundred to two fifty." "Just an eightball? How bout more?" "Much as you need, son." "How soon?" "Right now if you want."

Harlan didn't have the cash on him. He would need to take money out of the bank. But first he would have to go back home for his checkbook. Could Sanford meet him at the Mid-State parking lot in, say, thirty minutes? Sanford said he would be glad to, then asked if he could bring Keefer along. Harlan said sure, to go ahead. When he got home, he saw that someone had left a message on his telephone answering machine. On the off chance that Pat called, he played it back: "At the sound of the beep.... Hi Harlan, this is Tony Bolet from Harmony Heights. Your great-grandfather has taken a turn for the worse I am afraid. They think he went into congestive heart failure, but they're not sending him to the hospital to get him shipped right back. I thought you would like to know." Probably another false alarm. He should have suffocated him with a pillow when he had the chance.

Harlan withdrew $1000 from his savings account, the balance of what his mother had given him. He waited in the parking lot until the Fiesta pulled up alongside his Mustang, then rolled down his window and said, "I'll follow you." "Not a good idea, man," Sanford said. "The dude doesn't know your car, and he gets real paranoid." Harlan said okay but didn't want to leave his car in the bank parking lot. He didn't want a ticket, he said. So they followed him back to his building. Harlan put up the seat to crawl in the back with Keefer, but Sanford said, "I ain't no chauffeur. Sit up front." So Harlan did. It took them sixteen minutes to make the trip from Tyrone to 'Toona. As they drove through Tipton, Harlan stared at the S&L. Sanford parked on a side street near the Jaffa Mosque and took Harlan's money. "I didn't know you wanted that much. I thought maybe you were after a quarter," he said. "I don't know for sure how much he's holding. Maybe all he's got is a half, and if that is the case I don't think he'll want to get rid of all of it, but'll want to keep some for himself. I'll score what I can for you." Right after Sanford left, Keefer asked Harlan how work went, and Harlan told him that the new DON had fired him and that he now pumped gas for a living. They chatted about residents. Keefer inquired after certain favorites of his and he asked Harlan if he ever became emotional about his former patients or if one of the old folks or some event or happening at the Manor had ever really stirred and touched him, and Harlan without hesitation replied Anna's one hundredth birthday, her grand entrance from the hallway to a standing ovation in the dining room. "They sacked me before that," Keefer said. "A conversation I had with Miss Martha Munch, an exchange of only one or two words, almost made me cry. You never met her. She died the year before you came. She had Alzheimer's, would answer when someone called her Miss Munch but would not respond to Martha. I found out that she had taught grade school; I guess that's why she answered to Miss Munch. She remembered her students addressing her that way. Fausty had her recite the pledge of allegiance. She remembered all of it and several state capitals and some of the multiplication tables. One day she asked me where her room was. I pushed her back to it. 'No, no, no. Don't take me here,' she said. 'My room's the one with the little children in it.' It broke my heart. Mr. Tibbons' courage, the way he fought his cancer, moved me also. And a husband who refused to eat and drink for four days, so he could get himself admitted for dehydration and could stay with his wife while she died of terminal cancer. And remember Mr. Larna? He always came in and fed his mother lunch. End-stage Alzheimer's. Totally gone. But he enjoyed doing for her and saved us aides some work."

Apparently he has as many ghosts as I, Harlan thought.

They waited for close to forty minutes in the parked car. Harlan began to perspire all over just as he had that day at the Coronet Mall waiting for Al. He probably should have given this Sanford only enough money for half a gram. Al had always said you should test a connection one or two times before putting down any serious bread. Score small quantities first. That way you wouldn't get scammed or ripped off. Had his wits deserted him? He had only just met this nig and already he had handed him a thousand bucks. Never see any of that again. Gone just like that. And what would he get for it? Mostly baby laxative no doubt. "Keefer, Sanford's not the kind of guy that'd say someone hit him over the head or anything?" "Hell no. Don't worry. He's probably just jawing and jiving with the guy. He'll be along any moment now." Ten more minutes passed, and another possible reason for the delay occurred to Harlan. What if Sanford walked into a set-up? What if the po-pos had staked out the place and Sanford had got popped? And here they sat waiting in his car.

Spooked, he wanted to flee, to get the hell out of there. But if he left now, he'd never recover any of his cash. He felt a whole lot better when, a couple minutes later, Keefer said, "Here he comes now" and pointed across the street. Well at least, he didn't have to fret any more about getting busted and thrown in jail for sitting in some nig's car and very soon he'd know just how badly this coon gypped him, when he sampled the product. Sanford got in and they sped off. Five lights down he took a plastic bag and two syringes out of his inside coat pocket and handed them to Harlan. "It weighs out. One half ounce of pharmaceutical-quality blow." At his place, Harlan held a spoonful of cocaine over a flame until it bubbled and liquefied. Then he prepared a hypodermic and stuck himself in his stick arm. Sanford shot up also, but Keefer merely snorted four or five lines through a rolled up one-dollar bill. Afterwards he rubbed his nose on his shirtsleeve. Har experienced euphoria, delirium, rapture. He felt juiced up and supercharged. His heart pumped much too fast. He remembered Al saying that Indians in South America chewed coca leaves in order to impart endurance. He remembered his chemistry. A bitter crystalline alkaloid. $C17H21NO4$. Once he had looked at a few crystals under his dad's microscope. They had jagged spur-like edges, sawteeth that'd tear your nose to shreds. The stuff Sanford copped did the trick and if anything the bag weighed, if not right on, over. Sanford must have concluded that Har had bread coming out his ass. Must have decided to build up his confidence and trust, then take him down big time later.

The three of them drank half a bottle of bourbon and two six-packs, and watched low budget porn films Harlan had rented till two a.m., then Keefer and Sanford polished off their last two doubles and left, and Harlan watched either test patterns or the Advertisement/ Headline channel of the local TV cable company. He listened to his heart beat all night; it kept him up although sometimes he shut his eyes and watched orange-red-and-yellow-colored dots, cones and rhomboids gambol, frolic, and cavort behind his lids. Then he opened his eyes wide to see them on the walls. He stared at the TV: a black ribbon on top, a red band twice as big right below it, and on the bottom a much larger blue square that took up most of the screen. Now white letters raced by instead of green but they ran across the screen at as fast a speed as the green ones had done in '83 when he read about the death of Al Arretto. You had to read very quickly if you wanted to catch the last line in the blue-colored rectangle:

FRI NOV 10, 1989   TIME: 4:10:07 AM

HOLIDAY PARTIES, BANQUETS, LUNCHEONS. DINNERS ALL A SPECIAL-TY AT ALASKALAND STEAK HOUSE. CALL DALE AT 0839 FOR ALL EN-GAGEMENTS/BOOKINGS.

—EGON KRENZ, WHO REPLACED HARD-LINER ERICH HONECKER AS LEADER OF EAST GERMANY'S RULING COMMUNIST PARTY OCT. 18 AND INHERITED THE HELM OF A COUNTRY SPINNING OUT OF CONTROL, TODAY OPENED THE BERLIN WALL AND OTHER BARRIERS TO THE WEST IN A DESPERATE EFFORT TO REMAIN IN POWER AND STEM THE EXODUS OF EAST GERMANS FLEEING TO THE WEST. IN RE-CENT MONTHS, EAST GERMAN WORKERS HAVE BEEN INCREASINGLY TAKING TO THE STREETS TO DEMAND DEMOCRATIC REFORMS.

—FORMER NURSING HOME OWNER WILLIAM R. FALISEC HAS BEEN INDITED ON SEVENTEEN COUNTS OF MEDICARE FRAUD IN FEDERAL COURT. A TRIAL DATE HAS BEEN SET FOR NEXT MONTH. THE CHARG-ES WERE BROUGHT BY THE ATTORNEY GENERAL'S OFFICE AND THE GOVERMENT'S CASE WAS PRESENTED BEFORE A GRAND JURY LAST WEEK BY SPECIAL PROSECUTOR ERIC R. HARVESTROM. FALISEC, A FORMER BLAIR COUNTY COMMISSIONER, IS ACCUSED OF MISAPPRO-PRIATION OF GOVT. FUNDS. ALLEGEDLY HE USED <CON'T>

Harlan blinked as the red rectangle disappeared and one-by-one the lines in the blue box ran off the screen and were succeeded by others:

FRI NOV 10, 1989   TIME: 4:10:32 AM

MONIES INTENDED FOR IMPROVEMENTS AND RENOVATIONS AT THE FORMER COLONIAL COURT MANOR NURSING HOME IN EL DO-RADO, TO REFURBISH CERTAIN APARTMENT BUILDINGS AND PRI-VATE RESIDENCES OWNED BY THE FALISEC FAMILY CORPORATION IN THE ALTOONA AREA. STATE INVESTIGATORS ALSO DETECTED A "GHOST" EMPLOYEE. BI-WEEKLY CHECKS WERE MADE OUT TO A CER-TAIN RICHARD ANDREWS OVER A SIX-MONTH PERIOD IN 1987 FOR A GRAND TOTAL OF $22,000.00 DOLLARS BUT NO TIME CARD OR ANY OTHER RECORD OF MR. ANDREWS DOING WORK FOR THE HOME HAS BEEN FOUND AND NO EMPLOYEES REMEMBER HIM. COLONIAL COURT MANOR NURSING HOME WAS RECENTLY SOLD AND IS UN-DER NEW MANAGEMENT. IT IS NOW CALLED HARMONY HEIGHTS. NO CHARGES OF WRONG DOING HAVE BEEN MADE AGAINST THE CURRENT OWNERS. ALL VIOLATIONS HAVING OCCURRED PRIOR TO THE SALE.

  –PLANNING YOUR WEDDING? DON'T MISS THE ANNUAL BRIDAL SHOW NOV. 16, 1PM AT DAYS INN.

Fate keeps wanting to shit all over us, doesn't it Mr. Falisec. The bully will never relent or let up, just wants to hold our face down in it till we get a good long sniff. What can we do about it, Bill? I know my solution. Har bout you? Either take myself out with a lethal injection or rob the S&L at the Century Mall. If only he had a handy woman to slip his part into. His cock stood fully erect, hard for the last several hours. When he at last blanked out (thanks to a few more shots) about 6:00 a.m., he slept for fourteen hours straight. When he woke he eyed bag and syringe significantly. A lot less sloppy than putting a hole in your head. But he wouldn't want to waste, to use up, so much cola for a hot shot when it could yield utter ecstasy and fulfillment in lesser quantities. If he had to off himself he would use a bullet. After he injected and felt invincible. He preferred a bullet to his heart exploding. Unfortunately, he didn't have any H to shoot. Still that remained the easy, the coward's, way. Certainly he did not want to grow old and die from a stroke. Grandfather Otto said that all the Rausches died from effusions of the brain. But cancer had gotten him. Did Pap-pap really lie near death? Maybe the two of them would go out together.

He shoots up everyday for a week, sleeps only six or seven hours a night. First he gets a call from Bolet that his great-grandfather's condition has improved. Then several days later, Tony informs him that he has once again slipped back into a coma. Finally he decides to rob the bank after seeing that he only has enough coke left to last him through one more day. He loads the Ruger, puts on a red toboggan cap and black boots. He hears Al's voice reassuring him just as it had in the past when he needed steeling up—usually just prior to their pulling a job.

This will go just fine, it said. The first thing you'll need is a bike.

No I don't. You never used one until you had me for driver.

But you can get away from the bank faster on bike than foot.

Nonetheless I won't be parked at any great distance. Sure. Real close. I'll get back behind the wheel within five minutes. You could disappear in an eye blink right off the face of the earth. But, ah, you stole a teller's car. I remember reading all about it in the newspaper. But I won't do it right away this afternoon. I'll drive by then come back later. After all Tipton's pretty damn near. In my neck of the woods. Right in the back yard, you might say. It always took me half a day to drive to where you wanted to rendezvous. Today I'm only ten minutes away from my bull's-eye. It's not three hours down the pike like with you.

After giving himself an injection, he rolled a few numbers then got into the Mustang and drove out of Tyrone onto PA 220 and on through Bald Eagle Valley toward Tipton. For the first few miles barns and farmhouses stood on either side of the highway, but billboards and service stations, shopping malls and warehouses soon replaced them. It seemed like he had just left, but he had already reached Tipton. He saw Bland's Park, closed now for the season and remembered how he had taken the twins on their first Ferris wheel ride there last June. They wanted to ride the same miniature roller coaster his parents had taken him on years before, but they didn't stand tall enough. Maybe next summer, he said. That seemed ages ago now. He passed the Century Mall and the S&L and went on toward 'Toona as if driving to work at Colonial Court Manor. He would double back later after he had a chance to walk around some and steady his nerves. To his right, he saw the Adult World bookstore. A tiny hut-shaped building without windows. As usual cars crammed the parking lot. He took the exit off 220 and drove downtown to the business district and parked the car on Eleventh Avenue near the combination parking garage, Greyhound Bus terminal and Amtrak passenger station. It had opened several years ago. Back in '83 when he took train trips with Arretto to Miami, the passengers waited in a doublewide trailer. The warehouses all around stood just as empty looking today as they did back then. He walked down 11th Ave past the post office then stopped at a bar for a drink. After gulping down two shots, he sprinted up 10th Street to the Cathedral of the Blessed Sacrament, then ran down 13th Street until he reached Wopsononock Ave and followed it to the edge of town, about two-and-a-half miles from where he started. He stopped at Grandview Cemetery. It extended up a hill that rose higher into woodland, but no leaves hung from the trees now. His face cut and bit by the lashing, laughing wind, he sat down behind the wall of a mausoleum and lit a joint. Back in '83, he partied here before he embarked on the train to Pittsburgh, after putting his bags in a locker inside the stopgap trailer an hour and twenty minutes before his train arrived. Just like today he had run under the streetlights past endless row houses with porches and shudders, two barking dogs to every block, until he ended up in the boneyard where he could party out of everyone's view. Then after he got good and trashed, he headed back, not sure that he had given himself enough time to get to the depot before the choochoo departed toward the west. But he managed it and when the train arrived in Pittsburgh, he met Al in the terminal and several hours later they boarded the Southland Express.

He held each hit for at least thirty seconds. He looked up at the egg-yoke yellow sun, high and small in the white sky. A sharp-shinned hawk circled over the memorial park seventy feet above the ground, gliding in the wind currents on outspread wings. Pine trees swayed in the wind. The outsize town stretched out below him—he could see it in between two tree trunks. Wobbly on his feet, he nonetheless felt like running. He steadied himself then stubbed the spliff out on the crypt wall. He looked both to his left and to his right for a stone with the name of Hudak, Smeltzer or Hutchins chiseled on it as he jogged through the cemetery. He stopped at a marker with two wrapped gifts resting in front of it. Blue and gold tissue paper with green ribbons and red bows. But Christmas still stood a month away. A child's grave because of the cherub and lamb cut in the granite. OUR DEAR BOY. Ah, his birthday came round this week. He saw November 18 on the stone. Lived only to age seven. "Ctbed" three years ago this May. He dropkicked the boxes like footballs and lifted those knees as high as they could possibly go as he headed down the slope and into town. He saw the cathedral sitting on top of the hill very small in the distance. A far piece yet. But he felt like he could continue running indefinitely, just keep on putting one foot in front of the other forever. But booking up the long street leading back down town, he thought of his own children and how much he loved them and he also recalled the uncommonly strong bond he had shared with his grandparents and the even stronger one that existed between him and his great-grandfather Anton who outlived all four of the Grands and even Harlan's father. He took another stroke and again came close to joining the dead 'cept his heart refused to stop beating.

Har remembered his grandparents' features. Otto and Tillie: thin-faced and gray; Sid and Martha: brunette, plump and tan. His most natural and ready allies against a common enemy: ma or da. Quite effectual ones too, he might add.

No, you have to block those thoughts out. Forget them. Knock over the bank and walk away with all this bread you didn't have before which you can now blow any way you want. Easy come. Easy go. You deserve to have a good—no—tremendous time.

He began to sweat underneath his coat. Men and women moved on the sidewalk. He darted around people all the way up Wopsononock Ave. He ran up the steps to the cathedral—sprinting to the top then back down again. On he went past the old Gables department store (a high rise) and down to the Amtrak passenger station. When he reached the railroad tracks, he finally stopped. All out of breath, he had to bend over, put his arms and head on the roof of his car. Winded for roughly two minutes, he reached into his pocket for the keys and got in, turned on his radio and pulled out into traffic listening to a country music station as he cruised through town out onto the highway and back toward Tipton and The Century Mall.

Once more he thought about Anne Arretto and all she must have endured and withstood. Good. If he got wasted, Fat would suffer too, his stigma forever attaching to her just like Al's did to his Anne. How would she handle the media attention? She would crack for sure. Thinking about her falling apart, he almost wanted to get shot in the head. It would serve her right. But the kids. Remember the kids. Would you want them to grow up knowing that their father was a vicious criminal or worse a bungler who botched his first attempt at armed robbery and got shot down dead? A dumb motherfuck, in other words. And who will Ruby live on in if not in you? But why persist, why fight on. You won't ever get to see your kids, and they'll turn them against you anyway. He didn't particularly feel like fathering a new set. No indeedy. And at the very least you'll walk away with seven to ten G tax-free. Now you can keep yourself medicated for a good long time on that, Har. When disconsolate and morose, past saving, emotionally strung tight right to that snapping point where you're ready to let yourself out of your skin forever, why then, to stave off all that's black and insufferable instead you reach for a drink or snort some coke. Do anything to get off. Because getting off will get you through. That's my motto. When you worked as an aide you saw the nurses give "mood adjusters" to disturbed, agitated, and violent patients to mellow them out, to make everything shine just a little bit brighter for them. And what happens when your candy, your Peruvian nose brandy's all gone? Why, you break everything in your house, kick in every door and upset all the furniture. Then you collect yourself, take a few deep breaths, and prepare to walk into another bank to make yet one more withdrawal.

Cars filled the mall parking lot almost to capacity. He drove around the nondescript giant gray building twice before finally finding a space in front of J.C. Penny's. He patted the gun under his coat with a gloved hand, then got out, and went through the glass portals into the mall. He stared at the seventeen-year old slut puppies in apple-green or cherry-red sweaters, ski jackets and leg warmers, or designer jeans and cowgirl boots. They listened to Walkmans, sat in yielding postures with legs spread. One with her boyfriend. Love locks falling across her tits as she leans over him, lucky guy. A group of three or four sitting together beside the water fountain. Old men with canes talking to their buddies also recline on the wooden benches. Hot pretzel kiosk. Then a jewelry store, Walden Books, GNC, and National Record Mart. Mannequins outfitted in fur coats in the display window of Fenmore's. In the hall, a brand new car and pickup truck. Some sort of promotion. A raffle. A crowd gathered around the two vehicles filling out forms and stuffing them into a box. He passed them, went by three other stores.

He ducked into Aladdin's Castle arcade, put a dollar in the bill changer and received four tokens which he fed into the nearest available pinball machine. It lit up when he pushed the button then made a lot of peeping noises. He tried to shut everything out except ball and flippers. He would try to earn some bonus games by swatting the steel marble into the 1000-point depression? crater? cavity? out of which it would issue back at him at light speed. But as he looked at his face staring up from the glass top of the machine like a smiling ghost, he again saw the tears in Pappy's eyes that night he told the made-up story about Al's last bank robbery. Could he possibly have been getting through to him? Anthony Bolet had warned him that he would soon die. Could he hear?

Something deep inside him understand? A prospect too frightening to contemplate. He remembered how Pap-pap hugged and held him as a boy. How he always said *"Fressen, fressen,"* when Harlan sat down to table and how he laughed as Harlan went at it with great relish and Grandpap Otto later had to explain to him that animals *fressen* but people *essen*. He remembered seeing Otto laid out in the funeral parlor and Pap-pap shaking his head while looking down into the casket. Tears in his eyes. And how he always made such a big deal over him and every little thing he did and accomplished. How he spent a lot of time with him when he visited and spoiled him silly. How he loved children. Any child. He always asked mothers to let him hold their babies and stood attracted to little girls because he had lost one of his own. And if he stayed a week, Anton marched him to the Lutheran church for Sunday school and the 11 o'clock service. And afterwards at the supper table, Granddad Sid Houser, who never failed to come over for dinner, would start in again about Japan. Who says they don't have the bomb? We've let their technology advance too far, allowed them to build nuclear reactors. They say they don't have it, but who'd take a nip's word? I bet they've turned their entire island into one colossal bomb. When Japan explodes, they'll all die instantaneously, but the radiation released will poison all the rest of us, decimate the entire planet.

Yes, all sorts of personal memories sprang to mind in rapid succession, concerning either his grandparents or Pap-pap Anton playing and having fun with him when he was a little boy, maybe a teenager, or else about his own babies and how they liked to romp and caper and carry on in front of him. Carrie saying wellow instead of yellow. Stace pointing to a color and asking its name. Watching Mickey and Donald for hours on the VCR. The TV. The world's best babysitter. Tears started welling up in his eyes.

He left the arcade and went out of J.C. Penny's into the parking lot. He saw the S&L across the street. A glass and concrete box. He pulled the red toboggan down over his face as cars and trucks moving in both directions whizzed by. He tapped the gun underneath his coat and ran across when safe both ways. He had to dash. Cars came out of a Po' Folks Restaurant directly across from him and adjacent to the bank. He cut through its parking lot, watched people eating through the wide rectilinear windows, then turned his head, trudged over the embankment and onto the grass of the bank lawn. A row of cars lined up behind the Mac machine and the luxury of twenty-four hour banking. All out of breath, huffing and puffing, looking at at least twenty parked cars in the lot and people coming out the glass doors in groups of two and three, he got cold feet. Someone would see and recognize him crossing over to Century Mall or know his car. Now quit this silliness, turn around and get the hell out of here. You fucking coward. Now don't start. You went on by a couple of times as I recall. Just had a bad feeling. Well, I had one just now. You just need to get higher. You shouldn't have run around and tired yourself out but come straight here still sky high and ready to rock and roll. What will you do tomorrow when it's all gone? Then just go in and get it over so you can give that nigger a bunch of bills. He can find it. So hup to.

No he wouldn't do it. He had to drive this adversary out! People kept exiting the bank. They walked towards him to their cars, looked him over he felt sure, and he heard cars rushing by on the highway right behind him. He stood drenched in his own sweat.

So I'm an adversary now. No, you're nothing but a pussy, a dickless little girl. Hi honey.

I've got a monster.

Kaleena Kaleena Kaleena.

She turned you down.

They all turn you down, but at least I can always sleep with somebody. You're not half the man I am. Just stand there with a flashlight on your little dick for everyone to see. Call attention to yourself. That's it, run away now you pantywaist. Wimp out you paltry poltroon.

Harlan is a chicken harlan is a chicken harlan is a mama's boy.

Blot him out. Think of your children's faces. They will drive him away. Feel us inside you. Your Daddy bluefaced no longer, Sid and OT. Tillie. We love you Harlan. We love you. Go home. And do what? Shoot up? Yes Harlan it's me again. Then come back here prepared. Anesthetized, suitably shitfaced and just do it. Let yourself go. No. Instead experience the continuity of our love to you and through you to your children an umbilical cord that unites you to Otto and Sid, Martha and Tillie and above all to me. Harlan you serve as a conduit for that love. Let it flow on through you and reach its destination your children Stacey and Carrie and the boy Jethro. Don't do this.

He felt Pappy Rausch inside him, a sudden warmth. Al Arretto's hold on him was finally broken.

He does not know how to solve his problems, but somehow he'd get past all the obstacles, and he'd even win back his wife. How would he get through tomorrow and the day after that? For a start he'd call his mother and ask her for help. But he would live. Now he felt bone-tired, ready to fall in bed. He welcomed sleep. A little eternity of non-existence, a foretaste of death.

He staggered back to the car and drove back to Tyrone.

A light snow fell.

That day his great-grandfather died at Harmony Heights. Anthony Bolet had left him a message on his telephone answering machine as he was out.

THIRD

"When I'm not on the spot, it's like I'm lying face down on a sheet of glass that stretches out forever, and I can look down through it. Beyond that in the farthest ground, it seems like stars of outer space, but then there's a circle, a beam of light. It's almost as if it's coming out of my eyes because it is always in front of me. Around it, some of my people are lying in coffins. The lids aren't on them because they are not dead yet. They're asleep, waiting for something. There are some empty coffins because not everyone has come there. David and the other young ones want a chance at life. The older ones have given up hope."

"What is this place?" I asked him.

"David named it," he said, "because he made it. David calls it the dying place."

William Milligan, as quoted by Daniel Keyes in The Minds of Billy Milligan

For the transformation which had taken place was the transformation of outside to inside, the merging of the outer with the inner face, always striven for, never attained .... Oh dusk, oh interrealm, streaming and subsiding in the past, the inflow and outflow of soul! .... Not a star vanished, in spite of the increasing brightness of the advancing day by which their brightness was overtaken, they remained in their full number, starry-crystal in their dome, an enduring starry-countenance of an unspeakably clear expression, and flying on through the crystalline arch, flying to the sun, the seraphic apparition had finally freed itself, had finally separated from the dissolving, floating form that had been a boat; and, wrapped in the gleaming mantle of its own radiance, becoming more and more luminous in a final transformation, in a final gladdening, becoming more and more compelling, more and more lovable, the same face though with a new name, the nameless, transported boyish face became that of Plotia Hieria, the boy inseparable from her, she inseparable from the boy, identical in the blurred and fading gesture she had taken over from him, pointing, the ring on her finger, to the east.

Hermann Broch, The Death of Virgil

For the sleigh ride to correspond to what happened since, Lucetta Krolich should have fallen off just as they started down the slope, Albert Stipetig shortly thereafter and he—Anton Karl Rausch—no that name did not hold any significance for him—mean him—any longer. He had renounced it and had rechristened himself Cominious Aemilius Lepidus—impotent old man—he continued to hold on for dear life hurtling through space—swoosh—through time—not pausing to probe the mysteries of their interrelation, his bobsled exchanged for a Luminex recliner pushed by a nurse's aide or occasionally an LPN. Head cernuous. Nose running. Eyes shut or when not shut glued to wrist restraints with brass fasteners, blanketed knees, suprapubic and Foley catheters, slippered feet, the meal on the tray, the syringe full of pureed slop on its way to his mouth, the parquet floor—never the ceiling, the chandeliers, a shooting star. *Respice finem*. A breathing stiff limber only from the waist up.

But what matter the body? Only matter. No all there is the only thing that matters. Even so let it undergo disintegration. Like the ghetto let it catch flame and…. And the flame reduce it to ash for the river Ganges! Let it burn away like that of Mohandas K. Gandhi. Yes, dissolve into simpler compounds and constituent elements. Rot in the ground or smolder on the funeral pyre. For alack, the process had already begun. Indeed it is already well under way. So why halt from happening today what will occur tomorrow? Shuffle off this mortal coil and be done. Ah, but still to wait. After so so long still to wait the real rub the wrong way. Go in one's youth instead. But hold! Imagine it and it will start happening.

Brucknerian polytonalities canorously ring, resound in my ears as I enter the tunnel of universal love. I have waited long enough. I don't need to see through as many years as a Roman division had men only to grow sleepy every afternoon, to nod off then have someone roughly awaken me to take pills or eat or set me onto the commode or finally place me in bed to yes sleep. Yet each morning wind whistling through the pipes wakes me. Winter will soon turn to spring, a needle going round and round the same groove, and I keep having to say *adsum*, not *ad patres*. Yes, still holding on but quickly approaching whatever follows. Finally coming up on that big question mark. The secret divulged to Lucetta and Albert decades ago.

He lay in his hospital bed, the man on his left side's chief trouble senility, his name Frein; in the bed to his right a stroke victim like himself but worse, bed bound, named something Healy. He heard the night nurse (he did not yet know her name) say she had suctioned maggots out of his lungs. He learned the employees' faces first. Sometimes weeks or months went by before he got the name to be put with a face. Before someone finally called out to the person where he could overhear.

He waited for the daily routine to commence with the entrance of the morning aide. Either Shirley or Walker. On rare occasions his great-grandson substituting on the morning shift. But for weeks—or was it months?—now he had not seen him—not even at night when he usually always appeared to torture him with tales of his bank robberies and murders. Shirley would always smile when she greeted him: "And how are we today Mr. Rausch? Feeling okay? Let's get into our clothes and then I'll get you up and into the chair, and we will see about some breakfast." Awake by then, Mr. Frein would begin to shout: "I don't want to be here. Can't you hear? I wanna get out of here." Die then, Cominious thought. Within minutes, aides would whisk both of them from the room and into the elevator (all aboard, Shirley'd say when the bell went ting and the doors parted like the Red Sea) along with others not long for this world, to descend from the home of the gods, from the stratospheric heights of the residential quarters, to the Niffleheim depths hammering dwarfs smithying away of recreation, therapy, and dining rooms. Lying in bed Cominious Rausch began conjugating verbs—first in Latin (he taught that language, his bread and butter, for over thirty years in the public schools; began every class with each student standing and saying *adsum*—I am present—as he took roll) then in German (the tongue of his forebears) and finally if the aides came late and Mr. Frein had not yet started to scream he would surprise himself by recalling in their strict order the inflected forms of Russian and French verbs. Forms that had gotten rusty since he last pressed them into service. Even if he had only done so several hours beforehand. Since he couldn't move or speak, he preserved his sanity and made the time pass by conjugating verbs. Spent hours at it. Those fools thought nothing went on inside his head.

Ich bin. Du bist. Elle est. Il est. But you can't say I am in Russian I bet.

Or I am not.

Kapitulieren? Nein.

Mr. Rausch infinitely preferred middle-aged, stupid, but Aryan Shirley to the little nigger Walker, who would pull the geri-chair instead of pushing it so that old Aemilius Lepidus, drawing close to journey's end—the wait would soon be over—would only glimpse what receded behind him (the place Walker took him from) but never catch sight of what lay ahead, the destination where Walker carted him.

At least when Shirley "drove," he could see where he went.

Deposited in the dining room with the other second feeders who like himself sported catheters and whom the aides syringe fed, Cominious could overhear a "healthy" septuagenarian as she got up from the table (for Cominious healthy meant able to feed oneself, get up from table, speak) tell her messmate what, if she had it to do over again, she would do differently. Something trivial of course. Utterly inconsequential. The messmate's reply stood equally banal. She wouldn't change the least little thing. He knew immediately what he would alter. With complete determination of the will he would obliterate his past mistakes.

If only he had withstood the urge to return home, if they had stayed in Akron, if she that one day had not gone to school, if it had not rained during recess so that the teacher to make up for it had not let them go home early .... Anything so that the death of his daughter, struck down by a truck whose half-wit driver should never have sat behind any wheel, would never have occurred. As a little girl Hedi would come into their bedroom, crawl in bed and sleep between them like a cat or puppy. Four decades after the death of their daughter, he buried Helen to one side of her. Someday Hedi would once again sleep between them. But first he had to see his son Otto lowered into an adjacent plot alongside his wife Tillie. For years now they had lain waiting—for him.

If. Only if. Mr. Rausch refused to speculate further. It remained fruitless, futile. Every event in his life—being introduced to Helen at the church social, the move to Akron, the decision to return, Hedi's death—stood part and parcel of every other event—his life a thing multi-faceted yet somehow undivided, somehow whole. As if it had all happened simultaneously. But always the forward momentum, that sense of propulsion, of linear progression, from the moment of the little big bang—the eruption of a partial self into the mother there to achieve completion, to become whole—to that final apotheosis he rapidly approached, that he came closer to with each passing second. If he could only hasten it. If he concentrated hard enough on his objective ... but no he could not make it happen. He hated the whole human race. If wishing for it would bring it about, he would start the bombs falling right away. Exterminate everything and everyone.

Could he bring calamity on by profane oath or curse? He remembered Uncle Etters saying that the weed did not constitute a serious intrusion, but every year became an annoyance nonetheless.

Devil's flax grew to the height of about two feet and bore a yellow flower. The widows Lewis and Connelly squatted upon Houser's land and tenaciously held to what they claimed as their improvement rights. No Grette never should have married anyone with that surname. Look what sprang from the union? Look at that valueless troublesome plant of a great-grandson. Look at him! Growing wild and crowding out the desired crop of little Mozarts. The master race that he and Helen should have produced. Why did that seed reach the egg? And his children would become less Rausch-like yet. The two women held tenaciously to their claimed improvement rights, so Houser had to make formal ejectments and call the sheriff's men into service. In retaliation, the widow Connelly placed a *hechs* on the land, swore to put a weed on Houser's fields that he could not easily get rid of and Mary Connelly's flax did appear and it throve.

If he had such powers, oh what thorns, what thistles, would push up through the cracks of Colonial Court Manor. His community's Dachau. Briar bushes and prickly pears would rise everywhere, their tips and points stretching out as if to touch the sun. Too small to effect much harm. Like Devil's flax suitable only for laying to waste cropland. It would take forever to achieve *his* objective. Again he'd have to wait. Again the rub. Well then, a giant bean stalk, shooting forth as many stems and branches as the hydra grew heads, would with sudden violence break through the floor and soar skywards. A battering ram crashing through all impediments of steel, glass and brick. Higher and higher it'd climb, up through all six floors of the old Filmore Hotel. In his bachelor days he had eaten in this very same dining room when, at the end of one semester, his train arriving in Altoona late in the evening, he needed some place to stay before proceeding on to Houserville the next day. Much more appetizing fare.

Yes, through each hall and every room, its many limbs and boughs would spread, applying enough pressure on the walls of the building for them to first shift and crack, then finally explode, bricks flying in all directions! In the lobby at that moment, the glass chandelier would drop in slow motion through a fissure in the floor; invalid chairs and their occupants would, drawn down, also tumble in. But a phoenix would ascend from out of the rubble. His soul would break loose!

If he could wield such force!

If through mental exertion, he could bend people to his will, his great-grandson would rise like a sleepwalker and put bullets in both their brains!

What a time to live in, when Prussia and Saxony—yes even the beautiful Thuringian forest—had become part of a Russian fiefdom and Silesia lay behind Polish borders. Fate never fails to punish us for the sins of our forefathers. Since the German people stood willing to use other means to carry out their political objectives and of course because Schicklgruber gassed the Jews, angry that England and America refused to make peace with him so that he could conquer Russia. If a great race had to die then surely the Jews' lives also stood forfeit.

He could only look down, never lift up his head. Snot ran out of his nose in two long strands. First one then the other fell to the floor as the Bible verse kept repeating itself in his brain again and again like a broken record:

The Lord Jehovah visits the iniquity of the fathers upon the children and upon the children's children, unto the third and to the fourth generation.

He deserved punishment and reproof for his blindness and chauvinism. In the thirties, an old man even then, he became active in the German-American Volksbund and attended the meeting of U.S. Bund members in New York's Madison Square Gardens. He wore a dark suit, but the man sitting beside him came decked out in a storm-trooper's uniform, complete even to the swastikas. And children dressed in Hitler-youth regalia. Nazi and American flags flew side by side. A huge mural of George Washington hung at one end of the stage. One of Hitler at the other. Brass bands played, and everyone drank beer. He had joined the organization because he felt German-Americans had a duty to stand up for their former fatherland. The French, the English always had lobbied for their nations? So why not the Germans? And people had so many preconceived and unreasonable opinions about Germany. Hadn't the barber refused to cut his hair during the first war because he came from German descent? Hadn't they taken away his German class in the school? At least William Jennings Bryan stood up to that Anglophile Wilson. Being Irish, he had no great love for the Britishers. And many German men had taken Irish wives in the U.S. But that remained the Great War, the war to end all wars. Germany hadn't yet sold her soul to the devil. What a dupe to have viewed Hitler as Germany's saviour. Her greatest statesman since Bismarck. He cheered the incorporation of Austria into the German Reich, the defeats of Czechoslovakia, Poland, and France. It stood quite ironic, regardless, that he had adopted such a pro-German stance since his grandfather Casimir, a decorated lieutenant in the Prussian Army who had served under von Moltke, had deserted in 1871 right after the defeat of the hereditary enemy. The Prussians had captured Napoleon III and had forced Paris to capitulate. By treaty of peace, France agreed to cede virtually all of Alsace and part of Lorraine and to pay an indemnity of $100,000,000, German troops remaining in certain French departments pending payment! Casimir fled to England with his son just as Bismarck established the

German empire under Prussian leadership, and there he met his twin brother Eberhard, recently returned from India and grieving over the loss of his wife, and persuaded him to go with him to America where they both could start a new life. Anton's father Reinhold had always said that Casimir had become disillusioned with Germany, thought her on the path of destruction, even then at the height of her power. She will not remain content now, he had said, until she conquers every nation in Europe, dominates the entire continent, or her foes defeat her in the attempt which would mean her utter ruin. Just a few years before, the Americans had fought among themselves. Not for territorial gain but to end oppression, to abolish slavery. They sacrificed their young men in such numbers for something just. The future belonged to them. Casimir no longer desired to serve a king. He wanted to live in a country where all men stood equal. What foresight. What vision. Casimir had known when to change horses, but Anton, his grandson—he had other ideas. Manifest destiny and *Lebensraum* seemed to him the same thing. Look how the Anglo-Americans exterminated the Indians in America's westward push. Besides Stalin stood the scum of the earth. If the Germans rid the world of Bolshevism, the planet would owe them a great debt. He had argued cleverly, but then the Japanese bombed Pearl Harbor, and Hitler declared war on America. He took solace (but not too much) in the fact that sixty percent of the men in the American Army descended from German ancestors, that it took German Americans—Trumans and Eisenhowers—to bring down the Third Reich. No one else could do it. Then he saw the pictures from the camps.

Now he paid for his blindness, his guilt. He sat a prisoner. Like Rudolf Hess in Spandau. Or had Hess died? He seemed to remember having heard someone say so. Or did he only imagine it? At any rate, like the East Berliners, he lived behind a wall. If only he could burst forth from his confinement, go back to any other period of his life. Sometimes he strained enough that he almost broke through. For a time he did. He found himself with Helen on their wedding night. Or again his Great-uncle Etters and Granddaddy Cronemiller took him to Altoona as a boy to see a train turn round the horseshoe curve. But after a few minutes he would return to the glum generic room. The two old friends flesh and spirit simply wouldn't part. But he would try again and put more effort into it this time. Something began to give inside him. He felt Lucy's arms around his waist. Again he sat on the sleigh. No, only in the invalid chair. An aide pushed him yet again.

Both Lucetta and her mother perished five months after the bobsled crashed into the stone fence and he dislocated his shoulder, broke his collar bone, and went into shock, when they took a drive in the wagon, not realizing that the joists underneath the covered bridge's floor had begun to dry rot and could not bear the carriage's weight. The floor collapsed under them, and they fell through onto the rocks below, the carriage and horses on top of them. Stipetig died in France in 1918 brought down by machine gun fire as he headed across no man's land toward the enemy wire. But miraculously neither Lucetta nor Albert broke any bones when the bobsled gaining speed went out from under his control, like an unruly horse from under its rider. He saw the fence coming closer and leaned to his left, but the sleigh didn't swerve to the side, it continued straight ahead and he flew headfirst into the stone wall. The blow knocked him unconscious. Lucetta's father Reverend Mathias ran down the slope after them and, seeing that the other two remained unhurt, went on for help. They lifted him into the wagon and drove through town back to the Lutheran parsonage. Someone ran for the doctor. He wouldn't regain consciousness until nine hours had passed. His mother thought that they would lose him; his breathing became very irregular.

Don't you realize I can hear you?

Apparently not. He slipped out of himself, looked down at his carcass from the ceiling, saw his mother dressed in her best blouse and crinoline kneeling at the foot of the four-poster weeping as the physician put on his greatcoat and top hat, then stepped into the adjoining room and lit his cigar. Keep the boy warm, he told Krolich. It could go one way as well as the other. We'll hold a vigil then, Reverend Mathias said, raising his right hand on high. Ask for God's intervention.

The hum caused by the wheels coming closer and closer when he put his ear down on the rail and listened for the 11 o'clock train (it had just turned 10:45; he and Uncle Etters had hiked through the woods to the Beech Creek tracks; before leaving he would put a penny where he laid his ear) that hum, that vibration, could not compare to the cacophony that he now heard. And he saw thousands of people. Saw them going into the tunnel, each trying to outswim all the others and reach the egg first. One after another they went in and disappeared. He entered of his own free will. Moving at a great speed, he lost consciousness then regained it. He saw a bluish-white light triangular in shape and almost painfully bright. The vibrations in his head increased in their intensity. The *alte Herr* Grandfather Casimir stood waiting for him. They had buried him the previous summer. Now he pointed to the light, and then beckoned to him from inside it. He had white muttonchops and wore the beribboned, bemedaled uniform of his youth, the spiked helmet that Anton had put on, and had paraded throughout the house in, when but a few years younger (even though it didn't fit and remained far to big), now in its proper place atop the old man's head. It is your decision my son, he said. Papa Casimir will take you across. Or you can go back to them. Anton said no. It wasn't time. The figure wavered, vanished, and he heard indistinct female voices mumbling. No, it wasn't time! He opened his eyes and saw his mother and the ladies of the church kneeling at his bedside, their hands locked together and their heads bent. She still wore her Sunday best.

Now, all these years later, he still lived yet but led an entirely passive existence. Like all the other husks in their invalid chairs, he was pushed by attendants. From his room to other parts of the building. There and back and back again. A pointless Sisyphean circuit as repetitious as Mr. Frein's rambling speech. When the occupant of some other chair came toward him, the aide standing behind propelling it, it looked as if the aide rode a bicycle and the patient sat in front in some outsize basket. Yes, he raced with these other *basket cases* to achieve death, then transfiguration, new life. Or did he face only prolonged and painful death? He wanted to die first, next, saw it as his destiny. He had outdistanced the myriad others before for the honor of taking birth as Anton

Rausch. He could do so again. Leave them behind. Motion would immobilize and he would cross over to the other side to a new life beyond. Centuries would pass. They'd still remain here, frozen in their wheelchairs waiting. Caught at the moment space and time began to disintegrate. When all time strands, all time threads, cancelled each other out as they converged together in the Infinite where all lines met, intersected…. But he would stand free! Now he could barely see. Everything broke down to spots of color and streaks of white light. Movement and motion became line as present, past, and future began to fuse and coalesce, and Anton could no longer distinguish the near from the very far. Everything blurred. He could not speak. He needed someone to feed and dress and bathe him. He remained paralyzed on his left side. Yet he could hear (still hear!) and, yes, think. No one paid him the least kindness, the least courtesy, because they thought that only his body lived, that his brain had already died. His great-grandson talked about the bank robberies because he didn't think he comprehended anything he said. But fate had not reduced him to a mere husk living on after the person-soul-consciousness had gone. How he wished he did not have to listen, to hear him! If only he could stop his ears! His great-grandson, a rogue, a bandit, murderer. Worse than Robber Lewis. This the same little boy he had taken to the park to play on the slides and swings, who on his hands and knees crawled through the entire length of pipe?

Way at the other end, Anton stuck his head in and said boo.

He had crossed the line in the sand, the line of unbearability. But wishing his death no matter how persistently did not of itself bring forth the desired result.

For a long time every afternoon at one o'clock, a middle-aged woman with curly red-orange hair played classical music at his bedside on a cassette-tape player. A "greatest hits" recording containing only excerpts. And just music by French and Russian composers. Nothing by Wagner, Mahler, Bruckner, or Richard Strauss. Grette must have told someone at this place about his abiding love for classical music. Then the red-haired woman stopped coming. A tall blonde replaced her. One day he overheard her tell a nurse that he did not respond to sensory stim, and she never appeared again.

At two-thirty, they took him down to the lobby and wheeled him into the TV room (which had carpeting, chandeliers, drapes and leather chairs) for exercises. Occasionally they would bring him down early while a religious service went on in the room. They would leave him "parked" in the hallway with other low-functioning patients who all wore drooling bibs and mumbled nonsensical words. They had more people to fetch for the class. In one of the offices, he saw a woman writing at length in a patient's chart. They remained as officious record keepers as the Nazis. Several oriented residents walked by talking about their dead, people whom they had known but who had passed. One woman tapped him on the shoulder and asked if he could spare a cigarette. "Hazel stop that," the receptionist called out from her window. A portrait once hung on that wall. But now a landscape replaced it. "He hasn't got any. He doesn't smoke." "Yeah he does. Come on. Give me one." The receptionist got up from behind her desk, took her by the arm and led her away. Several weeks ago, he saw this same woman shaking her head and laughing like a hyena as she talked to herself about her old occupation. How she and the other girls liked it at the house where the men came every night of the week and paid them exceptionally well except for the cops whom they had to treat, one damn patrolman even bringing his damn dog with him. The service concluded. The door to the TV room opened and people came out. Someone pushed him in. The activities person told them to touch their faces then to pat their hair and clap their hands. Some did. He could not raise his arms up from off his tray, but if he had been able to, he wouldn't have done anything so demeaning anyway. Next she tossed a Nerf ball to the patients who could catch it and throw it back to her. She rolled it towards him on top of the tray. He would not use his good hand to push it back. Then she started to pull his left arm, attempted to straighten it out. This hurt so much he tried to yell but could not even manage a grunt. After she finished with him, she turned on the television. He and the others would sit here watching soap operas for two or three hours before they came to get them for supper. The television stood enough of a technical marvel that just staring at one playing was supposed to be stimulating. But invariably if something he found even just a little bit interesting happened to be on, an aide would remove him for any of a number of pointless reasons. Once he watched an interesting news story about birds evolving from dinosaurs. Five minutes into the program, an aide came and collected him. The doctor made his rounds and it was his turn to be oh-so-cursorily examined. On another occasion, he watched a program about persons who had multiple personalities. He learned most multiples were women who had been terribly abused as children. But males also could split into separate selves. Some of the people within remained little children, others grown adults. Some male, others female. They each had a different IQ. Either a genius or a retarded self could emerge and hold the consciousness, and each personality had a unique ability. Performed a special function for all the others who would allow him to manifest himself in the world whenever "the family" needed his particular skill. Often the inside people came in conflict with each other and fought among themselves for dominion of the family. He had difficulty hearing what the commentator said because the patients beside him howled and clapped. One lady sang. Another stripped off her clothes. He did make out the announcer saying that one multiple William Milligan of Ohio had one personality who spoke fluent Serbo-Croatian and another that could read, write, and speak Arabic.

That he found highly suspect. I don't believe it, thought Anton Cominious Rausch. If he could have mustered the power to do so, he would have shaken his head. But then he remembered Mathias Krolich telling his father that after the death of their son his wife had said to him that spirits from hell had invaded her body and tormented her but good people also came to help her battle the bad. He watched with renewed interest. *Stranger things in heaven and hell.* But then Harlan came and wheeled him to the dining room.

He began to doze in his chair more often and for longer intervals. Throughout the day, he would nod off and drowse at least seven or eight times. Often during an activity, his eyes would close, and, suddenly made heavy with sleepiness, his head would droop to one side—even when he would have preferred to remain awake, as when the church organist, each Sunday, performed Bach gavottes in the Activities lounge. Music for lively

Alpine dances in moderately quick duple measure, having two parts, the first of four measures, the second of eight ....

Soon they started putting him to bed everyday for a few hours in the afternoon. He would curl up in the fetal position and escape into his past. Loved ones would visit him in his dreams, call out for him to join them, their voices scarcely audible at first, as if they came from a great distance, but then suddenly clear, strong and direct. He saw his mother and father, wife Helen, daughter Hedi and son Otto. His grandfather Casimir and Casimir's twin brother Eberhard approached together. Behind them Eberhard's granddaughter, Anton's cousin Lucetta, very scared. Panic-stricken. His dreams seemed so real that he didn't realize that he dreamed. He forgot all that happened in the intervening years and he enjoyed the moment, again a boy of twelve or a young man in his early twenties. *Carpe diem, quam minimum credula postero.* But then he would wake up, find himself imprisoned in an old man's body lying in a hospital bed. Only once while dreaming did he realize his vision a chimera. An illusion. In that nightmare David Lewis and John Connelly pursued him on horseback deep in some forest. But Lewis had the face of his great-grandson Harlan and Connelly that of his boyhood friend Albert Stipetig, who had fallen in France. Now on his deathbed his days and nights filled with mirages from the past. As a babe in the womb did he picture illusions and apparitions from his future?

When up in his chair, he lost time (one moment he sat in the dining room and it was day, the next he found himself back on the sixth floor and it was night), and underwent periods of absence and blackness that conveyed him not back to some past moment in his own life where he would have desired measurable duration, the pocket watch's interminable ticking, to cease and some pleasure to abide perpetually, forever and a day, but to an eerie condition of paralyzed submersion in nothingness and no-time. Peering inward into the darkness he saw a bright, blinding wheel of white light. They stood, no, danced around it holding each other's hands. First moving clockwise but then abruptly stopping and shifting counter clockwise. An elaborate cotillion, executed under the leadership of his little cousin-german, and marked by the giving of favors and frequent changing of partners. He looked at their glassy faces one at a time as they frolicked and cavorted. Spectral, crystalline, glowing countenances permeable to the swimming light. He heard a buzzing in his ears like an angry swarm of bees but also a yodeler's warble reverberating off canyon walls. Chest voice to head voice (falsetto) and the reverse. They descanted and trolled to each other, their song garbled and indistinct, yet he knew that he himself remained the subject of their weird music. Then suddenly he heard only one voice. A soprano's. She sang *Das himmlische Leben* (Life in Heaven), a song from *Des Knaben Wunderhorn* which Gustav Mahler incorporated in his fourth symphony:

> No music is anywhere on earth
> that can be compared with ours.
> Eleven thousand virgins
> are bold enough to dance!
> Even St. Ursula laughs!

Cecilia and her relations
are excellent court-musicians.
The angelic voices
delight the sense,
so that for joy all things awake.

The light hurt his eyes. He turned his head away; everything darkened into shadow and eclipse. Mahler had given titles to the first two movements. *Die Welt als ewiger Jetztzeit* (the world as eternal present) for the first. The second, *Freund Frein spielt auf.* No, Frein was his roommate. *Freund Hein.* A folk name for death. Friend Hein begins to play. The symphony depicted the ascent of the soul to the Elysian Fields. A friendly figure, Death guides us from the present to the hereafter with music. We reach a final resting place where our every wish is fulfilled. *Yes.* Anton felt his cousin slip her hands into his. She led him into the light, into the circle's center. He felt an odd warmth surge through him, rise up from his feet through both legs then center in his vitals. He opened his eyes, saw a sweet face–his mother's, no it was his own countenance–reflected back in a mirror. He had breasts and wore a white blouse and a red crinoline. Yes a hoop skirt. Like Tiresias he had become a woman. Indeed he had recoiled backward to the mother, to the one affiliation that remained comprehensible, unclouded, and certain amid the baffling and unremitting mutability of life. But it was not his mother's face (or his own, transmogrified) which looked back at him. He had once known these features. But now could not place them. He saw a baby's cradle reflected in the glass in the room behind him. It rocked gently back and forth on two curving pieces of wood like the runners on which a sleigh slides. Suddenly overcome by a great fear, he shut his eyes tightly and again lost consciousness, then after a long pause, he perceived the negligible wobbling motion of the chair as an aide wheeled him yet again down the dark corridor. As they turned the corner, his eyes opened. The dark shadow of the aide's head and shoulders fell upon his lap and his blanket-covered knees. Then it extended forward onto the parquet floor ahead of them. His eyes glazed and drifted sidewards as the aide simply gave the chair a push and it rolled into his room with its acrid smells of human spoilage and putrefaction, coming to a stop at the foot of his bed.

One afternoon he awoke to find that he sat again in the TV room and saw on the screen people wielding sledgehammers and picks smashing holes in the Berlin Wall. Crowds pulled and yanked on cables to pull down sections of it. Thousands of men, women, and children streamed through checkpoints; cars remained backed up for miles. Horns honked continuously. The East German border had opened. People climbed up on top of the wall where they danced and sang and drank from wine bottles which they passed freely back and forth among themselves.

Surely this great event stood as a sign. A foretoken. Maybe now he could join the others. Casimir had died in 1898, the same summer they found Frederick Krolich, not even a year old, drowned in Spring Creek. He had almost succumbed himself that December on his sled. Cetta and her mother had gone next, perishing the following

May, seven months prior to the start of the new century. Eberhard gave up the ghost in 1910, and in 1912, the year Anton graduated from Franklin & Marshall College and married Helen Thiele, a debilitating stroke had laid low his father Reinhold August Rausch. All the men in the family died of cerebral hemorrhages. Two years later, Helen bore Hedi. Otto followed in 1916. He resigned the succeeding year in protest of the school board's decision to drop his German class following Germany's notification to the U.S. of unrestricted submarine warfare and Wilson's severing of diplomatic relations, taught in Akron from 1917 until 1920, then resumed his old post in Houserville. The moron ran over his daughter in '22 three days before her eighth birthday. His poor mother developed stomach cancer, died an agonizing death in '29. He buried Helen in '62. A heart attack. Otto in '73. Cancer .... Would he now outlive Grette? Even that wretched cur of a great-grandson Harlan! Why did he keep waking up? Why wouldn't the blackness last? He felt a sharp, stabbing pain in his chest and suddenly had difficulty breathing as the room began to spin. He closed his eyes and opened them to find himself in bed with the side rails up. A doctor in a white coat and brown slacks examined him—listened to his heart beating through a stethoscope. Dark-skinned, short but very thin, this man (whom Anton had never seen before) had a protuberant jaw, little black beads for eyes, and a square mustache beneath his aquiline nose. One at a time, he had opened Rausch's eyelids with his forefinger and thumb and had shone a tiny light into each eye. A nurse in a starched white dress stood beside him, also looking down. "A TIA, Dr. Sighn?" she asked. "I think so. Notice the glazed stare. Monitor him carefully for the rest of the day and check his vitals hourly." Sighn, Anton thought. An Indian name. These people and their religion had fascinated Uncle Eberhard, who had expatiated at great length about their beliefs to both Anton and his father. It seemed to Cominious that, somewhere inside his head, he heard him speaking now:

"Their religion embraces both philosophic pantheism and gross animism. Its central teaching is the unity and oneness of all existence and the relative unimportance of distinctions within the totality. Accretions from other religions and philosophies have imported into Hinduism all sorts of ethical and cosmogonical speculations, every variety of philosophical thought and supposition. Although the Brahmans drove out Buddhism from India, they incorporated Buddha's doctrines of metempsychosis or transmigration of souls and the existence of divine mercy. The various philosophical tenets and teachings became increasingly divorced from ritual practice which sank to the level of glorifying anthropomorphic deities through superficial though elaborate ceremonies. A trinity developed of Brahma creator, Vishnu preserver and Siva destroyer."

After the doctor and nurse left the room, he stared at the chipping paint on the wall. He hated and despised the wall. It wanted to close in on him and crush him to pulp! It laughed at him! He could not break through or dance on top of it like the Germans. As he eyed the white barricade, faces began to appear at the center of it. Grotesque, ravaged, faces. They disintegrated and reconstructed as if by witchcraft or black magic, and each face went through several different stages of maturation or growth, just like a fetus in embryonic development. These shifting and rapid-fire metamorphoses both frightened and fascinated Mr. Rausch. He saw a man's face with a narrow skull, a thin high nose and a well-shaped mouth. But abruptly, it seemed warped and twisted. As if in great pain, the man winced and gritted his teeth as an ugly purple scar appeared where, a minute before, Anton had seen a luminous pupil. Next a black patch covered the missing eye so the face resembled that of the Nordic god Wotan. Finally the cheeks, the entire face, turned bright blue. It dawned on Cominious then, to whom the face belonged—Grette's husband. The suicide. At the moment of recognition, Anton began hearing Harold Houser's voice though the lips on the face did not move.

Dr. Houser

My tongue fastens at the center and wags at both ends. While I talk to you about her, I simultaneously feed information to the rest of the omnium-gatherum about you. And to her too, of course, as hers remains the host body in which we all live. Just now I advised them to prepare for your arrival. They sent me because they wanted my professional opinion. Permit me now to give it to you. Mr. Rausch, you've just had a TIA or slight stroke. Not a full-fledged cerebrovascular accident. The blood supply to your brain became impeded or blocked. Probably a blood vessel in one of your cerebral arteries ruptured with hemorrhaging into surrounding tissues though cerebral thrombosis, or embolism might also have caused the obstruction. In any case, this hindrance, this impediment, whatever its origin, precipitated a reduction in cerebral circulation. The brain did not receive its normal blood supply. The greater the degree of the infarction—in other words, the more cell destruction that took place—the greater the severity of the stroke. You already know the more common stroke symptoms: loss of speech, paralysis of a limb or one side of the body, vision problems and difficulty in swallowing. You have experienced them all, and you realize that in your case the effects of your two previous CVAs remain severe and permanent. You haven't ceased to breathe yet, so your body has probably repaired the damage this time by restoring the blood supply via collateral circulation. But you remain prone to TIAs. The big CVA, I think, is just around the corner. It's only a matter of time. All Rausches die from effusions of the brain. Now let me tell you a little about the purgatory that awaits you. No, she or one of the others wants to do that herself. Someone forces me to yield the spot....

Taffy-colored hair rapidly grew from the back of the head which a moment before he had recognized as Dr. Houser's, until it reached the shoulders, or at least to where the shoulders would have been had they appeared on the wall. But a new face had begun to materialize out of the old. The nose shrank, the lips compressed into a beautiful cupid's bow, and the patch vanished to reveal an eye which like its mate had changed from cobalt blue to dark brown. Bushy eyebrows turned into narrow pencil lines. The eyelashes lengthened and twittered, and Anton saw a woman's face. He recognized it as the one which had stared back at him in his dream when he looked into the mirror. Then he could not identify it, but now he knew it immediately as Aunt Inga Krolich's. She spoke but not with her own voice. Her father the pedantic, ever-digressing Herr Eberhard Rausch lectured through her. When he finally came round to the matter at hand and alluded to his daughter, he referred to her in the third person. He spoke about himself and his own intellectual pursuits first, presumably to provide essential background, even though Anton had heard it all before.

Inga/ Eberhard

Linguist, Vedantist, Wagnerite, amateur archaeologist, Cambridge graduate and Methodist convert, I became a missionary and studied native customs in Mysore, India in the mid 1860s, where I married the daughter of the British Garrison commander, the former Fanny Boughton. As a student at Cambridge I grew intrigued and fascinated with the sub-continent. When I studied at the university, cordial relations existed between England and the many German states and kingdoms, the Queen of the United Kingdom of Great Britain and Ireland the German Victoria. *Ja*, we all experienced quite an India craze at that period. After all, in 1858, the Queen had only just appointed the first Viceroy. That year the governance of the country transferred from the East India Company to the crown, to the aforesaid Victoria of Saxe-Coburg-Saalfeld. Even with the assistance of an executive council and legislature, what a gigantic task the Viceroy had to oversee and govern that vast and multifarious nation.

My fascination with languages first drew me to India. I knew that with a few exceptions all the languages spoken in Europe belonged to a language group that originated in India and Iran. The seven principal branches of the Indo-Germanic tongues–Germanic, Slavo-Lettish, Celtic, Italic, Greek, Iranic, and Indic–showed by their structure, stock of words, number of features, and sounds themselves, that they descended from one common root, the Aryan proper. We speculated that the entire body of these languages derived from monosyllabic elements, and that there stood of course two classes of them, verbal and pronominal. From these two proto-grammatical forms then, there arose gradually the rudiments of all the separate grammars and vocabularies of the member languages. In some of the languages, constructions and syntactical arrangements lingered which had disappeared much earlier in others. We conjectured that, of all the Indo-Germanic tongues, Sanskrit preserved most of the original standards, so I taught myself the language and read portions of the Vedas and other religious texts in order to help myself better imagine and envisage the broad framework of that theoretical ur-language, Indo-European. But like Schopenhauer, Thoreau, Wagner and Emerson, I became fascinated by the contents of the texts I read, by the philosophic speculations enclosed in the Upanishads, Mantros, and Aranyakas, the depth of thought present in the sacred writ of such a primitive, backward people. Their theory regarding the creation of the universe particularly fascinated me. When Vishnu, the focal deity of the Trimurti (Brahma and Siva remained merely two of His aspects) exhaled, He created a universe. It took aeons for him to empty his lungs. During this immeasurable, seemingly unending period of time, He wore his Brahma mask, but finally He inhaled, destroying the universe, and at that moment He became Siva. But then he would exhale once more and a new universe would replace the old. Thus one breath of the god contained all of time. The Hindu version of the fall also intrigued me. Millions of separate souls all constituted the Super-soul, the great white light, the aforesaid Vishnu, but an individual essence could become infatuated with itself and grow to love its very individuality while envying the power, the wholeness, of the Totality. It desired to become the Whole but in itself and on its own. It would then fall ... first to become Brahma, the demigod of creation. The soul got what it ached for, the illusion of being God. But even Brahma died, and the soul would continue its descent. First into the ranks of the lesser demigods, then into the body of a man. Finally it traveled one at a time through the bodies of all the animals and plants that throve in the material world. Only then could it begin its slow ascent back to the deity or Godhead. Brahma grew so puffed up with pride that Lord Vishnu invited him to his house to undeceive him. He demanded that the porters announce his arrival at once. To his dismay, however, they ushered him into a room filled with countless other Brahmas, most of whom stood much more imposing than he. Dwarfed by these coevals hundreds of times larger and more potent than himself, he discovered that they all waited on Lord Vishnu's pleasure and that there existed not one but manifold material worlds.

Of course the long history of India also held its fascination for me. Here stood a land—the Hindus refer to their terra firma as "The Great Mother"—that throughout the centuries many conquerors had invaded. From the far north came the first marauders, the Aryans who drove the aboriginal people, the dark-skinned Dravidians, to the south and established the Hindu faith. The Greeks under Alexander the Great arrived in 326 BC. The first Mohammedan conquest—people coming from across the plains of Afghanistan—occurred during the eighth century, and the Moguls established their dynasty in the sixteenth. A number of independent states arose. The European powers established commercial organizations in the pursuit of trade with the English gradually gaining the ascendancy. Making the journey to India, I felt like I traveled backward into Time. I visited many ancient ruins and saw all sorts of architectural marvels. I wondered at tall pyramidal towers with their profuse ornamental carvings of gods and demigods and men, women, and animals, at monumental mounds with long corridors and masonry coverings and superstructures at the top. I saw ancient frescoes on cave walls. And of course I made a pilgrimage to Agra to see the Taj Mahal, the marble mausoleum erected by Mogul Emperor Shan Jahan in memory of his favorite wife, its inner walls inlaid with precious and semi-precious stones. I won't deny a spirit of adventure—something undoubtedly romantic—impelled me to journey to the east, but I also went to save souls, to win the natives over to Christianity—to share in the white man's burden. I did not realize that, when left alone with our daughter, my wife would do unspeakable things to her while our Indian servant watched and jeered. We had brought Sita into the home as Inga's wet nurse. Her own baby had been stillborn. For some reason I still can't fathom, Fanny had rejected our daughter at birth and would not hold her for weeks afterwards, but then she seemed to recover completely. She showered affection on the child, a charade, I guess, for my benefit. I had no idea that she could become such a monster. I never would have married her, much less fathered a child by her, had I known. But after my wife's death, I returned to England with Inga, totally in the dark as to what had happened to my little girl. She had turned eight when we left for home. Her mother had told her never to tell, and she never did. Even after we buried the witch in the ground. Maybe she thought I wouldn't believe her. I probably wouldn't have. But how could you not believe a little girl? Only after my own death—when I came here—did I find out. The great tragedy of the town of Houserville when we lived there, as you will remember, was first the drowning death of Inga's son Frederick Krolich and then only ten months later her own death and that of her daughter Lucetta, the accident on the bridge. Not one person knew that she murdered both children and committed suicide.

At this point, Anton heard Harold Houser's voice break through and say "A multiple." Then Eberhard continued.

She is, was, and will be haunted by ghosts from both the past and future, some of whom died very violent deaths, one a Delaware Indian woman killed by General John Armstrong's men at Kittanning, Pennsylvania, in 1756. The wraiths all become diminished once they enter her body—remain but shadows of their former selves—and once inside her, they forget their previous incarnations. When one arrives, he displaces someone else who came before him, and in turn another will displace him. They all stand around a white light. There exist coffins there for people who haven't yet been born—not even in 1989. Some souls enter her to cleanse and purify themselves by their own efforts. Others ....

Again Anton heard Dr. Houser's voice.

Like viruses they invade the living body whose own soul shattered when her own mother molested and tortured her as a little girl. The ghosts vie with each other for the control of the host body ....

But once more Eberhard's grew louder, drowned him out.

Inga sacrificed the children so that they would escape the cycle of birth and death. She thought that, by killing herself and them, she would, like Christ, take her children's future sins upon herself. They would die innocent, guiltless. When she put the little boy in the water, she thought that she became the child's saviour, a Moses' or Perseus' mother placing her son in a basket and letting the waves carry it out to sea and on to the bulrushes of a better world. She didn't perceive that she had turned into the person she hated most, her own mother. A sturdy, sensible Christian woman, she changed into a Medea, a hideous old crone feeding at the neck of her beloved boy! And Lucetta saw her mother throw her brother into the water!

The words ceased then the voice faded into that of a bewildered child's.

Why did she hurt me? What did I ever do to deserve such punishment? She would crack and hit me for nothing. Once she twisted my arm nearly off. And she yanked me by the hair, let me drop to the floor onto my back, and kicked me again and again. Once when I didn't come right when she called, she fed my puppy broken glass and I had to watch him squirm, whimper and yap and then die and she said that's what will happen to you if you ever tell. If you ever say anything. And she tied me up and locked me in a cedar chest. I gave you birth. I can put you into your grave. I banged on the lid over and over again with my fists, but she wouldn't let me out. And at night she put sharp things inside of me and said I better get used to it for when I grew up that's what men would do to me all the time ....

At that moment, another little girl started to speak.

When I turned six, I had a make-believe inner friend named Ilsa. I saw her the first time sitting across from me at table. Whenever my mother would catch me alone, I would close my eyes and leave, and Ilsa would come instead to feel the hurt. She would stand in my place ....

When this second little girl's voice trailed off, Inga Krolich's face split down the center, separated into two silhouetted profiles—one a man's, the other a woman's—which Anton could not identify. The woman's face had high cheekbones, and she had interlaced strands of her hair into a plait or braid which hung down at the side of her face and extended well below her chin. The man wore a tricornered hat, had a hooked nose and a prominent jaw. As Anton continued to stare at the wall, the faces suddenly switched places. No longer silhouettes, crude outlines filled in with a uniform dark color, they had transformed into miniature portraitures with lifelike delineation and deposition of pigment. The woman had dark eyes, brown skin, and coal-black hair; the man a pasty complexion, red-blond curls and ringlets, broad blubbery lips and a bloodshot pale-blue eye. Their noses almost touched, and they seemed to threaten each other with violence and murder. Anton did not recognize either face. He heard a masculine voice first, again from somewhere inside his own head.

Summerfield Cronemiller

You descend from me. I am a forebear of your dear mother Amanda. A colonial soldier who participated in the expedition led by Colonel John Armstrong against the Indian village of Kittannin, the largest Indian settlement in western Pennsylvania, a strategic point from which the stealthy bucks could quickly reach all the other Indian villages on the River Ohio either by water or else by the Great Trail or Main Road down the river through Logtown, Sawcunk, Kuskuski, and other prominent villages—the chief war path of the Iroquois to the Mississippi. Also a branch of the Catawba trail ran directly southward from this Indian town through Westmoreland and Fayette counties to Stewart's Crossings, where Braddock crossed the Youghioghenny River, and then southward into the Carolinas. At the commencement of the war between Great Britain and France, the village began to fill with Delaware and Shawonese who stood hostile to the English. The residence of the Delaware war chief Captain Jacobs, who took part in the Battle of the Monongahela and helped rout Braddock's army, Kittannin became the chief rallying point for Delaware and Shawonese forays and incursions into the Cumberland valley, the

Juniata region and to Virginia. Raiding parties carrying guns and scalping knives came down the Kittannin trail and its various branches to attack individual farms, kill or capture whomever they found in the fields or houses, destroy cattle, burn buildings, and disappear into the forest with their prisoners whom they carried back to the Indian town, where they made the adults run the gauntlet or put them to other torture, and where they adopted the children and raised them as Indians. The settlers had established a line of forts and stockades at strategic positions, some on waterways, others at the junction of important trails, and provincial troops patrolled the intervals between the forts, but the Indian parties could easily slip through the cordon by fanning out through the dense woods. They always approached their objectives with stealth. The patrols could not keep them back, so the Governor placed a bounty of $350.00 on both Captain Jacobs' and Chief Chingas' heads, but no one collected it. Then in July and August of 1756, Captain Jacobs and his men joined a French force under Louis Coulon de Villiers and attacked and captured Fort Granville on the Juniata, needless to say a very great shock to colonial confidence. The Indians stood good fighters. They could march abreast in concert, and in scattered order, though their line might extend more than a mile long, and they could perform various necessary maneuvers, either slowly or as fast as they could run. They would surround their enemies either in a circle, or a semicircle if the enemy had a river to one side of them, and if the enemy ever surrounded them, they would form a large hollow square, each man behind a tree trunk, to prevent themselves from making a target on either side. The expedition of Colonel Armstrong, for the purpose of restoring colonial trust by destroying Kittannin, the starting point for all these Indian war parties, set forth on the 30th of August. We left Fort Shirley on a forced march and reached Kittannin on the morning of September 8th. With the advantage of surprise and a superiority in numbers of three to one, we destroyed most of the town and rescued a number of the prisoners. We called on Captain Jacobs to surrender or that we would burn him alive. From within his log house, he screamed, "I eat fire," so I gladly put the torch to the hut's bark covering, and he perished inside as the cabin went up in flames. In face of Indian reinforcements from across the river, we retired. But we had achieved our military purpose. We drove the Delaware back to less exposed positions, and the news of their first major setback lifted English morale.

Immediately after he finished speaking, the Indian woman he faced began to chastise him.

The Woman

I lived by the great river. I lived by the Kithanne. I saw what you do. We a peaceful tribe. Whole tribe, even our men, take ceremonial role of women in the Iroquois longhouse. Let the other nations fight. We remember William Penn. How he kind. But other English not like him. Give us blankets infected with the smallpox. Send us away from the forks of the Delaware. Say Wyoming Valley will now be home for the six nations. Our home forever. But him lie. We remember the Walking Purchase. How English take away what he give. French remind us of these grievances. Say will treat us better. Never take our land. Offer us the French hatchet. Our men decide to remain women no longer. In longhouse they make up mind to lift hatchet ....

Anton blinked, and the faces disappeared. He must have dreamed it all. Summerfield Cronemiller was his grandfather's name. He had no ancestor who had fought in the French and Indian War. True, he had taught Pennsylvania history in the school, and colonial life had always fascinated him. Studying the past remained a hobby for many years. He knew all about John Armstrong's strong-arm tactics and the commando raid he had led against the Delaware at Kittanning. Also the colloquial expression Indian gift thoroughly disgusted him he found it so unjust. Throughout U.S. history, hadn't the white man constantly taken back land that he had previously conferred upon or granted to the Indian, and not the other way around? Likewise he knew, and had taught his students all about, the Indo-European languages, how in the nineteenth century, comparative and historic study of the Aryan tongues established their descent from a common ancestor, spoken in the late Stone Age, probably by a group of people of perhaps mixed race in Eastern Europe and how modern scientific philological method had hypothetically reconstructed this unrecorded language. He had taught generation after generation of dense and dull students—they didn't want to open their minds; they didn't want to learn, but he drove it into their heads anyway—all about this conjectural parent speech and about the two great divisions of the Indo-Germanic languages, the centum and the satem, indicated by the development of palatial gutturals into mutes or stops in the one, the western, division, and into sibilants or spirants in the other, the eastern, as illustrated by the word for hundred. Soon he would be one hundred! How could he have possibly lived for so long? It seemed to him that these voices he heard repeated old lectures of his and things that he had read out of books, but why had he thought about persons with multiple personalities? Ah, he remembered. Earlier in the day, he had recalled something that he had seen on the subject on television. He was looking at it when Harlan snatched him away to the dining room to be force-fed. If anyone in the family had opposite faces, it wasn't his dear Aunt Inga but Harlan himself. A demon named Al lived inside of him and played Hyde to his Jekyll. If he had met Al, this person who had so corrupted his great-grandson, by God, he'd have struck him down. Could Harlan really have done everything he said? It stood too horrible to contemplate, and Anton felt very tired and at the same time light-headed. As if he would once again drift off to sleep.

Throughout the afternoon, nurses came into his room and felt his pulse, listened to his respirations and to his heart, and repositioned him in his bed. He dozed in between their visits, and eventually slept soundly. Like a log. Blackness closed in on all sides. Yet he did not experience a complete diminution of sensation. His heavy slumber only superficially resembled a state of hibernation, a complete suspension of consciousness, for he felt someone give his shoulder a good hard shove and heard a woman say that he had now become totally unresponsive and then a man state that he had slipped into a coma and that it appeared that congestive heart failure would shortly set in and that someone had better inform the family.

Anton started to dream. He knew he dreamed because the colors around him became unbearably intense and the noises became amplified by many decibels. Someone shook him awake in his dream. He still lay in his hospital bed surrounded by the same four walls, but a twenty-year-old Albert Stipetig stood to one side, looking down at him, one hand gripping a side rail, the other clutching a paper to his breast. Tall and gawky, with closely cropped strawberry-blond hair with two or three prominent cowlicks, he had on army fatigues and wore a chaplet of glory on his brow. His eyes looked terribly sunken. He pressed his paper toward Anton, and, to the latter's great surprise and unbelievable delight, he could lift up his arm to reach out and take it. He found that he could also sit up in bed and that he could bend his head back so he could see the ceiling. But there was no ceiling, only the night sky. He could see endless stars and constellations. Diadems of all colors, each one sun bright. Still an old man, he could tell at once by glancing down at his hands, one of which held Stipetig's paper, but no longer a paralytic! He smiled, consumed with joy. He must try to speak. "Albert," he said. "My God I can!" "Yes, it's me. But why won't you look at what I brought you?" Immediately Anton read the inscription on the paper. He had seen it before. Albert's mother had shown it to everyone in Houserville, she had stood so proud of the posthumous honor bestowed by the French Government on her son, a German-American boy who died fighting against his ancestral fatherland:

A LA MÉMOIRE
DE
ALBERT STIPETIG
PRIVATE FIRST DIVISION COMPANY C 24TH INFANTRY
DES ESTATS-UNIS D' AMÉRIQUE,
MORT POUR LA LIBERTÉ
PENDANT LA GRANDE GUERRE
HOMMAGE DE LA FRANCE
LE PRÉSIDENT DE LA RÉPUBLIQUE

"While you stayed home and taught," Albert said, "I gave my all, never grew old like you." He sat down in one of the chairs beside Rausch's bed. "Since 1918, I have slept in a soldier's grave." Tears began to form in Anton's eyes. A poem he had once read began running through his head:

> In Flanders' fields, the poppies blow
> Between the crosses, row on row,
> That mark our place; and in the sky
> The Larks, still bravely singing fly,
> Scarce heard amid the guns below.
> We are the dead. Short days ago
> Loved and were loved and now we lie
> In Flanders' fields.

He couldn't remember the rest. "Now," Albert said, "I have come to tell you what happened during the second phase of the Meuse-Argonne Battle on that first day of November, 1918."

Albert Stipetig

I fought as a soldier in the First Division. We stood first in everything: the first in sector, the first to shoot Germans, the first to attack, to conduct a raid, to be raided, to capture prisoners, and, of course, we became the first military unit cited singly in general orders in number of division, corps, and Army Commander and general staff officers produced from our personnel. Naturally, we also suffered the first casualties. We stood weary and nerve-racked when we got word of the new offensive. We had returned to our old positions after a prolonged assault against the St. Georges-Landres et St. Georges section of the Kriemhilde Stellung when we received word from High Command that our forces would shortly undertake an all-out attack to blast the enemy from his stronghold along the heights of Barricourt. The line stretched from the northern edge of the Côte de Chatillion to a position one kilometer south of St. Georges. The men, I among them, all suffered from fatigue and exhaustion. We had become demoralized after our regiment had advanced through the woods and valleys of the Côte de Maldah. A number of our horses had been killed in the assault at St. Georges. Others had died from overwork and exposure. The ones still alive had all become emaciated. They looked just like the men, gaunt and skeletal. We stood the lucky survivors, and, like our bays and chestnuts, we bore an assortment of scars on our bodies and had far too little to eat. To a man, we had dark circles under our eyes. Scuttlebutt had it that command would launch the offensive at night. The final objective stood more than nine kilometers from the initial assault position, but a heavy gun barrage of at least two hours' duration would precede the infantry charge. A maximum-intensity bombardment of gas and shell from a number of heavy guns would cover our entire advance. The officers told us that the heavy calibers would obliterate every hidden enemy machine gun nest and that a sheet of machine-gun bullets would literally rain down on all his trenches and communications. At 3:30 AM, November 1st, the preparatory barrage commenced. As we waited in the trenches, we held our hands over our ears as explosions lit up the sky. At 5:15, we got the order to advance. A line of bursting shell fell one hundred fifty meters ahead of us; two hundred meters in front of the shell exploded shrapnel fired by one third of the light artillery; one hundred fifty meters beyond it all the machine guns of three divisions directed their barrage; and finally three hundred meters beyond the falling shrapnel bursts from our one hundred fifty-five-mm howitzers pounded the enemy lines. A cyclone of steel and bullets, in other words, moved inexorably in front of us, and extended as far as a thousand meters beyond our position at any given time. Still our progress remained slow. We gained ground but encountered obstructions—pockets of resistance. The batteries moved forward to maintain close support. A wall of smoke concealed our flanks, and high-explosive shell obstructed the Huns' frontal view. I ran in front of all the others. At the close of the day, we reached the enemy barbwire, and our men began to storm the heights. I heard the machine-gun bullets whistling toward me as I snapped the wire with my cutter. I fell backward into the mud, dead before I landed. For awhile, I hovered over my body. But then rose upwards as if I had become a balloon filled with helium. I saw our men break through the last enemy defenses as I ascended toward the starry dome. Most of the Germans had fled. I saw machine guns in their concealed positions with belts inserted but not a shot fired. Artillery stood with muzzle covers on the guns and piles of untouched ammunition beside them. Here and there fieldpieces reclined among the bodies of horses, drivers, and cannoneers. In the trenches lay the corpses of Germans who had risen to fire at the last moment. Who had resisted to the very end ....

At that instant I woke up in bed to the sounds of pitched battle, and I wondered if I had only dreamt the raid. Or if I lay wounded in hospital. Someone slept soundly beside me. I threw off the cover and went to the window and pulled back the curtain, and saw lightning; thunderclaps had awakened me, not shells. I noticed my reflection in the pane, gasped, and brought my hand to my mouth. A woman's face stared back at me.

Albert fell silent. Anton had turned his head away. He didn't want Albert to see him cry. The pause lasted for some time. Finally Anton looked around. His friend now stood dressed in a costume from another era. He wore white duck trousers and a double-breasted bottle-green frock coat, having skirts reaching about to the knees. His heelless black shoes had prominent square buckles on them, and he held a thin-stemmed clay pipe in his left hand. When he started to chat again, he prattled in another man's voice.

The public knew us as Lewis and Connelly, not the other way round. My name came first as well it should, for I, not John, planned our little ambuscades. Not that I found doing so in any wise difficult. The mountain roads remained rough, the haul long. While a number of springs ran along the way, water couldn't slake certain thirsts. More often than not, the wagoners and calèche drivers had drunken such large quantities of whiskey, they couldn't even draw their pistols. Be that as it may. What one man finds easy, another does not. Despite being nothing but a follower, a lemming in human flesh, Johnny Connelly now feels that he hasn't yet secured proper recognition for our robberies, that I received too much of the credit, whereas he acquired nought but the short end of the stick, and certainly not his due. All I can say is that the way it came down is absolutely correct. I exerted complete control over him. At the snap of my finger, he'd do my bidding. I won't pamper his pride and feed his insolence by saying otherwise. Had it not been for me he would have found himself in gaol long, long, before. He stood grossly incompetent, a bully who relied on brawn only. He did not have a single subtle bone in his body. By God, he would never have made a successful highwayman if not for me. Why once, left to his own devices, he robbed a wagon drawn by an ox team which had nothing in it but blankets, sheeting, calico, cotton, thread, needles, brandy-wine, lead and salt! Demoralizing currency or shaving bank notes stood completely beyond his ken. No, he did not have the wherewithal of the Noble Philanderer, the only person ever partnered with me who would have the right to claim that he stood on an equal footing with myself. So don't believe one thing he tells ye. It's all balderdash and poppycock!

With that, Albert snapped his fingers and disappeared in a cloud of smoke. At the same moment a ruby-red star fell out of the sky, plummeted towards the earth just over Anton's bed. But instead of landing on the ground and crushing him, it stopped in mid-air and hovered there. The face inside the star could have been Lucifer's but it was not. It was his great-grandson's. He recognized the bright blue eyes, as magnetic and misleading as Hitler's, the jet-black hair brushed forcefully to one side, the button nose, and the evenly spaced little teeth crowding and cramming a too-small mouth.

Abruptly, the face bounded back into the heavens, shrank to the size of a marble and then to the size of a pinhead which was exactly what his great-grandson was. But then it came again, this time stopping only several inches above Anton's face and ballooning in size at least seven fold. It drew so close that it seared Anton's cheeks and forehead. He had to turn his head and shut his eyes. Otherwise the star would have blinded him.

Harlan

I don't care what Al says. I'm the better bank robber. He may have brought me into the business. He may have taught me everything he knew, but in the end I grew more skilled at it than he. That damn Fed Schumann took him in. But he didn't trick me. I had my suspicions all along and don't forget Al wound up dead, a bullet in his head. Not Har. They didn't get me then, and they haven't got me since, and—you know what—they never will. Al bought the farm over six years ago, and subsequently I have held up an untold number of banks and have gotten away with it every single time. He started his bank-robbing career long before I did, but I think I have caught up with, or even surpassed him, in number of banks robbed. I've hit more than twenty in the last year alone. I enjoy pointing a gun in some hysterical woman's face and taking all the money in her register. I spend it on women and drugs. Shit, I can always get more, and if occasionally I have to do someone—well what the hell. Working here is a perfect cover. No one suspects me, and in the whole wide world not a single person knows except you, and I know for a fact that you'll keep your mouth shut, so I got it made in the shade, wouldn't you say? Oh I forgot you can't talk. See you around. ....

The heat streaming down on him gradually diminished then fell off altogether, and Anton opened his eyes to see the flaming face soaring and spiraling like a corkscrew upwards into the night sky where it finally went through a glowing and pulsating inverted bluish-white triangle, which suddenly appeared below the very apex of the heavenly dome and which opened at the center like a sheath, to give it admission to a long dark tunnel into which poured and teemed countless other shooting stars and pulsing comets with long nebulous trains and radiant comae, each one containing a human face—a little homunculus—in its coma or nucleus. Rushing in by the millions, gravity sucked them all upwards like liquid through a straw, toward a small oval, the canal's other end, far, far above: a tiny pin prick of white light towards which the many sons and daughters all raced at incredible speeds, as if to their inevitable, unavoidable destination. The whole sky it seemed was being drawn up into this whirling circular vacuum. But a cherubic voice lured Anton's eyes away from the spectacle. It belonged to an angelfaced little girl about eight years old who stood at the foot of his bed wearing a red bonnet, a pink dress with bows at the shoulders and ruffles at the ankles, and boots with pull straps, caps, and vamps. She thrust her hands into a white muff and asked him to come and play with her. As she spoke, his covers flew back of their own accord and the side rail went down. Anton swung his legs over the bed, put his feet on the floor and stood. By this time, the girl had already bounded out the door. Behind her, she pulled a sled, having taken one of her hands out of her muff to seize the umbilical-cord-like leader tied to its nose. "It lay under your bed, has always lain there," she said cheerfully. "Come on now. Follow me." He did, but he had trouble keeping up with her. He had never seen a more beautiful young girl, but she began shedding her clothes piece by piece like so many superfluous layers of skin—the muff and bonnet, red dress and shoes all disappeared—until she ran naked, and suddenly Anton, himself bare and exposed but not at all cold, grew confused as to her sex. Maybe a boy dressed in girl's clothing, he thought, for the tyke suddenly had broad shoulders and thickset legs like a boy and ran as fast as one. And her features also puzzled him. She had long yellow hair, which fell to her shoulders—the same color and length as Lucetta's. However, her little smile, the giggle in her voice, reminded him of his daughter Hedi, yet her eyes, two luminous sapphires, belonged to the small boy he had taken to play in the park and who used to love to crawl through the grooved culvert while he (Anton) stood at the other end and waited for him to emerge. She raced on ahead of him, outdistanced him by, he could not tell, how great a span, but he followed her footprints, and the two parallel lines made by the sled's runners, in the snow. For outside his ceilingless room it snowed. Tiny pink and blue flakes landed on his face while others swirled and danced in the sultry, sweltering—practically stifling—air before descending at last to the ground.

The terrain went up and down like whitecaps on a rough sea, and a few gnarled trees dotted the dream-landscape resembling cardboard stage props. The boy/girl would drag the sleigh up each swell, then climb onto it, and sail downward into the trough. This went on and on, hill after hill, until winded and on the verge of giving up the chase, Anton stopped. At the same moment the androgyne halted. She (?) had reached the next pinnacle but this time did not jump on the sled but instead, turned around, waved to Anton from the summit and called out, "It's your turn now." So once more the old man trudged up an interminable slope. When he reached the top, he wiped his brow, caught his breath and sat down on the bobsled; its two runners sank in the pink snow. From behind, Angelface tried to push him off—start him going. She toiled and sweated but did not budge him. Anton had to crouch forward before the sleigh began to move, but once it did start, it quickly gained more and more speed, and soon he soared so fast that he felt a tingle in his privates as the snow blew up into his face and he hurtled downwards. He saw the wall, the white wall in his room, and again he bore down on it. But this time it gave way, the sled went right through it, and he saw himself stretched out on the ground on the other side with arms outspread. As a boy, he used to lie down in the snow where he would raise his arms up from his sides until they made a V over his head, then would slap them back down, in order to raise them once more, so that when he got up, he left the impression of a winged angel in the snow. But now, he was sure the two old friends flesh and spirit had at last parted. He had shed his body like snake skin and had become pure consciousness. He experienced the true weightless condition of the soul as he rose upwards into blackness while watching his body, his former residence, recede below him. Next the earth itself grew smaller and smaller. Then the sun, the solar system, the Milky Way galaxy. Finally it seemed that he had reached the center of the cosmos when from all directions stars of every conceivable color—blue, orange, red, emerald, and canary—were pulled into the weightless core of his being where they combined and consolidated into pure white light. Each star enclosed the face of one of his ancestors. From the north and south came his father's people, the Rausches and the Trissenaars; from the east and west, his mother's, the Cronemillers and the Etters. Generation followed generation until all the successive stages of natural descent from the beginning of time had paraded by and Anton saw his entire antenatal history revealed as one by one his ancestors merged with him, but after the forebears and progenitors came the extended family of each of the ensuing generations of the four families—the aunts and uncles, the nieces and the nephews, the first- the second- and the forty-second cousins. From his mother's side, Frankie Etters approached. He had been one of Anton's earliest and most promising students, but he had become a Major in the United States Air Force during the Second World War and sacrificed his life, like so many others, on the altar of his country. Before he joined with Anton, a twelve-year-old girl from the Rausch side overtook him. Her eyes searched his out, accusingly. Etters spoke first.

Frankie Etters

In the operations room, the Intelligence Officer of the bombardment group, a wizen-faced old man, pulled back the curtain to unveil a large wall map of the continent on which stood marked our primary and secondary targets. Each of the three hundred combat crewmembers craned forward to better see the chart as the officer used his pointer to indicate our objectives. Some of the men had trouble focusing as they had drunk too much the night before and remained hung over. After we came back from the last mission over Schweinfurt, command issued us all—or I should say those of us who had returned, for many didn't—three-day passes to get tight and to visit our girls. After granting us liberty, however, the brass told us that we should prepare to fly on the fourth day, and now it had come round. Furthermore the weather forecast remained good for a deep penetration over Germany even though it remained overcast and drizzling here, so we knew the mission would receive a go. But some of the men just wouldn't lay off, kept on drinking until just several hours beforehand. The meeting took about a half hour. We made low whistles and catcalls when the briefing officer informed us that the purpose of our raid was to "dehouse" Germans in retaliation for a recent V-2 attack on London. Afterwards I glanced over the crew sheet pinned to the wall—I saw that I would sit in the pilot's seat of one of the B-17s in the lead squadron—then went to the mess hall for a three a.m. breakfast and gulped down cup after cup of coffee. I noticed, as I walked across the blacked-out airfield to the officers' mess, that in the last forty-five minutes that the atmosphere had started to haze over and that only the odd star remained visible in between cloud banks. We wouldn't get off on schedule—I knew it in my bones. As I ate, the Operations Officer walked up to my table from behind, tapped me on the shoulder, then informed me that due to the last-minute request of the Low Squadron Group Commander, he had transferred me from the lead to low group and that I would now pilot the Mary Lou instead of the Canned Heat. Though of course I did not realize it at the time, I had received my death sentence there and then. It took only one rub of the Operations Officer's eraser. I did grasp that my chances of getting back had just dropped. I had flown many missions and knew the score. The low group always made the easiest target for the enemy's anti-aircraft guns since, as its name suggested, it flew at the lowest base altitude over the target, and dropped its incendiary bombs after all the other squadrons delivered their payloads. I rode in a jeep in the semi-darkness part way round the five-mile perimeter track. About two miles down, we reached the flying fortress that command had assigned me to pilot. She appeared massive and bulky but above all impervious and indifferent on her plump tires. The crew stood inspecting those tires, the bomb-bay doors, and the oxygen pressure at each station. The gunners fingered the ammunition belts and field stripped the fifty-caliber machine guns in order to oil the parts. I introduced myself to each of the men then took my seat in front of the instrument panel in the nose of the plane and examined my oxygen mask, life vest and parachute. Thirty minutes before taxi time, command notified us that takeoff would be postponed for at least an hour due to the present poor visibility. We sat for nearly two hours before another jeep stopped at our dispersal point long enough to tell us that we would take off within the next forty-five minutes. One by one the B-17s rolled out onto the runway. Over sixty planes went before us. Finally our turn came. We sped down the track and took off, our glass nose tilted upward for the protracted climb to base altitude. We burst through the cloud tops into the glow of the rising sun. We continued to ascend slowly, our ample wings carrying the weight of a heavy load of incendiary bombs in our belly plus the additional onus of full main and wing-tip tanks, fuel that would not only keep the B-17 afloat in the air of the upper altitudes but would also get us both there and back home. After everyone had taken off, the planes of the three squadrons gradually assembled in close group stagger formations—high squadron up to the right of the lead; low squadron down to its left—groups converging into loose combat wings of several planes each along the wing assembly line by homing over predetermined positions with their radio compasses, so that the air division looked like a giant anvil-shaped swarm of wasps or hornets. The planes arranged themselves to allow optimum maneuverability but also so that every gun could be deployed in a firefight. As we soared over the channel, the gunners tested the fifty calibers by firing short bursts. I could see wisps of blue smoke from the guns of the group up ahead. We did not encounter any resistance on the way in until we bore down on our primary target, and the co-pilot spotted two Foche-Wulf 190s at two o'clock low. They rose above the horizon, arced in a bowlike curve and whizzed through the formation ahead of us in a frontal assault, nicking two B-17s in the wings and breaking away in half rolls over our group. I saw one of them glare past at a six hundred mile-an-hour rate of closure, its yellow nose smoking and small pieces of metal flying off from below its wing. Evidently the gunners of our group stood awake and at the ready. Nobody had fallen asleep at the switch. Smoke trailed from the two hit B-17s in the group in front of us, but they held their stations as they passed over the city below them, and we saw the first enemy flak burst below us light and inaccurate. Our bombardiers began synchronizing their sights. A few seconds later, they released their payloads. A red light on the instrument panel went out, and the Mary Lou gave a slight lift. We turned from the target, and I looked back to see a wonderful display: rectangular plume after rectangular plume rising above the city. We had smeared our objective. But then the cockpit burst into flames. A wing crumpled, and the Mary Lou began to lose altitude, the last thing I remember the smell of burning cordite. Two crewmen managed to bail out of the burning plane before it crashed. I did not.

Irmgard Rausch

No I won't go into the light. My life isn't over. It can't be. I am only twelve. I don't desire to come in yet. I want to stay here and experience all those things denied me, to mature into a woman, taste love, and learn the joys of motherhood. To grow old. To live my life. A good long one—through....

They built a house where ours stood and now a new family lives there. A husband and a wife and two little girls. Eva and Elsa have seen me. They have told their Mama, but she does not believe them even though she has also noticed my presence on occasion. But not with her eyes. She steps into a corner of a room where suddenly it is ice cold. It's that way because I stand there. She can feel me. And every morning I run through the grass toward the wine cellar one hundred feet back from the villa. But I always stop midway, turn around, and start back toward the house. In our haste, we had forgotten Arouette the cat. She must come too, so I will run and fetch her. Mother does not see me go. She bolts ahead with my baby brother Konrad cradled in her arms and my little sister Frieda in front of her. She thinks that I follow close on her heels and does not miss me until she reaches the cellar door. I have done this every morning since that first time I decided to turn back, that horrible day back in '44, when we heard the sirens start to wail and then the roar of bombers overhead as they came boring down the river. By then, we had grown used to them coming, British squadrons at night and American ones during the day. Sometimes the bombs started to fall before the sirens began to blow. We could hear them exploding in the distance. That noise would sometimes wake us in the middle of the night. The windows would begin to rattle. Something would fall down and break such as the pitcher and bowl on my night stand, and Arouette would spring from off my breast and hide either underneath my bed, or behind my dresser, or in my clothes closet. I would always find her before Mama got to my room. We would dash outside and across the yard, then down into the stale and dank cellar where we would wait often for as long as five or six hours until at last the all-clear signal sounded. Sometimes we would hear nothing for a long while. But then it would start again and we would hear more bombs detonating. Mother and I both hated waiting in the dark. Frieda would begin to sob and whimper and then the baby would start to bawl. But Mama said the war would soon end and that Papa and Johann would come home any day now. Afterwards, when we emerged from out of our shelter, we could see burning buildings in every direction. A conflagration blazed fiercely either to the north or to the south. The outlying areas usually suffered the heaviest poundings. But the raids threw the entire city into confusion and paralysis. Black smoke billowed over housetops just two blocks away, and fire trucks rushed and raced through the rubble-strewn streets. While firemen sprayed the burning buildings, other volunteers tended to the wounded and removed the dead. Hours—maybe even days—would pass before electric and telephone service came back on line. But our villa always stood undamaged. No bomb fell near it until that day I went back for Arouette when sticks of incendiaries bounced off the rooftop. The last thing I remember seeing before a balloon of fire engulfed and surrounded me.... Now Mr. Etters says Germany deserved to suffer. That the continued series of air bombardments finally brought the war home to her people. Paid them back for putting Hitler in power and starting yet another world slaughter ... for mounting blitzes against all the weaker nations of Europe. Launching rocket bombs at London which also killed children. For the starvation of millions of men, women and children in Soviet Russia. And the cruel medical experiments performed by the Nazi doctors in the camps and the mass murders of Jews, Poles, and anti-Nazis at their hands. I agree wicked people should receive punishment. But I stood innocent of their crimes. I was just a little girl whose life the bombs cut short. No I don't want to follow the voices into the light. I haven't yet accepted my death. And won't no matter what they say. Like all the little ones, I yearn for life. I want mine back. So no I won't leave.

Yet gravity pulled her in anyway, like all the others, and finally only one light remained in the heavens and it constituted his—Anton's—perfect essence ... his subtle substance. He groped for the right words, still had not found them. His epitome? Quintessence? Paradigm? No single word would do. Yet, swarms of comets or remnants of disintegrated comets had moved around him in definite orbits, attracted toward his weightless middle, at last entering into it with great velocity and incandescent with heat. Then it seemed that space itself had begun to collapse inwards and that he had become the nucleus into which it would all shrink, and, yes, it did happen. In a matter of seconds, no in the space of one breath, the entire celestial cosmos compressed itself into its midpoint—into him. For he stood the universe's heart, its hub! An ultra-dense particle of energy and light. But then the pressure, the tension could no longer be borne. At least not by him. He could not condense any further. So he split in two, like a cell undergoing mitosis, and saw his own face looking back at him from the other grain of light. Apparently he had a twin like Grandfather Casimir. But shortly thereafter he started to enlarge and expand. As he did, he heard his own voice emanate from the speck, now so much smaller than himself.

The Adversary

No, you can't have children. You mustn't. They will only disappoint you and bring you grief. It's immoral to bring sons and daughters into this world. If I could reveal to you the future that awaits them, you would stand appalled and not want them to live. For if they are born, they will have to die, a truism yes, but now is not the time for you to turn captious! Do you want your son to undergo an agonizing death on some god-forsaken battlefield? Do you want to see your daughter struck down by a runaway truck driven by a mental deficient? For they give licenses to dimwits with intelligence quotients as low as sixty-eight in that world out there, the one into which she will be born. You feed, clothe, and bring up your family, trying to instill in them your own values and codes of behavior, but in truth you do no more than raise cows for slaughter. Johnny will march off to the wars, to serve either President or Kaiser, or, if among the lucky ones who live out their lives in times of relative peace, he will have to see his body and mind wither away, perhaps have to spend his last years in a convalescent center like Colonial Court Manor and that rates almost as bad as dying in Auschwitz. Life remains nothing but suffering. All sorts of pain and misery await your children—the thousand natural shocks the flesh is heir to all lie ahead. Yes, the Bard said it better than anyone else. The slings and arrows of outrageous fortune. That's what they will have to face and look forward to. Remember your own sorrows and afflictions. Your own travails. How can you wish them, or others similar in kind, upon your offspring and progeny? And as I said previously, your children will do nothing if not disappoint and dissatisfy you. Your sons will become bank robbers and kidnappers, drug peddlers and tempters and seducers of little children. Your daughters drunks and wantons ....

But even as his Doppelgänger spoke these words, stars began to issue out of the white light that was Anton. Like the stars which he had attracted and which had earlier come racing to him, each bore a human face within its contours, the first sun to emerge his cherished baby girl Hedi, but her light—once it burst forth from his—shortly went out—extinguished all too quickly, indeed almost instantaneously. But Otto, Grette, and

Harlan followed her, and others succeeded them—many more, none of whom Anton recognized, but as each shot ahead, the white light that constituted his essence diminished until he himself became but a homunculus and the heavens filled up with as many stars as had shone there previously. The stars, Anton included, made for the distant oval, but he stood dead last in the cavalcade, yet he soon progressed with such speed that he began to overtake the others. He went by Grette and Harlan, then caught up to his great-great-grandchildren. They addressed him from either side.

Harlene

I will lead a life of idleness and dissipation. I won't read books or study languages. Such pursuits bore me. In fact, I will hate school. I'll daydream and yawn in the classroom—won't ever listen to what the teachers have to say. They always grate on and on and grow so dull and monotonous. You bet I'll chew my gum loudly, really smack it, because it annoys them, gets their goat, and I love to tick them off whenever and however I can. No, I won't even finish the ninth grade, much less go onto college. Not that my parents'll ever encourage me in that direction. I come from a family that doesn't think that much of higher education. It just isn't practical, doesn't have anything to do with life in the real world, my daddy says, and I agree with him. The teachers' bull won't interest me. But the boys in the classroom will. And in my time I'll get to know quite a few of then, but none'll ever marry me though four or five will knock me up. But I'll go to the doc's and get scraped. Thirty minutes in his office and my problem will be disposed of. Once or twice I'll even let myself get pregnant in order to trap a guy, but all he'll ever say is get an abortion. If he doesn't care, neither will I. I'll *gladly* kill his kid. Every night after work, I'll sit in front of my mirror, redden my nails and lips, apply the blue eye shadow to my lids with the little brush, and put on my artificial lashes and, if I have to, I'll touch up my hair, that is if the roots have begun to show. Then I'll get all dressed up and head out to the beer garden. I am. Oops I mean I will be an incredibly social person ....

Harlan Houser II

I stand fated to become a combat soldier in the third world war, named for where we'll fight it—throughout the third world, especially in the various nations of Central America. Our President'll say that the peoples of the south will hail our coming, lay offerings of fruit at our feet, and welcome us as liberators. He'll claim inevitable hemispheric triumph as our ultimate destiny. I hear him orate as I speak. History, he says, overflows with examples of superior nations with popular pluralistic political systems conquering lesser countries with dictatorships either of the right or the left; of noble crusades undertaken to suppress repugnant totalitarian ideologies wherever they might rear their ugly heads; of the inherent struggle between barbarism and the drumbeat of human progress toward perfection; of the clash between centralized government which allows no recognition of or no representation to other political parties and the fresh breezes of enlightenment. He cites the defeats, in Europe, of the fascist regimes of the 1940s and the communist ones of the 1980s. But now, he iterates, the challenge which faces us stands to the south, where the countries of Latin America—in which anti-USA, anti-colossus-to-the-North, sentiment runs rampant—all totter in confusion and instability. We have all watched the movement called the Peoples' Popular Front spread from nation to nation like an ominous dark cloud. We saw friendly regime after friendly regime topple, yet did nothing. But then the militants seized the Panama Canal and terrorists took United States citizens hostage, so now he has no choice but to send in the troops. He says that we will bring peace and plenitude to the region. Instead we'll kill, humiliate and conquer. The leader of our expeditionary forces—General Ulysses S. Walker—claims that in the fullness of time all the nations of South America will fall under the influence of the laws and institutions of the United States, that we will annex the entire southern hemisphere to the Cape of Horn. For it remains now, and in the future it will continue to remain, our back yard. I, myself, shall stand responsible for the slaughter of thousands ....

What these two had to say stung Rausch's ears, so he moved by them and also past the next several generations until he encountered a comet with a little girl's face which resembled that of his daughter Hedi's—the effect of atavism, no doubt—in its nebulous coma, behind which a long tail formed. She sang out to him as he came up on her, and her voice—so sweet, so mellifluous—a scientific and artistic combination of melodic, rhythmic, and harmonic tones—completely arrested him. He slowed his pace and for a while swam alongside of her.

The Little Mozartina

I am the wonder child that you and Helen wanted so badly to have. The good genes sometimes skip over a number of generations. Then they have a renascence. I will learn to play the piano and violin at age three, and at age four I'll begin to compose. I'll tour all the great cities of the world to give concerts starting at age seven, and before I die I will give mankind over seven hundred published works, comprising many sacred, instrumental, and vocal compositions; one hundred four symphonies and tone poems; and twenty-five operas. That is, if I am born. For if I am to live, you must not follow the adversary's advice. You must preserve Harlan's life, not destroy it. For in him now lodges the creative potential. His existence must go on so that the life cycle may continue.

Her words cheered him and he sped ahead of all the others and bore down on the wheel of white light which suddenly loomed in front of him. He had won the race once again. He remained the chosen one. Afresh he pierced and punctured the ovum and found admission therein.

"Karl's" vision blurred and clouded, but gradually the parlor he stood in began to come into focus. It seemed to him that he emerged from some sort of trance. He felt sure that his pupils expanded and gathered in greater quantities of light as more and more of the drawing room became visible, whereas a moment before when everything was still faint and indistinct they must have been only pinpoint in size.

A fire crackled on the hearthstone underneath a chimney in an open recess in the wall. The richly carved marble fireplace was decorated with composition eagles. A pair of candelabra flanked a Regency bronze and ormolu clock on its mantel. To the right of the fireplace and in front of a chesterfield with upholstered back and arms sat a small *étagère* on top of which a blue and white porcelain tea setting stood artfully arranged on an elaborate lace doily. In fact, Karl—at least that had been part of his name; he couldn't remember the balance of it, try as he might—held a half-full cup in his hand. He drained it, then set it down on top of the mantel. Behind the overstuffed sofa, a large window admitted light into the airy room. Lace draperies were drawn back to either side of it and four panes of glass set in its sash. Outside, the sky was overcast and snow fell. As his eyes trailed down from the casements and curtains to the floor, Karl noticed the royal-blue Wilton carpet he stood on and saw that he wore a pair of drab gray trousers and black oxfords. He didn't know where he was, whose house he stood in, though this particular sitting room looked vaguely familiar. He might have been in it once before. A cherry-wood desk with a flat top stood on the left side of the marble fireplace. A handsome nickel-center draft lamp with ten-inch opal dome shade and a Rochester chimney rested on the desk, and a framed oval-shaped portrait of a lovely lady hung on the wall above it. Karl stepped forward, took a spill of paper from off the desk, thrust it into the fire, then lit the lamp after removing the chimney and shade, and took a closer look at the painting. The woman had long light-brown hair drawn up in a coiled knot on top of her head. Underneath a dark green jacket with sleeves tugged to her wrists, she wore a taffeta blouse with pearl buttons. A gold locket hung from her neck on a chain. Her face was both narrow and long but her lips were ample, and her brown eyes large and limpid, seemingly serene. This queen's beauty rivaled Helen of Troy's, a face tailor-made for male adoration. He would wager that it had charmed and captivated more than one wayward Paris, perhaps had even driven several to the point of distraction. Karl himself had trouble turning his eyes away from the likeness. But in the end he did and looked across the spacious room (it had two more windows) at the wall opposite the fireplace. More paintings (landscapes not portraits) hung there. A tall, narrow chiffonnier of quarter-sawed bird's-eye maple with an oval French bevel-plate mirror, full-swell front top drawers, and one large compartment below, stood in the corner next to the doorway. A secretary with a carved bust in its pediment and seven shelves, each one full of books sat in the opposite corner, next to the third window. A blue settee and a piano varnished in French burled walnut and equipped with beautiful one-leg trusses, all polished in an attractive manner, reposed in between the two cabinets, underneath the paintings. A colonial-style library table in highly figured sawed oak with a golden finish, standing on four massive curved legs, rested in the middle of the room, and a Grandfather clock stood up against the wall between the second and third windows. Kismet, Lucille, and Romeo lamps sat on the various pieces of furniture, and a handsome black-and-gilt gas chandelier hung from the ceiling. Karl strode across the room up to the chiffonnier, then glanced at the mirror in order to glimpse his reflection. He had piercingly blue eyes, an egg-shaped head, and red wattles hanging from his throat. His scalp stood clearly visible underneath his thinning straw-colored hair. He had on a gray wool jacket cross-barred with narrow bands of various colors, a white shirt with celluloid collar, and a colored madras tie. He looked every inch a schoolteacher which was exactly what he was, even though he couldn't say with any degree of certainty what subjects he taught. He had forgotten, and they would not come to him when he tried to remember, just like his surname would not. Many things refused to yield themselves.

A newspaper lay on top of the bureau underneath the mirror. He unfolded it and saw the banner and the date—*The Centre Democrat*, Friday, December 9, 1898. He took a few steps to his left, then sat down in the settee and began to leaf through the daily, skimming through the headlines and the first paragraphs of several articles that especially caught his interest. A fire devours a Broadway Sky Scraper in New York. Mrs. Samuel Colgate weds Earl of Strafford. In Congress resolution introduced authorizing and directing the committee on military affairs to investigate the war department and the conduct of the Spanish American War. Hurricane does thousands of dollars worth of damage in Jersey City. Wind plays havoc all along Atlantic Coast. Colliery Breakers in Pennsylvania destroyed. Roofs torn off buildings. Church steeple toppled in Cranbury, New York. Panic created in the city hospital when large chimney over the lunatic ward falls down with a crash. Shower of bricks terrorizes inmates. Record snowfall in Pennsylvania.... Report on Hawaii. Congress now has the recommendations of the Commissioners. Three bills formulated. Main one outlines General Plan of Government for the islands.... The Buffalo, Rochester, & Pittsburgh Railroad begins turning out boxcars for its own use at DuBois shop. Every part of DuBois make.... News From Abroad. Emperor William opened the Reichstag. After announcing the introduction of a series of labor and social bills and the completion of the organization of the army, he stated that Germany's relations with all the foreign powers continued to be friendly and the principal object of his policy would be to contribute to the maintenance of peace. Alluding to the war between Spain and the U.S., his majesty said that the German nation would continue to conscientiously and loyally observe neutrality toward both belligerents.... Of Local Interest. Rev. Mathias Krolich gave an entertainment under the auspices of the German Lutheran church on Wednesday evening. He exhibited the marvelous Edison Projecting Kinematograph and gave a fine selection of music, vocal & instrumental, upon the phonograph of the above-named inventor. He exhibited to a large-size audience, which showed its appreciation by many favorable comments. They found the moving pictures astonishing and lifelike and maintain that they need to be seen to be appreciated. Price of admission, ten and twenty cents, was low for the entertainment....

As he turned the page, Karl heard voices—a great deal of bustle and commotion—outside the room, so he got up, stepped through the archway into a close hall with a black-and-brown looped-pile carpet with fancy geometric patterns and walls paneled in oak and immediately felt a gush of cold air. Down the corridor, through a pilastered vestibule chamber, he saw a man hold the entrance door open as two more men carried in a boy on a litter. The man standing at the doorway wore a Klondike cap made of heavy duck with a large visor, a nose protector, and a heavy flap held in place over his face by patent snap-glove fasteners. He stood dressed in a heavy Merton coat and wool kersey trousers and had on a neckerchief and gloves. The other two had mufflers covering the lower halves of their faces. One wore a felt hat and a close-fitting double-breasted jacket of thick cloth. The other had on a bowler and a sage-green hunting coat. After closing the door behind them, the first man conducted them down the hall straight toward Karl. On the way, the man in the green coat bumped into a rosewood table and almost knocked over the solid brass vestal parlor lamp sitting on top of it, its white shade embossed with pink roses entwined with dainty little forget-me-nots. Karl stepped back into the draw-ing room as the men went by. They carried the litter to the end of the hall then turned into a side room. After directing them in, the first man swung around, unfastened the face flap and tore off the cap. He had a fat, sweaty face and a curly brown beard. He looked straight at Karl, and fidgeted with his hands while rocking back and forth on his feet. Finally he spoke. "It's your cousin Reinhold's boy. Little Anton. He's had a terrible accident. I sent Albert to bring the doctor and Lucetta to fetch his mother. By God, Inga, the travails we've had to face this year. Our baby boy, little Frederick, stolen from his crib and thrown into the creek by some culprit who has yet to be apprehended. And now this. Our family might lose another child. And with Reinhold away, answering his nation's call to arms in the Philippine Islands." He shook his head and tears began to flow down his cheeks. Startled at the way he had been addressed, no words at first came to Karl. Then as he opened his mouth to disabuse the obviously overwrought man—to undeceive him and set him right—how could he possibly have mistaken him for his wife?—he heard an interior voice say, "We all answer to her name. You have been asleep for a long time. Naturally you are a bit bewildered. You don't yet know our rules. But whatever you do, you must not edify him, give us away. You must pretend you are this woman—put on a show for them." The voice sounded so peremptory that Karl decided to heed it. For the time being at any rate. He followed the brown-bearded man down the hall and into the end room, where at that moment, the two men lifted the boy onto the bed, one having first pulled back the quilt and covers. The room had purple flocked-stripe wallpaper, looped-pile carpet like that in the hallway, and two windows with green velvet draperies with green and gold tassels. Constructed of high-grade iron, the bedstead had corner posts with large brass knobs and vases. A white enameled steel washstand stood to one side of the bed. A bronze-mounted bureau veneered in fiddle-back mahogany sat at its head, pressed against the wall. The man in the green hunting coat took a match out of his pocket and proceeded to light a lamp that sat on the bureau. Karl stared at the shade after the man replaced it over the lit wick. Little lions' heads stood out prominently from the corners of small glass panels illuminated now by the flickering flame. Each one con-tained a depiction of an oriental landscape: camels and Bedouins in the desert; a domed mosque with many ogee and lancet archways and two slender lofty minarets; an oasis surrounded by date palms and women wearing veils, balancing pitchers on their heads.

The three men took off their coats and hats and laid them down on a lyre-backed chair sitting next to the bureau. The brown-bearded one had on a sweater with an all worsted zigzag weave. The other two wore military-style cheviot work shirts. They pulled down their mufflers to reveal their faces, one an older man with a red beard, the other a clean-shaven lad of twenty. The older man rubbed his hands together and addressed the teary-eyed, chubby-faced man with the brown beard. "The Stipetig boy should soon arrive with Doc Schoffer. Don't blame yourself, Reverend Krolich. You didn't intend for this to happen. You merely wanted to have some fun with the kids. The boy probably ain't seriously hurt. And Schoffer will know what to do." *Krolich*, Karl thought. *That was the name I just saw in the newspaper.* The redbeard now spoke to him. "Ma'am, do you think you might boil some water? The Doc will probably need some when he gets here." Karl nodded his head, and turned around to leave the room. Another man thought him a woman! As he stepped into the hallway, he realized that he didn't know where to find the kitchen, but an inner voice guided him. Following its directions, he went down the hall past the drawing room and into the vestibule, then swung left, going past the foot of a mahogany-balustraded staircase which mounted to the second story, and on through a doorway with a pediment above it into a spacious dining room. An octagonal walnut table with six slat-backed chairs sat in the center of the room underneath a fancy lamp with a polka-dotted cerise dome suspended from the ceiling, its shade band trimmed with glass prisms and pendants. A flat-chase punch bowl sat on the table surrounded by four candles. Karl saw a fireplace and marble-topped sideboard. Three great windows stretched from the floor to the ceiling's cornice, their frames ornamented with beautiful double-encased pilasters on either side. The voice told Karl the kitchen was through the next door. He grasped the knob protruding from the keyhole escutcheon, and pushed the wooden door open. A cast-iron coal stove with a pipe of sheet steel connecting to the flue stood in the corner next to the dry sink. Karl could smell food cooking in the oven. He lifted the kettle from off a nearby counter top and set it on the range. He heard his own voice: "That's right. Do every thing they want. But if you get a chance to be alone with the child, hold a pillow over his face and smother him." Again the voice seemed imperious. "You will spare him any further suffering, and he won't have the opportunity to bring others into this world. Suffocate him when the occasion presents itself."

Karl realized that he must do as the voice bid him. He had no will of his own. He found a basin underneath the sink and when the kettle began to whistle he filled it with hot water. On his way back to the bedroom, he met a woman and little girl in the vestibule. They had just come in the door. "Mama," the girl said and ran up to Karl. "Careful," he said, "I'm holding a basin full of hot water." He beheld a strikingly beautiful child, but he was not her mother. For a moment he wished that he could call her his own. She wore a perky little hat, her blonde tresses brought forward over her shoulders. She had an ermine scarf wrapped around her throat and both her hands thrust in a chinchilla muff. Attired in a plain brown cloth coat, she sported fancy Blucher-style boots. Karl looked up when the woman asked him where Anton was. She wore a blue flannel jacket, an embroidered *mousseline de soi* fichu, and a large *chapeau* hat with an ostrich feather and had a very worried look on her face. "Follow me," Karl said and led them down the hall. "Put your coats in there," he said, nodding his head in the direction of the drawing room. "I would take them, but, as you can see, I am holding this water." The lady and the little girl stepped into the room. A few moments later, someone knocked at the door. Karl spoke to the girl, who had rejoined him in the hall after taking off her coat. She had on a pink dress with bows at the shoulders and ruffles at the ankles. He didn't know her name. "Darling, would you get that." Then he addressed the woman, who just then came out of the drawing room, having removed her hat and coat and *La Perie* kid gloves. "That must be the doctor," he said. The lady had her dark hair styled in a pompadour and dressed in a white shirtwaist with embroidered collar and cuffs and a cerise-colored crinoline. The little girl opened the door, let the doctor in, then led him up the hall. Karl beheld an old man with a white Vandyke beard attired in a black reefer greatcoat with a storm collar and wearing a stovepipe hat. He gave Karl his bag, then took off his coat and hat and handed them to the lady with the pompadour, whom he addressed as Mrs. Rausch. He had on a dark suit, a white shirt, and a black silk puff tie. "Where's the boy?" he asked. Karl directed him back to the bedroom door. He wouldn't allow the little girl to go in. He told her to make herself useful and go to the kitchen and check on their meal but to be careful not to burn herself when she pulled down the oven door. He and Mrs. Rausch, who had not put down the doctor's hat and coat but held them to her bosom, followed the doctor into the bedroom, and Karl laid the basin of hot water down on the bureau. Schoffer did not seem to want it. The three men made way for him at the side of the bed. He opened his bag and took out a wooden tube with a widened end like a trumpet's bell, which he placed against the boy's chest while he listened at the earpiece at the hollow cylinder's apex. "His breathing is labored and his heartbeat is irregular. How long has he been unconscious?" "About forty minutes," Reverend Krolich answered. The doctor turned the boy's head from side to side and felt under his neck. "There is nothing I can do tonight." "Do you mean to say we're losing him?" Mrs. Rausch asked, her voice suddenly high-pitched and frantic. "Now, Amanda," the doctor responded, taking his hat and coat from her, "did I say that? You must remain calm and stay here with him. There is nothing I can do for him until he regains consciousness. Until then it sits in God's hands." Mrs. Rausch curtsied then dropped to her knees at the foot of the bed and folded her own hands and started to pray. As Schoffer put on his hat and greatcoat, he motioned to Reverend Krolich to accompany him. Karl followed them into the hall and watched them go into the drawing room. They walked up to the fireplace. The doctor took a cigar out of his pocket and lit it with the nickel-plated draft lamp sitting on the cherry-wood desk. He took a few puffs. "You know that painting does not do your wife justice. It makes her look too starched and stiff." "What about the boy?" the brown-bearded man asked. "He has sustained a dangerous concussion, and I believe he may have broken his collar bone. If he survives the night, I think he will make a full recovery. The next several hours remain critical. It really is in God's hands. All I can tell you to do is keep the boy warm. It could go one way as well as the other." He shook his head. "I just don't know. You may remain of more service to the child than I. His condition calls for your special province, not mine." "We'll hold a vigil then," Reverend Krolich said, raising his right hand. "Ask for God's intervention." "Good," Doctor Schoffer replied. "I'll drop by in the morning." The doctor let himself out. Reverend Krolich met Karl in the hallway, and they reentered the room together. The minister told the two men to go home to their suppers, but requested the older man to ask his wife Mrs. Wertz, the younger one his mother Mrs. Halderman, to stop at the parsonage later that night for a prayer vigil. Both ladies were members of the Sheridan circle at the church. He said that he would be especially grateful if Mr. Wertz could pass the word along to any other church members he might think of. Mr. Wertz said that he would be happy to. The two men took their coats and hats and left. Karl saw his opportunity fast approaching. Now if he could just get these other two out of the room. He spoke to the man, his purported husband. "Dear, you must be hungry. I've got dinner fixed. Why don't you and Amanda go to the dining room and help yourselves. I'll stay here and watch Anton." "I'm not leaving his bedside," the woman cried. "Why don't you bring us a tray," Reverend Krolich suggested. "All right," Karl answered. "I'll prepare one."

Bide your time, he thought. You may still get your chance.

He brought them the tray and stood and waited. One by one the members of the Sheridan circle began to arrive. He kept going back and forth from the bedroom to the front door. He took their large picture hats and *chapeaux*, their muffs and scarves of real ermine, mink, chinchilla, and squirrel, and their outer garments of flannel, serge, mohair, and cotton, and laid them on the oak table in the drawing room. Underneath their coats, the ladies of the church wore embroidered chiffon and taffeta allovers with insertions, flouncing effects, trimmings, and ruchings in all the latest designs and combinations. They had on ginghams and madrases; silk, satin, and pongee blouses; plain, striped, and plaid skirts; oxfords with bows, romeos, bluchers, and nullifiers, as well as felt-sole and flexible welt shoes. The group included a few ladies well up in years as well as middle-aged and recently married, youthful women. They all knelt around the bed, bowed their heads, and held one another's hands. Each lady offered a prayer out loud, then they entreated the Lord silently. Finally Pastor Krolich petitioned the Lord: "Almighty Father, spare your young servant Anton Rausch. In the name of Your son, our Lord and Savior, we beseech thee ...." For eight hours they remained at the boy's bedside. The women offered prayers again and again, and the boy's mother wept steadily. Karl hoped that they would grow tired and yearn to leave. Eventually they would want to go. Even Mrs. Rausch would have to retire, then Karl would stand alone with the boy. The ladies on either side of him squeezed his hands slightly. He felt fatigued and drained, himself. He yawned. Sooner or later the session would have to break off. But then the boy lying on the bed opened his eyes, and Karl closed his own.

He opened them to find himself sitting on a folding porch settee on the lawn anterior to a house on a warm summer day. He still wore his gray suit and pants and his black oxfords, and he held a sandalwood fan with a hand-painted floral design embellished with small colored spangles. He waved it in front of his face. Beside him sat a perambulator. The baby inside slept soundly.

Built of partly plastered stone, the three-storied house had an attractive Federal-style portico and a semi-circular north bay, its chimneys brick and its roof slate. Three dormer windows projected from the roof and were enclosed in little houselike structures. Camellias and azaleas bloomed in a formal brick-walled garden on the east side of the house. A cruciform church of quarried stone stood to its west side. A group of people clad in black garb indicative of grief came out the church doors; the woman Amanda Rausch and her son the boy Anton stood among them. Reverend Krolich exited the church last, accompanied by an elderly man with white muttonchops. He carried a crepe wreath under one of his arms. The group made for Karl. The old man bent over and kissed him on the cheek. "And how do you do today, daughter?" he asked. Caught off guard, Karl stammered. "I'm fine," he managed to say after a moment's hesitation. Reverend Krolich meanwhile had lifted the sleeping baby out of its carriage after having laid down the wreath alongside of it. "Frederick looks well, this morning, doesn't he?" he said to the old man. The child stolen from the house! Karl thought. The one they found drowned. What has happened? A moment ago it was winter. Now it's summertime. That baby should be dead. Didn't they just carry that woman's son into my parlor? I sat reading the newspaper. It was December 1898. He bent over and picked up the wreath, a small linen square fluttered at the bottom of it, a verse printed thereon:

ON THE DEATH OF
CASIMIR HENDRIK RAUSCH
July 17, 1898

We place, O gathering brothers! on the door
    This token sad of death's unpitying sway;
A signal that in fellowship no more
    Shall he we mourn be with us night or day.

He was the ready hand, the willing heart,
    A generous nature and a gentle soul—
Yet from our cherish'd brother must we part
    For he has reached death's goal.

Who, when humanity's appealing voice
    Call'd to the blazing scene of wild alarm,
Could, more than he, bid sinking hearts rejoice,
    And shield each drooping sufferer from harm?

Peace to his dust! and to his memory love;
    Long may his image dwell in every breast,
And live the hope that high in realms above
    Our 'parted friend may dwell forever blest.

Our trump no more the vanish'd one shall heed,
    Flames, grief, despair, and death may rage around;
No more to him shall stricken sufferers plead;
    Heaven's trump alone shall call him from the ground.

Then place, O sadden'd brothers! on the door
    This token dear of death's relentless sway,
A signal that in fellowship no more
    Shall he we mourn be with us night or day.

Karl had traveled backward in time! He set the wreath down and began to tremble all over. "A wonderful eulogy, Reverend Krolich," Amanda Rausch said. "The impoverished and needy will truly miss my father-in-law. He always stood willing to help anyone in distress. I only wish Reinhold could have been here. His troopship pulled away from a San Francisco pier two weeks ago. Casimir had begged him not to enlist, but Reinhold felt that it was his duty as an American to help reduce Spanish power in that quarter. Now that he's gone, I don't know who will manage the business." A man wearing a Roelof soft hat and a double-breasted coat broke in: "Yes indeed, Houserville has lost its leading philanthropist. The men at the Monarch Coal Company knew they could always depend on him in a pinch. No one was more indefatigable and successful in making the earth disclose her secrets than the Silesian—as the men liked to call him. The employees at the Mine Engineering Corps will certainly miss their chief. Before anyone else, he realized that the land in and about Houserville stood rich in coal, and he had an uncanny ability when it came to uncovering new beds. He knew where we should dig. Just recently he discovered a new seam at the Ophir mine under the water level, opening the way to thousands of acres as yet untouched and underlying the previously unworked sections. The mine remains a splendid one and puts out one thousand five hundred tons per day when working full time. I can assure you Mrs. Rausch that the business will stand well managed until Mr. Reinhold returns."

Karl listened in amazement. He knew what would happen, what the future would bring. The firm would remain prosperous until Reinhold's return. His mismanagement would bankrupt the concern, and the family would lose a fortune. But how did he know this? Everything remained so strange. What was happening to him? Through some magical process he couldn't even begin to fathom, he had taken this woman's place. Yet he was still himself. Still a man. When he looked into a mirror, he saw his own reflection. Right now he saw that he sported a gray suit. But he didn't appear in his own flesh and no doubt even in his own clothes to these people around him. When they looked at him, they evidently saw her. Her husband, daughter, and father all remained fooled. Had his soul somehow migrated into her body? What does it weigh? he wondered. And if so, for what reason? Why had the voice commanded him to smother that child? He loved children, would do anything to protect them. Now it appeared that some sort of time slip or displacement had taken place. He had traveled backward into the past. A second time. For it seemed to him that he originally came from even further in the future. Otherwise how would he know about the Monarch Mining Company going belly-up? Or did he come from the past? Did he have the gift of prophecy? He had read somewhere about a man in modern-day London who saw a division of Roman soldiers suddenly appear inside a newly quarried section of the underground below the street level of the city. They marched down the tunnel straight through a wall. While digging the tunnel, workers had unearthed Roman artifacts. It seemed as if the soldiers' images were freed and let loose from the rock itself, in which they lay somehow trapped. Sounds can be registered permanently on Mr. Edison's wax cylinders. One can mechanically reproduce them afterward just as one can play moving pictures over and over again on his kinematograph. Did some similar process stand at work in nature? Did ghosts exist? Was he himself one? At any rate, it was July 1898 where before it was December of the same year. What's more, he knew what would happen to this woman's baby boy. Perhaps he could prevent it. Conceivably divine providence had brought him here for a reason. To save the child? Yes, he had the answer. The small band of people around him began to disperse. They said their goodbyes and went their separate ways. They bid him farewell. Rather they bid Inga farewell, but he answered to her name. Reverend Krolich, who placed the baby—still asleep—back in its carriage, picked the wreath up off the ground, strode up to the house and hung it on the door. He came back down the steps and walked up to where Karl sat. "It's a lovely day my dear," he said. "Why don't we take a walk?" Karl pushed the perambulator. They walked past the church and by the little adjoining cemetery enclosed by an iron fence. "Each in his narrow cell forever laid," Reverend Krolich said, "the humble forefathers of the hamlet sleep." A few aged oaks and tall green pines kept constant vigil over their silent graves. Next they passed a tannery which consisted of two immense dry houses and a leach and a hide house. They went by a blacksmith and carpenter's shop, a beam house and a furnace. The streets of the town stood unpaved. Horses pulled buckboards and broughams down them. Karl and Reverend Krolich walked to the end of the lane then strolled up the Front Street of the town. Several people bade them hello. Hitching posts rose in front of each place of business. They passed the bank, a tonsorial parlor, a confectionary, and a steam laundry. Then they advanced up the opera house block, walking by a taxidermist shop and a dry goods emporium before they reached the theater. Everything looked vaguely familiar to Karl, yet he had the sensation that he had something yet to see, something yet to find. But he didn't know what.

He blacked out, then opened his eyes to see that he stood in the dining room of the house. He held a platter in his hands. It had a fancy arbutus floral pattern around its sides; a ham loaf sat in the middle of it. Reverend Krolich, his daughter Lucetta, and the old man with the muttonchops all sat at the table. All three of them still dressed in black. The old man wore a windsor tie, Reverend Krolich the same shield bow he had on earlier in the day when they took their walk. Karl had been one place—on the street. Now he was suddenly somewhere else. Time had passed, but he didn't know what had happened in between. Silverware, cups and saucers, light and thin dishes with a deep gloss and a milk-white glaze, an ornate sugar bowl, a blue sauce boat, a butter dish, and a creamer all sat on the table as did a covered pot from which he would serve coffee. The polka-dot cerise lamp cast a rich ruby glow on the ceiling. Karl laid the platter on the table and sat down in the empty chair between Reverend Krolich and the blonde-haired girl and opposite the old man. Reverend Krolich said the grace and they proceeded to eat the meal. After he put down his fork and knife, the old man addressed his daughter, "Inga, you asked me what I thought of the phenomenon of *déjà vu.* The reincarnationists, like the Hindus we tried to convert to the true faith in India, would say that, when we come to some place we have never traveled to, but feel as if we have been there before, that indeed we have—in a previous lifetime. I think that it is far more likely that we inherit the memories of our ancestors. If we accept this idea of memory inheritance, then we see more than ever the significance of the words, their works live after them. Yes, we owe it to our progeny that our lives and thoughts should stand well ordered, so that future generations shall not suffer through us." Again Karl lost awareness. The next time he opened his eyes two days had elapsed.

During the days and weeks that followed, Karl continued having blackouts. He remained unable to account for the lost time. Several hours would pass by, then whole days—even a week—would go by, in between his periods of perception and revelation. He heard other people complain, "Where did the day go?" But for them, he knew it remained only a way of speaking. They did not lose time, he was sure, like he did. Often he would emerge *in medias res.* Halfway through a conversation with someone or in the middle of some sort of action or activity. Once he opened his eyes to find himself seated at a desk, a pen in his hand. On the paper in front him, he saw a half-a-dozen sketches of a black-and-white cat. On another occasion he found himself in a seamstress shop, standing in front of a full-size maiden's form on roller castors with an extension upright and a heavy reinforced unbreakable wire skirt. Someone had just given the dressmaker an order, but it hadn't been him. Maybe it was the real Inga Krolich? One moment she would stand there, he construed. Then she would fade out and he would fade in. There had to be someone else, for whoever had been there before him had asked the seamstress how to remove yellow stains either from an article of clothing or possibly from her face and hands. The dressmaker started answering the question when Karl became conscious. "You take an ounce of dried rose leaves, add half a pint of white wine vinegar, then let the mixture stand ten days. Draw off the vinegar and add it to a half pint of rosewater. Apply it to the stain and it should come off. I sponge my face with the compound all the time." He learned to be fast on his feet. No matter how disconcerted he might be, he would strive to never let it show. No, his confusion must not manifest itself. He wanted the transition from Inga to Karl to remain imperceptible. Another time he opened his eyes to find himself sitting at the piano in the Krolich drawing room. He heard applause. He looked over his shoulder to see six or seven ladies and three or four gentlemen sitting on slat-back chairs. "Do you mean to say that you actually composed that lovely sonata yourself?" one of the men asked. "I wouldn't believe it, excuse me for declaring this, had it been anyone else than you who said so—I know you would never lie. But upon my honor that composition stands worthy of Haydn or Mozart. Why don't you give us another piece?" "You are very kind," Karl said. "But I feel rather tired." He had never learned how to play the piano. On still another occasion, he "awoke" to find himself falling backwards. It felt like someone had bumped him away. He hit the ground, saw a carriage's wheels rush by. The little girl who had worn the pink dress–his daughter–ran up to him. "Mommy," she said, "we were playing catch and the ball went out in the street. You ran after it just as that carriage came by. It almost hit you."

One day when he had remained conscious for eight or more hours, he came down the staircase to see Reverend Krolich and Dr. Schoffer standing in the vestibule talking. From what they said, he gleaned that Mrs. Krolich stood as the subject of their conversation. He sat down on a step and listened. "Ever since Frederick's birth, she has acted strangely. All of a sudden, for no reason, she will explode in rage. A moment before she seemed tender and responsive. Her face goes blank, and sometimes her lips move as if she talks in her sleep. Her eyes glaze and she stares straight ahead. It's almost like she is going into a trance. Then she blinks, opens her eyes, and her facial expression alters. Sometimes she looks at me with wide-eyed amazement and appears as befuddled and affecting as a lost little child. The next moment she waxes furious and storms up and down the carpet, cursing blasphemously. Then she turns witty and articulate. I just don't know what to expect next. At any given moment, her behavior, her mood, may shift dramatically." "Well Mathias," Dr. Schoffer said, "having a baby is a very emotional experience for a woman. Sudden changes in a mother's demeanor are not at all uncommon, vast hormonal modifications having taken place in her body. After a short while things will return to normal." Karl stood up and went upstairs. That night as he lay in bed, he watched Reverend Krolich undress and put on a muslin nightshirt. He turned over on his side, but Krolich crawled on top of him and kissed him full on the lips. He tried to push the Reverend away. What did he want from him? Didn't he realize that he was a man? Such intimacy could not exist between them. Karl shut his eyes and willed himself away.

The next time he came to, he sat in the drawing room staring at the portrait of the lovely lady. Suddenly he heard a voice.

I'm Albert.

He looked over his shoulder but did not see anyone. Who spoke to me, he asked.

I did.

Who are you? Where are you?

I'm sitting on the chesterfield.

No you aren't. I am.

I see a cherry-wood desk, a marble fireplace, and the portrait of a beautiful woman.

That's exactly what appears to me.

Would you answer a lone question?

If I can, I will.

Do the people here call you by the name Inga?

Yes. Do you know where the real Inga is?

I certainly do.

Karl watched his arm raise and the index finger of his right hand extend and point to his own chest.

She lives in here, but currently she sleeps. I live here also. We all share the same body. The old gentleman wishes to speak with you.

Who's he?

One of us. He determines which of us will come out. He stands smarter and stronger than all the rest of us combined. He has imposed order on our chaos. He tries to keep the family situation stable to insure our safety. He can even banish those of us who do not behave properly when out in the world. He's a strict disciplinarian. He has ordered me to trade places with you, so you and he might talk. He woke me up and told me to concentrate very hard. He said that I could picture everything you saw. That it would come into focus even though I hadn't stepped into the light but just stood on its periphery. I discovered that if I paid attention, I could see through your eyes. He told me to speak to you, that you would hear me. But I dawdle. You and I must trade places. Close your eyes, then open them.

Anton did. He saw that he stood at the edge of a large white circle of light. A face appeared clearly visible within the light, that of a young man. He wore a chaplet of glory on his brow and had closely cropped strawberry blond hair with several prominent cowlicks. His eyes looked sunken. Upright caskets and coffins stood around the light. They had no lids, and the men, women, and children inside them all seemed asleep. Behind the coffins, in the distance, he could see the stars of outer space. He looked at the faces one at a time. They all looked familiar. Karl felt like he had met each of these persons previously. In the recent past. Then he saw the old man with the muttonchops. He looked indistinguishable from Inga Krolich's father, the man at the supper table, except for the fact that he wore a military uniform and a polished steel helmet with a large spread-wing gilt-brass eagle front plate mounted in its center, gilt brass visor trim, studs, and a chin strap secured by gilt rosettes, a cloverleaf spike base and fitting, and, of course, a tall silver-fluted spike. Unlike the others, the old man appeared awake. His eyes stood open. Immediately Karl knew his thoughts. They communicated, as it were, internally. Neither one of them spoke aloud.

Well, you have finally arrived. As Albert told you, I determine who steps into the light and goes into the world. As a little girl, Inga Krolich decided that she didn't want to be herself anymore. Because she withdrew, we others could come. Except for the youngsters, each one of us has certain skills the others need. The women cook and clean and take care of Mrs. Krolich's two children, Lucetta and Frederick. They also sleep with Mr. Krolich. When he crawled on top of you that night, I sent out the Jezebel Harlene to satisfy him. If one of Mrs. Krolich's two children becomes ill, I call forth the physician. The little *Wunderkind* always plays the piano for the Reverend's wife, but only rarely do I allow the other children out into the world. The girl who calls herself Arouette held the consciousness when the ball rolled out into the street in front of the carriage. I let her enter the light so that she could play catch with Lucetta. She drew the pictures of the black-and-white cat. A number of soldiers stand under my command—the man in the tricornered hat; Albert, the infantryman who now holds the consciousness; the aviator, a Major, I believe; and the veteran of the wars in Latin America. They protect the others, especially the children. One rushed into the light to prevent Arouette from running under the horses' hooves. He knocked her away, and you took the consciousness as Mrs. Krolich's body fell to the ground. Do you understand what I say, or do you have any questions you wish to ask of me?

Yes. Who are we? Where did we come from before we arrived here? Are we ghosts?

I don't know. At first I didn't realize that there were others. All I knew was that I lost time. I observed other people closely and realized that what I experienced stood quite different from anything they encountered. I gathered that others had to exist, and over time I established contact with them and found that I had power over them. Once I thought us the spirits either of the dead or of the unborn, but now I'm not so sure. Possibly we remain only different sides of the same person. Perhaps Inga split apart into us? For a long time, I have pondered this question. I have also contemplated whether the different people inside her might solidify into one person, like the various kingdoms and principalities in central Europe joined together to form Germany. Indeed I have come to believe that all existence remains unified and that distinctions within the totality stand unimportant. But I have been unable to effect such a union. Even as we speak, my power diminishes. That is why I called you. Ever since you and the one who came with you arrived here, I have been losing control. He seems more powerful than I am. He can send people out into the world and call them back. He has even awakened Inga from her deep sleep. He steps into the light with her, and I cannot hear what they say, but I have a feeling, a foreboding, that he is up to no good. I am convinced that only you can do battle with him. The time will come when you will have to face him. But not now. Close your eyes and rest. You will need your strength for the struggle that lies ahead.

Karl's lids drooped shut, and blackness closed in on all sides of him.

He heard voices, opened his eyes, and saw two faces—a man's and a woman's—in the white oval, the female the woman whose portrait hung in the drawing room, and the man him! He recognized his reflection: the thinning straw-colored hair, the piercingly blue eyes, the red wattles hanging from the throat. He heard his own voice or rather the voice of his twin for he saw that he himself stood outside the light on the circle's periphery.

You must sacrifice your children and take their sins upon yourself. Like a Dickens' ghost, I will reveal the boy's and girl's futures to you. Frederick will become a bank robber and kidnapper. Lucetta will turn into a drunk and wanton. Better to take their lives now so that they will remain innocent, guiltless. Throw the baby into the creek.

No, Karl thought. He must stop his twin. He would have to drive this adversary out. He looked to the old man for help, raised his head, and saw that all the coffins faced outward. The adversary turned his attention to Karl and addressed him from inside the light.

I've put the others in cold storage. Sent them to limbo. Made them stand in the corner like *we* forced the pupils in our class to do whenever they misbehaved.

I will awaken them, Karl thought. And urge them to unite to oust you. He squeezed between two of the upright coffins, pivoted and saw that both caskets stood empty. He made a circuit around the light, looking into each coffin. They all stood empty. He peered outward into the blackness, the gloom. In the distance, he saw stars, but one by one they began to extinguish like candles in a Tenebrae church service, until only one remains burning behind or under the altar, leaving the church in darkness. Karl turned around and faced the light. He stood alone. He could expect no help from any of the others. He had to dislodge the adversary. He tried to enter the light, but his foe's will proved stronger than his own. He felt like he walked into a wall. He simply could not pass through. The adversary began to laugh. Karl closed his eyes and concentrated hard. When he opened them, he found himself out in the world standing on a bridge looking down. He saw the bundle fall, then strike the water which bespattered and splashed about it. He heard a scream behind him. He whirled around and saw his daughter—the girl with the blonde tresses. Both her hands clenched into fists. "Mother," she said. "You dropped Frederick into the water." He heard the adversary's laughter inside his head.

He turned away from the light and faced the darkness and sobbed and wailed. Again everything went black.

Anton Karl Rausch lifted his heavy, rheumy lids to see that he lay in his hospital bed. The side rails were up, and Mr. Frein sat in his invalid chair. Rausch could still hear the echo of many voices inside his head. He waited for the daily routine to begin with the arrival of the morning aide, either Shirley or Walker. This morning Shirley entered the room. She seemed surprised to see him awake and ran to his bedside. She pushed the call bell, and a few minutes later a nurse stepped into the room. "Mr. Rausch is alert," Shirley said, "He has come out of his coma! Look!" The nurse also appeared startled. She took his vitals and shook her head. "Just when we receive the order to send him to Mercy Hospital to have a gastrotomy tube inserted," she said, "he regains consciousness. Figure that. Well, I'll call Dr. Sighn and see what he wants to do." The nurse left the room, and Shirley pushed Mr. Frein out into the hall. Throughout the day, nurses checked in on him regularly. But they did not get him out of bed. An LPN applied creams, ointments, and a dry sterile dressing to the ulcer on his lower left shin. An RN listened to his heart with a stethoscope. An aide came in and fed him with a syringe. Later another aide undid his diaper and sat him on a bedpan, but he did not have to go. The aide also emptied the bag which contained the urine drawn off from his catheters. When the doctor made his rounds later that afternoon, he examined him. He, too, seemed dumbfounded. Everyone who entered the room, in fact, expressed amazement and disbelief at Anton's alert state. He heard everything they said. As usual, they spoke as if he did not stand present. One nurse said, "It's a shame he didn't die. When he went into congestive heart failure, we thought everything was over with him. But we guessed wrong. His heartbeat stabilized. Yet he remained comatose. Dr. Sighn said it remained likely that he would take another stroke or have a heart attack, but he didn't, so he wrote out the order to have the g-tube inserted, and then what happens? The old bugger opens his eyes. You know the three-to-eleven girls even had a pool going as to when he would kick off. I'm glad I didn't put any money down." "Yes," the aide standing beside her said, "it's a shame. Especially since he remains in a vegetative state and is disoriented times three. Think of what his family must feel like. He's been this way, what four-and-a-half years now? Every bit of money he saved has been spent for his care here, and he will never get any better. It really is sad to see them linger so." Neither woman noticed the tears coursing down his cheek.

That evening he had a visit from his granddaughter Grette. He hadn't seen her for years. She had aged. Her face had wrinkled and her blonde hair had grayed somewhat. She only stayed a few minutes. She didn't even sit down. She just stood at the foot of his bed, then turned around and hurried away. The odd thing was that an oriental man a head shorter than herself accompanied her. She held his hand. He looked like one of the mestizos, those people of mixed blood, that Anton's father had fought against while stationed in the Philippine Islands. Anton noticed the wedding ring glinting on his granddaughter's right hand. Could Grette actually have married this man? The prospect appalled and nauseated him. He could think of little else until finally he managed to drift off to sleep when an aide turned down the lights several hours later. How could a woman of northern European descent consent to give herself to a Malay or a Chinaman? She had passed the childbearing years. That partially mitigated her offence. At least no interbreeding of the races, no miscegenation, would occur. A voice in his dream had said that your children will always disappoint you. The truth of that statement rang home for him. Grette had remained unlucky in her choice of men. First she married a doctor, but he had turned out a drunk and adulterer. A curse had been put on his family generations before when his forebear ordered two widow women off Houser land. But now she had made an even worse mistake if indeed she had wed the mestizo. He hoped that she had not.

The following day, he also remained in bed. Every two hours, either two aides or else an LPN and an aide would reposition him on the mattress, move him from off his back onto his side or from his side onto his stomach. Once more they syringe fed him. He drifted in and out, slept fitfully throughout the day. Once or twice, he started to dream. He thought he heard voices. They seemed to come from far away. Someone told his great-grandson Harlan to put the barrel of a gun into his mouth, then to slowly squeeze—not jerk—the trigger.

It seemed to Anton that he could see his great-grandson doing what the voice bid. He remembered what the little girl in his dream —the one who so resembled his own daughter Hedi—had said. That Harlan must live in order for her to be born. No, Anton thought. Don't do it. He saw Harlan remove the gun from out of his mouth, then he awoke and beheld the white wall.

He had loved Hedi so much. Why did she have to die so young? He remembered the night she had been conceived. It was so strange. He and Helen had the same dream. They both visualized having a daughter who would grow up to be a musician. Their dreams it seemed were identical in every detail. He remembered that in both of them the little girl at a very young age picked up two sticks and began to draw the one across the other as if she held a fiddle and a bow. Now his dreams, his nightmares, seemed more real to him than the images that flooded though his eyes while awake.

Two more days passed before they got him up in the chair. Again the aides wheeled him through the hallways of Colonial Court Manor. Again he had to look at the other moribund. Once more they pushed him into the elevator and took him down to the dining room. Someone had taped cardboard cutouts of Tom Turkeys, Pilgrims and Indians to the walls. The first feeders got up from the tables and began shuffling out the doors, as the aides brought in the living dead in their invalid chairs. Beside each corpse sat a young man or young woman. A few of the patients were spoon fed like infants in high chairs. But most had to have their jaws pried open and then have a syringe inserted into their mouths. Once more an aide forced the pureed slop down his gullet. He had to swallow. He could do nothing else but swallow.

They wheeled him from the dining room to the elevator, then took him back to his room. The aide switched on his radio. Hell music issued from it. Harsh, cacophonous noise. Percussive and Negroid. Mercifully the volume remained low. For the next several hours, he had to listen to it and to Frein, who kept on saying, "I don't want to be here. Can't you hear? I wanna go home." Finally they came to take him down to lunch. Again they force-fed him. Afterwards someone pushed him to the activity lounge. Other sufferers wheeled themselves down the hallway. The room stood full of patients. A man walked in with a bundle of books under his arm, sat down at the table, and began reading poetry. Anton nodded, then awoke to find himself in the same room, but now a small jazz band performed before the guests. He listened wearily and hoped that the concert would end quickly. When it did, aides began to appear at the door. They wheeled the patients one by one out of the room. Anton watched the musicians pack their instruments into their cases. Finally an aide took him out. Instead of to the elevator, the aide wheeled him to the "beauty parlor" for a trim and a shave. As the beautician cut his hair, he looked at the two ladies sitting under the hair dryers. One had a tube coming out her nose. She had cataracts in both eyes and no teeth, and her mouth pursed open like a giant letter o. The other pounded on her geri-chair tray with both her fists and shouted over and over again, "God damn son of a bitch. God damn son of a bitch."

After the beautician finished with him, he had to wait twenty-five minutes before an aide finally arrived to take him up to his room. She and another aide got him out of the chair and put him into bed. One of them said: "We will wake you up at supper time." He never wished to go down to that dining room again.

Sweet Jesus, he thought. Take me home.

He shut his eyes and almost immediately went to sleep. After some time had passed, he again heard voices above him. He made out the words "again comatose" and "possible CVA" but then the voices faded and he heard nothing. He opened his eyes, but everything remained pitch black. He wondered if he was dead, but, after a few minutes, he thought he could make out his heart beating but that was the only sound that he heard. He knew time persisted. His heart thumped like a metronome. He did not lie paralyzed in nothingness and no-time. Measurable duration had not yet ceased. Yet while he knew that the clock continued to tick, he did not ever know at any given period or moment exactly how much time had passed. He had no way of gauging its progression. He started totaling his heart beats but would lose count and have to start over. Finally he gave it up, but time kept elapsing and expiring.

Was it only several hours, several days, perhaps a week, that had gone by? Or had an entire year rolled round? He had no way of knowing. Maybe he would sleep for twenty years like Rip Van Winkle. Or perhaps fifty or even one hundred years? He loved the blackness and was content to stay in it. He only hoped that one day he would not wake up and see the white wall yet again.

More time went by—how much he didn't know—then once more he began to hear voices. They came from far in the distance. He had to listen carefully to make out what was said. It appeared that two people planned to rob a bank:

This will go just fine. The first thing you'll need is a bike.

No I don't. You never used one until you had me for driver.

But you can get away from the bank faster on bike than foot.

Nonetheless I won't be parked at any great distance. Sure. Real close. I'll get back behind the wheel within five minutes....

Anton could see a pinpoint of white light in the distance. He stood up and walked out of the shadows toward it. But each step closer he took, the light bounced backwards, withdrew further into the distance. He had to concentrate very hard. It took an extreme effort of the will to secure the light in one place. But he had the willpower. The determination and resolution to fix the light, to rivet it down, and make it stationary, until he could traverse the distance between him and it and reach its rim. He saw two faces in the light. One a silhouetted profile, a shadow really. He could make out none of its features, yet he knew, he was certain, it was Al. The other face he recognized as his great-grandson's. He distinguished the coal-black hair, the button nose and the bright blue eyes. Anton found that through close mental application, exclusive attention, he could see through those eyes out into the world. He stared up at the yellow sun, high and small in the white sky, and saw a sharp-shinned hawk soaring seventy feet above the ground. Then he looked about him and saw that he, or rather Harlan, stood in a memorial park. Pine trees swayed in the wind. In between the trunks, he could see a town stretched out before him. But he could not hold the picture in focus. His eyelids drooped. He opened them to find that two-in-one he and Harlan walked through a shopping mall. He knew that Harlan must not rob this bank. He had failed in the past and had not saved Frederick Krolich. On that occasion, the adversary had defeated him. Now he was being given a second chance to redeem himself. He mustn't disappoint again. Although he did not open his mouth, he communicated with his great-grandson. He thought about the good times they had shared together when Harlan was a boy. He reawakened memories in

Harlan. But before long he began to nod off. It took a supreme effort to keep his eyes open. But at last they closed, and he found himself standing again at the lip of the white circle of light. The adversary again proved too strong. Now he taunted Harlan, called him a sissy and a coward.

Just go in and do it and get it over with.

You're nothing but a pussy. A dickless little girl.

Harlan is a chicken. Harlan is a mama's boy.

Blot him out, Anton thought. Think of your children's faces. They will drive him away. Experience the continuity of our love to you and through you to your children. An umbilical cord that unites you to your parents and grandparents and above all to me. You serve as a conduit for that love. Let it flow through you and onto your children. Remember the culvert you crawled through in the park ... crawled through to me.

Harlan made his decision. Anton watched as his great-grandson drove the adversary out of the light into the shadows. Then he turned his head away from the glimmer and faced the darkness himself. He felt very tired. Fatigued and exhausted. He knew that if he closed his eyes, he would never open them again. But he did not care. He would accept, he would rejoice in, annihilation and non-entity.

Just at that moment, on the verge, on the threshold, of his ceasing to be, as his eyelids began to droop, he had a last vision. A final epiphany.

He had led other lives. He had composed heroic operas and had written the greatest plays and music dramas the planet had ever known as well as served as Germany's most exalted statesman!

He had been Wagner, Bismarck, and Shakespeare. He had been everyone who ever lived.

The baser part of him would decay and rot, but that did not matter. His soul would persist and persevere. He would live on in his work. Life stood a refining process, and he had refined himself into sounds—such sounds and words. What glorious, magnificent words. That part of him would never cease to be.

Appendix

Two short stories and an honors essay by Michael Bolanger

The two prentice pieces and the University Scholar Honors Thesis that follow record Michael Bolanger's infatuation with the music and ideas of Richard Wagner. His enthusiasm and liking for the German composer developed gradually. As a boy, he preferred the playful and rollicking symphonies of Haydn and Mozart with their exuberant, joyous folk-inspired melodies, their imaginative use of instruments, innovative structures, predilection for contrapuntal textures, and the intensity of their emotional expression. Later the impressionism of Debussy enchanted him with its shimmering veiled sounds, and its parallel or gliding chords. The "program" symphonies of Hector Berlioz also captivated him. Berlioz believed in the necessity of tying a musical composition to a literary idea. The Frenchman showed great skill in arranging both sounds and words, and Michael especially admired the program notes for his great five-movement symphony of 1830: the most amazing first symphony ever composed. Wagner said that the work would have made Beethoven smile but added that the first movement of Beethoven's Fifth where Death came rapping on the door seemed an act of kindness in comparison. Berlioz had the notes for his *Episode in the Life of an Artist* printed and distributed in the hall on the day of the symphony's premiere. Michael considered Berlioz's sketch which clearly reflected the composer's infatuation with the English actress Harriet Smithson a literary composition of the first order. In the prose poem, the hero-composer pines for the love of an elusive, ideal woman who embodies everything he seeks. Every time the beloved's image appears before the mind's eye of the young musician, he links it with a musical thought whose character, passionate but at the same time noble, he finds similar to the one he attributes to the beloved. This signature motif or *idée fixe* representing Harriet Smithson recurs and is transformed in each of the symphony's five movements. As in Beethoven's Pastoral Symphony, each movement has its own title. During the course of the *Symphonie fantastique*, the musician experiences terrible visions under the influence of opium which he ingests in a suicide attempt, convinced that his love goes unappreciated. The narcotic proves too weak to kill him, but, as he plunges into a deep sleep, he dreams that he murders his beloved, receives a sentence of death and witnesses his own execution in an out-of-body experience. A frightful troop of ghosts, monsters and demons gather to celebrate his funeral and the musician hears strange noises, groans, and peals of laughter. The beloved's motif sounds a final time, but shorn of its character of nobility and shyness, it devolves into a mere dance tune, trivial and grotesque. If Berlioz aimed at a fusion of the arts in his symphony by insisting that his listeners read his extramusical program before they heard his work, Wagner spent his life trying to achieve the ideal of the *Gesamtkunstwerk*. Not only did he influence virtually every composer of the succeeding generation, he also had an enormous impact on the literature of both the nineteenth and twentieth centuries. Two of Michael's favorite authors Thomas Mann and Marcel Proust worshipped the composer and adopted his leitmotif technique in their fiction. Although he claimed that he did not care for Wagnerian opera, another titan of modern literature James Joyce remained perhaps the most Wagnerian author of all. He filled both *Ulysses* and *Finnegans Wake* with references to the composer's work, and the *Wake* itself stood perhaps as the ultimate realization of the *Gesamtkunstwerk*. French romantic composers and the literary geniuses of the twentieth century sparked Michael's interest in Wagner, as did his chance encounter with Delone Frailey, the first true Wagnerite of his acquaintance.

Michael had to agree with his beloved author Mann that Wagner's art remained "dubious" and "highly suspect" but also that once one had really drunk deeply of Wagner's music one became intoxicated for life. In his Honors Thesis at Herneshopple University, he attempted to show that of all Mann's works the great tetrology of his middle period the novel *Joseph and His Brothers* stood the most beholden to Wagner's art. Years later, he cannibalized from this essay, especially from the passages dealing with the opera *Parsifal*, when he wrote his novel concerning the death of Henry James *The Two Masters*.

Volsung's Song

The record dropped. The stylus rose automatically and lowered onto the vinyl. For a moment or two, only the surface noise—the ticks and the pops—could be heard. Then the music—the introductory orchestral passage followed by the singing of Kirsten Flagstad—began:

Zu neuen Taten
teurer Helde
wie lieb' ich dich.
liess ich dich nicht?
Ein einzig Sorgen
lässt mich säumen:
dass dir zu wenig
mein Wert gewann!

Was Götter mich wiesen
gab ich dir:
heiliger Runen
reichen Hort:
doch meiner Stärke
magdlichen Stamm
nahm mir der Held,
dem ich nun mich neige.

Des Wissens bar
doch des Wunsches voll:
an Liebe reich
doch ledig der Kraft:
mögst du die Arme
nicht verachten,
die dir nur gönnen,
nicht geben mehr kann!

Accompanied by the static, Flagstad's rendition of Brünnhilde's lines remained audible; Thomas could barely hear the Covet Garden orchestra. In actuality, the theater must have reverberated with sound when maestro Furtwängler lifted his baton and commenced conducting. An entirely different experience, Thomas thought, to have heard the performance live. Although loud, the sound, he felt, would not have been harsh or brassy, and in fact, during the soft passages, it would have had a smooth buoyant quality, floating up from the pit like a beach ball carried out to sea by a slow wave. And Flagstad? The strength and beauty of her voice must have astounded the audience. Even from this low fidelity recording, one could tell that she sang with icy, cold perfection. He'd have given anything to have actually sat in the stands. He had only this to listen to. Only this poor ghost of the classic performance had been captured for posterity, for him.

Immortal Siegfried heard Brünnhilde and answered her; the voice of Lauritz Melchior, the heldentenor of the century, issued from the speakers and rose momentarily above the static. But even this voice, perhaps the most powerful of all Wagnerian voices, could not conquer the ticks and pops for long. But Siegfried could conquer the world for his Brünnhilde. Her voice inspired and encouraged him:

> Willst du mir Minne schenken,
> gedenke deiner nur,
> gedenke deiner Taten,
> gedenk' des wilden Feuers
> das furchtlos du durchschrittest,
> da den Fels es rings umbrann.

His past accomplishments flashed before him. Once more he had confidence in himself. He could do it again. He'd convince himself that he could, that he must!

Siegfried! Siegfried! Think of the fire you walked through, of the dragon you killed. *Nicht geben mehr kann!* It's up to you, now. You're on you're own. What your father knew, he gave to you. No one could have prepared you better than he. You had all the advantages. Prove now that you stand worthy of them.

No, you have already done that, but you need to continue to effloresce, to produce and produce if you aspire to become the new superman of letters. You took the shards of Siegmund's sword and forged them back together. You utilized all that your father left behind for you. With that sword, with Nothung, you slew Fafner and won the ring. You can accomplish all that you want.

Listen to Brünnhilde. She speaks to you like those other goddesses of inspiration spoke to the two old blind men, the Greek and the Englishman, the poets of the fall of Troy and the fall of man! Magic fire surrounds you. The muses have heard and granted your request. This cockpit can hold the vasty fields of France. We can cram within this wooden O the very casques that did affright the air at Agincourt! Listen. Brünnhilde now addresses her fellow gods. She says that you and she have become forever joined. That you have spoken the vows of marriage and that even the deities themselves cannot now separate you. Listen to the muse. Listen to, follow, her instructions. She inspires you to go out into the world and win new glory, to bring fame and renown to her. That broader horizons, new adventures, await you. Give her the ring and take her horse Grane. Promise her that you will act as her arm. Everything that you win you will lie at her feet. Hail her as she hails you. Then go out into the world. Depart. Take up all the new challenges, and you will scale new heights. Do what you were born to do.

Heil! Heil! Heil! Heil!

Write the great American novel.

Once again the tone arm rested on the pick-up clip. Thomas opened the notebook and reached for his pen.

Thomas' eyes widened, and he sat bolt upright in bed. Both alarm clocks rang. They sat on his dresser on the other side of the room. He knew that he would simply turn them off and remain in bed if, like most people, he kept them beside his pillow. But by putting them where he did, he forced himself to get up. He hated nothing more than the sound of a ringing alarm clock. He had to stop it.

He kicked off the sheets, jumped out onto the floor and darted to the wall to find the light switch. On his way he tripped over his phonograph and fell on his face, bumping his knee on top of the portable record player and badly bruising it. He jumped up, swore, and hopped on one foot to the wall where he found the light switch, turned on the lights, and attacked the shrieking alarm clocks. The room again quiet, Thomas looked down at his knee to see that it bled. He wiped the wound with his hand. It would stop in a little while. He opened his closet door, took out a shirt and a pair of pants and slipped them on. He walked across the room, through the flotsam and jetsam of torn and crumpled up notebook paper. He picked up a page, read it, and tossed it back onto the floor. He picked up several more sheets and read them. One by one, he let them drop and shook his head. Then he sat down in a wicker chair and put on his socks and shoes.

All that work last night and for what—this? What did you do last night? Nothing, nothing, nothing but this?

He wanted to kick the pages in every direction, overturn his dresser, scream at the top of his lungs, and put his fist through his bedroom door. But he knew that his parents, sister, and grandmother all still slept. Perhaps his grandmother was right, and he should think of a more realistic career. What could he become? A teacher, a priest, an eye doctor? He could have such a rewarding life and do such significant things in any one of those wonderful professions. He had stepped out of his room into the hallway. He wanted to slam his door. He'd given anything to have been able to slam it. But he didn't. He ran down the hallway and down the stairs. He only had thirty minutes to get to his physics class, and Dr. Hammond didn't like stragglers. No breakfast today. He'd have to wait until lunch.

He heard his grandmother's voice behind him: "Tom, is that you?"

"Yes, Grandma."

"Getting ready to go to school?"

"That's right. Say, I didn't wake you, did I?"

"You didn't. Your alarm clocks did."

"I'm sorry about that. I only meant to get myself up."

"That's all right, but you haven't eaten yet. I'll come down and fix you some breakfast."

"No, that's all right. I don't have time. I'll pick something up after class."

"Drive carefully now and not too fast."

"I won't."

"You don't want to get into a wreck or anything?"

"Really, Grandma, I'll be careful."

"Nothing's worth risking your neck for. If you have to rush off somewhere today, you'll have to tomorrow too, and then the day after that. You'll end up putting your life on the line for things that really don't count. That's the truth, Tom. I wouldn't lie to you."

"Don't worry. I'll drive safely, but I really must go. I'll arrive late as it is."

"Okay, but remember—"

"I know. I know. To be careful."

Thomas skipped down the stairs into the living room, took a book out of his father's bookcase to read after class, opened the front door, stepped outside, then realized he had forgotten his keys. He swung around, went back inside, and scooped them off the mantle. Again he went through the door, this time pulling it shut behind him. Perhaps what he had written wasn't so bad after all? Even if he found the pages substandard, they represented only one night's work. He'd start back at it tonight. He unlocked the car, got in, pulled the door shut, and put the key in the ignition. He had, after all, written several very fine short stories. His teachers said that they had shown promise. He felt confident that he would again write well and with increasing ease. He backed down the driveway then punched the accelerator. He would certainly arrive late and incur his instructor's wrath, but, as he saw little traffic and no patrol cars, he put the needle in the red.

Son of the Sun

"You're not going to try and find those caves, are you?"

"No, I'm just going to take a hike through the woods."

"I don't want you to look for those caves. Do you hear?"

"I'm not going to look for them. I just want—"

"Well see that you don't."

"I said I wasn't. I just want—don't interrupt—to take one last look at the farm and woods."

"Dress warmly then."

"Don't worry, I will."

Thomas finished packing his knapsack. He had everything he needed—a baseball helmet, rope, chalk, an old coat, and two flashlights—as well as two sandwiches and a couple of apples. What did she know about spelunking? Besides, his grandfather had said the caves remained safe. He would have taken him to them.

Was it cold outside? The weather report called for a cold day. And for snow showers, but it didn't look like it would snow. The sun shone and yes clouds raced in the sky, but not snowclouds white fleecy clouds and not too many of them. It looked comfortable outside. In fact—the temperature hadn't dropped—except for last night—below fifty degrees in a month, strange highs for this time of year, but he had read somewhere—perhaps in his grandfather's copy of "The Farmers' Almanac"—to expect a mild winter, that it might not snow until after Christmas. That suited him fine. No snow, no snow days. Longer summer vacation, more time to read and write extensively.

No, it didn't look cold outside. But last night, temperatures dropped, and it got cold as hell out. But although it had rained almost everyday, it had remained warm for the last several weeks, exactly what "The Farmers' Almanac" or whatever he had read predicted for November: warm but wet weather, and it said that in December—today marked the first—the temperature would turn warm and sunny. And the sun did shine. It looked warm out too. He probably wouldn't even need a coat. He'd go out and check.

He rushed back into the house. In just that little time, he froze his ass off! It hadn't warmed up a bit. Cruel and deceptive sun! He'd need the coat. He'd need it inside the caves anyway. He lifted the jacket out of his knapsack—at least it wouldn't snow on a sunny day like today—and put it on.

"Tom, are you still there?"

"Yes, Grandmother."

"Can I talk to you for a moment?"

"Yeah, sure," he said and walked into the living room, where his grandmother sat on the sofa.

"Tom—your parents—they do want me to come live with you, don't they?"

"You know they do. You didn't have to ask me that."

"You're sure now, aren't you?"

"I'm sure I'm sure. Why do you have to ask such a silly question?"

"Tom, you're not just saying that to make me feel good? You're telling me the truth?"

Lines from a soap opera. She watches them everyday. Lives in a soap opera world. But go along. Play your part. Make her happy.

"Gram, you know how much we care about you. We want you to come live with us. We really do."

"Thank you, Tom. Thank you for saying that," she returned, and then for a moment or so the only sounds one could hear were the noises coming from outside and the ticking of the grandfather clock. "Grandma, I must go. It's hot inside with this coat on, and I want to get out in the woods before it starts snowing. You know they said it would today. Well, I'll come back in an hour or so. I'll see you then."

He walked back to where his knapsack sat, hoisted it over his shoulders, opened the door, and stepped outside. The grandfather clock struck ten.

"Tom, you're not going to try and find those caves?"

"No, Grandmother, I'm not," he said and shut the door.

Having walked through the former cornfields, he could see the woods and the hill ahead of him. The hill had never belonged to his grandfather, but he had found the caves there. Thomas had seen the hill before, but had never climbed up it.

His grandfather had cleared the land upon which he walked just last spring, but no one had planted corn in it that year. What a terrible waste. Already nature had begun to reclaim it. Timothy, ragweed and Queen Anne's Lace again abundantly sprung from the ground, and to his left, the pond—dug last May when his grandfather last plowed the fields; covered today by a thin layer of ice—never saw a fish stocked. All that work, sweat, effort for nothing, nothing. Damn God and Goddamn. It remained freezing cold, too cold for caving or hiking. This summer it would warm up though. That would be when to cave: during the summer. But he couldn't then; he wouldn't have time. Maybe it'd rain all summer like it did last year at Governor's School. Then he'd find it easy to work. But what if he had to start college? That would ruin everything.

He put his hands—he wished that he had brought gloves—into his pockets, but his fingers remained just as cold inside the pockets as out.

He found it hard to work now. School ate up his time and interfered. Whether A.P. English, Advanced Biology, or P.O.D., some subject always demanded extra effort. He had managed to begin, had managed to do the hardest thing, and he stood pleased, genuinely pleased with all that he had written. But carrying through would become increasingly difficult. TM characterized the process correctly when he called it a descent into hell in the prelude to his quadripartite work, the beautiful god invention of Joseph and His Brothers. What intellection. What massive erudition. And the ultimate humanism and geniality of his cosmogony, a soul-light man creating the universe; god—albeit a sympathetic, understanding god—only helping; his explanation wise and winsome of how the mythic past merges with the prophetic future to form an eternal present. A feast of life and death in which two conflicting principles, those of the Spirit and of the Soul, so contend with each other that it remained inconclusive which principle actually stood as the death principle. It all remained brilliant, breathtaking, and thought provoking. But calling the soul man's—Adam Qadmon's—creation of the earth a descent into hell, calling his own god invention also a descent into hell, meaning both a descent into the subconscious, the collective unconscious—the deep well out of which all creativity stems—and the struggle with stubborn, refractory matter, the form becoming more important than the idea—there TM came across an eternal truth. Yes, Thomas found it hard to continue writing. Damn hard. But if he had trouble making headway now, how would he get anything done while enrolled in college and taking university courses? Still somehow he'd make the sacrifice. Down, down, down into the depths he'd go. He saw it as his duty. While praising his writing one of his friends had proclaimed him hot shit. Which friend? He remembered: Jim. Jim, you're the rock on whom I will build my church. Make the sacrifice? Sure he'd make it. He considered it his duty to make it. Father please do not let this cup pass from me! People of Judea, spare Barabbas, crucify me! Thomas Mann said that his artist's sensibility resulted from the exotic admixture of his blood. No Portuguese/South American Indian blood coursed through Tom Englehardt's veins, but a little North American Indian did. And with a name like Englehardt, a lot of German burgher blood ran in him too. Maybe even some of the same blood. Then the two of them would have more in common than just their first names. Perhaps future, past, and present could fuse together in a single moment of time. After all a name stands all important. Tommy M. said so in his god invention, where all the Egyptian pharaohs upon ascending to the throne took the name Amun-is-satisfied. Once they wore the double crown, they all stood as sons of the Sun and rulers of the earth.

He reached the woods, and oaks, maples, and elms surrounded him. Ahead he could see the barbed wire fence that marked the end of his grandfather's property and beyond it the dirt road that led to the top of the hill. He had been named after his grandfather. He reached the fence, lifted up the lowest rung of the barbed wire in order to crawl under it, and cut the second and third fingers of his right hand on a barb. Goddamn, shit, fuck! Immediately, as hard as he could, he pressed the fingers (direct pressure, use direct pressure) into his thigh. Must stop the bleeding. Gotta stop it. Everything depends on stopping it. Still bleeding? Yes, it still bled. Press harder. Harder. Still not stopping. What should I do? I know, I know....

He opened the knapsack, took out a sandwich, put it between the bleeding fingers and the palm of the other hand, pressing fingers and palm together as tightly as he could; the bleeding stopped.

What, are you crazy? If someone saw you just now, they'd think that you had a screw loose or that you had gone off your nut. You're an idiot, a fool. Why does bleeding scare you so much? The time you hit your head on the wall, the ambulance? That happened seven years ago. You're an asshole, an idiot asshole.

He tossed what remained of the sandwich into the dirt. Body and Blood of Our Lord. But no hundred-handed or one-eyed monsters sprang up from it, but then again the blood had not come from the genitals. No one had snipped off his genitals and thrown them into the sea, nor did a starry-eyed Phallus Goddess arise from the waves. Disregarding a no-trespassing sign, he crawled under the fence and began to walk up the dirt road.

He was there. He was. He was finally there. It had taken him a long time, an hour, maybe an hour and a half, to climb to the top of the hill (he wasn't used to climbing hills this big—the hill had the highest elevation of any hill in the county—and had to stop several times on the way up). But he stood on the hilltop now. He remembered his grandfather had said something about three pines marking the entrance to the caves. There they stood. Three pines on top of a huge rock. A spring ran near the entrance too. He saw the water purl. He stood up. No, he'd sit back down and eat the remaining apple first. He had eaten the other one as well as the last sandwich on the climb.

The sky had progressively clouded over. The temperature had also risen a few degrees, and it had become more comfortable outside. Like a hand thrust in and out of a pocket, the sun came out from underneath then darted back behind a cloud. Again and again the sun vanished. Again and again it reappeared. Then the sun disappeared but did not reappear. Would Tom witness the Ragnarök? Did the twilight of the Gods stand near at hand? Has Apollo's chariot fallen from the skies? Has Fenrir the wolf's son—has Odin's bane's son—supped?

The atmosphere stood completely altered—he wished that the sun would come out. How he yearned to again behold it. Prometheus, embark on thy sacred journey; bring us thy subjects, Fire—the hill itself didn't seem especially pleasing to look at now. The absence of sunlight made all the difference in the world. The sunlight made the hill beautiful and attractive, lent it a special aura and magnetism, made it a thing which could engross a mind. But it could cause anything—broken coke bottles, rain rusted beer cans, worn-down tenement buildings, battlefield bodies (dead soldier boy bodies)—to appear that way. The right touch of sun will always bring out colors and make things captivating. Eyesores become eyesores only on sunless days. Cruel deceptive Sun! Deceptive lying Sun! But without the sun, without its magic life-giving fire, without light, nothing could be beautiful, nothing at all. Nothing could be born. Nothing could die. Without the daily golden shower of the sun's rays (Ancrisius shut Danae up in a brazen underground chamber in his palace, but Zeus loved her and entered the chamber in the form of a shower of gold and lay with her), no plant could sprout from out of the earth, nor any animal rise from out of the sea. Cold perpetual night. Sunlight! Sunlight! Needed. Necessary for life: $6CO_2 + 12H_2O + \text{light c-h-l-o-r-o-p-h-y-l-l}> 6O_2 + C_6H_{12}O_6 + 6H_2O$. And did not the sun out of itself give birth to the planets?

He wanted the sun to reappear. Please come out sun. Please, please, come out. He sat there waiting for it to reappear. Jim Morrison's song, how did it go? Since we came out of Eden, we have been waiting for the sun. Or something like that. He had heard it only once. Morrison wanted to sing his songs, and he wanted to write his books. He'd write many books, and all his books would succeed. He would have no failures. Indeed, some of his novels would rise to greatness. His twelfth book for instance. What would it be about? A woman. He'd create a great female character like Eustacia Vye or Rosalie von Tümmler or Potiphar's wife. He wanted to become a "great writer" and he wanted to see the sun, and suddenly the attainment of his greatest desire would stand determined by the gratification or non-gratification of his desire of the moment, his desire to see the sun. If the sun came out, he would realize his dreams. If it didn't? Well he did not want to think about that. Yes, the question of whether he would or wouldn't become a great writer would stand determined by the sun re-emerging or not re-emerging.

Come out sun, come out sun; please, please come out. Damn you, you're not listening to me. Why, why, why have you forsaken me? Don't you realize who I am? Your child, the soul-light man. Your son, your Phaethon. The boy who once drove your chariot. You're ignoring me. Why, why, why have you forsaken me?

He would remain perverse and keep behind the clouds, damn him. Fenrir swallowed him and the end of the world stood at hand. Thomas never had any luck! He couldn't lose this game. The stakes remained too high. He had to find a way to win. Had he gone insane? This was silly. But what if it did depend on the sun coming out? What could he do? Maybe he could do something else? If he could hit that tree in front of him with a rock ... no he'd probably miss.

He had it. If he could throw a rock past the tree, he could do something else. What would he put on the line? What would he give up? It would have to be something important. If he didn't throw the rock past the tree, in addition to not becoming a writer, he would never do well in school again. He picked up a stone and threw it with all his might. It passed the tree easily. Yes, now he could substitute something else. He'd make it depend on his tossing his apple up in the air and catching it ten times. He could do that. He knew he could. One. Two. Three. Four. Five. Six. Seven. Christ, almost dropped it. Eight. Nine. Ten. He did do it! He did. He did. He did. He could call himself Amun-is-satisfied.

If someone had seen him they'd think .... He didn't care what they would think. Some things should remain private. Yet he wanted the world to know all. Introvert or extrovert? Extrovert. Do I dare, do I dare? Yes, I do dare.

In a few minutes, he'd stand up and walk towards the pine trees. He unzipped his knapsack, took out one of the two flashlights and the baseball helmet. You had to have protection for the head. He looked up into the sky. It had gotten even cloudier, but it didn't really matter if the sky stood cloudy or clear. It would not matter in the caves. At least it had gotten warmer. Perhaps "The Farmers' Almanac" had it right after all. Perhaps it would be a mild winter.

It had turned much colder. It had gotten warmer, but then the temperature had again dropped. The sun had set and it had started raining. But he had dressed for the occasion. He had two sweaters on beneath his coat, and he wore gloves on his hands and a yellow cap on his head.

He had eaten, his grandmother having fixed him one of his favorite meals: spinach and chopped bacon served over boiled potatoes. He had read. He was rereading TM's novella *The Black Swan*. He had first perused the book last summer prior to going to Governor's School. He had finished it early in June while visiting his grandparents and had forgotten to take it home with him. So this evening he asked his grandmother where she had put it. She told him. He found it and began leafing through it. For an hour he worked on his new short story, made the journey downwards, had written. He might not complete this particular story. Maybe it would forever remain an unfinished fragment. But that didn't matter, for once again he plied pen to paper. And it seemed to him that he wrote well. If only it came so effortlessly all the time. It stood a good thing that he hadn't found any time to write last week when he first conceived his idea for the story. He could never have produced stuff as good as this. Never written these passages so well. And then his grandmother asked him to play the piano. She planned to sell her piano at an auction. She would auction off most of her belongings. And he complied. He played several works including her favorite piece, a composition which had been written in the twenties, "The Robin's Return," a Haydn sonata (he had loved Haydn's music ever since he started taking piano lessons as a little boy and sang *Papa Haydn's dead and gone, but his memory lingers on*, and later he had read somewhere that the father of the symphony had to wear a certain ring whenever he composed for if he did not have it on his finger he felt that he lost all his ability), and finally Liszt's transcription of Wagner's *Liebestod*. He closed his piano music and told his grandmother that he stepped outside to take another walk and came here to the pond.

If it had meant so much to him, goddamnit, he should have looked for the other caves. He should have done that in memory of Granddad. Perhaps more caverns and passageways existed? But how could he find them? And the cave he did locate; was that what Granddad meant when he said safe? Sealed shut? And behold no earthquake made the ground shake. For no angel of the Lord descended from heaven and rolled back the stone. What would have Theseus have done or wily Odysseus or the slayer of the Hydra? Or Anchises' son? Found another entrance. That's what he should have done. But if he hadn't come home when he did, he wouldn't have seen the girl, the blue-eyed girl, riding the horse up the hill. That made the whole trip worthwhile. And perhaps he wouldn't have done any writing.

But maybe there still stood a way. Maybe he could still find another entrance. Off the ground he picked up a stone (and David put his hand in his bag and took out a stone and slung it) threw it, threw it as hard as he could (and it struck the Philistine on the forehead; the stone sunk into the forehead), but the stone bounced off the ice.

Try again. Try again! He picked up another stone. Beware Nuliajuk, beware! For I with my battering ram, with my golden meteor, with my flaming stones stand ready to batter down thy fences, thy walls, thy gates! Icy gates that separate the Kingdom of Air from the Fluid Region. Beware sapphire-eyed goddess! Beware mother of seals, for I'm a Shaman and nothing in your kingdom frightens me. I shall swim down, down, down, to thy kingdom, to the bottom of the murky sea. For I remain Kiviok, the great warrior Kiviok, and as surely as Hermodr's mount Svadilfari overleapt the gates of Hell, so shall I enter thy kingdom. Thomas threw another stone, but the rock once again bounced off the ice.

You need a big rock. A heavy rock. There's one. Part of it remains embedded in the ground. Well dig it out then. It *is* heavy. Grasp it with both hands. Either side. Lift it above your head and fling it. Ha Ha Ha! Nobody, you stand deceived. The deceiver stands deceived. You blinded Polyphemus, but you did not blind me. And now I'm going to have my retribution. The rock thudded and bounced off the ice. Damn, you'll never do it. It's impossible. What can you do that you haven't already tried?

He sat down. The rain stung his face. His cheeks had become red. He could walk out on the ice and jump on it until he fell through. But what purpose would that serve? He'd only drown. His effort would remain fruitless, as fruitless as Wildeve's attempt to rescue Eustacia. Not even a pyrrhic victory. Hiawatha's brother, Wolf Twin! He sacrificed his life, but nonetheless he found his way there and became king of that realm. The Jew-Egyptian, he had no such difficulties. His brothers out of jealousy sold him into slavery and they—without him even asking him to do so—threw him into a well ....

What would he have done? He whose Blood is blood of my blood, whose Flesh is flesh of my flesh? Yet he had dark hair and dark eyes. I blond hair and blue eyes.

Tonio Kröger. The morbid and demonic do not interest him. Only that which remains healthy. The story *Tonio Kröger*, a defense of life over spirit—a Nietzschean parable. Opposites attract. Artists such as the dark-haired, decadent Tonio stand as outcasts, no matter how burgherly they remain in their work habits. They hanker after that which appears normal, healthy and ordinary, the blond-haired, blue-eyed Hanses and Inges of this world, realizing that it remains the object of love, and not love itself, which stands beautiful and superior. Did not the Nazi beast, the Austrian monster, the emperor Nero (Heil Hitler, Heil Hitler, Heil Hitler) say almost the same thing? They spoke and made their points in such different contexts, but did they not in end say the same thing? Could they represent two opposing aspects of the Godhead, of Ishvara? No, that's impossible. You don't believe that? Did they in fact resemble the duelists, the humanist and the irrational Jesuit, who remained polar opposites and espoused contrary positions, yet in the end, came to identical conclusions, their positions at last weirdly dovetailing? Didn't he write in an essay that the beast could have been his brother, that they both remained members of the guild? Didn't he feel that by writing the god invention, he somehow stood responsible for what happened in Germany? Could they have represented two aspects of Ishvara? One Brahma, the other Shiva?

Monism.

Mannism?

And what about Kafka and his novella *The Metamorphosis?* Did not Gregor the cockroach, the bed bug, the sperm lashing its tail—a fish out of water—as it dried on the bed sheet, did not he lust after his own sister Grete? Blonde Grete might have been a Sieglinde, but Gregor Samsa stood no Siegmund. Didn't he despise himself? Did he not turn into a horrible bug when he placed upon his head Mime's tarnhelm? Did not his father throw apples at him? Did they not sink into his back? Throw a rock at the pond's icy face. No, you won't crack that surface. Why torture yourself? It stood better when he died, when the charwoman swept his body into the fire. Did not blonde Grete feel relieved? Relieved of an awful burden? And why, why, why did they not fight back? Why didn't they tear their captors to pieces? They must have all stood Hungarian Turks, none of them true sons of David? Nothing but Shadrachs and Abednegos, or did they think themselves bugs?

Suddenly Tom Englehardt laughed out loud.

Kafka, Mann, Englehardt—they did not stand criminals. Mann distinguished himself as the spokesman of Weimar. He fled to America during the war. True, the demonic fascinated him, but the humanist won out. And Kafka himself was a Jew and hated all militarism. A prophet maybe, but certainly he did not share the fascists' views. And Tom Englehardt? A neophyte Nazi? Hardly. They stood avatars of Vishnu. Like Rama, Krishna, and the deceiver, the great deceiver Siddhartha Gautama Buddha—they stood incarnations of Narayana, one and the same person. Neither Brahma nor Shiva, but Vishnu, Vishnu the preserver. They stood incarnations of Narayana, avatars of Vishnu, providers of the Lotus--the forbidden fruit ... Messiahs, Jesus Christs!

The Lotus! Partake, partake! He thrust a hand into a pants pocket. Yes, yes, yes. He deserved it. He deserved it. He was the only one in his class who understood Tennessee William's poem about the boy sitting on top of a tower and shooting spitballs at the moon or truly understood the symbolism of "The Rocking Horse Winner." He was a writer. He had written several very fine short stories at Governor's School—he had gone to Governor's School!—his conquest of Anne, his good friend Anne the poet, and how difficult that was. How first she wanted to make love to him, but then she didn't. How he lied to his friends, lied to them about Anne. How he didn't go to the motel like he said but instead went to the library and wrote. And then, then she did give in to him but wouldn't buy the Encare ovals. He had to buy them. And Ilse, the German girl, how he enjoyed copping her cherries, and if he had enough time he could get his way with any girl—even the blonde-haired, blue-eyed vixen of today; never would have seen her if he had not tried to find the caves. His grandfather said that there were many caves, but he found only one, and it stood sealed shut, but that wouldn't matter if he could ... he knew, he knew he could! Another rock. Many rocks beside him. Use that one, the long white one. Pick it up. Pick it up. Pick it up, up, up! And by tomorrow morning the clouds will have passed, and he would see the sun and would stand as ecstatic as the Valkyrie when she heiled die Sonne and heiled das Licht. He would do what he had to do tonight, and tomorrow he'd see the sun. And he would not have to be meek or diffident, and, without any qualms, he could sit down and sup with his Brothers. They would be his brothers, wouldn't they! And he might shine, might shine so resplendently, prevaricate so well, that his brothers would throw him into a well.

Would his Brothers do that? Yes they might. They remained his brothers and he stood a son of the Sun. Hardy, Mann, Wolfe. Hardy, Mann, Englehardt! Sons of the Sun. Sons of the Sun. Hardy Mann Wolfe. Ragnarök, Götterdämmerung. Siegfried. Brünnhilde. Zu neuen Taten. Teurer Helde. His short story. An ending to his short story. Introduce a female character. Make her responsible for character Mark's demise. The girl in the woods. Green-eyed temptress. Succubus. Veeeeeeenussss!!!!!

He flung the stone, but like the other rocks had previously done, it bounced off the ice. He sat there stupefied, and it began to rain much harder—but it wasn't a summer or a spring rain—a rain that brings life out of the soil—nor was it snow. It was an icy rain. A "freezing" rain. And ice from the sky fell on the water ice.

Wagnerian Elements in Thomas Mann's Joseph Tetralogy

Probably no writer of world prominence in modern times was so inclined to enumerate the great personalities who had guided his own artistic life than Thomas Mann. Not only did he frequently allude to many German and European figures who had played vital parts in his own development, he also wrote many critical and laudatory essays on these (Goethe, Lessing, Schiller, Schopenhauer, Freud, Dostoyevski, Tolstoy, etc.), often while engaged in writing his longest fictional works. Of all the greats of German and European culture who played important roles in Mann's development, few would question that Richard Wagner's role—other than that perhaps of Goethe's—was the more pervasive one. Mann's characteristic emphasis on the questionable sources of the artistic impulse, his attraction to the neurotic and decayed as the basis of his aesthetics, his reliance on archetypes and myths as the revealers of ultimate meanings of life, his use of *leitmotif* and continuous melodic line as his preferred structure in the vast amount of his writing—all these exemplify Mann as a Wagnerite in the most profound and legitimate sense.

Mann's Wagnerian bent is made particularly clear by the writing of his Wagner essay *Leiden und Grösse der Meister* at the very period when Adolf Hitler and the Nazi party were grasping power in Germany. It is well known that Wagner was quite anti-Semitic, particularly in the last years of his life, those in which he was writing his Christian "consecration play" *Parsifal*, and that he expressed in his many quasi-philosophical and scholarly essays (which Wagner, too, incidentally, wrote as diversions while laboring on his mighty music dramas) and in his autobiography *Mein Leben* his anti-Semitic views quite clearly. It is also known that Houston Stewart Chamberlain and Joseph Arthur, Count de Gobineau, and later Hitler, among many others of their racist cult, were quite considerably influenced in the further development of pro-Aryan, anti-Jewish ideology by Wagner's condemnatory statements on Jews. Ironically, Mann's Wagner essay, so laudatory and so understanding of the overriding greatness of Wagner, was the immediate cause of Mann's expulsion from Hitler Germany in 1933. Mann had been too truthful in identifying the neurotic aspects of Wagner which to the Nazi intelligentsia—and to the musical world of Strauss, Furtwängler and Knappertbusch as well—was sacrilege. While certain German composers were now banished from the musical lexicon (Mendelssohn, Mahler, and Weill) and all others relegated to definite second place, Wagner had become the paragon of German composers in Nazi Germany. He was, of course, Hitler's favorite composer. Since the Nazi ideology was despicable to Mann, one would have thought that he would have turned sour on Wagner as artist, teacher, and man at this time. All the more so in that his wife Katia was half-Jewish and most certainly would as such have suffered death at the hands of the Nazi government during the war years and perhaps all Mann's sons and daughters as well had they remained in Nazi Germany. But Mann emphatically did not reject Wagner at this time. Much earlier as a young man, Mann had briefly done so, but as Tristan and Isolde once they had drunk the love potion were eternally bound to each other, once Mann had drunk of Wagner's music he was never able to free himself of the hold Wagner had on him. In his more dubious moments, Mann would joke that once one had really drunk deeply of Wagner's music one became intoxicated for a lifetime. This is borne out in his daughter Monica's book, *Past and Present* (1960) and also in his wife Katia's *Meine ungeschriebenen Memoiren* (1974) in which both testified to Mann's good ability as a pianist and his fondness for playing piano transcriptions of Wagner, particularly from Wagner's *Tristan und Isolde* and especially the *Liebestod*. The maturing Mann indeed submitted to the master, and the compelling presence of Wagner remained with Mann in the writing of all of his major works of fiction, from *Buddenbrooks* and *The Magic Mountain* down through the last ones *Doctor Faustus*, *The Holy Sinner*, and *Confessions of Felix Krull*. The great middle work, the one which occupied him steadily from 1926 to 1942, the Jewish Biblical tetralogy *Joseph and His Brothers* was perhaps the most Wagnerian of them all. In his preface to the 1948 one-volume edition of the American Knopf H.T. Lowe-Porter translation of the four volumes of the Joseph tetralogy (*The Tales of Jacob* and *Young Joseph* published in their German originals in 1933 and 1934 in Hitler's Berlin, and subsequently in German *Joseph in Egypt* in 1936 in pre-Anschluss Vienna and *Joseph the Provider* in 1943 in neutral Stockholm, Sweden by the German-Jewish Fischer *Verlag* publishers which had affiliates in all three cities), Mann admits that Wagner's great tetralogy of pre-Christian Germanic mythology *Der Ring des Nibelungen* was constantly with him as a guide and inspiration in his working out of his vast undertaking of Jewish and Egyptian myth, even to the extent of his extended interruption in his completion of it. Between the completion in Kusnacht, Switzerland of *Joseph in Egypt* in 1936 and *Joseph the Provider* in 1942 in Santa Monica, California, Mann wrote his Goethe novel *Lotte in Weimar* and the romance on earlier-day India *The Transposed Heads*. Just so Wagner wrote *Tristan und Isolde* and *Die Meistersinger* as "lighter" works between the conclusion of Act II of *Siegfried* and the beginning of Act III of the same opera and the completion of the entire *Ring* cycle *Götterdämmerung*, which, of course in its resolution of the *Ring* tetralogy is comparable to *Joseph the Provider* in the fourth volume of the Joseph Tetralogy.

Apart from the obvious structural similarities of the two vast undertakings, there are many other quickly recognizable similarities. Both offer extended explorations of myth, Wagner's of pre-Christian primordial Germanic culture undertaken decades before Jung, Freud, and Sir John Frazer, and Mann's of ancient early-Biblical and Egyptian times abetted by what these later figures could teach him as well as the intuitive insights he gained from Wagner's music dramas, particularly the *Ring* but others as well as we shall see. Both Wagner's *Ring* and Mann's Joseph tetralogy dramatize the mystery of human origins and the growth of religious and social structures, in Wagner as revealed in the conflicts between the Nibelungen and Walsungs tribes and among the Nordic gods on Valhalla, and in Mann through Joseph that astonishing contribution of the Hebrews in their very embryonic stage of tribal growth to the already aging Egyptian land, its pyramids and Sphinx erected long in the forgotten past and its religion and social structures so distantly developed that they are cloaked in superstition and priestly dogma by Joseph's time.

Both works concentrate on familial roots over several generations, the father Wotan, the son Siegmund, and the grandson Siegfried in Wagner's *Ring*, and in Mann's Joseph tetralogy Isaac, Jacob, and Joseph. The introductory work of each tetralogy, Wagner's *Das Rheingold* and Mann's *The Tales of Jacob*, deals with a theft, Wotan's of the *Rheingold* magic ring from Alberich the dwarf and Jacob's of the tribal birthright from Esau, which generates the problems of guilt and redemption and the ramifications thereof that enfold for the characters in the successive works. Jacob who had stolen the birthright from his brother Esau in later days is a victim of his father-in-law Laban's trickery and deceit over many years of his early manhood before gaining hegemony among the family herdsmen. Then in his old age, he suffers the loss of his favorite son Joseph through the vengeful acts of his ten older sons. Joseph, although he ultimately finds good fortune and recognition in Egypt is beset constantly by those who resent his uniqueness and his ability to win favor from his superiors. Wotan's selfish desire to regain the magic ring which he forfeited to Fafner, the giant in *Das Rheingold* and the dragon-to-be in *Siegfried*, brings a series of misfortunes on himself and his offspring Siegmund, Sieglinde, Siegfried, and Brünnhilde. His grandson Siegfried who grows up to kill Fafner as dragon and gain the ring is the ultimate sacrificial victim to Wotan's ambitions and selfishness, and he and his beloved Brünnhilde die in achieving the oblivion for Wotan which alone can bring him redemption and peace. Similarly, Joseph, the sacrificial victim of his troubled family, brings peace to Jacob in his last patriarchal days when Joseph, foremost among the mighty of Egypt, is able to save his father and renegade brothers when they journey to Egypt during the period of the great famine. Moreover, Joseph and his Egyptian wife live out their lives in tranquility and apparent happiness, unlike Wotan's progeny.

Among other similarities between Wagner's *Ring* and Mann's Joseph books perhaps the most striking are the presence in both of the godlike, abandoned youth, the incestuous union of brother and sister, and prominent dwarf characters who act as microcosms of the energies and pathos of human life. In Wagner's *Ring*, Siegfried at sixteen has always been bereft of all blood ties, has never had knowledge of his roots or his place in life. But he is godlike and egotistic, and in his parts of the *Ring* narrative *Siegfried* and *Götterdämmerung*, he sets outward on his journeys of discovery, first farther into the forest to kill the dragon, then surmounts the flames at the mountain top and finds his destined mate Brünnhilde, and last of all to proceed forth as a man down the German Rhine to the land of castles and forts and worldly strife. Joseph, on the other hand, up to his sixteenth year had basked in the love of his father Jacob, taking for granted his higher place in the affection of his father over his lesser brothers. Then suddenly he experienced the murderous fury of his brothers, no less jarring to him because he had long half expected it, and found himself sold to a caravan of Ishmaelite traders heading west to Egypt. His story then too becomes one of a journey forth, in his case through Canaan, across the desert, then up the Egyptian Nile past pyramids and sphinx to the forbidden gods, Pharaoh, and Thebes—to a world very different from his prosaic past of migratory Jewish herdsmen. Both Siegfried and Joseph in the fullness of time make a mark for themselves, gaining successes and then suffering betrayals and reversals, only to gain still further and lasting glory.

Next we quickly note in Wagner's work the twins Siegmund and Sieglinde, separated from each other throughout their childhood, brought together briefly by chance as young adults to fall in love and thereupon conceive Siegfried, Siegmund to die shortly thereafter at the hands of Sieglinde's boorish husband Hunding, and Sieglinde to die in pain and sorrow giving birth in the forest to Siegfried. The twin situation in Mann is somewhat different. In Mann's tetralogy the twins are the very aged brother and sister, the parents of Potiphar. It is while standing in the shadows of their evening gardenplace that the young Jewish slave servant Joseph, silently waiting to serve them food if they should want it, overhears the fretful words of the death-waiting pair. To his astonishment, he learns that in their reigning years in the household they had castrated their infant son Potiphar, feeling guilt that they had conceived their son in the muddy darkness of incestuous mixing—of unisexuality. They had come to see their relationship to each other as unisexual and to be compared with the self-regenerating abominations produced in the muddy depths of the Nile.

Last must be mentioned the most evident use of *Ring* material by Mann's tetralogy. In the third volume *Joseph in Egypt*, which is equivalent to *Siegfried* in the *Ring*, we encounter the dwarf servants in Potiphar's court, Bes-em-heb and Dudu. Clearly these two comic and important pivotal characters play roles quite comparable to those of Mime and Alberich in Wagner's *Ring*. Of the two dwarfs in Wagner's work Alberich is the indisputable villain. It is he who originally stole the gold from the Rhinemaidens in *Das Rheingold* and from it made the magic ring that would have enabled him to control all of human destiny and even the gods themselves. Alberich's villainy is constantly at work in the *Ring* to the detriment of all the major figures in the story, Wotan, Siegfried, Brünnhilde, Fafner, Hagan, Gunther, and Mime. Dudu, the scheming dwarf in *Joseph in Egypt*, attempts from the first to thwart Joseph's advancement in Potiphar's household, attempting to have him relegated to the lowest position of a field slave. Failing in that, he schemes over the passing months and years to find Joseph's weaknesses, and finally ensnares him with Potiphar's sexually deprived wife to bring about Joseph's downfall. In Wagner's *Ring*, Mime is also a villain, but he is an endearing character despite himself, having rescued the infant Siegfried after his birth in the forest and raising him both as father and mother in the ensuing sixteen years. Fully intending to poison Siegfried once the youth has forged the sword and killed the dragon to gain the magic ring and tarnhelm which would enable him to supersede the smarter dwarf Alberich, Mime is killed by Siegfried. His beheading by his adolescent ward in Act II of *Siegfried* almost seems ingratitude despite our awareness that Siegfried had learned of Mime's murderous intents toward him. Mime's mental inferiority to his brother dwarf Alberich and his life history of bondage to this craftier and more resourceful one softens the feelings of Wagner's audience toward Mime. Knowing this, Mann evidently realized his appealing, kindly, loving dwarf Bes-em-heb was essentially playing the Mime role in *Joseph in Egypt*. In contrast to Dudu's hostility from the beginning, Bes-em-heb welcomed Joseph's appearance at Potiphar's court. He advised him on how to ingratiate himself within the court and informed him of opportunities when they occurred. And he was quick to recognize the long-range scheming of Dudu against Joseph and to warn Joseph against him, warnings which it turned out Joseph did not heed sufficiently. The squabbling between these two dwarfs, often pitching to near blows over the handsome young Hebrew, is the most amusing element in Mann's third volume of the Joseph series. Obviously he used the dwarfs to create an amiable atmosphere in his long novel series, just as Wagner did in his sixteen-hour opera.

While the parallels between the two tetralogies mentioned this far hardly seem challengeable, it should be noted that in a broader sense *Joseph and His Brothers* is Wagnerian in technique, inclusive or exclusive of the *Ring*. Mann consciously used Wagner's *leitmotif* in his writings preceding *Joseph and His Brothers*, particularly so in *Death in Venice* and *The Magic Mountain*. These two preceding works established the Wagnerian *leitmotif* as a basic element in Mann's matured writing style. Thus the knowledgeable reader expects to encounter the *leitmotif* in the Joseph novels. It is definitely present. As with *Das Rheingold* in the *Ring*, the *leitmotifs* are established in simplest form in the introductory work, *The Tales of Jacob*. Then they are repeated, varied and expanded in the succeeding three Joseph novels. For instance, in *The Tales of Jacob*, an obvious initial *leitmotif* is the antagonism between the articulate and clever Jacob and the dull-witted and boorish Esau. In *Young Joseph*, Joseph becomes the parallel to Jacob, and his ten resentful brothers (whom Mann is careful to term a "collective Esau") are parallel to their father's supplanted brother. Young Jacob, once he had succeeded in stealing the birthright from his heedless brother, was obliged to flee his brother's wrath and live in exile for many years in Haran, the distant land of his uncle Laban. Likewise Joseph, too long flaunting his preferred position with the aged Jacob, is withheld from the land of his father and sold by his brothers into Egyptian slavery. Thus we have Jacob and Joseph, the exiled ones, and Esau and the other ten brothers, the agents of their exile. Since three of the four books in Mann's tetralogy are about Joseph, we see that *leitmotifs* established for him early in his story are recurrent still later on. The brothers had cast Joseph in a pit where he had stayed starving for three days, only then to be sent off to Egypt with the Ishmaelite caravan. Ten years would follow in steady ascendancy for Joseph in Potiphar's household. While there, however, he would beget both enemies and partisans, the drama with Potiphar's wife would be enacted, and Joseph once more would descend into the pit, this time a fortified Egyptian prison. In the fullness of time he would still once again be resurrected from the pit to rise to even greater responsibility and power in Egypt. That is to say, he would become chief advisor and administrator to the Pharaoh Ikhnaton, who would, interesting to note, seal Joseph's position by granting him the official "ring" of power. Of course, these patterns are for the most part already etched in the Biblical original of the Joseph story. Mann recognized that the Biblical storytellers were consciously using a technique roughly the same as Wagner's operatic one two to three millennia later. Mann expands his several thousand-page narrative (as compared to the Bible's score of pages), always with the "Biblical" *leitmotifs* in mind. His methods of concentrated expansion are obviously those from Wagner. One might briefly note the cycles of seven mentioned in the Biblical story and likewise emphasized, explicated, and expanded in Mann's monolithic account, the seven years Jacob worked for Laban to win Rachel and the seven more that Laban imposed on him when he was forced to marry the older sister Leah first. Mann manages to find other references in discussing Joseph's ten years of service to Potiphar which the Bible doesn't mention. But in the final book *Joseph the Provider* Mann's fabricated sevens of *Joseph in Egypt* have led significantly to the Bible's seven years of plenty and the seven years of famine, which, of course, represent Joseph's Egyptian career at its zenith.

Having established that *Joseph and His Brothers* has both general affinities to Wagner and specific ones to Wagner's *Ring*, now it can be pointed out that Mann's Biblical tetralogy also has many elements that relate to two other major Wagner works *Tristan und Isolde* and *Parsifal*, particularly in the third volume *Joseph in Egypt.* At first consideration, the Parsifal themes of sexual renunciation and spiritual purity would seem the more likely source of comparison. Joseph goes to Egypt with high regard for the sanctity of his body, of his obligations to Jacob and to the God of Jacob and Jacob's tribe to remain physically unblemished. Joseph's highest love is for the one God who guides and protects him, and who has brought him to Egypt with some as yet unrevealed design in mind. Comparably, Joseph's castrated master's life condition is highly inhibited. His family line will die with him, and the roles he plays as son to his aged brother-sister parents, as husband to Mut-em-enet, and father to his own household, and finally as titular high general of Pharaoh's armies and overall attendant at the imperial court are solely ritualistic. His wife, the beautiful and haughty Mut-em-enet, is the virginal priestess to the mighty god Amun, whose formalistic marriage to Potiphar presumably has been quite appropriate to her special priestess role among the entire coterie of Amun priestesses whose consummated unions with their husbands are properly conjunctive to their sexual associations with Amun. Nor should Mont-kaw or the good dwarf Bes-em-heb be neglected in alluding to Parsifalian sexual renunciation in Mann's Joseph saga. Mont-kaw, Potiphar's own overseer, purchased Joseph from the Ishmaelite nomads who had brought him from Canaan to Egypt, and quickly took to the beautiful youth. Recognizing Joseph's intelligence, he trained him in the succeeding seven years as his eventual successor, knowing his own failing kidneys would before too long necessitate his replacement. Mont-kaw is particularly noteworthy in the Joseph tetralogy. Not only does he suggest the surrogate father Leopold Bloom in Joyce's *Ulysses*, he is a further portrayal of the surrogate father figures Mann had himself previously provided for Tadzio and Hans Castorp through Aschenbach and Settembrini in his earlier *Death in Venice* and *The Magic Mountain*. Mont-kaw had married early in his years of service to Potiphar, but his wife had died in childbirth like Wagner's Sieglinde in giving birth to Siegfried and Mann's Rachel to Benjamin, Joseph's younger brother, only in this case the infant son was also stillborn. Following his wife's and infant son's deaths, Mont-kaw had chosen celibacy for his future leading a life of sacrificial service to Potiphar, his beloved master, emulating thus his superior in his thoughts on the ideal servant-master relationship. Bes-em-heb, the good dwarf, reinforces Mont-kaw's views. He too is a representative of celibacy. It was Bes-em-heb who had urged Mont-kaw to purchase Joseph when Dudu, his rival dwarf, had tried to dissuade Mont-kaw. While Dudu had married a normal-size Egyptian woman and had fathered full-size sons for Potiphar's household, Bes-em-heb remained unmarried and more pre-occupied with superficial niceties of worldly life and contemplation on the Gods of Egypt and other lands. He quickly accepts Joseph's Hebrew God in accepting Joseph, for so fine and good does the little man find Joseph, he concludes a very special God must have planned and made him. Understandably, Bes-em-heb, perhaps in part from his own possessive love for the glorious Joseph, constantly warns the young Hebrew against the dangers of Mut-em-enet and Dudu. In praising Joseph's God and encouraging his dedicated service to Mont-kaw and Potiphar in the seven years of apprenticeship, Bes-em-heb plays his part in the maintenance of Joseph's unblemished chastity, despite the many Egyptian women who looked upon him lustfully as he traversed the streets of Thebes and beyond in seeing to his master's business. Unfortunately, in the last crucial three years when Joseph had taken over Mont-kaw's position, Bes-em-heb could not completely circumvent the combined dangers of Dudu and Mut.

Two-thirds of Wagner's opera *Parsifal* deals with the celibate ideals of Christian knights in the monastery at Montsalvat. Therefore in those earlier parts of Mann's *Joseph in Egypt* that deal with Joseph's seven-year apprenticeship the parallels between *Parsifal* and *Joseph in Egypt* are very strong. When Mann arrives at the point in his story of Joseph's three years of household overseership, our attentions must turn to *Tristan und Isolde* as well as that third of *Parsifal*, Act II, which focuses on much more carnal matters. Attention to *Tristan und Isolde* parallels with *Joseph in Egypt* will be more useful at first. I

In the section of *Joseph in Egypt* which deals with the three-year overseership, Mann shifts in his concentration from Joseph to Mut-em-enet to develop one of modern literature's most extraordinary studies of an overwrought woman in the clutches of non-reciprocated love. In many respects, as we will see later, Mut's relationship can be compared to that of Kundry and Parsifal in Act II of *Parsifal*. However, in Mut's irrational, heedless, ever-growing ardor for Joseph, her emotions and behavior are particularly those of Isolde, and Mann evidently thought of Wagner's impassioned medieval Irish princess in his conception of Mut. It will be recalled Wagner's Irish princess had abundant reasons for hating Tristan. He was from Britain, the hated land that had attacked and vanquished Ireland. Tristan had also killed Morold, her Irish betrothed, in battle. Later, having nursed the wounded Tristan back to health, she had fallen in love with him despite her discovery of his role in Morold's death. Before her love for Tristan achieved physical consummation, love and hatred alternated in her response to him, reaching dangerously tumultuous levels when her royal parents complied with King Marke's wishes that his knight bring back Isolde to Britain as surety from vanquished Ireland to be his, King Marke's, bride. On the stormy Irish Sea voyage to Britain when the circumspect Tristan ignores Isolde, she has her maid servant Brangäne prepare a death potion. Commanding his presence, she has him join her in drinking it, not guessing Brangäne would substitute a love potion which would heighten the love of the ill-starred pair. Past nervous *Augenblicken* are now succeeded by a long, steadfast meeting of eyes, and when the ship arrives in Cornwall, Tristan and Isolde are totally unified in their love for each other and oblivious of those around them. At this point in Wagner's plot, Act I ends. Acts II and III deal with the tragic consequences of the adulterous love that ensues between Tristan and Isolde, for which the love potion nominally absolves them of moral responsibility to King Marke, Isolde's husband and Tristan's uncle and surrogate father. Like Joseph, Tristan too came in his youth from another land from the east, Brittany, and rose to prominence in his foster country.

Mann's Joseph and Mut never reach the Act II and III stages of Wagner's opera. Their relationship is never consummated and so their feelings toward each other are never refined to unalloyed love. Mut, like the Isolde of Act I is tormented by alternating love and hate, longing and revulsion for Joseph. Joseph, in turn, feels veneration and compassion for the wife of his eunuch master, plus growing physical attraction for her which he equates with Sheol (hell) and, should he surrender to her, alienation from his earthly and heavenly fathers.

In Wagner's *Tristan und Isolde*, Tristan's retainer Kurvenal and Isolde's Brangäne act as go-betweens for the title characters. Kurvenal's loyalty is entirely to Tristan and Brangäne's to Isolde. They would prefer master and mistress were free of the disastrous bond. Nevertheless, the two are obedient. Brangäne's rash act in preparing the love potion instead of the death potion aptly illustrates her love for her mistress. In Act II she receives Isolde's confidences on the love affair with Tristan, the joys that Frau Minne the goddess of love had brought to her. Brangäne watches from the palace tower while Tristan and Isolde have their garden tryst, and she calls forth her warning to them as dawn approaches and with it the return of King Marke to the palace from the hunt. Brangäne is a finely conceived character, who projects vividly the emotions of loyalty and guilt toward the woman who is her *raison d'être*. Similarly Kurvenal, the strong and resourceful retainer who had fought alongside Tristan in the Irish wars, in Act III projects deep anguish and unavailing solicitude for his beloved master as he dies of his bodily and spiritual wounds.

In *Joseph in Egypt* the bluff and hearty Kurvenal is not matched by a character of similar masculinity. The advisory role he plays for Tristan regarding Tristan's liaison with Isolde are paralleled by the roles the two dwarfs Bes-em-heb and Dudu assume toward Joseph in the three years of Joseph's overseership in Potiphar's household. It is then that Mut's feelings had progressed much beyond the disdain and coolness toward a physically attractive foreign servant whom she had casually observed in the flow of days over seven years, at most irked that he should hold the affection of her eunuch husband with whom she maintained only respectful, formal communications. The infrequent *Augenblicken* that she and Joseph had exchanged at the evening dinners had not seemed so very significant. In the three years of Joseph's stewardship they had become much more direct and piercing. In short, Mut then became very enamored of Joseph and she repeatedly consulted with Dudu on her strategies to bring the chaste Joseph to submit to sexual relations with her. He was all too eager to comply in his determination to bring Joseph to disgrace before Potiphar. Despite his grotesquely peacock manner (his manly swaggering, his pride in his potency and fatherhood in the household of his eunuch master), Dudu in a sense plays a reverse Brangäne role as well as a reverse Kurvenal one. In any case, he frequently confronts Joseph with arguments that he should grant his favors to Mut interspersing them with descriptions of Mut's many amatory attractions. He also serves as messenger between them overtly conveying the desires of his mistress which Mut in the routine private sessions with Joseph over household matters could not in all propriety voice so directly, at least not in the first year and more of her self-confessed desire for Joseph. 2 The good dwarf Bes-em-heb, having Joseph's best interest at heart and therefore being most truly Kurvenal's counterpart, is all the while engaged in warning Joseph of Dudu and Mut with adjurations that he not forget his avowed chastity to his father and his Hebrew God. If Dudu acts as messenger to Joseph (Joseph responding ambivalently to him knowing his insincerity but also gratified to hear of Mut's undiminished ardor), Bes-em-heb, in contrast, on many occasions acts as spy for him, hiding behind curtains in Mut's chambers and hearing the schemes Mut and Dudu contrive for Joseph's submission. Obviously, Bes-em-heb prefers to keep Joseph for himself. He recognized Mut as a potential threat to Joseph's security in the seven training years, and he struggles in the three following years to circumvent Joseph's downfall. In the end, both Kurvenal and Bes-em-heb are for all their precautions helpless to prevent their young man's doom, Tristan's final one and Joseph's temporary one.

If Dudu plays the Brangäne part as much as Kurvenal's as intercessor and messenger, there are females who do function in Brangäne capacities for Mut. In the first years of Mut's determination to gain Joseph as lover, before ruthlessness and increasing depravity overtook her, her two young maids Hedjes and Me-et would accompany her in her first relatively sedate encounters with Joseph, such as an evening walk in the garden outside the summerhouse such evenings when Joseph as overseer would check there. The two maids waited deferentially as Mut detained Joseph in lengthy exchanges on the care of the summer grounds, noting Mut's undisguised delight in Joseph's presence, and later once more with her in her chambers, heedless of their presence, hearing her impulsively speak aloud to herself, recalling something about Joseph especially pleasing to her. Indirectly, here, Mann is describing the type of confidence that Isolde exchanges with Brangäne at the beginning of Act II of *Tristan und Isolde* preceding Isolde joining Tristan in the garden. Apparently, since their sole role in life was to serve their mistress, Mut later described to them more directly her all-consuming love for Joseph. Mann suggests that these two maids helped Mut maintain emotional equilibrium during her first year as "the smitten one." By the third year, however, the once pristine Mut had progressed to deranged frenzy, shorn of all decorum and restraint, neglectful of her prescribed observations to Amun at his temple in Thebes. Instead she indulges in basest witchcraft with Tabubu, a bitch sorceress, a Kushite from nether Africa who in the black of the night while the household sleeps performs her heathen rites to gain demonic intervention to effect Joseph's submission to Mut's desires. Bones and bloodied, putrid flesh and knots of hair from the remains of animals and executed Thebans, interspersed with grain and crumbs of bitumen, are arranged as an offertory table garlanded with twigs of ivy and blades of corn, reflected gruesomely in the burning torches that Mut and a concubine bear to assist the Negress in summoning the bitch demon from the night. Mut's base role in these dark supplications contrasts pathetically to her customary role in Amun's temple. The proud mistress of the household is here reduced to eager anticipation of the black bitch demon who Tabubu in terrible, contemptuous candor, as priestess here, calls out loudly to aid "the supplicant, a fool for love and a trollop bewitched." The tower heights from which Tabubu works her seamy magic suggest Brangäne's special service to Isolde in the progression of Isolde's illicit relationship with Tristan. Like Tabubu, Brangäne is a consorter with magic and potions, and she works out solutions in her own way, substituting a love potion for Isolde's requested death potion. Also from the tower's height she stands searching throughout the dark night of Isolde's and Tristan's tryst in the garden waiting for the first glimpse of dawn and a return to the proprieties of day. Brangäne is by no means so disturbing a figure as Tabubu in her black magic and her lack of moral scruples, but for medieval Ireland and Britain, she functions in sufficiently similar fashion. Admittedly, the offertory feast that Tabubu prepared the black bitch demon is more suggestive of the vaporous, poisonous broth that Mime concocted in *Siegfried* to poison Siegfried once his young ward had killed the dragon and gained the ring. Still another Brangäne passage, this one in the section dealing with the second intermediate year of Mut's bondage to her passion, might be found in the woman's party sequence, a scene modeled in part on a passage from the epic poem *Yüsef and Zuleikha* by the Persian poet Firdusi. Mann called Joseph's vindictive brothers a "collective Esau." Here we might call the woman at the party a collective Brangäne. True, the women assembled in Mut's reception hall were of the aristocratic, wealthy ladies of Thebes and many of them, like Mut, priestesses to Amun. Unlike Mut, however, they represented less lofty functions to the god Amun as they were wives of husbands who had not been sacrificed in the extreme fashion of Potiphar, and thus were spiritually on a lower plane than Mut in the complexities of Theban religious practices. Indeed, several of the women not only had the favors of their husbands but those of high-ranking soldiers of the Egyptian army or male servants of their households. In this second year, Mut's desire to match the domestic infidelities of some of these ladies indicates her willingness to relinquish her higher spiritual role toward Amun, although not so drastically as she would in the third year in consorting with the black arts with the Kushite sorceress. In this intermediary stage, Mut had summoned the Theban ladies in her need to confide to her sex her incipient affair with Joseph, whom she knew to be the most desirable of all males in Thebes. Her longstanding, subconscious awareness of their contempt for her unawakened sexuality and her pride in her slave servant Joseph led her to the expedient of the women's party. She had the finest meats and fruits prepared, and the ladies' little carving knives sharpened to the finest point. Simultaneously with the serving of the food and the distribution of the knives, she had Joseph called to serve them wine. All of them, without exception, cut themselves with the little knives once they eyed the godlike Joseph, his own male beauty especially blossoming in the presence of all the assembled high-placed beauties of Thebes. In this passage, Mut gives vent to her need to confess her state of love and at the same time establish her superiority. She alone will have Joseph, not they. In making Joseph her lover she will forfeit her virginal status with Amun, but she will still maintain a superiority none of them could challenge, the bleeding hands of all the assembled ladies clear evidence of their mutual reactions to him. Understandably, the women now react to her in a salutary fashion, which they otherwise might well not have. They gush enthusiastically at the joys they foresee for Mut. Joseph, however, undergirded by Bes-em-heb and soured by Mut's complicity with Dudu, continued to see the beckonings of Sheol in Mut's blandishments and successfully resisted her. At least, well into the third year.

Mann's use of Isolde-like confidences to Brangäne can be seen three times over in *Joseph in Egypt*. With justification, however, some might consider the party sequence much more representative of Kundry and one of her chief strategies to seduce Parsifal. Kundry had, of course, surrounded Wagner's young blond knight by lovely flower maidens to work on his physical susceptibilities so that she could more easily win him. Mut's ladies' party definitely recalls them. Actually, the larger part of Act II of *Parsifal* involves the unsuccessful attempts of Kundry the enchantress and Klingsor the magician to corrupt the pure, young Christian by gaining his submission to Kundry. From that standpoint, Klingsor and Kundry are obviously equivalent to Dudu and Mut.

Certainly from the first Dudu was not acting out of concern for Mut's emotional and physical needs. Quite the contrary, he carefully maneuvered her first signs of interest in Joseph to set the crisis to effect Joseph's dismissal. But Mut's desire for Joseph was genuine, not motivated as Kundry's was to destroy Parsifal in her Christ denial. Nevertheless, Kundry's frustration and vindictiveness over Parsifal's successful denial of her, and her underlying guilt—she was a creature who lived on century after century unable to die as God's punishment for having scorned Christ on his way to Calvary—have many dramatic facets that suggest Mut's situation. Certainly the decline from dignity and beauty to frenzy and ugliness of both women is much the same. Isolde's hurt pride and spirit of vengeance disappear after Act I of *Tristan und Isolde*, and her role in Acts II and III expresses her generous love and commitment to Tristan, shorn of all resentment or desire to dominate. Even though Act II is interrupted before coitus is completed for the lovers, Isolde's comments to Brangäne earlier in the act make manifest that she and Tristan had consummated their physical love on numerous occasions between Act I and II. Interrupted in Act II by King Marke and his retainers returning from the hunt and mortally wounded by Melot before he and Isolde had arrived at the peak of sexual rapture, nevertheless Tristan, now exiled with Kurvenal to his native Brittany across the sea, lives on between Acts II and III long enough to realize the long delayed resolution of that last interrupted meeting in the garden. Isolde arrives by ship from Britain in the nick of time. Tristan dies at her approach, and she then sings her *Verklörung* (transfiguration) and her *Liebestod* (love death). Isolde thus cannot be compared to Mut in the latter's final encounter with Joseph in *Joseph in Egypt*. Isolde's arrival has brought Tristan ecstatic release, and she quickly follows him in death, her spirit so united with Tristan in love, she cannot separate from him.

577

If there is release for Mann's ill-matched pair, the release is of quite another sort than that of Tristan and Isolde, a much more realistic, non-operatic one. Joseph and Mut both achieve release from one another. Joseph is sent down the Nile to prison, and Mut has revenged herself on him, regained a measure of her dignity, and is freed of Dudu's corrupting influence. Potiphar, aware of the domestic crisis for much of the three-year period of Mut's disturbed state, recognizes Dudu as the chief culprit, and, at the impromptu trial convened in his house at Mut's insistence to try Joseph, Potiphar informs the trouble-making Dudu that he will lose his position as attendant in the household and have his tongue cut to nullify the main instrument of his maliciousness.

The penultimate encounters with Mut and Joseph and Isolde with Tristan do have very suggestive similarities, however. Mut's one last attempt to seduce Joseph, subsequent to her tower vigil with Tabubu, occurs on the New Year Day's festivities in Thebes, the procession of the holy image of Amun and the Pharaoh and his family throughout Thebes. Mut, oblivious to her priestess function, remains alone in the vacated household, expecting the demonic forces Tabubu had summoned to draw Joseph back from the festive city ahead of Potiphar and the others of the house. Joseph does reappear early, ostensibly to make ready for a household celebration later in the day of Pharaoh's still further advancement of Potiphar in palatial rank, but aware that Mut will be alone in the house waiting for him, determined yet once more to argue her out of all her professions of love and entreaties that he lie with her. Mut had long since passed the stage where she had bitten her tongue in an attempt to suppress her urge to beg Joseph to make love to her, or had sent him via Dudu *billet doux* in which the innuendo of the Egyptian hieroglyphics of her desire to sleep with him was clearly manifest.

With great dramatic tension, Mut calls Joseph to her when she hears him return to the vacated household, vacated save for the presence of Potiphar's aged parents in their own distant quarters, they who had set the scene decades before when they had desexed their infant son. As before, on innumerable occasions, Joseph again approached in lengthy argument Mut's reason, her morality, and her conscience. Nevertheless, the excitement of a house only temporarily vacated of its inhabitants, the fever pitch of Mut, her enticing beauty, and perhaps now the demonic force of the bitch goddess Tabubu had recruited working to her advantage, Joseph, despite himself, at long last, experiences tumescence in Mut's presence. Momentarily, Mut is triumphant. She had won. Joseph, the Hebrew slave, had not in reality rejected her. He did desire her. But if Joseph's body quite unmistakably demonstrated willingness to oblige Mut, father images flash before him, and at the decisive moment he turns and flees. In Mann's continuance of the torn garment *leitmotif*, introduced ten years earlier in the story when, as in the Biblical account, the angry brothers had torn the coat of many colors from him, as Joseph flees, Mut grasps his outer garment and tears it from him. Then, both in the spirit of revenge and in her desire to proclaim the truth to the returning household members—this final interlude between Joseph and Mut has been a lengthy one in which Joseph's genius for elaborate discourse and argument almost succeeds in avoiding the crisis both for himself and Mut—flaunting his garment she accuses Joseph of assaulting her.

Mut's three-year wait did not result in her much-sought coitus with Joseph, but at least, at the end of the three years, she had the gratification of knowing that she had the power to enflame Joseph's senses which his endless opposing intellectual arguments had led her to doubt. Even so, Tristan had the satisfaction in death knowing that the ultimate resolution of their mutual love was Isolde's willingness to pursue him to the after realm of death. Tristan's situation in the weeks and months of physical and emotional suffering between the hunting party's interruption of his lovemaking to Isolde and the arrival of Isolde at his death is dramatically speaking very much like that of Mut's longing for coitus with Joseph and the failure to achieve it when she was so near success. Likewise, Isolde and Joseph are similar in Isolde's near failure to lead Tristan to full ecstasy in death and Joseph's fleeing when Mut's eyes saw so clearly his body's willingness to unite with her. In *Tristan und Isolde*, Wagner wrote an opera of heady romanticism, and the great overwhelming tide of his music leads his audience into realms of passion, ecstasy and spirit that are not quite so accessible to literature, at least not prose literature. Mann has Joseph in one of his stratagems at midpoint of his three-year love game with Mut extrapolate on how scornfully men of literature would deal with them as notables of Egypt if they gave way to their carnal impulses. Their "saga" would only live in their higher selves, his the spirit of Abraham's Hebrew God and hers of Amun determine their relations to each other. Mann takes literary license in the use of the term "saga," and even of *"leitmotif"* at one point, though this last not through the lips of Joseph, but Mann's disciples accept Mann's moments of humorous comment on his tale just as much as those when he philosophizes very seriously—as a corollary, say to the serious intellectual and scientific concerns he portrayed earlier in his novel about the twentieth century German youth, Hans Castorp, in *The Magic Mountain*—on Joseph's God-involvement and, in turn, the god-involvement of the entirety of Egypt in which the larger part of Joseph's tale unfolds. Mann writes in an age that witnessed the emergence of Darwin, Marx, Freud and Jung, not to mention Lenin and, more recently, Hitler in Germany at the very time Mann had begun work on his Joseph stories. Joseph's tale might have found full poetic expression in the somewhat more heady atmosphere of early nineteenth-century German literature. Goethe had expressed admiration for the Biblical tale of Joseph and implied the story would benefit from greater expansion, no doubt as an epic poem, but Goethe preoccupied himself with *Faust* instead. Mann spent sixteen years writing his prose saga *Joseph and His Brothers*, and then went on to write what many feel his masterpiece *Dr. Faustus*. Twentieth-century rationality and skepticism are present in both works in a proportionally large degree, more so in the latter which is a portrayal of the forces that led Germany in the mid-twentieth century to shame and destruction. Nevertheless, while very much a member of the twentieth century, Mann, as a writer, was always equally convinced that his creative perceptions were an outgrowth of the German and European artists who had preceded him, particularly those of nineteenth-century German Romanticism. He was inspired to write the Joseph stories because of Goethe's comments. Wagner was equally, and in my view a greater influence on him on the choice of Joseph as a literary subject. At least, the "disease" of later nineteenth-century

Wagner, like that of Darwin and Marx, relates more easily to the disease Mann saw in his own day than does Goethe's healthier mentality. Also Mann knew that Wagner had through much of his life intended to write a Biblical opera on the lives of Christ and Mary Magdalene. Wagner did not carry out his New Testament opera, just as Goethe set aside any intentions he had for an Old Testament epic poem on Joseph. Wagner did turn the Semitic Jesus into the medieval Aryan knight Parsifal, and he transformed the Jewish Mary Magdalene into a still Semitic Kundry. Thus we have every reason to pursue an investigation of Wagnerian concepts in Mann's working out his stories of Joseph, an archetype of Christ, particularly as Mann portrays him in his various elevations, falls, and rebirths. However, as a twentieth-century skeptic and irrational rationalist and enthusiastic student of post German-European romanticism, and as a writer of very long German prose sentences, equally long in English prose translation, Mann's tendency to explore the humor and irony and sometimes absurdity of his Joseph story is understandable and also quite appropriate. We have already seen that recognition of the *Tristan und Isolde* undertones of his Joseph and Mut story is necessary to our understanding of Mann's authorship. Now we can center our attention on the mother-son (Mut's name interestingly suggestive of the German word *Mutter*) witch-temptress, guileless knight, Kundry-Parsifal aspects of it.

Wagner's final opera on Christianity, a strange work of genius and a cornerstone of Western civilization, synthesizes the Semitic roots of Christianity and its Aryan adaptations. It reflects, too, the aberration of Christian anti-Semitism which is all too clearly documented in Wagner's autobiographical writings and philosophic and music treatises. The instruments of evil in the opera are the brunette, Semitic Kundry and the Judas-like Klingsor. The pure and godlike characters are the blond, blue-eyed Parsifal and presumably not much less physically Aryan Gurnemanz, Amfortas, and Titurel. The opera is highly pious in Acts I and III, but Act II focuses on Kundry's and Klingsor's strategies to bring about Parsifal's ruin, abetted by their coterie of flower maidens, perhaps all Eastern and Semitic, some maybe proselytized by Kundry and Klingsor to lives of sensuality from their Western Christian habitats. The settings of the opera are a holy Christian monastery and a magician's castle in and about Montsalvat in medieval Spain (a country whose history interestingly enough involved the blending of various ethnic cultures, Basque, Aryan-Celtic-Latin, and the Semito-Negroid Moorish, but which Wagner seems to be describing at a point in medieval Spanish history before the blending of the three separate streams into one national river). Considering these factors, we can see how *Parsifal* might have influenced Mann in his conception of *Joseph and His Brothers*. In it Mann, the Aryan, too was describing in his German-language work, Semitic, Egyptian, and Negroid racial elements, although his attitude toward Jewish beliefs and motivations were not nearly so fuzzy as Wagner's. Wagner's wife Cosmia was one-fourth Jewish on her mother's side, and one of the many myths about Wagner was that his natural father was Ludwig Geyer whom Wagner's widowed mother married not many months after his own birth. Geyer was frequently a Jewish name although the Geyer family from which Wagner's stepfather descended had been Christian over many generations, as far back as church and municipal records were extant. Mann's wife Katia was half-Jewish, thus his children one-fourth. Wagner philosophized negatively about Jewish influences in Europe and doubtlessly played a considerable part in paving the way for the Nazi persecutions of Jews in Europe in the 1930s and 1940s. Mann's ties with the Jews were closer than Wagner's in family and culture—Mann's most highly regarded contemporary in music was Mahler, and the father-son partnership between the scientists Freud and Jung played a great part in the development of Mann's "modern" thought—and certainly the ever-advancing, foreboding trends toward activist anti-Semitism in Germany in the late twenties and early thirties led Mann to a humanistic reaction that Wagner's present-day admirers hope Wagner would also have evinced had he lived to see how dangerous and evil self-centered Jewish animosities could be.

In any case, Parsifal's affinity to the *Joseph in Egypt* novel has already been clarified from the standpoint of the extended portrayal in both works of attempted seduction by a determined older woman of a self-contained young man. From this aspect the affinity of Mut to Kundry seems much closer than to Isolde. Perhaps instead of attempting to determine which of Wagner's two women come closest to Mut in concept, one should consider Mut as a composite of Wagner's two characters, Isolde in her initial disturbed state in Act I of *Tristan und Isolde* and Kundry in all her facets throughout *Parsifal*. Considered thus, in a solely literary sense, Mut comes out a more complex, fuller characterization. Obviously Mann's prose, despite his use of *leitmotif* and "extended melodic line," cannot compete with Wagner's musical revelations of character and personality. His words in prose do, of course, exceed Wagner's word devices in poetry. 3 We can understand an inclination of Mann to view Mut as a character worthy of, say, Tolstoy's Anna, even if Tolstoy, unlike himself, did not school himself in Wagnerian methods to guide him in producing his well-known heroine.

Mut reflects the Act I Isolde, of course, in her allegations-aspersions aspect. Isolde's most dramatic moments in Act I take place when she sings to Brangäne during her sea journey from Ireland to Britain her long narrative and curse, in which she recalls how she inadvertently nursed back to health the wounded warrior whom she discovered killed her betrothed in battle. Despite herself, she had fallen in love with him only to later have him return from Britain to arrange her own marriage to King Marke, who now held Ireland in subjection. Following her narrative, Isolde commands Brangäne to summon Tristan to her from his ship quarters. Next, in a long colloquy between Isolde and Tristan, Isolde at length mockingly reiterates to him their past experiences with each other, of her compassion and generosity to him which he returned with dalliance and insincerity. Mut on several occasions is seen in very much the same manner. Before actively courting Joseph, she had attempted to warn her husband, Potiphar, albeit in not nearly so candid self-revelations as she did with Dudu and her concubines, of the dangers posed by Joseph's presence in their household. Later, her appeals whether direct or indirect to Joseph to become her lover alternate with colloquies with him in which she recollects the first seven years in the household in which he grew from adolescence to his present virile manhood. She discloses to him her interest in his past life in Canaan and what she has learned from others, Dudu and the like, of his family and its God. In such narratives and colloquies, Mut clearly plays the basic Isolde role of Act I of Wagner's opera of first unrequited, then requited and transfigured, love. Again we note Mut's remained the unrequited love of the larger part of Act I of *Tristan und Isolde.* Mut's Kundry aspect admittedly has its narrative side also. As a part of her total strategy to seduce Parsifal, the latest of the Christian knights from Montsalvat to attempt to retrieve from Klingsor's castle the holy spear that had pierced Christ's side at Calvary that the older knight Amfortas had years before lost to her and Klingsor, Kundry tells Parsifal her secret knowledge of his boyhood. She tells him how his mother had reared him in the forest in hopes of saving him from the world of men which was responsible for his father's death, and how she died in heartbreak after he grew tired of her loving protection and thoughtlessly left her. Parsifal, whose wanderings had most recently led him to Montsalvat, had not known of his mother's death, and Kundry counts on his remorse and sudden need for motherly comfort and forgiveness to win her to him, just as Mut (whose name Mann surely chose to suggest the German word *Mutter*) had tried to do in informing Joseph of her awareness of the beloved and long-dead mother Rachel. Parsifal was at his most vulnerable when Kundry revealed her sorceress vision of his mother's death, and indeed she does succeed in getting him to accept her kiss, unlike Mut's repeated failures with Joseph. The success is of short duration however. Parsifal draws back, his first reaction changing to pity, pity for all suffering things—the mother who had died in sorrow when her son had left her, pity for Amfortas and all the other knights of Montsalvat whom Kundry and Klingsor had dishonored, and even pity for Kundry. Despite the surface powers and confidence Kundry had gained from the magician Klingsor, she had deeply embedded in her soul the guilt of spitting on Christ when centuries before he bore the cross to Calvary. Parsifal becomes Christ-like in his reaction to Kundry, and she becomes in her frenzied arguments self-defensive and distraught. At the end of Act II, the young innocent knight has fully repulsed Kundry and defeated Klingsor. He has retrieved the holy spear that Klingsor in fury throws at him, and as he makes the sign of the cross over it, the spells and magic powers of Klingsor and Kundry end forever, the beautiful garden becomes a desert, and as Parsifal departs the castle itself fades into nothingness.

In the intricacies of Wagner's plotting, Parsifal much later returns on a Good Friday to the order of Montsalvat. He brings with him the spear with which a Roman soldier had pierced Christ's side at Calvary on the first Good Friday and with which Klingsor within his castle many centuries later had also pierced Amfortas' side in finalizing the effects of Kundry's seduction. The wound that Amfortas took back with him to Montsalvat had never healed, and as the years passed the success of Klingsor over all the knights who had attempted to retrieve the holy spear had demoralized the order. Even the Holy Grail which had also passed on over the centuries to the order no longer radiated its holy splendor. Parsifal, however, places the spear on the wound of Amfortas, and the wound is at long last healed. A humbled, unprepossessing Kundry had also worked her way to Montsalvat before Parsifal's return, seeking redemption. She falls dead as

Amfortas' wound is healed. The opera ends with Parsifal's unveiling the Holy Grail from its long dormant state, and the repurified knights are able once more in good conscience to pray.

At the end of *Parsifal*, Kundry's soul is at peace after many centuries following Calvary. Mut also presumably finds peace during the time period of *Joseph the Provider*, the final novel of the Joseph tetralogy which deals with Joseph's experience in Pharaoh's court after his release from the underground prison from which he had been sent as the result of Mut's accusations. Perhaps she did suffer somewhat from guilt for the part she played in Joseph's downfall in her husband's household. More likely, the unsettling presence of Joseph no longer there, and Dudu's power to stir up mischief ruined, Potiphar's house returned to normal, at least within the religious and domestic spheres. In the years Joseph would remain in prison the elder Pharaoh would die, and Potiphar would in honor be retired from his formalistic service to the deceased ruler. Mut having retained her virginity would return for a time to her duties as Amun priestess, and Potiphar's parents eventually finding the courage to die and face the judgment of the Egyptian gods would be gradually replaced in their roles as the honored elders of the household by Potiphar and Mut, they too in their childless state anticipating oblivion. But that story no longer applied to Joseph, and Mann, the Biblical chronicler, does not tell it in *Joseph the Provider*. In any case, after three years of Mut's mounting passion and rage, frenzy and guilt, she is finally relieved of all her tensions. She either forgets Joseph or can come to view him in afterthought in the chaste aspect he had struggled so steadfastly to maintain. So Kundry after many centuries of inner torment from rejecting Christ and alternately seeking and rejecting atonement—in Act I of the opera we learn that she had been a penitent pilgrim arriving at Montsalvat always antecedent to another knight taking off on a private mission against Klingsor's castle—so Kundry is freed at long last to die and find acceptance in a better world beyond. Mut had died to the world of desire and sensuality when she willingly married Potiphar.

Her gradual, tentative withdrawal from her dead world to consideration of the one of living flesh and blood occurred over the first seven years of Joseph's presence in Potiphar's household. Her determined efforts to become a part of it lasted for only three. These three were so filled with frustrated love and hatred and pain, Mut no doubt was once again confirmed in her earlier acceptance of her dead world. Kundry sought and after a millennium finally achieved the death beyond the physical world.

Wagner's *Tristan und Isolde* and *Parsifal* are often compared. Wagner wrote *Tristan und Isolde* when he was immersed in his love affair with Mathilde Wesendonk. While living as a guest at the house of her Swiss husband in a rather Joseph-Mut-Potiphar type of relationship except that Wagner was considerably into middle age and Mathilde was his junior. The opera is often considered to be a paean to physical love, and certainly Wagner like Tristan (as well as Tannhäuser, and even Siegmund and Siegfried) for long periods of his life found sex a demanding element in his life that he had to accede to and indeed had to express in music. We recall Wagner's passionate love affair with Liszt's daughter Cosima that led to their living together out of wedlock and producing illegitimate children while Cosima was still the wife of the pianist Hans von Bülow. However, in his last years, Wagner often professed sympathy for sexual abstinence and celibacy, and *Parsifal* was the opera that he completed just before his own death. Even earlier he had considered sexual abstinence as an alternate life style. As a young man, he wrote *Lohengrin* which implies such ideas long before he had met either Frau Wesendonk or Frau von Bülow. It is significant to note that Lohengrin was the son of Parsifal and that the opera about the father's youth was written as the coda to Wagner's own musical life. Both men for the most part valued chastity over sexual pleasure. Lohengrin deserts Elsa on their wedding day after she had asked him in the bridal chamber the forbidden question about his identity. Parsifal apparently fathered Lohengrin in a brief relapse from chastity during his wanderings between Act II and III of his opera, after he successfully resisted Kundry's enticements and before he returned to the order of knights at Montsalvat. Perhaps Parsifal's fathering of Lohengrin might be the decisive factor in convincing many of Mann's personal identification of his Joseph character with Wagner's Parsifal. After marrying an Egyptian of the appropriately high status due the chief advisor of Pharaoh, Joseph fathers two sons Manasseh and Ephraim. But in his intellectual exchanges between himself and Ikhnaton, Joseph seems to convey even in his middle years an attitude of sexual independence very similar to his youthful chastity. Perhaps Joseph's marriage had the drawbacks of a negotiated one, just as certainly Potiphar's and Mut's had, and most likely Ikhnaton's and Nefertiti's as well. Young Ikhnaton while under Joseph's influence becomes progressively more concerned with religious matters, his evolving concept of the one god, Aton. It seems evident, in any case, that Joseph had not forgotten his observations of the family history of Potiphar's household over two generations, that of the twin parents of Potiphar and Potiphar and Mut, and his own complicated and disturbing relationship to the second.

Interestingly enough, castration is an emphasis in both *Parsifal* and *Joseph in Egypt*. As a solution to the sexual demands of the body, it is not endorsed by either Wagner or Mann. Wagner's Klingsor had at first been a fledgling knight of the order of Montsalvat which Amfortas' father Titurel had established to perpetuate the guardianship of the consecrated grail and spear. Disturbed by his own carnality, Klingsor had resorted to self-castration only to experience contemptuous rejection by his fellow knights. In bitterness, Klingsor plotted to destroy the order and the spiritually healing properties of its holy relics. He, like Mut in turning from her priestess role of veneration to the spirits of light of the upper world, resorted, like her, in his extremity of humiliation to the powers of darkness. Subsequently, the non-castrated knights of Montsalvat were beckoned separately to his mysteriously emerged castle and to Kundry and the flower maidens to their shame. Only Parsifal succeeded in resisting the maidens' attractions and loosening the fetters by which Klingsor had bound the young women in loyal service to him. Being castrated, Klingsor himself had been invulnerable to the women in his castle. Without the capacity for sexual experience, Klingsor became bereft of all feelings of love and compassion and the ability to forgive. Evil took him over completely and instead of serving goodness, his life's sole aim had been to destroy it. Wagner's Klingsor is a very apt portrayal of frustrated decency turned sour. Perhaps in Hitler, Wagner would have recognized a twentieth-century corollary.

Mann's Potiphar, however, is not the destructive, vindictive man that Klingsor became after his self-castration. Potiphar's incestuous parents, of course, had decided on his castration, not Potiphar. In his evident consideration of *Parsifal* concepts in working out his own Joseph narrative, Mann may well be making a significant distinction. Unlike Klingsor, Potiphar seems a man of an unusually obliging nature, dutiful to his parents, his wife, servants, Pharaoh, nation and its gods. He was trained from childhood to be a functionary and each day he applied himself to all the ritualistic observances expected of him. In him, the promptings of the ego never impeded his ability to act as intermediary for the confluence of all the social orders of Egypt. In a purely formalistic manner, he clarified his Pharaoh's involvement with the military, religious, economic, cultural and social levels of Egyptian life. A large, tall, strong man, he often engaged in dangerous hunting of hippos and lions to set standards of valor and courage for Egyptian manhood. Still there was a sadness to his life; he felt obliged to serve the interests of high and low within and beyond his household, and he did not understand the emotions of love. To Joseph he took a great fancy, but this was because Joseph had sympathy and insight into Potiphar's situation within the complicated social structures of Egypt. Also Joseph, though not castrated, evidently valued chastity and chose higher service to the God of his Hebrew nation. For many years, Joseph was an intelligent student to Potiphar and a convenient amanuensis. When at the end of his ten-year stay he had become embroiled in the embarrassing business with Mut and Dudu, Potiphar can recognize the not totally unresponsible role that Joseph has played. Disinterested from the sexual standpoint and not partisan in his feelings because of his inability to understand love, he can in justice send Joseph off to prison (but not to the crocodiles), reinstate Mut to her proper and restricted role as ritual wife and Amun's virginal priestess, and demote and detongue the mischief-causing Dudu. No doubt, recognizing the unusual nature of Joseph's abilities, and Joseph now obviously no longer able to serve his household constructively, Potiphar may well have concluded, in any case, that only by Joseph descending once more to another pit could he again rise to even higher levels of service in Egypt. 4 And so Joseph does. As Potiphar served the elder Pharaoh, in future years Joseph would serve Ikhnaton. During the seven years of famine that would follow in the score of years to come, Joseph would rise to challenges greater than those with which Potiphar ever had to deal.

Still other instances of male chastity are present in *Joseph in Egypt* which can also be paralleled to *Parsifal*. In Gurnemanz, Wagner portrayed one of the older knights of Montsalvat who throughout the long assault of Klingsor on the order that had disowned him had remained loyal to the precepts of the order and hopeful for its return to sanctity and happy service. Indeed Gurnemanz explains to the novice Parsifal in the early stages of the opera the history of the order's troubled times, and much later prepares him for his acceptance of his role as leader of the order when he returns in the closing Good Friday scene with the long-absent holy spear. Gurnemanz too shows his acceptance of the suppliant Kundry at Montsalvat in Act I, although her departures from the monastery had always preceded the departure of another knight embarking to Klingsor's castle in hopes of succeeding where others failed in retrieving the holy spear. Gurnemanz has apparently always the ability to see good at work in people. It is he who receives back Kundry at Montsalvat in Act III before Parsifal's long-delayed return, a Kundry who through Parsifal's victory over her and Klingsor is now free of Klingsor's magic spells and also drained of any power to betray again the brotherhood. Gurnemanz like Parsifal is instrumental in setting up the scene for her long-sought release in death.

Mont-kaw, Joseph's predecessor at Potiphar's court, plays a role to young Joseph that is quite similar to Gurnemanz's to Parsifal. It was he who gave approval to Joseph's purchase at the urgings of Bes-em-heb over the protests of Dudu. When he first saw Joseph, he was jolted by his unusual beauty, and later he was impressed with his knowledge and his ability to write. Soon Joseph became, as he had in his boyhood for his father Jacob and more recently for the crafty Ishmaelite merchant who had bought him from the brothers intending to sell him to this very Mont-kaw, the pleasant and uplifting conversationalist at the end of Mont-kaw's busy and responsibility-laden day. He recognized Joseph's organizational skills and his ability to take in the general scheme of things. Like Bes-em-heb, he saw Joseph was not suited to be a common slave worker as Dudu would have had him be on the household lands. Before long Mont-kaw not only begins training Joseph to be his assistant, but prepares him, even though Joseph is not Egyptian, to become his eventual successor as overseer. Joseph's gift for languages and his inclination to identify with the intriguing broader world as well as the restricted one of his Hebrew heritage help him to develop an authentic Egyptian manner. His Eastern differences are just sufficient to keep him interesting. Mont-kaw, too, has trouble with his kidneys and he realizes his days of total dedication to his revered Potiphar may be running short. So for seven years he supervises Joseph's apprenticeship and plays a father surrogate role to Joseph in a specific sense just as does Potiphar more generally in his position of master of the household. Preferentially serving Potiphar and his wife and the aged parents at the dining hour and at prescribed daily intervals reading to Potiphar from literature on papyri scrolls and engaging with him in intellectual discourse of a properly proprietary nature, late in the evenings Joseph discusses the practical matters of household business and, more personally, matters on life and goals with the wise and generous Mont-kaw. When frequently the older man's physical debility and the pressures of his daily work make sleep difficult for him, Joseph's soothing manner enables him to submit to the conditions that enable him to fall asleep. When at the end of the seven-year apprenticeship, Mont-kaw catches a fatal chill to his kidneys after appearing at a Theban temple for Potiphar, Joseph is there to soothe him into submission with the sleep of death. Mont-kaw dies after many years of devoted service to Potiphar, choosing a life of celibacy after the death of his young wife, as if in final deference to his master. His example, no doubt, enforces Joseph's unbudging celibacy during the three years of Joseph's own overseership of the household.

Mont-kaw's debility works effectively as a complement to Potiphar's physical incompleteness. In Mann's own service to Wagnerian methodology, it also neatly parallels

Tristan's mortal wound in *Tristan und Isolde* or Amfortas' unhealing one in *Parsifal*. In the latter case, Parsifal by touching Amfortas with the order's long-absent spear makes Amfortas whole once again, physical purity once more restored to him. Joseph, on the other hand, helps the long-suffering and patient Mont-kaw finally submit to death and the presumed rewards for his long-imposed celibacy, joining his beloved bride and the son who had died with his mother at birth and for whom Joseph over seven years evidently served as a comforting surrogate.

Perhaps Wagner's *Meistersinger* should also be mentioned. In this opera of apprenticeship, Wagner's treatment of Hans Sachs is very suggestive likewise of Mann's treatment of Mont-kaw, and young Walther von Stolzing, the stranger who has thrown in his lot with the sturdy citizens of Nürnberg, also resembles young Joseph, the "naturalized" Egyptian. Hans Sachs, the town shoemaker, poet, and musician, prepares Walther for the contest of song in Nürnberg, the winner of which will not only become the town's reigning mastersinger but the winner of the lovely Eva as his bride. Sachs recognizes in the stranger Walther a gift in music more promising than that of the other young music makers native to Nürnberg and, like Mont-kaw to Joseph, he facilitates Walther in becoming his own successor. Sachs abdicates to Walther as musician of the future and even forfeits Eva to him. The middle-aged Sachs, a widower, had in his Indian summer considered the possibilities of winning young Eva as his bride, and in the course of the opera Eva's love for Sachs as well as for Walther is amply shown. In time, however, Sachs too comes to recognize continued celibacy as his proper state, and Walther wins Eva as well as the title of mastersinger. Like Joseph, the good and purely motivated if somewhat egotistic Walther will experience physical love but not of the unrelenting sort that would come with Isolde, Kundry, or Mut. Eva is a pleasing little bourgeoisie, and Joseph's eventual mate in *Joseph the Provider* is an ideally chosen woman happy to serve as wife and mother to Joseph and his children.

Not to neglect the less pleasant tones of Wagnerian and Mannian portraits, Beckmesser, the musical pedant, should perhaps be mentioned. Assumed to be a depiction in *Die Meistersinger* of Wagner's chief opponent in musical circles, the Jewish critic Hanslich (as often the calculating, vindictive Alberich of the *Ring* and Klingsor of *Parsifal* are as well), we can confidently step further and identify Beckmesser with Mann's Dudu, the arch trouble maker for the very pleasing and productive Jewish youth in Potiphar's household.

At this point, probably there has been enough identification of character and thematic devices in Wagner that Mann utilized in writing his Joseph tetralogy, surely in many cases in full knowledge of the source of his methodology, but possibly just as likely in many instances resulting from experiencing in his early years so much Wagner in the opera house and absorbing the methodology by cultural osmosis. He may have consciously rejected Wagner's art for a time, but he later accepted it. This Mann admitted in his maturity in discussing his artistic creed. This granted, a reemphasis of Mann's use of Wagnerian *leitmotifs* in his Joseph stories should be considered further.

The incident in *Joseph the Provider* of the placement of the valuable cup in his brother Benjamin's traveling gear at Joseph's command is, while from one perspective simply expanded by Mann from the same cup incident as recorded by the original Biblical scribe who wrote the Jewish version of the Joseph story, as elaborated by Mann, it can just as readily be viewed an allusion to the cup roles in Acts I of *Die Walküre* and *Tristan und Isolde* and the Holy Grail motif of *Parsifal*. Also the reiteration by Mann at intervals in the Joseph stories of Reuben's copulation with one of Jacob's concubines compares strongly with the incest motif of brother and sister in *Die Walküre* of Wagner's *Ring*, compared in these pages to the brother-sister mating in Mann's reconstruction of Potiphar's family background. Reuben's incest with Jacob's concubine also functions within Mann's writings as a *leitmotif* relating to Joseph's three-year shifting balance on a tight rope between self-confident celibate service to the father of the Egyptian household and narcissistic curiosity regarding Mut's erotic declarations. We should not forget of the ten half-brothers Reuben was the brother who spared Joseph from death and therefore that he identifies more with Joseph than do the others.

Constantly in Mann's tetralogy the leitmotival pattern suggests Wagner. Even the time Mann expended in writing it and the psychological delays he experienced at a crucial point suggest an overriding *leitmotif* guiding Mann. Like the long delay between Wagner's conclusion of Act II of *Siegfried* and the composition of Act III of that opera and the entirety of *Götterdämmerung*, there was Mann's long delay between *Joseph in Egypt* and *Joseph the Provider*. Mann explains that one reason he delayed for some four years in taking up pen and resuming *Joseph* writing *Lotte in Weimar* and *The Transposed Heads* instead was because he feared that he could not balance the two elements which he had dealt with repeatedly in the preceding works—young Jacob's physical desire for Rachel and his enforced marriage with Leah, the widowed celibate Jacob and the lustful Reuben, Joseph and his temptations with Mut—in the predominantly intellectual and pragmatic concerns of the final stage of Joseph's history. He finally resolved the dilemma by including the story of Tamar to precede his account of Jacob and his progeny migrating to Egypt in the period of famine.

In Tamar, Mann again describes a woman of great physical determination. Jacob had eventually designated his son Judah as heir to the tribe after Joseph's reported death. Tamar, a foreign Canaanite woman who had joined herself to Jacob's tribe, in her desire to play a major role in the future of the tribe manages to obtain Jacob's approval to marry Judah's eldest son, Er. Er dies soon after their marriage, and so does Onan, Judah's second son after he in turn also becomes her husband. Both had evidently worked excessively to impregnate the woman bent on motherhood. When Judah would not permit the sacrifice of his third son Shelah in marriage to her, she tricked Judah himself into sleeping with her, the encounter resulting in the birth of twin sons, fittingly replacing the two sons she had deprived him of in her too zealous determination to perpetuate his line. She subsequently becomes Judah's wife. In Tamar, Mann provides a primitive woman in a herdsman society who manages to subject sexually three Jewish men, while the aristocratic, much more finely grained Mut over three years had failed so pathetically to do so with the equally fine-grained Joseph. Expansion of the Biblical account of Tamar was a happy inspiration of Mann. It is fine enough to stand alone as a novella. Indeed, in Germany it has been published separately in lavish format as a separate work under one cover. Not to be forgotten also is Mann's very suggestive use of dreams throughout the Joseph novels as a *leitmotif*. Of course, again the majority of the dreams were already there in the brief Biblical accounts of Jacob and Joseph—Jacob's wrestling with the angel and his vision of the ladder into heaven, the boy Joseph's dream of his brothers bowing down before him, the dreams of the elder Pharaoh's butler and cook, and finally the dreams of the younger Pharaoh of the fat and skinny stalks of corn and the fat and skinny cows. These are confidently expanded and reinterpreted by Mann and readily fitted into the leitmotival, Wagnerian pattern. Interestingly, Mann needed a dream emphasis for *Joseph in Egypt* which the Biblical story did not supply. He therefore contrived a very eloquent and impressive dream for Mut based on an incident in the Persian poet Firdusi's epic *Yüsuf and Zuleikha* which not only functions in the tetralogy as a needed bridge between the early and later dream motifs but of equal importance prepares the reader for an understanding of Mut's seminal stages of susceptibility to Joseph. Here Mann worked simultaneously as he had over two decades earlier in writing *Death in Venice* with both Wagnerian and Freudian materials. In Mann's "original" dream creation, after many days, perhaps months or even several years, of scarcely observing the Jewish youth who stood in the dining quarters to serve Potiphar, his aged parents and herself at their evening meals, occasionally by merest coincidence casually glancing at him at the very moment his eyes turned on her—the *Augenblick* of Tadzio and Aschenbach in *Death in Venice* and also of Wagner's Tristan and Isolde—Mut dreamed that at dinner she had cut herself with one of the eating utensils. While Potiphar and his aged parents responded with shocked dismay, Joseph rushed to her side and stanched her spurting blood with his lips, certainly a commendable action on the part of Joseph in her dream but hardly suitable to the proprieties of the inner circle of the household and certainly not in the manner in which he would have managed to help her had such an accident actually occurred at the dining hour. Mann splendidly uses his knowledge of Freudian dream imagery in devising a believable dream for Mut in this early stage of her Joseph mania, and through it makes quite convincing Dudu's manipulation of her emotions to stage Joseph's downfall. Mut's much later party of the ladies in which she dramatizes her passion for Joseph and challenges them to scorn her fall from virginal grace can be understood now not only in its Brangäne-confidence aspect but as an extension of Joseph's stanching of her blood in her earlier disturbing, uncomprehended dream. By the time of her party, Mut has a sophisticated understanding of her dream, and she verifies it for herself by her setting the scene for all the self-cutting instances that Joseph precipitated when he appeared to serve the Egyptian ladies at Mut's command (the incident recorded in Firdusi's poem). Among many brilliant touches in *Joseph in Egypt* the episode of Mut's dream and her studied reenactment of it later are among the best. How paradoxical and yet how necessary, too, are Mann's synthesis of Wagnerian and Freudian elements in the novella *Death in Venice* and book three of *Joseph and His*

Brothers. By now the purpose of this attempt to go beyond Mann's own admission that *Joseph and His Brothers* was his Biblical *Ring* tetralogy has probably been taken far enough. If only the *Ring* associations were considered certain limitations would obviously be apparent. Certainly Brünnhilde's rage at Siegfried's betrayal might in some ways be compared to the growing wrath of Mut at Joseph's lack of responsiveness. When Mut lists to Joseph all the terrible modes of execution which might befall him if she should accuse him of attempting to seduce her, from casting him to the crocodiles to a succession of increasingly more refined, time-tested Egyptian modes of agonizing death, her threats could well be compared to the revenge Brünnhilde actually carried out when she informs Siegfried's enemies Hagen and Gunther of the vulnerable spot on his back that the dragon's blood had failed to touch. On the other hand, Brünnhilde as actual sister-aunt-cousin of Siegfried hardly would represent the separation of blood and nations that exists between Kundry-Isolde-Mut and Parsifal-Tristan-Joseph. The physical love consummated between Brünnhilde and Siegfried also would suggest amiable, happy, non-neurotic love which would certainly not be the case for the other pairings. It would, however, be unfair and unjust to Mann's admission of parallels between his and Wagner's tetralogies if one last interesting parallel between the last work of each were not mentioned. It is a frequent judgment even among devoted Wagnerians that in *Götterdämmerung*, Wagner failed to maintain his objectives of creating four separate art dramas. In *Götterdämmerung* despite its vastness and complexity and the richness of its music, Wagner allegedly abandoned the restrictions he had imposed upon himself in writing the preceding three operas. Instead he included many standard arias and separate orchestral pieces (such as the Rhine Journey, the vassal chorus, the hunting music, and the funeral march) and as a result produced a much more standard, German-type opera of the pre-Wagner Meyerbeer style. There seems to be a measure of truth in these observations. Equally interesting is the information Mann gives his reader in the 1948 introduction to the American edition of the four Joseph novels under one cover. He tells us that German critics of *Joseph the Provider* had concluded that in it, unlike the first three volumes, he had become so liberated in his use of German that it was "really not German any more" and that the spirit of its telling had become "untrammeled to the point of abstraction." Mann admits the truth of these assertions. He had written the first three books in Germany and Switzerland and *Tales of Jacob* and part of *Young Joseph* even before having taken a vacation in 1930 to Egypt and Palestine to gain a greater sense of place. Then came the war, his family's migration to the U.S. and eventually their settlement in California. As previously mentioned, Wagner had taken time off to compose *Tristan und Isolde* and *Die Meistersinger* between the completion of Act II of *Siegfried* and the writing of Act III and all of *Götterdämmerung*. After *Joseph in Egypt*, Mann wrote *Lotte in Weimar* and *The Transposed Heads* (notable works it might be added but hardly comparable in scope to Wagner's intervening operas). Finally Mann summoned the courage to pick up pen and begin the last volume of the tetralogy, *Joseph the Provider*. Now it was the radiant sun of California that inspired his description of ancient Egypt, less so his observations of Egypt in his visit there in 1930.

His interest in the New Deal politics of Roosevelt and his own friendship with the wartime president also colored his concepts of Joseph's economic planning in the seven famine years of Old Egypt as well as the friendship between Ikhnaton and Joseph that he described. Most important of all, Mann's way with German necessarily was affected by the changed linguistic climate of America with its non-British English. Thus Mann's implications have the final word. *Joseph and His Brothers* and Wagner's *Ring* in their closing parts whether through exhausted wills near the end of such long creative undertakings or because of circumstances beyond their creators' control had similarly not worked out in the final parts quite as their authors had originally planned them.

Endnotes

1

Mann was particularly indebted to Wagner's *Tristan und Isolde.* In the short story "Tristan" and in the long novel *Buddenbrooks* the destructive effects of the inordinately beautiful music of Wagner's opera are portrayed. The tubercular wife of the short story and the delicate boy Hanno of the novel die following their too intense association with the music of the opera through transcriptions of the love and death music which they played on the piano at emotionally and physically precarious periods of their lives. In *Death in Venice*, Aschenbach's and Tadzio's secret, platonic love relationship is maintained over several weeks through a series of eye glances that parallel those exchanged by Tristan and Isolde at various key points in Wagner's opera. The use of the *Augenblick leitmotif* to portray the love impulse, is similarly if less emphatically used in *The Magic Mountain* and *Confessions of Felix Krull*, and, of course, in *Joseph in Egypt*.

2

It is interesting to note that Thomas Mann in 1923 wrote in collaboration with his brother Victor a film scenario based on Gottfried von Strassburg's *Tristan*, in which the Aquitanian dwarf Melot plays a role almost identical to Dudu's. See Allan Blunden, *Thomas Mann: Pro And Contra Wagner*, p 73.

3

Mann was inclined to consider music an irrational creation, a production of the dark and even the demonic. Writing, on the other hand, was a rational creation, a product of the light. He loved music and wrote about it confidently, but as was stated earlier in this paper, his Wagner essay, despite its noble intentions and profound sympathy for Wagner as an artist and genius, aroused the wrath not only of the Nazis but the irritation of German luminaries of the musical world–Strauss, Pfitzner, Furtwängler, and Knappertbusch. In 1950, Mann's great novel of the corrupted German musician and contemporary of Hitler Adrian Leverkühn, *Dr. Faustus*, aroused Harold C. Schonberg to expose Mann's faulty understanding of the twelve-tone system which Mann attributed to his fictional Leverkühn. Perhaps Schonberg disliked Mann's association of Leverkühn's moral decline with his so-called Faustian musical experimentation in atonality as much or more than Mann's imperfect understanding of the system. See Harold C. Schonberg, "Music Meta-physics …its Cause and Cure," *Etude*, LXVIII (March 1950), 12, 13.

4

Joseph the Provider is, of course, the novel of the tetralogy that conclusively demonstrates the life of service that was Joseph's destiny. It should be noted that ultimately "service" in the noblest sense is the life direction of all the worthy characters in *Parsifal* just as it was in the households of Potiphar and Pharaoh in *Joseph in Egypt* and *Joseph the Provider*. Wagner makes the predominant thematic *leitmotif* of service particularly evident in the opening dialogue of Act III of *Parsifal* where the aging Gurnemanz once more rescues a repentant Kundry, now tattered and nearly frozen following her exposure to a long and difficult winter. Gurnemanz, somewhat less tolerant and forgiving than he had been to the faithless woman in the past, chastises her. Kundry, now for all time freed of Klingsor's evil magic and truly repentant, bows her head and begs in a rough and broken voice, "*Dienen, dienen!*" (to serve …to serve!)

Author's Note

At Last The Distinguished Thing, my novella concerning the death of Henry James, is indebted to Leon Edel's five volume *Henry James: The Complete Biography* and his later one volume revised and condensed *Henry James: A Life*. I wish to acknowledge that I have not only liberally sprinkled many of Henry James' own words, including whole sentences from his works and personal letters throughout my text, but that I have also relied heavily on Edel's recounting of certain pivotal conversations between James and his family members, servants, and familiars. Edel's traditional view of James as a sexually repressed, pallid individual has been challenged by subsequent biographers, most notably by Sheldon Novick and Fred Kaplan. While I find these revisionist portraits of James fascinating, the fictional James of my novel is cut from Edel's cloth.

The essay "Wagnerian Elements in Thomas Mann's Joseph Tetralogy" attributed here to my fictional character Michael Bolanger was in actuality a collaborative effort between my father Frederick W. Seinfelt and myself and dates from the early 1980s. My father, a noted Wagner scholar, first introduced me to the works of Thomas Mann. He gave me a copy of *Buddenbrooks* when I entered the seventh grade. I read *Joseph and His Brothers* for the first time while in college, and it struck me that Mann had patterned pivotal scenes in the work on Wagner's *Tristan und Isolde* and *Parsifal*. I relayed my discovery to my father, who had not read Mann's tetralogy for many years. He again immersed himself in the book and agreed with my analysis. Subsequently he wrote the first draft of the essay. Later I revised and added to it. The essay in its present form is the result of both our work.

Finally I would like to express my thanks to Jeni Fowler for her kind assistance in transfer of data and in the preparation of the manuscript for delivery to the publisher.

Mark Seinfelt is the author of several books. He holds a Bachelor of Arts degree in English from the Pennsylvania State University, where he received the Henry Sams Memorial Award for his thesis and where he studied under critically acclaimed author and Lannan Lifetime Achievement Award winner Paul West and novelist and screenwriter Robert C.S. Downs. He also holds a Master of Fine Arts in writing from Washington University in St. Louis, where he worked with the noted fiction writer, philosopher, and essayist William H. Gass, who served as chairman of his dissertation committee. Seinfelt's fiction and non-fiction has been featured in numerous publications. Currently, he resides in Philipsburg, Pennsylvania.

45925632R00336

Made in the USA
Lexington, KY
15 October 2015